The Magic Circle

ALSO BY KATHERINE NEVILLE

The Eight

Calculated Risk

KATHERINE NEVILLE

BALLANTINE BOOKS • NEW YORK

A Ballantine Book
Published by The Ballantine Publishing Group

Published in the United States by The Ballantine Publishing Group, a division of Random House, Inc., New York, and simultaneously in Canada by Random House of Canada Limited, Toronto.

Grateful acknowledgment is made to the following for permission to reprint material:

Henry Holt and Company, Inc.: "Fire and Ice" from *The Poetry of Robert Frost* edited by Edward Connery Lathem. Copyright 1951 by Robert Frost, Copyright 1923, © 1969 by Henry Holt and Company, Inc. Reprinted by permission of Henry Holt and Company, Inc.

Houghton Mifflin Company: Excerpt from *J.B.* by Archibald MacLeish. Copyright © 1956, 1957, 1958 by Archibald MacLeish. Copyright © renewed 1986 by William H. MacLeish and Mary H. Grimm. Reprinted by permission of Houghton Mifflin Company.

Tom Lehrer: Excerpt from the lyrics of "Pollution" by Tom Lehrer. Copyright © 1965 by Tom Lehrer. Used by permission.

Thomas Nelson, Inc.: Scripture from the King James Version Scripture. Copyright © 1976 by Thomas Nelson, Inc. Publishers. Used by permission.

New Falcon Publications: Excerpt from *AHA* by Aleister Crowley. Reprinted courtesy of New Falcon Publications, Tempe, AZ.

http://www.randomhouse.com

Library of Congress Cataloging-in-Publication Data

Neville, Katherine, 1945–
The magic circle : a novel / Katherine Neville.—1st ed.
p. cm.
ISBN 0-345-40792-X (alk. paper)
I. Title.
PS3564.E8517M34 1998
813'.54—dc21 97-38613
CIP

Text design by Ann Gold

Manufactured in the United States of America

First Edition: March 1998

10 9 8 7 6 5 4 3 2 1

The Age Returns. —Motto of Lorenzo de' Medici

Time itself is a circle; everything recurs.
—Friedrich Nietzsche

What goes around comes around.
—Motto of the Hell's Angels

THE CAVE

And they do not know the future mystery,
or understand ancient matters.
And they do not know what is going to happen to them;
and they will not save their souls from the future mystery.
—*The Dead Sea Scrolls,* prophecy of the Essenes

Now has come the last age of the song of Cumae.
From the renewed spirit of the Ages a new Order is born.
Now the Virgin returns, the reign of Saturn returns.
Now a new generation is sent down from heaven on high.
—*Virgil, Fourth Eclogue,* messianic prophecy of the Sibyl

Cumae, Italy: Autumn, A.D. 1870

It was just before dusk. The volcanic Lake Avernus, high above Cumae, seemed to float in the air, partly veiled with a thin metallic haze. Between the patches of mist, the lake's glassy surface mirrored opalescent clouds scudding across the crescent sliver of the moon.

The walls of the crater were wild with scrub oak, changing color from bloodred to purple in the descending twilight. The aroma of the dark sulfurous lake filled the air with a sense of danger. The very landscape of this ancient, hallowed spot seemed to be waiting for something, something that had been foretold for thousands of years. Something that was about to happen tonight.

As the darkness deepened, a figure slipped stealthily from the trees bordering the water's edge. It was followed swiftly by three others. Though all four were dressed in sturdy leather breeches, jerkins, and helmets, it was clear by form and bearing that their leader was a woman. Over her shoulder she carried a pickaxe, a roll of oiled tarpaulin, sturdy rope, and other climbing gear. Her male companions followed silently, skirting the rim to the far side of the lake.

The woman moved back into the shadows, where a thick cluster of trees camouflaged an overhanging cliff. In darkness, she felt along the sheer face of vine-covered rock until she'd once more found the hidden crevasse. Pulling on heavy gloves, she loosened the rubble she'd so carefully replaced earlier. Her heart pounded as she slipped sideways through the narrow cleft in the rock, followed by her three companions.

Inside the cliff, the woman quickly unrolled the tarpaulin and, with the help of the others, stuffed it into the crack. When not even the smallest trace of light from the cave could be observed outside, she pulled off her metal helmet and lit the carbide miner's lamp affixed to it. Tossing back her mane of blond hair, she gazed at her three rugged companions, whose eyes glittered in the lamplight. Then she turned to look at the cave.

Carved from the lava rock, the walls of the vast cavern rose more than one hundred feet above them. It took her breath when she realized they stood at the edge of a sheer cliff that dropped off into the pitch-black void. She could hear the sound of rushing water, from what seemed hundreds of feet below. This was the passage that had once led those seeking the mysteries deep within the bowels of this extinct volcano. This was the legendary place sought by so many over so many centuries, the cavern that had once served as home to the most ancient of all prophets: the Sibylline oracle.

Now, as she shone the lamp across the glistening walls, the woman knew there could be no mistaking what she'd found. The cave was exactly as described by those who'd visited here from earliest times—Heraclitus, Plutarch, Pausanias, and the poet Virgil, who'd immortalized this grotto in verse as the site of Aeneas's entry into the underworld. Indeed, she knew that she and her three comrades could well be the first to have laid eyes on this fabled spot in two millennia.

When the emperor Augustus had seized power in Rome in 27 B.C., his first act had been to round up all copies of the books of her prophecies, called the Sibylline Oracles. He'd burned any he deemed "inauthentic"—those that did not support his tenure, or that prophetically heralded the return of the Republic. Then he'd ordered the Cumaean grotto sealed. Its official entrance, located not here but at the base of the volcano, was buried beneath a mountain of rubble. All trace of the famous cave's existence had been lost to mankind. Until now.

The young woman set down her gear and once again pulled on her mining helmet with its small beacon of light. Extracting from her leather jerkin the crudely drawn map she'd brought, she handed it to the tallest of the three men. She addressed him aloud for the first time.

"Aszi, you will come with me. Your elder brothers must remain here and guard this entrance. If we can make no progress below, this crevasse will be our only avenue of escape." Turning to the sheer cliff, she added undaunted, "I shall make the first descent."

But he'd taken her by the wrist. His handsome face searched hers with great concern. Then he drew her to him and he gently kissed her forehead.

"No, let me go down first, Clio," he said. "I was born on the rocks, you know, *carita*; I can climb like a goat. My brothers will lower you after me." When she shook her head, he told her, "No matter what your father sketched out on this map before he died, it's just one man's scholarly opinion, formed from reading dusty books. Through all his travels, your father could never find the place. And you know well that oracles are often dangerous. The one at Delphi kept a brood of deadly pythons in her cave. You can't know what we'll find in the shrine you imagine is down there, in the dark."

Clio shuddered at the thought, and the two strapping men nodded in support of their brother's bravery. Aszi lit a second lamp, which he clipped onto his own helmet. The men secured the heavy rope to a rock and their younger brother, with only his bare hands on hemp, used his hobnailed boots to clear the wall and vanished with a brief, flashing smile into the darkness.

After what seemed a very long while, the rope swung loose, so they knew he had touched bottom. Clio passed her own rope between her legs to form a harness, which the brothers secured to the main line as double protection if she slipped. Then she, too, went over the side.

As Clio descended the sheer rock face, alone in silence, she studied the schist in the light of her lamp as if it contained the key to some riddle. If walls had ears, she thought, this one might reveal thousands of years of mysteries. Just like the Sibyl herself, a woman who could see all of the future and the past.

The oldest oracle in history, a woman who lived in many lands over dozens of generations, the Sibyl was born on Mount Ida, from which the gods once overlooked the war on the plains of Troy. More than five hundred years before Christ, the Sibyl traveled to Rome, where she offered to sell to King Tarquin the books of her prophecies spanning the next twelve thousand years. When he refused to meet her price she burned the first three volumes, then the next three, until only three books were left. Tarquin did buy these, and he enshrined them in the Temple of Jupiter, where they remained until that structure, too, burned to the ground, in 83 B.C., along with its precious contents.

The Sibyl's vision was so profound and far-reaching, she had been granted any wish by the gods. She asked to live for one thousand years, but she forgot to ask for youth. As the end of her life approached, she had shrunk so small that nothing remained but her voice, which still prophesied from a little glass ampulla placed in this ancient cave of the mysteries. People traveled from far and wide to hear her song—until Augustus silenced her, for eternity, with Neapolitan clay.

Clio hoped beyond hope that the information her father had gleaned from his wealth of readings in ancient texts, a vision he'd only really understood on his deathbed, would prove true. Whether true or not, to follow the overriding wish of a dying man had already cost her everything she'd known in her young life.

When she reached bottom, she felt Aszi's strong hands grasp her waist, helping her to gain her footing on the slippery rocks that bordered the onrushing underground river.

They made their way for more than an hour through the caverns beneath the volcano, following the directions her father had laid forth on the map. At last they came to the hollow, high in the rock, beneath which the Sibyl's successors, young country girls, had for centuries sat on a golden throne—now a mass of crumbled stones—transmitting the prophecies passed down through them from the mind of the ancient goddess.

Aszi stopped beside Clio, then he unexpectedly bent to her, and he kissed her on the lips. He smiled. "You are nearly free," he said.

Without another word he bounded up the crumbled pile of rock to the hollow, scaling the last length of cliff with his hands. Clio held her breath as he gained purchase against the rock with his boots and she saw him stretch his arm to reach his hand into the high hollow, feeling about in the dark hole above his head. After a long moment he drew something out.

When he returned, he handed it to Clio. It was a shimmering object, like a tiny vial, not much larger than her palm. Clio had never believed that the Sibyl's voice was contained in an ampulla, but rather that the ancient vial held her prophetic *words*. Her prophecies, Plutarch had said, were written on small bits of metal, so light and fragile that, when released, they were borne away on the wind.

Clio carefully opened the vial and the tiny leaves tumbled out into her palm, each the size of a fingernail and each inscribed in Greek. She touched one leaf and looked into Aszi's dark purple eyes gazing into her own.

"What does it say?" he whispered.

"In Greek, this one says '*En to pan*,'" she told him. "It means 'One is all.' "

The Sibyl had foretold what would happen at each critical turning point in history—and, more important, how it was connected to each critical event of the past. It was said that she'd predicted the dawn of a new celestial age immediately following her own—the age of Pisces, the fish, whose avatar would be a virgin-born king. The Sibyl could see mysterious connections, like spider threads spanning thousands of years, connecting the age of Pisces with that of Aquarius, the water-bearer, an age that would not dawn until twenty centuries later—which would be just about now.

Clio slipped the leaves back into the vial. But as she and Aszi began their long trek through the caves, back toward the surface, she feared she knew what this moment really meant. It was as her father had always imagined. By unearthing a bottle like this, a bottle filled with time—by uncorking the long-mute voice of the past—she'd opened a door that perhaps should have remained closed. A Pandora's box.

Tonight, the Sibyl's song that had lain mute in darkness beneath the volcano had been reawakened, to be heard once more by humans for the first time in nearly two thousand years.

ENTERING THE CIRCLE

So [Jesus] told us to form a circle, holding one another's hands, and himself stood in the middle and said, "Answer Amen to me." So he began to sing and to say . . .

> *Dance, all of you. . . .*
> *To the universe belongs the dancer.*
> *He who does not dance does not know what happens. . . .*
>
> *Now if you follow my dance, see yourself in me who am speaking,*
> *And when you have seen what I do, keep silence about my mysteries.*
>
> *I leaped: but do you understand the whole?*

—Acts of John, New Testament Apocrypha

Jerusalem: Early Spring, A.D. 32

MONDAY

◆ ◆

Pontius Pilate was in trouble, deep and serious trouble. But it seemed to him the most bitter of ironies that—for the first time in the seven years of his tenure as Roman *praefectus*, governor of Judea—the bloody Jews were not to blame.

He sat alone high above the city of Jerusalem, on the terrace of the palace built by Herod the Great, overlooking the western wall and the Jaffa Gate. Below, the setting sun turned the leaves of the pomegranate trees of the royal gardens to flame, highlighting Herod's legacy of golden cages filled with doves. Beyond the gardens the slope of Mount Zion was thick with blossoming acacias. But Pilate couldn't focus on his surroundings. In half an hour he would have to review the troops brought in to be quartered there in preparation for the week of the Jewish festival. Things always went wrong at these events, with so many pilgrims in town, and he dreaded a debacle like others they'd seen in the past. But that was far from the greatest of his problems.

For one holding so important a post, Pontius Pilate was a man of surprisingly humble beginnings. As his name implied, he was the descendant of former slaves, having somewhere an ancestor who'd been granted the *pileus*—the cap distinguishing a freed man who, through noble acts and personal endeavor, was made a citizen of the Roman Empire. Without education or advantage, but only through a combination of intelligence and hard work, Pontius Pilate had risen to join the ranks of the equestrian order in Rome, and was now a knight of the realm. But only when he'd had the great fortune to be discovered by Lucius Aelius Sejanus had Pilate's star, along with his patron's, soared like a meteor in the firmament.

These past six years—while the emperor Tiberius had been in

resplendent retreat, diverting himself on the isle of Capri (rumor had it that his sexual appetites ran to young boys, unweaned infants, and an exotic zoo of imported beasts)—Sejanus had become the most powerful, hated, and feared man in Rome. In his capacity as coconsul, with Tiberius, of the Roman senate, Sejanus was free to govern as he chose, arresting his enemies on trumped-up charges and extending control abroad by furthering his own candidates for foreign assignment—such as Pontius Pilate's appointment here in Judea. In a nutshell, that was Pontius Pilate's problem, for Lucius Aelius Sejanus had been killed.

Not only was Sejanus dead, he'd been executed for treason and conspiracy by order of Tiberius himself. He was accused of seducing the emperor's daughter-in-law, Livilla, who'd helped him poison her husband, Tiberius's only son. When the document from the emperor in Capri had been read aloud before the Roman senate last autumn, the ruthless, cold-blooded Sejanus—taken completely off guard by the betrayal—had crumpled and had to be helped from the chamber. That same night, by command of the Roman senate, Lucius Aelius Sejanus was strangled in prison. His lifeless body was stripped naked and tossed on the Capitol steps, where it remained three days for the amusement or retaliation of the Roman citizenry, who spat, urinated, and defecated upon it, stabbed it, turned their animals loose upon it, and finally threw it into the Tiber for the fish to finish whatever was left. But the end of Sejanus was not the end of the story.

All members of the Sejanus family were hunted down and destroyed—even his little daughter who, as a virgin, couldn't be put to death under Roman law. So the soldiers raped her first, then slashed her throat. Sejanus's estranged wife committed suicide; the complicitous Livilla was locked in a room and left to starve by her own family. And now, less than half a year after his death, any allies or colleagues of Sejanus not yet executed had committed suicide by taking poison or falling on their swords.

Pontius Pilate was not horrified by such acts. He knew the Romans intimately, though he would never be one of them. That was the error Sejanus had made: he'd wanted to be a noble Roman, to marry into the imperial family itself, to supplant their rule. Sejanus had believed his blood would enrich the blood of kings. Instead, it was enriching the silt of the river.

Pilate had no such delusions about his own immediate situation.

However qualified he might be for his position, however remote from Rome was this provincial outpost of Judea, he was deeply stained by his indebtedness to his late benefactor, and there were other associations linking them as well. Pilate's actions regarding the Jews, for instance, might be seen as patterned after those of Sejanus, who'd begun his own political career with purges of the Roman Jews and had ended it by banning Jews from Rome altogether—an order recently rescinded by imperial command. Tiberius protested that he'd never wanted intolerance toward any of his subjects, that it was all Sejanus's doing. This made Pontius Pilate extremely nervous, and with excellent cause. These past seven years, Pilate had often pitted himself against the Judean rabble he so loathed.

For a reason unclear to Pontius Pilate, the Jews, unlike other colonized peoples, remained all but exempt from Roman law—from service in the Roman armies and from nearly all forms of taxation, including those paid by Samaritans and even Roman citizens within these provinces. Under legislation by the Roman senate, a full Roman citizen could be put to death just for trespassing on the Jewish Temple Mount.

And when Pilate had to raise funds to complete the aqueduct, to bring lifeblood to these hinterlands, what had the damnable Jews done? They'd refused to pay the aqueduct levy, claiming it was the job of the Romans to provide for the people they'd conquered and enslaved. (Enslaved—that was amusing. How quickly they'd forgotten their sojourns in Egypt and Babylon.) So he'd "borrowed" the required funds from the temple tithe, finished the aqueduct, and that was the end of the whining. It was not the end of the Jews and their missives to Rome, but he'd prevailed. Of course, that was while Sejanus was still alive.

Now a new event was on the horizon. It was something that might save him, and turn the wrath of Tiberius, whose arm was long and grasp viselike when it came to retaliation against subordinates who'd lost his favor.

Pilate stood up and paced the terrace restlessly.

He had it on good advice from his authorities—that nest of spies and informers essential to the colonial governor of any subject people—that there was a Jew who was wandering about in the wilderness claiming, as so many of them did, to be the *inunctus*—the anointed one. This was the one the Greeks called *christos*, meaning covered with chrism, or oil, and whom the Jews called *mashiah*, which meant the same, as he understood it. This was a very ancient thing, he was told, in the history of their faith: that a person was coming, would suddenly arrive, that they believed fervently would deliver them from whatever bondage they thought they were in, and turn the entire world into a Jewish-ruled paradise. Of late, the desire to see this potential king anointed seemed to have reached fever pitch—and to Pontius Pilate, it was the blessing he'd been hoping for. It was the Jews themselves who would save him!

As the situation stood, the Sanhedrin, the Jewish council of elders, supported this new candidate, as did a vast discipleship from among the Essene colony, followers of that madman a few years back who'd gone about dipping people in water. Rumor had it he'd gotten himself executed by Herod Antipas, Jewish tetrarch of Galilee, for calling Antipas's wife Herodias a whore—that Antipas had beheaded the fellow at the request of his stepdaughter, Salome. Was there no end to the perfidy of these people? Antipas feared this new anointed one; he believed he was the reincarnation of the water-dipper he'd beheaded, returned to exact revenge against the tetrarch.

But there was a third contender in the game, placing Pilate in an even better position: the Jewish high priest Caiaphas, a puppet of Rome with a larger police force in Jerusalem than Pilate's, quite as dedicated to getting rid of rabble-rousers who were out to topple the Roman Empire and civilized governance. So Caiaphas and Antipas hated and feared this Jew, and the Sanhedrin and the bathers supported him. Better and better. When the fellow went, he would take them all down with him.

Pilate looked out over the plain beyond the western wall where the sun just now was setting. He heard the new troops assembling in the courtyard, as they did each festival. They would handle the overflow of pilgrims here to celebrate the spring equinox, which, as usual, the Jews insisted upon equating with their own unique experiences: in this case, the passing over of their houses by some spirit in Egypt more than a thousand years ago.

Pilate listened to the commands of the drill officer calling the new troops to order and putting them through their paces. He heard the sounds of their leather soles moving across the marble tiles of the courtyard below. At last Pilate turned to look over the terrace wall at the troops beneath, who squinted up at him—directly into the western sun blazing behind him like a fiery aura, so they could see only the vaguest outline of his form. He always chose this hour and this location for that very reason.

"Soldiers of Rome," he said, "you must be prepared for the week ahead, for the crowds that will enter this city on pilgrimage. You must be prepared to deal with any events that might place an undue burden on the empire. There are rumors of rabble-rousers whose goals are to turn what should be a peaceful festival into a riot, to bring down law and order. Soldiers of Rome, the week ahead may be a time when the actions of each of us will change the course of empire, perhaps even the course of history. Let us not forget that our first obligation is to prevent any act against the state or the *status quo* by those who wish, for reasons of religious fervor or for personal glory, to alter the fate of the Roman Empire—to change the course of our destiny."

◆ ◆

TUESDAY

It was not yet dawn when Joseph of Arimathea, bleary-eyed and exhausted from his journey, arrived at the edge of Jerusalem. In the darkness of his mind he could still hear the sounds of last night—the water lapping against the sides of the large ships, the oars dipped into water, the whispers across the surface of the moonless sea—as the small boat approached his merchant fleet that lay moored outside the port of Joppa, awaiting first light to enter the harbor.

Even before Nicodemus's messenger identified himself and boarded the ship, even before Joseph saw the note he had come all this way to deliver, he felt a sense of impending doom. It came as no surprise that the note was cryptic, to protect against its contents being seen and understood by others. But for Joseph it raised a thousand specters merely by what it did *not* say. Even now he could see the words before him:

Make haste. The hour is come. *Nicodemus*

The hour had come, it said. But how *could* it have come? Joseph had thought in anguish. It wasn't time!

Throwing judgment and caution to the winds, Joseph had roused his sleeping crew and given the command to cut his flagship loose from the others—right now, in the dead of night—and to bring this one ship, alone, into the port of Joppa.

His men had argued hotly against it, no doubt thinking him mad. And upon docking in port, Joseph had demonstrated further madness. Leaving the crew to secure his precious cargoes—an unheard-of act for the owner of so large a merchant fleet—he'd violated Roman curfew, storming through the streets, having servants awakened and his horses brought out and harnessed, and he'd headed off alone into the night. For the Sanhedrin, the Jewish council of elders, would meet at dawn. And when they did, he must be there.

On the dangerous roads of the backcountry—in the black silence broken only by the sounds of horses' hooves on broken stone, their hot lathered breathing, the cicadas' chirping in the distant groves—Joseph heard the silent thought whispered over and over in the depths of his own mind:

What had the Master done?

As Joseph of Arimathea entered the city, the first faint haze of red was bleeding into the sky above the Mount of Olives, picking out in silhouette the twisted shapes of the ancient olive trees. Hammering with his fists to rouse the stableman from bed, Joseph left his horses to be watered and groomed. Then he quickly went on foot, two steps at a time, up the flights of stone stairs to the upper city.

In the damp predawn darkness around him, he noticed the stirrings of the acacia trees in the early morning breeze. Their fragile boughs laden with blooms, these trees drowned Jerusalem each spring in a sea of rich gold. Arising from alcoves and archways, they seemed to permeate each pore of this labyrinthine city. Even now, as Joseph moved through the crooked alleyways and ascended the hill, he inhaled their dark perfume, like incense wafting from a censer, soaking into the shadowy crevices of the sleeping city and swirling in drunken pools around the base of Mount Zion.

Acacia: the sacred tree.

"Let them make me a sanctuary, that I may dwell among them," Joseph recited aloud.

Suddenly there was the tall, regal Nicodemus standing before him, and Joseph realized he had arrived already at the familiar gates of the park surrounding Nicodemus's palace. A servant was locking the gates behind him as Nicodemus, his mass of unbound hair swinging round his broad shoulders, threw open his arms to welcome his friend. Joseph warmly returned the embrace.

"When I was a boy in Arimathea," said Joseph, looking out over the sea of golden boughs, "all along the river there were embankments of *chittah*, which the Romans call *acacia* for their sharp thorns—the tree of which Yahweh instructed us to build his first tabernacle, the lattices and altar, the Holy of Holies, even the sacred ark itself. The Keltoi and Greeks hold it sacred just as we do. They call it 'the golden bough.' "

"You've remained far too long among pagans, my friend," Nicodemus said, shaking his head. "Even your appearance is nearly blasphemy in the eyes of God."

It was hard to deny, thought Joseph ruefully. With his short toga and high-laced sandals, his muscular, tanned limbs, his shaven face—the skin crackled and leathery from the burn of salt sea air—and his hair uncut in the prescribed fashion but braided up off his neck like a Norseman's, he knew he must look a good deal more like a Hyperborean Celt than what he actually was: a distinguished and respected Judean merchant and, like Nicodemus, an official council member of "the seventy," the common name for the Sanhedrin.

"You encouraged the Master, when he was still a boy, to follow these foreign ways that can only lead to destruction," Nicodemus pointed out as they started downhill. "Even so, the last few weeks I've prayed for your arrival before it's too late. For perhaps only you can undo the damage that's been done this past year in your absence."

It was true that Joseph had raised the young Master as his own child, ever since the boy's father—a carpenter also named Joseph—had died. He'd taken him abroad on many voyages to learn the ancient wisdom of the diverse cultures. Despite this parental role, Joseph of Arimathea, having by now attained the forty years required to sit in the Sanhedrin, was only seven years older than his surrogate son, whom he could not help but think of as *the* Master. Not just a *rabbi*, meaning *my* master or teacher, but as the great spiritual leader he'd become. Yet Nicodemus's comment was still unclear.

"Something I could undo? I came as soon as I could, upon receiving your note," Joseph assured him, dismissing the risks to his fortune and his neck. "But I assumed a political crisis—an emergency—some unforeseen incident that caused our plan to change. . . ."

Nicodemus stopped on the trail and regarded Joseph with his sad dark eyes that seemed to penetrate to the very depths—though today they were ringed red from exhaustion, perhaps from weeping. Joseph suddenly saw how much his friend had aged in the one short year of his absence. He put his hands on Nicodemus's shoulders and waited gravely, feeling the chill creeping upon him again, though the air was warming and balmy and the sky had turned from lavender to peach as the sun approached the rim. He wasn't sure he wanted to hear the answer.

"There is no political crisis," said Nicodemus, "at least, not yet. But something perhaps far worse has taken place; I suppose one might call it a crisis of faith. He himself is the crisis, you see. He has changed until you'd scarcely recognize him. Even his own mother doesn't understand it. No more do his closest disciples—the twelve he calls 'the magic circle.' "

"He has changed? Changed how?" said Joseph.

As Nicodemus searched for words, Joseph looked down over the city where the acacias stirred in the breeze like fingers, stroking him with rustling sighs. And he prayed—prayed for some kind of belief, for faith to brace him against what he sensed was about to come. Just as he felt a glimmer of hope, the sun burst over the Mount of Olives in an explosion of light, glittering from the facades of the villas and palaces that rose above them high on the hill of Mount Zion, penetrating even the twisted puzzlelike passageways of the lower city. Beyond, in the distance, lay the majestic outcropping of the Temple of Solomon and, beneath it, the Chamber of Hewn Stone where the Sanhedrin would meet this morning.

The temple had been conceived in a dream by Solomon's father, David, the first true king of Israel. Rebuilt or restored after any kind of disaster, embellished from the treasuries of many great kings, it was the soul of the Jewish people. Rising from a sea of open courtyards, its white marble pillars glowing like forests of ghost trees in the morning light, the temple shone from the valley like the sun. The shimmering roofs of pure gold tiles—the gift of Herod the Great—dazzled the eye at dawn, as now, and nearly blinded one with refracted light at high noon.

As this radiance filled Joseph's heart, though, he heard the voice of Nicodemus murmur in his ear.

"My dear Joseph, I can think of no other way to explain it. I think—we all fear—it seems likely that the Master has gone completely mad."

◆ ◆

The Chamber of Hewn Stone was always cold and damp. Water oozed from the walls and fed the lichen that grew there in iridescent colors. Carved from the very rock of the Temple Mount, the chamber formed an egg-shaped vault beneath the court of priests and the high altar, once the threshing floor of David. It was reached by a spiral stairway of thirty-three steps carved from the ancient rock. Joseph had always felt that entering this chamber was in itself a form of ritual initiation. In the days of summer its clammy chill came as a relief. But today, it only added to the presentiment of doom that had already settled in Joseph's spine at Nicodemus's words.

Though the council was commonly called "the seventy," there were actually seventy-one members when the high priest was counted, in keeping with the number of such councils since the time of Moses.

The corpulent high priest Joseph Caiaphas, swathed in his purple prayer shawl and yellow robe, descended the stairs first. Upon his staff was an opulent pineapple of pure gold, symbolizing life, fertility, and the rejuvenation of the people. As all high priests before him, Caiaphas was official president of the Sanhedrin by virtue of his religious stature, which meant his legal stature as well, for law and Torah were one.

From ancient times, high priests had descended from the line of Sadducees—Sons of Zadok, the original high priest of King Solomon. But after Roman occupation, the first act of the Roman-appointed puppet king Herod the Great had been to execute the scions of many princely families, replacing them in the Sanhedrin with his own appointees. This house-sweeping had significantly improved the situation of the Pharisees, the more liberal and populist party comprised of Torah scholars and scribes, the party of both Nicodemus and Joseph.

The Pharisees controlled the majority vote, so the leader of their party, Gamaliel, grandson of the legendary *rabb* Hillel, was effectively leader of the Sanhedrin, a bitter thorn to Joseph Caiaphas. The Pharisees couldn't refrain from pointing out that Caiaphas had attained his position neither by birth, like the Sadducee aristocracy, nor by learning, like the Pharisees, but by marrying the daughter of a *nasi*, a prince.

There was one individual the high priest hated more than a Pharisee, thought Joseph with foreboding as he followed his companions down the stone stairway into the chamber. That person was the Master himself. These past three years Caiaphas had kept his temple police busy, like a dog pack, sniffing out the Master's every move. He'd tried to have the Master arrested for agitation, after that business of overturning the tables in the temple courtyard where, for generations, the family of Joseph Caiaphas had held the lucrative dove concession. Indeed, it was the wealth he'd raked in from the sale of sacrifices during holy days and pilgrimages that had paid for Caiaphas's current sinecure and the dowry of the Jewish princess he'd married.

When all the seventy-one had filed down the spiral stair and taken their seats, the high priest Caiaphas gave the blessing and stepped aside as the noble *rabb* Gamaliel, his long hair and rich robes billowing about him, came forward to open the council meeting.

"A grave assignment has been given us by God," Gamaliel intoned in his dramatic voice, rich with the resonance of a bell. "Whatever our mission, whatever our desire, and whatever the outcome of today's gathering, I feel I speak for all of us when I say that no one will leave this room with a feeling of complete satisfaction, in this sorry case of Jesua ben Joseph of Nazareth. Because our burden is a heavy one, I should like to begin with a more inspiring topic. There has just returned to us, as you see, the most wandering of all our nomadic brethren—Joseph of Arimathea."

The men at the table turned to gaze at Joseph. Many nodded in his direction.

Gamaliel continued, "One year ago today Joseph of Arimathea agreed, upon private assignment from the tetrarch of Galilee, Herod Antipas, and myself, to attempt a secret mission to Rome in behalf of the descendants of Israel. This mission was to be embedded within his ordinary travel plans, his merchant fleet engaging in trade as usual in Britannia, Iberia, and Greece. But when the order was given for the expulsion of Jews from Rome, we asked Joseph instead to go directly to Capri—"

No sooner had Gamaliel mentioned Capri than a buzzing of whispers was set up, as the council members turned with excitement to their neighbors.

"I will not keep you in suspense, for most of you have guessed what I am about to say. Through the instrumental assistance of the emperor's nephew Claudius, who's known the Herods well from early times, Joseph of Arimathea secured a meeting with the emperor Tiberius at his palace on Capri. During this meeting, and aided greatly by the timely death of Lucius Sejanus, Joseph of Arimathea was able to persuade the emperor of the wisdom of approving the return of the Jews to Rome."

There was an unusual outburst of pounding on the table, and a few hearty squeezes of Joseph's arms from those seated nearby, including Nicodemus. All the council members had heard months ago of the favorable Roman edict. But until now, with Joseph returned safely from his voyages, his personal involvement had remained a closely held secret.

"I realize my request will seem rather unusual," Gamaliel continued, "but as Joseph of Arimathea has performed us so great a service, and in view of the unique nature of his relationship with Jesua ben Joseph of Nazareth, I should like to begin by asking how *he* would like this meeting to proceed. Joseph is the only one among us here today who may be unaware of all the circumstances that have led up to the crisis."

He did not glance at the high priest Caiaphas, who was scowling behind his back at this change in procedural policy. But the others were nodding their heads in assent, so Joseph replied.

"I thank you all warmly, from my heart. I've just arrived this morning before dawn, and as we sit here, my fleet will not yet have completed entry into port, nor have I had time to sleep or bathe or dress. That is the urgency with which I approach the matter before us. Indeed, I've had no time to learn what *is* the matter before us, only that Jesua, the Master—whom, as many of you know, I regard as my entire family—is in some deep and serious plight involving us all."

"Then we must tell you the story," said Gamaliel, "and each of us must speak out in turn, for most of us have had a share in a part but not all. And the telling shall begin with me."

◆ ◆

THE TALE OF THE MASTER

He arrived alone last autumn in Jerusalem, at the Festival of Tabernacles. It came as a shock to everyone who knew him. The disciples had asked him three times to come down with them from Galilee, to spread the word of God as he did at all holy events, and to perform healings for the festival crowds. He refused thrice, and sent them off without him. But then he came down secretly by himself, arriving suddenly, unexpectedly, in the outer courts of the temple. He seemed strange and mysterious, not at all like himself—as if following some inner pattern of his own.

The Festival of Tabernacles during the autumn equinox, celebrating that first tabernacle of acacia boughs ordained by God in our exodus from Egypt, also commemorates the crude tabernacles or tents constructed in the wilderness and lived in during that pilgrimage. At the festival last autumn, each garden, court, and private park in Jerusalem was filled as always with hastily improvised tents of boughs festooned with flowers, through which the stars can shine, breezes blow, and rain sprinkle upon our families and visitors that live and feast all week, until the festival ends with the last chapter of Torah, the death of Moses, being read aloud in the temple to mark the end of an old cycle, just as Moses' death did for our people.

At the close of the eighth night feast, when the host rises from dinner in each court or garden, the prayer he recites is the oldest in haggadic tradition, older than the festival itself. What does he pray for? He asks one favor from God for having "lived in a booth" for a week: that next year, he might be counted worthy to sit in the booth of Leviathan. And what does the booth of Leviathan signify? The coming of a new age, the age of the messianic kingdom that begins with the appearance of a *mashiah*, an anointed one who will defeat the sea beast, using its hide for the booth of the righteous and its flesh for the messianic banquet. He will release us from bondage, unite us under one kingdom, bring back the ark and glorify the temple like David and Solomon. As the natural successor of these mighty princes, he'll lead the Chosen People to glory and bring about the golden dawn—not just of a new year, but of a new aeon.

As you see, it could therefore be no accident that the Master came down from Galilee, alone, to attend this specific festival.

◆ ◆

It was in the garden of Nicodemus that he appeared that eighth night, for the Simchath Torah. Nicodemus's park was large and well stocked with trees. As always on this occasion, there were many tents of boughs and flowers, and torches illuminated the feast so the gates might remain open for pilgrims and others to drop in.

At the end of the feast, when Nicodemus stood to give the blessing and ask for the honor, next year at this time, to sit in the tent of the sea beast, the Master himself arose from his seat in one of the booths not far away. In his flowing white robes, his hair whirling wildly around him, he crossed to where Nicodemus was standing and, sweeping the platters and goblets to one side, he climbed onto the low brass table.

He held up an urn of water and, holding on to the branches of the bower with the other hand to steady himself, he began to pour water everywhere—on the table, on the ground—splashing the guests still reclining there, who leapt to their feet in alarm. Everyone was amazed or flustered; no one knew what he meant by this action, or could even imagine. Then the Master tossed down the urn. His arms aloft, he cried,

"I am the water! I pour myself out for you; whoever thirsts should come and drink from me! If you believe in me, rivers of living water will flow from you. . . ."

And, as it was recalled afterward by those present, his voice was so rich, his command of words so inspiring, that it wasn't until later that they realized no one had the vaguest clue what he was talking about.

As the supper was adjourning and people drifted from the gates of his grounds, Nicodemus happened to overhear a conversation among a few of his fellow Pharisees. A clandestine council had been hastily called for later that night at Caiaphas's palace across town. Nicodemus, though uninvited himself, resolved to attend, for it was clear that even the Master's strongest supporters had been shaken and confused by his strange performance.

The next morning, Nicodemus went early to the temple court seeking the Master before others found him. He wanted to protect him from whatever he might do or say, for his words were often misconstrued even by his own disciples. The previous night, despite heated objections by Nicodemus and others—even by his own temple police—Caiaphas had insisted that some pretext be created to secure the Master's arrest as soon as he appeared in the morning.

The Master arrived just after Nicodemus. He was wearing the same white robes as before. No sooner had he entered the temple court than a large circle formed about him—including many of those from the secret meeting. This time they were more prepared. At the prompting of Caiaphas, today they'd brought an adulteress with them. They shoved her before the Master and asked whether *he* thought they should stone her, as the law, of course, required. This was a trap: it was well known that—like Hillel, who was liberal about marriage rulings, especially with respect to women—the Master believed in forgiveness when there was repentance of such sins.

But to the astonishment of all, the Master said absolutely nothing. Instead, he squatted in the dirt in silence and started to draw pictures in the dust with his fingertip as if he hadn't heard a word. By then, a real crowd had begun to form around him to see what he would do and to jeer at the woman, whom they held just before him like a dangling piece of meat on a hook.

When they'd pestered him for what seemed a very long time, he stood up and looked around at the crowd in silence—deep into each pair of eyes, as if in final judgment on each person's individual soul. At last he spoke.

"He who is without sin among you," he told them, "then let him cast the first stone at her."

Again he squatted in the dust without a word and drew pictures with his finger. After a very long while, he glanced up and saw the woman standing there before him. She was all alone.

"Go, and sin no more," he told her.

With those words Nicodemus, who had observed all this from afar, understood the importance of what the Master had done. He had risked his life for a woman he knew to be guilty as accused, for he'd said "no *more*." The Master had forced each person present to judge himself—including the woman, for she too would have to recognize the magnitude of what had been done in her behalf.

When the woman departed and the Master was left there alone, Nicodemus came up to stand beside him as he still drew with his finger in the dust. Nicodemus was curious to see what the Master drew. He looked down, and there in the dust was drawn a kind of knot—a very complex knot, for one couldn't make out the beginning or the end; it just seemed to go round and round.

The Master sensed Nicodemus's presence and arose from the dust. With his foot he scraped out the image he'd drawn. When Nicodemus broached the topic of the risk taken by the Master in coming down alone from Galilee with no warning, the Master smiled and said only,

"My dear Nicodemus, do I seem alone to you? But I'm not: I came here with my Father. Don't forget, the *shofar* blows also in Galilee."

This of course referred to the Day of Atonement the week before while the Master was still in Galilee, when the ram's horn was blown as it was each year-end, signaling all men to reflect in the coming year on how they might act more in keeping with God's will. But it was the casual way the Master mentioned this age-old tradition that gave Nicodemus the uncomfortable feeling that it might have taken on fresh meaning within the Master's feverishly active and fertile mind. What was he really up to?

Before Nicodemus could pursue the matter, the Master headed off briskly to the court of the money changers just within the temple precincts. Nicodemus had to puff to catch up with him. There, those who'd taunted the Master outside surrounded him again—as he might have expected and seemed to want—accusing him of bearing false witness. And that was when he did it, the thing that started the rumor he might be mad.

When these men said they were descended from Abraham's seed and didn't require the Master to give them all this guidance he loved to hand out, and particularly they didn't like his pretentious claims that he was the messiah and heir to the Davidian branch, the Master had the audacity to say he knew Abraham personally. Furthermore, he told them, when Abraham had heard of the Master's mission here on earth, he'd rejoiced. They said the Master hardly was old enough to know a man who'd been dead, like Abraham, for thousands of years. The Master silenced them with a look. Then he told them that God Himself had introduced them, personally! He said that he, the Master, was himself the son of God—the flesh of God! But this was not the end. He told them, and many here in the chamber were present to witness it:

"I and my Father are one. Before Abraham was . . . *I am!*" He used the sacred name to describe himself, a blasphemous act worth a lashing or even a stoning.

But that was only the beginning. Just three months ago, long after the festival, the Master was called to Bethany, to the home of young Lazarus, brother of Miriam and Martha of Magdali, among the Master's closest disciples. The boy was gravely ill and longed to see him before he died. But according even to the twelve, the Master behaved badly, refusing to go down from Galilee and see the family although the situation was critical and the women begged him to try to heal the boy, to save him from certain death. By the time he finally came, the child had been dead for three days. Miriam told them that the corpse was rotted and stinking, and she and her sister refused to grant the Master the access he requested to the crypt.

So he stood outside. He stood outside and called to Lazarus—young, dead Lazarus—until he raised him. He raised him from the tomb of his fathers. He raised him in his decaying condition, wrapped in the rotted burial cloths with maggots already working on the corpse. He raised him from the dead.

◆ ◆

"Dear God," whispered Joseph of Arimathea when this tale was over. As he stared at the others around the table with glazed eyes, he couldn't bring himself to speak. What could he possibly say? The Sadducees preached that death was simply the end of life; the Pharisees taught that for the good man, for the life well lived, there could be the reward of eternal life in heaven. But *nobody* believed in the concept of resurrection, of bringing a rotted corpse from the grave back to existence on earth. It was a horror beyond imagining.

Many of those around the table, seeing Joseph's consternation, tried to avoid his gaze. But the high priest Caiaphas, who'd contributed nothing to the story told by the others, now interjected a thought of his own.

"It would seem your nephew, our beloved Jesua ben Joseph of Nazareth, son of a humble carpenter, has developed delusions of grandeur, my dear Joseph," he said in his annoyingly unctuous voice. "Instead of being the leader—the teacher, the *rabb* or master, the anointed king or whatever it was—that our companions here had hoped for, it seems he's degenerated into a madman who thinks he's genealogically descended from the one true God and can decide who shall live or die. I wonder how such an idea could have arisen in his confused brain?" He looked at Joseph with a sneering smile.

Joseph knew full well that many there, though silent, must share the high priest's opinion. For God was ineffable and intangible: He could not be incarnate. How could this have happened? thought Joseph. In one short year, his world had turned inside out.

Joseph had to see the Master in person, at once. He knew him better than anyone—he always believed that he alone could see the purity of his soul. He had to see him before the others, before it was too late.

◆ ◆

FRIDAY

Joseph's own beautiful but wildly overrun estate on the Mount of Olives, which he rarely saw these days, owing to his travels, was called Gethsemane. He felt certain the Master would not take his disciples to Gethsemane, nor even go alone, without Joseph's permission. So there was only one place he would stay in that part of the hill country, and that was in the town of Bethany—at the home of Lazarus of Magdali and his sisters, Miriam and Martha.

At the very thought of the sisters of Magdali, Joseph always had to grapple with difficult emotions. Miriam of Magdali, or Maria as the Romans called her, brought back to him all the failures of his life, as a Jew and as a man. He loved her—there could be no question of that—and in every sense, he loved her as a man should love a woman. Though at forty he was old enough to be her father, if he had his way he would fulfill his infernal Jewish responsibility to God and litter the earth with the fruits of his seed—as Nicodemus might put it.

But Miriam loved another. And only Joseph of Arimathea knew for certain, though many certainly suspected, that the object of her love was the Master. Joseph could not fault her for that, for he loved him too. Which was why he had never declared himself openly to her. Nor would he, for as long as the Master lived. But he did send a messenger to Bethany to invite himself to dinner.

The Master would come down from Galilee on Thursday, and a

formal dinner and a light supper were prepared for Friday when, according to Martha's confidential reply, the Master would have something important to announce. Since the Master had raised the young head of the household from the grave upon his last visit, Joseph wondered with a kind of dark humor what he planned to do to follow that performance.

On Friday morning Joseph drove out to Bethany, a few miles beyond Gethsemane. When he pulled up below the house, he saw the vision—or rather an apparition in white—coming down the hill with open arms. It was the Master, but he seemed somehow transformed. He was surrounded by as many as a hundred people, as usual most of them female, all dressed also in white and bearing armloads of flowers, and singing a strange but haunting chant.

Joseph sat speechless in his cart. When the Master came up to him, his robes flowing like water over his limbs, he looked into Joseph's eyes and smiled. Joseph saw him, just in that instant, as the little child he once had been.

"Beloved Joseph," said the Master, taking him by the hands and drawing him from the cart, "how I have thirsted for you."

Then, instead of embracing him, the Master ran his hands up Joseph's arms, across his shoulders, over his face, as if examining an animal, or committing his features to memory to execute a pagan sculpture. Joseph scarcely knew what to think. And yet—he felt a kind of warm tingling deep beneath the skin, down in his flesh, his bones, as if some physical action were taking place. He drew away uncomfortably.

The chanting people drifting about them were annoying to Joseph, who recognized none of them and longed to draw the Master away. As if he had grasped his thoughts, the Master said,

"Will you stay with me, Joseph?"

"For dinner, you mean, and the night?" said Joseph. "Yes, it's all been arranged by Martha. And I'll stay for as long as you like; we really must speak."

"I mean, will you stay with me," the Master repeated in a tone Joseph couldn't identify.

"Stay with you?" said Joseph. "Why, yes, you know I'll always be with you. That's why we must—"

"Will you stay with me, Joseph?" the Master asked again, almost as if repeating a mnemonic phrase. Though he was still smiling, a part of him seemed to be looking off into a deep distance. Joseph felt a horrible chill.

"We must go indoors," he said quickly. "We haven't seen each other for a very long time; we have much to discuss in private."

Shooing away the others, he ushered the Master up the path to the house. He would send someone down to tend to the horses. They reached the portico of the large and rambling stone building.

As Joseph entered the dark recesses of the courtyard with its tree-shaded pool, he took the Master by the arm. His attention focused for a moment as his fingertips touched the cool linen sleeve—that new white garment he recalled having been mentioned by Nicodemus and several others. Joseph, as a knowledgeable importer of foreign wares, could recognize by touch that this was not the world-famous but affordable linen of Galilee, the production of which had built the fortunes of the Magdali family and so many other Galileans. Rather it was the far costlier Pelusian linen of northern Egypt—one might almost say precious, for its cost rivaled that of another fabric also made by some mysterious secret process: Chinese silk, a fabric sufficiently rare that in Rome it was forbidden to be worn by any but the imperial family. How on earth had the Master come by such a treasure? Stranger still, given his message of renouncing the trappings of worldly wealth, why had he kept the garment instead of selling it and giving the money to the poor, which had always been his policy even with far less extravagant gifts?

They found Martha, the older sister, her braided hair covered by a cloth, her neck damp from perspiration, bustling among the servants around the clay hearths at the back of the house.

"I'm making a real feast-offering for today," Martha said proudly as the two men came to embrace her, carefully picking their way among servants bearing food-laden platters. "Pickled fish in wine," she went on, "breads and gravies, chicken broth, roasted lamb, and the first spring vegetables and herbs from here in our garden. I've been cooking for days! Since the Master, as usual, has adopted this visiting crowd, I've had to prepare more food than planned. Though Pesach isn't until next week, this is a special thanks offering from our family—not only for your safe return from the sea, Joseph, but also in gratitude for the miracle that the Master's faith brought about only three months ago, as I'm sure you've heard, with respect to our young Lazarus."

Martha beamed upon the Master with familiar affection, and seemed to notice nothing amiss. In surprise Joseph glanced at him too, and indeed the former feeling of otherworldliness had vanished. In its place was that warm compassion that Joseph had always felt went far to explain the powerful and tremendous following the Master had acquired within the very short period of his ministry. The Master seemed to possess a knowledge of every dark secret buried within one's bosom, but with it the ability to forgive and absolve all.

"Dear Joseph," the Master was saying, smiling as if about to share some private jest, "please do not believe a word this woman has told you! It was her own faith and that of her sister that brought young Lazarus from the earth. I assisted in the delivery as a midwife might, but God alone performs the miracles of birth and rebirth, whether from womb or tomb. And only for those who have true faith."

"Our brother Lazarus can share his experience with you himself," Martha assured Joseph. "He is out on the terrace now, with the other guests."

"And Miriam?" asked Joseph.

"You really should do something about her, Master," Martha said, working herself into a small fit. "She's been cavorting all morning on the mountain with you and the others; and now she's in the orchard with the disciples and their families from out of town. She's only interested in philosophical chitchat, while life goes on and reality is tossed like a saddle over the shoulders of us beasts of burden. She needs your reprimand."

The Master held Martha away to look at her, and when he spoke it was with an urgency, a passionate intensity, that Joseph found positively dizzying.

"I *love* Miriam," the Master told her sister in a tone that sounded more angry than loving. "I love her more than my mother, more than I love Joseph here, who raised me. I love her more than any of my brothers, even those who've been with me from the very beginning. There is a bond, a *knot*, that links the understanding of Miriam and myself, which must be strong enough to transcend anything—even death. Do you imagine that Miriam's importance will be increased by helping you cook a meal, even if for a thousand, rather than by sitting at my feet for one more hour while you have me with you?"

Joseph was astounded at the Master's cruelty. How could he upbraid a woman who'd just exalted him to the skies for saving her brother's life, and who'd spent three days cooking for him, his disciples, and a hundred uninvited guests?

Joseph saw Martha's chin tremble and her face begin to crumple. But as he started forward to intercede, the Master changed again. As Martha was trying to cover her teary face with her hands, the Master seized her wrists, bowed his head, and kissed her upturned palms, which were still covered with pastry dough and flour. Then, folding her once again into his arms, he kissed Martha's head and rocked her gently, until she seemed to relax and the tears subsided. Then the Master held her away and looked at her.

"Miriam has chosen the right path, Martha," he said softly. "Let each of us give according to our own capacity. Never ask that anyone be chastised for doing the Father's will." Then, before Joseph knew what was happening, the Master took him by the arm and slipped outside to the terrace.

Below in the walled gardens, the invited guests were milling about where tables, carpets, and other arrangements had been set up for them beneath the grape arbors that led to the orchard. Beyond the gardens were weathered stone walls upon which uninvited but welcome guests could dine in shade beside a small creek.

Beneath the grape bowers where the first vine shoots were just unfurling, Joseph saw the fishermen down from Galilee: Andrew and his brother Simon huddled whispering together with their partners, Johan and James Zebedee, whom he called "thunder and lightning" for their impetuous, stormy personalities. Nearby was young John Mark, who'd come out for today's feast from his mother's house at Jerusalem.

It frightened Joseph to see so many of the important disciples and their families gathered together in one place. Especially here in Judea, where they were now under Roman jurisdiction and within reach of Caiaphas. If they intended to stay longer, he must move them to his estate of Gethsemane, where he always had servants securing his property.

Shaking these thoughts aside, he stopped the Master and drew him within the shelter of the grape trellises before the others beneath could notice them.

"My beloved son," said Joseph softly, "you've altered so in the one short year of my absence that I don't know you anymore."

The Master turned his gaze to Joseph. His opalescent eyes, that strange mixture of brown and green and gold, had always been unreal to Joseph. They were the eyes of one accustomed to other, fantastical worlds.

"*I* have not changed," the Master said sadly, with a smile. "It is the world itself that's changing, Joseph. In such times of change, though, we must all focus upon the one thing that's unchanging and imperishable. The day is now dawning that has been foretold since the time of Enoch, Elijah, Jeremiah. And just as I helped bring young Lazarus from the grave, it's now our task to deliver the world into this new age: that's why I'm here. I hope you will join me, all of you. I hope you will stay with me. Though you needn't all follow me to where I must go."

Joseph didn't understand this last remark, but he pressed on.

"We're all concerned about you, Jesua. Please listen. My fellow Sanhedrin members told me of your coming down from Galilee during the festival last fall. Jesua, you know that the Sanhedrin is your strongest supporter. I thought it was all arranged when I departed last year, that they would anoint you at the festival this coming autumn. They planned to anoint you themselves as *mashiah*—as our chosen king and spiritual leader! Why have you changed it all? Why are you trying to overturn all that was planned by so many wise men for so long?"

The Master rubbed his hand across his eyes. "The Sanhedrin is *not* my strongest supporter, Joseph," he said. His voice sounded weary. "My Father in heaven is my strongest supporter; I do His bidding alone. If His ideas happen to conflict with those of the Sanhedrin, I'm afraid they'll have to take the matter up with Him." Then he gave Joseph that same wry smile and added, "And as for what's unchanging and imperishable—it's a knotty problem."

The Master liked to hide secrets in riddles, and Joseph had noticed his constant reference to knots. Joseph was about to pursue that topic when the veil of vine tendrils surrounding them parted and Miriam was there before them, smiling the warm, sensual smile that always made Joseph weak with emotion.

Her richly abundant hair, in a rainbow of colors, tumbled loose about her shoulders with the suggestion of wild wantonness that had driven the elders—and even many of the disciples—to consider her a politically costly and unnecessarily dangerous bauble within the Master's entourage. Joseph thought there was something primal about her, like a force of nature. She was like that ancient Lilith whom the oldest of Hebrew texts called Adam's first wife: a ripe fruit that spilled forth life, withholding nothing.

"Joseph of Arimathea!" she cried, and flung herself into his arms in an enthusiastic embrace. "We've all missed you, but I have longed for you most of all." She drew back to look at him gravely with those large grey eyes beneath a thick canopy of lashes. "The Master and I have discussed it often. When you're here, there's never any bickering or whining or complaining. You sweep it all away and make everything seem so simple."

"I wish I understood what it is that's changed since my departure, for something surely has," Joseph told her. "There was never any bickering in the past."

"No doubt *he* has told you that nothing has changed?" Miriam asked Joseph, glancing at the Master in mock irritation. "Everything's going along nicely, thank you—was that what he said? Not so; he's been in hiding for months, even from his own followers. And all so that he can make a triumphant entry into the city at Pesach next Sunday, surrounded by—"

"You'll not go into Jerusalem now, as things stand?" Joseph asked the Master, alarmed. "I don't think it's wise. The Sanhedrin will surely refuse to anoint you next autumn if you stir things up more now at the Passover."

The Master put one arm around Joseph and the other around Miriam, and drew them close to him as if they were his children.

"I cannot wait until autumn. My time has come," the Master said simply. Then, pressing Joseph lightly, he whispered in his ear, "Stay with me, Joseph."

◆ ◆

As the sun was setting, the mobs of followers went over the hill peaceably, leaving behind in the gardens and orchards a snowy carpet of strewn flower petals.

As darkness descended, Martha lit fires in the clay oil lamps on the terrace and the servants set out a light supper before retiring for the night. The twelve were there, and young Lazarus, who looked pale and wan and had hardly spoken all day, and a few older women, and the sisters themselves. The Master's mother had sent her regrets, saying she could only come down from Galilee at the end of the Pesach.

When this small group was seated in the flickering light, the Master had given thanks, and all were breaking bread over generous helpings of hot soup, Miriam stood and picked up a beautifully carved stone box that rested beside her at the table. She went to where Joseph sat near the Master and asked him to hold the box for her. Then without a word she opened the lid and dug both her hands deep inside as the others at the table stopped speaking and looked up at her form where she hovered there, like an angel of doom or prophecy, in the firelight.

As she withdrew her full hands, at once the terrace and vineyard and gardens were saturated with a cloud of the overwhelmingly voluptuous aroma of spikenard. The ointment, as Joseph knew, was extravagantly dear. Hefting fistfuls of rubies and gold would have been less prodigal.

One by one the diners understood what was about to happen. Simon pushed away his meal and struggled to rise from his place; James and Johan Zebedee reached out to try to stop her; Judas leapt to his feet—but they were all too late.

Joseph held the alabaster box and watched in amazement as Miriam, her face almost beatifically beautiful in this light, let the liquid ointment pour from her cupped hands over the Master's head, where it trickled down his face and neck into his robes: the traditional, sacred rite of anointing a king. Then she knelt before the Master. She gestured to Joseph for the box and, pulling free the Master's sandals, she took another double handful, again worth a king's bejeweled crown, and poured the liquid over his naked feet. In a gesture of complete submission and adoration, she tossed forward her magnificent silken tresses and, using them as a cloth, she wiped the Master's feet.

Joseph and the others sat frozen in shock at this strange and horrid travesty—an almost sexual inversion of the time-honored ritual of anointment, but here conducted without the authority of priest or state, and on profane ground. And by a woman!

Judas, the first to speak, expressed a mild version of what was felt by all: that above and beyond the rest, there was the horror of throwing away, with such abandon, a complete fortune in rare ointment. "We might have sold that ointment to aid the poor!" he cried, his face black with anger.

Joseph turned to the Master, trying to understand.

In the firelight, the Master's eyes glittered dark green. He was looking at Miriam, who knelt on the ground just beside Joseph's knee. He was looking at her as if he would never have the chance to regard her again, as if he were committing her features to memory.

"Why are you so concerned about the poor, Judas?" the Master said, never taking his eyes from Miriam. "The poor, you will always have with you. But me—you have not always."

Again Joseph felt that awful chill. He felt helpless sitting beside the Master, ineffectually holding the ointment box. But as if he'd read Joseph's thoughts, the Master turned to him.

"Miriam will explain later what you need to know," he told Joseph in a low voice, his lips hardly moving. "But for now, I want you to procure an animal for me to ride into Jerusalem next Sunday."

"I beg of you, do not go forward with this ill-advised scheme," Joseph whispered urgently. "It is dangerous—and not only that, it's downright unholy. You profane the prophecies. Though I love Miriam, I must point out that no king of Judea has ever been anointed on profane ground, nor by the hand of a woman!"

"I am not come here to be king of Judea, my beloved Joseph. I have another kingdom—and, as you've seen, I've another method of anointment as well. But I have also another request of you, my friend. By the time of the Pesach supper, many will be searching for me. It is dangerous to reveal where we will meet for that night's meal. You must come to the temple, and bring the others with you. There, near the marketplace, you will see a man bearing a pitcher of water. Follow him."

"Those are your only instructions? That we come to a place and follow an unknown person?" said Joseph.

"Follow the water-bearer," said the Master, "and all will happen as planned."

◆ ◆

SATURDAY

It was just after midnight when it happened. Caiaphas would never forget the moment when they came to awaken him, the knock on his chamber door as he stirred beneath the bedclothes, wondering what time it was. The sensation he felt then was one he'd heard of but had never before experienced: the hair actually rose up on the back of his spine! He knew something dangerous and exciting was about to happen. He knew, without being able to name it, that it was what he had been waiting for all along.

The temple police, who guarded the high priest's palace and his person, too, stood outside his chamber door and told him that a man had come to the palace gates—here, in a secured quarter of the town, and now, in the dead of night, hours after the Roman curfew was in effect—asking to see him. It was a darkly handsome man, they said, strong, with a craggy face and heavy brow. He refused to speak with any but the high priest Caiaphas, on a very private matter of utmost urgency. He had no credentials, no appointment, and no explanation for his visit, and the temple police knew that it was their duty to arrest and interrogate the man or send him away. Yet they somehow hesitated to do either.

Caiaphas knew, deep in his soul, that he need not ask further questions. As one betrayer understands another, Joseph Caiaphas understood that he had known this man always, perhaps through all eternity.

His servant wrapped him in the cocoonlike folds of his lush green dressing gown and, followed by the temple guard, he padded along the stone corridors in silence toward the chamber where the stranger awaited him. Caiaphas knew in his private thoughts that this was the moment of destiny. He knew that his hour had come.

But later, when he was asked about that night—interrogated, really, by the Romans and the Sanhedrin—it was odd, for that was all he could recall. His awakening in the dead of night, that march down the long hall—and the sense of personal destiny, which he never mentioned, of course, for it was nobody's affair but his own. The stranger himself, the encounter, was just a blur to Caiaphas, as though his mind had been clouded with drink.

After all, why *should* he recall him, when they'd met only for a moment, just that one night? The police took care of the rest: they paid out thirty pieces of silver for the job. How could Caiaphas be expected, so long afterward, to remember his name? Some fellow from Dar-es-Keriot, he believed, though he wasn't even sure of that. In the larger perspective, thought Caiaphas, in the great tapestry that was history, what difference did it make? Only the moment was important.

Two thousand years from now, their names would be like specks of dust blowing across a vast plain. In two thousand years, no one would remember any of this at all.

◆ ◆

SUNDAY

Tiberius Claudius Nero Caesar could see in the dark.

Now, as he stood in the black night on the parapet, a night without moon or stars, he could still see clearly the clean lines and veins of his own strong hands resting on the parapet wall. His large dark eyes surveyed the sea; he could make out whitecaps all the way to the Bay of Napoli, where the coastline lay in inky darkness.

He had been able to do so practically since infancy, and was thus able to help his mother escape, across meadows and mountains and through a raging forest fire that licked so close it singed her hair, when the troops of Gaius Octavian were pursuing her, trying to catch her so that Octavian could seduce her. Then Octavian became Augustus, the first emperor of Rome. So Tiberius's mother divorced his father, a *quaestor* who had been commander of Julius Caesar's triumphant Alexandrian fleet. And she became Rome's first empress.

That was Livia, a remarkable woman, key sponsor of the *pax romana*, honored by the vestal virgins and thought of as a treasure by nearly everyone in the empire. Herod Antipas built a city named for her up in Galilee, and it had been proposed several times that she receive the status of an immortal, as had been decreed for Augustus.

But Livia, at last, was dead. And thanks to her, Tiberius was emperor—since, to further her son's ambitions, she'd poisoned every legitimate heir standing between himself and the throne. Including, it was privately rumored, even the divine Augustus. Or perhaps one should say, to further *her* ambitions, which had been plentiful. Tiberius wondered whether Livia—wherever she happened to be now—could also see in the dark.

He remembered when he'd stood here at this very spot, only last year, through most of the night, awaiting the bonfires he'd arranged for them to light at Vesuvius on the mainland as soon as it was certain in Rome that Sejanus was dead.

He smiled to himself, a bitter smile full of deep and unending hatred for the one who'd pretended to be his best and only friend. The one who had betrayed him in the end, just as all the others had done.

It seemed a thousand years ago that Tiberius had stood on that other parapet of his first self-imposed exile—in Rhodes, where he'd fled from his slut of a wife Julia, Augustus's daughter, whom he'd been forced to divorce his beloved Vipsania to marry. The week Augustus banished Julia herself and wrote to beg his son-in-law to return to Rome, an omen was seen: an eagle, a bird never previously sighted at Rhodes, perched on the roof of his house. By this, the astrologer Thrasyllus correctly predicted Tiberius would succeed to the throne.

Tiberius believed that the world was ruled by fate, that destiny could be learned through astrology, omens, or the traditional methods of divination, reading bones or bowels. Since our destinies were foredrawn, in vain were any supplications to the gods, appeasement by sacrifice or by the costly erection of public temples and monuments.

Of no avail were doctors, either. At the age of seventy-four, having received no treatment or medication since the age of thirty, Tiberius was strong as a bull, well proportioned and handsome, with the skin tone of a young athlete. He could poke through a fresh, crisp apple with any finger of either hand. And it was claimed that in his military days in Germany he'd actually killed men that way. He had been, indeed, a great soldier and a statesman par excellence—at least at first.

But those days were over. The omens had altered, and not in his favor. He could never return to Rome. Only a year before the Sejanus affair Tiberius had attempted to sail up the Tiber—but his small pet snake, Claudia, whom he carried in his bosom and fed from his own hand, had been found one morning on the deck, half eaten by ants. And the omens said: Beware the mob.

Now he stood each night on this high cliff of his palace, on the overgrown rock whose very history lay steeped in antiquity and mystery. It was named Capri: the goat. Some thought it was called so for Pan, half man, half goat, fathered on a water nymph by the god Hermes. Others believed it was named for the constellation of Capricorn, a goat that rose like a fish from the sea. And some, he was sure, said it was named for a goatlike emperor in rut, hoarding child concubines on an island, riddled with sexual depravity. He didn't care what they said.

The stars that guided his destiny had still been the same at his birth. There was no changing that.

Though Tiberius had been lawyer, soldier, statesman, emperor, he was, like his nephew Claudius, in his heart of hearts a lover of history. In the case of Tiberius, especially the history of the gods which most in these modern times regarded as myth. Best of all he loved the tales of the Greeks.

And now, after all these years of exile on this pile of stones—years when he'd heard of little but tragedy and betrayal in the day-to-day affairs of the outside world—now suddenly a new myth had surfaced at the far edge of the Roman Empire. It wasn't really a new tale, as Tiberius knew. Rather it was a story of great antiquity—perhaps, indeed, the oldest myth in the world—and was found in each civilization since the dawn of recorded history. It was the myth of the "dying god," a god who makes the ultimate sacrifice: to become a mortal. A god who, through the surrender of his own life as a mortal being, brings about the destruction of an old order and its rebirth as a new world order, a new aeon.

As Tiberius stood listening to the dark sea breaking against the rocks below, he looked across to the dim glowing outline of Vesuvius, where hot lava had churned and boiled from time immemorial, though it only erupted, so they said, one time at the end of each aeon.

But were they not entering a new age now? Was this not the new aeon the astrologers had been awaiting? Tiberius wondered if he himself would live to see the force of the vulcan god unleashed from the belly of the earth—soon now—the one time it would happen between the past and future aeons of two millennia each: only once in a span of four thousand years.

Just then, near the breakers at the mainland, he saw the flash of an oar, which must be the ship he was awaiting. He'd been watching half the night, and now, as it approached in the thinning darkness that spoke of imminent dawn, he gripped the wall before him. It was the ship bringing the witness to him. The witness who had been present at the death of the god.

◆ ◆

He was tall and slender, with olive skin, almond eyes, and hair like a raven's wing that hung in a straight glassy panel to his shoulders. He wore a white linen tunic, wrapped once and cinched loosely with a rope belt, and the bronze arm cuffs traditional with those from the South. Before him, across the terrace, Tiberius sat on his marble throne on an elevated marble dais overlooking the sea. Behind the man stood the imperial guard and the captain and crew who'd brought him there by sea. As he crossed the terrace and knelt on one knee before Tiberius, it was clear that he was afraid—but proud.

"Your name is Tammuz, you are Egyptian," said the emperor, bidding the other to rise from his knee. "And yet, they say you are the pilot of a merchant ship that plies between Judea and Rome." When the witness stood in silence, Tiberius added, "You may speak."

"It is just as Your Excellency—Your Imperial Highness—states," Tammuz replied. "My master owns a fleet of merchant sailing ships. I pilot one of his ships that carries not only freight but also many passengers."

"Tell me what you saw, in your own words. Take your time."

"It was late one night, after dinner," said the Egyptian Tammuz. "No one was sleeping; most passengers were talking on deck and finishing their after-dinner wine. We were just along the coast of Roman Greece near the Echinades Isles. The wind had dropped, and the ship now drifted near the darkly forested outline of the camel-humped double isles of Paxi. Just then, a deep voice floated out across the waters—a voice from Paxi, calling my name."

"The name of Tammuz," murmured the emperor, as if recalling some half-forgotten melody.

"Yes, my lord," replied Tammuz. "At first I was distracted, steering the ship, and did not realize at once that it was I who had been called. But upon the second call, I was surprised, for no living soul on that small Greek isle knew me; nor did even the ship's passengers themselves know my name. By the third time my name was called, the passengers were looking about them, for ours was the only ship at all in this part of the dark sea. Therefore, collecting myself, upon the third call of my name I replied to the hidden voice that called out to me across the waters."

"And what happened once you'd answered?" asked Tiberius, turning his face away from the first dawn light toward the shadow, so the sailors and guards standing nearby couldn't read his thoughts when he heard the Egyptian's reply.

Tammuz said, "The caller cried out: 'Tammuz, when you come opposite to Palodes on the mainland, announce that Great Pan is dead!' "

Tiberius leapt to his feet, his height towering over all, and he looked Tammuz in the eye. "Pan?" he snapped. "Which Pan are you speaking of?"

"My lord, he is not one of the Egyptian deities, those in whom I was raised to believe. And though now, as a resident of the great Roman Empire, I have done with those pagan ideas, I fear that I'm not well schooled in my newly adopted faith. But it is my understanding that this lord Pan is the half-divine son of a god named Hermes, whom in Egypt we call Thoth. And therefore, as a half-divine, perhaps the lord Pan is available to death. I hope I do not commit a sacrilege by saying so."

Available to death! thought Tiberius—the greatest god in thousands of years? What kind of absurd tale was this? With a masklike face, he rubbed his jaw as if nothing were unusual, resumed his seat, and nodded for Tammuz to continue, though he felt the first tingling presentiment that something might be very, very wrong.

"The passengers and crew were as astounded and confused as I," Tammuz went on. "We debated among ourselves whether I should do as the voice had demanded, or whether I should refuse to be involved in this strange request. At last I resolved the problem thus: If, when we passed Palodes, a breeze was blowing, we would sail on by and do nothing. But if the sea was smooth, with no wind, I'd announce aloud what I had been told. When at last we came opposite Palodes, there was no wind and a smooth sea—so I called out, 'Great Pan is dead!' "

"And then?" said Tiberius, leaning out from his shadow to look the pilot again in the eye.

"At once there was an outcry from the mainland," said Tammuz. "Many voices, weeping, lamenting, and many loud wailings of amazement and astonishment. My lord, it seemed as if the whole coastline and the deep interior beyond were in mourning at some hideous family tragedy. They cried out that it was the end of the world: that it was the death of the sacred goat!"

Impossible! Tiberius nearly screamed aloud as he heard those phantom cries in the darkness echoing through his mind. It was completely mad! The first soothsayer had cast the first lot for Rome's fate in the time of Remus and Romulus—who were raised by wolves, as was also prophesied. From that age down to the present moment, no dark event such as this had ever been hinted at by anyone. Tiberius felt his skin cold and clammy despite the warmth of the morning sun.

Wasn't this era merely the dawning of the Roman Empire, which, after all, had just begun with Augustus? Everyone knew the "dying god" was a god in name only, for the gods themselves could never actually die. A surrogate was chosen: a new "god" to rejuvenate, regenerate the old myth. This time it was to be a poor shepherd, farmer, or fisherman—someone who drove a wagon or a plough—not one of the most ancient and powerful gods of Phrygia, Greece, and Rome. The great civilization of Rome, suckled at the teats of a she-wolf, would not be brought down by one old, heirless, hermit king ending his days in exile on an isle named for a goat. No, it must be a lie, a trick launched by one of his many enemies. Even the name of the pilot himself, Tammuz, smacked of myth, for this was the name of the oldest god who died—older than Orpheus, Adonis, or Osiris.

The emperor drew himself together, signaled for the guard to give the pilot some silver for his trouble, and turned away to signify that the audience was ended. But as the money was handed to Tammuz, Tiberius added: "Pilot, with so many passengers on your ship, there must be other witnesses available to confirm this strange story?"

"Indeed, my lord," agreed Tammuz, "there were many witnesses to what *I* heard and did." Deep in the unfathomable black eyes Tiberius thought he saw a strange light. "Regardless of what we believe we know," Tammuz continued, "there is one witness alone who can tell us whether that Great Pan was a mortal or a god, and whether he is alive or dead. But that sole witness is only a voice, a voice calling across the waters—"

Tiberius waved him away impatiently and departed for the isolated parapet—his prison. But as he watched the pilot being led down the slope to the harbor, the emperor called his slave and handed him a gold coin, motioning toward the Egyptian on the trail below. On swift feet the slave descended the trail and handed the coin to the pilot, who looked up to the terrace where Tiberius stood.

The emperor turned away without a sign and went into his empty quarters in the palace. Once there, he poured aromatic oil into the amphora on his altar and set it alight in the service of the gods.

He knew he must find the voice—the voice crying in the wilderness. He must find it before he died. Or Rome itself would be destroyed.

THE WITNESS

I only am escaped alone to tell thee . . .
My thought
Darkened as by wind the water . . .

There's always
Someone has to tell them, isn't there? . . .
Someone chosen by the chance of seeing,
By the accident of sight,
By the stumbling on the moment of it,
Unprepared, unwarned, unready,
Thinking of nothing . . . and it happens, and he sees it . . .
Caught in that inextricable net
Of having witnessed, having seen . . .

It was I.
I only. I alone. The moment
Closed us together in its gaping grin
Of horrible incredulity.

I only. I alone, to tell thee . . .
I who have understood nothing, have known
Nothing, have been answered nothing.

—Archibald MacLeish, *J.B.*

God always wins.

—Archibald MacLeish, *J.B.*

Snake River, Idaho: Early Spring, 1989

◆ ◆

It was snowing. It had been snowing for days. It seemed the snow would never end.

I had been driving through the thick of it since well before dawn. I stopped at midnight in Jackpot, Nevada, the only pink neon glow in the sky through at least a hundred miles of rocky wasteland in my long ascent from California back to Idaho, back to my job at the nuclear site. There in Jackpot, against the jangle of slot machines, I sat at a counter and ate blood-rare grilled steak with fries, chugged a glass of Scotch whiskey, and washed it down with a mug of hot black coffee—the multi-ingredient cure-all my uncle Earnest had always recommended for this kind of stress and heartache. Then I went back out into the cold black night and hit the road again.

If I hadn't stopped back in the Sierras, when the first fresh snow came down for the day of skiing I'd suddenly felt I needed to soothe my aching soul, I wouldn't have been in this predicament now, sailing along on black ice in the middle of nowhere. At least this was a nowhere I knew well—every wrinkle of road along this trek from the Rockies to the coast. I'd crossed it often enough on business, for my job as a nuclear security expert. Ariel Behn, girl nuke. But the reason for this last jaunt was a business I'd as soon have missed.

I could feel my body slipping into autopilot on that long, monotonous stretch of highway. The dark waters of my mind started pulling me back to a place I knew I didn't want to go. The miles clicked away, the snow swirled around me. The studded tires crunched on the black ice that flowed beneath.

I could not erase the dappled image of the grassy slope back there in California, the smoothly geometric pattern of those tombstones moving across it, those thin, thin layers of stone and grass. All that separated life from death—all that separated me from Sam—forever.

◆ ◆

The grass was electric green—that shimmering, wonderful green that only exists in San Francisco, and only at this time of year. Against the brilliant lawn, the chalk white gravestones marched in undulating rows across the hill. Dark eucalyptus trees towered over the cemetery between the rows of markers, their silver leaves dripping with water. I looked through the tinted windows of the limousine as we pulled from the main road and doubled back into the Presidio.

I had driven this road so many times when in the Bay Area. It was the only route from the Golden Gate Bridge to the San Francisco Marina, and it passed directly by the military cemetery we were entering. Today, observed up close and in slow motion, it was all so beautiful, so ravishing to the eye.

"Sam would have loved being here," I said, speaking aloud for the first time during the ride.

Jersey, sitting beside me in the limo, said curtly, "Well, after all, he *is* here, isn't he? Or what's all the hoopla about?"

At these close quarters, I caught a whiff of her breath.

"Mother, how much have you had to drink?" I said. "You smell like a brewery."

"Cutty Sark," she said with a smile. "In honor of the Navy."

"For God's sake, this is a funeral," I said irritably.

"I'm Irish," she pointed out. "We call it a wake: drink the buggers on their merry way. In my opinion, a far more civilized tradition . . ."

She was already having trouble with the three-syllable words. Inwardly I was cringing, hoping she wouldn't try to give part of the eulogy that was to be delivered by the military at graveside. I wouldn't put anything past her—especially in this state of incipient inebriation. And Augustus and Grace, my well-starched father and stepmother who disapproved of everything, were in the car just behind.

The limousines pulled through the iron gates of the Presidio cemetery and slid on past the funeral parlor. There would be no indoor service, and the coffin was already sealed for reasons pertaining, we'd been told, to national security. Besides, as we had also been told somewhat more discreetly, it might be hard to recognize Sam. Families of bombing victims usually preferred not to be afforded that opportunity.

The cortege moved along Lincoln Avenue and pulled up the drive sheltered by brooding eucalyptus at the far end of the cemetery. Several cars were already parked there, all with the recognizable white license plates of the U.S. government. Atop the small knoll was a freshly dug open grave with a cluster of men standing around it. One was an army chaplain, and one with a long thick braid of hair looked like the shaman I'd asked for. Sam would have liked that.

Our three limos pulled up in front of the government vehicles: Jersey and I in the family car, Augustus and Grace behind us, and Sam in the black limousine up front. In a lead-lined coffin. We all got out and started up the hill as they unloaded Sam from the hearse. Augustus and Grace stood quietly aside, not mingling—which I frankly appreciated, so Jersey's breath wouldn't be a problem. Unless someone lit a match near her.

A man with dark glasses and a trenchcoat separated from the gaggle of government types and moved over to speak a few words to the other two family members. Then he approached Jersey and me.

I suddenly realized we weren't dressed for a funeral. I was wearing the only black dress I owned, one with purple and yellow hibiscus all over it. Jersey was in a chic French suit, that particular shade of ice blue that was her trademark when she was on the stage because it matched her eyes. I hoped no one would notice our lapse in protocol.

"Mrs. Behn," the man addressed Jersey, "I hope you don't mind waiting a few more minutes? The president would like to be here for the ceremony."

He didn't mean *the* president, of course, but a former president: the one Jersey called the Peanut Farmer, whom she'd performed for when he himself was in the White House.

"Hell no," said Jersey. "I don't mind waiting if *Sam* doesn't!"

Then she laughed, and I got another waft. Though I couldn't see the man's eyes behind those glasses, I noticed that his mouth tightened into a thin line. I stared at him in stony silence.

The helicopter was coming down across the road, settling on the Crissy Field landing strip beside the bay. Two dark-paned cars had driven out to meet it and collect our distinguished guest.

"Mrs. Behn," the shaded one went on *sotto voce*, as if in a spy movie, "I'm instructed to tell you that the president, acting in behalf of our current administration, has arranged this morning's agenda. Although your son, as a civilian adviser, was not technically a member of the military, his death took place while he was performing a service for—I should say, rather, operating in an advisory capacity to the military. Our government therefore plans to honor him appropriately. There will be a small ceremony; a military band will play; then the deceased will be given the seventeen-gun salute in farewell. After that, the president plans to present to you the Distinguished Service Medal."

"What for?" said Jersey. "I ain't the one who died, sugar."

◆ ◆

The ceremony did not go exactly as planned.

After it was over, Augustus and Grace retired to their suite atop the Mark Hopkins on Nob Hill, sending a message that they were "expecting me" to join them for dinner. Since it was just lunchtime, I took Jersey to the Buena Vista to drink her lunch. We found a wooden table at the front windows, overlooking the wharves and the bay.

"Ariel, honey, I'm really sorry about what happened," said Jersey, tossing down her first glass of Scotch as if it were milk.

"Sorry doesn't help," I said, repeating a line of hers from my childhood when I'd done something wrong. "I'm having dinner with Augustus and Grace tonight. What the hell am I supposed to say to them?"

"Fuck them," said Jersey, looking at me with those famous icy blue eyes, which seemed surprisingly clear, given her recent dietary habits. "Tell them that I was startled by the guns. It's true. I was startled by those damned guns going off in my ear."

"You *knew* they were going to give a seventeen-gun salute," I pointed out. "I was there when the security agent *told* you. You were as drunk as a skunk. *That's* why you fell into the grave—good God—in front of all those people!"

Jersey looked up at me in injured pride, and I glared back.

But all at once I felt it coming over me, and I just couldn't help myself. I started laughing. First Jersey's expression changed to surprise; then she started laughing, too. We laughed until tears were streaming down our faces. We laughed until we could no longer catch our breath. We were choking with laughter and holding our sides at the thought of my mother sprawled, ass up, six feet down in a hole in the ground, before they even had a chance to lower the coffin.

"Right in front of the Peanut Farmer and everything," Jersey practically screamed, and this set us off on another peal.

"Right in front of Augustus and Grace," I gasped between hysterical sobs.

It took a long time to run down, but at last we subsided into moans and chuckles. I wiped my tears with my napkin and leaned back with a sigh, holding my stomach, which was raw from laughter.

"I wish Sam could have seen what you did," I told Jersey, squeezing her arm. "It was so bizarre—just what tickled his funny bone. He would have died laughing."

"He died anyway," said Jersey. And she ordered another drink.

◆ ◆

At seven o'clock I arrived at the Mark in the limo Augustus sent for me. He hired a car whenever he visited any city so he'd never have to degrade himself flagging down a cab. My father was into appearances. I told the driver to collect me at ten and take me back to the little Victorian inn where I was staying across the bridge. Three hours of Augustus and Grace, as I knew from experience, would be more than adequate.

Their penthouse suite was large and filled with the lavish flower arrangements Grace required in any surroundings. Augustus opened the door when I knocked and regarded me sternly. My father was always elegant, with his silvery hair and tanned complexion. Now, in a black cashmere blazer and grey trousers, he looked every bit the part of the feudal lord he'd been rehearsing for all his life.

"You're late," he said, glancing at his gold wristwatch. "You were to arrive at six-thirty so we could speak privately before dinner."

"This morning was enough of a family reunion for me," I told him.

I instantly regretted having alluded to the earlier events of the day.

"And that's something else I want to speak with you about: your mother," said Augustus. "First, what can I fix you to drink?"

"I had lunch with Jersey," I said. "I'm not sure I need anything much stronger than water."

Wherever Augustus went, he had a well-stocked bar set up, though he drank little himself. Maybe that's what went wrong when he and my mother were married.

"I'll fix you a spritzer; that's light," he said, and squirted the soda from a mesh-encased bottle, handing the wineglass to me.

"Where's Grace?" I asked, taking a sip as he mixed himself a light Scotch.

"She's lying down. She was quite upset by that little debacle your mother pulled this morning—and who can blame her? It was unforgivable." Augustus always referred to Jersey as "*your* mother," as though I were responsible for her very existence, rather than the other way around.

"Actually," I told him, "I felt her display provided a well-needed touch of brightness to the entire morbid affair. I mean, I can't really imagine providing brass bands, shooting off guns, and giving someone a *medal* all because, in the service of the U.S. government, he got himself blown into pieces like a dismembered patchwork quilt!"

"Don't change the subject on *me*, young lady," my father reprimanded me in his most authoritarian tone of voice. "Your mother's behavior was absolutely shocking. Deplorable. We were fortunate that reporters were not permitted."

Augustus would never use words like "disgusting" or "humiliating." They were too subjective, involving personal emotion. He was only interested in the objective, the remote—things like appearance and reputation.

In that regard, I was a good deal more like him than I cared to admit. But I still couldn't bear the fact that he was more interested in my mother's comportment at a social event than in Sam's brutal death.

"I wonder if people scream when they die like that?" I asked aloud.

Augustus turned on his heel so I couldn't see his face. He went across to the bedroom door. "I'll wake up Grace," he informed me over his shoulder, "so she'll be ready in time for dinner."

◆ ◆

"I don't see how we can speak," said Grace, blotting her eyes, which were swollen with tears, and brushing a wisp of stark blond hair from her forehead with the back of her wrist. "I don't see how we can eat. It's truly incredible to imagine how we can all be sitting here in a restaurant, trying to behave like human beings."

Until that moment it had never occurred to me that someone like Grace had ever visualized the concept of attempting to behave like a human being. Things were starting to look up.

I glanced around at the walls of the restaurant, which were done up with lattices covered in painted vines. They were scattered with a few tiny red painted lizards, which seemed to be basking in invisible sunlight. The table groupings were separated by large plantings of fresh chrysanthemums—flowers that are offered in tribute to the dead in all Italian cemeteries.

I'd begun and ended the day in a cemetery. Only that afternoon, I'd looked up the word in a bookstore. From the Greek *koimeterion*, a sleeping chamber; *koiman*, to put to sleep; or Latin *cunae*, a cradle. It was nice to think of Sam, wherever he was, as cradled in sleep.

"He was so young," Grace was saying between little sobs as she took another bite of steak tartare. She adjusted her diamond bracelet, adding the telltale words "Wasn't he?"

The truth of the matter was, Grace had never met Sam in her life. My mother's divorce from Augustus had been nearly twenty-five years ago, and he and Grace had been married for little more than fifteen. In between was lots of proverbial water beneath the bridge, including how Sam got to be my brother without actually being the son of my mother or father. My family relations are rather complex.

But I had no time to think of that, for Grace had moved on to her favorite topic: money. As she switched to it, her tears miraculously dried and her eyes took on a luminous glow.

"We phoned the lawyers this afternoon from the suite," she told me, suddenly filled with buoyant enthusiasm. "The reading of the will, as you know, is tomorrow—and I think I should tell you that we got some good news. Though they won't give out the details, of course, it does appear that *you* are the principal heir!"

"Oh, goody," I said. "Sam hasn't been dead a week, and already I've profited. Did you dig out exactly how rich I'll be? Can I retire from my labors right now? Or are the tax folks likely to take most of it?"

"That's not what Grace meant, and you know it," said Augustus, who was designing forms in his *crème de volaille* as I jabbed at the capers on my Scottish salmon. They rolled around the plate and evaded my fork. "Grace and I are only concerned for your own interest," he went on. "I didn't know Sam—at least not well—but I'm sure he cared a great deal for *you*. After all, you practically grew up as brother and sister, didn't you? And as Earnest's only heir himself, Sam must have been very—well, comfortable financially?"

My late uncle Earnest, who'd been in the mining and mineral business, was my father's older brother, and rich as Midas. On top of that, he died with every cent he'd made, because spending money was of no interest to him. Sam was his only child.

When my parents, Augustus and Jersey, divorced I was still very tiny. My mother ran around with me for a number of years, visiting all the capitals of the world. She was welcome in such places, since she'd been a famous singer long before marrying my father—which is how she met the Peanut Farmer and nearly everyone else of high social visibility. The Behn men had always liked flamboyant women. But, like my father, they often had trouble actually living with them.

Jersey had been drinking for years, but everyone expected opera singers to be swilling champagne as if it were water. It wasn't until Augustus announced his betrothal to Grace—a clone of Jersey at a similar age, but twenty years her junior—that the bottle came out of Jersey's closet. She fled with me to Idaho, to consult my widowed, hermitlike uncle Earnest about financial matters—my father had invested all her earlier musical income in himself, another Behn male trait—and to everyone's surprise, Jersey and Earnest fell in love.

And I, a child who'd grown up like Eloise at the Plaza, eating *pâté de foie gras* before I could pronounce it, suddenly found myself in the middle of a nowhere that I now, nearly twenty years later, called home.

So my father's question, seemingly vague, was really direct and to the point. My mother, married to two consecutive brothers, had actually stopped drinking during Earnest's lifetime. Knowing her as he did, though, Earnest left all his money to Sam, with a proviso to take care of her and of me "as he deems best." And now Sam himself was dead. In all likelihood his death made me a multimillionaire.

Uncle Earnest died seven years ago, when I was off at college, and none of us had seen Sam since. He simply vanished. Jersey and I got our checks every month. She drank hers, and I put mine into an account and left it there. Meanwhile, I did something radical, something the Behn family women had never done. I got a job.

It was when I started working as a nuclear security officer, my first week on the job, that I heard from Sam. He phoned my office, though God knows how he knew where I was.

"Hi, hotshot," Sam said—his favorite name for me ever since we were children. "You've broken a family tradition: no high notes or high kicks in the chorus line?"

" 'Life upon the wicked stage ain't ever what a girl supposes,' " I quoted from my vast, unsolicited musical repertoire. But was I ever happy to hear his voice. "Where have you been all these years, blood brother? You don't need gainful employment, I gather, now that you're the full-time family benefactor. Thanks for all the checks."

"In fact," Sam corrected me, "I'm gainfully employed by a variety of governments that shall remain unnamed. I provide a service no one else can—with the possible exception of those who've been hand-trained by me: a group of one. Maybe one day you'll consider going into a joint venture?"

And the cryptic hint of a job offer was the last I'd heard of Sam until my phone call from the executor.

◆ ◆

I felt the tires start to suck under the snow. The whole car was sliding, pulling with a riptide force off the road.

Adrenaline gushed as I snapped to and gripped the steering wheel. Throwing my whole weight behind it, I yanked those massive tons of steel back from the edge of the shoulder. But now I was hurtling in the opposite direction, out of control.

Bloody hell, I *couldn't* run off the road! There was nothing out there but snow and more snow. It was so black, the snowfall so thick, I couldn't even see what was beyond the road on either side—maybe a sheer drop. I heard my mind, as if inside a well, screaming "Fool! Fool!" while I racked my brain trying to recall when I'd passed the last light in the abyss out there. Fifty miles back? A hundred?

As these panicky thoughts ran through my mind I was still able, with that dual processing ability we come equipped with, to marshal my muscles and juices to bring the car back under control. I rocked it back and forth like a yo-yo, trying to prevent it from spinning out, trying to feel beneath me—as I would under a pair of skis—the tires hydroplane on the new snow that had now formed a slick, waxy surface atop the deeper, and lethal, layer of diamond-hard black ice.

It seemed forever until I felt I was winning the wrestling match, and the rhythm of the thousands of pounds of steel started to move toward a center of balance. I was shaking like a leaf as I let it slow to thirty, twenty-five. I took a deep breath and nudged it back up, knowing like every mountain girl that you never stop completely when the snow's coming down like that, or you may never get momentum again.

As I moved on into the black and empty night, casting up prayers of gratitude, I slapped my face a few times, hard, and rolled down the car window to let the blizzard come in and swirl around inside. Needles of snow cut my skin. I took a deep breath of icy air and held it in my lungs for a minute. I wiped my stinging eyes with the back of my glove, then yanked off the ski cap I'd been wearing and shook my hair around wildly in the whirling wind that was battering around inside the car, blowing bits of paper in its wake. By the time I rolled the window back up, I had returned to reality, greatly sobered. What the hell was wrong with me?

Of course, I knew what was wrong. Sam was dead, and I was having trouble visualizing life on this planet without him. It was what a schizophrenic might call being "beside yourself" with grief. Though I hadn't seen or heard much from Sam these past seven years, he was always there in everything I did. In a way, he was the only really close family I'd ever had. For the first time I realized that in his absence I had conversations with him in my mind. Now I had no one to talk to, even in my head.

Still I wasn't about to join Sam in the happy hunting grounds this moment. Certainly not by flunking an intelligence test out here on the midnight road. It was then that I noticed a glow in the distance that I could just make out through the thick lacy curtain of snow. It was large enough to be a town, and there weren't that many out here in the high desert. It looked like home to me.

◆ ◆

But the adventure was not quite over.

I pulled up on the road above the house that contained the charming root cellar I called home, and looked down in exhausted frustration. The driveway had disappeared, vanished in the whipped-cream snow that was drifted above the first-floor windows. It seemed that after miles of grueling combat driving, I now had to face a dig-in to reach the house at all, much less to uncover my fathoms-deep basement apartment. That's what I deserved for living in a cellar in Idaho—just like a goddamned potato.

I turned off the ignition and sat looking in gloomy silence down the steep hill where the drive used to be and trying to figure out what to do. Like all mountain folk, in the back of my car I carried emergency supplies in all seasons—sand, salt and water, thermal clothes, waterproof footgear, firemaking supplies, jump-starters, ropes and chains—but I had no shovel. Even if I had, I'd be incapable of moving enough snow myself to get my car down that drive.

I sat there, mindlessly numb, watching the soft, sifting shroud of falling snow dropping silently around me. Sam would say something funny just now, I thought. Or maybe jump out and start dancing in the snow—a snow dance, as if he were taking credit for the handiwork of the gods. . . .

I shook my head and tried to snap out of it. I heard the phone ringing in my apartment below. The lights were off in the main house, suggesting that my eccentric, if adorable, Mormon landlord had gone off to the mountains to catch the fresh powder for tomorrow's skiing—or perhaps over to the temple to pray for the driveway to clear itself.

Much as I hated mucking about in deep powder, I understood that the only way to traverse the steep gap between the house and the car was to ski. Luckily, my lightweight cross-country boots and skis were in the back of my hatchback with the other survival gear. Now if I could only manage to follow the line where the drive should be. Our yawning chasm of a front lawn, nearly invisible beneath the drifts by now, might seem as bottomless and lethal as quicksand if I fell in to it. Also I'd have to abandon my car up here on the road for the night, where it would vanish too if the snowplows came through at dawn before I could rescue it.

I got out and yanked the skis from the back of the car, as well as my duffel bag and a few belongings I thought I could carry over my shoulder, and set them out on the flat road. I had slipped in back to rummage for my boots when, through the side window, I saw my mailbox—identified by the little flag rising like a gay beacon from a drift—and suddenly recalled I'd forgotten to stop my mail when I'd left so hastily for the funeral. Slamming the back car door shut and hanging on to its handle for balance, I swept the mound of snow off the box and extracted the mail that must have been building up all week. It was more than I'd imagined. So with my other hand I let go the door handle and reached for the duffel bag, unintentionally stepping slightly away from the car.

With that first step I sank into snow up to my waist, and I kept on sinking. I felt the fear clutching at me as I struggled to keep from panicking. I knew that thrashing about would only make me sink faster. I'd lived in these parts long enough to hear of many folks who'd been smothered, sinking into bottomless snow where they couldn't move arms or legs to free themselves. And the second I started to sink, it also occurred to me that I'd departed for the funeral with little fanfare, only telling my boss there'd been a death in the family and leaving a cryptic note for my landlord. It was entirely possible, even though my car would be found, that no one would find *me* until after the spring melt!

I tossed the disabling pile of mail up onto the road—under the car so it wouldn't sink into the drifts and vanish too. I managed to get one elbow propped on the solid surface, clawing with my other hand until I could twist enough to get both arms flat on the road. When I pushed myself up, it felt like vaulting from a swimming pool with fifty-pound weights on my legs: it wrung out every ounce of energy I had. I lay flat on my stomach on the road, shaking and hot with fear and exhaustion. It didn't last long; soon the chills set in as the clinging ice from my full-body dip in that snowbank saturated my inadequately waterproofed clothes.

I staggered to my feet and yanked the car door open. Cold, soaked, thoroughly wiped out, I was furious with myself. Wasn't Jack London's *To Build a Fire* required reading for mountain children? About a chap who goes out in the tundra at sixty below, against all advice. He freezes to death. Very slowly. Not what I had on my agenda.

I pulled the cross-country boots from the car, laced them with stiff fingers in soggy gloves, snapped on my long, featherweight Nordic skis, stuffed the bundle of mail in the duffel, slung it over my shoulder, and slalomed down to the back door. Why hadn't I tried that as my first idea, and bypassed Mr. Postman until morning?

The phone was again ringing as I shed my skis, threw open the door, and half tumbled—along with a mess of powder—down the steep stairway to my cozy dungeon fortress. At least, it *had* been cozy when I'd left it a week ago.

I flicked on the lights, and saw ice caking the inside of the windows and patterns of crystals formed on the mirrors and picture glass like something out of *Dr. Zhivago*. Softly cursing my landlord, who turned down my heat to spare expense whenever I left the building, I yanked off the dripping boots before I stepped onto the orientals, raced across the open, book-lined living room, and made a dive into pillows to grab the phone on the floor.

I kicked myself at once for even picking it up: it was Augustus.

"Why did you leave?" were the first words out of his mouth. "Grace and I have been nearly at our wits' end, trying to find you. Where have you been?"

"Having fun playing in the snow," I told him, rolling over on my back in the pillows and cradling the phone to my ear. "I thought the party was over; were there other treats in store?" I unbuttoned my wet trousers and tried to wriggle out of them so I wouldn't get pneumonia down here in this bitterly cold dungeon—or, more likely, develop mold. I could see my breath in the air.

"Your sense of humor has always seemed to me ill placed, at best," Augustus informed me coolly. "Or perhaps only your sense of timing. When you vanished just after the reading of the will, we phoned your hotel and were told you had checked out earlier that same morning. But once we'd heard the will, of course, Grace and I had agreed to a press conference—"

"A *press* conference?!" I said, sitting bolt upright in astonishment. I tried to keep the phone to my ear as I yanked myself out of my wet parka and pulled off my sweater, but I only caught Augustus's last words:

"—must be yours as well."

"What must be mine?" I asked. I rubbed my hands hard over my goosebumpy body, stood up, and dragged the phone over to the fireplace. I was tucking pinecones and paper under the pile of logs already stacked as Augustus replied.

"The manuscripts, naturally. Everyone knew Sam had inherited them, how very valuable they must be. But after Earnest's death no one could locate Sam. He seemed to have been swallowed up. When I tried to discuss it during dinner after the funeral, you seemed to want to avoid the issue. But now that it's known you're not only Sam's principal heir but his sole heir, naturally matters have changed—"

"Naturally?" I said with impatience as I lit a match under the kindling and watched with relief as the flames leapt up at once. "I have no idea what manuscripts you're talking about!"

And stranger still, I thought, regardless of what they might be worth, why on earth would someone with my father's predilection for privacy ever dream of agreeing to a press conference? It was more than suspicious.

"You mean you don't know of them?" Augustus was saying in an odd voice. "How can that be, when the *Washington Post* and the *London Times* and the *International Herald Tribune* were all here? Of course, there was nothing we could say, since the manuscripts were not in the hands of the executor, and you had vanished as well."

"Maybe you could clue me in, before I freeze to death," I said between chattering teeth. "What are these manuscripts Sam left me—no, let me guess: Francis Bacon's letters to Ben Jonson, admitting that Bacon really did, as we've always suspected, write all Shakespeare's plays."

To my surprise, Augustus didn't miss a beat. "They're worth a good deal more than that," he informed me. And my father was a man who understood the meanings of words like "worth" and "value." "The very moment you learn anything about them, as I've no doubt you will," he went on, "you must notify me or our attorneys at once. I don't think you quite appreciate the position you are in."

Okay, I thought, I'll give this one more try. I took a deep breath.

"No, I suppose not," I agreed. "Could you see your way to share with me, Father, what the whole world already seems to know? *What are these manuscripts?*"

"Pandora's," Augustus said curtly, the name sounding bitter as acid in his mouth—as well it might.

Pandora was my grandmother—my father's loving mother, who'd abandoned him at birth. Though I'd never met her, by all accounts she'd been the most colorful, flamboyant, and outrageous of all the Behn women. And with our family tree, that was going some.

"Pandora had manuscripts?" I asked my father. "What kind?"

"Oh, diaries, letters, correspondence with the great and near great, that sort of thing," he said in a dismissive tone. Then, casually, he added, "It's possible she might even have written a memoir of sorts."

I might not see eye to eye with my father on most things, but I knew him well enough to know when he was pulling my chain. He must have been calling here every fifteen minutes for the past two days; that's why I'd heard the phone ring twice during my brief time outside. If he was in so much of a panic to reach me, and this stuff was so hot that he had to give in to a press conference, why was he playing footsie with me now?

"Why all the belated interest?" I asked. "I mean, Granny dearest has been dead for years, right?"

"It's generally believed that Pandora left these manuscripts in trust to the . . . other side of the family," my father said stiffly. I started thinking just how complex my family relations actually were. "Earnest must have had them under lock and key for decades, for he had many offers," Augustus went on. "But he couldn't evaluate their true worth because apparently they were all written in some sort of code. Then your cousin Sam . . ."

Holy cow!

I stood there before the fire in my skivvies, phone in hand, as my father's voice flapped on like meaningless noise in the background. Good lord—they were in code!

Sam had vanished just when his father Earnest died. He was out of touch for seven years, and now he was dead. And what coincided with that hiatus? Sam's inheritance—including, perhaps, that of these manuscripts. What was Sam's profession and calling? What had he lavished his time upon teaching me even since childhood, that got me my very well-paying job?

Sam was a codebreaker, one of the best in the world. If Sam knew about these manuscripts of Granny's, it would have been far too hard for him to resist having a look, especially if his father wanted to determine their value. He must have seen them—perhaps broken them—long before Earnest died. Of that I was certain. So where were they now?

But there was a question more crucial to me at this moment, given my own unique situation:

What was in my grandmother's diaries, which I had now technically inherited, that was so dangerous it had gotten Sam killed?

Alexander, finding himself unable to untie the [Gordian] knot, the ends of which were secretly twisted round and folded up within it, cut it asunder with his sword.

—Plutarch

The secret of the Gordian knot seems to have been a religious one, probably the ineffable name of Dionysus, a knot-cipher tied in the rawhide thong. . . .

Alexander's brutal cutting of the knot, when he marshalled his army at Gordium for the invasion of Greater Asia, ended an ancient dispensation by placing the power of the sword above that of religious mysteries.

—Robert Graves, *The Greek Myths*

It was nearly three A.M. when I turned on the taps of the big claw-footed tub, praying that the pipes hadn't frozen, and watched with relief as the hot water splashed into the bath. I dumped in some salts and liquid bubbles, stripped, and climbed in. The tub was so deep, the water went up to my nose, and I blew the bubbles away. Lathering up my road-wrecked hair, I knew I had lots of thinking to do. But my brain was engaged in fuzzy logic—not surprising, given the week's events and the trauma of my trip home.

As I soaked there, the bathroom door swung open on squeaky hinges and Jason came strolling in unannounced—which probably meant Olivier, my landlord, had also returned. Jason barely gave me a glance with those penetrating green eyes. He sauntered over and regarded with disdain my soggy silk undergarments on the floor. He started to paw at them, as though he thought my long johns would make a nice litter box, but I reached over and yanked them out from under him.

"Oh, no, you don't!" I said firmly.

Jason jumped up on the wooden rim of the tub, stuck out his paw, and batted at the bubbles. He looked at me inquisitively. This was my hint to douse him. Jason was the only cat I knew that loved water—any kind of water. It was normal for him to turn on a sink tap to fetch himself a drink; he preferred a toilet to a litter box; and he was known to jump into the Snake River below the falls to retrieve his favorite little red rubber ball. He could swim in current as well as any dog.

But tonight—this morning, rather—I was too tired to dry him, so I flicked him off the side of the tub, got out, and toweled myself instead. In my big fluffy bathrobe, my hair wrapped in a towel, I padded to the kitchen and heated some water to make myself a hot buttered rum before bed. I picked up a broom and banged on the ceiling to let Olivier know I was back—though my car abandoned on the road should have been his first clue.

"Dearest one," Olivier's voice soon came floating down the stairway, with his recognizable thick *québecois* accent. "I snowshoed in from my Jeep, but I wasn't sure it was proper to send the little argonaut down to you yet—you might already be sleeping. And what about me?"

"Okay, come down and join me in a quick buttered rum before I crash," I called back up. "And let me know what's been going on at work."

Olivier Maxfield and I had met some five years back, when we were assigned to a project together. He was a strange amalgam: nuclear engineer and gourmet chef, devotee of Yankee slang and cowboy bars, and unrepentant "Jack" Mormon. He'd been born a French Canadian Catholic in a household devoted to *la cuisine française*, and now as a latter-day culinary genius himself, those no-alcohol-no-caffeine dietary restrictions of the Latter-day Saints hardly mixed with Olivier's *nouvelle* persona.

The first time he met me, Olivier told me he'd already known I would soon enter his life, for I'd just appeared as the Blessed Virgin in a dream involving a pinball competition between myself and the prophet Moroni. By the end of the first week that we'd worked together, Olivier received a sign that I should be offered cheap rent to move into his downstairs apartment. The actual pinball machine upon which I, as the Virgin Mary, had beaten the prophet had miraculously appeared as a new acquisition of the cowboy bar down the road from our very office.

Perhaps it was the result of my kooky upbringing, but I found Olivier refreshing at a nuclear site stacked with engineers and physicists, all of whom brown-bagged their lunches and went home by five o'clock so they could watch wholesome TV reruns with their children. I went all the time to parties at the homes of "site families." In summers they barbecued hamburgers and hot dogs in the backyard; in winters it was spaghetti, salad, and prefab garlic bread in the family room. It was as if no one here in this remote high desert had ever heard of any other manner of dining.

Olivier, by contrast, had lived in Montreal and Paris and had passed a summer workshop in the south of France with *Cordon Bleu*. Though perhaps a tightwad about providing landlordly services such as heat and driveway clearing, he did have assets. While mincing, dicing, *mouli*-ing, and clarifying butter in his enormous industrial kitchen upstairs to prepare the designer meals he cooked for Jason and me at least once a week, he regaled me with tales of the great chefs of Europe, interspersed with the latest fads on the cowboy bar scene. He was, as the French say, "such a one."

"What was this huge emergency that called you away?" Olivier's handsome, dimpled smile appeared around the half-open door from the steps, as he ran his fingers through his curly mop of brown hair and regarded me with large dark eyes. "Where did you disappear to? The Pod was asking after you every day, but I knew nothing."

"The Pod" was the widely used nickname of my boss, the director and general manager of the whole nuclear site. It was used behind his back, for though his actual name was Pastor Owen Dart he was anything but shepherdlike. Indeed, the monogram was recognized also as his description: the Prince of Darkness.

I'd like to argue that this moniker was inappropriate to my boss. But to be perfectly frank, of the ten thousand employees working at the site—or even among the industry muckety-mucks in Washington he hobnobbed with—I was the only one I knew who hadn't been scalded by the man. At least not yet. The Pod seemed genuinely to like me, and had handpicked me for my job while I was still in university. As a result of this unexpected affinity, not all my colleagues trusted me—another reason why Olivier, the dashing Québecois Mormon cowboy gourmet, was one of my few close friends.

"Sorry," I said to Olivier, pouring hot water over the mush of brown sugar, butter, and rum in the two glass mugs and handing one to him. "I had to leave suddenly. There was an unexpected death in the family."

"Oh gosh, no one *I* know, I hope?" said Olivier with a gallantly supportive smile—though we both knew that he knew no one in my family.

"It was Sam," I said, trying to wash down the stick in my throat with the buttery hot liquor.

"Heavens! Your brother?" said Olivier, sinking onto the sofa near the fire.

"My cousin," I corrected. "Actually, my stepbrother. We were raised as brother and sister. In fact, he's more of a blood brother. Or I mean, he *was*."

"My goodness, your family relations *are* somewhat complex," Olivier said, mocking my own retort whenever anyone inquired about my family. "Are you quite certain you were related to this fellow at all?"

"I'm sole heir to his estate," I told him. "That's enough for me."

"Ah—then he was rich, but not really close, is that it?" Olivier said hopefully.

"A bit of each," I told him. "I was probably closer to him than anyone in my family." Which wasn't saying much, but Olivier didn't know that.

"Oh, how dreadful for you! But I don't understand. Why have I never heard of him, then, except for the name? He's never been to visit, nor called that I know of, in the many years we've worked together and shared this humble abode."

"Our family communicates psychically," I told him. Jason was slaloming around my legs as if he were trying to braid a maypole all by himself, so I picked him up and added, "We have no need of satellites or cell phones —"

"That reminds me," interrupted Olivier. "Your father's been calling here for *days*. Wouldn't say what he wanted—just that you must phone him at once."

Just then the phone rang, startling Jason, who jumped out of my arms.

"They *must* be psychic to pick up our vibes at this hour," said Olivier. As I reached for the phone, he finished his drink and headed for the door. "I'll make you some pancakes before work, as a welcome home," he tossed over his shoulder. Then he was gone.

"Gavroche, darling" were the first words I heard as I picked up the phone.

Good lord, maybe my family members *had* suddenly become psychic. It was my uncle Laf. I hadn't heard from him in ages. He always called me Gavroche: French for a Parisian street urchin.

"Laf?" I said. "Where *are* you? You sound a million miles away."

"Just now, Gavroche, I am in *Wien*," meaning he was at his big eighteenth-century apartment overlooking the Hofburg in Vienna where Jersey and I used to stay—and where it was now eight hours later than it was here, or eleven A.M. his time. Apparently Uncle Laf had never gotten the hang of differing time zones.

"I was so sorry, Gavroche, to hear about Sam," he told me. "I was wanting to come for the service, but your father, of course—"

"That's okay," I assured him, not wanting to open that can of worms. "You were there in spirit, and so was Uncle Earnest, even though he's dead. I found a shaman who did a little ritual at the ceremony, then the military gave Sam honors, and Jersey fell into the open grave."

"Your mother fell into the grave?" Uncle Laf said with the enthusiasm of a five-year-old. "Oh, but that is marvelous! Did she plan it, do you think?"

"She was drunk, as usual," I told him. "But it was still fun. I wish you could have seen Augustus's face!"

"Now I am *really* sorry I was not able to attend!" Laf said with more tickled enjoyment than I would have believed a man of his age, pushing ninety, could muster.

There was no love lost between my father, Augustus, and my uncle, Lafcadio Behn—perhaps because it was with Laf, my grandfather's stepson by a previous marriage, that my own grandma Pandora had run off when she'd abandoned my father at birth.

This was the thing my family never spoke of, in public or private. Well, at least it was *one* of the things. It suddenly occurred to me that I could probably make a fortune—if I hadn't just inherited one from Sam—by designing an entirely new model of complexity theory, based solely upon my family's interactions.

"Uncle Laf," I said, "I want to ask you a question. I know we never talk about the family, but I want you to know that Sam has left everything to me."

"Gavroche, this is just what I expect of him. You are a good girl, and everything good should come to you. I have plenty of comfort on my own—do not you fear for me."

"I'm not worried about you, Laf. But I want to ask you about something, something involving the family. Something maybe only *you* know about. Something that Sam apparently also left to me—not real estate or money."

My uncle Laf was so silent, I wasn't sure he was still on the line. At last he spoke. "Gavroche, you do understand that international telephone calls are recorded?"

"They are?" I said, though in my profession I knew it very well. "But that doesn't affect our conversation," I added.

"Gavroche, there is the reason why I called," said Uncle Laf in a voice that sounded very different than a moment ago. "I regret I could not attend the funeral of Sam. But by coincidences, I will be quite near you on the next weekend. I will come to the big hotel at the Valley of the Sun—"

"You'll be at the Sun Valley Lodge next weekend?" I said. "You're coming from Austria to Sun Valley?"

I mean, the routing from Vienna to Ketchum was probably not ideal under the best of circumstances—but Laf was almost ninety years old. In fact, what with high mountains and erratic weather, it was hard enough just to get there from the next state. What on earth was he thinking?

"Laf, much as I'd love to see you after all these years, I don't think that's a very sensible idea," I told him. "Besides, I've missed a week of work already because of the funeral. I'm not sure I can get away."

"My darling," said Laf. "The question you want to ask me—I believe I know what it is. And also, I know the answer. So please be there."

◆ ◆

Just as my eyes were about to close, I remembered something I hadn't thought of in years. I remembered the first time Grey Cloud cut me. I could see the thin line of beaded blood, like a necklace of tiny rubies on my leg where he drew the sharp blade. I didn't cry, though I was very young. I recall the color: a beautiful, surprising red—the lifeblood leaving my body. But I was not afraid.

I hadn't dreamed the dream even once since childhood. Now, as I drifted off into a troubled sleep, it came upon me unexpectedly, as if waiting all along in the shadows of my mind. . . .

I was alone in the forest. I had lost the way, and the dark, dripping trees closed in about me. From the steamy forest floor, smoky moisture was rising and swirling in the few remaining shafts of light. Damp pine needles formed a spongy carpet beneath my feet. I was only eight years old. I'd lost sight of Sam, then I had lost the trail. It was growing too dark to follow his markings as he'd taught me. I was alone and frightened. What was I to do?

I'd waited up for dawn to arrive that morning. My small backpack was already packed with all I knew to take along: granola, an apple, and a sweater against the cold. Though I'd never been on a serious hike, or more than backyard camping overnight, I was filled with eager excitement about following Sam secretly on this, his first day of *tiwa-titmas*.

Sam, only four years older than I, had started these journeys when he was the age I was right now. So at age twelve, this journey would be his fifth—and all with no results. Everyone in the tribe was praying that this time it would be successful, that he would have the vision. But few had real hope. After all, Sam's father (Uncle Earnest) was a white face from afar. And when Sam's mother, Bright Cloud, had died so young, the father had taken the child from the reservation at Lapwai, so he'd been unable to receive the proper training by his own people. Then the father had done the unspeakable: taken as his new wife an Anglo woman (Jersey) who drank too much firewater. No one was deceived when she showed up with a daughter of her own, stopped drinking, and insisted in a spirit of generosity that both children spend each summer with Sam's grandparents on the reservation. No one was deceived by tricks like these.

The *tiwa-titmas* was the most important event to a Nez Percé youth. It was his or her initiation into life and the universe. Strong measures were taken to ensure that one could receive the vision—hot baths, steamings in the mud hut, purgation with birchbark sticks inserted in the throat—especially if the vision was a long time in coming, or if it took many trials.

Sam had grown up in these mountains, and was able to greet each rock, brook, and tree as if it were an individual, as if it were a friend. Furthermore, having been on four such quests before, he knew how to find the place by himself whether in darkness or blindfolded—while I, bloody little idiot that I was, couldn't even find the trail.

So here I was: deplorably lost, soaked through from a sudden mountain shower, cold and hungry and weary and footsore and small and young—and terrified by my own stupidity. I sat on a rock to consider my situation.

The sun hovered at the lip of the far range, barely visible through the thick fringe of trees. When it set, I'd swiftly find myself in total blackness, ten miles or more, as near as I could guess, from the place I'd left this morning. I had no sleeping bag, waterproof clothes, matches, or extra food. If I'd brought a compass I wouldn't know how to use it. Worse yet, I knew that when the sun vanished, there would be rodents and snakes and insects and wild beasts moving in the darkness beside me. As the sun sank lower the temperature dropped quickly and the damp chill began to penetrate my bones. I started to cry—huge, hot sobs of unleashed fear and anger and desperation.

The only skill I had, which Sam had taught me, was to send and receive coded messages as the Indians had always done: by smoke signals or flashing mirrors against the sun. Now that it was nearly dark these talents were useless. Or were they?

I gulped back my sobs and peered through my tears at the bicycling reflector strips on my little backpack. Wiping my eyes with my hand, my nose with my sleeve, I stood on wobbly legs and looked around.

Through the darkening forest mist I saw that the sun was not yet gone. But it soon would be. If I could get up high enough before the last beams departed, I'd be able to see a great distance. I could scan the hilltops for the kind of place, the high place, that I knew Sam himself must reach before sunset: the magic circle. It was a wild scheme, but it seemed the only chance I might have to reflect a message from the last light, to send my code into the heart of the magic circle. Forgetting how tired and frightened I was—forgetting that Sam had told me it was more dangerous above timberline at night than here in the protection of the wood—I raced on my little legs uphill, high into the rocky crags that rose above timberline. I raced against the setting sun.

In the dream, I hear the sounds of the forest closing around me as I scramble frantically over rocks, cut by twigs and grasses, the crunch of something large moving behind a tree. In the dream, the forest grows darker and darker, but at last I reach the high ground and clamber to the very top of the highest point. I flatten myself to crawl to the edge, and I peer out across the mountain peaks below.

And there on a mountaintop beneath me, across a wide abyss, is the magic circle. At its very center is Sam. In the dream, he sits on the ground in his fringed buckskins, his hair tumbling loose about his shoulders, his legs and arms folded in meditation—but his back is to me! He is facing the setting sun. He can't see my signal.

So I shout his name aloud, over and over, hoping an echo will bring it back to him. And then the shout turns into a scream. But he is too far, too far. . . .

◆ ◆

Olivier was shaking me by the shoulders. I could see light coming through the high windows of my dungeon, which meant that some of the snow covering the windows had melted. Just how late in the day was it? My head was pounding. Why was Olivier shaking me up and down?

"Are you all right?" he said when he saw my eyes were open. He looked frightened. "You were screaming, you know. I heard it all the way upstairs. The little argonaut crawled under my refrigerator when he heard you."

"Screaming?" I said. "It was just a dream. I haven't had it in years. Besides—it didn't really happen that way."

"Happen what way?" said Olivier, looking puzzled.

But then it suddenly dawned on me that Sam was really dead. The only way I could see him again was in a dream, so even if the dream was an incorrect memory, that was all I had. Shit. I felt as if I'd been kicked in the head by the mule of karma.

"The pancake batter's all ready," Olivier told me. "I'm making you buttermilk flapjacks, with gallons of chicory coffee and some of those cute, disgusting little pig sausages—enough cholesterol to plug your pipes permanently—and just for good measure, eggs over tenderly—"

"Over easy," I corrected Olivier's Yankee slang, a pastiche of *patois*. "Exactly what time is it, landlord?"

"Time for brunch, not breakfast," said Olivier. "I waited to give you a ride to work. I'm afraid that your car has been buried by the snowplow."

◆ ◆

I decided to put on some warm clothes and thick gloves after brunch and dig out my car before checking in for work. I needed physical exercise after two days of driving. And sometimes, after a melt like this one, we'd have a deep freeze, which would mean a month of hacking at automobile glacé. But also, I needed the time to be alone, to make the mental transition from funeral to factory.

So I dragged out my "ghetto blaster" portable radio and took it outside where, surrounded by sparkly snow dunes and icicle-tinseled houses, I hand-dug the slush from my little Honda to the rhythm of Bob Seger cranking out *The Fire Down Below.* And I thought about the various kinds of tissues we choose from which to weave our dreams and our realities.

The truth was, I never *had* found Sam in those woods, he had found me. In the real story—not the dream—I got up above timberline, where the air was too thin for trees to survive and where no animal, so they say, ever chooses to sleep. There was a full moon and I stood atop a rock, bathed in the bright white light. The sun had long gone, and the sky was a purple-black spangled with stars. Thick, dark forest circled me below on every side.

I don't think I've ever known terror like that, standing alone in that milky white light, staring up at the whole universe. I was too terrified to remember my pangs of hunger. Too terrified to cry. I have no idea how long I stood unable to move, knowing that—whatever the danger to a small animal like me, being exposed and defenseless up here—any move I made would be a move closer to that black and impenetrable forest full of night sounds from which I'd just escaped.

Then he came through the wood, in the dead of night, to find me. At first, when I saw a movement at the forest fringe, I backed away in fear. But when I saw the flash of Sam's white buckskins, I raced across the vast space and threw myself into his arms and wept with relief.

"Okay, hotshot," Sam said, pulling me away to look at me with eyes turned a silvery grey by the moonlight. "You can tell me later what gave you the crazy idea to follow me like that. You were lucky I doubled back on my own trail and found your tracks. But I hope you realize you've interrupted my very important meeting tonight with the totem spirits. And here you are, above timberline, where I thought I taught you never to go at night. Didn't my grandfather, Dark Bear, ever tell you why even the wolf and the cougar will never spend the night above timberline?"

I shook my head and gulped tears as he tossed one arm around my shoulders and picked up my backpack from the ground. We went back into the wood. Sam took my hand and I tried to act brave.

"It's because the totem spirits themselves live above timberline," said Sam. As we moved through the dense foliage I could hear the padding squish of his moccasins on the damp ground before me. "Animals sense that the spirits are there, even if they can't see or smell them. That's why if you *want* to meet the spirits, you must wait in a place where not even trees can live. But the place where I'm going is protected by great magic. Since it's too late to take you back, you have to stay up there with me tonight. So I guess we'll do our *tiwa-titmas* together, you and I. We'll wait up there in the circle for the spirits to enter us."

Although I was flooding over with relief at being rescued from a night alone on Bald Mountain, I wasn't sure about this business with the totem spirits.

"Why do we want the spirits to . . . *enter* us?" I found it hard even to ask.

Sam didn't reply, but pressed my hand to show he'd heard as we began again to climb through the dark forest. After what seemed a very long time, we came at last to the circle. It was still dark here within the woods, but up there a shower of white moonlight fell upon the place, lighting the bare, domed crest and the circle of rocks. It looked like the amphitheater where Jersey had once performed in Rome.

Side by side and hand in hand, Sam and I stepped out of the wood. Something strange happened as we entered the circle. The moonlight had a different quality here: sparkling and shimmery, as if bits of silver were hung suspended in the air. And a slight breeze sprang up, bringing with it a chill. But I was no longer afraid; I was truly fascinated by this magical place. I felt that, somehow, I belonged here.

Sam, still holding me by the hand, led me to the center of the circle and knelt before me. He untied the satchel on his belt, and from it he pulled out things I knew must be talismans—brightly colored beads and "lucky" feathers—and, one by one, he tied them into my hair. Then he arranged logs and branches at the center of the circle and swiftly built a fire. As I stood there warming my hands, I suddenly realized how horribly cold I was—wet and chilled to the bone. Hot flames licked the sky as sparks leapt into the blackened night, mingling with the stars. I heard autumn crickets in the brush, and above I could make out the Big and Little Dippers.

"We call them the Large and the Small Bears," said Sam, following my gaze. He sat cross-legged beside me on the ground and stirred the fire. "I believe the bear may wind up being my own totem spirit—though I've never seen her face to face."

"Her?" I said, surprised.

"The bear is a great *female* totem," said Sam. "Like the lioness, the female protects the young—sometimes even from threats by the father—and she gets their food."

"What happens when your totem spirit . . . enters you?" I asked him, still worried about the process. "I mean, does it *do* anything to you?"

Sam smiled his ironic smile. "I'm not sure, hotshot. I've never been 'entered' myself—but I think we'll know if it happens to us. My grandfather, Dark Bear, has told me that the totem spirit approaches you softly, sometimes in human form and sometimes as an animal. Then the spirit determines whether you're ready. And when you are, it speaks to you and gives you your very own secret, sacred name—a name that no one else will ever know but you yourself, unless you decide to share it with somebody else. This name, my grandfather says, is each brave's own spiritual power, separate from, and in many ways more important than, our eternal soul."

"Why hasn't your totem spirit ever entered you and given you your name?" I asked him. "You've been trying so hard, and for so long."

Sam's jet black hair, hanging in a shimmering fall to his shoulders, shaded his eyes as he stirred the fire, so that I could only make out his profile: dark lashes, strong cheekbones, straight nose, and cleft chin. All at once, in this light, he seemed much older to me than just my twelve-year-old big stepbrother. All at once, Sam himself seemed like an ancient totem spirit. Then he turned to me. His eyes in the firelight were as clear and deep as diamonds, and he was smiling.

"Do you know why I always call you 'hotshot,' Ariel?" he asked me, and when I shook my head, he said, "It's because, even though you're only eight years old, the age that I was when I went on my first *tiwatitmas*, you're much smarter than I was then. Maybe you're *still* smarter than I am now. And that's not all; I think you're braver than I am, too. The first time I came to these woods by myself without a guide, I already knew every stick and stone on the path. But you weren't afraid just to launch out all alone today, to trust blindly in what would happen to you. That's what my grandfather calls the necessary faith."

"I was following *you*," I pointed out. "And *I* think maybe I'm just *stupid*!"

Sam threw back his head and laughed. "No, no. You're not stupid," he said. "But maybe, hotshot," he added with his wonderful smile, "just maybe your getting yourself lost in the woods and nearly killed will be some kind of a talisman to me—my lucky rabbit's foot." He yanked my pigtail. "Maybe finding you will change my luck."

And it did. That was how Sam became Grey Cloud, and how our totem spirit blessed us with the light, and how I became part Indian, by the mixing of our blood. From that night forward, it was as if a knot had been untied inside me, and my path through life would be forever straight and clear.

From that night until now, that is.

◆ ◆

The U.S. government has been accused of wasting taxpayer dollars, but never on lavish work facilities for its employees. Especially not out here in the provinces, where every nickel that might have provided comfort in the work environment was squeezed tightly or, better yet, put back into the till. As a result, more cash had been spent on paving the six acres of parking lots surrounding our work site, where government workers parked their cars, than on constructing, furnishing, repairing, cleaning, or heating the buildings where actual humans had to work.

As I pulled into the vast parking lot just after lunchtime, patches of snow still clinging to my car, I surveyed the lots as far as the eye could see. As I'd suspected, by this late in the day the only slots left in the official employee parking areas seemed to be located in western Wyoming. And at this time of year and after a melt like this morning's, the late afternoon wind chill could drop to sixty below; ice pebbles were already kicking against my windshield. I decided to risk a penalty and leave my car at the front of the main complex, where a small strip of official visitor parking was located. Employees were forbidden to park there, or to enter through the guest lobby. But I could usually talk a security guard there into letting me sign the logbook instead of making me hike outside all the way around the vast complex to enter through the official mantraps for employees at the rear.

I slid into one of the open spaces, pulled up my sheepskin coat, wrapped the long fringed cashmere scarf around my face, and pulled my wool ski cap down over my ears. Then I leapt from the car, locked it up, and made a dash for the glass front doors. Not a moment too soon, for the gust that came through as I stepped in nearly ripped the door off its hinges. I managed to yank it shut, then went through the next set of doors into the lobby.

I was unwrapping my scarf and wiping my windburned eyes when I saw him. He was standing at the reception desk, signing out. I froze.

I mean, how could I forget the lyrics of "Some Enchanted Evening"—"you will see a stranger . . ."—when Jersey used to play it over and over, that recording of herself singing it with Dietrich Fischer-Dieskau onstage at the Salle Pleyel?

So here was the stranger. And while the setting was not exactly idyllic—the visitors' lobby of the Technical Science Annex—I knew beyond the shadow of a doubt that this was the one human being on earth who'd been created just for me. He was the gift the gods had sent me in consolation because my cousin Sam was dead. And to think I might have entered by another door instead. How subtle are the mysteries the fates have in store for us just around every corner.

He actually looked somewhat godlike—at least, like my picture-book image of a god. His dark hair swept back in abundance to his collar; he was tall and slender, with the chiseled Macedonian profile one always associates with heroes. The soft camel coat and tasseled white silk scarf he wore swung loose from his broad shoulders. He carried a pair of expensive Italian leather gloves lightly between long, graceful fingers. This was no cowboy engineer, that was for durned tootin', as Olivier would say.

There was in his posture and demeanor something of aloof, regal composure that bordered upon arrogance. And when he turned from the security guard Bella—who was looking at him with her mouth open like a fish—and headed toward me, I saw that his eyes, beneath dark lashes, were the purest dark turquoise, and of an amazing depth. His eyes swept me, tightening for a moment, and I realized that in this getup I had the sex appeal of a polar bear.

He was coming toward me to the exit. He was leaving the building! I felt in a panic that I must do something—fall on the floor in a faint or hurl myself spread-eagled across the door. But instead I closed my eyes and inhaled him as he passed: a mixture of pine and leather and citron that left me a bit dizzy.

It may have been my imagination, but I thought he whispered something as he passed me: "enchanting," or perhaps it was "exquisite."

Or maybe it was only "excuse me," for it seemed I was partly blocking the exit. When I opened my eyes, he was gone.

I went to have a look at the logbook, but as I got to the reception desk, Bella, having recovered her composure, slapped a piece of paper over the open page. I looked up in surprise to find her glaring at me in non-security-guard fashion. It was more the look of an angry cat in heat.

"You're to use the mantraps, Behn," she informed me, pointing at the door that led back outside. "And the logbook is confidential to management."

"All the other *visitors* can read the book and see who's been here when they sign in," I pointed out. "Why not the other employees? I've never heard that rule."

"You're in *nuclear* security, not premises security; that's why you don't know," she retorted with a sneer, as if my field were some kind of primitive throwback compared with her own.

I yanked the paper out from beneath her mauve lacquered fingernails before she knew what was happening. She grabbed at it, but too late. I'd already read his name:

Prof. Dr. Wolfgang K. Hauser; IAEA; Krems, Österreich

I hadn't the vaguest where Krems, Austria, was located. But IAEA was the International Atomic Energy Agency, the group that patroled this industry worldwide—not that it gave them very much to do in recent years. Austria itself was a nuclear-free country. Nevertheless, it trained some of the top nuclear experts in the world. I was more than interested in having a serious look at the *curriculum vitae* of Professor Dr. Wolfgang K. Hauser. And that wasn't all.

I smiled at Bella and scratched my name on the log. "I have an emergency appointment with my boss, Pastor Dart. He asked me to get over from the other building as quickly as possible," I told her as I took off my wraps and hung them on the lobby coatrack.

"That's a lie. Dr. Dart's still out to lunch with some visitors from Washington," Bella informed me with a snotty expression on her face. "I know, because he signed out here with them over an hour ago. You can see for yourself—"

"Gee, so I guess the log isn't confidential to management anymore," I told her with a grin, and I swept through the inner doors.

Olivier was sitting in the office we shared in this building, playing with his computer terminal. We were the project directors in charge of locating, recovering, and managing "hot waste" such as fuel rods and other transuranic materials: that is, materials that had an atomic number higher than that of uranium. These were tracked by programs designed to our requirements and developed by our computer group.

"Who is Professor Doctor Wolfgang K. Hauser of the IAEA in Austria?" I asked when Olivier glanced up from his machine.

"Oh lord, not you too?" he said, shoving back his swivel chair and rubbing his eyes. "You've only been back at work for a few minutes. How could you have picked up the sickness so fast? He's like the site plague, this fellow. To date, not one woman has failed to succumb. I really thought you'd be the one to resist. I have serious money riding on you, you know. We've opened a table to wager the odds."

"He's absolutely gorgeous," I told Olivier. "But it's more than that. There's some kind of—I don't know what to call it—not really an animal magnetism—"

"Oh *no*!" cried Olivier, standing up and putting his hands on my shoulders. "It's far worse than I imagined! Maybe I've lost the grocery money too!"

"You didn't wager the exotic gourmet herbal tea budget?" I asked with a grin.

He sat down again with his head in his hands and moaned. I suddenly realized that Professor Doctor Wolfgang K. Hauser was the first thing in a week that had made me smile and forget, for an entire ten minutes, about Sam. That in itself made up for Olivier's lost wager and a few pounds of glamorous herbal teas to boot.

Olivier jumped to his feet as the alarm system started hooting and a voice came over the loudspeaker between bursts:

> *"This is a test of the emergency alarm system. We are conducting our winter fire drill. This drill is being timed both by local fire officials and federal safety officials. Please proceed in haste to your nearest emergency exit and wait in the parking lot well away from the building until the all-clear signal is blown."*

Holy shit! During fire drills, we could only use the emergency exits. They sealed all mantraps and doors that led back into the building, where people might get trapped in a real emergency—including the door to the lobby where my coat was. The outside temperature, well below zero when I came in, would be colder by now. And a fire drill could last thirty minutes.

"Come on," Olivier said, pulling on his parka. "Get your things—let's go!"

"My coat's in the lobby," I said as I started walking briskly in his wake toward the exit across the vast floor of already vacated desks. A sea of people was flowing out the four exits into the bitter wind I could see outside.

"You're completely insane," he informed me. "How many times have I *told* you not to use the lobby? Now you'll be transformed into a block of ice. I'd share my coat, but we can't both fit inside it—it's snug. But we can each pass it back and forth until the other starts to turn blue."

"I have a down parka in my car, and my car keys are here in my handbag," I told him. "I'll sprint to the car and turn the heat on. If the drill goes on too long, I'll go over to the cowboy bar and have some hot tea."

"Okay, I'll come join you," said Olivier. "I guess if you came in the front doors, that means that you parked illegally, too?"

I grinned at him as we burst out the doors with the crowd, and we jogged around the side of the building.

When I went to unlock the car door, I saw that the button locks were already up. That was strange; I always locked my car. Maybe I was just so distraught today I'd forgotten. I crawled in, put on my parka, and turned on the ignition as Olivier got in at the other side. The engine turned over sluggishly, so it was good that I'd been forced to come out and start it. In weather like this, with little protection, the oil in your crankcase could turn into a snow cone.

And then I noticed the knot, hanging from my rearview mirror.

Sam and I as children had a pet project of learning all kinds of knots. I'd become an expert of sorts. I could tie most knots single-handed the way a sailor could. Sam said the Incas of Peru had used knots as a language: they could do mathematics or even tell a story with them. As a child I used to send knot messages to people—or even to myself, to see if I could recall later what they meant—like tying a string around your finger.

I had the habit of leaving pieces of yarn or rope in different places—like the rearview mirror. Then when I was under stress or working out a problem, I'd tie and untie them, sometimes even working up a complex macramé. And as the knot pattern was worked out, miraculously, so would be my problem. But I didn't recall seeing this piece of yarn on my drive home, or even this afternoon coming in to work. My memory was getting pretty flaky.

I touched the knot as I felt the car warming. It was actually two knots, if you included the part wrapped around the mirror bar: a Solomon's knot, signifying a critical decision, and a slippery hitch, meaning exactly what it sounds like. What did I have in mind when I'd put that there? I undid the yarn and started playing with it.

Olivier had turned on the radio and located some of the awful, twangy cowboy music he loved so much. I regretted inviting him to share my vehicle retreat; after all, we spent ninety percent of our lives under the same roof, as it was. But then I recalled that I'd seen no traces of Olivier's entry and exit, or, indeed, anyone's snowprints when I'd pulled up last night—correction, this morning—before the house. Though the snows and winds might well have been constant and heavy, there should have been *some*thing to show he was there. Indeed, why hadn't he brought in any of my mail if he'd been in residence the whole time? The plot thickened.

"Olivier—where were you while I was gone?"

Olivier looked at me with dark eyes, and he kissed me lightly on the cheek. "Darling, I must confess," he told me, "I met a cowgirl I just couldn't resist."

"You passed the blizzard with a cowgirl?" I said, surprised, for Olivier had never been the overnight-pickup type. "Fill in the blanks. Is she pretty? Is she a Latter-day Saint like yourself? And where was my *cat* while all this was going on?"

"I left the little argonaut with a large bowl of food; he fixes drinks on his own, after all. As to the lady, the past tense would best describe our relationship. It melted away along with the snow; by now, I'm afraid it's as frozen as the ice outside."

Very poetic.

"I have to go to Sun Valley next weekend," I said. "Are you going to desert Jason in that frigid basement again, or should I take him with me?"

"Going skiing?" said Olivier. "Why don't you take us *both* with you? I was just trying to figure out where to go to catch this new snow. In

Sun Valley they have forty inches of base on the slopes, and in the bowls sixty inches of powder." Olivier was an excellent skier and floated like a feather in the powder. I could never get the hang of powder myself, but I loved to watch him from afar.

"Well," I said, "I probably won't be able to be on the slopes much. My uncle's coming to visit. He wants to discuss family matters."

"I should imagine!" Olivier agreed. "You seem to be getting plenty of attention from your formerly absent family, now that you're an heiress." Then he suddenly looked sorry for having mentioned it at all.

"It's okay," I told Olivier. "I'm getting over it. Besides, my uncle's very wealthy himself. He's a famous violinist and conductor in—"

"Not Lafcadio Behn? Is that your uncle?" said Olivier. "With so few Behns in the world, I always wondered if you were related to any of the famous ones."

"Probably to all of them," I said with a grimace. "It's the *Behn* of my existence."

The all-clear signal blew just as I was telling Olivier he could come along this weekend if he liked. Reluctantly I turned off the warm engine to go back out into the bitter cold again. As I was locking the car door, I remembered that I *had* locked it on my way into the lobby. It wasn't my imagination—someone had broken into my car.

I looked in the hatchback where the backseat was folded down. Everything I usually had was still there, but it was slightly rearranged. Someone had searched the car, too. I locked the door anyway, a kind of reflex action. I followed Olivier around to the back entrance, almost bumping into my boss, Pastor Dart, as he was going in.

"Behn—you're back!" he said, a grin crossing that pugnacious face of his. "Come to my office in about half an hour, when I'm free. If I'd known you were coming back today I'd have cleared the decks. There's a lot I need to discuss with you."

Bella the security guard, filing back in just in front of us, turned and smirked over her shoulder. I told the Pod I'd be there, and went back to my office just as the phone started ringing.

"You get it," Olivier said. "I forgot: Before you came, a lady from a newspaper phoned about some documents she said you'd inherited. But the rest of the morning, every time I answered the phone they just hung up. Probably some crank."

I picked up the phone on the fourth ring. "Ariel Behn, Waste Management," I answered.

"Hi, hotshot," said that soft, familiar voice—a voice I'd believed I would never hear again except in a dream. "I'm sorry. Really, truly sorry that it had to be done this way—but I'm not dead," Sam said. "However, I might be, soon, unless you can help me. And fast."

THE RUNE

MARSYAS:
Black, black, intolerably black!
Go, spectre of the ages, go!
Suffice it that I passed beyond.
I found the secret of the bond
Of thought to thought through countless years,
Through many lives, in many spheres,
Brought to a point the dark design
Of this existence that is mine.
I knew my secret. All I was . . . all I am.
The rune's complete when all I shall be flashes by
Like a shadow on the sky. . . .

OLYMPAS:
Through life, through death, by land and sea
Most surely will I follow thee.

—Aleister Crowley, *AHA*

I had to sit down, and fast. The blood drained from my brain like the vortex in a sink, as I dropped like a rock into my chair. I ducked my head until my forehead was grazing my knees, to keep from blacking out.

Sam was alive. Alive.

He *was* alive, wasn't he? Or maybe I was dreaming. Things like that happened sometimes in dreams—things that could seem very real. But Sam's voice was still there, humming in my ear, though I'd just returned from his funeral. It was clearly time for a sanity check.

"Are you there, Ariel?" Sam sounded worried. "I can't hear you breathing."

It was true: I had stopped breathing. It required conscious effort to begin again, to jump-start even this most basic autopilot function. I swallowed hard, gripped the arm of my chair, straightened up, and forced myself to squeak out a reply.

"Hi," I said into the mouthpiece. I sounded ridiculous, but what on earth was I *supposed* to say?

"I'm sorry. I know what you must be going through right now, Ariel," Sam said: the understatement of the century. "But please don't ask questions until I can explain. In fact, it's dangerous for you to say anything at all unless you're completely alone."

"I'm not," I told him quickly. All the while, I was still trying to harness my runaway brain and bring my biorhythms under some semblance of control.

"I figured," said Sam. "I've been phoning since this morning, but I just hung up whenever somebody else answered. Now that I've got you, the first thing we have to do is find a clean phone line so I can fill you in right away on what's happened."

"You could phone me at home," I suggested, trying to be careful in my choice of words. I also slid my wheeled desk chair a bit farther from where Olivier, with his back to me, was still tapping away at his terminal.

"No good; your home phone is bugged," said Sam, who would

know such things. "This office line's clean, at least for the moment—long enough for us to work out a plan. Your car isn't safe, either," he added, anticipating my next question. "Someone broke into it and did a thorough search. I left those knots there to warn you. I hope you haven't stashed anything of significant value in your car or your house: I'm sure you're being watched by real professionals, and most of the time."

Real professionals? What was that supposed to mean: that *I* was somehow embroiled in this spy thriller, too? That was about all I needed to hear, on top of everything else I'd been through in the past twenty-four hours. And though I did wonder what Sam meant by "anything of significant value," I had to restrict myself to: "I didn't notice anything . . ." Instead of "missing" I added, ". . . out of order."

Now Olivier was standing up and stretching. When he glanced over toward me, I swiveled my chair away to face my own desk and started acting as if I were taking important technical notes on my phone conversation. The blood was still pounding in my head, but I knew I had to get Sam off the phone, and quickly. I asked him, "What do you suggest?"

"We need to arrange a way that you and I can talk at appointed times, without letting on to those watching you that you're trying to conceal anything. Like, no ducking into phone booths out on the street."

Which, in fact, had been my first idea. Scratch that.

"On the computer?" I asked, still scribbling on my pad. I wished to God that Olivier would take a hike.

"Computer?" said Sam. "Not safe enough. Any asshole can hack into a government computer—especially a *security* computer. We'd have to work out a multilayered code for protection, and we don't have time. There's a cowboy bar called the No-Name down the road from your office. I'll phone you there in fifteen minutes."

"I have a meeting with my boss in fifteen minutes," I told him. "I'll see if—"

Just then, with immaculate timing, the Pod poked his head in at the door. "Behn, I've cleared the decks a bit earlier than I'd expected. Come to my office as soon as you've finished here. We have something important to discuss."

"Okay, I guess you've gotta go," Sam was saying in my ear. Olivier started to follow the Pod to the meeting as Sam added, "Let's make it an hour from now instead. If you're still tied up, I'll just keep phoning over there every fifteen minutes or so until I reach you. And, Ariel? I'm really, really sorry about all this." Then the line went dead.

My hand was shaking as I put the receiver back in its cradle, and I tried to stand up on wobbly legs.

The Pod had halted at the door and was telling Olivier, "You won't be needed at this meeting, just Behn here. I'm borrowing her for an emergency project for a couple of weeks. A little 'firefighting,' helping Wolfgang Hauser of the IAEA."

He went out the door, and Olivier sank back to his seat with a groan.

"What did I ever do to deserve this, my prophet Moroni?" he asked, casting his eyes toward the ceiling as if expecting to find the Mormon prophet hovering there. Then he looked at me angrily. "You *do* realize this means I've also lost the whole year's budget for multicolored vegetable pastas from northern Italy, *and* my allowance for gourmet wine vinegars with herbs and spices?"

"Oh, Olivier, I'm so sorry," I said, patting him on the back as I went out the door in a kind of daze.

Holy shit—this was shaping up to be an extremely interesting day.

◆ ◆

The Idaho site where I worked was the premier site in the world when it came to nuclear safety research: that is, we studied how accidents happened, and how they could be prevented.

The topic in our field that had recently gained particular prominence—waste management—dovetailed, as it happened, with the exact project Olivier and I had been working on for the past five years. Olivier and I controlled the largest database in existence to identify and monitor where toxic, hazardous, and transuranic materials were stored or buried. As pioneers in the field, we felt it only right that we'd also accumulated the world's largest stockpile of scatological humor—quips like "Other people's waste products are our bread and butter."

But Olivier and I were small fare. The real bread and butter of the research done here in Idaho consisted of the wide-ranging tests on meltdowns and other types of accidents at our reactors out in the lava desert. Though it wasn't surprising that the International Atomic

Energy Agency, watchdog to the world, would send a representative like Wolfgang Hauser to Idaho to share ideas on such topics, I was unprepared for what the Pod was now telling me about this forthcoming mission.

"Ariel, you're aware of the problems going on just now in the Soviet Union" were his first words when I was seated in his office and he'd shut the door.

"Um—well, of course. I mean, it's on the six o'clock news every night," I replied. Gorbachev had hell to pay, introducing freedom to a country that had imprisoned or slaughtered millions of people just to keep them from discussing it over tea.

"The IAEA is concerned," the Pod went on, "that the Soviet Union might lose control of some of its republics—permanently lose control, that is—that there might be large stockpiles of nuclear weapons and materials in these places, not to mention the breeder reactors they're so fond of, many of which are antique with inadequate control systems. All that falling into the hands of untrained provincials with no centralized authority, nothing to lose, and everything to gain by the situation."

"Holy . . . Moly," I said. "So what can I do to help out?"

He threw back his head and laughed, a surprisingly warm and open laugh. Despite his well-deserved reputation, much of the time I couldn't help but genuinely like Pastor Owen Dart. A wiry, rugged former army boxing champ and Vietnam vet, he wore his shaggy bronze hair and leathery, battered face as badges of his inner nature. Though he was barely taller than I, the Pod was a scrappy fighter who only did better coming out of tight corners. But I was still relieved that I'd never had to cross him. Unfortunately for me, all that was about to change.

"Your assignment, you mean?" the Pod was saying. "I'll leave that to Wolf Hauser, when he returns. Had I known you were back already, I would have detained him long enough to meet you, but he's out doing field work for the rest of this week. I can tell you this much, though not for publication: Your involvement will require that you accompany Dr. Hauser to Russia in a few weeks. The arrangements are already under way."

Russia? I couldn't go flitting off to Russia. Not with Sam newly resurrected from the grave, dodging a squad of hit men from God knew where, and lurking only a few yards from here in the parking lot leaving messages for me on bits of string. Sam and I thought we were having trouble communicating *now*, but as far as I knew, they didn't even have working phones in the Soviet Union! Much as I fancied the idea of an intimate foreign boondoggle with the gorgeous, pine-scented Dr. Wolfgang Hauser, I knew I must put a stop to this at once.

"I'm grateful for the opportunity, sir," I told the Pod, "but frankly I don't see how I can help with this project. I've never been to Russia, and I don't speak the language. I'm not a Ph.D. chemist or physicist, so I wouldn't know what I was classifying if it walked up and bit me. My job has always been security—tagging and tracking what other people have already dug up and identified. Besides, you told Olivier Maxfield this job would only last a few weeks and wouldn't take me away from our own project."

I was out of breath from this back-paddling, but it seemed my canoe was going nowhere.

"Don't worry," the Pod assured me in a non-reassuring voice. "I had to tell Maxfield something, or he would have wondered why he wasn't included in this. After all, you're codirectors on your project."

I wanted to ask why, indeed, Olivier had *not* been included. But the Pod's voice had taken on that detached tone he often used with those whose funeral oration he had already prepared. He was on his feet and seeing me out. I felt a chill in my bones at what I still had to do.

"The fact is," he added before we reached the door, "the IAEA handpicked you months ago, based on your record and my recommendation. It's been discussed fully, and finalized. And frankly, Behn, you should leap at this chance. It's really a plum assignment. You ought to be kissing my hand for ensuring that you got it."

I was reeling from the number of blows that had been delivered just since lunchtime. As he opened the office door, I blurted, "Besides, I don't even have a Russian visa!"

"That's been arranged," the Pod said coolly. "Your visa will be handled by the Soviet consulate in New York."

Curses, foiled again. Well, at least I had learned the bad news *before* my private phone chat with Sam. Maybe he could figure out something—along with everything else we had to unravel—to bail me out of this trip.

"By the way," the Pod added in a more conciliatory tone as I was about to take my leave, "I understand that the reason you were absent last week was to attend a family funeral. No one really close, I hope?"

"Closer than I can say, just now," I replied with a noncommittal expression. I touched the Pod's arm. "But thanks for asking."

As I went off down the hall, I glanced at my watch and wondered exactly how close to this spot Sam actually was. Then I went to put on my thermal gear and headed for the No-Name cowboy bar.

◆ ◆

The dark wood-paneled interior was steeped in beer and smoke. The jukebox was playing. I arrived about twenty-five minutes early, sat at a table near the wall phone, ordered a Virgin Mary, and waited. Finally the phone jingled. I was on my feet and grabbing it by the end of the first ring.

"Ariel." Sam's voice sounded relieved when I answered the phone. "I've been crazy since the funeral, wanting to explain everything, to let you know what's happened, what this is all about. But first—are you all right?"

"I think I'm recovering," I told him. "I don't know whether I want to laugh or cry. I'm hysterical with joy that you're alive, but I'm furious that you put all of us—especially me—through all that shit. Right now, I have to take your word for it that you really had to pretend you were dead. Who else knows about this but me?"

"Nobody can know about me, just now, but you," said Sam, his voice tight as a guitar string. "We're in tremendous danger if anyone else learns I'm alive."

"What's this *we*, paleface?" I quoted Tonto's reply to the Lone Ranger when they found themselves surrounded by hostile Apache.

"Ariel, I'm serious. You're in more danger right now than I am myself. I was so afraid you wouldn't come directly back to Idaho—that you'd go off somewhere to be alone and you wouldn't get the package. After I found out your phone was tapped and your car had been ransacked, I kept praying that you'd had the presence of mind to put it somewhere safe. . . ."

The waitress was scooping her tip from the table and raising her eyebrows to inquire if I wanted a refill.

I shook my head and said to Sam on the other end, "I don't understand." I was afraid I did, though. When the waitress was out of earshot, I added in a hoarse whisper, "What package?"

The line was stony silent for a moment. I could feel the tension over the line. When Sam finally did speak, his voice was trembling.

"Don't tell me you didn't get it, Ariel," he said. "Please God, don't tell me that. I had to get rid of it, and fast, before the funeral. You were the only one I could think of that I could rely on completely. I tossed it in a mailbox, addressed to you. I sent it third class parcel post. I was sure no one would ever imagine anything as overt or baldfaced as that: sending it by common mail. I hoped you'd get back just after it arrived, that it would be waiting in the post office for you. How could you not have received it, unless . . . maybe you haven't gone yet to pick up your mail?"

"Holy shit, Sam," I whispered. "What have you done to me? What did you send me in the mail? Not my 'inheritance,' I hope?"

"Did anyone mention it during the funeral?" he asked, whispering back as if someone were listening on the line.

"Anyone?!!" I had to throttle my voice. "It was read aloud in the *will*. Augustus and Grace gave a *press* conference! The *news* media have been telephoning trying to find it! Uncle Laf is flying here from *Austria*! Are those enough anyones for you?"

My throat was getting raw from this full-blast wind-tunnel whispering. I couldn't believe what had happened to my recently calm, well-organized life, which now looked like confetti. I couldn't believe Sam was alive and that I wanted to kill him.

"Ariel, please," said Sam. His voice sounded as if he were pulling his hair. "Did you pick up your mail, or not? Is there any possible explanation we can think of, why you haven't"—he choked a little—"seen the package?"

I felt sick to my stomach. It hadn't taken much to guess what must be in that parcel: Pandora's manuscripts. The manuscripts everyone was so hot to get hold of. The manuscripts I had believed had gotten Sam killed.

"I forgot to stop my mail," I told Sam. I heard his sharp intake of breath at the other end, so I added irritably, "I was a bit distraught! I had to attend the funeral of someone very close to me. I just *forgot*."

"So, if it was in your mailbox all this time," said Sam, still whispering, "then where is it now?"

Terrific. It was in a pile of mush on my living room floor—or maybe buried in a seven-foot snowdrift. Then the image came back of my sinking in snow and tossing my mail up onto the road beneath my car.

"I pulled all the mail out of my mailbox when I got home last night," I told Sam, "and I threw it inside on the floor. I didn't go through it last night. It's still lying there."

"My God," said Sam. "If your line was bugged even before you got home, then it's positive that the place has been searched thoroughly by now—maybe more than once, but surely again since you left to come to work today. Ariel, I nearly got killed for that package, and your only insurance is if they believe you haven't received it yet. But I didn't think of your danger when I sent it to you."

"How sweet," I told him. "Sort of like a chain letter, where you're cursed with a thunderbolt and eternal damnation if you don't pass it on?"

"You don't understand—we *will* be cursed," said Sam. I'd never heard this note of despair from him. His voice sank, and when he spoke it was as if he were at the bottom of a well. "It's so important, Ariel, not to let this fall into the wrong hands. It's more important than we are—more important than your life or mine—"

"Pardon *me*?" I said. "Have you gone completely bonkers? What are you trying to tell me? I should put my life on the line for something I've never even seen? For something I don't even want to know about?"

"It is part of you, and you are part of it," said Sam, for the first time becoming testy. "And although I am very, very sorry I involved you in this, Ariel, what has been done cannot be undone. You are the only one who can find this parcel—and I'm telling you that you *must*. If you fail, the lives at stake won't just be ours, I assure you."

I had no idea what to do. I just wanted it all to go away. I wanted to hide under the bed and suck my thumb. But I tried to pull myself together.

"Okay, let's start from scratch. What did this parcel look like?" I asked Sam.

He seemed to be trying to focus his own thoughts. His words were brittle. "It was about the size of a couple of reams of paper," he said.

"Wow, that's great! There was nothing like that in my mailbox." I knew, because I'd been holding all my mail in one hand when I'd started drowning in snow, and I was able to toss everything up on the road as I sank. "There's only one explanation," I told Sam. "The parcel hasn't arrived yet."

"That gives us some kind of reprieve, but not for long," said Sam gloomily. "It may come today, and you're not at home. But very likely *they* are—or at least they'll be keeping an eye on the house."

I longed to know who "they" were, but I wanted to get the basics down first.

"I could stop the mail now, today—" I began, but Sam interrupted.

"Too suspicious. Then they'd know it was coming by post. As I said, it's my opinion they won't touch you until they're *positive* you have the parcel—or they have it themselves, or they know for sure how it's going to arrive—so for the moment you're okay. I suggest you go home at the normal time and check the mail casually, the way you usually would. I'll try to get a message to you somehow. But to be on the safe side, I'll phone you here again tomorrow, at the same time."

"Roger," I said. "But if you need to reach me quicker, my computer address is ABehn@Nukesite. You can encrypt the message any way you want. Just give me a clue, in another message, what it might be, okay? And, Sam? Uncle Laf is flying in this weekend. I'm going to meet him at the Sun Valley Lodge. He said he was going to tell me the history of . . . my inheritance."

"That should be extremely interesting, coming from Laf. Take good notes," Sam said. "My father was always pretty closemouthed about family history, same as yours was. Then too, if you're staying at the Lodge, maybe we can shake your watchers and meet up on the mountain. We both know it like our palms."

"That's a great idea. I'm afraid my roommate and my cat are coming too," I told him, "but no matter what, we'll figure a way. Assuming we live that long. God, Sam, I'm happy you're—um, around." I seemed unable to yank myself from this umbilical connection of sound, though I saw the waitress approaching my table again, and knew I must.

"Likewise, hotshot," said Sam. "I hope we're both going to be around for a very, very long time. And again, sweetheart—please forgive me. I had to do things this way."

"Time will tell," I told him.

I just prayed there'd be enough of it left for both of us. At least enough to get our hands on Pandora's deadly files.

◆ ◆

Olivier had to work late to catch up enough to take off for a weekend of skiing, so I dropped by the grocery store to pick up a steak and fixings for Jason's and my dinner. It was dark by the time I got home, but the moon was out amid drifting clouds, and enough snow had blown off that I could almost make out the drive. I got out and threw some salt and gravel on the rest. Then I pulled my car in and let Jason out into the dappled darkness to check out the snow.

After putting away the groceries I hiked up the drive as casually as possible to check my mailbox. I could hear Sam's voice in my mind telling me to behave normally, though my heart was thudding. I mindlessly watched Jason jumping around on the crusted snow still covering the sloping lawn. I was praying to find it waiting up there—no matter what dire consequences might result—just to put an end to the clammy terror I felt whenever I thought of it.

As I pulled the mail from the box, scudding clouds suddenly effaced the moonlight, drowning the road in darkness. But just by feel, I knew there was no large package. My heart sank. This meant another suspense-riddled day ahead, and perhaps another and another after that, with my life and Sam's both in danger until we could get our hands on that package. But now it would be a thousand times worse since I was no longer in ignorant bliss.

It was at that precise instant the flashbulb exploded in my brain: I knew what was wrong with this picture.

No one had taken that mysterious package of Sam's. It had never been in my mailbox and never *could* be! My mailbox was smaller than even one ream of paper. And since the snows had prevented anyone reaching my door to leave a parcel, as I'd discovered myself only last night, it meant my postman had been unable to deliver it at all. When that happened, he'd have left a little yellow postal slip notifying me to call at the main branch during office hours to pick up the parcel myself.

Whoever Sam's "professionals" happened to be, I knew that even a criminal or a spy wouldn't be fool enough to stand out here in the open road, in a rural area like this where everybody knows his neighbor, just waiting to rifle through my mail looking for a yellow slip of paper. Especially if he had no inkling that the "valuable" item would come by uninsured parcel post.

Even if someone *had* found this postal slip, would he try to claim the parcel at the post office? It would be taking a huge risk in a town this size, where a stranger trying to call for somebody else's mail would be not only remembered but probably questioned right on the spot. We Idahoans are naturally suspicious of strangers. If the package had indeed arrived, the yellow slip of paper could still be in the damp pile of mail inside my house, where it could have been found if they searched this afternoon. Even if I didn't find the paper tonight, I could go to the post office when it opened first thing tomorrow morning and collect the parcel myself—paper or none.

I headed back to the house, today's mail in hand, intent on sorting through my entire week of soggy mail on the floor. But halfway down the drive the clouds parted briefly, showering the snow-laden lawn with milky moonlight. I saw Jason sitting on the mounded whipped-cream waves of snow out there, batting at a leaf with his paw. I started to call for him to follow me back into the house for dinner. Then I froze. It wasn't a leaf he was batting at, it was the corner of a yellow piece of paper half buried in the snow—blown perhaps from my tossed pile last night.

It was right there in plain sight, yet hopelessly out of reach. The crust of that snow might be strong enough to support one small cat, but there was no way it could support one hundred ten pounds of healthy girl nuke. If I tried to cross to where Jason was playing with the paper, I'd crash through the crust and repeat last night's sinking experience. Nor could I clamp into my Nordic skis, as I had last night. If I was being watched, that would be even more obvious than leaping into phone booths. Sam would not approve.

There was only one choice: I had to hope that Jason's obsession and talent for retrieving would work on something more than his little red rubber ball.

"Jason, fetch," I whispered, as I crouched in the drive and reached my hand out.

Jason looked at me and flicked his tail. The clouds closed in again, plunging us into darkness. I could still make out the outline of Jason's small black body against the stark white snow, but in this light—or lack of it—I could no longer see the paper. I prayed to God he wouldn't decide playfully to bury it so I'd have to excavate the whole garden tomorrow to find it. That would be hard to do "casually," as Sam had enjoined me—and worse yet than the Nordic ski idea.

"Come on, Jason," I whispered a little louder, wondering whether my invisible snoopers were just across the road in the woods.

I stood up, trying to act like an ordinary woman calling her ordinary cat in to dinner. I continued down the drive, not wanting to be overly obvious. Besides, Jason himself would grow suspicious if I started acting *too* normal. He was accustomed to life in a highly eccentric milieu. Nevertheless, he got the message. Before I reached the back door I felt him rubbing against my boots as he did when he wanted to be picked up. I crouched again in the inky darkness, yanked off my gloves, and took Jason's face in my hands so I could feel what I couldn't see: in his mouth was a bit of paper.

Thank God, I thought—choosing not to dwell on what might follow immediately on the heels of this discovery. My heart was thudding again as I carefully removed the paper, holding it gingerly between my trembling fingertips.

"Good cat!" I whispered. Jason purred back, and I patted his sleek head.

At that instant the driveway was flooded with blinding light; I was drowning in light, frozen like a jackrabbit in the brilliant glare as the scream of a giant engine bore down from above, barreling toward me. I panicked, unable to see where to dive for shelter. Jason had ducked behind me as if for protection from a ravening monster. But somehow, in that split second, I found the presence of mind to tuck the piece of yellow paper in the sleeve of my sheepskin coat.

The high beams and growling engine bore down on me, penetrating the drive and shutting off any exit. I stood there riveted by the noise, trying in blindness to feel for my car as a buffer. Then all at once the lights and motor were shut off—though I still couldn't see—and we were plunged back into darkness. A car door opened and slammed shut, and I heard Olivier's voice with its *québecois*-soaked accent calling:

"Jiminy Crickets, do they *never* grow weary of playing in the snow?"

"What is that monster?" I called back up into the void. "The headlight beams alone look ten feet high! You frightened me out of my wits."

"You mean I frightened your wits out of *you*," Olivier said as his voice moved toward me in the darkness. "My crankcase oil froze before I left work. I guess the temperature had dropped more than I knew. Larry the programmer loaned me his truck till tomorrow. I dropped him at his apartment in town before coming home."

I was curious how Olivier could have approached down our dark, deserted road without my having seen or heard the truck, but I was so relieved it was Olivier, not the gang of spy-thug-murderers I'd been expecting, that I hugged him when he came within range, and we three went into the house together.

"I only got one steak," I told Olivier at the landing where our two stairways diverged. "I thought you were planning to grab fast food at the office."

"Tish, tish." He waved his hand in dismissal. "I've been exhausted since our breakfast this morning; I couldn't eat a bite. I'll turn in for the night, if you and the argonaut don't mind dining without me. Maybe a healthy sleep will work a miracle."

From below we heard my phone ringing. Olivier raised an eyebrow. It was rare for me to get so many calls.

"I hope my phone isn't forming bad habits," I said. "I may have to join the twentieth century and get one of those evil answering machines."

Olivier and I parted ways; I raced downstairs and grabbed it on the sixth ring.

"Ariel Behn?" said a woman with a strident voice and an affected mid-Atlantic accent. "This is Helena Voorheer-LeBlanc, of the *Washington Post*." Holy cow, that was some moniker. But I'd never liked newspaper dames: too pushy by far.

"Ms. Behn," she went on without awaiting a reply, "I do hope you don't mind my intrusion during this time of grief, but I've tried to reach you on several occasions at work, and your family *did* give me this private number. They assured me you wouldn't mind speaking with me for a few moments. Is now a good time?"

"As good as any," I agreed with a sigh.

I was getting a headache, no doubt fueled by the number of times I'd had to jump-start my heart this afternoon. My steak was getting warm, my house was getting cold, and I had a piece of yellow paper stuffed up my sleeve that was hotter than nobelium, with a half-life a good deal longer than my own if I didn't do something about it, and soon. Interview with the *Washington Post*? What the hey, why not?

"What would you like to know, Miss—um, LeBlanc," I asked politely, pulling out the yellow sheet Jason had retrieved and looking at it as I spoke. Yup, this was it: Zip code, San Francisco. The square that was checked read: "parcel too large for box."

I sat on the leather sofa and stripped off my coat. Then I stuffed the paper in my back pants pocket and started to make a fire in the fireplace where I usually cooked my dinner. Jason jumped up on the mantel and tried to lick me in the face, so I boxed his ears a little. And I wondered, for just one fleeting moment, whose body was lying in pieces in that coffin under the deep dark earth. Or had they just buried a piece of lead or a rock instead of Sam?

"Your late cousin must have been a very brave man" was Ms. V-LeBlanc's segue into our conversation.

"Look, ma'am, I don't really feel up to chatting too much about my late cousin just now," I told her, tossing logs on last night's cold ashes. "Why this sudden interest in me and my family? I'm afraid no one has made that very clear to me."

"Ms. Behn—Ariel—may I call you Ariel? As you must realize, for three generations your family has produced individuals renowned for their talents and . . ." Greed, I longed to suggest, but she found a more diplomatic term. ". . . world socioeconomic and cultural influence. And yet, no one has ever accomplished an in-depth study of a family whose contributions—"

"The *Washington Post* wants to do an in-depth study of my family?" I cut in. What a joke. "You mean, like a series in the Sunday supplement?"

"Ha, ha," she tinkled. Then, recalling my "time of grief," she settled down. "No, of course not. Ms. Behn, shall I come to the point directly?"

I wished to Christ she would—we both knew what she was digging for—but I simply said yes.

"It's the manuscripts, of course, that we are interested in. An exclusive to publish them is what the paper would like. We're prepared to pay a large sum, of course. But we don't want to get into a bidding war."

A *bidding war*?

"Exactly what manuscripts are you referring to?" I said naively. Let her work for it.

Touching the inflammatory yellow ticket in my pants with my fingertips, I closed my eyes; then I lit the kindling, thinking all the while how life might be simplified if I accidentally dropped it into the flames. But Ms. Helena Post's next words snapped me back to reality.

"Why, the letters and journals of Zoe Behn," she was saying. "I thought your family had spoken with you—"

"*Zoe* Behn?!!" I said, nearly choking on the name. This was worse than my darkest imaginings. "What does Zoe have to do with any of this?"

"It seems impossible you don't know exactly what you are heir to, Ms. Behn." Helena's formerly forceful voice was nearly mellow with amazement.

"Why don't you fill me in?" I suggested.

She had my complete attention now. There'd been plenty written about my horrid aunt Zoe—my father's estranged half sister and the true black sheep of the family. Most of it Zoe had written herself. But this was the first I'd heard of any letters or journals. Besides, what could Zoe have to say that was worse than what she'd already told in worldwide print?

"I was at the press conference in San Francisco, Ms. Behn." Helena took a deep breath. "We were told that as sole heir to your late cousin Samuel Behn, you are entitled also to the estates to which *he* had fallen heir—including those of your grandmother, the famous opera singer Pandora Behn, and your uncle, the mining magnate Earnest Behn. When questioned by the press at this recent conference, both your father and Mr. Abrahams, the estate executor, said it was their understanding this estate might have included not only Pandora Behn's correspondence with world figures and her private writings but also those of her stepdaughter Zoe, the noted . . ." Tart? The word hovered on my lips, but she finished: ". . . dancer."

As I said, my family relations are rather complex.

"It seems, Helena," I told her, "that since you learned so much at this press conference which I unfortunately missed, someone there must have had a clue as to where these important manuscripts actually *are*?" They certainly weren't mentioned at the reading of the will, as I could attest.

"Why, yes, Ms. Behn," she told me. "That's the reason I've phoned so soon, of course, because time is of the essence. According to the executor, in the event of your cousin's death all his property was to be placed in your hands no more than one week after the date of the reading of the will."

Holy shit. My life had been put in danger—I'd been completely set up—and all by my own true blood brother, Sam.

◆ ◆

Actually, it was not totally impossible to delineate my familial relationships for others. It was just a damned unpleasant experience.

My grandfather Hieronymus Behn, a Dutch immigrant to South Africa, married twice, first to Hermione, a wealthy Afrikaner widow who already had one young son, my uncle Lafcadio, whom Grandfather Hieronymus adopted and gave the Behn name. This marriage of Hieronymus and Hermione produced two children: my uncle Earnest, who was born in South Africa, and my aunt Zoe, born in Vienna, where the family moved just after the turn of the century. Therefore these two children were half siblings to my uncle Laf, since all three shared the same mother.

When Hermione became ill in Vienna and the children were still small—so the story goes—my grandfather, at Hermione's request, hired an attractive young student from the Wiener Musik Konservatorium to serve as a sort of nanny or *au pair* to the younger children and to provide their music education. After Hermione's death this young woman, Pandora, became in swift succession: my grandfather's second wife; mother to my father, Augustus; and, after deserting them both to run off with my uncle Laf, the most famous opera singer in post-Secession Vienna.

To further tangle matters came the complex issue of my black-sheep aunt Zoe. Zoe—who'd supposedly been practically raised by Pandora and who had barely known her own sick and dying mother, much less her busy father—elected to run off *with* Laf and Pandora, thus creating, in a single blow, what later became known as the "family schism." Zoe's subsequent life as Queen of the Night, the most successful *demimondaine* and camp follower of the great and famous since Lola Montez, would take some describing.

What I now was dying to know, so to speak, was how much Uncle Laf, a key actor in the family drama, knew about these manuscripts I'd inherited; whose they actually were, Pandora's or Zoe's; and what role they played in the overall picture—information I hoped I'd glean this weekend. If I lived that long.

It was clear that Sam, too, knew far more than he was able to communicate. But why some decades-old letters and diaries were still too hot to handle, or why my father had said they were all in code, which no one else had mentioned, or why Sam had faked his own death with the aid of the U.S. government and set me up as the fall girl at a last-will-and-testament-blabbing press conference—all these remained to be seen. This last item still left me speechless with impotent rage. But for now, since I wouldn't be able to confront Sam even by phone until tomorrow afternoon at the No-Name cowboy bar, I would have to figure out how to hedge my bets and stay alive.

My first step was to ring off the phone with Helena, star investigative journalist for the *Post* (who'd told me a good deal more than I'd told her). I said I'd let her know first thing, if I got the manuscripts.

My next step, critical to events in the days ahead, was to decide whether to let the parcel lie a bit longer in anonymity at the post office, leaving me with only this tiny claim check to conceal, or to pick up the package and try to figure out what to do with it until I could get it to Sam. He certainly deserved to have it returned with equal zeal, like the hot potato it actually was. Whatever the contents—and I was certain by now I didn't want to know—they'd probably have been better left buried. What a fool I'd been ever to believe I could escape my awful family by burying *myself* here, potatolike, in Idaho.

That night before bedtime I lifted my woven, feathered "dreamcatcher" down from the place where it always hung, keeping away bad dreams, just above my bed. I put it in a drawer instead. I thought if I planted the idea in my psyche, just before falling asleep, I might catch a dream that would place in my hand the thread I needed to guide me through the labyrinthine nightmare that was swiftly becoming my life.

◆ ◆

I awoke before dawn in a frantic sweat.

I'd dreamed I was running—not upright, but on all fours—as fast as I possibly could through canelike underbrush so dense I could barely see. Behind me I could feel the hot breath of a large dark animal with ravenous, slathering jaws, its gnashing teeth snapping at me. I saw through the cane that I was coming to an open space of meadow with a wall just beyond. Could I cross it fast enough to leap up and escape the pursuing beast? I gave one extra push of power, though my lungs were already bursting; I crossed the patch of grass and leapt for the wall.

Just then, I woke up and sat bolt upright in bed. Jason, who'd crawled into the bed and somehow wedged himself flat beneath me and the warm pillow, was lying on his side, his eyes shut tight. But his feet were paddling back and forth as if he were running fast to escape something fearful. I started laughing.

"Wake up, Jason," I said, shaking him until he opened his eyes. How dizzy could you get, I thought, tuning in to the dreams of your *cat*?

But I *had* awakened with at least today's first decision resolved in my mind. I'd pick up the package from the post office. I had no other choice. I'd never recover if I put it off and the damned thing vanished. Where to hide it was another question. My office wasn't safe: too many people in and out all day. And until I actually saw the parcel I wouldn't be sure I could even put all the documents in one place—a drawer or briefcase, for example—since it hadn't fit into my mailbox.

When I went out, I was relieved to find that Olivier's huge borrowed truck was no longer blocking the drive, so I could back my car out without going off the side. He must have had to pick up Larry the programmer extra early.

I pulled up before the post office about ten minutes after they opened for the morning. There were no cars yet parked in front as I pulled into the lot. I got out and nodded greetings to the postal worker who was scattering rock salt on the steps. The pounding of my heart and my head sounded from inside like a tympani section hooked on Latin American rhythms. Why was I so uptight? Absolutely no one here could have any idea of the contents of what I was about to collect.

I went up to the desk and handed George the postal clerk my yellow slip. He went in the back room and came out carrying a large parcel—bigger than a ream of paper, wrapped in brown paper with twine tied around it.

"Sorry you had to come all the way down here to pick this up, Miz Behn," said George between wide-gapped teeth as he handed it to me. He scratched his head. "I'd a been happy to give it to that fella you sent for it just now, but he said you lost the claim slip. I told him then you'd have to come in person or send a signed note that it was okay to give it to him. But I guess you found your claim slip anyway."

I was standing there deaf and dumb, as if all sound had been shut off, as if I were in a glass jar. I held the package in my hands, not speaking. George was watching me as if maybe he should give me a drink of water or fan me or something.

"I see," I managed to choke out. I cleared my throat. "That's okay, George, I had to come this way anyway. It's no inconvenience." I started for the door casually, trying to think of a way to ask the question I desperately needed the answer to. Just at the door, I found it.

"By the way," I said to George, "I mentioned to a couple of folks to pick it up if they came this way. Who finally came by, so I can tell the others not to bother?"

I expected him to say "new fellow in town" or some such. But what he said made my blood run cold.

"Why—it was that Mr. Maxfield, your landlord. His postal address is just down from yours. S'why I felt bad not to be able to give him the parcel. But rules is rules."

Olivier! The bottom fell out of my stomach. In my mind flashed the image of those truck high beams last night—and the drive empty of anything but tire tracks when I left this morning. I tried to smile, and thanked George. Then I went out and got into my car, and I sat there with the parcel on my lap.

"It's all your fault," I told it.

I knew I shouldn't, but I had to do it. I reached into the glove compartment and pulled out the bone-handled deer knife I kept there, that had never touched a deer. I cut the twine and pulled the paper open. I was desperate to know the brand of my hemlock before I had to drink it. When I saw the first page, I started laughing.

It was written in a language I couldn't read, with letters that weren't even letters of the alphabet, though they did seem oddly familiar. I riffled through the rest like a deck of cards: about two reams of paper, and all alike, each page printed in black ink by the same hand. The pages were filled with feathery stick figures with little circles and bumps protruding here and there like forms dancing across the pages, like the symbols painted on an Indian teepee. What did they remind me of?

And then I knew what they were. I'd seen them in a cemetery once in Ireland, where Jersey had taken me to visit her ancestors. They were runes: the language of the ancient Teutons who'd once lived all over northern Europe. This bloody manuscript was written entirely in a language that had been dead for thousands of years.

Just as that knowledge dawned, from the corner of my eye I saw the flash of something dark moving in the parking lot. I glanced up from the manuscript and saw Olivier walking across the pebbly, salted ice, headed for my car! I tossed the manuscript on the passenger seat, where it slid partly out of its wrapper and a few pages fluttered to the floorboard, which I ignored. I was trying to jam the key into the ignition, but in my hysteria I missed twice. By the time the engine turned over, he was almost at the passenger door. Frantically I shoved down the door lock with my elbow, which caused all the car doors to lock in tandem, as I threw it in reverse.

Olivier grabbed the handle of the passenger door and tried to yell something through the window, but I ignored him and threw the stick forward. I tore out of the lot, dragging Olivier along until he finally let go. I glanced at his face for one instant before I took off down the street. He was staring through the glass at the manuscript!

Now that I was out on the street driving, and I knew Olivier was really after the manuscript, and I knew he knew I had it, I was becoming even more hysterical. The chances of hiding it anywhere in town, at this point, were absolutely nil. I knew I had only one choice, and that was to get it somewhere out of town to hide it. But where?

Olivier knew I was meeting my uncle at Sun Valley this weekend, so that was too obvious. I *had* to get on a road in some direction—and fast, before he got back to his car to follow me. The absolutely worst thing that could happen was for me to get trapped with this manuscript in my car.

With no time to think, and with no thoughts leaking into my brain anyway, I headed full speed down the road to Swan Valley, to run over the Teton Pass into Jackson Hole.

THE SNAKE

THE SERPENT:
The serpent never dies.
Some day you shall see me come out of this
beautiful skin,
a new snake with a new and lovelier skin. That is birth.

EVE:
I have seen that. It is wonderful.

THE SERPENT:
If I can do that, what can I not do? I tell you I am very
subtle.
When you and Adam talk, I hear you say 'Why?'
Always 'Why?'
You see things, and you say 'Why?' But I dream things
that never were; and I say 'Why not?'

—George Bernard Shaw, *Back to Methuselah*

It would be a good two-hour haul, with winter road conditions what they were, across the Idaho border and into Wyoming. But it would be my first chance to think things through since my return from San Francisco—was it only yesterday morning?

I had a job I'd already been absent from for more than a week, and a boss who wasn't too happy just now because I had cold feet about leaving for Russia. If I went AWOL at work on my second day back, I might not *have* a job. Then too, there was my critical arrangement to wait by the phone at the No-Name cowboy bar this afternoon. But now, with this unexpected loop, I had no idea how I'd ever contact Sam again. The final disaster struck my beleaguered mind just before I reached the end of the valley: I couldn't leave my cat in the same house with a villain—especially a villain I still owed for this month's rent!

At the end of the valley, the road spiraled down like a corkscrew to meet and follow the curving sweep of a river that seemed to appear from nowhere out of the dense undergrowth. I knew every twist and turn by heart. I took the dips like a slalom course. Dropping beneath the crashing two-tiered waterfall, I descended to the chain-linked valleys carved out by the rushing waters of the Snake.

The Snake is one of the most beautiful rivers in North America. Unlike the broad, complacent rivers that water the Midwest, the Snake behaves more like its namesake: a dark, mysterious reptile that only feels at home in wild and inaccessible crevasses of the mountains. It winds in a narrow zigzag for most of the thousand-mile meander from Yellowstone in Wyoming through Idaho, Oregon, and Washington State, where it joins the massive Columbia in its headlong sweep to the ocean. But the glassy sheen of most of the river's surface hides the underlying serpentine treachery, which strikes swiftly and often lethally. These waters are so rapid, the current so strong, the hidden pools so deep, that few of the bodies swept away are ever found. Indeed, even whole automobiles have been swallowed and never recovered. This may explain the rumors of the enormous water beast lurking there, who devours everything he drags to his underwater lair.

As usual at this time of year, the valley below was buried in thick marshlike fog formed as the warmer water of the river impacted the ice-cold air. Just before the last descent, while the road could still be seen, natives usually checked fore and aft for other cars they might collide with when they got down there in the soup. It was then that I saw it, slipping out of sight around the curve behind me—a plain grey government car with standard white plates identical to a hundred others in our fleet at the nuclear site, which any of ten thousand employees might borrow for site visits or other official business. What was it doing out here, en route to no place? There was a hefty penalty, even job probation, for using government vehicles in personal or recreational activities.

But maybe this *was* official business, I thought. Sam had said I was being watched all the time, hadn't he? If even Olivier had his hands in the cookie jar, who knew how many others might be in it too? Though I couldn't see the driver through the windshield, when I saw the car reappear around the last corner I was certain he was tailing me. There was nobody but me out here.

But I knew every bend and wrinkle along this road, and I knew that the best place to ditch him would be in the soup. So as soon as I reached the last steep decline, I accelerated and dove in. Behind me, I saw him pick up his pace and do likewise. Then the blanket of dense white fog closed around us, and we were isolated within its embrace. I heard only the sound of silence as my car slalomed on the sharply curving road, moving like the serpent itself through the mist.

It seemed hours that I swung through the whipcrack curves of the road, through that smothering whiteness like the inside of a pillowcase, but my car clock told me it was really only twenty minutes. I knew the road would soon come out of the fog again as it approached the pass. Up there the road would fork, giving a choice of several routes heading into Jackson. So at the first turnout sign that appeared, almost invisible in the swirling mist, I cut my wheels and pulled off the road. Then I turned off my engine and cracked open my window a bit to listen.

Less than a minute later the government car swept by. I could hear the engine and see its outline, dark silver through the mist, but that was all. I waited a full five minutes before starting again on my way.

The road was clear over the pass, so I had a brief respite enabling me to think. I wondered what this manuscript was that had fallen into my hands, why everybody wanted it, and how it was that it had come to be written in runes. It surely wasn't any correspondence belonging to Granny Pandora or my nefarious aunt Zoe. Nor did these pages resemble mementos of any of those great and famous legends with whom they'd reportedly trafficked throughout their long lives. And though the Celtic language itself might be thousands of years old, the document on the seat beside me wasn't even beginning to yellow: it seemed to be written in pretty fresh ink. It was quite possible, I knew, that Sam had written in a rune code himself, trying to transcribe key elements of the original, and possibly more dangerous, documents—and maybe also to give a clue where the real ones were located, in case something happened to him.

It didn't make sense why Sam "had to get rid of" the manuscript. If his death was faked, if everyone on the planet knew I was about to inherit the goods, if journalists knew enough to demand a press conference and ask for exclusive rights, and if even my own landlord was set to spy on me, then this whole situation had been designed to flush someone out of the woodwork: someone who wanted the real manuscript for whatever reason. And I was the bait.

I also now understood exactly what it was I must do: I had to hide this document in such a difficult place that no one but me—including Sam—could find it. And I knew precisely where that was going to be.

It was lucky I'd brought my skis.

◆ ◆

At Jackson Hole I pulled into the parking lot facing the Grand Tetons—or "big tits," as French trappers had dubbed these showgirl-breasted mountain peaks pointing at the sky. I stuffed the manuscript into one of my dog-eared canvas knapsacks from the back, grabbed my silvery moonsuit and parka and the thermal socks and gloves I always kept there, and went inside the lodge to the powder room to transform myself into the Snow Queen. Then I bought a cup of coffee, got some change at the cafeteria, and made the de rigueur long distance call to the Pod to explain my absence on this, my first full day back at work. I wanted to be sure he hadn't gone ballistic when, after our slight unpleasantness yesterday, I'd failed to show up this morning at the office.

"Behn, where are you?" he said as soon as his secretary put me through.

"Last night I suddenly realized that I needed to collect some data out here at the western site, where I'm phoning from," I lied.

The nuclear site at Arco out in the high desert, where the government's fifty-two experimental reactors were located, was a three-hour drive in the opposite direction, past town and the post office I'd so hastily quitted. But the Pod's next words made my lie seem absurdly unnecessary.

"I've had Maxfield beating the bushes for you since he first came in this morning. Wolf Hauser unexpectedly came back to town and dropped in here quite early. He was overjoyed to hear you'd be joining his project and wanted to meet you at once, since he was about to depart again on out-of-town business. We phoned you at home, but you'd already left. So I had Maxfield dash over to try to catch you at the post office—"

"The—post office?" I interjected, in what I hoped was a casual tone, though my ears were ringing and my head had started pounding again. Why on earth the post office? I pulled my psychological cards close to the chest to take a peek: Was the Pod in on this, too? I was beginning to trust no one, a prescription that hardly seemed the antidote to paranoia. But he was still speaking.

"After you left work yesterday I got a call from someone representing the *Washington Post*," he explained. "She said she'd been trying to reach you for several days about some valuable papers she learned at a press conference were en route to you; that the *Post* urgently wanted to speak with you about acquiring them. I said I'd be sure to have you phone her today.

"Then when Hauser came through in such a rush this morning, it occurred to me that you might be over picking up mail—especially if you were expecting important documents. So I sent Maxfield at once. But when he found you—well, he's told me the most astounding tale of your behavior."

I knew what was coming next: how I drove off with some of Olivier's body parts still attached to my car, and nearly glued the rest of him to the pavement. I looked like a fool, and worse. Yet though this seemed straightforward enough, there were a few things dangling here. For instance, whether it was the Pod's idea or Olivier's to try to pick up that package. But I could think of no way to ask, without letting the Pod know that the parcel was now actually in my possession.

"All this trouble just because I missed Dr. Hauser again," I told him apologetically. "Well, it couldn't be helped. I was in a big hurry too, so I didn't realize Olivier was standing so close to my car. Tell him I'm sorry I almost drove over his foot." Then I added, more cautiously, "Dr. Hauser and I seem to keep passing like two ships in the night. Things have gotten pretty confused, but I'm sure we'll meet up soon enough. I did think over this project last night. I agree with what you said, that it might be the shot in the arm my career could use right now."

I wasn't just cranking up the Pod's ego. Maybe my brain *was* getting scrambled and soggy after all this stress and hysteria, pushing me into believing everyone I'd ever known was out to get me. Maybe I *did* need a short retreat in the USSR to introduce me to a different reality than my own, which was starting to look pretty "virtual." It was time for a *schuss* downhill to flush out my microprocesses.

I told the Pod I'd be back from the site before quitting time, and rang off. I felt relieved that Olivier was an unlikely candidate for the spy, hit man, and potential cat assassin I'd been visualizing. But I was still going to take the appropriate precautions and hide this manuscript where no one could ever find it—maybe not even me.

◆ ◆

I had to wait half an hour for the tram to get hooked up. By the time it finally did, there were so many passengers queued up that they had to jam us in like sardines and weigh the fully laden tram before letting it take off over the deep gorges on that spindly-looking high wire. Packed in with all those restless midwesterners and Japanese tourists, my face was squashed against the windowpane by the mass of bodies, affording me a lovely view of the two-thousand-foot drop we'd experience if the load did prove too heavy for this orange crate. It would have been faster and simpler just to catch a chair lift instead. But I wasn't sure I could locate the spot I was looking for without starting from Scylla and Charybdis.

Scylla and Charybdis were my two pet rocks: giant pinnacles of stone, side by side, that you were forced to ski between when you first came off the gondola—unless you decided to circumvent them and go into the deep powder, something I rarely did, and especially not today when I had to keep my balance on this treacherous slope with close to ten pounds of illicit manuscript strapped on my back.

The passage between the thirty-foot-high black rocks was narrow, steep, and always icy from the constant wear of many skis. It was like a blind tunnel, with light coming in only from a narrow crack at the sky. There wasn't room inside there to brake or angle your skis, and nothing soft enough to dig your edges into for control.

Once, in high summer, I had hiked to this meadow and tried to climb up through the gap between Scylla and Charybdis. It was too steep to negotiate on foot: pitons and ropes were called for. But going down in snow was a lot simpler: all it took was nerves of stainless steel. You had to tuck down, knees locked, hands on your ankles, stay balanced, *schuss* through the gap, and keep praying that you hit no bad ice or rocks when you exited again into daylight.

I pried myself out of the gondola along with the rest of the sardines. From the forest of skis and poles hanging on the side of the tram I found and extracted mine. I took my time waiting beside the upper warming hut, knocking snow off my boots, clamping on my skis, defogging my goggles—giving my trammates, who were champing at the bit to hit the mountain, the right of way. I wanted to have a clear hill when I came out of the chute, not only to avoid dodging the bodies that were usually littering the slope beneath Scylla and Charybdis but, more important, so I could go prospecting for my hiding place without being observed.

I knew there wouldn't be another gondola for half an hour, so when things quieted down and the crowds had vanished, I shoved off alone across the hill. The only sound was the swish of my skis on the snow as I dropped into the fall line and plunged through the gorge between the glittering and mammoth black forms of Scylla and Charybdis.

I managed to keep on track until I came out the other side, when a blast of wind hit me sideways, catching my backpack with full force. I wobbled and started to go down, but I picked up my left ski and swung my weight down into my right knee until the tips of my glove brushed the earth. Then I bounced back up and swung down again into the left knee like a skater, still plummeting with the fall line until I recovered the rhythmic center of balance.

Taking a deep breath as I skied on, I scanned the line of hills—the Grand Teton rising majestically in the distance as my marker—searching for the ridge I knew I had to drop from to find the crevasse I was seeking, and the cave. Just then, I thought I heard the soft swish of skis behind me. Odd, since I was on the highest ski slope of the mountain with no other lifts above me, and I thought I'd waited for everyone coming off the gondola.

"Your *wedeln* is a bit off," said a gravelly voice with a German accent from a few yards behind me.

There were plenty of Germans prowling around ski areas, I told myself. It couldn't be.

But it was. He skied up beside me, and again I went a little weak in the knees as I swung to a halt. He pulled off his goggles, wrapped them like a rubber band around the sleeve of his stark black jumpsuit, and smiled at me with those amazing turquoise eyes.

"Good morning, Dr. Hauser," I managed to say. "What brings you up here for midweek skiing?" Then I pulled myself together. After all, this could hardly be a coincidence. Which meant it might be dangerous. So I took off again down the slope.

"I might ask you the same question, Mademoiselle Behn," he called out behind me as he double-timed to catch up. "I *do* have an extremely important project. But *you* seem to be what is holding things up."

Glancing over, I thought how beautiful his mouth was, and those cheekbones . . .

We pulled our eyes away from each other just in time, only seconds before we would have hit a mogul. We split up around the bump, and when we swept together again Dr. Hauser was laughing. We floated on down the hill, side by side in perfect rhythm. Suddenly, with a strength and agility that took me by surprise, he planted his poles as we ran, lifted both skis in midair, and hopped over a fallen tree in the path. It didn't seem to faze him; he was still moving like flowing water over the sea of billowing moguls.

It was simple to explain how he'd recognized me on sight. After all, as the Pod had said, he'd reviewed my files, so he'd seen not only my vital statistics but my security photos as well. Still that didn't explain what he was doing here on this mountain, one hundred miles from town. As if tracking these thoughts, he skidded to a halt where the trails forked, throwing up a spray of snow, and turned to me.

"I've already followed you across two states and up this mountain. That's quite enough for one morning. What if we go to the ski lodge just downhill from here, the upper *Schloss,* where I can buy you a nice hot lunch. Then perhaps we can talk, get to know one another a bit. Unless," he added, "you've already brought a lunch for yourself in your backpack there?"

"No, I'd love to join you," I said, I hoped not too hastily. "And I'm very sorry. I didn't know it was you following me."

"I accept all apologies," he said with a bow. "But that trick in the mist was quite something. When you vanished I tried roads in three directions until at last I understood what you'd done. Tell me, how does a young woman like you learn to—as I believe you Americans say—'lose a tail' with such competence?"

"I guess that's why I went into the security field," I told him. "I've always had an interest in things that are hidden: in the idea of pursuit and discovery and capture."

"So have I," said Professor Dr. Wolfgang K. Hauser with an enigmatic smile.

◆ ◆

By the time we'd finished lunch at the bird's-nest restaurant and warming house at midmountain, Dr. Hauser was calling me Ariel and insisting I call him Wolfgang. He'd shown me how to make swing chairs of our parkas by stretching them over our skis and poles, which we planted in the snow. We hung there in the sun just beyond the deck, dipping crusty dark bread in our oyster stew and drinking fruity *Glühwein* spiced with cloves and dusted with cinnamon.

Wolfgang had given me plenty of ski tips as he'd followed me down to the restaurant. He was an incredible skier, even better than Olivier. I'd skied mountains all over the world since childhood, and I knew a master when I saw one. There were very few who had that combination of strength and fluid grace that made everything they did on the mountain seem effortless.

Now, as we reluctantly started collecting our things to go down the mountain, my new colleague turned to me with a bemused look. "I wonder: what should I collect from you in repayment for giving you all those free skiing lessons this morning?"

"You shouldn't charge anything," I told him, tying my parka around the waist of my jumpsuit. "Everyone knows it's in the very nature of the Austrian to give ski instruction, it's as natural as breathing. You don't charge for what comes naturally."

He laughed, a little uncomfortably I thought.

"But I have to ask you a serious question," he said. "You know, I actually *did* recognize you from your photos—it was really from your eyes alone—when you came into the building yesterday, although you were all bundled up and looking like a polar bear." Wow, those had been my thoughts exactly. "I wanted to speak with you then, but I felt somewhat awkward doing so in front of others."

He took my backpack from my hands as I was about to pull it on, and he set it on the ground; then he put his hands on my shoulders. I felt the heat moving from his fingers into my flesh. This was the first man I'd ever met, or even dreamed about, who could make me limp just by looking at me—and now he was *touching* me. But I was rendered totally speechless by what came next.

"Ariel, you know we'll soon be working together closely on a critical assignment. Under the circumstances, I realize that what I'm about to say to you is probably inadvisable—but I really can't help it. I must tell you that it's going to be very, very hard for me to maintain a professional relationship with you—the kind of relationship that is needed for us to carry out this project. I assure you I didn't plan what's happened. Indeed, this sort of thing has never happened to me before . . ." He trailed off, as if expecting me to speak. When I held my breath, waiting for the other shoe to drop, he added, "I don't know how to say this exactly, but, Ariel, I'm extremely attracted to you. I am very . . . very attracted to you."

To *me*? Holy shit. I was in deep water and I knew it. I could have drowned in the depths of those turquoise eyes as he stood there looking so *intense*. This guy was dangerous in more ways than one—and I had plenty of danger in my life already without taking any extra free ski lessons. If only he weren't so . . . attractive.

Forget it. He wasn't attractive, he was charismatic: he was magical. I knew it, and so did everyone else who ever laid eyes on him. But this couldn't be happening to me—not on top of everything else. Not now. Why in heaven's name had the Pod decided to dish up this poison to *me*? I had to do something to get myself back to reality, such as it was.

I closed my eyes and took a deep breath. Marshaling all my reserves, I stepped backward so that his hands fell from my shoulders, snapping the link. I opened my eyes.

"So what's the question?" I asked.

"Question?" he said, momentarily confused.

"The serious question you said, only a moment ago, that you needed to ask me," I explained.

Wolfgang Hauser shrugged his shoulders and looked a little pained. It seemed that he hadn't thought through what kind of response he himself had really expected of me—nor what might come next in the scenario.

"You don't trust me," he said. "And you're perfectly right—why should you? I follow you like an idiot through the fog, I chase you down a ski mountain and drag you to lunch. I blurt out unsolicited feelings for you that I bloody well should have kept to myself. For all this, I deeply apologize. But I do want to say one thing. . . ."

I waited. But I was totally unprepared for the broadside when it came.

"I am a personal acquaintance of your uncle Lafcadio Behn, from Vienna," he informed me. "I've been sent here to Idaho to protect you as best I can. Before you came back from that funeral in San Francisco I flew here to be sure you'd be placed on my project—not only for your professional expertise, I admit, but because the documents you are heir to *must not* fall into the wrong hands. Do you understand?"

Holy Mother of God and all the saints. What was he saying?

"Ariel," he said, "I assure you that when I took this assignment, I didn't expect to find . . ." He paused and looked me in the eye for a moment. "Oh, *Scheiss,* how I've messed this up," he said finally, and he turned away to pull his skis from the snow, so I couldn't see his face. "Let's just go back to town, shall we?"

◆ ◆

This wrench in the works had altered my freshly formed plans. I tried to think up some excuse: that due to my grief, or whatever, I wanted to be alone so I could have some time to think. But now that Wolfgang and I had been so chummy over *Glühwein*—now that he'd disclosed his acquaintance with the black-sheep branch of my family, and had hinted at his burning passion for me, and also, I'd noticed, had eyed my backpack more than once—I felt it might seem too obvious a ploy. And although he had never actually asked me what *I* was doing up here, I understood that my only option was to play for time, ski down the rest of the mountain, and worry about where to stash the manuscript while I drove back alone.

By the time we'd suited up and snapped into our bindings, Wolfgang had recovered enough of his former charm and self-control to suggest that this time I follow him down the mountain. As good skiers learn early, if you can pattern your own form—the rhythmic combination of weight-shifting and pole-planting—after that of a superior skier, it will be worth more than ten thousand lessons with some instructor yelling in a foreign tongue: "Bend zee knees! Stop dragging zee poles!" I was delighted to get this education—at least, until he cut into the powder.

He dropped from the side of the groomed slope and slashed down through a grove of aspen thick with snow, slaloming in and out among the trees. It took a moment before I realized he was headed for a big bowl of sugary powder of a quality that drew tourists by the thousands each year. It was at the far end of these woods. But in all the years I'd frequented this mountain, I myself had avoided it like the plague.

Powder skiing requires a completely different approach from basic Nordic or Alpine techniques. You lean back on your haunches, as if in a rocking chair, which forces your ski tips high above the snow so they don't bog down and stop you dead in your tracks. This takes enormous flexibility of the knees and strength in the thighs. If your tips get buried, if you stop, if you catch an edge and fall, you start sinking.

Because I'd never found that special rhythm, I felt completely helpless in the powder. But now I also had a heavy backpack adding awkward weight, which explains why I balked in the aspen grove—why I swerved instead to thread my way back to the groomed slope I'd just left.

And that was when it happened.

I had reached the edge of the wood when I knew something was wrong. I felt it coming above me long before I could hear it. There was no sound, but perhaps, like a whisper, the earth breathing a long, shuddering sigh. I think the palms of my hands, tingling with pinpricks inside the warmth of my gloves, sensed it before my conscious brain did. The moment I understood what was happening, I also understood that I had no idea what to do.

The ground was moving under my feet—not the ground itself, but rather the snow! The mountain was shedding its skin: ripping away, in one brutal slash, that five-foot-deep blanket, an accumulation of leaden snow that had taken all winter to fall. I was in an avalanche.

And then the noise began, first a rumble, then quickly a roar, as snow started churning over itself and pebbles and rocks started spinning down the mountain around me. I was speeding just along the forest hem, as fast as I could safely go without falling, but unsure whether to duck into the woods and risk a tree falling on me or to take my chances here, with this mountain of heavy snow moving down like a load of cement.

My mouth was dry from terror and my hands were growing numb. I prayed I wouldn't black out—then I thought maybe I should, so that when I went under, the angry onslaught would be painless. I was moving, but I knew the snow was moving faster. To my left, out on the open slope, it was tossing big rocks in the air like children's beachballs. At my right, from the corner of my eye, I saw trees going down, their roots flung up toward the sky. The avalanche was a living, breathing thing, devouring whatever fell into its maw, like the beast of the Snake River.

I couldn't outrun it. I was no downhill racer, and better skiers than I had tried to beat avalanches in the past, with small success. There wasn't a thing in my bag of tricks that would save my ass. And I still had this bloody backpack on my back.

Just at that second, two things flashed into my mind. The first, knowing the mountain as I did, was that I was about to run out of woods on my right-hand side, woods that separated me from the powder bowl just at the base of the slope, where the bowl emptied out. The second was, what had become of that bowl? And since powder moved quicker than packed snow toward uncontrollable avalanche, what had happened to Wolfgang Hauser?

These two questions were answered together.

Beneath, I could see the spot where the snows met in a cauldron of violence, where the groomed slope to my left and the powder bowl to my right unloaded masses of snow, rock, and debris. At their impact point a funnel of snow was flung into the sky.

My legs were shrieking with pain from the strain of my flight, every sinew screaming to stop and rest, but I knew that to stop now meant certain death. Then, in a blur to my right, I saw a black form cutting through the trees. Timber was being ripped from the ground as the snows hurtled down without respite, but still he came.

"Ariel!" he screamed above the crashing roar all around us. "Leap! You must jump!" I scanned frantically, trying to see what he meant—and then I knew.

Just below, where the line of forest ended, was the lip of a crevasse that jutted into the air like a ski jump. I couldn't see over the top, but I already knew what was beyond it. Many times in the past I'd gone off that edge, letting my ski tips tilt over the lip so I slid like a teardrop down the sheer cliff face and into the chasm; then I would slalom through the forest of rock littering the floor of the gorge.

But at the speed I was now moving, I couldn't slow down at the edge of the gorge to drop safely over the side. If I did try to slow down, I'd be crushed by moving snow. I either had to bypass the gorge altogether, taking my chances on the open slope, which were now practically nil with the avalanche closing on me, or take the jump, as Wolfgang had told me to, and pray I'd land upright on my skis, more than a hundred feet below, and on snow instead of hard, sharp rock.

I had no time to think, only to act. I yanked off the wrist straps, dropping my ski poles in my wake so I wouldn't get skewered by one of them when I hit bottom. Then I shed the parka tied around my waist for the mobility I'd need to get enough loft. I knew I couldn't unbuckle the damned backpack in time to make the jump, so it had to come with me: the flying hunchback of Notre Dame.

I crouched into my boots to increase speed and control. As I shot off the cliff, I lifted my body, stretching out full length into the wind with my arms pinned back and my chin thrust forward, so I could completely clear the cliff and make a clean landing.

My skis were resting on bottomless space. I was hurtling into the gorge, falling. It was free fall, and I knew I had to concentrate and not panic. I struggled to keep my tips high and together for the landing, as snow and rubble flew from the cliff, tossed like a sea of confetti around me. I fell and fell. As the ground loomed toward me, I saw how truly narrow was the ribbon of snow beneath, how many and massive were the rocks. And again I thought of the serpentine beast, and the open jaws of death.

After what seemed the eternity of a bad dream, my skis struck snow—and simultaneously my arm smashed into rock. The jagged edges ripped through the sleeve of my silver moonsuit like a serrated knife; I felt the slash of flesh parting, ripped from elbow to shoulder. The impact knocked me sharply sideways, off balance. Though there was no pain yet, I felt a sickening throb as the warm, wet blood soaked into my sleeve.

The forest of rugged rock flashed by me in a blur. I struggled frantically to stay on my feet. But I was moving too fast, without poles for balance. I caught an edge and spun out, whirling sideways and then flipping head over heels. I was somersaulting out of control, my skis striking rocks, knocking the binding locks open. But to my surprise, more than once when I smashed into a boulder, the thickness of the backpack actually protected me.

My shoulders and shins weren't so lucky: they were smashed into rock after rock. I felt the deep bruises blossoming as I tried to protect my head with my ragged and bloody arm. One loose ski flipped up and whacked me on the forehead. Blood splashed into my eye. In the end I was hurled up against a megalith, and I came to a stop—but not to a rest.

I was battered and bleeding, the pain was starting to throb, but the pounding roar above me told me I had no time for a tuneup just now. Snow and debris were flying into the gorge from up the mountain. The air was so dense with rubble, it darkened the sky. Whole trees, roots and all, were hurled into space above me. My jump had given me enough of a head start downhill that I did have a *chance* to beat it, but only if I kept moving.

I struggled to get up and set my skis—still dragging from my ankles by their loose safety thongs—beside my feet as fast as possible. I snapped into my step-locks and started to skate off down the *couloir* of ice and snow, threading swiftly between the rocks, just as Wolfgang Hauser caught up with me, breathing hard.

"Christ, Ariel, you're a mess," he said between gasps.

"I'm alive, and nothing's broken," I told him as we raced side by side to avoid the coming onslaught that was drowning our voices. "How about you?"

"I'm fine," he yelled back. "But thank God you jumped. The entire bowl collapsed. Once you ran out of woods, you'd have been trapped between two avalanches with nothing to stop them."

"Holy shit!" I said, glancing at Wolfgang.

He laughed and shook his head. "My sentiments precisely."

At the far end of the gorge was another sheer cliff rising above us. But a curved ramp of snow-covered rock led to it, which we herringbone-stepped our way up, on our skis. Halfway up this ramp, Wolfgang stopped and looked back toward the end of the gorge we'd just come from. As I came up, he laid his gloved hand on my shoulder in silence, and nodded in that direction. I was already a little giddy from loss of blood, but when I followed his gaze, I felt my stomach heave. I hunkered down and wrapped my arms around the ankles of my boots.

The entire valley had disappeared. The sea of black stones we'd just ribboned through had completely vanished. What had been a gorge was now stuffed nearly to the brim with dirty white rubble, roots and branches sticking up clawing the sky. The only landmark left was that lip of cliff we'd jumped from, protruding less than six feet above what was now the valley floor.

I felt Wolfgang's hand stroking my hair as I quivered in horror. We watched a last dusting of snow sift from the cliff and saw the raw, dark earth of the open slope beyond, raped of its white cover, where a few pebbles still tumbled down the hill. It was total devastation, all in less than ten minutes. I started to cry. Wolfgang pulled me to my feet without speaking and put his arms around me, stroking me until my sobs subsided. Then, pulling me away, he wiped the blood and tears from my face with his glove and brushed my forehead with his lips as if healing a frightened child.

"We'd better get you cleaned up and mended. You're a valuable creature," he told me with a gentle smile. But the next words of the beautiful Dr. Hauser, though just as tender and solicitous, terrified me.

"And more than valuable," he said. "You're quite amazing, my dear—to outski an avalanche without once losing hold of that manuscript in your backpack." When I looked at him in genuine horror, he added, "Oh, I don't have to *see* it to know what it is. I followed you to the mountain to be certain you wouldn't hide it or lose it. If that's the rune manuscript you have there, as I believe it is, then it belongs to me. I sent it to you myself."

matrix *(Latin=the womb) . . . that which encloses anything or gives origin to anything. A source, origin, or cause. From Greek=meter, mother.*

—*The Century Dictionary*

In tragedy the tragic myth is reborn from the matrix of music. It inspires the most extravagant hopes, and promises oblivion of the bitterest pain.

—Friedrich Nietzsche

All that openeth the matrix is mine.

—Exodus 34:19

Anyone can make a mistake, but this was a humdinger. And *mea culpa, mea culpa,* the conclusions I'd leapt to were all mine. Sam had said nothing about runes, or even that what he'd sent me was a manuscript—only that it was the *size* of a few reams of paper. In a single day I'd nearly run over my landlord, fled across two states, and almost gotten run over myself, by an avalanche, while dallying with a gorgeous Austrian scientist. And all for the *wrong* parcel. I promised the gods I'd stop batting so many strikes if fate would stop throwing those curve balls. But that didn't help solve my new crisis: the *real* package from Sam was still missing. And now, thanks to my overreaction, maybe Sam was, too.

As I made my battered and bleeding way down the mountain, Wolfgang tried to fill me in about the rune manuscript he'd sent me—not an easy task on skis, especially since we were both anxious to reach the base camp clinic where I could get patched up. He did manage to explain en route that when he'd come to Idaho to start me on this project he'd intended to give me the manuscript first thing, but he found I was still off at Sam's funeral. When I stayed away so long and his other professional commitments called him out of town, he put the runes in the mail so I'd get them when I returned. Then this morning when the Pod sent Olivier to look for me, Wolfgang took a drive by the post office himself. When he saw me take off in panic like that, he decided to round me up on his own.

When Wolfgang and I got down the mountain, I asked him what the runes in my backpack were, and what I was to do with them when I couldn't even read them. He explained they were a copy of a document he'd been asked by my family in Europe to bring me, and that it was his understanding that the runes were connected somehow with the manuscripts I'd just inherited from my cousin Sam. He said as soon as I got medical attention and we could sit down and talk in confidence, he'd explain everything else he knew.

We spent an hour at the base camp clinic surrounded by astringent-smelling bottles and the pandemonium of the ski patrol dashing about with stretchers and beepers, hauling injured parties from the wounded mountain. In their midst I let the medicos slap me on a metal table, shoot me up, bandage my head, and put fourteen stitches in my arm.

All chitchat between Wolfgang and me naturally had to be curtailed here in the chaos of the surgical theater. But I could still think private thoughts. I knew that our nuclear project couldn't be a front for Wolfgang Hauser's junket to Idaho. For starters, it was a given that he was a high-level official of the IAEA, or he couldn't obtain clearance to set foot inside our site, much less to eyeball the U.S. government security files of somebody who had high-level clearance herself. So there was no question: he was legit.

One key unanswered question still remained: How was it that Professor Dr. Wolfgang K. Hauser arrived in Idaho while I was off in San Francisco at Sam's funeral? How had anyone *known*—as someone must have, in advance—that Sam's death would place those other, still missing, documents in my hands?

◆ ◆

With me shot up with drugs by the surgeon and my stitched-up arm in a sling, Wolfgang and I agreed it would be best if he drove me home in my car and had someone from the office come over to Jackson Hole and collect the government vehicle.

The journey back home was rather a daze. The pain kicked in as soon as my anesthetic wore off. Then I remembered—too late, after taking the pill the doctor had given me—that I usually overreacted to codeine. In short order I felt as if I'd been hit over the head by a hammer. I was out cold for most of the trip, so my question was left unanswered.

When we got back it was well past dark. Though later I couldn't recall giving directions to my house or how we arrived there, I did remember sitting in the car in the driveway and Wolfgang asking whether he should keep my car to get himself to his hotel or come inside and phone for a taxi. My reply, and everything else, remained a blur.

So imagine my surprise, upon awaking at dawn the next morning, to find myself tucked into my own bed, and my backpack and yesterday's clothing—along with a stark black ski suit I suddenly realized, with a jolt, was not my own—all piled on a chair across the room! Under the covers, I seemed to be wearing nothing but my stretchy silk long johns, which left little to the imagination.

I sat up with the covers spilling about me and saw the shaggy head, tanned arm, and bare muscular shoulders of Professor Dr. Wolfgang K. Hauser protruding from my sleeping bag on the floor. He stirred and rolled over on his back, and I could just make out his features in the early morning light sifting through the high transom windows: those thick dark lashes shadowing strong cheekbones, the long narrow nose, cleft chin, and sensual mouth, combining to suggest the profile of a Roman sculpture. Even in repose, he was the most beautiful man I'd ever seen. But what was he doing half-naked in a sleeping bag on my floor?

Wolfgang Hauser's eyes opened. He turned on his side, propped himself on one elbow, and smiled at me with those incredible turquoise eyes, like dangerous tidal pools with hidden currents. Like the river.

"As you see, I stayed here overnight," he said. "I hope you don't think it was too forward. But when I helped you out of the car last night, you passed out in the driveway. I caught you just before you hit the ground. I got you down the steps somehow, and out of those torn and bloody clothes, and I put you straight to bed. I was afraid to leave here until the drugs wore off and I could be sure you were all right. And are you?"

"I'm not sure," I said, feeling my head still full of cotton wool and my arm still throbbing with heat. "But I'm grateful you stayed. You saved my life yesterday. If it weren't for you, I might be at the bottom of that canyon right now under a mountain of snow and rubble. I'm still pretty shaken."

"You haven't eaten a bite since last noon." Wolfgang sat up and unzipped the sleeping bag. "But I have to leave town; thanks to yesterday I'm behind schedule. Why don't I make you breakfast? I know where things are kept in your kitchen: your cat showed me last night. He seemed to expect me to make him dinner, so I did."

"I don't believe it," I said, laughing. "You saved my life, and you even fed my cat! By the way, where *is* Jason?"

"Perhaps he's being discreet," said Wolfgang with a complicitous smile.

Then, his back turned, he crawled out of the sleeping bag wearing nothing but his undershorts, grabbed his black jumpsuit from the chair, and pulled it on quickly. I couldn't help but notice, even in just this brief glimpse from the back, that Professor Dr. Wolfgang K. Hauser had a truly magnificent physique. All sorts of dark, erotic visions suddenly flooded my brain. With these, to my horror, came the telltale hot flush of blood. Before he could turn and see hidden thoughts spelled out on my burning cheeks, I picked up a pillow and buried my face in it.

Too late. I heard the sound of bare feet padding across the cold concrete floor. The springs squeaked as he sat on the edge of my bed. He pulled the pillow down and looked at me with those fathomless eyes. I felt his fingers brush my shoulder, and he drew me to him and kissed me.

It isn't as if no one had ever kissed me before. But this was nothing like any kiss I knew: no meaningful sighs, biting of lips, saliva, groping, or histrionics, as too often in my less than quotable past. Instead, when our lips met, a flood of energy was unleashed, spreading from him to me and leaving me filled with a hot, liquid desire. It was as if we'd already made love, and needed to do it again. And once more.

I wondered if Professor Dr. Wolfgang K. Hauser could be siphoned off and bottled?

"Ariel, you're so beautiful," he said, touching my hair with his fingertips and looking at me with those cloudy indigo eyes. "Even now, when you're covered with cuts and stitches and bruises—a disastrous wreck—I want to do things with that sublime body of yours that I've never done with anyone."

"I think . . . I don't think . . ." I blithered mindlessly. Lobotomized, no doubt, by an overdose of hormones. I tried to pull myself together enough to speak coherently. But Wolfgang put his fingertip to my lips.

"No, let me go on. Yesterday, everything went wrong between us because I tried to rush into things when I ought not. I don't want that with you. I admire you greatly, my dear; you're very strong and brave. Do you know that your name was once an ancient name for Jerusalem, now the holy city of three religious faiths? In its oldest form, Ariel meant 'lioness of God.' "

"Lioness?" I said, regaining my real voice for the first time since that kiss. "That's some reputation to live up to."

"So is 'Wolf,' " he told me, again with a cryptic smile.

"I get it—we're both hunters," I said, smiling back. "But *I* work solo, while your kind travel in packs."

He released the strand of my hair he'd been playing with and regarded me with a serious expression. "I'm not hunting you, my dear. Though you still don't trust me. I'm here to help and protect you, nothing more. Any feelings I may have for you are my problem, not yours—and they shouldn't interfere with the goals or mission of those who sent me here."

"You keep saying 'those who sent you,' but you never say *who*. And why hasn't anyone told me anything about it?" I demanded with impatience. "Yesterday, you claimed you were my uncle Lafcadio's friend, but he's never mentioned your name to *me*. I think you should know I'll be seeing him this weekend at Sun Valley. It won't take much to learn the truth."

"I said an acquaintance, not a friend," said Wolfgang Hauser, turning away with no expression. He looked at his hands. Then he stood up and looked down at me where I still sat in the rumpled bedclothes. "Have you finished?"

"Not quite," I said, warming to my theme. "How does it happen that everyone seems to have known I was getting that bloody inheritance in the first place—even before my cousin was dead?"

"I'll tell you the answer to everything, if you really want to know," Wolfgang said quietly. "But first I must say I fear such knowledge can be very, very dangerous."

"Knowledge is never dangerous," I told him, feeling my anger uncoiling. "*Ignorance* is dangerous. Especially ignorance of things that affect your own life. I'm sick of everyone hiding things from me, claiming it's all for my own good! I'm sick of always being kept in the dark!"

As I said it, I suddenly realized how much I meant it. It was, at the root of things, what was wrong with my whole life. It wasn't just fear of the unknown, of a mysterious parcel—even if the contents of that parcel might get people killed. It was ignorance *itself*: it was never being able to ferret out the truth. It was this compulsion for secrecy, rife through my industry, dominating even my own family—the idea that nothing could ever be done openly, that everything required conspiracy and collusion.

Thanks to Sam, I'd become a real master of this game. Thanks to Sam, I trusted no one on earth. Nor could anyone trust me.

Wolfgang was watching me with a strange expression. My sudden, passionate outburst had surprised me too. Until now, I hadn't realized how deeply these feelings had lain buried in me—or how quickly they could rise to the surface.

"If that's what's required to win your trust, then I'll always tell you whatever you want to know, regardless of the danger to either of us," he said, with what seemed great sincerity. "For it's vital that you trust me completely even if you don't like the answers. The person who sent me here is also the one who asked me to give you that manuscript of runes." He motioned to my backpack sitting on the chair. "Although you have never met her, I suppose you will recognize the name. It's your aunt: Zoe Behn."

◆ ◆

I wondered about my compulsion to say "holy shit" all the time whenever anything startling or upsetting happened to me. I mean, what exactly *is* holy shit? Do gods or saints eliminate waste like the rest of us? And furthermore, was I so creatively bankrupt that I could think of no more imaginative exclamation to use, even within the privacy of my own mind?

But in my business, as I said, it was a way of life to make up witty sayings about waste—probably because the chore of constant cleanup after an ever expanding and ever more wasteful population living on this ever shrinking planet was in itself a pretty mind-bogglingly depressing task to confront each and every day.

So it was not unusual to be greeted, as I was by Olivier that morning when I came into the office, with a rousing round of the Tom Lehrer song "Pollution," an industry favorite for phrases such as "The breakfast garbage that you throw into the Bay, they drink at lunch in San Jose." Olivier was clicking his fingers like castanets as he spun around in his chair and caught sight of me.

"Oh, my blessed prophet Moroni!" he cried. "You *do* look like something the argonaut dragged in, if you don't mind my saying so. What happened to you? Did you crash into a lamppost in your zeal to run down pedestrians yesterday?"

"I ran into an avalanche, in my zeal to get away from my life," I told him, knowing that the pickup of Wolfgang's government car would engender tongue-wagging around the site anyway, when it was learned that we'd been off together skiing all day. "And I'm sorry about what happened at the post office, Olivier. I'm just a bit crazy these days."

"An avalanche? On your way from the post office to work? My, things must be picking up around here in the adventure department," Olivier said, standing up to help me solicitously to my seat. He settled my arm on the arm of the chair. "But you never came in to work all day, and when I got home last night at seven, your car was in the drive, and the whole house was dark and silent. Jason and I dined alone, wondering where you could possibly be."

So Jason had wangled himself two dinners—one downstairs and another from Olivier's gourmet cat stockpile. What a little conniver. I wished he were human enough that I could put him to work on some of *my* problems. But I knew Olivier was waiting for an answer. I closed my eyelids and pressed my fingertips against the bandage above my throbbing eye. Then I opened them and looked at Olivier.

"I hope you haven't speculated with the budget for free-range chickens and farm-reared venison, too," I commented.

Olivier stared at me, his mouth open. "You didn't?" he gasped. "You didn't actually—"

"Spend the night with Dr. Hauser? Yes, I did," I said. "But nothing happened."

After all, with the kind of attention Wolfgang Hauser attracted, and in a town this size, everyone would know about it soon enough.

"Nothing *happened*?!" Olivier nearly screamed. He slammed the door shut and flung himself into his chair. "Just what is that supposed to mean?"

"The man saved my life, Olivier," I told him. "I was injured, as you see, and he brought me home. I was unconscious, so he stayed with me." I held my aching head.

"I think I need a new religion," said Olivier, standing up. "The prophet Moroni doesn't seem too connected to the impulsive behavior of women. I've always admired the Jewish faith, for the power of that Hebrew word of theirs: *Oy!* What is the etymological derivation, do you think? Why does it *feel* so good, just to run around, saying: *oy?*" Olivier started pacing around saying "*oy-oy-oy.*"

I thought it was time to intervene. "Are we going to Sun Valley this weekend?" I asked him.

"Why else am I working late every night?" he asked me back.

"If Wolfgang Hauser has returned from his trip by then, he's coming with us," I told him. "After all, I start work on his project on Monday—and he did save my life."

"Oy," said Olivier, looking at the ceiling. "My prophet, you've really screwed up."

◆ ◆

I hoped Olivier would come up with the meaning of that word *oy*, and soon. Because it was starting to sound like a pretty good description of my life just now.

Earlier that morning, since I still couldn't move my arm without tearing stitches, Wolfgang had driven me to work. I'd asked him to stop en route at the post office and keep the engine running while I went inside for a minute. I signed a postal form so George, the clerk, could hold my mail for a few days until my arm healed. I asked him to phone me at work if any large parcels arrived—not to have the route driver leave claim slips in my mailbox. Then if there was something important, I told him, I could come by the post office on my way home from work and the postal folks could load it into my car.

"I hope you weren't too shocked to learn about your aunt Zoe," Wolfgang had said at home that morning as I'd wolfed down the sour-cream-and-caviar omelette he'd thrown together from the bizarre fixings in my fridge. "Your aunt would very much like to know you, and have you know her. She's a fascinating woman of great charm—though she understands why the rest of your family thinks of her as the black sheep."

And well she might, I thought. Most details of Zoe's life were widely known from the did-all-schmooze-all books on herself she'd already published. For instance, her legendary vocation as one of the most famous dancers in Europe, along with her pals Isadora Duncan, Josephine Baker, and the Nijinskys. Or her legendary *avocation* as one of the most famous *demimondaines* in Europe, along with her role models Lola Montez, Coco Chanel, and the fictional *Dame aux Camélias*. And so on, and so on.

But until this morning's breakfast with Wolfgang, I hadn't heard some other details, such as the fact that during World War II my infamous aunt Zoe had been a member of the French Resistance, not to mention also acting as an informant for the OSS—the Office of Strategic Services, America's first official international spy group.

I wondered precisely how much of this could be true. Though such endeavors were in keeping with *our* part of the family tree, I found it incongruous that a group like the OSS—which broke codes, encrypted messages, and operated in an environment of presumed secrecy—would have any traffic whatever with a gushy, gossipy, world-class blabbermouth like my aunt Zoe. But on closer consideration, a reputation like hers might prove the best cover—in the long run, clearly a superior one to that of her philosophical predecessor and fellow dancer Mata Hari.

Indeed, if current reports of Zoe were correct, now at eighty-three she was alive and kicking in Paris, swilling down champagne and living as bawdy and scandalous a life as ever. I was curious about how she'd gotten hooked up with someone like Wolfgang Hauser, a high official of the IAEA in Vienna.

Wolfgang explained that last March, a year ago, at a fiftieth-anniversary reunion of international World War II "peacekeepers" in Vienna, he was recruited by Zoe when the two became chummy during a welcoming gathering at a local *Heuriger*: one of those typically Austrian garden pubs where first-picked grapes just culled and pressed are drunk. According to Wolfgang, after a few gallons of new wine Zoe trusted him enough to speak of the rune manuscript. Then she solicited his aid.

Wolfgang said Zoe had acquired the manuscript, of which I now had a copy, decades ago—though she didn't reveal where or how, just that it dated to the Wagnerian era before the turn of the century, when interest had sprung up in Germany and Austria in reviving the roots of their supposedly superior Teutonic culture. Societies were founded, he explained, that dashed all over Europe recording and deciphering runic inscriptions from ancient stone monuments.

Zoe thought her document was rare and valuable, and that it might form some connection with the manuscripts Sam had inherited from Zoe's estranged brother Earnest. It was even possible, she'd suggested to Wolfgang, that Sam might possess other runic documents, and help her identify and translate her own. But after Earnest's death, Zoe's efforts to find Sam and discuss this with him had proven unsuccessful.

Because of Wolfgang's position in the international nuclear field, Zoe hoped he might be able to get in touch with Sam through *me* and to discuss the thing without involving the rest of the family—though it wasn't clear to Wolfgang why she'd chosen him, a total stranger, to confide in.

Knowing Auntie's reputation, her reasons seemed clear enough to me. Zoe might be eighty-three but she wasn't stone blind. The men she'd dallied with hadn't always been rich but they *were* extravagantly handsome, some as smashing as Herr Wolfgang Hauser himself. If I hadn't actually held this fabled manuscript in my hands, I might have guessed the batty old broad cooked it up just to add Wolfgang as the last bauble to her already heavily bejeweled crown.

Though he'd agreed to Zoe's request to end-run our family, with whom she wasn't on speaking terms, and to find Sam and me and sell us on this project, Wolfgang hadn't acted at once—not until he found a legitimate reason that would bring him here to Idaho. He couldn't know that Sam would be dead by the time he arrived—nor what my reaction would be to trafficking with one more relative among those I'd habitually avoided like the plague.

It was pointless to explain to Wolfgang that if my cousin Sam, even for a short time, had ever possessed such a document, it already would be decoded. The only unbroken encryption system in this century was designed during the Second World War by the Navajo. Native American culture engenders a penchant for such things, and I knew Sam lived and breathed encryption too.

But, as I had to keep vividly reminding myself, I was the only person on the planet who knew that Sam *himself* was still living and breathing. Now, in order to undo this knot I'd tied around myself, all I needed was to find him.

◆ ◆

For the rest of the week things were frustratingly quiet. It wasn't that I was hoping for a follow-up car chase or another avalanche to rescue me from boredom. The problem was, no package had arrived yet. Nor had I been able to contact Sam.

I cruised by the No-Name cowboy bar, inquiring as casually as possible about phone calls. The bartender told me he'd noticed the pay phone on the wall across the room ringing a few times earlier that week. But nobody picked it up, and nothing since.

I scanned my mail messages on the computer each day, coming up empty.

Olivier and I had to coordinate our driving schedules for a few days until I could operate my car again, and Wolfgang was still out of town. So in a way I felt lucky that the parcel didn't arrive until I could be alone when I went to fetch it. Meanwhile I hid the rune manuscript in a place where no one could find it, right beneath ten thousand United States-government-employed noses: inside the DOD Standard.

The Department of Defense Standard was the bible of all research and development branches of the federal government: thirty-five massive bound volumes of rules and regulations that had to be consulted in order to do anything from developing a computer system to constructing a light-water reactor. It cost the taxpayers a fortune to produce and update this key document. We had many sets around the site: one was kept on the six-foot bookshelf just outside my office. But in the whole five years I'd worked here, I'd never once seen anyone stroll idly across the floor to peek at it, much less really consult the thing for the purpose intended. To be blunt, we could have papered the latrine walls with the DOD Standard and I doubt, even then, anyone would have noticed it.

I was the only one I knew who'd actually tried to read it—but once was enough. What I saw was less comprehensible than the revised Internal Revenue Service tax code: government service writing style, par exellence. I was sure no one would find the rune manuscript if I hid it there.

So on Friday, the first day I was able to drive myself to work, I stayed until after Olivier left the office. It didn't surprise him. We were off to Sun Valley at dawn, so any work I'd need to finish before the weekend had to be done now. As soon as he left to get his things together for the trip, I started hauling volumes of my nearby set of the Standard down from their shelves and unfastening the sliding bindings. I inserted a page of runes about every forty or fifty pages along, throughout the set.

It was ten o'clock when I'd finished. I felt lucky I hadn't hurt my arm, hefting those heavy binders for such a long time. As I sank into my desk chair to relax for a minute and collect my thoughts, I bumped the mouse pad on my desk. The test patterns that had been revolving on the screen vanished and a clean screen came up, illuminating the half-darkened room.

I stared at it. A symbol I'd never seen, like a giant asterisk, half filled the screen.

Beneath this symbol was printed a question mark.

How did this get on my computer screen? No one here in the office could have done it; I'd been right at my desk all day.

I tapped a question mark into my terminal, for Help. The Help screen gave me a message it had never given me before, and one I felt certain it wasn't programmed to produce: it said I should check my mail.

I called up my message file, though I'd swept it out completely only a few hours earlier this evening. Nonetheless, there was one new document out there. I pulled the message up on the screen.

```
B L O N G A N O U H A U R E S N O U S S A F X M V C
O F Q O A E F O G S J O B E E Y T U I T I B P Z G A
N A J U N R S I N A P N R G N I N I D A N T D K R T
E D D N A H C C S I I O O M O T L O M E T H O H A G
S E M C S C W T S F O G R A H C F N I E G R I S E T
H P S A A W I O N M C U O A F G A O R O O D J L T E
A W O L L E Y R N E E A L D P H U O R H T O A I S E
R L E A R O A A A I S I F D A S T N I M T L C N I V
A O I E N I R E I G G L I L N E T Y Y A S R K E D A
E L L F H T H W L H A G I E A P O A E A A U S A B L
T E C T T G E M P T N I L C M M W D V R L D O I Y L
R Y I T T H R E E F O U R D R S T & E L O H N E R E
U V L A M B W A S A I P T O D O C Y L M I R S A A T
W R H G R A N D T T M S U N L O O E L Y M L H I A I
E A E M O A A S I S E T O E C C W M L A C C H T S N
E T R O F N M Z N E L R T H H A Y N T L & T S E T A
I T G E B D H O A J E B Y H L I V L B H A C A O N A
I T F L A M L D G K L O T O D U D L I W I V A O E B
O R T H O T H D W J T O L N E B A G K B X R N O V T
Y L A H T E Z I L O F N E H T C T X C H A L T U E E
Q F L W E V N F L O W T T M D K C H L Y E I N Y S S
S D R A R O B A Q E O S H U N D S P Q D U A F E T U
D O F N U R C U A P S I R X O I W P A L Y Q W E C I
O O S G M H K T N O H Y P O M A R B K E A G M S F R
J W H N S T H W R Q L O Y U O M L I K Z Y Y Z I O A
L P U P T T A V R O E X Z H N I N O G H I P S H L K
```

It started to build across the screen slowly, as if there were a hidden hand within the tube itself drawing the picture from inside out. As the letters drew themselves magically, I watched with a kind of dazed fascination. Before it had finished I knew, of course, who had put it there. It could only be Sam.

At the laser printer beside my desk, I printed out a few copies to mess with by hand, and I studied them.

Although I knew that the first rule of security was to delete an incoming encryption from the machine as fast as possible, I also knew Sam. If Sam wanted something destroyed at once, it would have been programmed to self-destruct when printed. The fact that it was still sitting there on my screen meant there were more clues contained in it, other than the sequence of the letters themselves. In fact, I might already have received one: the asterisk.

From my desk drawer I grabbed three of those cheap transparent government pens. I wound a rubber band to hold them together, then fanned them out in a snowflake pattern, in the shape of the asterisk. I slid this across the page to see whether, along any of the three axes, acrostics could be ferreted out. No luck—though I didn't expect any. It would be too simple a clue, and therefore too dangerous, for Sam to leave on my computer.

While scanning this page of letters, I drew back for a few seconds to get perspective. In breaking an unknown code, it's always a huge advantage if the person who encrypted the message is *trying* to communicate with you. And clearly even more so if you happen to have been hand-trained by him, as I was by Sam.

Right now, for example, I could make some fair assumptions about the hidden message before me: Sam would never have sent it, or any message, via computer, which he hotly opposed as unsafe, unless the message itself was important or urgent or both. That is, unless it was something I vitally had to know before I left, as he knew I'd planned to, for Sun Valley on the weekend. Even so, he'd waited all week to send it—right down to the wire, almost the final hour of Friday night. Obviously he'd been unable to find another way to communicate, and was therefore forced to use a method he didn't trust. This told me two critical things about the "personality" of the code he'd used.

First, since he believed it might be vulnerable to the snooping of others, the code would have to be many-layered, with red herrings dropped on every trail costing time and labor to anyone else also trying to decipher it.

Second, since Sam had taken a risk that must have been forced on him by time constraints and urgency, he would have to use a code simple enough for *me* to unlock quickly, accurately, and all by myself.

The combination of these two vital ingredients told me that the key to this code must be something that *only I would be likely to see*.

Using a ruler as my guide, I searched the page. The first clue popped out at once. There were two items, and only two, on this page that were *not* letters of the alphabet: the two ampersands (&) in lines twelve and sixteen. Since an ampersand is a symbol for the word "and," perhaps they formed some connections between parts of the message. Though this could be guessed by anyone, I felt sure that was where the trails—both the false and the true trails—began: that is, in the middle. And I felt even more certain that I would find a clue "for my eyes only" that would tell me where to look for the place to branch off from the obvious path.

```
B L O N G A N O U H A U R E S N O U S S A F X M V C
O F Q O A E F O G S J O B E E Y T U I T I B P Z G A
N A J U N R S I N A P N R G N I N I D A N T D K R T
E D D N A H C C S I I O O M O T L O M E T H O H A G
S E M C S C W T S F O G R A H C F N I E G R I S E T
H P S A A W I O N M C U O A F G A O R O O D J L T E
A W O L L E Y R N E E A L D P H U O R H T O A I S E
R L E A R O A A A I S I F D A S T N I M T L C N I V
A O I E N I R E I G G L I L N E T Y Y A S R K E D A
E L L F H T H W L H A G I E A P O A E A A U S A B L
T E C T T G E M P T N I L C M M W D V R L D O I Y L
R Y I T T H R E E F O U R D R S T & E L O H N E R E
U V L A M B W A S A I P T O D O C Y L M I R S A A T
W R H G R A N D T T M S U N L O O E L Y M L H I A I
E A E M O A A S I S E T O E C C W M L A C C H T S N
E T R O F N M Z N E L R T H H A Y N T L & T S E T A
I T G E B D H O A J E B Y H L I V L B H A C A O N A
I T F L A M L D G K L O T O D U D L I W I V A O E B
O R T H O T H D W J T O L N E B A G K B X R N O V T
Y L A H T E Z I L O F N E H T C T X C H A L T U E E
Q F L W E V N F L O W T T M D K C H L Y E I N Y S S
S D R A R O B A Q E O S H U N D S P Q D U A F E T U
D O F N U R C U A P S I R X O I W P A L Y Q W E C I
O O S G M H K T N O H Y P O M A R B K E A G M S F R
J W H N S T H W R Q L O Y U O M L I K Z Y Y Z I O A
L P U P T T A V R O E X Z H N I N O G H I P S H L K
```

I wasn't disappointed. The ampersand on line sixteen connected the words *Scylla* and *Charybdis*, and led to the complete message *Jackson Hole two p.m. Scylla & Charybdis*. That was a red herring, not only because it was my private nickname for those rocks—others might know that too—but rather because I'd told Sam I was going to Sun Valley this weekend, not Jackson Hole, to meet Uncle Laf. But herring or no, it *did* tell me that the message I was seeking would explain where Sam would try to meet me this weekend. Thank God.

There were a few other scattered messages that leapt from the page, like the one starting with *Grand* on line fourteen, saying he'd meet me Sunday at Grand Targhee, lift three, at four P.M.

But I thought it far more likely that Sam's real message would be buried in the crop of conflicting messages that branched from the other ampersand. And all of those dealt with places at Sun Valley.

The ampersand on line twelve connected the two words *valley* and *day*. Backing up, it read from southeast to due north: *Sun Valley & (Sun)day*. Then the bifurcations began, and were difficult to follow.

One said *noon*, after which I got lost in the maze. After a while I found a backwards *ten* and followed it around in a circle, reading: *ten a.m. room thirty-seven*. Fat chance Sam would be so complex, just to deliver so simple a message. More complex by far was the word *eve* that I finally found branching up from the ampersand. Its message danced all over the page: *Sunday eve at lodge dining room eight p.m. wear yellow scarf*—as if I needed to be identified by a flag. Hmm.

Besides, though Sun Valley lay near three towns, two mountain ranges, and miles of open, skiable tundra where we might meet, I was sure Sam had said we should meet on Baldy, the ski mountain itself, because we both knew it so well. Given my armload of stitches and my current physical condition, I wasn't too anxious to clamp on my Alpines again. But it seemed I might have little choice.

I was sure I hadn't encountered the right message yet. It had to be the one following the word *noon*—so where did it lead? I found the word *met*, which connected with a long passage that seemed part of a bigger picture, but the word didn't lead contextually into that sentence. I looked again. I found *on*, beside which were *in* and *to*. My eyes began to cross, even though I was now using my finger to trace the labyrinth of letters on the page before me.

Just then, I found a real word: *Toussaint*. It went north from the word *on* and turned east, then south again. Toussaint—All Saints' Day—though that was where my limited religious expertise ended. Having attended churches in my youth only when Jersey was booked to perform at one, I couldn't recall whether that was near All Souls' Day or Carnival—neither of which fell within spitting distance of this coming Sunday, anyway. And though all ski slopes have names, there wasn't a run at Sun Valley named either Hallowe'en or Mardi Gras. As it happened, however, most of the slopes on Baldy *were* named for festive occasions: Holiday, Easter, Mayday, Christmas. Probably no coincidence.

I squinted and studied the grid again. I'd now spent an hour on this eye-crossing puzzle, and my starting-to-heal arm throbbed and itched like crazy. I was able to connect the word *Toussaint* with some words I'd found earlier, such as *go* and *through*, but then I was lost again. Damn it, Sam! *Get to Toussaint, go through*—go through *what*?

There were dozens of trails and lower slopes branching off those four I'd mentioned. But I took a deep breath, closed my bleary eyes, and tried to visualize the three-dimensional layout of the mountain. For instance, if you came off the top of the chair lift at Lookout, which fed onto three of the aforementioned slopes—all but Mayday—and if you then skied down around behind the lift, you'd be following a path that from a bird's-eye view would very much resemble the way the letters that formed this message were laid out on the page! Indeed, even if I backtracked to the very beginning of the message, the words *Sun Valley* were placed on the page, if memory served me, at the same angle as the ski lift itself was laid out on the mountain!

I knew I was on to something, so I kept my mind focused on the mountain. When you came off the lift, you dropped over a small ledge, then went through a wide mogul field. I opened my eyes and searched for the word *mogul* near where the field would actually be. It took a minute, but I found it—a zigzag pattern, exactly the way you'd have to ski it—with the word *field* just after. My heart started pounding.

There was still some deciphering to be done, though.

I had found the word *down* just after *field*, but I knew there were five other slopes branching off that mogul field, and I couldn't recall their names any more than I would have recalled the first bunch if I hadn't found *Toussaint*. All I ever recalled were geographical features, lift numbers and where the lifts took you, and the levels of difficulty marked on each run: green, blue, or black; circle, square, or diamond. None of these seemed to help here.

I reminded myself how well Sam knew me. Just after the word *down*, I saw the letter *b* and traced it through a sharp switchback pattern that formed two words: *black diamond*. The black diamond run below the mogul field emptied out at the base of another lift. If I took that I would arrive atop the next slope. I followed the words on the page just there. They read *then follow this path through*, and the word then going north was *woods*. Since the end of a word at an edge of a page meant "exit," I assumed this was the end of the message. And that it marked the spot where I'd meet Sam at noon on Sunday.

So I could see the whole pattern now: I would take chair lift three to Lookout, ski through the mogul field, and take the early branch to my left onto a black diamond, or most difficult, run. Everything was

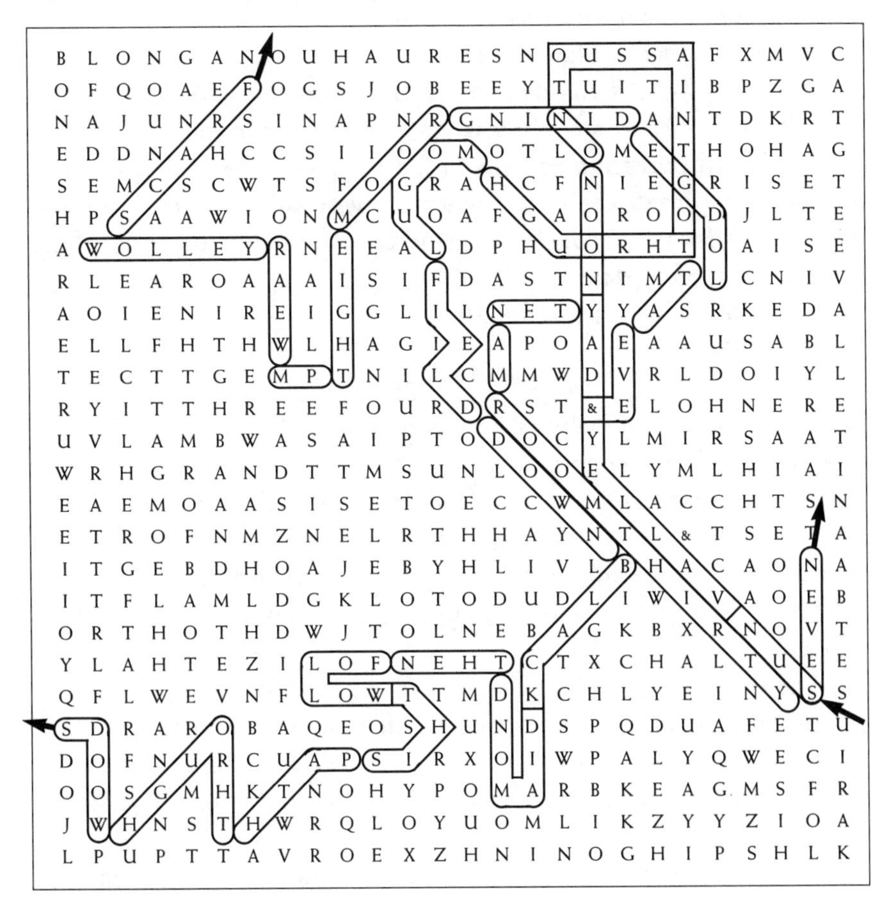

simple—except for the steepness of that slope, if I happened to fall with my bad arm. This run, I knew, would put me over around the side of the mountain, away from the tourists, in a backwoods where tracks were narrow and where markers left by Sam could be easily read by me, so he would feel safe to change them at the last moment, if necessary, to redirect my path.

I felt highly proud of myself, deciphering all this from a 26-by-26 matrix—though I knew it was Sam who was brilliant, putting it into geographical context only to be read by someone who knew the lay of the land as well as he himself did.

Just as I was about to erase the matrix still looming on the screen, I remembered to hunt for another, deeper layer. I double-clicked my mouse on the asterisk, to no avail. Then I tried the first letter of Sun Valley, and finally I clicked on the exit letter *s* in *woods*. The screen vanished at once and a message popped up:

Keen gnosis of gnosis. Signed: *Reg du Coly.*

Reg du Coly was an anagram of Grey Cloud, Sam's sacred spirit name known only to me—just as were *C. G. Loudyer* and *Lou D. Grecy* and all the other rearrangements of letters of our names that we used to make up to dazzle each other when we were kids. So this meant that the other half was an anagram too, and contained the other half of the message from Sam to me.

It was going to be a long night.

◆ ◆

Not all *that* long, actually. I was very good at cryptic anagrams—something Sam had counted on.

The first word of his anagram was *keen*, which the dictionary at my fingertips told me was a mourning cry or lament for the dead. Highly appropriate, considering that Sam was technically dead and that's what I felt like doing right now, keening, even if I knew he was actually alive.

The other word, *gnosis*, I knew meant knowledge—especially the secret, hidden, esoteric kind one needed in transformations. Once again contextually appropriate to my genealogical bent, my career, and the situation in which I seemed to have found myself while sitting in front of my computer just at this moment.

The easiest and quickest way to decipher an anagram is to take all common letters and sort them into clumps, then see what words they produce in common. For instance, in Sam's eighteen-letter message *Keen gnosis of gnosis*, there were the following numbers of vowels and consonants: e=2, i=2, o=3, f=1, g=2, k=1, n=3, s=4. There weren't that many meaningful sentences you could construct from so limited a set. To simplify even those options, he'd provided two clues in the words *keen* and *gnosis*.

If a keen was a lament or moan, then it was a sound, a cry, maybe even music. And given that my mother and grandmother had each been among the top singers of her day, it was a good bet that by *keen* Sam meant a song.

With the letter set Sam had given me there were enough letters to spell *song* not once but twice—which was all it took. Of the letters left over, after borrowing from my crop to create two *songs*, I quickly spelled the words *seek* and *in*. Ergo: *I Seek in Song of Songs* was my message.

So that's what I would do.

Olivier had the Book of Mormon in his top desk drawer, though there was no Bible. But good lord, there were so many religious fanatics here at the site that they even had brown-bag scripture readings at lunchtime. There must be a copy of the Bible somewhere. I dashed around a few offices until I found one. Then I flipped through and located the book.

And I read: "The Song of Songs, which is Solomon's . . ."

It didn't escape me that this wasn't the only reference Sam had made to Solomon. The first was the Solomon's knot he'd hung from my rearview mirror: his first contact with me since being born again. Not feeling I really had time, tonight, to decipher the hidden meaning in a seven-page poem that had inspired zeal on the part of so many over the millennia, I slaked my immediate interest just by flipping to the last stanza:

"Make haste, my beloved, and be thou like to a roe or to a young hart upon the mountains of spices . . ."

And I knew I must make all due haste, to the mountain.

THE MERRY-GO-ROUND

Woe to Ariel, to Ariel . . . yet I will distress Ariel, and there shall be heaviness and sorrow . . .
For the indignation of the Lord is upon all nations and his fury upon their armies: he hath utterly destroyed them; he hath delivered them to the slaughter.

—Isaiah 29, 34

One cannot say it is pleasanter to look at a battle than at a merry-go-round, but there can be no question which draws the larger crowd.

—George Bernard Shaw

Sunlight glittered like black diamonds off the volcanic cones of the Craters of the Moon National Monument. Wild, twisted lava beds sprawled across the valley floor as the car shot down the deserted road heading toward Sun Valley.

We'd taken my car because Olivier's was still on the fritz, but he did the driving. Jason sat, or stood with front paws on the dashboard, checking out the panoramic view and keeping close tabs on the navigation. My arm had recovered enough to drive, so Olivier was surprised when I asked him to drive the whole 150-mile trek so I could sit in the backseat and read the Bible. Maybe he thought my recent troubles had driven me to find solace in the Good Book, but that's not what I was seeking in the Song of Songs, now lying open on my lap—nor did it seem a likely tale to provide much solace.

I found it odd that Sam would pick the Bible to hide his message in. Neither of us had much expertise in the religion department, and this particular chapter, which I'd never actually read, was about as steamy as you could get in a book with no brown paper wrapper. The torrid, heavy-breathing account of a romance between King Solomon and the Shulamite, a young woman who works down in the vineyards—it's more or less in the same league as the Kama Sutra. By chapter seven, he's even drinking liquor from her belly button. I tell you: a real bodice ripper.

It's hard to imagine such verses being read aloud from a pulpit, especially falling as they do, in biblical sequence, between the ashes-to-ashes of Ecclesiastes and the hellfire and brimstone of Isaiah, both of which I skimmed for perspective, hoping they'd give a hint of what Sam was trying to tell me. To no avail.

When we reached Sun Valley, Olivier unloaded the few bags and our skis, and we checked in at the front desk. Then I took Jason to my room and rang up Laf to let him know we'd arrived. Earlier in the week I'd left a message here at the Lodge for Laf, saying I might bring two friends this weekend. Laf had wired back saying he'd await our arrival and take us all to brunch. But Wolfgang's later message said he had been detained in Nevada, so today it would just be Uncle Lafcadio, Olivier, and me—or so I thought. After dumping our gear upstairs in our respective rooms, Olivier and I went together to the Lodge Dining Room to meet Laf.

The dining room's massive stone fireplace, richly paneled walls, high ceilings with crystal chandeliers, crisp damask tablecloths laden with place settings of heavy silver and steaming coffee urns, and its vast windows displaying snowy meadows beyond—all spoke of a time of quiet elegance between the wars, when Sun Valley was built by the railroad to attract the rich and famous to the unknown, therefore exotic, wilderness of the Idaho Rockies.

The maître d'hôtel escorted Olivier and me to a large circular table reserved for our party at the prime location before the windows. A bowl of bloodred roses graced the center of the table, the only one so ornamented in the room. A few diners discreetly glanced our way as we were seated, our water glasses were filled at once, and a basket of fresh warm breads magically appeared. The maître d' himself took the Dom Pérignon from the icer beside our table and filled our crystal champagne flutes.

"I've never been treated this way here before," Olivier said when we were alone. "It's generally cold shoulders and colder food."

"You mean the instant wine and roses?" I asked. "It's all for my uncle Lafcadio; he's the prince of splash and panache. That's just the audience warmup."

Just then, with impeccable timing, Laf swept through the double doors across the vast dining room. His entourage included the maître d' as well as Laf's personal valet and an unknown woman and several waiters. He paused, removing his gloves finger by finger, before advancing toward us, his trademark floor-length cape billowing in waves, sucking in its wake the attention of the other diners. Uncle Laf didn't care to be lost in the crowd—nor was it likely: he enjoyed a brand-name recognition enhanced by the fact that his mug shot appeared on as many album jackets as Franz Liszt's.

Crossing the room with long strides, Laf swept his gold-handled cane before him as if scattering wildfowl from his path. I rose from the table to greet him. As he threw his arms wide to embrace me, the cape slipped from his shoulders. It was caught from behind (on one finger, before the hem touched earth) by Volga Dragonoff, Laf's impeccable

Transylvanian valet, who swirled it in midair with a flourish, then dropped it over his own arm—a choreography so artistically executed I knew it had been rehearsed.

Ignoring the byplay behind his back, Laf embraced me. "Gavroche! What a sight for the sore eyes!" he said, beaming and holding me away, the better to see me.

In unison, the waiters pulled out our chairs and stood there holding them, waiting for us to take our seats. That meant we'd be standing awhile, because Laf disliked being dictated to—even in body language—by those in the serving classes. He tossed back his shoulder-length mane of white hair, looking at me with sharp blue eyes.

"You are even more beautiful than once your mother was," he told me.

"Thanks, Uncle Laf. You look terrific, too," I said. "I'd like you to meet my friend Olivier Maxfield."

Before Olivier could speak, the young woman who'd arrived with Laf stepped from the group behind him. As if proffering assistance to ford a stream, Laf crooked his arm and she rested one long, elegant hand there—a hand almost ostentatiously devoid of paint or jewels—and smiled at us.

"Delighted," Laf said. "Gavroche, I present my companion: Bambi."

Bambi? I mean, this chick was some item, as by now everyone in the room had noticed.

I really had to hand it to Uncle Laf. This was not your ordinary run-of-the-mill exotic sleeve decoration of the sort Laf had watered in his stable ever since Pandora, the great passion of his life, had died. *Au contraire,* this one was a thoroughbred, one of the most breathtakingly beautiful women I'd ever laid eyes on. She had a face that managed to be at once both sculptural and sensual, with languid eyes, full lips, and high cheekbones framed by long blond hair. She was wearing a creamy, clingy, one-piece velour body suit that was unzipped sufficiently low to reveal plenty of what was beneath—which in itself was truly astonishing. But it wasn't only her voluptuous beauty that had vacuumed the room into total silence. She had a rarer quality still. She exuded a kind of glimmering luminescence, as if she were made of living, breathing gold. Her hair shimmered like a waterfall when she moved; her flesh had the glow of a rich, ripe fruit; the wide-set eyes glittered from the depths with a sea of little gold sparkles. Yep, this was definitely the face that launched a thousand ships and sent the fabled towers of Ilium up in smoke.

Okay, maybe it was sour grapes, but—there had to be *something* wrong with her. Then she opened her mouth and spoke.

"*Grüss Gott,* Fräulein Behn," she said. "Your *Onkel* hass told me so much about you. It hass been my lifelong dream to meet you."

Hmm: her lifelong dream. Not a major contender in the goal-setting department. And despite the *hochdeutsch* accent, her manner exuded the vacuous wispiness of a none too clever child. She offered her fingertips like a limp washcloth to me; her eyes, which a moment ago had seemed of impenetrable depth, now seemed only impenetrably vacant. I glanced at Olivier, who shrugged and grinned back a little sadly. There was definitely room for rent upstairs.

"I hope you two will be like sisters," Laf said, pressing Bambi's arm.

Laf turned toward our table of waiting waiters, at last prepared to be seated, the signal for the rest of us to do likewise. The Transylvanian factotum Volga Dragonoff—who could divine Laf's every whim as if they were connected at the frontal lobes—found himself a chair across the room by the door and sat there holding Laf's cape on his lap. I'd never known Volga to take a meal with my uncle or any of the family, even when stranded for two days inside a lean-to in the Tyrol with nothing to eat but trail mix. I tapped my brow to Volga and he nodded back, not smiling. Volga never smiled.

"Bambi is an *extremely* talented cellist," Laf was telling Olivier, which got my attention. I knew what *that* meant. "Everyone knows," he went on, "that deft fingering and the action of the bowing wrist are hallmarks of all great string artists. But very few realize that, when it comes to the *cello*—"

"It's how you grip it with your thighs that really counts," I finished up.

Olivier glanced at me, choked, and reached for the water.

"Yes, indeed," Uncle Laf agreed as the maître d' arrived with the menus. "The performer's body *itself* must become the instrument, completely enfolding the music in a hot and all-encompassing embrace of passion."

"I can see that," Olivier managed to croak. His eyes were riveted in astonishment on Bambi's Olympian body.

"I'll have the *oeufs Sardou,*" Uncle Laf was telling the maître d'. "But with béarnaise, and plenty of extra lemon."

Olivier leaned toward me and whispered: "I *am* breaking out in hives."

"Gavroche, perhaps you young people will like to go skiing this afternoon, after brunch?" Uncle Laf asked when he'd finished ordering for Bambi as if she were a child.

I shook my head and pointed to my injured arm.

"Then we two can have our private chat while the others ski. But just now, while we have our meal, I thought I might tell a story of more general interest—"

"A family story?" I asked, with what I hoped was a tone of cautionary reserve. Hadn't Uncle Laf told me on the phone that what he had to say was confidential?

"Not really *family*," said Laf with a smile, patting my hand. "Actually, this is my own story, a story I'm sure you've never heard, for your father doesn't know it any more than did my half brother Earnest. Nor does Bambi here, who thinks she knows every dark and hidden secret behind my transparent and public life."

This seemed an odd characterization of the vapidly beautiful Bambi, whose demeanor suggested an incapacity for sustained interest in any topic.

"Despite my long and full life, Gavroche," Laf continued, "I still recall every sight, every taste, every scent. Sometime I must discuss my philosophy that aromas are indeed the keys to unlock such early memories. But the strongest memories are those associated with either the greatest beauty or the greatest bitterness. The day when I first met Pandora, your grandmother, was a combination of the two."

The procession of waiters arrived, set down our dishes, and simultaneously whipped the lids off with a flourish. Laf smiled at me, and went on, "But to explain how it all began, I must tell you first of the bitterness—then the beauty.

"I was born, Gavroche, toward the end of the year 1900, in Natal province on the east coast of South Africa. The place itself was named four hundred years earlier by Vasco Da Gama to commemorate the Nativity, for he'd sighted the place on Christmas Day. The astrological portents at the time of my birth were extraordinary: five planets at once were passing through the sign of Sagittarius, the archer. The most important of these was Uranus, bringer of the new world order, the planet that was expected to usher in the new age of Aquarius nearly upon us. Or one might call it, rather, a new world *dis*order, since from ancient times it was prophesied that the Aquarian age would begin with the violent destruction of the old order, crushed and washed out to sea as though by a tidal wave. For my family there in Natal, that upheaval had already begun: I was born at the very height of the Boer War, the event that baptized this century in fire and blood.

"For two years after my birth, this war had been raging between the more lately-come English settlers and the descendants of earlier Dutch immigrants who called themselves Boers, like the German word *Bauer* or farmer—those whom we English call simply boors or country bumpkins—"

"*We* English, Uncle Laf?" I interrupted in surprise. "But I thought our family was descended from Afrikaners."

"Perhaps my stepfather—your grandfather Hieronymus Behn—had the right to claim such *boor*-ishness," Laf agreed with a dark smile. "But my true father was English and my mother Dutch. My mixed parentage, and my birth into a country torn by such a war, go far to explain what bitterness I felt toward the bloody Boers. This war was the match touching off a chain of events that would soon engulf the world, and propel our family into the very heart of chaos. I have only to *think* of those events and I cannot choke down my gall, nor quench my unrelenting, burning, and fathomless hatred for those men."

Holy shit. Unrelenting, burning, and fathomless hatred? Until this moment, like everyone, I'd regarded Laf as a brilliant violinist but a dilettante nonetheless, whose problems were about as pressing as trying to decide what piece of music to fiddle while Rome burned, or under what social circumstances it was appropriate for a gentleman to keep his trousers on. This change in tone revised that impression.

Olivier and Bambi too, I noticed, were staring at him and barely touching their food. Laf had picked up the cheesecloth-wrapped lemon from his plate and stabbed it with his fork, squeezing some extra juice into his béarnaise sauce. But his eyes were focused on the snow that was just beginning to trickle down from the skies outside beyond the picture windows.

"It's hard to understand the depth and bitterness of such feelings, Gavroche," said Laf, "until you know the history of the strange country of my birth. I say strange, for it began not as a country but as a business enterprise—a company. It was known as *the* Company, and this company created from the start a private, completely separate world of its own, upon a dark and little-known continent. It created an isolation as impenetrable as the one created by the thorny hedge of bitter almond, which itself grew into the very symbol of the Boers and their desire to live apart from all the rest of the world. . . ."

◆ ◆

THE HEDGE OF BITTER ALMOND

For hundreds of years, since the Dutch East India Company had first set up garrisons along the Cape of Good Hope, many Boers engaged in animal husbandry, keeping flocks of sheep and cattle, an occupation that made them more mobile than farmers who worked the soil. If they chafed under the greedy and tyrannical whims of the Company, they would simply pull up roots and trek to greener pastures—as it soon became their preference to do, no matter who else might already be occupying the new lands they coveted. Nor did they intend to share.

Within less than a century, these *trekboers* had taken most lands formerly inhabited by the Hottentots, enslaved them and their children, and tracked down the Bushmen like wild prey, hunting them nearly into extinction. When the Boers did settle in a place for long enough, believing themselves a superior race chosen by Divine Providence, it became their practice to wall themselves into compounds hedged with sharp-thorned thickets of the bitter almond tree—the first clear symbol of *apartheid*—designed to prevent the natives both from poaching and from intermingling.

Thus the story might have continued. But in 1795 the British captured the Cape. At the request of the exiled Prince of Orange (Holland itself having fallen to the French revolutionary government), Britain purchased Cape Colony from the Dutch for six million pounds. The resident Boer colonists were never consulted in this matter; it would scarcely have been customary in that day. But it rankled them nonetheless, for they were now to be treated as an actual colony, and subject to law and order quite inconsistent with their former way of life.

Then too, more colonists began arriving from Britain: planters and settlers with their wives and children, and the missionaries who went into the bush to minister to the natives. The missionaries were quick to protest, and report back to England, the treatment they observed of local tribes. After fewer than forty years of British rule, in December of 1834, the Slave Emancipation Act freed all slaves within the British Empire, including those impounded by the Boers, an action completely unacceptable to them. And so the Great Trek began.

Thousands of Boers participated in this trek across the Orange River, through Natal, and into the wilderness of northern Transvaal, fleeing British rule, claiming all of the Bechuana territory for themselves, fighting the warlike Zulus. These Voortrekkers existed as an armed camp, hovering always at the brink of anarchy but still believing themselves the chosen of God.

The Boers' faith in their racial superiority was a concept fanned to white-hot flame by the Separatist Reformed—or 'Dopper'—Church, one of whose most fervent adherents was the young Paulus Kruger who later, as president of Transvaal, would foment the Boer War. The leaders of such Calvinist churches were determined to ensure that Boer hegemony would prevail and endure: forever chosen, forever pure, forever white.

To preserve racial purity, the church itself arranged to loot orphanages back in Holland of young girls with no other prospects for their futures. Boatfuls of these, many little more than children, were shipped to the Cape colonies as brides for unknown Boers in the wilderness of the veldt. Among these, in the late winter of 1884, was a young orphan girl with the name of Hermione, who was to become my mother.

◆ ◆

My mother was barely sixteen when she was told she would be sent to the African continent, along with other young girls, to be married off to men whose names they were not even told. Nothing is known of Hermione's parentage, though she was likely illegitimate. Abandoned in infancy, she grew up in a Calvinist orphanage in Amsterdam, and she prayed often to the Deity for some bizarre accident of fate, some adventure to come her way and break her free of a strict, colorless existence. But it wasn't her idea that God's response would mean being hauled halfway around the world and bartered off like livestock. Nor did her Calvinist training inform her precisely what the marriage bond entailed. What she gleaned from the whispers of other girls only increased her fear.

As the young women arrived at the port of Natal—shaken from the stormy passage, ill nourished, and sickened by anxiety at leaving behind what little they had known of reality—they were greeted by a mob of drunken Boer farmers, the intended husbands, who were unwilling to wait until the church elders selected each a specific mate. They had come to grab prizes of their own choosing and haul them home.

On deck, Hermione and the others huddled like frightened animals, gazing down in horror at the sea of screaming faces that pushed toward the lowered gangplank. The ministers aboard cried out for the ship's crew to raise the ramp again, but their voices were drowned out by the mob. Hermione closed her eyes and prayed.

Then pandemonium broke loose. The drunken, unruly Boers swarmed onto the ship. Screaming girls were plucked from their feet and tossed over burly shoulders like sacks of flour. A child clinging to Hermione was torn from her and vanished silently into the roaring swirl of bodies. Hermione herself was desperately pressing toward the railing, thinking she still might act upon her earlier thought of wedding herself to the sea instead of to one of these reeking, brutal men.

Just then, from behind, two arms pinned her own arms to her sides and she was swept off her feet. She tried kicking and biting, but her unseen assailant shoved through the mob, tightening his grasp, and screaming profanities in her ear. She became lightheaded as she was carried down the ramp toward the muddy streets of the port, and began slipping from consciousness. Then something smashed into her assailant and she was hurled to the ground. Freed from her captor, she clawed at the mud and crawled to her feet to run away—though she'd no idea where—when she felt a hand grasp hers. It was a firm, cool hand with a confident grip, unlike the rough paws that had dug into her. For some reason, instead of yanking herself away and making that dash to freedom, she stopped and looked at the owner of the hand holding hers.

His eyes were the same color of pale blue as her own, and they crinkled at the corners when he smiled down at her with the sort of smile she'd never seen: a smile of possession, almost of ownership. He brushed a lock of hair from her face—an intimate gesture, as if they were alone, as if they'd known one another for years.

"Come with me," he said.

That was all. She followed him without a single question, stepping daintily over the prostrate body of her assailant. The stranger lifted her onto his waiting horse and climbed up just behind, holding her close.

"I am Christian Alexander, Lord Stirling," he said in her ear. "And I've been waiting for you, my dear, for a very, very long time."

◆ ◆

It was fortunate for my mother, Hermione, that she was one of the most astonishing beauties of her day. That silvery blondness served her well in her debut on the shores of Africa. My father, however, was nothing like the lofty lord he pretended to be—though few at the time, including my mother, knew so.

Christian Alexander was the fifth son of a minor yeoman from Hertfordshire, and stood to inherit absolutely nothing. But as a young man, he did go up to Oriel at Oxford along with a childhood friend of his, the son of a clergyman. And when the friend went off to Africa each year for his health, my father had both the opportunity and the foresight to follow him. Eventually, my father would become his most trusted business partner. The name of the childhood friend was Cecil John Rhodes.

Cecil Rhodes had been seriously ill when young, so ill that during his second trip to Africa he believed he had fewer than six months to live. But working and often even living outdoors in that warm dry air restored him to health a bit more with each passing year. It was during their very first trip, however, in the late spring of 1870, when both boys were seventeen, that diamonds were discovered at the De Beers farms, while they were working on the land. Then Cecil Rhodes had a vision.

Much as Paul Kruger believed in the Divine Providence of the Boers, so Cecil Rhodes came to believe in the Manifest Destiny of the British in Africa. Rhodes wanted the diamond fields consolidated under one company, a British company. He wanted a British railroad built "from Cape to Cairo" to join Britain's African states. Later, when South Africa's vast reserves of gold were discovered, he would claim those for the

British Empire, too. In the interim Rhodes became powerful and my father—thanks completely to their friendship—became rich.

In the year 1884, when sixteen-year-old Hermione arrived from Holland, my father was thirty-two and had been a millionaire in diamonds for more than a decade. By the date of my birth, in December of 1900, my mother herself was thirty-two. And, thanks to the Boer War, my father was dead.

Everyone had believed that the war was over when the sieges of Mafeking, Ladysmith, and Kimberley were lifted. The Transvaal was annexed by the British and Paul Kruger fled to Holland, barely two months before my birth. Many British packed up then and went home. But the guerrillas fought on in the mountains for more than another year; the English rounded up women and children from the rebellious Boer colonies and incarcerated them for the duration in the first concentration camps. My father died of complications of a wound incurred at Kimberley, as Rhodes was to die two years later, his health broken by the same siege. Kruger would be dead in Holland a mere two years after that. It was the end of an era.

But as with every end, it was also a new beginning. This one marked the beginning of terrorist and guerilla warfare, concentration camps, and the practice of genocide: the dawn of a bright new age for which we have largely the Boers to thank, though the English swiftly caught up, with many dire contributions of their own.

When my father died, Cecil Rhodes settled a huge estate in cash and ancillary mineral rights upon my mother, in exchange for my father's shares and interest from building the De Beers diamond concession. And he gave yet another generous amount from his own vast wealth toward my upbringing and education, in thanks for my father having given his life in the service of a British-controlled South Africa.

In settling all this on the bereaved widow Hermione Alexander, Mr. Rhodes did not think of several important considerations, to wit: That my mother was not the well-bred, sensible Englishwoman the name Lady Stirling might suggest but a poor Dutch waif raised in a Calvinist orphanage. That her entire subsequent experience of life was to be kept in lavish estate by an older, doting husband. That she was still only thirty-two years of age, and still a great beauty, with only one dependent newly born child (myself). And that she was now one of the richest women in Africa, perhaps in the world—which could only make her the more appealing.

Mr. Rhodes did not think of these things, nor probably did my mother, for hers was not a material or grasping nature. But there would be others, quite soon, who would think of such concerns *for* her. The one who moved quickest, of course, was Hieronymus Behn.

Today it is impossible for those familiar with Hieronymus Behn as industrial magnate and ruthless deal-carver to imagine that in the year just after my birth, 1901, he came into my mother's life in the guise of a poor Calvinist minister sent by the Church—undercover, even as the war raged on—to console her in her grief and bring her back to the fold of her own people and their faith.

My mother was brought to the fold, it would appear, almost as soon as they got up off their knees from that first prayer session. Not into the safe, protective fold of any church, however, but rather into the waiting arms of Hieronymus Behn. Three months after they met, when I was less than six months old, they were married.

It must be added that, religion aside, Hieronymus Behn's appeal to a grieving widow was palpable. The tintype photographs taken at that time do not do justice to the man I knew as a child. I used often to try to contrast the pictures of my late father, to his advantage, with those of my new stepfather—but in vain. My father looked out of the frame with pale clear eyes, a handsome mustache, and, whether in military clothes or those of a gentleman, a romantic, swashbuckling air. Hieronymus Behn, by contrast, was what would have been described in those days as a magnificent piece of horseflesh: today we would call him a stud. He was the sort of man who, when he set his eyes upon a woman, seemed to be setting his hands on her instead. I've no doubt Hieronymus Behn knew precisely where and how to use those hands: he would use them often and well, reaching into others' pockets as he amassed his great fortune. How could I know, at the time, that he'd already begun with ours?

When the war was over and I was two years old, Mother gave birth to my brother, Earnest. When Earnest was two and I was four, I was shipped off to a *Kinderheim*—a children's boarding school—in Austria, a country to which I was told my family would soon relocate. When I was six, I received news there at my school in Salzburg that I now had a new little sister named Zoe.

It was only when I was twelve that I finally got word I would see my family, along with a train ticket to Vienna. It was the first time in nearly eight years that I had seen my mother. I did not know it would also be the last.

◆ ◆

I learned that my mother was dying before I saw her.

I was sitting opposite large double doors in the big drafty hall, on a straight-backed chair upholstered in hard leather—and waiting. Beside me, to my left, waited two new acquaintances: my half brother and sister, Earnest and Zoe. The sister, Zoe, was fidgeting in her chair, yanking at her blond corkscrew curls, and trying to pull the carefully arranged ribbons out of her hair.

"Mummy doesn't *want* me to wear ribbons!" she was complaining. "She's very sick, and they scratch her face when I kiss her."

This child's rather odd personality was hardly that of a six-year-old girl. She was more like a Prussian officer. While the serious Earnest still had an awkward trace of that South African twang I'd lost in eight years at an Austrian boarding school, this little terror spoke in a bossy, patrician High German and possessed the self-containment of Attila the Hun.

"I'm sure your nanny wouldn't want to displease her mistress by letting your ribbons scratch her," I replied, trying to appease her so she'd settle down.

Though it seemed inappropriate to say "her mistress," I found it hard to refer to the woman I knew was lying in a bed just beyond those doors as "Mother." I wasn't sure what I would feel when at last I saw her. I scarcely remembered her at all.

Our brother Earnest wasn't saying much, just sitting there beside Zoe with his hands folded in his lap. His was a pale, almost flawlessly handsome version of the more ruggedly chiseled profile of his father, combined with that glorious ash blond coloring of our mother. I thought him really beautiful, like an angel from a painting—a combination that, in a rough boys' school like mine, he would not have found an asset.

"She's dying, you know," Zoe informed me, pointing with her small hand toward the forbidding double doors across the hall. "This may be the last time any of us will see her—so the *least* they could do is make it so she can kiss me goodbye."

"Dying?" I said, hearing the word echo in the darkened corridor. I felt something hard and numb forming within my chest. How could my mother be dying? She was so young the last time I'd seen her. And all those pictures of her on my dresser at school: so beautiful and so young. Illness, perhaps. But death was something I was totally unprepared for.

"It's awful," said Zoe. "Really *disgusting*. Her brains are spilling out. Not just her brains—there's something hideous and creepy growing in the dark inside her head. They had to cut a hole in her head bone, so she wouldn't get squashed—"

"Zoe, stop it," said Earnest softly. Then he looked sadly at me, his pale grey eyes shadowed by long, thick lashes.

I was in shock. But before I had time to collect myself, the large doors opened and Hieronymus Behn stepped into the corridor. I hadn't seen him earlier that evening when I'd been collected from the train. I hardly recognized him in the full muttonchop whiskers then in fashion, but underneath, the outline of his handsome, sculptural face remained virile and strong, lacking the soft complacency one often found in the Austrian upper classes. He seemed in complete command of the situation, unmoved by any such horrors as Zoe described that might lie beyond those doors.

"Lafcadio, you may come in now and see your mother," Hieronymus informed me. But when I tried to stand I found my legs were trembling, and the cold lump moved into my throat, where it stuck like a block of ice.

"I'll come too," Zoe announced, on her feet beside me, her small hand thrust into mine. As she marched toward the doors with me in tow, my stepfather remained in our path. His brow furrowed slightly and he seemed about to speak. But just then Earnest stood up and joined us.

"No, we'll all go in there together, we children," he said quietly. "I know Father will think that best, since it will tire our mother the very least."

"Of course," said Hieronymus after only a heartbeat's pause, and he stepped aside for all of us children to pass through the high paneled doors.

This was the first time, but it was not to be the last, that I would see the quiet self-possession of Earnest prevail over the clear and strong-willed intentions of Hieronymus Behn. No one else could ever do so.

Despite my late father's wealth, the grandeur of our plantations in Africa, or the resplendence of the many estates I'd since seen around Salzburg, I had never once in my young life set foot inside a room as grand as the one that lay behind those doors. It was as awesome as the interior of a cathedral: the high ceilings, lavish furniture and accessories and hangings, the rich, jewellike colors of imported stained-glass lamps, the silky, liquid lines of crystal bowls filled with flowers, the mellow sheen of polished pieces of costly Biedermeier.

Zoe had told me, as we'd waited in the hall, that the lower floors of our house had already been converted to that new energy source electricity, which I knew had been installed a decade ago by Thomas Alva Edison himself, at the Schönbrunn Palace right here in Vienna. But my mother's room was lit by the soft yellow glow of gas lamps, and warmed by a fire that flickered behind the panels of a low glass screen set before the hearth across the room.

I hope never to see such a sight again as that of my mother lying in the enormous canopied bed, her face bleached whiter than the lace counterpane. She weighed next to nothing. She was like a sucked-out husk about to crumble to dust and blow away. The cap covering her head could not conceal that her hair had been shaved—but thank God it hid the rest of the story.

I should never have believed this was my mother. In my childish memory, she was the beautiful woman who'd sung me to sleep with her lovely voice until the age of four. When she turned those watery blue eyes on me now, I wanted to cover my own eyes and to run, sobbing, from the room; I wanted not to think again of my lost childhood, of an abandonment that now could neither be undone nor atoned for.

My stepfather leaned with folded arms against the dark wainscoting beside the entry doors, his cold, immobile eyes focused upon the bed. A small group of servants hovered near the hearth, some silently sobbing or holding each other's arms, watching as we children crossed the room to our mother's bedside. God help me, but I only wanted her to vanish as if swallowed by the earth. As if in support, Zoe's tiny hand squeezed mine, and I heard Earnest's voice beside me as we reached the bed.

"Lafcadio is here, Mother," he said. "He would like your blessing."

Our mother's lips were moving, and Earnest again helped by lifting little Zoe up onto the bed. He poured out a glass of water and handed it to Zoe, who fed it drop by drop between our mother's parched lips. She was trying to whisper something, so Zoe took it upon herself to translate. I found it eerie and unnatural to hear what were perhaps the last words of a dying woman emerging from the rosebud lips of a six-year-old child.

"Lafcadio," my mother said via little Zoe, "I give you my blessing with all my heart. I want you to know I feel the greatest pain that we've been parted for so long. Your stepfather thought . . . we believed it best for your . . . education."

Even whispering through Zoe seemed a great effort, and I was frankly praying she'd find herself too weak to go on. Of the many reunions with my mother I'd naturally imagined over the years, none had been like this: a leave-taking before teary onlookers, being barely welcomed at the last possible moment into a family of complete strangers. It was positively ghoulish; I could barely wait for it to end. I was so distraught, I nearly missed the critical words:

". . . so your stepfather has generously offered to adopt you, taking responsibility for your well-being and education, as if you were one of his own children. I pray you'll embrace and care for one another as such. I've signed the papers only today. You are now Lafcadio Behn, full brother to Earnest and Zoe."

Adopted me? Good lord! How could I become the son of a man I scarcely knew? Was I given no choice in the matter? Was this horrid opportunist, who'd tricked his way into my mother's bed, now to be in control of my education, my life, my family's property? Aghast, I suddenly realized that when my mother died, I would no longer *have* any family. A rage struck me, that dark, despairing rage that can perhaps only be so deeply felt by children, who are completely impotent over their own destiny.

I was about to dash from the room in tears when a hand touched me lightly on the shoulder. I expected my stepfather, who'd been behind me only moments before. Instead, there stood the most astonishing creature, regarding me through eyes of a deep, clear green, with mercurial fire burning in their depths—the eyes of a wild animal. Her face, framed by an unbound mane of dark hair, seemed the sort found in paintings of Ondines, creatures arisen from the sparkling magical realms of the sea. She was absolutely ravishing. And despite my youth, I was well prepared to be ravished by her, having forgotten all about Hieronymus Behn, my future, my despair—even my dying mother lying on the bed.

She spoke in a strange foreign-sounding accent, and a voice so musical that it seemed rich with hidden bells. "So this is our little English lord Stirling?" She smiled at me. "I'm Pandora, your mother's friend and companion."

Was it only my imagination that she'd stressed the word "mother's"? She didn't look old enough to be her companion—perhaps she meant paid companion—but she'd also said friend, hadn't she? When Hieronymus came forward to address her, Pandora slipped past him as if she hadn't noticed, and went instead to the bed where my mother lay.

Plucking little Zoe like a loose pillow from the counterpane, she casually tossed the child over one shoulder. Zoe twisted her head to look at me upside down, and she raised one eyebrow in wise judgment, as if we shared an interesting secret.

"Frau Hermione," Pandora said to my mother, "if I were a fairy here at your bedside, and I said that you could make three wishes before you died—one wish on behalf of each of your children—what would your wishes be?"

There was whispering amongst the servants—no doubt shocked, as I was, at the cavalier manner in which this new arrival had brushed aside the master of the household and was treating the mistress's impending death and last wishes almost as a parlor game.

But far more surprising was the change in my mother. Color infused that deathlike pallor, flushing her cheeks with a rosy glow. As she and Pandora locked eyes, a beatific smile lit her face. Though I shall always swear that neither woman spoke a single word, it seemed that a communication passed between them. After a long moment, Mother nodded. When she closed her eyes, she was still smiling.

Pandora, with Zoe swinging from her shoulder like a fur neck-piece, turned toward the rest of us. "As you children know, it's bad luck to cast wishes abroad on the winds: it breaks the spell," she announced. "So I'll tell each of you in secret your mother's wish."

Perhaps Pandora *was* a fairy or sorceress, as she seemed. She slid

Zoe from her shoulder onto the bed and tugged the starchy hair ribbons, shaking her head. "My poor girl, you've been trussed and trimmed like a Christmas goose," she told Zoe. And as if she knew of our earlier conversation outside in the hallway, she pulled the stiff ribbons from Zoe's hair while whispering Mother's wish into her ear. Then she said, "Now you can go and give your mother a kiss, and thank her for your wish."

Zoe scrambled across the bed and did as bidden.

Then Pandora went to Earnest, whispered to him likewise, and the same procedure was followed.

I found it hard to believe that, where *I* was concerned, there'd be much more to say in the wish department. How could my mother make a wish for me when she'd just admitted that, behind my back, I'd been sold like chattel to Hieronymus Behn, who'd waste no time demolishing my future hopes as thoroughly as he'd done to my present and my past?

Maybe it was my imagination that my stepfather, who was still standing near me, stiffened as Pandora approached us in her rustling grey silk gown. For the first time since she'd entered the room, she not only seemed to take notice of him, she looked him directly in the eye, but with an expression I couldn't fathom.

Putting her hand on my shoulder again, she leaned to my ear so her cheek brushed mine. I could smell the warm aroma of her skin and I tingled with the same excitement as before. But her next words, spoken with great insistence, made my blood run cold.

"You must show no reaction to anything—you must go along with whatever I say," she whispered urgently. "We're all in great danger because of your presence here—you most of all. I cannot explain until I can get you outside this house filled with spies and lies and pain. I will try to arrange this for tomorrow, understood?"

Danger? What sort of danger? I understood nothing, but I nodded my head to show I would make no reaction. Pandora pressed my shoulder firmly and went back to the bed, taking Mother's hand as she addressed the servants.

"Frau Behn is happy to see her children together at last," Pandora informed them. "But even so brief a visit has taken her strength. We must leave her to rest now."

But before the servants had filed out, Pandora called to my stepfather across the room, "Herr Behn, your wife would also like you to have the carriage prepared first thing in the morning, so I may take the children for an outing around Vienna together before Lafcadio returns to his school."

My stepfather's eyes flickered for a moment as he stood beside me, halfway between the bed and the door. He seemed to hesitate before bowing his head slightly to her.

"With pleasure," he said, though it didn't sound it. He turned and left the room.

◆ ◆

It was snowing when we left the house the next morning, but dark skies and inclement weather did little to daunt Zoe, who was excited by being in on some kind of mystery—especially one involving a new brother whom she could instruct and bully. She could barely contain herself long enough to be bundled up by the servants before dragging me off to the stables where we children, I discovered, had our own conveyance: a carriage and four. It was already rigged by instruction of my stepfather, the harnessed horses pawing and the driver waiting high in his box. Nearby stalls held surreys and traps, and the family's sparkling new motorcar.

I'd tossed sleeplessly all the night, filled with questions about Pandora's cryptic communiqué.

This morning, in the warmth of the closed cab, as we clopped through the cobbled streets and I got my first good view of Vienna, I saw Earnest turn several times to glance at the rigid back of our driver through the isinglass window separating us. So I held my tongue and waited, becoming more overwrought moment by moment. But no matter how hard I tried, I couldn't imagine what sort of actual danger—in a rarefied atmosphere like that of the Behn household, surrounded by servants and wealth—could befall a twelve-year-old child.

Pandora interrupted these thoughts. "Have you ever been to an amusement park before?" she asked with a smile. "The *Volksprater*, or people's park, used to be the hunting preserve of the emperor Joseph II, the one who was the brother of Marie Antoinette and also a patron of Mozart. Today it has many interesting rides. There's the carousel: English children call it a merry-go-round because it spins about in a circle. You sit on horses and they go up and down as the wheel turns, so it seems as if you're riding. This one at the Prater hasn't got only horses but an entire *Tiergarten* of animals."

"Papa doesn't permit us to go to the Prater," said Zoe, sounding more than disappointed at this sorry fact.

"He says it's filled with low-class workers who drink beer and eat sausages," Earnest explained. "And when I said maybe they wouldn't go outdoors to such a place in winter, Father said the Prater is closed in the winter—even the giant Ferris wheel."

"As usual, your father is half right and half wrong," Pandora said—a cheeky remark for a girl her age to make about a man of my stepfather's position, whatever the nature of their relationship, which itself was shaping up as a real complexity. "The park may be closed for the winter, but I have special connections that don't shut down in bad weather."

By the time we reached the park, the weather had grown bitterly cold. The place did look awfully barren and deserted, completely shut down for the season. There were barriers at the gate that prevented our carriage from passing inside to the area where the big mechanical rides were located. Zoe was crushed.

"It isn't far," Pandora told us. "Lafcadio, you carry Zoe on your shoulders through these drifts. It will be easier going once we're inside the park."

We had the driver pull the carriage and horses beneath the shelter of a train trestle. Pandora tucked up her heavy skirts, I hefted Zoe onto my shoulders, and we marched through drifts around the barricades and into the silent white arcades of the park. When we reached the broad *Hauptallee* with its chapel of groomed trees where the paths had been cleared, I set Zoe down.

"Lafcadio, now we can all tell you what we couldn't say last night," Earnest said. "You see, Father didn't want you to come here to Vienna at all; there were awful rows over it. If it weren't for Pandora, you wouldn't be here."

There were rows over *me*? I looked at Pandora.

"How much do you know of your stepfather?" she asked.

"Practically nothing. I haven't seen him or my mother in nearly eight years," I said, with a bitterness I tried to suppress. Although I felt sick at the very idea that I was now the legal son of Hieronymus Behn, I felt awkward saying so before his two blood children walking beside me.

"Zoe and I don't know Father well ourselves," Earnest told me, kicking at the snow with his perfectly polished knee boots. "He's always off at meetings or away on important business. We're never alone with Mother either: my tutor or Zoe's nanny or the servants are always about, just like last night."

"Your mother is little more than a prisoner in her own house," agreed Pandora. Then, when she saw my expression, she added, "I don't mean to say she's been chained up in the attic. But ever since moving here to Vienna eight years ago, she's never been permitted to be alone. She's watched by a complement of servants who read her mail. She has neither friends nor visitors, and she never goes outside the house unescorted."

"But you said *you're* her friend," I pointed out.

I'd probed my mind a thousand times all these years, trying to make sense of my mother's desertion of me, a desertion the more bitter in that she'd kept her other two children at her side. I'd believed—or longed to believe—that my stepfather was the cause behind it all. Was he really as evil a blackguard as I'd imagined? But Pandora's revelations had just begun.

"After your mother married Hieronymus Behn, twelve years ago," she said, "he parlayed your father's fortune, including the mining interests your mother still held, into an international mineral and industrial consortium with holdings so broad they could no longer be managed from provincial Africa but only from a world capital like Vienna. Your stepfather soon learned that in Vienna it was not enough merely to have a rich and beautiful wife whose assets he could exploit with impunity. In order to gain access to the best drawing rooms, impeccable social credentials were needed. In prosperous Catholic Austria, any poor Dutch Calvinist roots must be quickly buried, along with stories about the unknown parentage and orphaned upbringing of your mother. Then too, there were cultural attainments expected of a woman in Hermione's position: a command of the fine arts and music that she didn't have.

"But this situation was to prove a great boon. For though, within the house, there was always some watchful eye, Hermione was permitted to help select tutors to give lessons to her and the children—lessons that would provide her first chance to be alone, if for just a brief time, with someone not under her husband's total control. This was how your mother and I met: before me, she'd already interviewed a large number of tutors. But after spending only a few minutes with each, one after another, she found none who could meet the one criterion she secretly wanted."

"Secretly?" I asked, surprised.

Pandora looked me in the eye with a strange expression and said, "You see, your mother was convinced she would be satisfied only with an instructor who came from Salzburg."

"Salzburg!" I cried, as the truth suddenly struck me. "My mother wanted to find *me*—but *he* wouldn't let her?"

Pandora nodded and went on: "I had a friend named August—Gustl for short—a young viola player who was studying at the Wiener Musik Konservatorium and giving music lessons on the side to help pay his rent. Gustl came from a town not far from Salzburg, and he knew I had family there. When your mother was interviewing tutors and she brought the conversation around to Salzburg, Gustl mentioned me, and that's how I became music teacher to the Behn household."

"And that's how Pandora found you in Salzburg," chimed in Zoe, "and how Mother and Earnest and I know so much about you!"

"But you never came to see me at Salzburg," I pointed out.

"Did I not?" said Pandora, raising a brow.

We had reached the center of the park. There, where the hub of paths united, was the giant Ferris wheel Earnest had spoken of, dressed like tinsel with little dangling silver chairs, and so high that it disappeared into the heavy clouds. From the top, on a clear day, I was sure one could see the entire Ringstrasse, the magic circle that surrounded the city of Vienna. Beyond this was the carousel: prancing ostriches, giraffes, and wild stags that seemed strangely out of place in this dark wilderness of drifted snow. It was moving in silence, the circle wheeling mysteriously round and round without anything seeming to push it, as if the animals had been awaiting us.

Not far away on a stone bench sat a man wearing a peacoat and knit nautical cap, his back to us. He started to turn, as if expecting us. I grasped Pandora by the arm there on the path.

"*Why* has my stepfather kept me from my mother for so many years?" I demanded. "What sort of mother would permit it? Even if she was a prisoner as you say, surely she might have smuggled a letter or two in all this time—"

"Hush," Pandora said impatiently. "I told you last night you were in danger. We're all in danger, even here in this solitary place, if we're overheard. It's the money, Lafcadio—your father Christian Alexander's money—the equivalent of fifty million pounds sterling in gold Krugerrands and valuable mining interests I spoke of. These were left in trust, for your mother to live from their income during her lifetime—and the balance to come to *you* upon her death. Don't you see, she's about to die! He's seized control of the money; he forced her to sign those adoption papers, threatening to cut off all of the children if she refused. The woman is suffering tortures of remorse, not knowing what may become of any of you—"

"And Earnest and I want to run away with *you*," Zoe completed her sentence.

"With me?" I objected, my mind racing madly. "But I'm not running anywhere. Where would I go? What would I do?"

"I thought you could keep a secret," Pandora told Zoe firmly, tugging at a lock of hair that peeked from the child's fur-trimmed bonnet. Then to me she said, "I want you to meet my cousin Dacian Bassarides, who will help explain the plan we have in mind. In winter he's park custodian here at the Prater. In the summers . . ."

But my mind had completely stopped functioning. The young chap in the peacoat came up, took my gloved hand in his two, and smiled warmly as if we shared an intimate secret—as indeed we did! I was completely flabbergasted. Then, slowly, the pieces began to fall into place through the hazy forest of my thoughts.

I had never spoken to anyone of my private obsession, which I'd nurtured like a flame through all those lonely days of childhood. Ever since arriving at my school in Salzburg, after my classes each day I would go into the nearby woods and play for hour after hour on a small violin—almost a toy—that I'd been given as a child. Even the masters at my school didn't know.

But there were limits to what even the most burning desire could accomplish given so inferior an instrument—not to mention that the extent of my instruction had been sneaking to listen outside the doors of the Mozarteum. All this changed one day, nearly a year before, when a darkly handsome young man came walking through the woods playing his own violin—and in strains at once so sweet and yet so transcendental, one forgot there was a violin at all, as if sounds emitted by his soul were merging with the air in a long, passionate embrace. He made love to the wind.

And that same day, the young man I'd just met as Pandora's cousin Dacian Bassarides—whose name I'd never known till now—had become my master. Several times a week we met in the woods, and with few words he taught me how to play. So he must have been the go-between sent by Pandora and my mother to find me in Salzburg.

"Your mother *does* have a 'last wish' for you, Lafcadio," Pandora said as she lifted little Zoe up onto the revolving carousel platform. "Once she learned from us of your gift, she prayed that you should become a great violinist—even the greatest in the world. To that end, she's kept a private fund, set aside for you by your godfather, Mr. Rhodes, a fund your stepfather knows nothing about—not a huge sum, but ample to pay for your musical education when you are ready. In these next few years, Dacian has agreed to help you prepare for the conservatory. If your stepfather stops your schooling, we'll find you a place to live. Is this plan of your mother's at all to your liking?"

A plan to my liking? In one day, my world had turned inside out—from a future that resembled a prison camp with my stepfather as jailer, to a sweet-scented bed of rose and narcissus where all my fantasies would soon be fulfilled.

It seemed only moments, though it must have been an hour or more, that we whirled on the snowy carousel. Dacian played snatches on the violin with cold fingers—there was no steam, he explained, to run the calliope—and Pandora hummed the counterpoint through her muffler from which steamy breath emerged. Zoe danced and pranced about the circle as it whirled, and Earnest and I rode up and down proudly on our chosen steeds, a wolf for me and a soaring eagle for him. In between, my siblings spoke to me in whispers of what the future might be like without our mother—an interesting proposition from my viewpoint, since it described my entire past.

As to what Pandora's role was in it all, or why she'd chosen our family on whom to bestow her fairy magic, this still remained a mystery. I felt so euphoric at the thought of realizing my true dream that it never occurred to me it might be years before I learned the answers to such critical questions.

My first family outing was now disrupted by a new arrival, who approached down the *allée* in the opposite direction to the one we'd come.

"Goodness, it's Lucky," Pandora said, pulling down her muffler and taking her cousin's arm. "But how did he find us here?"

I didn't find this intrusion on my fantasies to be in any respect lucky. Perhaps he'd come to collect us and take us home. From my perch on my wolf I studied him as he came.

He was slender, with a long, pale, clean-shaven face, and older than Pandora—perhaps even twenty or more. He wore a threadbare but well-pressed suit with an artist's long fringed scarf, yet he had no topcoat in such weather! His mop of silky brown hair was cut in the popular "romantic" fashion, so he had to toss it back from time to time. He slapped his gloved hands against his chest for warmth, his breath streaming behind him. When he came close enough, I could see eyes of such startling blue intensity, it was hard to pull one's gaze away.

He called to Pandora, "I've been searching for you long enough to become a block of ice in this weather, Fräulein."

Zoe piped up, "Please, please, Lucky—come up here on the carousel and dance with me." So I now understood that Lucky was the fellow's name.

He regarded Zoe with mock derision. "Real men don't dance, *Liebchen*," he told her. "Besides, I've something of importance I must show you all. We have to see it today. The Hofburg museum will close up for cleaning and repairs next week, and these Viennese are so *gemütlich*, who knows *when* it will reopen? I'll be long gone by then. But I've got today's tickets for the Hofburg already for all of us, yes?"

"I'm sorry you've come out in the cold like this, Lucky," Pandora said. "But I promised Frau Behn I'd show her son around Vienna today. He must be returning to school quite soon."

"So this lad is the other Behn son—the English one, part Boer?" said Lucky.

Though I didn't correct him about my Boer-ness, I wondered how such a lower-class person who didn't possess an overcoat, or even a peacoat like Dacian's, could possibly be acquainted with my family here in Vienna.

"Lucky was the roommate of Gustl, Lafcadio," Pandora explained. "Gustl is the musician I told you about, the one who introduced your mother and me. They've known each other from high school, and have even written an opera together."

"But I haven't seen Gustl in ages," Lucky told her with a smile. Swinging himself up onto the carousel as it whirled, he made his way around to my wolf and added almost privately, as if we two shared a secret: "Our paths are so different. Gustl has diverged toward the mundane, I toward the divine."

Now that Lucky was so close, I saw his eyes really were extraordinary. I found myself nearly hypnotized. He studied me as if his appraisal would decide my total life worth, nodding to himself as if well satisfied, which made me strangely happy for some reason. Then he turned to Pandora, taking her hands in his and raising her fingertips to his lips. But he kissed the backs of his own hands instead—an odd, uniquely Austrian custom I'd sometimes seen in Salzburg.

"I don't write librettos anymore," he went on. "I've been working on paintings again; my watercolors have achieved some success. While I was engaged last Michaelmas for a small job of touching up gold leaf in the Rubens gallery at the Kunsthistorisches Museum, one night I went across the street to the Hofburg just before closing. And that's when I found this thing of enormous interest. I've been studying it intensely each night at the library ever since. I've been up the river to Krems, also to the monastery of Melk, using their library too, one with quite interesting manuscripts—and even once to Salzburg for more research." Then he turned to me.

"I don't believe in coincidences, young man," Lucky told me. "I believe only in destiny. For example, I find interesting the animals you boys have chosen from all this enormous menagerie. The name for eagle in Old High German is *Earn*, and Earnest sits astride an eagle—while the beast *you've* chosen is a wolf. Pandora's cousin Dacian here, his name comes from Daci, the wolfmen of ancient Thrace, one of the oldest hunting tribes in Europe. You see, study enhances not only the intellect but the very way in which we perceive ourselves and our history. *My* nickname, Lucky, is something of a private joke among my friends. My Christian name in Old High German is Athal-wulf, meaning highborn or fortunate wolf—Lucky Wolf, do you see? And my family name originally must have meant the same as Boer: Heideler, or 'heath man,' like Bauer, one who lives from the land—"

◆ ◆

"Whoa," I cried, stopping Uncle Laf's life story in midstream with a wave of my hand as we sat there in the Sun Valley Lodge dining room. "Rein up there, partner—you mean to say this guy was *Adolf Hitler?*"

When Laf merely smiled, I looked at Olivier and Bambi, who both had glazed expressions like a trout that's just realized it's no longer breathing water.

"Gavroche, the story was almost over," Laf said.

"It's definitely over for me," I told him, pushing aside my half-eaten *saumon fumé* omelette and getting to my feet.

"Where are you going?" asked Laf pleasantly.

Olivier was wrestling with his napkin, trying to figure out whether he was my guest or Laf's. I motioned him to stay seated.

"Outside for a walk," I told Laf. "I need to swallow some fresh air before you ask me to swallow anything else."

"I ask you to swallow nothing but a bit more champagne," he said, still smiling and patting me on my good arm. "Then I shall go for the walk *with* you—or perhaps even have a swim?—while your friend here shows Bambi a bit of the mountain. That is, if you don't mind." Laf raised his brow in question to Olivier, who leapt to his feet.

After a flurry of waiters and coats and thanks and hugs, Bambi and Olivier vanished to the slopes and Laf and I headed off to the glass-walled outdoor thermal pool, surrounded by the mountains, its roof open to the sky. Volga Dragonoff met us there with bathing suits.

"Uncle Laf," I said when we two were alone at last, ensconced in the steamy relaxing mineral waters, "how could you have told a ridiculous story like that one at breakfast? Olivier's a friend of mine, but he's also my colleague. After this morning, he's going to think my family's even crazier than you all actually are."

"Crazy? I see nothing crazy about my story," Laf objected. "Every single thing was completely truth."

He ducked his head under the water. When he came up, the

silvery mane was slicked back, accentuating the magnificent bone structure of his face and those sharp blue eyes. I thought how truly handsome he must have been when he was young. No wonder Pandora had fallen for him. But wasn't that part of the problem?

"Everything you said was a myth," I pointed out to Laf, "especially the parts about our family. That's the first I've heard of your father being English—much less having a fortune of something like a hundred million dollars! And if Pandora really hated my grandfather Hieronymus as much as you say, why did she wind up marrying him that same year, when you were still only twelve, and staying married long enough to have a child by him?"

"I can imagine what Augustus's version must be of the story," Laf said with the first note of cynicism I'd heard so far. "But I'll be direct, now that we're alone. Though I hate to be the one to tell you of your own grandfather, Gavroche, you asked the question—and a good one—why Pandora might marry so despicable a man.

"When we returned that afternoon to the house in Vienna, we learned my mother had died in our absence. The younger children were distraught, beside themselves, and we were all sent early to bed. Next morning, in the predawn light, I was taken by several strong male servants to the train and forcibly escorted back to Salzburg.

"That day would be the last I would see of Pandora in nearly five years, for she was taken from Vienna and then the First World War intervened. Only five years after would I learn how she had been raped by my stepfather that very night—more than once. How he forced her to marry him, under the threat that he would reveal things about her that might bring great danger, to her and to her family as well."

"He what?" I gaped at him. "Are you mad?"

"No—but I thought I might go mad, back then," Laf told me with a bittersweet smile. I knew by the way he said it he was telling the truth, and I wondered whether he'd ever told anybody of this before now.

"Why don't you finish your story, Uncle Laf?" I said, moving over through the water to put my hand on his shoulder. "I'm sorry about what I said. I really do want to know everything."

"Let me begin anew, with Lucky going with us in our carriage to the Hofburg to see the weapons collections and his discovery there of a mysterious and fascinating ancient treasure. . . ."

◆ ◆

THE SWORD AND THE SPEAR

Over many centuries, the Austrian Habsburgs had cut and glued together their vast empire through a series of brilliant marriages to women who were heiresses to countries like Spain, Hungary, and so on. Now a part of the Hofburg, the Habsburg winter palace, had been converted to a museum to show to the public the royal jewels, the silver, the many collections accumulated over centuries.

The collection, one of the world's most extensive, was of special interest to Lucky. He had said he believed in destiny, and en route to the museum in our carriage, he stressed to us children that the destiny of the German-speaking people should never have included rule by this dynasty of motley intermarriages, spawning the ragtag population we saw around us in the streets of the capital. But that is another story about Adolf, which by now everyone unhappily knows.

More to our point, Lucky had discovered within the Hofburg two relics that dazzled him: a sword and a spear. These items which he believed to be so ancient and valuable were placed, strangely enough, off in a corner in a plain glass case, almost as if abandoned. The sword was long and curved, with a grip that appeared more medieval than ancient. The spear was small, black, and unobtrusive, with a crude brass-colored collar holding together the handle and shaft. We children looked at them for some time, until Earnest asked Lucky to tell us their significance.

"These pieces," Lucky said in an almost dreamlike voice, "go back at least two thousand years, and possibly much more. It's a well-known fact that they existed already in the time of Christ, and were very likely handled by his own disciples. It's thought the sword was the one carried by Saint Peter, who wielded it in the garden at Gethsemane and cut off the the temple guard's ear. Jesus told him to put it away, for 'They that live by the sword shall die by the sword.'

"But the spear is even more interesting," Lucky went on. "It was carried by a Roman centurion, one Gaius Cassius Longinus, who was under the command of Pontius Pilate. Longinus pierced Christ's side on the cross with this very spear, to be certain he was dead, and they saw the liquid flow from the wound. . . ."

I could see Lucky's long, pale face reflected in the glass of the case before us. He still seemed lost in a dream as he gazed upon these weapons. His pupils were dilated, exaggerating the hypnotic quality of those intense blue eyes beneath his thick dark lashes. But Pandora, who was standing at the opposite side of the case, broke the spell.

"On the printed card here inside the case," she coolly informed us, "it says it's reputed that this sword once belonged to Attila the Hun, and the spear to Frederick Barbarossa, great figures of Germanic history and of Teutonic myth. And it also says there's a legend that whenever these two weapons have been combined in the hands of a single warrior, as they apparently were by Charlemagne, that same warrior has become the leader of all of the civilized world."

"Is that why the Habsburgs rule over so many countries?" I asked her, excited by this peek into the mysteries of ancient legend. "Because they *do* own both of them right now, don't they?" But Lucky, his trance apparently broken as well, answered for her.

"It says a *warrior* must possess them both," he snapped. "The so-called Habsburgs are just like their name: a hawk's-perch but not a hawk. They roost wherever they alight, and they feather their nest. These are not hunters, nor leaders of a proud, brave people. And merely possessing two of these objects, as I have learned, is insufficient for the kind of power you speak of. There are many such relics, ancient with the dust of the aeons—and only when *all* are reunited in one man's hands will the world itself be transformed. I believe that such a time is nearly upon us."

We children gazed with new respect at the two weapons in their glass case. But I privately wondered how such a profound transformation might take place if all the other "ancient treasures" were so crumbling, fragile, and unimportant-looking as these.

"If the time is nearly upon us," said a soft voice from behind my shoulder, "then surely you must know what these other objects are that you seek?"

We turned, and I saw that the speaker was Pandora's young cousin, my violin master Dacian Bassarides, who'd been so silent throughout our entire trip that we'd nearly forgotten him.

Lucky nodded his head in excitement. "I believe there are thirteen in all. Some are serving dishes, some garments, some tools or implements of war—and one gemstone, and a gaming board of sorts. Although my studies have told me how each might have been disguised throughout the ages, the last time I feel *certain* they were together was at the time of Christ: in other words, at the last New Age. That's why I went to pursue my studies at Melk and then at Salzburg, for here on the river and high in the mountains of the Salzkammergut are the places in our land where the ancient peoples dwelt, and I knew the message I sought would be found near there. There is information there, written in the runes . . ."

◆ ◆

"The runes?" I said uncomfortably. I saw that Laf not only had paused but seemed to have drifted off into another world.

"A manuscript written in runes. I suspect this is the 'something' your cousin Sam left you in his will," said Laf, returning from the sea of his nightmare memories. "Lucky, or Adolf, was trying to assemble and decipher it even then, on the eve of World War One in Vienna—a task at which I feel confident he never completely succeeded. But someone else did."

"I don't think I got that from Sam," I said, though I could hardly reveal that Sam was still alive or that I'd spoken to him of it. "But I did get a *different* document made of runes from a friend of yours, though I haven't had a chance to look at—"

"A friend of mine?" said Laf. "What friend?"

"Wolfgang Hauser—a fellow Viennese—"

"Gavroche, what are you saying?" Even in the steam I could see Laf's face grow pale beneath his leathery tan. "Wolfgang Hauser is no friend of mine. How could he obtain that manuscript? Where would he get it?"

I don't know if my expression revealed exactly how sick I felt, but when he looked at me Laf said, "Oh, Gavroche, what have you done?"

I prayed the answer wasn't going to be "fucked up royally," though it was starting to look that way.

"Uncle Laf, I want you to tell me exactly who Wolfgang Hauser is, and how you know him," I said, choosing my words carefully even if I was pretty sure I didn't want to hear the answer.

"I *don't* know him," Laf said. "I've met him once or twice. He's a minion of Zoe's—one of those good-looking boys she likes to keep as ornaments on her wrist."

I applauded myself for not flinching at his callous description of the recent great lust of my life—and also for passing over the obvious fact that one might make the same observation of Uncle Laf and Bambi.

"I do know your aunt Zoe, however," Laf went on. "She was never the queen of the night as she liked to portray herself—far from it. That was clever salesmanship, a program of propaganda conceived and tailored for Zoe, the most famous dancer of her day, by the cleverest salesman of our century. She and this benefactor spent decades trying to get the manuscript from Pandora, the one who actually collected it. Perhaps by now you have guessed that Zoe's own mentor, best friend, and closest confidant for twenty-five years was none other than Adolf Hitler."

Laf paused and looked at me. My heart was well below my stomach by now, and I felt I must get out of the steamy heat of the pool before I blacked out. Laf's next words seemed to echo across the water.

"There is no way on earth that either Zoe or Wolfgang Hauser could have a copy of that manuscript. Anything belonging to Earnest, he guarded all his life." Then, after a pause, he whispered, "Gavroche, I pray you have not trusted Hauser with it—or even left him alone with it in the same room. If you have you've surely endangered everything Pandora and Earnest risked their lives for—what indeed may have cost them their lives, and your cousin Sam's, too."

If circumstances lead me, I will find
where truth is hid, though it were hid indeed
Within the centre.

—Shakespeare, *Hamlet*

JESUS:
To this end was I born, and for this cause came I into
the world, that I should bear witness to the truth. Everyone that is of the
truth heareth my voice.

PILATE:
What is truth?

—Gospel of John 18:37–8

Therefore the effort to arrive at the Truth, and especially
the truth about the gods, is a longing for the divine.

—Plutarch, *Moralia*

It's sort of a hobby of mine: the truth.

—Cary Grant, as master thief
John Robie in *To Catch a Thief*

Judea: Spring, A.D. 33

THE FIRST APOSTLE

◆ ◆

> *Now when Jesus was risen early the first day of the week, he appeared first to Mary Magdalene . . . and [his disciples], when they had heard that he was alive, and had been seen of her, believed not.* —Gospel of Mark 16:9–10

"But what is the truth?" Johan Zebedee asked his older brother James. "How can Joseph of Arimathea expect any of us to remember something that took place more than a year ago?"

The brothers had left behind the port of Joppa and the ship on which James had just returned from his year-long mission abroad in Celtic Iberia. They took the rocky high road out of town.

"When I visited with Joseph in the isles of Britannia," said James, "he told me it was his belief that some key element was missing from the story of the Master's last days. You know the Master always said his legacy would be to share his 'mysteries' with his truest disciples. It occurred to Joseph that maybe the Master, realizing his time on earth with us was short, actually *did* impart these secrets, but because he spoke in parables none of us grasped the hidden meaning in his words. That's why I've hurried here from Celtic Iberia, to bring Joseph's letter asking Miriam of Magdali to look into this matter. And he hopes that we—you and Simon Peter and I, as the Master's three chosen successors—will lend her our support."

James and his younger brother Johan Zebedee, along with their business partners, Simon Peter and his brother Andrew, had been the first disciples recruited by the Master for his mission. When he'd found them along the shores of Lake Galilee, he'd told them to put down their fishing nets and follow him: he would teach them to become "fishers of men." So the Zebedees, as first-chosen, had come to expect preferential treatment. And they'd always received it—until recently. This year had cost them everything, Johan thought bitterly. His older brother had stayed away too long and there was much he needed to learn.

"Perhaps you can explain to me what Miriam of Magdali has to do with any of this?" he asked James. "Why should *she* be the official messenger?"

"Joseph has always supported Miriam's claim that she was the first apostle: first to see the Master after death, risen from his tomb that morning in Joseph's garden at Gethsemane," said James. "Whenever Joseph refers to Miriam, he still calls her the First Messenger—apostle to the apostles. And whether or not we want to believe the Master really honored Miriam so greatly, in all honesty we must recognize such a thing was not wholly out of his character. The truth is, it would be no different from the honors the Master constantly bestowed on Miriam throughout his life."

"Honors and kisses!" snapped Johan. "The world knows *I* was the Master's most beloved disciple. He treated me like his child and embraced me even more often than he did Miriam. Didn't he entrust me with his mother's care when he died, as if I were her own son? And the Master said you and I would sip from his chalice when the kingdom of heaven came—as great an honor as any he gave Miriam."

"I fear that cup, Johan," James said softly. "Perhaps you'd be wise to fear it too."

"Everything has changed since you left Judea, James," said the younger man. "Even our triumvirate no longer exists. Peter says that only one 'rock' can be a foundation stone, and that he was chosen by the Master. There's factionalism, jealousy, resentment, friend against friend. If you'd stayed here in Jerusalem this past year, things might not have arrived at such a sorry state."

"I'm distressed to hear that," said James. "But surely things haven't changed so much that they can't be salvaged."

He set his hands on his younger brother's shoulders just as the Master used to do. Johan felt a pang of sorrow. How he missed the Master's simplicity and strength!

"You don't understand, James," said Johan. "Miriam has become Peter's particular thorn. She's been sequestered with her family in Bethany these many months, and no one ever sees her. Peter resents her more than he ever did me, for her special closeness to the

Master. He's changed everything because of her: the women don't preach or heal—or even go abroad on missions now, unless they're accompanied by a male apostle. And they must cover their hair, for it's said that the temptation of such openness and liberties as were permitted when the Master was alive is too great, and will turn most women to wantonness—"

"But—do you mean to tell me Simon Peter has created such rules by his own decision?" James interrupted.

"With the support of others—though I assure you I'm not among them! James, you must understand that while you and Joseph may *want* the truth, there are those who believe they already *have* it. A saga is being spun to explain the Master's every word and deed, and often by those who never understood him or even knew him at all. These stories are confusing, contradictory, and sometimes totally baldfaced lies! It's been suggested, for instance, that those 'seven devils' the Master cast out of Miriam were not merely sins of pride or vanity in her education or beauty, but something far worse—something venal—"

"But how can they say such things?" cried James. "How can Peter permit it? Doesn't he fear the Master will shut him out of the kingdom altogether?"

"Please remember," said Johan with a bitter little smile, "it is Simon Peter himself who holds the keys to that kingdom. They were given him by the Master, as he permits no one to overlook. As you see, my dear brother, you have returned not a moment too soon."

◆ ◆

Brigantium: Summer, A.D. 34

THE WORDS

For nation shall rise against nation, and kingdom against kingdom . . . false Christs and false prophets shall rise . . . the sun shall be darkened, and the moon shall not give her light, and the stars of heaven shall fall, and the powers that are in heaven shall be shaken . . .

But the gospel must first be published among all nations . . . Heaven and earth shall pass away. But my words shall not pass away.

Jesus of Nazareth
—Gospel of Mark 13:8–31

Joseph of Arimathea stood high on a cliff above the Bay of Brigantium, watching in the last waning western light as James Zebedee's ship moved into the fog and slipped out to sea. Brigantium, once the center of worship of the great Celtic goddess Brighde, was the last Celtic seaport on the continent still in existence since ancient times. Most of Iberia had been in Roman hands for hundreds of years since the Punic Wars. But this remote northwestern section had been taken, in bitterness and bloodshed, only as recently as Augustus's time, and the spirit of the natives was far from obliterated.

Whether they were called Celts, Keltoi, or Galtoi, Galicians, Galatians, Galli, or Gauls, these tribal pagans, as the Romans considered them, had left their mark on civilizations from here to far-flung Phrygia, indeed they themselves had founded many of these civilizations. Brilliant Celtic craftsmen still influenced artisans from Scandinavia to Mauretania; wild Celtic warriors had harried the continent with so many invasions over the years that, just to hold them back, the Romans had designed the system of legions that today controlled most of the world. And the lot of preserving their history and faith, keeping alive their words, fell to the Celtic *druid*—men like the one who at this moment stood beside Joseph on the cliff.

The ship below was swallowed into the bank of cold, dark fog that always encased this coast, even, as now, in summer. But from up here, Joseph could still make out the beach, its surface unmarred but for the lapping waves, each narrow silken line disappearing beneath the next—much like the Master's words, he thought. Though the Master had always told them not to carve his words in stone but to hold them in their thoughts, perhaps those words had already vanished from the minds of men—because there was no *drui*, like his companion, who was trained to keep them alive in his heart.

If this were so, then the only remnants of the Master's words might be those gathered by Miriam of Magdali over the past year, which now lay sealed within the clay amphorae here in the fishing net at his feet: the memories of those who'd seen and heard the Master in his final week on earth.

Joseph and the *drui* had climbed from the dark, dank summer fog below to this isolated lookout to watch the ship depart before discussing their own mission. Now for the first time Joseph turned to his companion.

In the slanted light of the setting sun, the *drui*'s rugged, angular face took on the hard cast of burnished copper. His red-gold hair was plaited into many complex knotted braids that tumbled over his broad shoulders and powerful chest. Though he wore the same loose Celtic tunic as Joseph wore himself, over one shoulder and held by a golden brooch was a throw made entirely of the soft, thick pelts of red foxes, the badge of a high official of the fox clan. His muscular neck and upper arms were encircled by the thick, intricately wrought gold torques he always wore, which marked the status of a prince or a priest: as a *drui*, he was considered both.

He was Lovernios, Prince of Foxes, a man Joseph had trusted all his life—and, except for the Master, the wisest man he'd ever known. Joseph prayed that his great wisdom would bring them through the crisis he felt impending.

"It is nearly over, Lovern," Joseph said.

"Over—perhaps," Lovernios replied. "But each ending is a new beginning, as Esus of Nazareth told me when you brought him to live among us when he was but a boy. He said during his travels with you he'd learned everyone resists change." Lovernios added with a questioning smile, "I wonder if you understand exactly what that means?"

"I'm afraid it means," said Joseph, "that just like Miriam of Magdali you believe the Master is really alive: that he went through the transformation of death, yet somehow he still walks among us."

The *drui* shrugged. "Recall his statement: 'I am with you always, even unto the end of the world.' "

"In spirit, yes, that's possible," agreed Joseph, "but hardly by taking off and putting on flesh like a cloak, as some would have it! No, my wise friend, it wasn't primitive superstition that brought me here. I'm after the truth."

"What you seek, my friend," Lovernios said, shaking his head, "you'll never find in these clay vessels at your feet: they contain only words."

"But it's you yourself," objected Joseph, "who first told me of the magic with which the *druid* invest words. You said words alone have the power to kill or to heal. I pray some of these memories will reveal the Master's last message to us—just as he prayed his words would not be forgotten."

"Writing does not aid memory but destroys it," said Lovernios. "That is why our people restrict the use of our written language to sacramental functions: to protect or sanctify a spot, destroy an enemy, raise the elements, work magic. Great truths cannot be put into writing, nor ideas be set in stone. You may open your clay vessels, my friend, but you'll find only memories of memories, shadows of shadows."

"Even from boyhood the Master had the memory of a *drui*," said Joseph. "He knew Torah by heart and could recite from it hour after hour. During long sea voyages I used to read him stories, and he committed those to memory too. His favorite was the *Pythian Odes* of Pindar—especially the phrase '*Kairos* and tide wait for no man.' In the Greek tongue, there are two words for 'time': *chronos* and *kairos*. The first means time as the sun passes through the heavens. But *kairos* means the 'necessary moment'—the critical instant when one must catch the tide or be swept under and utterly destroyed. It was this second meaning that was so important to the Master.

"The very last occasion when I saw him—when I went to tell him I'd arranged for the white ass he'd requested to ride on his entry into Jerusalem the next Sunday—he said to me, 'Then all is done, Joseph, and I go to meet my *kairos*.' Those were the last words he spoke to me before he died." Joseph blinked tears from his eyes and swallowed hard. "I miss him so much, Lovernios," he whispered.

The Celtic prince turned to Joseph. Though the two were of the same age and of nearly equal height, he put his arms around Joseph and rocked him like a child, as the Master used to do when words seemed inadequate.

"Then we can only hope," Lovernios said at last, "that these glimpses of words, even if they are not all of them true, will at least take some pain from your heart."

Joseph looked at his friend and nodded. Then he stooped to the net and extracted the amphora that bore Miriam's mark as the first of the series. Breaking the seal of the clay container, he pulled out and opened the scroll, and he began to read aloud:

To: Joseph of Arimathea
at Glastonbury, Britannia
From: Miriam of Magdali
at Bethany, Judea

Dearly beloved Joseph,

Many thanks for your letter, which James Zebedee brought after his visit with you. I regret it's taken one whole year to fulfill your request, but as you've no doubt learned from James by now, everything here has changed—everything.

Oh, Joseph, how I miss you! And how grateful I am that you've asked me to carry out this undertaking. It seems you alone recall how much the Master relied upon women. Who but women financed his mission, provided him shelter, traveled and taught and healed and ministered by his side? With his mother Miriam we followed his path to Golgotha; we stood weeping beneath the cross until he died and we went to the sepulchre to wash his body, to prepare it with rare herbs and fine Magdali linen. In short, we women were the ones who stayed with the Master from beginning to end. Even beyond the end, until his spirit ascended to heaven.

Joseph, forgive my pouring out these turbulent feelings. But when you reached across the waters through your letter, I felt like a drowning woman rescued at the final hour. I agree that something significant happened in the Master's last days, and I'm the more frustrated since I can't come at once to Britannia as you wish. But this delay could prove a blessing—for I myself may have discovered something that hasn't been hinted at in any of the memoirs I've collected for you: it's related to Ephesus.

The Master's mother, who's been like a mother to me, is as disturbed as the rest of us at what's become of her son's legacy in so short a time. She's determined to move to Ephesus on the Ionian coast, and has asked me to accompany her there and to stay out the year until she's fully settled.

Her protector, young Johan Zebedee, whom the Master used to call *parthenos*, or 'blushing virgin,' now seems a grown man. He's built us a little stone house on Ortygia, Quail Mountain, in the outskirts of the city: perhaps you recall it from your travels? I'm sure the Master did, for he selected the location himself and told his mother of it shortly before his death. It's an odd choice of site: the house, I'm told, is only a stone's throw from the sacred well the Greeks believe marks the spot where their goddess Artemis (or Diana, as the Romans call her) was born. But there is more.

Each year at their festival of Eostre—the spring equinox when the goddess's birth is celebrated—Ortygia becomes the focus of pilgrimages from all over the Greek world. Small children tramp across this mountain searching for the fabled red Eostre eggs, symbols of luck and fertility, sacred to the goddess. Ironically, this celebration takes place just during our Pesach: the very week, two years ago, when the Master died. So this pagan goddess and her rites seem strangely linked with the memory of the Master's death, and also with the one thing I told you was missing from all the other accounts: a story the Master told us up on the mountain, the same day you came to my house two years ago, just home from your year at sea.

"When I was young," the Master told us that morning, high in the wildflower meadow, "I went abroad among many foreign peoples. I learned that the people of the far north have a word for something they hold true: 'dru,' which also means belief, and 'troth'—a pledge. So just as in our Judaic tradition, truth, justice, and faith are one: priests are also lawgivers. When one of their priests dispenses justice, as our own ancestors did in ancient times, he stands beneath the duru, a tree we call oak. Their priest is therefore called *d'rui* or *d'ruid* in plural, meaning 'giver of truth.'

"Also like the ancient Hebrews, these northerners hold most sacred the number thirteen, the number of months in a year of the lunar calendar. Because the thirteenth moon marks the end of the year, it's the number we identify with change, the number of a new cycle, the number of rebirth and of hope. This number itself is the kernel of truth in the story of Jacob, who wrestled with the angel of God and was transformed into 'Isra'el.' As everyone tends to forget, our forefather, Jacob, did not have twelve children—he had thirteen."

Then, as if he'd explained everything clearly and the session were at an end, the Master seemed to drift back toward an inner realm, and turned from us as if to depart.

"But, Master!" cried Simon Peter. "Surely there's some mistake? I admit I know nothing of these oak-men you speak of. But among our own people it's an established fact of Torah that there are *twelve* tribes of Israel—not thirteen as you said. Such a thing has never been questioned!"

"Peter, Peter, God gave you ears. You should pay Him back by using them!" said the Master, laughing as he squeezed Peter's shoulder. When Peter looked crestfallen, the Master added, "I didn't say thirteen tribes but thirteen children. Listen to the story with new ears: ask yourself why this fact should represent the kernel of truth I was seeking."

The Master came over to where I sat with the others in the broad ring of grassy meadow, and he placed his hand on my hair and smiled down at me.

"One day Miriam may find the answer," the Master told Peter. "I've always thought of Miriam as my thirteenth disciple. But one day she'll also be my first apostle: thirteen and one, the completion of a cycle. Alpha and omega, the first and last." Then he added, almost as an afterthought, "Jacob's forgotten child that I spoke of was named Dinah. As I see it, Dinah herself embodies the kernel of truth in the story. Her name, like that of her brother Dan, means judge."

Smiling that strange smile, the Master turned away again and went off down the mountain, leaving all of us to follow in his wake.

Joseph, you know as well as I that the Master never used parable or paradox to confuse, or merely to titillate: there was motive behind his method. He thought that only if we quested after truth, and arrived at it ourselves, would the truth we found be completely understood, thoroughly absorbed, and become a part of us.

That morning the Master made clear the number thirteen was related to the Hebrew lunar calendar, therefore to the concept of seasonal change. But why didn't he also mention what he must have known: that the Roman name for Dinah is Diana? And why didn't he tell us the plan I've just spoken of: that he intended one day for his own mother to live in a famous oak grove in Ortygia? That her house was to be built beside a well on the very spot where the moon goddess Artemis—also called Diana of the Ephesians, patroness of springs and wells, whose rites are conducted in oak groves throughout the Greek world—was born? No, it could be no accident that this was the last story the Master told his flock, on what proved to be the last day we were all together. The only mistake was mine, in not seeing it before.

Joseph, I know that this story and the reports I've sent will give rich fodder to your mind, and that before we meet again, you'll have digested them fully. I myself, meanwhile, shall strive to learn more about the Master's private motives—for such, I'm convinced, they were—in sending his mother to the home of this famous Ephesian goddess. Perhaps, together, you and I can find the missing link that will knot together all these seemingly diverse and scattered events of the Master's last days.

For now, Joseph, I pray that you walk with God; and I send you my eyes, my ears, my heart, and my blessing—that you may see, hear, love, and believe as the Master wished us to do.

Miriam of Magdali

◆ ◆

When Joseph looked up from this letter, the sun had dipped below the horizon, staining the sea bloodred. The churning fog rolled over the waters like sulfuric fumes rising from the depths. Lovernios stood beside him, his eyes on the fiery vista as if lost in thought, and did not speak.

"There's something in this tale Miriam hasn't mentioned," said Joseph. "While it's true Jacob's daughter, Dinah, was one of thirteen children, she wasn't the thirteenth child born to him. In Torah, birth sequence—at least among the sons of a tribe—is quite important. Dinah was the last child born to Jacob's elder wife, Leah, but not the last of Jacob's thirteen."

"He had more than one wife, then, your ancestor?" asked Lovernios with interest. Polygamy among the Keltoi was rare, and unacceptable within the elite class of Druid.

"Jacob had two wives and two concubines," said Joseph. "I told you the Master's memory was remarkable, especially regarding Torah. All the numbers in Torah are significant—for the Hebrew alphabet, like the Greek, is based on numbers. I agree that the Master wanted the story of Dinah to be seen from many angles."

"Tell me then," said Lovernios.

It was dusk, and the fog had encased the beach below. It would quickly grow dark, so Lovernios collected some nearby brush and a few branches and twigs, and chopped at the flint he'd extracted from his thong-tied sack, to make a hastily improvised fire. The two men sat on a nearby rock plateau as Joseph recounted the tale.

◆ ◆

THE THIRTEENTH TRIBE

The story begins with our ancestor Jacob as a young man. Twice Jacob had tricked his older twin brother Esau out of his birthright. When he learned Esau had threatened to kill him as soon as their father died, Jacob fled the land of Canaan and headed north, to the country of his mother's tribe. Arriving in the mountains near the Euphrates River, the first thing Jacob saw was a beautiful young shepherdess who brought her sheep to a well, and Jacob fell in love with her. As it proved, she was his own cousin Rachel, the younger daughter of his mother's brother, Laban. At once Jacob asked for her hand in marriage.

Jacob worked seven years for his uncle to earn Rachel as his bride. But the dawn after his wedding night he learned he'd been tricked: the woman he'd lain with that night—substituted under cover of darkness for Rachel—was her squint-eyed older sister, Leah, for it was the custom in the north to marry off the eldest first. When his uncle Laban offered Jacob Rachel as a second wife, Jacob agreed to pay her dower by toiling seven years more in his uncle's fields. The number seven is also a key number in our people's history. God created the world and took his rest within seven days. The number seven marks the fulfillment and completion of all creative undertakings, the number of divine wisdom. It is therefore significant that seven is the birth sequence of Jacob's only daughter, as are the key events leading up to her birth:

While God ignored Rachel's desire to have children, her sister Leah gave birth to four sons. Rachel offered to her husband her servant

Bilhah, who gave birth to two more sons. Because Jacob no longer came to Leah's bed, she offered her own servant, Zilpah, who likewise had two sons by Jacob—while the unhappy Rachel still remained barren. But things were about to change.

One day the eldest son, Reuben, found some mandrakes in the wheat fields and brought them to his mother, Leah. Mandrakes, like May-apples, promote conception and are associated with the temptation of Eve. Rachel asked Leah to share them, but Leah would agree only in exchange for Jacob's restored services as a husband. The desperate Rachel said yes, after which Leah gave birth to two more sons. And then the vital event was about to occur. Leah's *seventh* and final child—the eleventh of Jacob's children—was a girl, who was given the name of Dinah.

Upon Dinah's birth, Leah's fertility and Rachel's barrenness were both at an end. Rachel's firstborn son Joseph, later viceroy of Egypt, therefore became Jacob's twelfth child. And the final child was Benjamin, whose birth resulted in Rachel's death and the end of the family cycle. His number was thirteen.

The sequence in which the children were born, the way each was blessed by Jacob before his death, and even the way in which the tribes were later blessed by Moses in the desert, are all known to be important in the history of our people. But Dinah herself does not reappear in the story until her father Jacob returns from self-imposed exile in the north, and brings his family back into the land of Canaan.

Jacob bought land from the local prince, Hamor, and dug a well that's still there today at the foot of the sacred Mount Gerizim, and settled in with his family in the land of Canaan. When Dinah went through the wheat fields one day to meet some of the local maidens, Hamor's son Shechem saw her and wanted her, and he defiled her there in the field. But when Shechem realized he was in love with Dinah, he took her home and asked his father Hamor to arrange that they might marry.

When Hamor went to Dinah's father and her brothers, he offered to share half his estates if they'd permit this marriage. Jacob and his sons agreed, only if all males of the Canaanite clan would agree to be circumcised, as Jewish covenant requires. But two of Dinah's brothers were lying—for no sooner had the Canaanite men undergone surgery than Simeon and Levi fell upon their households, killing all the men, removing Dinah forcibly from the house of her captors, looting and destroying the houses, and making off with the women and children, sheep and oxen and material wealth. Jacob's family was forced to flee Canaan in fear of retribution for this deception and bloody massacre.

We know two more things regarding this tale:

Jacob and his family left Canaan, never to return. Near the well he'd dug there—Jacob's well—grew the Oak of Shechem, where Moses would one day instruct the Hebrews to build their first altar upon their return from Egypt to the promised land. Beneath that now famous tree, Jacob buried all the clothes and jewelry and treasures, and even the statues and idols—all the belongings of his wives and concubines and servants and the captives from Canaan—so that each might put on clean clothes and begin a new life before starting into the land of his father's people.

Between the land of Canaan they'd left behind and the land of Judea that lay before them, near Bethlehem, Rachel gave birth to the thirteenth and last child, whom she called Benoni but whom Jacob named Benjamin—and then she died.

◆ ◆

"And what of Dinah, the cause of all these changes in fortune, these beginnings and endings and reversals of fate?" asked Lovernios when Joseph had finished his tale.

"We'll never know how she felt about the treachery that had been done by her brothers in her name, for this is the last time she's mentioned in Torah," said Joseph. "But the objects that were buried beneath that oak are often called 'Dinah's legacy,' since they changed the destiny of the Hebrew people from what it might have been, stripping them of their past and even their identities. From that day nearly two thousand years ago when they left Canaan—modern Samaria—and entered Hebron—now Judea—they were reborn into a new and different life."

"Do you think this was the hidden message of Esus of Nazareth?" Lovernios asked. "To strip ourselves of our past and be reborn to a new way of life?"

"That's what I hope to learn from the contents of these cylinders," Joseph replied.

"I believe by this woman's letter I can already guess what was in the mind of Esus of Nazareth, and why he told that tale to his disciples," said the prince. "It has to do with the well of Jacob you spoke of, and the tree."

Joseph looked into those deep blue eyes, nearly black pools in the firelight.

"My people have oak trees too, my friend," said Lovernios, "groves of them, each with its sacred well, fed by a sacred spring. And in each of these holy spots we pay tribute to a special goddess. Her name is neither Dinah nor Diana. But it *is* Danu—my own tribe, for instance, the *Tuatha De Danaan*, are the people of Danu—which seems rather too close for chance. Danu is the great virgin, mother of all 'found waters'—that is, fresh waters like those of springs and wells. Her very name means 'the gift,' for such water is life itself. And we pay tribute to her much as your ancestor Jacob did, only we don't bury our treasure under an oak, we throw it down the well near the oak, where it's received into the waiting arms of the goddess."

"But you can't really think the Master's final message was—" Joseph began.

"What you might call heathen or pagan?" Lovernios finished for him with a wry smile. "I fear you never understood him, any of you, even since his boyhood. You saw him as a great philosopher, a mighty prophet, a saviour king. But I saw him as one *fili*, or seer, regards another, with unveiled eyes: naked, as it were. Naked as when we come into the world, and naked as when we die. A *fili* can see the raw soul of another—and his soul was ancient, your Esus of Nazareth. But there was something more. . . ."

"Something more?" said Joseph, though he was half afraid to ask.

The Prince of Foxes gazed into the fire, watching the sparks that crawled like living things across the ground before slipping soundlessly into the black night sky. Joseph felt his skin prickle in anticipation before hearing the *drui*'s whispered words:

"He has a god in him."

Joseph felt his breath let out suddenly, as if he'd been struck a sharp blow.

"A god?" he said. "But, Lovern, you know for our people there can be but one God: King of Kings, Lord of Hosts, the One whose name is not spoken, whose image is never graven, whose breath created the world, and who creates Himself simply by saying 'I am.' Do you suggest this God might actually enter into a living human being?"

"I'm afraid I saw his resemblance to another god," the prince said slowly. "For even his name is that of the great Celtic god Esus, lord of the netherworld, of wealth sprung from the earth. Human sacrifices—or, more properly, those who sacrifice themselves to Esus—must hang upon a tree in order to gain true wisdom and the knowledge of immortality. Wotan, a god of the far north, hung for nine days from a tree to obtain the secret of the Runes, the mystery of all mysteries. Your Esus of Nazareth hung for nine *hours*, but the idea is the same. I believe that he was a shaman of the highest degree—that he sacrificed himself to enter the magic circle where truth resides, in order to achieve divine wisdom and spiritual immortality."

"*Sacrificed* himself? And for wisdom? For some kind of immortality?" cried Joseph of Arimathea, leaping to his feet in agitation. It was true that the Romans spoke of human sacrifice among the Keltoi, but this was the first he'd heard a *drui* mention it. "No, no. It simply isn't possible. Jesua may have been a Master, but I raised him—I thought of him as my only child. I knew him better than anyone. He could never have turned his back on mankind, or turned away from his life's mission of seeking the salvation of his fellow beings through love, right here on earth! He strove always toward life and light. Don't ask me to believe that the Master would engage in some dark, barbarian ritual to invoke the bloodthirsty gods of our ancestors."

Lovernios had stood too. He put his hands on Joseph's shoulders, searching his eyes deeply before he spoke.

"But that's exactly what you *do* believe, my friend," he said. When Joseph stepped back in protest, Lovernios added, "It's what you've feared all along, isn't it? Or why did you wait until James Zebedee's departure before opening those clay cylinders? Why bring *me* from the isles to be here beside you when you opened them?"

Without awaiting Joseph's reply, the prince reached down and picked up the net filled with clay amphorae, holding them near the fire to study them.

"Our only question now is whether to read these or to burn them," he told Joseph. "Your master has taken a path I know well, you see. Among our people, only those who are chosen by destiny may follow the path of a *drui*, of a messenger to the gods. It's a path that prepares one for the self-sacrifice that I think your Esus always intended to make in behalf of mankind. Such a path, as I said, also confers upon the messenger the wisdom and truth essential to the completion of such a goal. But there is another path, a path of far greater danger but bringing with it—if successfully carried out—vastly greater knowledge and power."

"What sort of power?" asked Joseph.

Lovernios set the net down and regarded Joseph grimly. "We must find out exactly what those objects were, the ones buried by your ancestors beneath the roots of that oak tree in Samaria, and where they are today: whether they have indeed remained underground throughout these past two millennia, as I greatly fear they have not. For I suspect the story Esus of Nazareth intended to tell is not as simple as the rape of Dinah and the revenge wrought by her brothers. I think the kernel of truth in his story relates to a larger kind of transformation—and that the objects Jacob buried may be the key to the mystery."

"But it was *I* who told you about those things," said Joseph. "The Master never spoke of them. Besides, they were only clothes and jewels and personal treasures and the servants' household gods, and they've been buried for two thousand years. So how could they relate to transformation, much less explain the Master's actions?"

"You said the *place* they were buried was beside a sacred well and beneath a sacred oak, and the *reason* they were buried was to change the identity of the tribes descended from Jacob. This suggests they were not merely personal goods but talismanic objects invested with the *charism* of each individual member of the tribe," said Lovernios. "The initiate who's chosen that more difficult path I spoke of must first have possession of such talismans. They must be united in communal force during his invocation of the ancient mysteries. I feel certain this was your master's objective. And if he elected to follow this path in behalf of your people, he himself must have obtained possession of your ancestors' talismans. But whether he failed or succeeded in his final goal of transformation, now these objects must be returned to the earth again at once, to propitiate the gods."

"I don't understand," Joseph protested. "You suggest the Master dug up objects that may have been buried for millennia—or perhaps never even existed—in order to gain for himself some mysterious power. But, Lovern, during his life the Master was capable of such feats as raising young Lazarus from death. And after his *own* death, he appeared to Miriam as in real life. What greater powers could there be than those he already held?"

The last flickers of fire had burned low, and by unspoken agreement the men started to break up the coals and prepare to return to Joseph's ship. Lovernios hefted the net filled with clay amphorae, slinging it over his broad shoulder. Joseph could now see only the outline of the other's muscular form. Lovernios's voice came softly out of the darkness.

"When I told you that your master was possessed by a god, I fear I was not completely clear," he said. "Instead, the *druid* believe that one is required to *be* a god—in order to bring forth a new Age."

◆ ◆

Syrian Antioch: Autumn, A.D. 35

THE TIME FOR TRUTH

◆ ◆

And why do they consider Saturn father of Truth?

Is it that they think . . . Saturn (Kronos) is Time (Chronos), and that Time discovers the truth? Or because it is likely that the fabled Age of Saturn . . . an age of the greatest righteousness, participated most largely in truth?

—Plutarch, *The Roman Questions*

Lucius Vitellius, newly appointed imperial legate of Roman Syria, paced the floor of his chambers. These vast official rooms, where the business of Syrian Antioch's Roman legions was conducted, overlooked the courtyard that connected them with garrison barracks for officers of the third legion. Whenever Vitellius passed the windows looking onto the court, he muttered a curse beneath his breath. Each time he did so, his scribe glanced up for an instant—then back quickly to the dictation before him, to see if he'd blotted anything. He was trying to clean a blotch just as the chief tackman came in.

"Where the *devil* is Marcellus?" Vitellius exploded. "I sent for him nearly an hour ago! Haven't I enough on my mind, having just arrived to this state of chaos: first the damned Parthians and now the Jews?"

"Excellence, he sent me to say he'll be only a bit longer," the tackman apologized, dropping on one knee as he did so. "It's the other officers: they're haranguing him. They don't want him to go to Judea if there's going to be anything beyond just the hearings, they say. They don't want a public trial—"

"*They* don't want a public trial?" Vitellius's face grew florid. "Be so good as to remind them just who is Roman legate!" Behind him the scribe, twisting in his seat, glanced anxiously toward the portal as if to escape. "Never mind," Vitellius added furiously. "If I must, I'll refresh my officers' memories myself of who's in charge here now!" He headed for the door, nearly colliding with the legionary officer Marcellus, just coming in.

"Sire, I'm sorry to be late," the officer said, adjusting his mantle and bowing. "But as you must know, ever since Rome's annexation of Cappadocia the officer corps has been tremendously taxed to maintain order among the troops, what with the Parthians harrying us the entire length of the northern border. And now this affair with the *praefectus Iudaeae* Pontius Pilate . . ."

Marcellus ran his fingers through his short-cropped hair and shook his head. "Quite frankly, our officers fear that if we place Pilate on public trial as planned, civil unrest may rock the whole of the southern region. The man is a political hot coal. From the beginning his actions have been provocative. He's looted Jewish temple funds, profaned the temple grounds and priestly garments, run an aqueduct through a Jewish cemetery. A few years back he actually crucified a popular Jewish preacher alongside some common criminals. It's all Jew-baiting, which is insupportable in the chief administrator of a Roman province—and now this massacre in Samaria. Please understand that the officers are justified in their concern. It's a terrible quandary. If the court finds Pilate guilty, the Jews will be emboldened by at last having scored a triumph over Rome. But if he's found innocent of ordering the slaughter of those hundred-odd Samaritan Jews, then open riots can hardly be unexpected."

"My dear Marcellus, believe me, I have made myself well acquainted with the facts of the case," said the legate, motioning him to have a seat. "You might have spared us both a good deal of time and frustration by coming here when I first called for you, since I have already taken my decision. There's little that can or need be done regarding Pilate's past transgressions. But for this latest offense, Pilate will be sent to Rome and tried there."

"Before the senate?" said Marcellus in amazement. "But how can that be? Pilate is subject to you, the imperial legate. He's a provincial military governor."

"And a member of the equestrian order," Vitellius added. "He can therefore be tried before a military tribunal of his peers, and then receive his censure or his sentence from the Roman senate."

Marcellus smiled broadly at this incredibly clever solution to a problem he'd believed until that moment was insurmountable. But then he realized that the tackman and the scribe were still with them in the room.

"You may leave us," Vitellius told the tackman, who departed at once. To the scribe he said, "I want you to read to Officer Marcellus what I've given you so far of my communiqué to Capri."

The scribe stood up and opened the scroll, and read aloud:

To: Tiberius Caesar
Emperor of Rome
at Capreae
From: Lucius Vitellius
Imperial Roman Legate
at Syrian Antioch

Revered Excellence—
This is to notify Your Excellence that upon my authority as colonial legate of Roman Syria I have hereby removed Pontius Pilate from his post as prefect of Judea, relieving him of all further duties in the eastern provinces of the empire. Due to the severity of charges and weight of evidence against Pilate and the heat of popular feeling toward him, I've ordered him back to Rome to stand trial before a military tribunal of the equestrian order, and to be censured as found suitable by the Roman senate. I am replacing the former prefect with one Marcellus, a long-serving senior officer of the third legion, whose record I think Your Excellence will find impeccable.

I attach the report of a one-month investigation, by our regional military board, of a complaint lodged with the legion by the Samaritan council at Shechem, charging Pilate with crimes against the civilian populace and some of its leaders. I believe this report will thoroughly justify and support the action I have taken.

I offer my prayers to the gods for Your Excellence's continued health, and that of the imperial family. And I beg leave to send my warmest regards to my son Aulus, for whose sake I shall burn a cone of myrrh that he may continue to please Your Excellence as cupbearer, dancer, and companion to the other youths there on the isle of Capreae. I remain the devoted and grateful servant of the Roman Empire:

Lucius Vitellius, Imperial Legate, Syrian Antioch

Report of the Third Legion at Antioch investigation of charges in the matter of:

The Council of Shechem, Samaria,
versus
Praefectus Iudaeae Pontius Pilate

A written complaint has been brought by the civilian council of Shechem against Pontius Pilate, Roman prefect of Judea, for ordering the violent repression last month resulting in the deaths of one hundred twenty-seven Samaritan civilians—men, women, and children—during a religious pilgrimage of more than four thousand to the Hebrews' sacred mountain of Gerizim. The complaint further charges that prefect Pilate ordered the subsequent detention, torture, and execution of some of Samaria's most prominent citizens, most of whom had earlier been arrested by his instruction at the site.

Samaria is the politically important central region of Roman Palestine separating the province of Roman Judea from the tetrarchy of Galilee governed by Herod Antipas. The chief city, Shechem, is situated between two important religious sites: Mount Ebal and Mount Gerizim. A long-standing hatred exists between the Judeans and the Samaritans. For centuries, the Samaritans alone have maintained an ancient form of Hebrew worship centered on Mount Gerizim, which includes reverence of the dove and the sacred oak tree. All Hebrews, including the Judeans, agree that Mount Gerizim is a holy site of importance in the history of their faith. It is called by them *Tabbur Ha'ares*, meaning the absolute geographical center of the land, the spot on which the four quarters turn, or what we would call the *Axis Mundi*.

By legend, certain sacramental vessels and other treasure from the first temple of King Solomon in Judea were removed during the destruction of the temple and buried there, and upon the Jews' return from Egyptian bondage their spiritual leader Moses instructed that sacred relics be placed there from their first tabernacle built in the wilderness, including the well-known Ark of the Covenant and even the tabernacle itself. The various branches of Hebrews also are in accord in their belief that the freshwater well near Shechem, still famous for its health-giving properties today, was dug by their ancestor Jacob, and that upon arriving in this land he built his first altar at that spot.

It has also long been believed among Hebrews of all persuasions that these sacred relics would come to light at the dawn of the millennium following Moses, which they reckon by their calendar is very close. So last month, after a Samaritan prophet foretold that the objects would surface just at the time of the autumn equinox, a crowd of four thousand gathered and made toward the mountain.

Hearing of this, Pontius Pilate called up a garrison of Roman soldiers stationed at nearby Caesarea, and had them disguise themselves as pilgrims and go to the pilgrimage site. When the pilgrims began their ascent of the sacred mountain, by Pilate's order the soldiers cut many down. Others, especially the wealthy and prominent among them, were afterwards taken hostage and carried off to Caesarea, where they were interrogated regarding the motive of the pilgrimage, and then summarily executed, also at Pilate's command.

When questioned by this tribunal, Pilate maintained he was trying to prevent civil disturbance, having learned beforehand that many of the pilgrims would be carrying arms. But as Samaritans and others customarily go armed against the brigandry rife in the region, and as many of those massacred at Gerizim were unarmed women and children, this explanation was deemed unsatisfactory. The prefect has been remanded into confinement at Antioch pending further action.

The inquisitors of this tribunal were in agreement, based on accounts by Roman soldiers present during the interrogations of captured Samaritans, that the prefect Pilate's real interest was to learn where the aforementioned objects of Hebrew lore might be buried. In view of this possibility, we ordered an auxiliary phalanx of the third legion into the region to search Mount Gerizim. Their report states they found numerous spots on the mountain where earth had been freshly turned. Since the pilgrims had not yet begun their ascent when they were set upon by Roman troops, clearly this work had been done by others, perhaps under order of Pilate himself. But the ancient, sacred relics were not found.

◆ ◆

Rome: Spring, A.D. 37

THE VIPER

◆ ◆

I am nursing a viper for the Roman people,
and a Phaeton for the whole world.
—Tiberius, speaking of Gaius

Let them hate me, so long as they fear me.
—Gaius "Caligula"

"What fascinating little surprises life springs upon us, just when we least expect them!" the emperor Gaius remarked, with seeming pleasantry, to his uncle Claudius.

They were strolling arm in arm across the Field of Mars and along the Tiber toward the mausoleum of Augustus, its half-completed temple to Augustus the God left unfinished at Tiberius's death. Gaius smiled to himself as if at a private joke. Deeply inhaling the scent of fresh spring grass, he went on:

"To think that only a month ago I was still regarded as 'little *Caligula*'—Bootsie—'born in a boot,' raised by my father like a camp follower among soldiers," he said. "And that at eighteen I was just another of those dancing-boys Grandpa kept for pleasure along with his harem on that dreadful rock of Capreae. Yet look at me today—at twenty-four I'm ruler of the whole vast Roman Empire! Wouldn't Mother be proud?" Then his face suddenly clouded black with rage, and he snapped viciously, "If only she'd been permitted to live long enough to see it!"

Given the imperial family's history, Claudius was hardly startled by this swift and violent mood change. He patted his nephew gently on the arm as they walked. Like the young emperor, whom everyone still fondly called Caligula, Claudius had spent his life wondering which of them, including himself, would be murdered next, and what other family member might be the one to arrange it.

It was widely rumored, for instance, that before Tiberius succeeded to the throne he'd murdered Germanicus—Caligula's father and the brother of Claudius—in order to prevent Germanicus, as Tiberius's legally adopted son who was favored by Augustus, from inheriting in his place. But that was the last family member whose cause of death remained merely a rumor—including Caligula's own two brothers and his mother Agrippina, whom Tiberius had openly ordered to be exiled, beaten, and starved to death.

"Naturally, I'll be suspected by some of complicity," Caligula added, referring to the death of his adoptive grandfather. "It's true I was there when Tiberius stopped at the country house in Misenum. I *was* there that night when he suddenly died. It was a case of indigestion following three days of banqueting along the road. But I admit it does look suspiciously like poison—and heaven knows I had as much motive as anyone to do the old goat in. After all, the man arranged the slaughter of nearly everyone he ever dined with."

"Well, if that's the case, and they all believe you did it," said Claudius with a twinkle, "I wonder what wonderful awards the senate and citizens of Rome are planning to heap on you? Did you know, during your inaugural festivities there were mobs in the streets crying 'To the Tiber with Tiberius'? Just like the good old days of Sejanus—what goes up must also come down."

"Don't say that!" cried Caligula. Pulling his arm away, he looked at Claudius with eyes strangely devoid of human expression. Then, with a smile that sent chills up Claudius's spine, he said, "Did you know that I fuck my sister?"

Claudius was completely dumbstruck. Caligula had been known to have fits as a child, falling on the ground and frothing at the mouth, a symptom common to the Caesars. But now, as he stood there in the fresh air on the bright green lawn of the Field of Mars beneath the brilliant blue sky on this seemingly normal spring day, Claudius realized that this was no ordinary madness. He knew he must make some response to his nephew's remark, and make it quickly.

"Good heaven!" he chortled. "No, no, I hadn't guessed such a thing at all—and what a surprise! Indeed, how *could* I have guessed? I mean, you've said 'my sister,' but in fact you have three of them, and each one lovelier than the next!"

"Everyone in the family is right about you, Uncle Claudius," said Caligula coldly. "You *are* a complete fool. Now I'm rather sorry I've made you my first co-consul, to rule the state with me. Though I've always liked you better than anyone in the family, I really might have chosen someone more astute."

"Now, now, that appointment can always be changed at any time—though of course I'm pleased and overjoyed at the honor," said Claudius hastily, wondering what on earth to do. He waited, praying for divine guidance, until at last his nephew spoke.

"I'm not talking about my *sister*!" Caligula hissed under his breath, though the guards posted around the field weren't even within shouting distance to overhear them. "Don't you understand? I was speaking of the *goddess*."

"Ah—the goddess," said Claudius, trying hard not to avoid Caligula's gaze, though his dark eyes were burning into him like awful coals.

"The *goddess*!" Caligula screamed. His hands were balled into fists in fury. His face had resumed its blackened color. "Don't you understand? I can't make a mere *mortal* my empress! *Mortal* brothers and sisters cannot marry! But gods *always* marry their sisters—it's always done—that's how they do it! That's how we know that they're really *gods*, you see: because *they all fuck their sisters*!"

"Of course," said Claudius, tapping his head as if he'd just had a revelation. "But you didn't *say* it was the goddess, that's why I was confused. Your sister the goddess. Of course. So you're speaking of—Drusilla!" he finished, praying wildly to all the *real* goddesses he could possibly think of that this was the right answer.

Caligula smiled.

"Uncle Claudius," he said, "you're a fox. You knew all along, but were just pretending in order to make me have to tell you. Now, let me share with you all my ideas on what I think we should do to save the empire."

◆ ◆

Caligula's ideas on how to save the empire were astounding even to Claudius, whose predilection for expensive women and lavish, drunken banquets was well known. In the one hour they spent touring the Augustan mausoleum and temple together, discussing how the structure might be completed, Claudius quickly calculated what such ideas must represent in terms of cost.

Caligula had already bestowed rare jewels upon the comedian Mnester and many of his other favorites. And when Herod Agrippa, brother-in-law of the Galilean tetrarch Herod Antipas, was released from the prison where he'd languished by order of Tiberius these past six months, Caligula had made a public display of replacing the iron chains he'd worn in prison with gold ones of equal weight. If only a small portion of his other projects went forward as planned, Claudius calculated, it would consume all of Tiberius's private fortune—a legacy of twenty-seven million gold pieces—and would substantially deplete the state treasury as well.

"Here at Rome, I'll complete the Augustan temple and the theater of Pompey," the young emperor said, ticking it all off on his fingers. "I'll expand the imperial palace across Capitoline Hill, connect it with the temple of Castor and Pollux, add an aqueduct for the gardens, and create a new amphitheater for Mnester to perform in. At Syracuse I'll rebuild all the ruined temples. I'll dig a canal through the isthmus to Greece, restore the palace of Polycrates on the isle of Samos, bring back the statue of Olympian Jupiter to Rome where it belongs—and I also plan to create a new temple to Didymaean Apollo at Ephesus, the design and construction of which I shall personally supervise myself. . . ."

It went on this way the whole of the morning until they reached the palace. It was only then, once they were within Caligula's private apartments, that Claudius was able to ask a question that had been nagging his mind all morning.

"What a paragon of altruism you've proven to be to the Roman people, my dear Gaius!" he told his nephew, who had seated himself on a bejeweled throne atop a small flight of steps that placed him several feet above his uncle, so Claudius had to strain to be heard. "They will surely be gratified for their love and the faith they've placed in you. And you say you've even arranged to resume the bread and circuses, as resplendently as in the days before Tiberius put a halt to all such things! But the role of tax collector hardly seems your style. Therefore, it's clear you've hatched some clever way to replenish your coffers?"

"You'd speak to a *god* about grubbing after money?" Caligula replied disdainfully.

Taking up the golden Thunderbolt of Jove he liked to carry about at public affairs of state, he meditatively began cleaning his fingernails with its tip.

"Very well, since you're my co-consul, I suppose I should tell you," Caligula said, looking down at Claudius from his golden perch. "You recall Publius Vitellius, the aide-de-camp to my father Germanicus? He was there when Father died, at only age thirty-three, on his last campaign in Syria."

"I knew Publius very well," said Claudius. "He was my brother's most trusted ally, even in death. You were only a child at the time, so perhaps you don't know it was he who brought Piso—an agent and friend of Tiberius—to trial on charges of poisoning your father. Tiberius too might have been charged in the murder, if he hadn't burned Piso's secret instructions when they were presented before him. But Tiberius had a long memory for such betrayals, and did not soon forget the Vitellii. Publius was later arrested and accused of being a member of the Sejanus conspiracy. He tried to slash his wrists, then fell ill and died in prison. Later his brother Quintus, the senator, was publicly degraded in one of those senatorial purges Tiberius demanded."

"So doesn't it make you wonder," Caligula said slowly, "why Grandpa would destroy two brothers in a family—and then, not long before he died himself, he'd turn around and appoint their youngest brother as imperial legate to Syria?"

"Lucius Vitellius?" said Claudius, raising his brow. "I suppose, like everyone else in Rome, I assumed his appointment was more of a . . . personal favor." Then he added awkwardly, "Because of young Aulus, that is."

"Well, really, who might deserve such high honors better than a father of someone like Aulus?" said Caligula sarcastically. "After all, the lad generously gave up his virginity to Tiberius when he was only sixteen. I should know, I was present upon the occasion. But that's not my point."

Caligula arose, came down the steps, and paced about the room, slapping his thunderbolt in the palm of his hand. Then he set it on a table and picked up a full pitcher of wine, poured some in a goblet, and rang a nearby bell. The taster, a boy of nine or ten, entered at once and drank the wine off, while Caligula filled two more goblets to the brim. Taking one and motioning his uncle to help himself to the other, he waited until the taster bowed and left the room. To Claudius's astonishment, his nephew then unlocked a large box on the table and plucked out two costly pearls, each the breadth of his thumb, and dropped them into the wine goblets to dissolve.

"I've had Tiberius's papers brought over from Capreae, and I've read them all," Caligula resumed after having a swallow from the goblet and wiping his mouth. "There was one of great interest from Lucius Vitellius, written just after he took up his appointment in Syria more than a year ago. It refers to some objects of great value once belonging to the Jews, which were buried atop a kind of holy mountain in Samaria—objects that it seems the former protégé of Sejanus, Pontius Pilate, had been after. Apparently Pilate murdered a number of people in trying to lay his hands on them."

Claudius, the only genuinely poor member of the royal family, privately wondered if he could fish out the pearl and rescue it behind his nephew's back before it dissolved. But he thought better of it and took a sip of the rarely enhanced wine.

"What exactly did Vitellius say these objects were? And what's become of them and of Pilate?" he asked.

"Pilate was removed from his post, but was held at Antioch under guard for at least ten months, waiting for a troopship that would be returning directly to Rome," said Caligula. "It arrived here the same week Grandfather died, so I arranged to have Pilate detained here for questioning—though I didn't really need to, for I'd been able to put a few pieces of the story together on my own some time ago, and make a few guesses. As you know, my first act as emperor just after the funeral was to release Herod Agrippa from prison, and I bestowed on him the tetrarchies of Lysanias and his late uncle Philip in Syria, as well as the title of king. I've instructed, when he returns there, that he perform a service for me."

Claudius began to think his mind had really cleared a bit with that first sip of wine, for he'd just come to understand that this god-obsessed nephew of his might not be as mad as he seemed. *In vino veritas,* he thought, and he had another healthy swallow.

"One must recall," Caligula said, "I lived six years with Grandfather at Capreae, where I saw and heard a good deal—not all of it mere debauchery. Five years ago something happened. Perhaps you'll recall it. Tiberius had an Egyptian pilot brought here to Rome, then he met with the fellow himself out on Capreae—"

"You mean, the same Egyptian who appeared before the senate—the one who claimed he'd overheard, while sailing near Greece one night around the spring equinox, that the great god Pan was dead?" said Claudius, quite interested. He took another swig.

"Yes, that one," said Caligula. "Grandfather was secretive about the meeting, and never discussed it. But I knew whatever he'd learned from the Egyptian had changed him. I spoke of this one day, with the husband of my sister Drusilla—"

"The goddess," suggested Claudius with a hiccup, but Caligula ignored him.

"Five years ago," he went on, "when my brother-in-law Lucius Cassius Longinus was consul here in Rome, his own brother—an officer named Gaius Cassius Longinus—was serving with the third legion in Syria. On the very same week of the spring equinox he was the duty officer assigned to Pontius Pilate, in charge of a public execution at Jerusalem. Something happened there he recalled as very strange."

"You mean to say this rumor about the death of the great god Pan may have to do with these valuable objects Pilate was seeking?" said Claudius, a bit foggy from the wine. "And because of something you learned about them from your brother-in-law, you've let Herod Agrippa out of jail and appointed him king, so he can help solve the mystery of what's become of them?"

"Precisely!" cried Caligula, picking up his thunderbolt and thrusting it high as if about to hurl it to the ceiling. "Uncle Claudius, you may be every bit the drunkard everyone believes you are, but you're no fool—you're a genius!"

Taking Claudius by the arm, he drew him back to the throne, and they sat on the steps together as the younger man leaned toward his uncle.

"As I say, five years ago, on the Friday before the equinox, Pilate ordered a rabble-rousing Jew to be crucified along with some criminals, knowing the bodies had to be taken down before nightfall by law, since it was just before the Jewish sabbath when they couldn't be removed. The way to hasten death, I'm told, is to break their legs so the lungs collapse and they smother."

Perhaps it was the drink, thought Claudius, but it seemed the light had dimmed in the room and his nephew's eyes had taken on an odd gleam while describing this unappealing procedure. He had another swallow.

"This was Gaius Cassius Longinus's first crucifixion," Caligula went on, "so when it was time to dispatch the bodies he simply rode up on his horse and stabbed the one in the middle to get it over with. But once done, Gaius noticed something odd about the spear in his hand. One of the troops must have handed it to him just before they went to the execution site, for it wasn't his. It was old and battered and seemed made of some primitive metal. He remembers that the hilt was hand-tied to the blade with something like fox gut. He thought little of it until the bodies were hauled away and he returned to Pilate's headquarters before heading back to Antioch. Pilate asked Gaius if he had the spear, suggesting it was some bit of official regalia he needed back—though I doubt that was likely. Only then did Gaius realize it had vanished."

"You think this was one of the objects?" said Claudius. His eyes had begun to ache, perhaps from the wine or the sudden odd darkness in the room. "But it hardly sounds precious or mysterious to me, and where did it come from?"

"What tells me it's mysterious is that it has disappeared, never to be found," said Caligula. "What tells me it's precious is that Pontius Pilate wanted it several years before that massacre on the mountain—which also means he believed at least some of those objects had already surfaced from the ground. As to where it came from or where it's gone, I suspect my grandfather was trying to find that out just when he died, as he was hastening home to Capreae and stopped at Misenum. And I've every cause to believe that he had the answer within his grasp right before his death."

"Tiberius?" said Claudius. Setting down his goblet at last, he peered at his nephew in the oppressively gloomy light. "But he possessed twenty-seven million in gold. Why should he go to such lengths for greater wealth?"

"When I said I believed these objects were valuable," said Caligula, "I didn't mean mere material wealth but something far more—something I've not shared with anyone, even Drusilla. It was no accident, you see, that I was at Misenum when Tiberius arrived the night of his death: I'd been waiting there to meet him. Though he rarely left

Capreae, he'd been away this time for months, but no one could learn exactly where. I discovered Tiberius had gone to those isles called Paxi, the very ones where the Egyptian pilot heard that eerie cry. And I think I know what he hoped to find there.

"On the isles of Paxi, near the Grecian coast, stands an enormous stone like those in the Celtic lands. On it are writings in a lost tongue which it was believed no one could decipher. But Tiberius thought he knew someone who could—someone who might have as deep an interest in doing so as he himself, and who owed him a great favor. You know who it is, Uncle Claudius. You yourself brought him to Capreae some years back to ask that favor: that Grandfather overturn the Sejanus decree and permit the Jews to return to Rome."

"Joseph of Arimathea! The wealthy Jewish merchant and friend of Herod Agrippa? What does he know of any of this?" cried Claudius.

"Joseph of Arimathea seems to have known enough to meet Tiberius on Paxi and spend these past few months deciphering those codes in stone," Caligula replied. "When Grandfather took ill at dinner that night, I stayed in his room to look after him, and I heard what he said in his sleep—or rather what surfaced from his nightmares in those last feverish throes of misery. Shall I say? For I wrote it all down. I've been the only one in the world who knows—until now."

When Caligula smiled, Claudius tried to smile back, but his lips felt numb. He had few illusions at this moment about the cause of Tiberius's death. He only prayed that at least the wine he himself had just guzzled wasn't also poisoned. He felt truly ill.

As Caligula took his uncle by the hand, the room seemed to Claudius to grow ever darker. The only light he could focus on any longer was the strange gleam that emerged from the depths of Caligula's eyes.

"By all means," Claudius managed to whisper as the darkness descended.

◆ ◆

THE THIRTEEN SACRED HALLOWS

Each aeon, when during the vernal equinox the sun starts to rise against the backdrop of a new astral constellation, a god descends to earth and is born into the flesh of a mortal. The god lives to maturity among mortals, then permits himself to be sacrificed, shedding his prison of flesh to return to the universe. Before his death, the god passes on universal wisdom to only one chosen mortal being.

But in order for the divine wisdom to become manifest within chronological time on earth, it must be woven into a fabric of knots representing the intersections of spirit and matter throughout the universe. Only the true initiate, the one indoctrinated by the god, will know how to do this.

To make this connection, thirteen sacred objects must be brought together in one place. Each object fulfills a specific purpose in the ritual rebirth of the new age, and each of these objects must be anointed in the divine fluid before it is put into use. The objects for the next age are these:

The Spear	The Platter
The Sword	The Garment
The Nail	The Loom
The Goblet	The Harness
The Stone	The Wheel
The Box	The Gaming Board
The Cauldron	

He who unites these objects without possessing the eternal wisdom may bring forth, not an age of cosmic unity, but one instead of savagery and terror.

◆ ◆

"You see?" said Caligula when he'd finished this diatribe. "What I told you about the spear at the crucifixion in Judea—why, a spear was the very first object on that list. Do you see what it means? Tiberius thought *Pan* was the god who'd permitted himself to be sacrificed in order to bring about the new aeon: the goat-god, the god most closely identified with the isle of Capreae, or with himself.

"But when that stone at Paxi had been translated, it proved it was the Jews, my dear, who'd provided the necessary fleshly cadaver for this transition. Isn't it the Jews who are running all over the world studying ancient languages so they can translate the mysteries? And maybe also collecting these objects of infinite power. Do you think for one moment your Joseph of Arimathea didn't know what he was doing when he begged Tiberius for the return of his people to Rome? Do you imagine he didn't know what he'd done when he stole the body of that crucified Jew in Judea? For that's what he did—and took the spear Gaius Cassius Longinus had plunged into it, as well."

"Good heaven, Gaius! Please desist!" cried Claudius, dropping his spinning head to his lap as his stomach churned with too much emotion and wine. "Bring me a feather. I need to be sick."

"Can't you concentrate for one tiny moment on anything?" said his nephew, getting up and bringing him a bowl and an ostrich plume from a nearby stand.

Claudius lifted his head and waved the plume through the air to loosen its tendrils. Then he opened his mouth and tickled the back of his throat until he retched and the wine from his stomach splashed out into the bowl.

"That's better. Now I'm clearheaded," he told Caligula. "But in the name of Bacchus, tell me what all this means."

"It means," said Caligula, "that while Herod Agrippa goes to Judea to find out where the other objects may be, you and I are going to Britannia to find Joseph of Arimathea—and get that spear!"

THE RETURN

Fu/Return: The Turning Point
Hexagram 24

The time of darkness is past. The winter solstice brings the victory of light. After a time of decay comes the turning point. The powerful light that has been banished returns. There is movement, but it is not brought about by force. . . .

The idea of return is based on the course of nature. The movement is cyclic and the course completes itself. . . . Everything comes of itself at the appointed time.

—Richard Wilhelm, *The I Ching*

The more one knows, the more one comprehends, the more one realizes that everything turns in a circle. —Johann Wolfgang Goethe

I was still jangled, despite steeping myself in the steaming hot pool for more than an hour. What with Uncle Laf's informative report on the Nazi collaborationist storm troopers and Boer rapists ornamenting my genealogical tree—not to mention my adorable grey-haired Auntie Zoe in Paris, who'd danced her way right into Adolf Hitler's heart—my family history was starting to look more and more like the stuff of my chosen career: a mess that was plowed under and kept buried for half a century, and just starting to ooze out of containment.

When Laf went off for his afternoon siesta, I went back to my room to be alone and do some thinking. I sure had plenty to think about.

I knew my cousin and blood brother had faked his own assassination and set me up as the public patsy, but it now seemed he'd done it using the very manuscript that was so zealously guarded by his own father, Earnest, and my grandma Pandora too—a manuscript my father and stepmother, aided and abetted by the world press, were conniving to snatch and publish for profit. And though I still wasn't clear what this mysterious manuscript was all about, it *did* seem beyond the shadow of a doubt that the document I'd interspersed throughout the DOD Standard last night must have been sent by Sam.

I'd thrown away the brown paper wrapping, so I couldn't examine the postmark. But the moment Laf mentioned it, a vivid image flashed before my eyes: that yellow postal slip Jason had retrieved from the snow, with a sender's zip code that began with 941, meaning it was mailed from San Francisco. So Wolfgang Hauser's claim that he'd mailed it to me from Idaho was a myth, like maybe everything else he'd told me.

I kicked myself for falling for just another gorgeous face, and I vowed that even with the aid of an avalanche he'd never catch me off balance again. It might already be too late to undo the damage, now that I knew the document was sent by Sam. Wolfgang had been with it all night, and since I was asleep I had no way of knowing if he'd examined it, or even microfilmed it or made some other kind of copy. So basically I'd come full circle to where I had been a week ago—between Scylla and Charybdis, a rock and a hard place.

As I unlocked the door to my hotel room, I realized I'd forgotten completely about Jason. He was sitting in the middle of the king-sized bed looking angry as hell.

"Yow!" he said in a tone that packed a wallop of feline fury.

Of course I knew exactly why he was furious. Though he had plenty of food, I'd gone swimming without him! The telltale scent of chlorine gave me away.

"Okay, Jason, what about a nice bath instead?" I suggested.

Instead of dashing into the bathroom to turn on the tap, as he usually did when he heard "bath," he trotted past me and plucked from the floor a slip of pink paper I had nearly stepped on—he was really good now at the paper-fetching trick—and, planting his paws on my knee, he presented it to me: a phone message that had been shoved under the door. When I read it, my heart sank.

To: Ariel Behn
From: Mr. Solomon

Sorry, can't make lunch at noon as planned. To book again, please phone (214) 178–0217.

Terrific. Sam was suddenly changing our noon agenda. And this bogus phone number—as I assumed it was—would fill me in on how.

This was Sam's third mention of King Solomon, whose biblical verses I still hadn't had time to scan closely for hidden meaning. But this note seemed a hasty last-minute change rather than a major decoding job. And Sam could safely assume that the name—after my little deciphering job of last night—meant something to me that no one else would grasp at first glance: that is, that the "phone number" for Mr. Solomon pointed to the Song of Songs.

With a sigh I opened my bag, hauled out the Bible I'd brought along, and took it into the bathroom, where I plugged up the tub and started the water running for Jason. As I waited for the tub to fill, I looked at the note again and flipped open the book. The Song of Solomon has only eight chapters, so "area code" 214 referred to Chapter 2, Verse 14:

O my dove, that art in the clefts of the rock, in the secret places of the stairs, let me see thy countenance, let me hear thy voice; for sweet is thy voice, and thy countenance is comely.

Sam would never get to hear my sweet voice or see my comely countenance unless he got a mite more specific in his instructions. He did—in Chapter 1, Verses 7–8. There the young woman I recalled, the one with the attractive belly button, asks her lover where he'll be lunching at noon the next day, and he explains how to find him:

Tell me, O thou whom my soul loveth, where thou feedest, where thou makest thy flock to rest at noon: for why should I be as one that turneth aside by the flocks of thy companions?

If thou know not, O thou fairest among women, go thy way forth by the footsteps of the flock, and feed thy kids beside the shepherds' tents.

Now, there was no place up on the mountain that had a name relating to shepherds, goats, or other flocks. But there was a pastureland down the road from here called the Sheep Meadow where, in summer, music and art tents were set up. In winter, it was a popular area for Nordic skiing: a flat open field with easy access from the road. So this must be the new locus of my rendezvous with Sam.

But it seemed more than strange that Sam would opt to change his former complex, trail-covering scenario to a high-visibility spot along the main road. It seemed odd, that is, until I read Chapter 2, Verse 17, saying *when* we were going to meet.

Until the day break, and the shadows flee away, turn, my beloved, and be thou like a roe or a young hart upon the mountains. . . .

Daybreak? Like, before *dawn*? I could certainly see why Sam might consider a meeting at high noon too conspicuous. And ski lifts up to the mountain, to reach the spot of our original assignation, wouldn't even open until nine. But how could I *in*conspicuously drive three miles to the Sheep Meadow before sunrise, haul my cross-country skis from the car, and go for a spin all by myself in the predawn darkness? I thought Sam had gone completely out of his mind.

Luckily for me, everyone in my ménage wanted to make it an early night too. Apparently Olivier, once he'd seen how well Bambi could ski, had outdone himself trying to impress her, dragging her onto black-diamond slopes all over the mountain. He returned exhausted, unaccustomed himself to such intensive *Sturm und Drang*.

Since Bambi had been away skiing all day, the only time she and Laf had for the daily practice that musicians compulsively need was a two-hour break before dinner. The management loaned us the Sun Room and its piano. I muddled through what little Schubert and Mozart accompaniment I could still play, with Olivier staring at Bambi, and Volga Dragonoff turning pages. Though Laf often winced at my rusty technique, he played as beautifully as ever—while Bambi astounded us with the kind of virtuosity one rarely hears off a concert stage. I gave her points for more than just a good grip with her thighs. It made me wonder if my first impression had been correct.

When we all left the room to head off for dinner, the balcony outside was filled with eavesdropping hotel guests who applauded wildly, flooded Laf with a lengthy flurry of I-saw-you-when's, and asked for his autograph on hastily proffered restaurant menus, hotel envelopes, and even lift tickets.

"Gavroche," said Laf when at last the hurrahs died away and the guests had drifted off, "I am thinking I shall perhaps be dining with myself in my suite tonight, and leaving you young people to yourselves. I am not as young as I once was, and my body did not wholly agree with this trip from Vienna. Let us meet at the breakfast. I can then tell some more of the story."

"Okay, Uncle Laf," I said, wondering just how much more of "the story" I could take. "But not too early—let's make it for brunch again. There's something I need to work on in the morning." Like a five A.M. whisk through a sheep pasture, I thought.

Bambi declined to join Olivier and me, and departed with Laf and Volga for their suites. As I was about to turn in to the dining room, Olivier surprised me by bowing out of dinner too.

"I admit it," he told me. "*My* body didn't 'wholly agree' with my trip up the mountain today. I ache everywhere. I thought I might hit the hot pool before it closes, then just order some soup in my room and crash for the night."

Checking my watch, I saw it was already almost ten, so I decided to do likewise.

By eleven, Jason and I had shared some seafood pasta and garlic bread, listened to the weather report that said sunrise tomorrow would be at six-thirty, and were tucked into bed where I was drowsily reading, sipping the last of my room-service wine and about to turn out the light.

Suddenly Jason's head popped up from where he'd been curled on the pillow. Ears erect, he stared at the door to the corridor as if waiting for someone to enter. He looked at me for a moment, but I'd heard nothing outside. Without a sound, he crept across the bed, dropped to the floor, padded to the door, and turned back to look over his shoulder at me again. There was definitely someone out there.

I took a deep breath. Then I threw back the covers and stood up, grabbed the robe that was lying on a nearby chair, pulled it on, and crossed to the door myself. Jason, standing there on the alert, was never mistaken about a visitor who was about to call. On the other hand, if someone was about to call—why didn't he?

I put my eye to the peephole and saw a familiar if unexpected face. I grabbed the knob and yanked open the door.

There, in the soft yellow light of the corridor, stood beautiful blond Bambi, her pale eyes wide and guileless, her shimmering golden hair framing her face. She was dressed for *avant le boudoir,* in a long black velvet robe cut along the stark lines of a man's smoking jacket, displaying cascades of antique lace and ribbons at throat and wrist. But I noticed she had one hand held behind her back.

Suddenly, in a panic, an insane but very real-seeming notion flashed into my head: She was hiding a gun! I was poised to leap back and slam the door in her face. At that instant she brought forth the other hand. In it she held a bottle of Rémy Martin and two small brandy snifters.

She smiled. "Will you join me in a cognac?" she said. "It's a kind of peace offering, though not only for myself."

"I have to get up quite early—" I began.

"So do I," Bambi said quickly. "But what I have to tell you, I should prefer not to say while standing out here in the corridor. May I come in?"

I stepped back reluctantly and let her pass.

Despite this woman's major beauty and her demonstrated artistry, there was still something bothering me—and not only her dippy demeanor. In fact, given those other qualities, it had occurred to me that her vagueness might well camouflage vulnerability, much as with Jersey and her drinking.

I went over to the table where Bambi was pouring, but stayed on my feet. I lifted my snifter, and she and I clinked glasses and sipped.

"What couldn't you tell me, outside in the corridor?" I asked.

"Please sit down," Bambi said in a low voice.

Her tone was so soothing, it wasn't until I was halfway to the chair that I realized the effect had actually been that of a rein being expertly snapped in by an extremely practiced hand. I decided to listen up to Ms. Bambi a bit more attentively.

"I don't want you to dislike me," Bambi assured me. "I hope we'll be friends."

In the dim light of my room, those clear eyes swimming like Goldwasser with little gold flecks were half shadowed by her lashes. I couldn't for the life of me make out what she was actually thinking, but I suddenly felt it was very, very important that I find out—and that honesty was the best policy to adopt.

"It isn't that I dislike you, but I don't really understand someone like you," I admitted, "and that makes me uncomfortable around you. You appear one way, but speak in another, and behave in a third. I feel you're not at all what you seem."

"Perhaps you aren't either," said Bambi, reaching down to touch Jason on the head with those long, slender fingers. He didn't purr, but he didn't dart away either.

"We weren't discussing me," I said. "But as I'm sure you gathered from our conversation this morning, I grew up in a family that's never been very close. If I seem mysterious when I'm around them, maybe I just want to distance myself from their controversies. That's why I've chosen to go my own way—to take a different path from the others."

"Do you believe so?" she asked cryptically. Then she added, "But you see, we actually *were* discussing you. And your opinion of me is important to me. When I said I didn't want you to dislike me, I did not mean I hoped we would be like real sisters, as your uncle expressed. I only wish to explain that under the present circumstance, I feel it would be—how shall I say?—quite difficult if we could not, at the least, be friends."

"Look here," I told her, having another swallow of brandy: it was excellent. "There's really no cause for the two of us to worry about whether we're going to be pals or not. After all, this is the first time in many years I've been around Uncle Laf, so it's unlikely that after this weekend you and I will even see each other again."

"In that, you are mistaken," she said with a smile. "But before I explain, I should like you to say what it is about me that has made you feel 'uncomfortable.' If you wouldn't mind to do so."

I looked into those clear, open eyes again, but they still seemed veiled to me. This chick was some item, but I decided that if that was what she wanted, she was going to get precisely what she asked for—even if it was a slap in the face.

"Okay, maybe this will seem too personal," I told her, "but you're the one who arrived in the middle of the night with the brandy, asking to chat. My uncle Laf's life is hardly a sealed book, so you must be aware he's been with plenty of women, each one more beautiful than the last, and many of them, like my grandmother Pandora, possessing great talent as well. But you're different from the others: I believe you're truly gifted. Really, your playing tonight was extraordinary, world class—as I think, given my upbringing, I am in a position to judge. It's not clear to me why someone with such skill would be willing to be just an arm decoration, a trinket, even of someone as talented and famous and charming as my uncle Laf. My grandmother wouldn't have done it, and I frankly can't imagine why you have. I guess that's what makes me uncomfortable about you: I feel there's another scenario behind the story that hasn't been revealed."

"I see. Well, perhaps that's true," said Bambi, looking down at her hands. When she looked up at me, she wasn't smiling. "Your uncle Lafcadio is very important to me, Fräulein Behn: he and I understand one another completely," she told me. "But that is another situation altogether. That is not why I have come here alone tonight to ask for your friendship."

I waited. Those gold-flecked eyes were trained on me. The news, when it came, dropped me like a thunderbolt.

"Fräulein Behn," Bambi said, "I'm afraid for my brother's interest in you. If you don't do something soon, I fear this involvement of his will endanger us all."

I sat there completely numb. This was the very last thing I could have imagined—but I suddenly grasped with a horrible certainty why everything about Bambi had seemed so familiar to me.

"Your brother?" I said weakly, though it didn't take a rocket scientist to figure out who that might be.

"Permit me to introduce myself properly, Fräulein Behn," she said. "My name is Bettina Braunhilde von Hauser—and Wolfgang is my only brother."

◆ ◆

Heilige Scheiss, I couldn't help but think when confronted with this turn of events. So Bambi was just Uncle Laf's nickname for Bettina, as Gavroche was for me. In fact, I had heard of a Bettina von Hauser, a young cellist who was starting to make a stir on the world concert circuit, though it would never have occurred to me that Bambi was Bettina, or to link either of them with my own rather dangerous passion, Wolfgang Hauser.

This far-from-welcome surprise made me suspect everybody even more than before—especially my uncle Laf, whose behavior in hindsight seemed suspicious. If Laf was so cozy with Bambi he could say anything in front of her, as he told me, then why did he wait until she was absent to discuss Hitler and the runes in the hot pool? When I mentioned Wolfgang, why did Laf actually *warn* me against him, while never even hinting that those two were related? And if Laf thought Aunt Zoe the *Schutzstaffel*-supporter was so chummy with Bambi's brother, why would he bring Bambi herself halfway around the globe to visit me?

Now here was Bambi tiptoeing around the lodge in the dead of night in her lavish lingerie, popping in with a bottle of brandy to reveal to me—behind Laf's back—a few things he might not have known himself, and a lot he hadn't bothered to mention. Since Bambi pointedly said she and Laf "understood one another completely," I had to assume *I* was the only one in this cross-family matrix who didn't have a clue what was going on. But I was damned well going to find out.

Luckily, I possessed a valuable secret weapon: my hollow leg. That is to say, despite my inferior age, weight, and experience, I could drink any number of cowpunchers under the bar, tossing down two-shot tequila bangers all night, and still stand up, walk out the swinging doors, and recall the next morning everything that was said the night before. So a half-bottle of Rémy Martin posed no challenge to me. I was hoping this talent would prove handy in my interrogation of Bambi. I poured us another round of drinks.

◆ ◆

By three A.M. the brandy was gone, and so was Bambi. She'd passed out in midsentence, sitting bolt upright in her chair, but I got her on her feet again and walked her back to the maze of suites at the far side of the lodge. I couldn't leave her in my room and risk having her wake up in a few hours to find me gone. But in three hours of sisterly if drunken cross-examination, I'd learned more than expected, including some real eye-openers.

Wolfgang Hauser wasn't Austrian; he and his sister were Germans born in Nürnberg, raised there and in Switzerland, and later educated in Vienna, he in science and she in music. Their family, though not wealthy, was one of the oldest in Europe. They'd had the *von* in their name for hundreds of years, though Wolfgang had dropped his, Bambi explained, because he felt it was inappropriate to use in his business dealings. Their lives, as described by her, seemed idyllic compared with my own—until they got involved with the family Behn.

Bambi, it turned out, had been my uncle Laf's protégé for more than ten years, from the age of fifteen. When everyone realized how gifted she was, and when he'd offered to hire the best coaches and structure her education and training himself, Bambi's family had let her go live at Laf's house in Vienna. Wolfgang had often visited his sister there, so Laf's assertion that he hardly knew him couldn't be true.

But something happened only seven years ago that changed even this limited familial relationship. Wolfgang had finished his degrees some years earlier, and his first job fresh out of school, as a nuclear industry consultant, took him away more and more often from Vienna. Then one day seven years ago, on returning from a trip, Wolfgang dropped by to visit his sister at Uncle Laf's apartment overlooking the Hofburg. Wolfgang told Laf and Bambi he was leaving his old job for a new one he'd accepted with the International Atomic Energy Agency. He wanted to take the two of them to lunch at a nearby restaurant to celebrate.

"After lunch," said Bambi, "Wolf asked that we will go with him to the Hofburg. He took us to the *Wunderkammer* to see the jewels, and then we visited the famous collections from ancient Ephesus that are now there, and to the *Schatzkammer* to look at the *Reichswaffen*."

"To the treasury, to look at the royal armaments," I said.

I hadn't forgotten the story Laf told me in the hot pool only that morning about his visit, more than seventy-five years ago, to these same chambers of the Hofburg—in the company of Adolf Hitler.

"*Ja,*" said Bambi. "My brother took us to see a sword and a spear, and he asked your uncle, 'Did you and Pandora know all about the sacred hallows?' But Lafcadio said nothing, so Wolf said that he'd for a long time been interested in these objects himself. The story was well known in Nürnberg: Adolf Hitler had taken many of them out of the Imperial treasury in Vienna—for example, the First Reich insignia, the Imperial Crown, the Orb and Scepter, the Imperial Sword, and so on—and he carried them off to the Nürnberger Castle. It was the first thing Hitler did just after he made the—how one says?—the *Anschluss*."

"Germany's 'annexation' of Austria in 1938," I said.

Was it only coincidence that exactly one year ago—in March of 1988, on the fiftieth anniversary of this same coup—my aunt Zoe arrived in Vienna with her fellow World War II "peacekeepers," and there made the acquaintance of Herr Professor Dr. Wolfgang K. Hauser? I thought not, especially when Bambi told me Laf had violently turned off the tap on Wolfgang and refused to see him again or let him in the house after Wolfgang insisted that if, as a favorite of Hitler, Pandora had kept her costly Hofburg apartment throughout the war, and kept performing at the Vienna Opera, it might be because of something important that Pandora herself knew about the hallows. Something connecting them with Nürnberg, even with Hitler himself.

"You and Wolfgang grew up in Nürnberg, where all the Nazis were put on trial just after the war. Were these objects mentioned in the hearings, then?"

"I don't know," Bambi said, resting one elbow on the table to steady herself. "The judgments at Nürnberg—the war—this all happened before Wolfgang and I were born. But even after the war everyone in Nürnberg knew about the relics. They were kept in a chamber in the castle. Hitler believed they were somehow sacred and contained mysterious powers connected with the old German bloodlines. Hitler had an apartment there at Nürnberg, just for when he visited to attend the rallies. The apartment was near the center of town beside the opera house, and its windows faced the castle so he could always look across from his rooms, toward where the hallows lay. They were often put on public display at those big Nazi Party political rallies at the zeppelin field. They stayed at Nürnberg and they weren't returned back to Austria until after the war—"

"Of course—Nürnberg!" Until that moment I'd completely forgotten, but now it suddenly flashed into my mind: All that film footage of nighttime rallies with flags and huge banners and strobe lights against the night sky, and thousands of people lined up in squared-off blocks to form a living chessboard—all those famous rallies had been held in Nürnberg. This raised another question.

I looked at the cognac and saw that the bottle was nearly empty, but I didn't want Bambi to conk out before I learned what I needed to know, so I poured the rest into my own glass.

"Why Nürnberg?" I asked her. "It's just a provincial city a bit off the beaten path, hundreds of miles from anywhere, isn't it? Why would Hitler bring these objects to such an out-of-the-way spot—or hold his rallies there, for that matter?"

Bambi looked at me, her eyes still wide but now clouded a bit from the cognac.

"But Nürnberg is the axis," she said. "Didn't you know?"

"Axis? You mean it's where the Axis powers met during the war? I thought they usually met at Rome or Vienna or—"

"I mean it is *the* axis," she said. "The World Axis, the spot where all geomantic lines of power are thought to meet. Its ancient name was *Nornenberg*—the Mountain of Norns. In our history, the three Norns, goddesses of Fate—Wyrd, Verthandi, Skuld: Became, Becoming, Shall Be—are said to have lived since the dawn of time within this very mountain. They hold the spindle of fate; they weave the story of our destiny in a fabric made entirely of runes. These women are like judges, and their runic tapestry is the real Judgment of Nürnberg, for the tale they write will decide the world's fate in the last days: *die Gotterdammerung*—the twilight of the gods—the tale of what will happen at the end of time."

◆ ◆

Maybe it was naive to imagine I could unkink knots in so tortuous a labyrinth, just by trying to untangle my own familial relationships. But I couldn't help noticing that my nearest relatives did seem to be plunged up to their eyeballs in this National Socialist-mythological-cosmic *Scheiss*.

It wasn't surprising that someone who was a stranger to me, like Bambi, would know so many repugnant things about my family of which I myself had been wholly unaware. After all, I'd spent a lifetime trying to distance myself from them. It now appeared I'd had plenty of legitimate, if hitherto unknown, reasons to have done so.

But I had to wonder—if what Bambi said was true—how Laf, Pandora, and Zoe had fared so well after Hitler's demise. In postwar Paris, Frenchwomen who'd been too palsy with the Gestapo got their heads shaved and were marched through the streets and jeered at. Musicians in many countries, if they'd even *performed* before the Nazis during the occupation, were publicly disgraced after the war, their reputations ruined. And those who'd been really close to power, as Wolfgang believed that Pandora had, got long prison terms or were hanged. This raised an important question: If Pandora *did* stay in Vienna, and was even Hitler's favorite opera star throughout the war, as Bambi said, why would Laf have mentioned her name in the same breath—much less stress the fact that Zoe knew the Führer well, too—instead of distancing himself and his branch of our family as far as possible?

There was yet another odd and almost frightening coincidence in this interfamily saga. It was the last thing I glimpsed in my mind, just before grabbing a few hours of shut-eye in preparation for my date in the meadow with that flock of sheep.

Bambi had told me it was seven years ago, therefore in 1982, when this confrontation between her brother Wolfgang and my uncle Laf took place in Vienna. But it was also exactly seven years ago, 1982, when my uncle Ernest died: the very year when Sam had inherited the rune manuscript and then suddenly vanished, never to be heard from again. Until now.

◆ ◆

In the predawn light the expanse of snow glimmered an eerie bluish white against the backdrop of dark and sinister woods. The moon still hung like an ornament in the star-spangled Prussian blue sky. The air smelled cold and dangerous, as it always did at this time of year just before dawn. It had continued snowing well into the night, and there were no fresh tracks in the meadow. I skated to the center of the open space, whipped backward on my skis, and peered into the woods.

Just then, a snowball struck me in the back with enough force to knock my cap loose and send a cold shower down my neck. When I turned, I saw a form cut briefly from the forest line; it passed for a flicker through the moonlight and then slipped back into the woods. But one upraised arm told me it was Sam, and that I should follow him. I grabbed my hat, stuffed it in my pocket, two-footed it across the pasture, and plunged in among the mesh of silvery fir and birch where I'd seen him vanish.

I stopped to listen. An owl hoot came from up a slight embankment, so I followed it deeper to where the darkness was nearly impenetrable. When I stopped again, unsure where to go next, I heard his whisper close by:

"Ariel, take this and follow me."

I felt him take me by the wrist and place the basket of his ski pole in my hand, and he went before me in darkness. With my two poles clutched in my other hand, I followed blindly, unable to see where he was leading me. We slalomed through trees for a long while, then started our ascent to the high meadow. When at last we came out into the wide space, the sky had lightened to cobalt blue and I could almost make out Sam's outline ahead of me.

He swung around on his skis and slipped his ski tips between mine like interlocked fingers, and he threw his arms around me just as I'd done to him on that mountain nearly eighteen years ago. He smelled of leathery tanned skin and woodsmoke. He buried his face in my loose hair and whispered,

"Thank God, Ariel. You're alive, you're safe—"

"No thanks to *you*," I muttered against his shoulder.

Then he held me away and peered at me in the predawn darkness, the only light the milky moonglow and that strange shimmer from the snow beneath.

I hadn't seen Sam in more than seven years. He was still so boyish then. It should have occurred to me that he might have changed in all that time. But here he stood: tall, broad-shouldered, ruggedly good-looking, with Earnest's chiseled profile, his mother's long dark hair tumbling about his shoulders, and the mysterious beauty of those silvery eyes that seemed to be lit from within. I realized with discomfort that this was no longer my youthful mentor and blood brother who stood before me, but an incredibly handsome man. And the surprised way Sam was looking at me just now told me that his reaction to me must be pretty much the same.

"What happened to that little stringbean with the scuffed knees who used to follow me around everywhere?" he said with a strangely awkward smile. "Good lord, hotshot—you're a knockout!"

"You almost knocked *me* out with that snowball," I said, feeling just as awkward. I actually found it hard to look at Sam until I could get used to the idea that he and I were suddenly completely grown up.

"I'm sorry," he said, still regarding me as if I were almost a stranger. "I feel that's all I can say to you anymore, Ariel—how truly sorry I am that all this has happened. How sorry I am that I ever got you involved."

"Sorry doesn't help," I said, quoting Jersey's line once again. But I smiled, and he smiled back. Then I knew I had to tell him at once.

"Sam," I said, "I have something to be sorry for, too, something I'm sorrier for than I've ever been about anything in my life. I hope it hasn't ruined everything for you or put us both in greater danger, but I've done something really stupid and foolish and awful and wrong. I left someone else alone all night with the rune manuscript—"

Sam had been looking at me with a growing expression of horror as I read out this lengthy litany of abject remorse—until I got to the specifics at the end. And then the surprise was mine.

"What rune manuscript?" said Sam.

◆ ◆

I had this really interesting fantasy that if my heart took enough of these sudden deep plunges into my lower abdomen, it would sooner or later stop ticking altogether and just keep bouncing up and down like a yo-yo. But a few miles of Nordic skiing with Sam through the high meadows worked like a thorax message. By the time we reached the cabin, I was okay—or at least I'd regained my ability to speak.

And I'd learned the reason Sam had changed our meeting plan for today. He'd felt himself in enough danger lately to avoid hotels, so ever since his "death" he'd been sleeping in hunting cabins, duck blinds, and field lean-tos scattered all over Idaho, abandoned or in disuse at this time of year. Arriving at Sun Valley a bit earlier than I, Sam had learned there wasn't that sort of shelter near the ski mountain, so he'd scouted until he found this one, about a two-mile ski from the main road. But most of the area was so open I could easily have been tailed, unless I arrived so early there was barely light enough to see.

Once we'd reached the deserted cabin where Sam spent the night, we snapped off our skis, banged the snow from our bindings, planted our skis and poles in the snow around back, and went inside, where Sam stirred up the dying coals of last night's fire and threw on a few more logs. The place had no other heat nor any plumbing, only pump water just outside the door. Sam jacked the handle to fill a tin pot with water, put it on the fire for instant coffee, and drew up a stool beside the rump-sprung chair where I'd already taken a seat.

"Ariel, I know you may not understand a lot of what I've done, or why I've done it," he began, "but before I begin to explain about all that's happened, I need to catch up on last week: why you didn't show up for our phone call, what you know about the missing package, and whatever you've learned so far from Laf."

"All right," I agreed reluctantly, despite the million questions I needed to ask. "But first—if you didn't send the manuscript I spoke of, then I need to know something right now, because I've met someone who told me he sent it to me himself. Have you ever heard of a Dr. Wolfgang K. Hauser?" Seeing Sam's quick twist of a smile, I added, "So you *do* know him!"

But Sam shook his head. "It was just—I don't know—I guess it's just the way you said his name." Sam was looking at me with an oddly closed expression. "I think I imagined you always as my little blood brother, my twin soul," he went on. "But just now I felt . . . What I mean is, who exactly is this guy, Ariel? Is there something going on here you'd like to tell me about?"

I could feel the hot blood suffusing my face. That damned Irish skin I'd inherited from Jersey showed every pulsating emotion the second it happened. I put my hands over my face. Sam reached over and pulled them down. I opened my eyes.

"Good lord, Ariel, are you in *love* with him?" he said. He jumped up and started pacing around in a circle, rubbing his forehead with his hand, while I sat there not having a clue what to say.

Sam sat down again and leaned toward me with urgency.

"Ariel, apart from anything else I may privately feel about the situation, this is hardly the moment for a blossoming romance! You've said you just met this man. Do you know anything about him at all? What's his background? Have you any idea just how dangerous this untimely 'friendship' of yours might prove to us both?"

I was so upset by this outburst, I felt like throwing something at him. I jumped to my feet just as the coffeepot boiled over. Sam grabbed a glove to rescue it from the fire. This gave us both a quick moment to settle down.

"I didn't say I was in love with anyone," I told Sam in the calmest voice I could muster.

"You didn't have to," said Sam.

He was fiddling with the coffeepot, not looking at me. Then he turned so I couldn't read his face, and he started to measure instant java into cups. As if he were speaking to himself, he finally said:

"I've only just realized that I understand your emotions, right now, far better than I seem to understand my own."

When he turned back to me with the two cups of coffee, he was wearing a slightly strained smile. He handed me my cup and then ruffled my hair as he used to do when we were kids.

"God, I'm sorry, sweetheart," he said. "I have no right to tell you who to care for, or to cross-examine you the way I've just done. I guess I was surprised, that's all. But you're smart enough not to fall for someone who might put us both in danger. And who knows? Maybe there's some link in this situation that will help us out of the mess I've gotten us into, once we can figure it out. By the way, this Wolfgang K. Hauser—I'm simply curious—did he tell you what the 'K' stands for?"

Surprised, I shook my head. "No, he didn't. Why? Is it important?"

"Probably not," said Sam. "But the next time you see him, you might just ask. Now let me hear your story about this past week."

So I took a deep breath and we sat down again, and I filled Sam in on everything that had happened. Well, almost everything. After

Sam's reaction to the way I'd even spoken Wolfgang's *name*, I did leave out the detail that he'd spent the night with me as well as with the manuscript. But about all the rest I was straight.

By the time I'd finished the exhaustive summary, I myself had begun to see just what a pivotal role Wolfgang Hauser seemed to play in the story. But maybe that was because so far the plot had hinged on the wrong parcel. The real parcel sent by Sam remained missing. I was about to find out just how dangerous it really was.

"I can't believe it's still missing," Sam said grimly, reading my thoughts. "But there's something here that just isn't adding up."

I asked Sam why the contents of the missing parcel were so valuable that everyone on the planet seemed to be after it—including members of our own family who hadn't spoken to one another in years—and so dangerous he'd had to fake his own death.

"If I knew all the answers," said Sam with a grim smile, "we wouldn't need to be holed up here in an isolated cabin just to speak to each other, after a week of having to mess around with secret codes."

"Mess around!" I said in frustration. "You're the one who's been messing around, with your rigged funerals and biblical anagrams and secret meetings! But after what I've been through this past week, I want answers and I want them right now. What's in that missing package, and why did you send it to me?"

"It's my inheritance," said Sam, as if it were clear. "Please listen to me, Ariel. You *must* understand everything I have to tell you. Seven years ago, just before he died, my father told me for the first time what Pandora had left him. He'd never discussed it before, he said, because by the terms of Pandora's will he'd agreed to keep the bequest confidential. So Father put it in a box in a bank vault in San Francisco, where our family's law firm was located. When Father died, I retrieved the box and brought it here to Idaho to study. It contained many old, rare manuscripts Pandora had collected over her lifetime. The package I sent you contained copies of these—"

"Copies?" I cried. "You had to fake your death—our lives are in danger—over a bunch of *duplicates* of something?"

"These are the *only* copies." Sam spoke a bit impatiently, it seemed to me, for someone who'd taken so long to explain himself. "When I said the originals were old and rare, I should have said ancient. They were stored in a hermetically sealed box against decomposition. There are scrolls made of papyrus and linen, or of metals like copper or tin. A few are written on wooden boards or metal plates. My judgment, based on the materials and languages used—Greek, Hebrew, Latin, Sanskrit, Akkadian, Aramaic, and even Ugaritic—is that these manuscripts originated in many regions of the world and were written over a long span of time. I knew at once that what I held in my hands was incomparably valuable. But I also sensed, as my father might have, that they were somehow dangerous. Many have disintegrated badly with age, nearly crumbling into dust, and can't be photographed easily without complicated, expensive equipment and processes. So I've made copies of each—myself, by hand, a labor that's cost me many years—so I could begin to translate them. Then I put the copies in the vault and I hid the originals where I don't believe they'll be found. At least, certainly not until my translations into English are complete."

"And have you been able to translate many?" I asked.

"Quite a few," Sam replied. "But it's all an odd ragbag of seemingly unrelated things. Letters, stories, testimonials, reports. Bureaucratic administrivia from imperial Rome. Celtic and Teutonic legends. Descriptions of Thracian festivals and dinner parties in Judea, tales of pagan gods and goddesses from northern Greece—and nowhere a thread that connects it all. Yet there *must* be something or Pandora wouldn't have collected them to begin with."

My mind was racing, but it was going in a circle. How could documents like these be connected to the neo-Nazi conspiracy plot I'd expected after listening to Laf and Bambi? All the events they'd described happened in this last century, while languages like Ugaritic, so far as I knew, hadn't been spoken in millennia. I thought of the Norns in their hidden grotto inside that mountain at Nürnberg, weaving and spinning the fatal game plan for the world's last days. But what if no one could read it when it was done?

As Sam took a swig of tepid coffee, I could sense the frustration a codebreaker as good as he must feel at removing the skin of the onion and contemplating the layers remaining to reach the core.

"If you haven't been able to find any connection among these manuscripts of Pandora's after years of trying," I said, "why does everyone think they're so valuable and dangerous? Could they be related to the objects in the Hofburg—the ones everyone says Hitler was trying to collect?"

"I thought of that, even before you mentioned it just now," said Sam. "But more important to me was figuring out where the documents came from, how Pandora obtained them, and why she wanted them in the first place. And perhaps *most* significant was to understand why—of all people—she bequeathed them to my father."

"I've wondered the same thing myself, since I learned about the documents," I admitted. "Do you know?"

"Maybe," said Sam. "But I want to know what you think. Before now, I've had nobody to discuss my theory with. It has to do with Pandora's will. When Pandora died, my father was called to Europe for the reading of her will, as a principal heir. He was surprised. After all, she was his stepmother only while she was briefly married to Hieronymus. She hadn't seen him since the 'family schism' took place. In fact, as I'm sure you'll agree, Ariel, Uncle Laf's story of our family must be filtered through a different prism from that of our fathers Earnest and Augustus. They could hardly have held her in such high regard, when she ran off and left them in Vienna to be raised by their father."

Sacrée merde, I thought, when confronted once more with my complex and bitter family history. But suddenly something occurred to me: Was it possible Pandora had actually *counted* on the deep bitterness and complexity of our family interrelations? I said as much to Sam.

"I already had more than a strong feeling," said Sam. "But when you told me your stories just now, everything fit. I think it's been at the root of everything from the beginning—I mean the family schism itself. Let's look at it closely. At the start, it was Pandora who created the split at one blow by going off with Laf and Zoe. It's been a sharp thorn in our side of the family that Pandora abandoned your father almost at birth, an act that might well explain the man's coldblooded, self-serving demeanor today. Throughout her life she did a good deal more to *keep* things severed. Then we know she left my father these rare and ancient documents I described. And according to your friend Hauser, Zoe has the original of some sort of rune manuscript of which you now possess a copy. We don't know what Laf may have inherited from Pandora besides the apartment overlooking the Hofburg—which in itself is probably significant—but we do know he was aware of the existence of a rune manuscript, though he seemed not to know Zoe had it."

Sam paused and smiled at me.

"So you see, hotshot, all this points to a single question: If *you* were the one who needed to hide something, and you wanted it to stay hidden even well after your death, can you think of any better insurance than to divide it among four siblings like Lafcadio and Earnest and Zoe and Augustus, whose hostility toward one another dates back, in some instances, even to the cradle?"

Right on the mark. From the moment they believed I'd "inherited," everyone in my family was sending emissaries hither and thither, or arriving themselves from Europe or phoning past midnight to interrogate me. Even Olivier had noted my relatives' uncustomary behavior. And in a family like ours with ancient wounds, operating in an environment of suspicion and resentment, it was a perfect way for Pandora to divvy up that loot so no one could guess who got what.

But something else bothered me.

"What prompted you to take the drastic step of pretending you were dead?" I asked Sam. "Not just dead, but staging that high-profile funeral—the family, the military band, the important dignitaries, the press—why make so huge a splash? How did you get the government to go along with it? And why on earth would you threaten *my* life by sending me those documents and letting everyone learn you'd done it?"

"Ariel, please," said Sam, taking my hand in both of his. "I swear on my life I wouldn't have put you in such danger if I'd had a choice. But I've known for over a year now that someone was following me. Then last month in San Francisco, someone overtly tried to kill me. There can be no mistake. A bomb was planted in my car—"

"A *bomb*?" I cried.

But just as that hit, something struck me with even greater horror. I'd already asked myself, if Sam wasn't dead, *what* was buried in that coffin at the Presidio in San Francisco. Now I asked Sam, my voice quavering, "My God, are you saying somebody else got killed in your place? Is that it?"

"Yes," he said slowly, "someone was killed in my rental car in Chinatown."

Sam's eyes were flat and his tone strangely distant, as if his memory were being filtered through a screen of fog. "You must understand, Ariel, that although I've never worked directly for the government or military, over the years as an independent consultant I've trained most of their in-house cryptanalysts, and even assisted the State Department. I've often helped various branches of the service, too, with sensitive decryption jobs that need to be fast and clean and quiet, in-and-out. As a result, I know a great many people and a great many secrets.

"The man who was killed in that car explosion was a friend, a high-level government official I've worked with for years. His name was Theron Vane. At my request a year ago, Theron assigned an agent in his employ to try to learn who was following me, and why. Last month Theron asked me to come at once to San Francisco: the agent he'd assigned to my case had died mysteriously. The agency had sealed off the small rented apartment he'd used as an undercover office. It's government policy to clean out such places anyway, to collect or destroy records before they fall into anyone's hands. But in this case, Theron thought whatever we found might be related to me as well as to the agent's death. We went over the place carefully. I broke everything, including what was inside the computer, and then destroyed the data.

"Based on what we'd learned, we agreed it would be faster and less conspicuous if I went on foot to the next stop and Theron took my car around the block to pick me up. But once outside, at the top of the steep flight of steps from the apartment house, I paused, as Theron had asked, to check the mailbox and be certain no new mail had arrived while we'd been inside. I was halfway down the steps when Theron started the car below, and it exploded. . . ."

Sam paused to put a hand over his eyes and rub his temples. I didn't know what to say. I didn't move till he took his hand down and looked at me in pain.

"Ariel, I can't explain how awful it was," he said. "I'd known Theron Vane for nearly ten years; he'd been a true friend. But I knew that bomb was really meant for me, so I had to leave him there as if it *was* me, splattered in pieces across the pavement for others to come and collect in bags like refuse. You can't imagine how that felt."

I could imagine it so vividly that I myself was quaking like an aspen. But unlike two weeks ago, when I'd believed it was Sam who was dead, the danger to us both suddenly came home to me in force. This was no faked funeral we were talking about—not even an accident—but a real murder, a violent death that was meant to have been Sam's. And if Sam's late mentor was a high-level official, clearly in the intelligence community, he must have known how to protect himself better than *I* did. Now it was plain that the many precautions Sam had taken were hardly overkill—so to speak.

"What made you sure the bomb was intended for you?" I asked.

"I found in the computer in that apartment a number that, until that moment, I'd believed I alone knew: the number of a vault located in a bank only a few blocks away," said Sam. "Clearly, whoever tried to kill me had already learned where I'd hidden the copied manuscripts in that Chinatown bank, and felt confident he could obtain them—perhaps even with greater ease if I were dead.

"When the bomb went off as I was headed for that very bank to retrieve the manuscripts, the coincidence was too great. I fled to my bank, got the manuscripts and a big padded mailing pouch from them, then slapped on postage from a stamp machine and tossed it into the nearest mailbox to send to the only person I knew I could trust with absolute certainty: you. Then from a pay phone I called Theron's superior and reported the whole story. It was the government's decision that we go on pretending I was dead. Indeed, I've broken both my word and my cover by contacting anyone—especially you, a member of the family." Sam looked at me with strangely veiled eyes.

"The family?" I said. "What does this have to do with the family?" I was again beginning to feel certain I really didn't want to know.

"There's only one thing that links this puzzle together, and also links it to our family," Sam said. "And to my mind, it's still Pandora's will. Since we've already agreed that she probably bequeathed something important to three of our relations, the question remains—what did she leave to the fourth, her only child?"

I choked a little and felt myself turn slightly green.

"To Augustus? My father?" I said. "Why would she leave him anything? After all, she abandoned him at birth, didn't she?"

"Well, sweetheart," said Sam with an ironic smile, "he's the only one in the family except you and me that we haven't discussed. I was only four and you weren't yet born when Pandora died, so I'd like to put a few things into perspective. Doesn't it seem odd that my father, Earnest, the *eldest* child of Hieronymus Behn, inherited only the Idaho mining interests—while yours, the youngest, wound up with a worldwide empire of mineral and manufacturing concessions—"

"Are you trying to tell me you think my *father* has something to do with all this?" I said in disbelief, withdrawing my hand. When I stood up, Sam remained seated, still watching me closely. My mind was reeling, but he wasn't quite through.

He said, "I think you need to come up with some answers—if only for yourself. Why do you imagine, the moment he thought I was dead, Augustus contacted my estate executor, as you told me, to learn what I'd left you? Why did he hold a press conference in San Francisco to drag out in public the contents of my will? Why did Augustus phone you in Idaho for days and days, and once he reached you, why did he alert you to the fact that you should alert *him* the moment you received the manuscripts from my trust? How did Augustus come to know anything whatever about any manuscripts?"

"But we *all* knew about them!" I cried. "They were mentioned in your . . ."

I had started to say ". . . in your will." Then I suddenly realized, with a cold and horrible shock, that throughout the reading of the will *nothing whatever* had been mentioned about the specifics of any such papers in the inheritance, only that I was to be sole heir. But this item raised an even bigger specter. If I *was* Sam's sole heir, why was Augustus present at the reading of the will? Why *did* he hold a press conference? And since my father hadn't seen Sam in years, nor his own brother for many years before Earnest's death, *why was Augustus even at Sam's funeral?*

Sam was sitting there nodding—but he was no longer smiling.

"So now, based on your observation of his behavior during and after the funeral, have you guessed why it was so important that everyone in our family, especially your father, believe I was really dead?" Sam asked me. He got to his feet and looked me right in the eye.

"Are you crazy?" I said. "Okay, I admit Augustus is an asshole and his behavior needs some explaining. But you can't really imagine he'd hunt you down and try to *kill* you for those manuscripts, regardless of what he might think they're worth. Even wildly assuming what you suggest is true, that Augustus were capable of such a thing, why wouldn't he have acted sooner to lay hands on the manuscripts? After all, Earnest inherited them decades ago and had them for nearly twenty years."

"Maybe Augustus never realized my father had them," said Sam. "No one seemed to know *I* did, until one year ago when I started being followed myself. . . ."

One year ago. One year ago someone started following Sam. One year ago Sam contacted his friend in the government and, possibly because of that, two of their employees were now dead. But what other important event had happened just one year ago? It was right at the edge of my mind. I racked my brain. Then all at once I knew—and a few more things got hammered into place as neatly as nails in a coffin.

The event that happened exactly one year ago, in March of 1988, was that Wolfgang Hauser met my aunt Zoe at an *Anschluss* reunion in Vienna. And Zoe revealed that she possessed another manuscript—a manuscript written in runes!

So Sam was right about one thing: If my father *had* inherited something from Pandora twenty-five years ago, and then somehow learned Zoe had inherited something too, it wouldn't take much to figure out—as Sam and I had just done—that there was more than one piece to this puzzle. Or to arrive at the conclusion that other pieces, likewise, had passed through Pandora's will to various members of our family.

Augustus had actually *told* me the manuscripts were Pandora's, and that they were written in some kind of code. Swiftly followed, a bit too coincidentally, a call from Ms. Helena Lengthy-Moniker of the *Washington Post*—who'd obtained my private phone number directly from my father, and who told me the manuscripts might be Zoe's instead. How did I know she really worked for the *Post* and not for my father? Still, none of this proved that Augustus was the culprit trying to piece together these divided manuscripts—much less that he might be a mad bomber.

"Do you know who was the executor of Pandora's estate?" I asked Sam.

"Exactly! That's the critical point." He grasped both my arms. Pain shot up to my shoulder; I winced and couldn't keep from crying out. Sam released me quickly, in alarm.

"What is it?" he said.

"Fourteen stitches. I almost collided with an avalanche," I told him—one of the less dramatic of last week's events that I'd managed to leave out of my earlier account. I drew in my breath and gingerly touched my twinging arm beneath the fabric.

Sam was looking at me with concern. He reached over to stroke my hair tenderly, shaking his head.

"It's almost healed; I'm okay," I said. "But it did occur to me that Pandora would have to be pretty confident to let anyone hand out documents, after her death, that she'd spent her life collecting and protecting."

"The exact conclusion I arrived at—more so, given the odd circumstances," said Sam. "My own mother, Bright Cloud, had died only a few months before Pandora did. Father and I were both in shock and in mourning, and I'd never traveled so far away as Europe. Father therefore requested he be sent by mail any legal papers he needed to sign for the bequest. To his surprise, he was told it wouldn't be possible: that under the terms of Pandora's will, he must sign for and receive his legacy from the executor in person. So father and I went to Vienna."

"Then the executor did have an important role," I said. "Who was he?"

"The man we've just learned was Laf's first violin teacher," said Sam. "Pandora's dark, romantic cousin Dacian Bassarides, who joined her and the children on the merry-go-round at the Prater, then went with them to the Hofburg to see the weapons. When my father and I went to Vienna for the will, I was only four years old and Dacian Bassarides was in his seventies, but I'll never forget his face. It was wildly handsome. Wild—just as Laf described the young Pandora.

"It's interesting, too, Laf's mentioning that business on the merry-go-round about Hitler telling the children that *Earn* meant eagle in Old High German, and *Daci* meant wolf. Such words seem important. Quite a few of the manuscripts I've translated involve the family of the Roman emperor Augustus. I'd love to learn who it was that gave your father that same name. And of course, you know what Pandora's family name, Bassarides, means in Greek?"

I shook my head.

"The skins or pelts of foxes," said Sam. "But I've learned that the root is from a Libyan Berber word, *bassara,* which means vixen—the female fox. Very much as Laf had described Pandora, a wild animal. Ironic, isn't it?"

" 'Take us the foxes, the little foxes that spoil the vines, for our vines have tender grapes,' " I quoted from the Song of Songs which is Solomon's.

Sam glanced up in astonishment, followed by the dazzling smile of approval that always made me feel, as a child, that I'd just done something intolerably clever.

"So you *did* understand my message!" he said. "I knew you could do it, hotshot, but I didn't think you'd have time to put it together that quickly."

"I didn't," I said, though my mind was still racing. "I only deciphered enough to figure out our meeting place this morning—not whatever else it was you wanted me to know."

"But that's *it*, don't you see?" said Sam. "That's the irony. The cunning little vixen, Pandora, actually *did* spoil the grapes—for at least the last twenty-five years—by keeping these manuscripts so successfully apart. I didn't begin to realize what she'd done until after I'd already sent you that parcel." Then his smile faded as he looked at me in the dim light of the fire with his silvery eyes. "Ariel," he said softly, "I think we both understand what we must do."

My heart sank, but I knew he was right. If this puzzle was so dangerous and ancient that everyone wanted it, we wouldn't be safe till we knew what it was all about.

"If the parcel you sent never shows up," I said, "I guess you'll have to reconstruct everything from those originals you've hidden; and Zoe's runes—"

"That can wait, since at least we know there *are* originals," said Sam. "But, Ariel, if someone has been so desperate to get these manuscripts that our lives are in real danger, our first priority is to learn what the four divided parts are, and why Pandora collected them in the first place. I need to go see the one person who can answer that question: her cousin and executor, Dacian Bassarides."

"What makes you believe Dacian Bassarides is still alive?" I said. "If he was close to Pandora's age, way back in Vienna, by now he's pushing a century. And how do you expect to find him? After all, twenty-five years have passed since you saw him. The trail's a bit cold by now, I should think."

"To the contrary," Sam said. "Dacian Bassarides is alive and well at ninety-five, and still remembered in some quarters. Half a century ago, he was a noted violinist in that tempestuous Paganini style: they used to call him Prince of Foxes. If you haven't heard of him, it's only because for some reason, though he performed in public, he refused to record. Until this morning, I'd never known he'd taught Laf, too. But as to where he can be found today, I'd have thought your friend Hauser might have told you. It's my understanding that for the past fifty years, even throughout the war, Dacian Bassarides's permanent base was in France, and that he's great chums with Zoe, who's now in her eighties. If anyone could arrange a tryst with him, she should be able to."

I knew it was too dangerous for Sam to go to Paris seeking Dacian Bassarides. He'd have to clear immigration and security in two countries using false IDs. But I soon found the solution to the problem:

Hadn't Wolfgang Hauser said he wanted to help "protect" my inheritance, and that he hoped I would meet my aunt Zoe in Paris to learn more about it? Since the Pod was sending us to Russia on government business, maybe we could arrange a layover for the two of us to visit with Zoe in Paris. Though Sam didn't sound thrilled at the idea of my April-ing in Paris with Wolfgang, it was after all Sam's idea that we interrogate Dacian Bassarides. This seemed the simplest way to do it.

We concurred that Sam should spend the next weeks, while I got my Franco-Russian trip set, shaking our family tree on the sly to see if he could knock down a few rotten apples—and that it would be a good idea to visit his grandfather, Dark Bear, on the Nez Percé reservation at Lapwai. Though neither of us had seen Dark Bear in years, we thought he might provide insight into Sam's father, when Earnest lived at Lapwai before Sam was born—information that might shed more light on at least one member involved in the family schism that we knew had inherited manuscripts.

But I understood that my family added up to more than eccentricity, fame, and feuding war parties. There was something mysterious that seemed to lie buried at its very core. To explore that core we needed fresh data gathered through an impartial outside source. It was then that I thought of the Church of Jesus Christ of Latter-day Saints.

Few outsiders or "gentiles" are aware that the Mormon Church maintains extensive genealogical facilities near Salt Lake City, containing records on family lineage that date back to the time of Cain and Seth. Olivier told me these records were kept on computers, the world's bloodlines woven in microchip technology, hidden deep in bomb-proof caves within a Utah mountain—like the rune tapestries of those fabled Norns of Nürnberg, I thought.

Though we had our missions laid out, Sam and I still had the problem of how to make contact after we left this cabin and parted ways—not easy, when we couldn't guess where either of us might be tomorrow morning. Sam had a plan: Each day, wherever he happened to be, he'd find a copy center and fax my computer at work leaving a fake name but a real number where I could fax *him*. I'd go to a copy shop and send him any new info with a key to decrypt it and a number where he could reply. This would work in the short haul, since there were copy shops in every town around the globe—except maybe in Soviet Russia, once I got there.

When Sam extinguished our fire and we came out of the cabin, though we'd been inside little more than an hour, the sunlight glittering from the snow in the high meadow was already dazzling. Just before I put on my dark glasses against the glare, Sam tossed his arm around my neck, drew me to him, and kissed my hair. Then he held me away.

"Just remember I love you, hotshot," he told me seriously. "Don't run into any more avalanches; I'd like to get you back in one piece. And I'm not at all sure about this business of your going to Paris. . . ."

"I love you back," I told Sam, smiling. Putting my glasses on, I took his hand. "Meanwhile, blood brother, may the Great Bear Spirit walk in your moccasin prints. And before we part, you must swear to me on her totem you'll take care of yourself the same way."

Sam smiled too, and held up his hand, palm toward me.

"Honest Injun," he said.

◆ ◆

I was coming over the top of the high meadow when I saw his outline against the shadowy blue snow in the lower meadow, an athletic form in a sleek dark ski suit and goggles, his shaggy hair moving in the morning breeze. I didn't need to see his face. No two people could move with that grace and agility on the snow. It was definitely Wolfgang Hauser. And he was headed toward me, following my tracks, the only ones that had yet been cut down there, I was sure, in last night's new snow.

Holy shit. Thank God we'd decided to take separate routes out. But at the speed Wolfgang was moving, it would only be moments before he reached the place in the woods where Sam's tracks and mine joined this morning. How in hell was I supposed to explain why and with whom I'd decided to go skiing in this isolated spot before dawn? The question of what Wolfgang himself was doing here, when he was supposed to be six hundred miles away in Nevada, would just have to wait.

In panic, I bolted off the rim and slashed down through the woods. It had never occurred to me that I should return by the same path I'd used that morning. I wasn't even sure where my old trail was in these woods, or—since it had still been dark—exactly where Sam and I had met. My only ambition was to find Wolfgang before he himself reached that spot and we would have something very, very difficult to discuss. I was moving so fast through the blur of woods that I skied right past him.

"Ariel!" I heard with a Doppler effect, and screeched to a halt, nearly wrapping myself around a tree.

I gingerly crosshatched back through the woods. Wolfgang, skating between the trees, pulled aside fir branches laden with last night's snow as he passed. As he released each branch, the load dropped on the ground with a soft *plump*. When we met in the dappled light, he regarded me with a questioning but stern expression, so I thought I'd better get in the first word.

"Why, Dr. Hauser, what a surprise," I said, trying to coax out a smile, though I still wasn't sure if he'd found our tracks. "We run into each other in the oddest places, don't we? I thought you were in Nevada just now."

"I told you I would come if I possibly could do so," he said in a tone of mild irritation. "I've driven all night to get here."

"So I guess you decided to loosen up from your trip by going for a spin on skis out here in the middle of nowhere?" I commented dryly.

"Ariel, please don't play games with me. I went to your room as soon as I arrived at the Lodge—the sun wasn't even up yet. When I learned you weren't there, I was horribly worried about what might have become of you. But before sending up a general alarm, I went to the car park and saw that your car was missing too. It snowed last night: the only fresh tracks from the car park headed in this direction, so I came and found your car in the woods. I followed your ski tracks here. Now it's your turn to explain what you thought you were doing skiing all by yourself, miles away from the Lodge, before dawn?"

Whew—so he thought I was skiing by myself, which meant he

hadn't reached our tracks. That rescued me from the next step, something I'd already been braced for: lying without compunction. But it still didn't get me out of the woods.

"I was hoping a little exercise would help me work off some of that cognac your sister and I slugged down in my room last night," I told him. And it was true.

"Bettina?" he said in amazement—so I knew I'd pushed the right button. "Bettina is staying here at the Lodge?"

"We tied one on," I said, but when Wolfgang looked puzzled I translated, "We got drunk together, and I pumped her for information about you. Now I understand why you told me my uncle Lafcadio was just an acquaintance of yours, not a friend. But in our lengthy conversation on the topic of *my* family, you just might have mentioned that your sister has been living with my uncle these past ten years."

"I'm sorry," said Wolfgang, shaking his head as if he were just waking up—as he might well feel, if he'd truly been driving all night. He looked at me with cloudy deep blue eyes. "I haven't seen Bettina in rather a long time. I suppose she explained that to you, too?"

"Yes, but I'll bet I'd like your explanation better. I mean, why would two people like you and Bamb—like your sister—become strangers to one another, just because of the overdramatized histrionics of somebody like Uncle Laf?"

"Actually, I still see my sister from time to time," said Wolfgang, not really answering my question. "But I am surprised to learn that Lafcadio brought her here from Vienna like this. He must not have guessed that I might be here, too."

"He'll know now," I told him. "Let's all have breakfast together and see what kind of fireworks start popping."

Wolfgang stuck his poles in the snow and put his hands on my shoulders. "You're very brave to plan such a meal. Have I said that I missed you, and that Nevada is a truly awful place?"

"I thought Germans always loved all those neon lights," I said.

"Germans?" said Wolfgang, taking his hands from my shoulders. "Who told you—oh, Bettina. It appears you *did* get her drunk."

I smiled back and shrugged. "My favorite interrogation technique: I learned it at the breast of my mother," I admitted. "By the way, since it now seems that you and I are practically related, through this attachment of my uncle and your sister, I thought I might get more personal and ask things I want to know about you—like for instance, what does the 'K' stand for?"

Wolfgang was still smiling, but raised one brow in curiosity. "It stands for my middle name: Kaspar. Why do you ask?"

"Like Casper, the friendly ghost?" I said with a laugh.

"Like Balthazar, Melchior, and Kaspar—you know, those three wise Magi who brought gifts to the infant Jesus." Then Wolfgang added: "Who suggested that you ask me that question?"

Boy, I might be terrific at interrogating the incredibly soused, but it seemed I was the world's worst, myself, at handling unexpected questions. I tried a punt.

"I guess you don't know I have a photographic memory," I said—not really answering *his* question. "I saw your name logged into that sign-in book at the site, including all that *Herr Professor Doktor* business, and the fact that you're stationed at Krems, Austria. Where on earth *is* Krems, anyway?" I rattled on blithely, hoping I could wriggle from beneath Wolfgang's penetrating and rather suspicious gaze.

"Actually, it's where you and I will be heading together on Tuesday," Wolfgang said. "So you'll be able to see for yourself."

I tried not to do a double-take, since my head was starting to throb with the effect of what liquor I hadn't managed to ski off.

"You mean *this* Tuesday?" I said, feeling slightly hysterical. This couldn't be happening again—not now. Not after I'd just found Sam, and had no way to find him again until he found *me*. "Like, the day after tomorrow we're heading to Austria?"

Wolfgang nodded, and when he spoke it was with a certain urgency.

"Pastor Dart phoned me in Nevada yesterday. He'd been trying to find us both—you and me—and he was relieved to learn I knew where you could be reached," he told me. "Our plane to Vienna will leave New York late Monday night—tomorrow. In order to catch that flight, we must fly all day; that's why I drove last night from Nevada to get here, pick you up en route, and get us both back in time to pack. I thought, since you'd told me Maxfield would be here anyway, he could bring your car later and you'd come with me. There are many things you and I need to discuss in private before we leave the country. We'll have time for breakfast here, of course, but we must—"

"Whoa!" I cried, holding up my ski mitt. "May I ask exactly *why* you and I are suddenly jet-setting off to Vienna together? Or has something escaped me?"

"Oh, didn't I say?" he said, smiling somewhat abashedly. "Our Soviet visas have been approved by the embassy. Vienna is our first stop en route to Leningrad."

◆ ◆

Wolfgang had brought me a little phrase book of Russian for travelers, and I read it as he drove back from Sun Valley. I wished I could find some Russian words right now that would truly reflect my current state of mind. I did find words for constipation *(zahpoer)*, for diarrhea *(pahnoes)*, and for bowel *(kyee-SHESCH-nyeek)*—this last, in my view, about as close as I was likely to get to the feel of the thing. But though I'd learned Wolfgang himself was fairly fluent in Russian, I felt somehow awkward asking him to translate the expression "holy shit."

To describe brunch as rather strained would be more than an understatement. Laf glared at me when I blew in with Wolfgang, and Bambi and her brother embraced. Then Olivier spent the entire *meal* glaring at me when he learned in swift succession that: a) Bambi was Wolfgang's sister; b) Wolfgang was driving me back home today, while Olivier chauffeured my car and my cat; and c) Wolfgang and I were leaving at the crack of dawn to depart for an idyllic journey together to the USSR.

But Laf perked up a bit when I informed him our first stop was really Vienna—where he himself was scheduled to return from San Francisco Monday night—and that I'd come see him there in the event we'd left anything still unsaid. Before I left the dining room, though, I took Laf aside.

"Laf," I said, "I know how you feel about Bambi's brother. But since he and I will be together in Vienna on business, I'm asking you to make an exception in this one case, and invite us both to your house. Is there anything else about our family situation that you believe I need to know right now?"

"Gavroche," said Laf with a sigh, "you have the eyes of your mother Jersey, those ice blue eyes she has always been so proud of. But yours are more like Pandora's—wild leopard eyes—because yours are made of the pure *green* ice. I don't blame Wolfgang: I don't really know how any man could resist eyes like these. I surely could not. But,

Gavroche, you must be certain that you will resist the *men*—until you learn exactly in what kind of situation you are involved."

That was all Laf would tell me, but I knew he was being straight with me. He was worried about me, not about some feud with Bambi's family or with ours.

I kissed Laf, hugged Bambi, handed over Jason to Olivier, and shook hands with the silent Volga Dragonoff who never smiled. As we headed back the hundred fifty miles to my basement apartment along the Snake River, I wondered what in hell I really was getting myself into. And I wondered how on earth I could contact Sam before I left and let him know.

Wolfgang gave me an earful on the way home about our impending trip. At the last moment he'd arranged this brief layover in Vienna for us en route to Russia, and for a reason—but not the one he had given to the Pod.

Though the IAEA was based in Vienna, Wolfgang's office was in Krems, a medieval town just up the Danube at the beginning of the Wachau, the most famous wine-growing valley in all of Austria. Wolfgang had told the Pod we'd need to check in there and go over a lot of paperwork, involving IAEA philosophy as well as our specific mission in the USSR, before he could take me into Russia. And it seems the Pod bought this scenario.

I hadn't remembered Krems earlier, but once Wolfgang mentioned the Wachau, I recalled it from my childhood. Just beyond it was another part of the Danube Valley, the *Nibelungengau*, where the early, magical inhabitants of Austria once lived. It was part of the setting of Richard Wagner's *Ring of the Nibelungenlied*, the cycle of four operas of which my grandmother Pandora's recordings were today world renowned. I also remembered that in the Wachau, Jersey and I had once climbed the steep trail leading up through the woods overlooking the blue-grey Danube to the ruins of Dürnstein—the castle where Richard the Lionhearted had been captured while returning home from the Crusades, and where he was held prisoner for ransom for thirteen months.

But Wolfgang's private reason for going to Krems was centered around another spot in the Wachau: the famous monastery of Melk. Once the castle-fortress of the House of Babenberg, the Habsburgs' predecessors, and today a Benedictine abbey, Melk possessed a library of nearly one hundred thousand volumes, many of them very ancient. According to Wolfgang, whose story jibed with Laf's in the hot pool, it was at Melk that Adolf Hitler first did his own research into the secret history of the runes, like those in Aunt Zoe's manuscript. Apparently it was Zoe who'd asked him to bring me to Melk for our own research.

We got back about five, and Wolfgang dropped me at my cellar door. We agreed to meet at the airport at nine-thirty to catch the ten A.M. connecting flight to Salt Lake. That left this evening to get ready for the trip. I tried to concentrate on what I needed to take for a two-week trek, most of it in the Soviet Union where I'd never visited at this time of year. But I kept feeling I was forgetting something. The travel leaflet Wolfgang gave me recommended bringing bottled water and plenty of toilet paper, so I packed those first. And though I didn't know much about Leningrad in early spring, I did recall that Vienna in April was no Paris—it was bitterly cold, requiring "thermal chic."

All the while, I was trying to collect my thoughts and to figure out what I could do about contacting Sam. It occurred to me that Sam might actually dial into my computer *before* tomorrow morning, to test out our new technique up front. I could pick up any such message on my way to the airport, and even if I had no time just then, at least I'd know where to fax back a message when I got to Salt Lake, or from Kennedy when we got to New York. It would be a good idea anyway, I realized, not to just dash off with no farewells, but to check in at work for any last-minute instructions from my boss, Pastor Dart.

I'd set my packed duffels beside the front door and was about to turn in when I heard Olivier upstairs. He was banging around with the skis, so I went up in my robe and fur-lined moccasins to see if I could help.

"You probably haven't had anything to eat since brunch" was Olivier's first comment. Which was perfectly true—I'd forgotten. "I was going to make smoked trout mousse on dilled rye bread for dinner, for the little argonaut and me, to commiserate over your departure tomorrow. I guess it will be just the two of us, dining as bachelors after that—but would you care to join us in a bite right now?"

"I'd love to," I told him. Though I was dead on my feet, I suddenly realized I might have no time for breakfast tomorrow, and there'd likely be no food but peanuts on my flights till well past noon. "Shall I whip us up a hot toddy to wash it down?" I suggested. I wanted to apologize to Olivier for how our weekend had turned out, though I soon learned it wasn't necessary.

"*Bien sûr,*" Olivier said with a grin, tossing the skis on the cold-room rack and hanging the poles up by their loops. "You've been forgiven some of my anger, my darling one, now that you've introduced me to the beautiful, bountiful Bambita," he went on. "I think I'm in love—and she isn't even close to being the cowgirl that I've always imagined I pined for in my heart."

"But she and my uncle Lafcadio *do* seem to be an item," I pointed out. "And they live in Vienna, pretty far from here."

"That's okay," said Olivier. "Your uncle's skiing days are over, even if his fiddling ones are not. I'm willing to follow this woman down the slopes like a slave forever, just to watch the way her *wedeln* swings—you know? And now that you're so chummy with her brother, she might come here again to visit us one day soon."

I went downstairs to heat some burgundy and soak a few *Glühwein* bags from my perpetual cache, to make my short-cut version of hot spiced wine. But as I was watching it heat up, something popped into my head that I'd nearly forgotten.

I crossed the vast, cold living room to the wall of books and flipped through the heavy volume H of my frayed *Encyclopedia Britannica* until I found the entry I sought. I was surprised to learn that, indeed, there *had* been a real person named Kaspar Hauser. His story was more than strange:

HAUSER, KASPAR

A youth whose life was remarkable due to the circumstances surrounding it, of apparently inexplicable mystery. He appeared, dressed in peasant garb, in the streets of Nürnberg on May 26, 1828, with a helpless and bewildered air. . . .

Two letters were found on his person: one from a poor labourer, stating that the boy had been given into his custody in October of 1812, that according to agreement he had instructed him in reading, writing, and the Christian religion, but that up to the time fixed for relinquishing his custody he had kept him in close

> confinement [and another letter] from his mother stating that he was born on April 30, 1812, that his name was Kaspar, and that his father, formerly a cavalry officer of the 6th regiment at Nürnberg, was dead.
>
> [The youth] showed a repugnance to all nourishment except bread and water, was seemingly ignorant of all outward objects, and wrote his name as Kaspar Hauser.

The article went on to explain that Kaspar Hauser had attracted attention from the international scientific community when it was learned he'd been raised in a cage, and that neither his family nor the laborer who raised him could be found. At the time, there was apparently a huge flurry of scientific interest throughout Germany in things like "nature children" raised by wild beasts, as well as "somnambulism, animal magnetism, and similar theories of the occult and strange." Hauser was put up at the home of a local schoolmaster there in Nürnberg, but:

> On the 17th of October 1829 he was found to have received a wound in the forehead which, according to his own statement, had been inflicted on him by a man with a blackened face.

The British scientist Lord Stanhope came to see the boy and, taking an interest, had him removed to the home of a high magistrate at Ansbach where he could be studied more closely. His case was almost forgotten by the public when, on December 14, 1833, Kaspar Hauser was accosted by a stranger who wounded him deeply in his left breast. Three or four days later he died.

It seemed many books had been written about Kaspar Hauser in the ensuing hundred and fifty years, with wild surmises ranging from his having been assassinated by Lord Stanhope himself all the way to the belief that Kaspar Hauser was a legitimate heir to the throne of Germany, whose kidnapping at infancy led to upheavals in the political order. The encyclopedia hinted the entire story was "humbug," dismissing its historical facts as "in any case in complete confusion."

But *I* was confused about why Wolfgang K. Hauser—who was from Nürnberg like his namesake—would give the misleading impression that his middle name was related to the biblical Magi, with no mention of an historical figure sufficiently well known to deserve a full-page entry in the *Encyclopedia Britannica*. As for further connection with a boy who'd been raised like an animal—didn't the name Wolfgang translate as "one who runs with the wolves"?

I glanced across the room and spotted Jason there, sniffing my bags beside the door. He could tell from two packed bags that I was going away longer than just a weekend trip—so I was afraid he might flagrantly piss on them, as he'd done in the past when he guessed he would not be coming along.

"Oh, no, you don't," I said. Scooping him up, I grabbed the bubbling *Glühwein* from the stove and trotted back upstairs to Olivier's warm kitchen. "Olivier, you'd better keep an eye on my roommate here when I'm gone," I told him. "I think he's nursing a grudge about my leaving, and you know what *that* means."

"He can stay up here in my place," Olivier said, slathering a toast point with mousse and feeding it to Jason. "It will save on the heating bill downstairs. And what about your mail?" he added. "Will you have time to go stop it tomorrow yourself? Or would you prefer that I—what's the matter?"

Bloody damned hell! I *knew* I had forgotten something! I opened my mouth for the proffered mousse point and chewed it so I couldn't speak. I poured the steaming wine into mugs for us and swallowed a stiff slug of it as my brain did loop-the-loops trying to figure out this disaster fast.

"It's okay," I finally told Olivier. "I suddenly thought of something I forgot to pack, that's all. But I'll have time tomorrow to handle all that, and to stop my mail, and to run by the office, too."

Thank the merciful heavens it was actually true—the post office opened at nine o'clock, and I didn't have to be at the airport to board my flight until nine-thirty. But it might have been otherwise, in which case I would have been in deep and serious trouble, with another two weeks of mail piling up while I was cavorting around in Soviet Russia. What in God's name had I been thinking?

When we finished eating and I went back downstairs, I cursed myself colorfully for having had the presence of mind to pack an alarm clock and pajamas—while again nearly forgetting the one thing that might have gotten Sam and me both killed. What good was it to possess a photographic memory for trivia, I thought, when all the important stuff ended up getting squeezed out of your brain?

◆ ◆

I went to the office at eight-thirty the next morning, bags and passport stashed in the back of the car. This time I parked at the far side of the building and went through the mantraps for site employees. I didn't plan to get stuck outside again, with my warm coat inside, when I was about to take off for Soviet Russia. But when I got through the first set of doors and placed my badge on the monitor, there was no click to indicate that the security guard at the entrance across the building had opened my next set of doors. I was freezing. I swiveled to look up at the seeing-eye camera and yelled: "Is anybody there?" The damned guards were supposed to be on duty around the clock.

I heard a scratchy sound, then Bella's voice coming through the intercom. "I can't see you well enough to ID you against your badge," she informed me in that snotty official tone. "You have to turn to the camera: you know the rules."

"For Christ's sake, Bella, you know who I am," I said. "It's freezing out here!"

"Turn your face the proper way and keep your badge flat on the monitor so I can complete my identification—or you're not getting in," her voice insisted.

Damned bitch. I contorted myself to "assume the pose." Bella was undoubtedly one of those who'd learned that I'd been off skiing at Jackson Hole with Wolfgang Hauser last week, and was getting even by delaying me here. She sure took her time to complete the identification of somebody she saw every single day. When I heard the door click at last, I yanked it open. But as I went through, I smiled back at the camera and flipped my middle finger right into the camera's eye. I heard Bella gasp; she was babbling hysterically behind me until the glass doors shut out her voice.

There was little she could do, as I knew. Premises security officers couldn't leave a post until their shift ended. If she was on duty now, she'd be stuck at her post until ten A.M., when I'd already be in the air.

I went to my office and checked the mail messages. As I had hoped, there was one from Sam—"Great Bear Enterprises"—followed by a phone number with an Idaho area code, probably somewhere between Sun Valley and the reservation at Lapwai. I committed it to memory, deleted it from the computer, and was about to go visit the Pod to say goodbye when he popped his head in with a puzzled expression.

"Behn, I've just received a call from security asking me to send you to the director's office at once," he told me. "I'm surprised to see you here at all. Aren't you supposed to be leaving with Wolf Hauser on the ten o'clock flight? But the director says there's an infraction of some sort. Maybe you can tell me what this is all about?"

"I . . . yes, I'm on my way to the airport," I said with a sinking feeling. "I just dropped in to say goodbye to you."

Goddamned Bella—was she writing me up? I knew what a security infraction meant at a nuclear site. It could take hours just to go through the initial review. A security officer's word was law. If her accusation stuck, I might be suspended from my job. What in God's name was *wrong* with me? Why couldn't I have let it go, just walked through the mantraps and forgotten her? Why did I have to flip her the goddamned bird?

Now the Pod was escorting me to the office of the director of security and I was wondering how on earth, even if I got out of this in time to catch my plane, I would ever get to the post office first to stop my mail. I wondered if you could get an IQ transplant or some kind of hormone supplement that would reduce female aggression. I wondered if I could fall on the floor and pretend I was having a fit.

Peterson Flange, the security director, was sitting behind his desk when we came in. Since I'd never seen Peterson Flange when he *wasn't* sitting behind his desk, I'd often wondered if he had any legs.

"Officer Behn," said the security director, scowling at me, "an extremely serious charge of security infraction has been brought against you this morning."

The Pod looked at me with raised brows, clearly wondering just how I had incurred a serious infraction when I'd only been on the premises a few moments. I was wondering the same thing myself: I'd definitely flunked another intelligence test. "Behn is scheduled to leave this morning on a critical project," he informed Flange, checking his watch. "Her plane leaves in less than an hour. I hope this isn't as serious as you suggest."

"The security officer who reported the infraction is being relieved right now at her post, and will join us shortly," Flange said.

Just then Bella came storming in. "You flipped me off!" she screamed, waving one long mauve lacquered fingernail in my face the moment she saw me.

"I did exactly what *you're* doing right now," I pointed out. "Only I might have used a different finger."

"What is this woman taking about?" the Pod asked, indicating Bella. He had that dangerous don't-mess-with-me edge to his voice as he glared at the security director.

But I knew I was in trouble. Though the Pod was head of the whole nuclear site, security personnel reported directly to the FBI's National Security wing. Peterson Flange could override the Pod and stop me cold if he decided to make it an issue, and that would incense the Pod with me too, since he'd have to lecture me and fill out reports and a lot of other nonsense. I really had to think fast.

"Officer Behn," said Peterson Flange, "our security officer here has charged you with making an obscene and threatening gesture to her through the security camera in the mantraps, when she, in her line of duty, was only trying to ID you against your badge."

"I have it on film," Bella sneered at me, "so don't bother to deny it."

Her attitude really pissed me off. I turned to Peterson Flange and asked pleasantly, "What exactly did your security officer think that, by my gesture, I was threatening to do to her?"

He stared at me in astonishment, jumping to his feet. So he did have legs, after all. "Security is the most serious business of this site, Officer Behn!" he stormed. "It's hardly a subject for levity!"

I was trying to recall exactly what levity was, whether it was something heavy or something light, when the Pod interrupted our interesting chat. "What is it you did to her, Behn?" he asked me directly.

"I flipped her the bird through the security camera, sir, when she wouldn't let me in through the mantraps," I said. "She was being a pain in the ass, and I was afraid if we screwed around much longer, I might be late for my plane."

"A *pain* in the . . . !!!" Peterson Flange was hyperventilating. He collapsed back into his chair—so maybe he just had springs under there.

Pastor Dart was staring at me with his hand covering his mouth. If I didn't know better, I might have guessed he was laughing. Finally, things settled down and the Pod took command.

"My opinion," he announced in his best screw-with-me-and-I'll-fuck-you voice, "is that Officer Behn deserves a verbal warning but nothing more. Speaking privately, I feel I must mention that she's just had a death in her family, only to return from the funeral and learn she was scheduled to leave in one week for an important assignment overseas in support of Doctor Hauser, our liaison with the IAEA. She pleaded not to go on this assignment, but I—" He stopped, for Bella had thrown herself across the director's desk and was screaming in his face.

"You have to let me write her up! You can't let her go on this trip with him!"

Peterson Flange shot Dart an embarrassed look and waved his hand. "I'll look into this further myself," he conceded, as the Pod and I turned and went out the door.

"Behn, you'll explain this later to my satisfaction," said the Pod, "but you'd better be on that plane this morning with Hauser." As I was leaving, the Pod shook his head with a grin. "I really can't believe what you did. But please, just don't try it again."

◆ ◆

I had only twenty minutes to get from my office to the airport, which was a good ten minutes away not counting the detour I still had to make. I screeched up to the front of the post office and didn't bother to park. I jumped out of my car and ran up the steps. George the postal clerk was behind the counter when I came in, but there were a few people already standing in the queue.

"George, I have to stop my mail for a few weeks," I called over their heads. "I'll just fill out the form, but is it too late to stop it for today, too?"

"Oh, Miz Behn, I'm sorry," said George, weighing and stamping things for the other customers. "I got to tell you this was all my fault, but I tried to make it up. Jest wait here fer a minute, and I'll get it right quick."

He tapped a bell on the counter as I got that horrid sinking feeling again. What had gone wrong? What did I need to be made up for by George? What was he going to get for me "right quick"? I was horribly afraid I knew, but I filled out my form anyway and handed it to him.

The assistant clerk, Stuart, came out from the back and started taking slips from those who'd come to collect parcels. George disappeared in the back and returned with a package. It didn't look much like the one I'd received last week—but it *was* in a large, battered, padded mailing pouch such as Sam had described, about the size of two reams of paper.

"I gave you the wrong parcel last week," said George. "*This* was the one what matched your yellow claim slip, but I didn't check. That other one come in the very day you was here; we hadn't filled out a slip to you about it yet. This Saturday, we was going through packages down here, to send unclaimed ones back to the sender—and lucky I was here jest then, and I seen my mistake. I sure am sorry about that, Miz Behn."

He handed me the parcel, and I gritted my teeth before looking at it. I knew I had only ten minutes to get to the airport for my flight to Europe with Wolfgang Hauser. I forced myself to look at the package. The postmark was San Francisco, just as on the original yellow claim slip I'd found in the snow. And this time there could be no mistake: the handwriting scrawled across the mailing pouch was Sam's.

THE GIFT

The danger [to giver and receiver is] nowhere better sensed than in the very ancient Germanic law and languages. This explains the double meaning of the word gift *in all these languages: on the one hand a gift, on the other poison. . . .*

This theme of the fatal gift, the present or item of property that is changed into poison, is fundamental in Germanic folklore. The Rhein gold is fatal to the one who conquers it, Hagen's cup is mortal to the hero who drinks from it. A thousand stories and romances of this kind, both Germanic and Celtic, still haunt our sensibilities.

—Marcel Mauss, *The Gift*

[When Prometheus stole fire from the gods, in retaliation] Zeus told the fabled craftsman Hephaestus to create a gift: to combine dirt and water and form a beautiful maiden just like the immortal goddesses . . . then Zeus instructed Hermes to fill her full of shameless trickery and deceit. . . . Hermes named this female "Pandora": she who gives all gifts.

Epimetheus had forgotten that his brother Prometheus had warned him never to accept a gift sent by Olympian Zeus, to return it in case it should prove an evil to mankind. But Epimetheus took the gift. Only later, when the evil was his own, did he comprehend.

—Hesiod, *Works and Days*

Timeo Danaos et dona ferentes. (I fear Greeks, even those bearing gifts.)

—Virgil, *The Aeneid*

I fled the post office, jumped in my car, and headed at breakneck pace for the airport. I screeched into the parking lot, jumped out, grabbed my stuff, and tore across the icy drive. Inside, I frantically scanned the two gate areas. Down at the end near Gate-B security I saw Wolfgang, waving his arms in heated debate with a guy from the ground crew.

"Thank God," Wolfgang said with relief the moment he saw me, but I could tell he was angry. To the crewman he said quickly, "Are we too late?"

"One sec," the man said, picking up the phone to call the cockpit as, behind his back, Wolfgang glared at me. The man listened, then nodded. "The steps are still there—but you better hop to it, buddy. We got a schedule."

He ran our bags through the scanner and pulled our ticket stubs. We dashed across the tarmac and up the metal steps. The instant our seatbelts had clicked into place, the plane was moving.

"I hope you have a good explanation for this," Wolfgang said as we taxied toward the runway. "You knew there wasn't another flight to Salt Lake for three hours. For the past half-hour I've talked and talked to convince them to hold the plane; we might have missed all our connections! What did you think you were doing?"

My heart, still pounding from that run, was hammering in my ears; my breath came in short hard bursts; I could barely speak.

"I—um—I had to run an important errand en route."

"An errand?" Wolfgang said in disbelief.

He was about to add more, but just then the propjets started revving for takeoff. His lips were still moving, so I gestured that I could no longer hear him. He turned away in anger and pulled some papers from his briefcase, leafing through them as our plane raced down the runway and gained altitude. We didn't speak again during the smooth but deafening forty-minute flight to Salt Lake. That was okay with me. I had plenty of thinking to do.

There was no question the parcel inside my canvas shoulder bag now stuffed under my flight seat was the gift my grandmother Pandora had bequeathed Uncle Earnest, which then passed from him to Sam—a gift so dangerous the body count included not only a few of Sam's colleagues but maybe Pandora and Earnest as well—a gift so destructive that, given a difference of only seconds, it could have killed Sam too. Now the gift was mine.

Since I no longer trusted friends, colleagues, and most members of my own family to be anywhere near this poisonous parcel, I'd been understandably reluctant, under the eyes of a dozen postal patrons, to leave it with George behind the post office counter. Unable to locate a cache in the scant time left between post office and airport, now I was stuck with the problem of what to do with my lethal inheritance before getting to Soviet Russia, where I knew it would be thoroughly examined and probably confiscated, posing greater danger to all concerned. Especially to me.

With that in mind, my first idea had been to destroy it. I'd thought of various methods if I had to dispatch it quickly: death by water, death by fire. But by the time we reached Salt Lake, my options seemed greatly diminished. It was far from practical to flush a thousand pages down a toilet, or to ignite a ten-pound bonfire at any of the airports I'd be passing through in the next twenty-four hours. Nor was destroying it any guarantee I'd breathe more freely, since I hadn't a clue who wanted these manuscripts or why. How could I announce that the object of everyone's desire was no longer on the scene? And if I did, it might prove deadly to Sam, the only one who knew where the original, ancient documents were hidden.

The solution seemed to be to hide the parcel as I'd done with the first one, where no one would think to search for it.

I knew that the lockers at the Salt Lake airport, unlike those where characters in movies stash their loot, worked more like a parking meter, renting for just a few hours at a stretch. Even if I had time to break the package up into smaller parcels and post it back to myself, it seemed as risky a proposition as just leaving it at the post office, what with Olivier, the Pod, and God knew who all else sniffing about the place. I was fast running out of ideas.

At the Salt Lake airport, I apologized again to the still-disgruntled

Wolfgang for my tardiness. Once we'd checked the larger bags through to Vienna, I made a trip to the lavatory and opened Sam's parcel: strange squiggles in foreign characters, but recognizably in Sam's hand. I stuffed it among the working papers inside my satchel, slung the heavy duffel over my shoulder, and tried to clear my mind until our flight. Before I left the lounge, I used the phone to call a Fax 800 number and sent a brief message to Sam: *Got your gift. It is more blessed to give than to receive.* A message from the Salt Lake airport would clue Sam in that my trip with Wolfgang was under way. I added the tip that any messages faxed in my absence would be forwarded.

Wolfgang was waiting for me at the entrance to the cafeteria, as we'd agreed. He was holding two steaming paper mugs. He said, "I got us some tea to drink at the gate. It's too crowded to wait here."

Over his shoulder I saw rows of tables already packed, so bright and early, with teams of Mormon "elders"—scrubbed, rosy-cheeked young men who sipped ice water while they waited for their flights—in crisp white shirts, dark suits, and ties, their uniform backpacks crammed with proselytizing materials. Day after day, year in and year out, such young elders were scattered across the globe like dandelion fluff, on missions to spread the good word cranked out by the Church of Jesus Christ of Latter-day Saints straight from its heart here in Salt Lake City.

"They don't convert many Austrians to their faith," Wolfgang said of them as we headed down the hallway to our gate. "In so Roman Catholic a country, conversion to new faiths is rare. But in this airport there are always so many of them coming and going, these young men. To me they seem quite foreign and strange."

"Not so strange, just different," I told him, taking the lid off my tea and trying to sip it: it was scalding. "For instance, you've met my landlord Olivier. He's a Mormon. But he's more what they'd call a 'Jack' Mormon: that is, he doesn't follow all the rules. He sometimes drinks coffee or alcohol, though they're prohibited. And while he isn't exactly a womanizer, he says he hasn't remained a virgin either—"

"A virgin?" said Wolfgang askance. "Is that customary?"

"I assure you, I'm not an expert," I said, laughing. "But according to Olivier it's more or less on a volunteer basis—keeping yourself pure in body and soul, I mean. It seems that's how they're preparing themselves for salvation, at the millennium."

"The millennium?" said Wolfgang. "I don't understand."

"It's sort of the drill," I told him. "Catholics have a catechism, right? Well, as I understand it, this is theirs: Today marks the beginning of the end, time is grinding to a halt. These are the Last Days, when the world as we know it is about to cease. Only those who've been purified and confessed their faith that 'Jesus the Christ,' as they say, is the Light and the Way will be saved when he returns to earth to judge and punish, and to bring forth the New Age. They're preparing themselves with baptism, cleansing, and purging in these, the last days, so that each one will be resurrected into a new, ethereal body and given eternal life. Hence the name *Latter-day* Saints."

"The Last Days is a widespread, ancient idea," Wolfgang agreed. "Throughout history, it's been the core belief of nearly all peoples on earth, eschatology, from *eschatos*—the farthest, the uttermost, the extreme. In Catholicism the doctrine is *Parousia*: the 'presence' or second coming, when the saviour reappears and makes the final judgment." Then he added unexpectedly, "Do you believe in it?"

"You mean believe in the Apocalypse—'I come quickly' and all?" I said, always uncomfortable flirting with faith. Wasn't reality tough enough? "That promise was made two thousand years ago and a few folks I know are still holding their breath. I'm afraid it takes something a bit more tangible to get me hooked."

"Then in what do you believe?" Wolfgang asked me.

"I'm not sure," I admitted. "I grew up around the Nez Percé Indians. Their wisdom is the nearest to a religious education I've had. I guess I believe what they do, when it comes to an idea of a new age."

I elaborated as we continued down the hall. "Like most tribes, the Nez Percé believe that Native Americans are the people chosen to bring the transition about. Late in the last century there was a prophet named Wovoka, a Nevada Paiute. During an illness, he had a vision that revealed to him what would happen at the end of time—which for the Paiute would mark the dawn of this new aeon. Wovoka was shown an inspired and visionary dance that enabled the people to cross the boundary between themselves and the spirit world. The people would hold hands and dance in a circle for five days, nonstop, each year. He called it *Wanagi Wacipi*, the Ghost Dance.

"The dancers invoke the son of the Great Spirit; he'll arrive as a whirlwind and all *Wasichu*—you fork-tongued sons of Europeans, who trash everything you touch—will be totally blown away. The ancestral spirits will return to earth, along with all the bison that were slaughtered by white men. Mother Earth becomes bountiful once more and we live in harmony with nature, as it was seen in all the ancient visions."

"It's very beautiful," said Wolfgang. "And this is what you yourself actually believe, this harmonic image of paradise regained?"

"I think it's time for *somebody* to start believing in it," I assured him. "Here on the third planet we've really fouled our own nest. That's why I do the job I've chosen. Waste management is sort of my own purification ritual: helping clean things up."

Sam had once observed that no civilization in history, however powerful, had survived for long without decent plumbing. Rome kept control of half the world through its aqueducts, water and waste systems. When Gandhi wanted to liberate India from the British, the first thing he did was to make everybody get down on hands and knees and scrub the toilets. When I said as much to Wolfgang, he laughed.

We'd reached the gate. He set down his briefcase inside the waiting area, and he touched his paper cup of tea against mine as if we were having a champagne toast. "Saving the world by controlling its waste *is* very much in keeping with the mission of my employer, the IAEA," he said with a smile. "But at root, men are still everywhere the same. I fail to see how purifying oneself as the Mormons choose to, or cleaning up after others as Mohandas Gandhi did—or dancing on the grassy plains, as your American Indians recommend—will change human behavior very much or bring about global reform."

"But we were talking about belief, not behavior," I pointed out. "When things are brought down to earth, the results are never exactly as we'd planned. For example, to you the idea of the Ghost Dance seemed beautiful, but look what really became of it. The dance incorporated so many paradisical elements it was quickly embraced by the Arapaho, the Oglala, the Shoshone—and most especially the Lakota, who were the ones destroyed by it in the end."

"What do you mean, destroyed?" said Wolfgang, looking confused.

"Why—they were killed," I said in amazement. I found it hard to believe there was someone who knew nothing of the story at all. "It's one of the bitterest subjects in the history of the Native Americans, but at base it resulted from conflicting beliefs. The people were prevented from hunting; they were rounded up and put on reservations and forced to farm. Then just before the turn of the century the great famine came. Thousands were starving, so they danced and danced. The dances became wild and ecstatically hysterical; the people went into trances, trying in desperation to bring back the idyllic, Arcadian past when the earth and her children were one. They believed the magical shirts they wore would repel soldiers' bullets. White settlers were frightened by the new religion—they took these to be war dances—so the Ghost Dance was outlawed. When the Lakota found a more remote site to continue the dance, government troops rode in and cut down whole families, shot and butchered them: men, women, children, even tiny babies. You must have heard of the 1890 massacre of all the Ghost Dancers, at Wounded Knee?"

"Massacred?" said Wolfgang in horrified disbelief. "For *dancing*?"

"It does seem hard to imagine," I agreed, adding with sarcasm, "but the federal government *has* usually taken a hard line on these regional issues."

Then I kicked myself for seeming glib about something that was, as it deserved to be for Sam and most Native Americans, their own personal vision of the Holocaust and the Apocalypse rolled into one.

"That's a truly astounding story," said Wolfgang. "Then it seems that descendants of civilized white Europeans are the villains of the piece?"

"You've no idea," I concurred. "But you did ask what I believed in, so I guess I'd have to go with conventional tribal wisdom: I wish there could be something like a Ghost Dance that would bring a renewal of harmony between us and our grandmother the earth, as Native Americans call her. Of course, I wouldn't be much help myself in bringing it off: I'm not a very good dancer."

Wolfgang smiled. "How can that be," he said, "when your aunt Zoe was one of the greatest dancers of the century? And it seems you have many similar qualities. You're designed like a dancer: your bones, the movement of your muscles, the way you ski, for example—"

"But I'm afraid to ski in the deep powder," I pointed out. "I'm a control freak. You can't be a control freak and be a really good dancer too. Sam's mother—though I never met her—was full-blooded Nez Percé,"

I said. "When we were young, Sam and I did the ceremony to become 'blood brothers.' I wanted to join the tribe and be an official Nez Percé, but Sam's grandfather disapproved because I'd refused to dance. A newcomer to the tribe must become what the Hopi call *hoya*, which itself is the name of an initiation dance. It means 'ready to fly off the nest'—just like a baby bird."

"But I've seen you jump off a cliff," said Wolfgang, still smiling. "Yet you imagine you cannot release yourself enough to dance in the deep powder. Do you see what a powerful thing belief can be—that in fact it's really through your own choice you've decided you can do the one thing but not the other?"

"At least I know what I believe about Sam's grandfather," I said, avoiding Wolfgang's observation. "I think his real hope was to distance Sam, his only grandchild, from my side of the family. We *are* a bit peculiar. But from Dark Bear's point of view Sam and I may have been becoming too close for comfort. The Nez Percé are strict about bloodlines. As Sam's cousin, I would have been considered forbidden fruit: intermarriage isn't permitted even among more distant relations—"

"Marriage?" Wolfgang cut in. "But you said you were only a child at the time."

Damn. I could feel the hot blood creeping into my cheeks as I tried to duck my head. Wolfgang put his finger under my chin and tilted my face up to his.

"I have a belief of my own, my dear," he told me. "If this cousin of yours were not prematurely deceased, I believe I'd be quite alarmed by this blushing confession."

Just then—thank heaven—over the loudspeaker they called our plane.

◆ ◆

During the long flight to New York, Wolfgang filled in some of the blanks he'd skimmed over yesterday with respect to our impending mission inside the Soviet Union for the International Atomic Energy Agency. But when it came to the background of the IAEA, I already knew quite a bit.

Anyone who toiled as I did in the nuclear field was known as a "nuke" and was almost universally disdained and loathed. Note the popularity of slogans such as No Nukes Is Good Nukes or The Only

Good Nuke Is a Dead Nuke—deep wisdom of the bumper-sticker school of philosophy.

The chief mission of Wolfgang's employer was channeling nuclear materials into peacetime and positive uses. These included diagnosis and treatment of disease, elimination of the toxic pesticides of the past century through programs like insect sterilization, and the development of atomic energy, which now supplied seventeen percent of the world's electricity while significantly reducing pollution from fossil fuels and cutting down on strip mining and deforestation. All of which gave the agency the necessary clout to enforce the safeguarding of weapons-grade materials as well. And a recent nuclear fiasco might have pushed that door open a crack wider.

Six months after the 1986 accident in Ukraine, the IAEA began to require early information on all accidents that threatened to have "transboundary effects"—like that mess at Chernobyl, which the Soviets had tried to deny until radiation was being detected all across northern Europe. A year later the IAEA created a program to counsel member states about waste hazards of the sort Olivier and I tackled daily in our jobs. Then only a few months ago, the agency added far tougher provisions against illegal transport and dumping of radioactive waste. But though the Chernobyl disaster triggered many of these changes, to the public at large it had never been made clear why.

Chernobyl was a breeder reactor, the kind the Soviet and U.S. governments, among others, had long supported, but which the public instinctively and universally feared. Perhaps with good cause. As the name suggests, a breeder reactor actually produces more fuel than it consumes—like the technique of the legendary Mountain Men of the Rockies that I'd once taught Olivier for growing a "sop," the sourdough starter used in leavening bread. You take a little nuclear leaven, a fissile material like plutonium-239, and add batches of ordinary stuff like uranium-238, which is in itself unsuitable as a fuel. You wind up with a bigger load of leaven—more plutonium—that can either be recycled as nuclear fuel or be diverted into making bombs.

Because breeders are so commercially viable, the Russians had run them for decades, and so had we. Where had all that plutonium gone? Well, as for the U.S. during the Cold War, there was little mystery: It was recycled into warheads, enough for everybody in America to have a few in his garage. But when it came to the Russians' hot waste, I had the feeling we might soon find out—when we got to Vienna.

◆ ◆

The International Atomic Energy Agency sits on Wagramer Strasse beside the Donaupark, on an island enfolded by the arms of the old and new forks of the Danube. Across the glassy expanse of river lies the Prater with its famous giant Ferris wheel—the same amusement park where, seventy-five years earlier, my grandmother Pandora spent the morning riding on that carousel with Uncle Laf and Adolf Hitler.

At nine A.M. on Tuesday, Wolfgang's colleague Lars Fennish was waiting to collect us and our bags at the *Flughafen* and to drive us into town for today's meetings. After my long, exhausting journey with little sleep, I sat in the backseat, not really wanting to talk. So while the two men conversed in German about our schedules and plans for the day, I gazed out the blue-tinted windows at the dreary suburban view. But as we approached Vienna nostalgia swept me, and I was plunged into the past.

It was nearly ten years since I'd been in Vienna, but till this moment I never realized how I'd missed the city of my childhood: all those Christmases and holidays spent with Jersey amid the musical milieu at Uncle Laf's—eating sugar cookies, opening ribboned gifts, and hunting for Easter eggs. My personal image of Vienna was richer and more multilayered than the schmaltzy image the city presented to the rest of the world: as Uncle Laf put it, "the town of *Strudel und Schnitzel und Schlag*." I saw a different Vienna—one steeped in many traditions, drenched in the flavors and aromas of so many diverse cultures that I could never think of Vienna without being flooded, as now, with that sense of its magical history.

Since its beginnings, Vienna has been the cultural gateway that at once unites and separates east, west, north, and south: a point of fusion and fission. The land we today call Austria—Österreich, or the eastern kingdom—in ancient times was named Ostmark: the eastern mark, the boundary where the fresh new Western world ended and the mysterious East began. But the word *Mark* also means "marshes"—in this case, those misty marshlands along the Danube River.

Running seventeen hundred miles from the Black Forest to the

Black Sea, the Danube is the most important watercourse connecting western and eastern Europe. Its Roman name *Ister*, or the womb, is still used to describe the alluvial delta separating Romania from the USSR. But whatever the river's name in many tongues over many centuries—Donau, Don, Danuvius, Dunarea, Dunaj, Danube—the more ancient Celtic name from which they all derived was Danu: "the gift."

The gift of water recognized no boundary, freely bringing its gift of life to all peoples. And there was another gift that had been harvested for millennia along the banks of the Danube—a treasure of dark gold upon whose riches Vienna itself was built, and for which the city had been named: *Vindobona*, good wine.

Even today, on the hilltops overlooking Vienna, I could see row after row of grapevines grown from gnarled old stock, interpatched with yellow corn sheaves from last autumn's harvest—gift of the goddess Ceres. But wine was the gift of another deity, Dionysus. His gift eased pain, brought dreams, and sometimes drove people mad; he invented dance, and his most conspicuous followers were frenziedly dancing women. So to me it seemed, if any city belonged to this particular god, it was Vienna, land of "wine, women, and song."

I myself, at an early age, had a run-in with this same divinity right here in Vienna, when Jersey sang a matinee at the Wiener Staatsoper of the Richard Strauss opera *Ariadne auf Naxos*.

Abandoned on the isle of Naxos by her great love Theseus, Ariadne contemplates suicide—until Dionysus arrives on the scene to rescue her. The lyric Jersey, as Ariadne, was singing that afternoon, "*You are the captain of a sable ship that sails the dark course . . .*" Ariadne believes the figure suddenly before her is the god of death, who's come to take her to Hades. She doesn't realize it's Dionysus himself, that he's in love with her and wants to marry her, to carry her to heaven and toss her wedding tiara among the stars as a bright constellation.

But I was so young, I didn't understand the situation any better than Ariadne. I guess that's why I threw the first and only public performance of my life—one that, within my family at least, I've never managed to live down. I really believed this awful Prince of Darkness (the tenor) was about to carry off my mother to an eternal torture of hellfire and brimstone, so I ran up onstage and tried to rescue her! It literally brought down the house. With unforgettable indignity, I was forcibly removed by stagehands. Thank heavens Uncle Laf was there to rescue *me*.

Afterwards we left Jersey signing autographs in her flower-filled dressing room and, no doubt as soon as we'd gone, apologizing to her astonished public for her child's unrehearsed behavior. Laf took me off to cheer me up with *Sachertorte mit Schlagobers*, followed by a stroll on the Ring encircling Vienna. When we came to a fountain, Laf took a seat on the rim of the basin and, pulling me to him, regarded me with a wry half smile.

"Gavroche, my darling," he said, "I offer a little advice: You should never sink your pretty teeth into the leg of someone like Bacchus, as you did back there today. I mention it not only for the reason that this particular tenor may not wish to appear onstage ever again with your mother. But also because Bacchus—or, by his other name, Dionysus—is a great god. Although," my uncle reassured me, "that singer was only pretending to be him."

"I'm sorry that I bit that man who sang to Mama," I admitted. But I was intrigued. "You said he was only pretending to be the god, so does that mean there's a *real* . . . Dy-oh-ny-soos?" I tried to sound it out. When Laf smiled and nodded, I was full of questions: "Have you ever seen him? What's he like?"

"Not everyone believes he exists, Gavroche," Laf told me earnestly. "They think he is only part of a fairy tale. But to your grandmother Pandora, he was very special. I'll tell you what she believed: the god comes only to those who ask for his help. But you must truly need his help before you ask. He rides on an animal which is his closest companion—a wild black panther with emerald green eyes."

I was very excited. The image of the tenor whose calf I'd bitten only an hour ago had completely melted away. I could hardly wait for this living god to come, padding up the Karntner Strasse astride his steaming jungle beast, into the very heart of Vienna.

"If I really need his help, and if he comes to rescue me, Uncle Laf, do you think he'll take me away, like Ariadne?"

"Gavroche, I'm quite sure of it, if that's what you wish. But first there is something I must tell you. The god Dionysus loved Ariadne, and because she was a mortal he came to earth for her. But you see, when a great god comes to earth, it can cause all kinds of trouble. So you must be sure never to ask for his help unless you really, truly need it—not like the little boy who cried wolf. Do you see?"

"Okay," I agreed. "I'll try—but what kind of trouble? What if I make a mistake by accident? Will something bad happen?"

Laf took my hand in his and looked into my eyes as if he were peering across the aeons.

"Gavroche," he said. "With eyes like yours, the color of the sea, I assure you that if you ever did make such a mistake, even a god would hesitate to blame you. But your grandmother believed his time was coming quite soon now, this Dionysus. And since he is the god of moisture, of springs and fountains and rivers, if called upon he will come and free the waters. The rains will pour down as in the time of Noah, and rivers will flood their banks. . . ."

Suddenly I flashed in panic to the boy who'd cried wolf when there was no wolf. Suddenly I dreaded those powers that Laf had said my grandmother could summon and he'd hinted I might, as well.

"Do you mean the world could be flooded and wrecked if somebody just *asked* for help before they really needed it? Somebody like me?" I said.

Laf was silent a moment. When he spoke, he did not reassure me.

"I think, Gavroche, you will know the right moment to ask," he said softly. "And I'm quite certain the god himself will know precisely when to come."

I had rarely thought of this episode from my childhood in the past twenty years. But now, as we crossed onto the island and neared our destination, I glanced once more at the canvas satchel on the backseat beside me, the bag containing Pandora's manuscripts.

We pulled through security and up before the International Atomic Energy Agency. As I stepped from the car still clutching the lethal bag, in my mind echoed, just for an instant, what Uncle Laf had said so long ago in Vienna: that I'd know exactly when to call upon the god. And I wondered if the critical moment was now.

◆ ◆

Maybe I wasn't sure about the critical time, but by lunchtime I had a pretty clear idea where the critical place was located: it was back in the USSR, in a region commonly referred to as the Yellow Steppe. In the geography books it was known as Central Asia.

To hear Lars Fennish tell it—as he and his colleagues *did* tell it, locked with us in an IAEA conference room for our "brief" multiple hours of briefing—it was one of the most mysterious and volatile regions of the world.

This slice of the globe we were talking about, displayed on a four-color map on a nearby wall, included the Soviet Republics of Turkmenistan, Tajikistan, Uzbekistan, Kyrgyzstan, and Kazakhstan—a group that together possessed some of the world's highest mountains, a recent record of polycultural and religious ferment, and an ancient history of intertribal warfare and violence.

They possessed some noteworthy neighbors too. Those just across the fence included China, a member of the league of "big five" weapons-wielding nukes; also India, a nation that claimed it possessed no nuclear weapons but had only "exploded a peaceful device" a few years back; not to mention Pakistan, Afghanistan, and Iran—a trio I'm sure would have been delighted to join the club. Not the most relaxing spot to pay a visit.

The item most crucial to the future of humanity was also the International Atomic Energy Agency's chief mission: ensuring that weapons-grade materials weren't diverted toward "proliferation," or more bombs in the hands of ever more countries. It hadn't occurred to me until our briefing that this was a goal that could never be achieved by the IAEA, even with the full support of the United States and all our allies, without the added cooperation, even the steel-fisted clout, of an equally supportive and on-board Soviet Union to balance the east-west axis. That the USSR had actually shown such support over the past several decades was my first surprise. My second, a real humdinger, was that it was not the IAEA who'd initiated Wolfgang's and my mission inside the USSR—the Soviets had invited us in themselves.

It's true that in recent years, especially in the wake of a catastrophe of Chernobyl's magnitude, the Russians might have grown a bit more mellow about outside intervention from folks like the IAEA. But *glasnost* and *perestroika* aside, Soviet external relations weren't quite as cozy as their public relations might suggest. Why would the Soviets suddenly be reversing their earlier cold-war stance and coyly asking us in to inspect their lingerie?

By the time our heavy briefing was completed, I had learned the answer to that and a number of other questions having to do with a mysterious clique I'd never heard of. They were called the Group of 77 and their ambition, it seems, was to join the club that controlled all the weapons-grade material in the world.

◆ ◆

It was one P.M. when Wolfgang and I finally escaped from the conference room, graciously thanked Lars and friends for torturing us these past three hours, and headed off to have lunch. With little sleep or breakfast followed by hours of intensive briefing, I was more than ready for some solid food and a little *gemütlich* atmosphere. Luckily, Viennese coffeehouses almost never stop serving chow.

We left our luggage at IAEA headquarters to be picked up later, and got a taxi. We were dropped at the canal and headed on foot to the landmark Café Central, where Wolfgang said he thought they'd still be holding our reservation for lunch. Though I felt awkward lugging my heavy shoulder bag through the cobbled streets of Vienna, at least I'd worn comfortable shoes. And it helped to walk. Before we'd gone far, the bracing fog from the canal had cleared my head enough so I could focus my thoughts a bit.

"Fill me in a bit more on this Group of 77," I suggested to Wolfgang. "They sound like some kind of Third World hit squad trying to grab all the liquid plutonium they can get their hands on. Where did they come from?"

"Here in Vienna we've known about them for a long time," he told me. "They began as seventy-seven developing countries, all members of the UN, who drew together in the early sixties as a lobbying group to promote cooperation among Third World countries. Today, though they still call themselves the Group of 77, they have nearly doubled their membership and have learned to vote as a bloc; as a result they've grown much more powerful. Although many of them also belong to the IAEA, the agency is insulated from such special interest groups by the fact that its board members mainly come from highly industrialized nuclear nations who remain prudent about with whom to share or not share atomic expertise."

"So you think the Soviets are worried the Group of 77 may churn up the Central Asian republics?"

"Perhaps," said Wolfgang. "There's a person who could tell us a great deal more, if he chose to do so. He knows these people well. He was to join us at lunch, and I hope he's waiting there now. The timing was extremely difficult: he's old and obstinate, and he refused to speak about the matter with anyone but you. That's why I was upset to think you'd missed that flight from Idaho. A good deal of effort has gone into the coordination of this trip on everyone's part, you know."

"It's starting to look that way," I agreed. I hadn't a clue what was going on. As we went through the streets, the fog around us had thickened. Though Wolfgang was speaking, his voice seemed distant, and I only caught the last words.

". . . from Paris last night, just when you and I ourselves were traveling here. He thought it was essential to see you in person."

"Who came from Paris last night?" I asked.

"We're going to meet your grandfather," Wolfgang said.

"That's impossible. Hieronymus Behn has been dead for thirty years," I said.

"I don't mean the man you think is your grandfather," he said. "I mean the man who flew from Paris last night to meet you, the man who sired your father Augustus upon your grandmother Pandora—perhaps the only man she ever deeply loved."

Maybe it was the fog, maybe my lack of sleep and food, but I suddenly felt dizzy, as if I'd just stepped off a carousel and things were still whirling. Wolfgang put his hand beneath my arm as if to steady me, but his voice went on.

"I wasn't sure how much to say earlier, but this was the real reason I came to Idaho to find you," he told me. "As I explained that first day on the mountain, the documents you are heir to *must not* fall into the wrong hands. The man we're about to meet knows much of the mystery behind them. But first, I thought I must prepare you, for you might be—well, there's something about him that's hard to describe, but I'll try. He seems like an ancient figure possessed of magical powers, like a magus of sorts. But perhaps you already suspect who it is, this grandfather of yours. His name is Dacian Bassarides."

Magus is derived from Maja, *the mirror wherein Brahm, according to Indian mythology, from all eternity beholds himself and all his power and wonders. Hence also our terms magia, magic, image, imagination, all implying the fixing in a form . . . of the potencies of the primeval, structureless, living matter. The Magus, therefore, is one that makes the operations of the Eternal Life his study.*

—Charles William Heckethorn, *The Secret Societies*

He it is who may owe his bond to the world of images and appearances—be sensually, voluptuously, sinfully bound to them, yet be aware at the same time that he belongs no less to the world of the idea and the spirit, as the magician who makes the appearance transparent that the idea and spirit may shine through.

—Thomas Mann

Man is superior to the stars if he lives in the power of superior wisdom. Such a person, being master over heaven and earth by means of will, is a magus. And magic is not sorcery, but supreme wisdom.

—Paracelsus

In his own magic circle wanders the wonderful man, and draws us with him to wonder and take part in it.

—Johann Wolfgang Goethe

Wolfgang wanted to "prepare me" to meet Dacian Bassarides. But how could anything have prepared me for the events of my past two weeks? And now this—the revelation that my insufferable, arrogant father might actually be the spawn of my grandmother's illicit lover rather than the legitimate son of Hieronymus Behn.

As we headed through the maze of cobbled streets to the Café Central, Wolfgang seemed to understand I needed a little peace and quiet. I was fed up with all these surprises about my awful family. And it hardly helped that every new fact raised a new question. For instance, if Dacian Bassarides really was my grandfather and Hieronymus Behn knew it, why would Hieronymus have raised my father Augustus as the apple of his eye, preferring him not only to his stepson, Laf, but to his own legitimate children, Zoe and Earnest, too?

In the larger picture, Dacian Bassarides had played a pivotal role in each and every scene. For instance, if Pandora's estate was parceled out—as Sam and I surmised—among members of the Behn family without anyone knowing who got what, then as executor of that estate, Dacian might well be the only person alive who could say how these manuscripts were connected, and to whom.

I recalled that when Uncle Laf gave me his version of the family saga, he'd described Dacian as his own early violin teacher, Pandora's handsome young cousin who'd let them ride the carousel at the Prater and who'd later accompanied Pandora, with her friend "Lucky" and the children, to the Hofburg to view the spear of Charlemagne and the sword of Attila the Hun.

That was the basic story without filling in any blanks. One blank, however, might be a connection Laf had failed to make. Based on his eyewitness account, during that Prater merry-go-round ride Dacian seemed on as intimate terms with Lucky as Pandora herself was. Then later at the museum, it was his unobtrusive but well-timed question about "these other objects you seek" that elicited what Hitler thought the sacred items were—platters and tools and such—and revealed how and where he'd conducted his search for them.

But if Pandora's cousin really was at the center of the plot, as Sam had hinted and as I myself was starting to believe, just how had this starring role fallen to Dacian Bassarides?

◆ ◆

The Café Central had recently been redone. Some construction at the back was still under way, as a bit of dust and intermittent sawing attested. But since my last visit the old dark paneling, flocked wallpaper, and dingy wall sconces had been banished, and the place was now a bright open space.

As we crossed the room, the fog outside lifted; pale light poured through the big windows and glistened on the glass-and-brass display case filled with rich Viennese pastries. At small marble tables scattered across the floor, people sat on the stiff chairs reading papers attached to polished wooden sticks, as crisp as if they'd been freshly laundered and pressed. The painted plaster figure of a middle-aged Viennese sat alone at his usual table near the door, a plaster cup of coffee on the table before him.

Wolfgang and I crossed to the raised dining area in back, where tables in open booths were each graced with a crisp white cloth, sparkling silver, and a pitcher filled with freshly cut flowers. The maître d' led us to ours, removed the Reserved sign, and took our orders for wine and bottled water. When the drinks had arrived, Wolfgang said, "I hoped he'd be here already."

The wine made me feel more relaxed, but Wolfgang's mind was elsewhere. He glanced around the open space of the room, then sat back, folding and refolding his napkin with some impatience.

"I'm sorry," he said. "Since we've come late, it's possible that he *is* here already. Let me try to find out. Meanwhile why don't you order some appetizer or fish for us to begin with? I'll send the waiter to you." Standing, he looked around once more, then left me alone at the table.

I sipped some more wine while I studied the menu. I'm not sure how much time passed, but just as I was wondering whether I ought to go on my own to find the waiter, a shadow fell across the table. Glancing up, I saw a tall figure bundled in a green loden greatcoat. His broad-brimmed hat shadowed his face against the light pouring from the windows behind, so I couldn't make out his features. His leather satchel, much like my own, was slung casually across one shoulder. He set the bag down in the far side of the booth that Wolfgang had recently vacated.

"May I join you?" he asked in a soft voice. Without waiting for a nod from me he'd unbuttoned the coat and was hanging it on a nearby hook. I glanced around nervously to see what was keeping Wolfgang. The soft voice added: "I saw our friend Herr Hauser back in the kitchen just now. I've taken the liberty of asking him to leave us."

I turned to object, but he'd slid into the booth opposite and removed his hat. For the first time I got a clear look at him. I was absolutely riveted.

His face was like nothing I'd ever seen. Though weathered like ancient stone, it seemed a timeless mask of sculpted beauty and enormous power. His long hair, nearly black but mixed with strands of silver, was pulled back to reveal his strong jawline and high cheekbones, then tumbled in ropes of braid about his shoulders.

He wore a quilted leather vest and a shirt with loose white sleeves, open at the throat to reveal a string of intricately carved beads in various colored stones. The vest was embroidered with bird and animal motifs in rich and vibrant colors: saffron, carmine, plum, cerulean, scarlet, pumpkin, viridian, colors from a primal forest.

His ancient eyes, beneath brooding brows, were of a depth and hue that might be equaled only in the rarest of gemstones, pools of mingled color, midnight purple and emerald green and ebony, with a dark flame burning in their depths. Of all the descriptions I'd heard of him, I thought Wolfgang's seemed the best.

"The way you're looking at me makes me quite self-conscious, my dear," he said.

Before I could reply, he'd reached over and casually plucked the menu from my hands, commandeering my wineglass too. "I've taken another liberty," he told me in that soft, exotically accented voice. "I've brought some Côtes du Rhône from my vineyards at Avignon. I put them in the kitchen earlier to—how you would say?—help them breathe. Before our friend Wolfgang agreed to leave, he insisted you hadn't eaten all day and must have some food to go with it. You're fond of *Tafelspitz*, I hope?"

The waiter unobtrusively set the new bottle on the table with fresh wineglasses, poured, and quickly vanished as Dacian went on.

"Since you're my only heir, my vineyard and its wines will one day belong to you, so I'm pleased for you to make their acquaintance—as I'm delighted to make yours. Shall I introduce myself formally? I am your grandsire, Dacian Bassarides. And I regard so lovely a granddaughter as a better gift than all the wines in the Vaucluse."

Holy shit, I thought as we clinked glasses—that's all I need, to be heir to one more bequest. If all my inheritances turned out like the *last* one, I wouldn't be around long enough to collect on anything!

"I'm delighted to meet you, too," I told Dacian Bassarides—and I meant it. "But I want to explain that I learned of our relationship only moments ago, so I hope you can appreciate that I'm still in shock. My grandmother Pandora died before I was born. She was rarely discussed by my family, so I know as little of her as I do of you. But if you're truly my grandfather as you say, I have to wonder why it's been hidden from me all these years. Do others know it?"

"Of course, it must be a shock for you," Dacian said with a sweep of his long, graceful fingers, the fingers of a violinist, I recalled. "I'll explain everything—perhaps even a few things you'd rather not learn—though I myself always prefer even the rawest of facts to the prettiest of fiction. But you must tell me what you've already heard, before I can provide the rest."

"I'm afraid I know very little," I told him. "All I've heard about that side of the family is that you and Pandora were cousins; that she was a music student in Vienna who worked as a companion or tutor in the Behn household; and that you taught my uncle Lafcadio to play the violin. He says you were young, but a great master."

"Quite a compliment—but, here, our meal arrives," he said. "As we eat, I can explain everything. It's not so much a mystery as one might suppose."

I watched as the waiter set down an array of covered platters. When he lifted the lid of my *Tafelspitz*—that traditional Austrian dish of hot boiled beef accompanied on its divided plate by cold applesauce and horseradish, hot vinegary potatoes, creamed spinach, fresh green salad with white beans—it looked and smelled fabulous. But Dacian's lunch was unfamiliar. I asked him what it was.

"It's the best way to find out about people: to learn how they eat," he told me. "For example, in this tureen we find a Hungarian cold soup of sour cherries. Then the dish you asked me about is *ćevapčići*, a kind of kebab made from ground beef, lamb, garlic, onion, and *paprikesh*; it's smoked over charcoals of smoldering grapevine so it has a taste of the vineyard. In Dalmatia they claim the Serbs invented it, but it's older than that. This dish was really invented by the Dacians—my namesakes—an ancient tribe that once inhabited Macedonia, now part of Yugoslavia. They were known even as far east as the Caspian, where they called themselves *Daoi*: the wolves. We wolves, it's how you recognize us—we very much like to eat meat." And he stabbed one of the patties with his fork and closed down on it with those magnificent white teeth.

When the first bite of *Tafelspitz* melted in my mouth, I realized how truly hungry I was. Dacian plucked choice items from various dishes and passed them across to me. I wanted to wolf down everything I saw, but I forced myself back to the topic.

"So you come from the Balkans, not Austria?" I asked.

"Well, I'm named for the Dacians, but my people are really of Romani descent. And who can say where the Rom originally come from?" he said with a shrug.

"The Romani?" I said. "Are they named for Rome? Or did you mean Rumania?"

"Romani is the name of our language, rooted in Sanskrit, and also what we sometimes call ourselves—although we've been called many names by others over the years: *Bohémes, Cingari, Tsiganes, Gitanos, Flamencos, Tartares, Zigeuner*. . . ."

When I still looked perplexed, he explained, "Most would call us by the common name Gypsies, because it was once believed our origins were in Egypt, though there are plenty of other opinions: India, Persia, Central Asia, Outer Mongolia, the South Pole—even places of magical belief that have never existed at all. There are those who think we came from outer space. And those who think we should be shot back there as soon as possible!"

"Then you and Pandora are Gypsies?"

I admit I was confused. One hour ago I had an Irish mother and a father I'd thought part Austrian, part Dutch. Now all at once I was illegitimately descended from a pair of Gypsy cousins who'd abandoned my father at birth. But befuddled as I might be about *my* ancestry, I had little reason to doubt Dacian Bassarides's description of his own: he looked every bit as wild as everyone described.

"The details of our family are never to be shared with the *Gadje*—

the others, the outsiders," Dacian cautioned me seriously. "This is why I have sent our friend Hauser away. But to your question: yes, we were Rom. Though Pandora grew up and lived partly among the *Gadje*, in her heart and blood she always was one of *us*. I knew her from childhood. She sang so wonderfully that she already had the marks of a great *diva*. Perhaps you know that in Sanskrit this term describes an angel, while in Persian it means a devil? Pandora was a little of each.

"As for the origin of the Rom, our sagas say we came to earth aeons ago from an aboriginal home which can still be found in the night sky: the constellation Orion, the mighty hunter. Or more precisely, the three stars forming a belt at its center—the *omphalos*, the navel or umbilical cord of Orion—called the Three Kings because they shine like the star the Magi followed to Bethlehem. In Egypt, Orion was equated with the god Osiris, in India with Varuna, in Greece with Ouranos, and in Norse countries with the Spindle of Time. In all cultures he is known as the messenger, the chief guide for each transition into a new age."

I wasn't about to get sidetracked just when the plot was thickening. And there was more than stardust clouding Dacian's story. How could he and Pandora have been Gypsies when, by all the accounts I'd heard, the Nazis considered Gypsies lower on the evolutionary totem pole than Catholics, Communists, homosexuals, or Jews?

"If you and Pandora were Gypsies," I said, "how could she have lived as she did, and *where* she did, running around with the kinds of people she did, both before and during the Second World War?"

Dacian was regarding me with an odd half smile. "And how did she live? I thought you knew almost nothing about her."

"No," I agreed. "But what I meant was, how could Pandora and Laf have stayed in that luxurious apartment in Vienna all during the war—I've been there myself, so I know what it's like—and lived such a lavish lifestyle? How could she have mingled with Nazis and such? I don't mean just being able to pass herself off as an upper-class Viennese rather than a Gypsy. I mean, how could she have permitted herself to stay here in Vienna when her own people were being"—I dropped to sotto voce—"I mean, *how could she have stayed on here as Hitler's favorite opera star?*"

Dacian was looking at our wineglasses as if he'd just noticed they were empty; he replenished them himself. Knowing the punctiliousness of Viennese waiters in such matters, I could only assume he'd instructed them all to stay away.

"Is that what you've been told?" he asked, as if to himself. "How interesting. I should like to know where you heard it, for it appears this tale must have been the collaboration of a number of creative minds." He looked at me and added: "*Very* creative. Completely appropriate for a descendant, such as yourself, of a family line originating in the constellation Orion."

"Are you saying none of it is true?"

"I am saying that every half truth is also a half lie," he said carefully. "Never confuse people's beliefs with reality. The only truth worth exploring is one that leads us closer to the center."

"The center of what?" I asked.

"Of the circle of truth itself," Dacian replied.

"So are you going to help rid me of those half truths and beliefs I've collected, and shed a little light on my own reality?"

"Yes—though it's hard to answer questions properly unless they are put properly."

Unexpectedly, he reached out and put his hands over mine, which rested at either side of my plate. I felt electricity moving into my flesh, my bones, suffusing me with warmth. But before I could speak, he motioned for the waiter, rattling off something in German I couldn't make out.

"I've ordered us a sweet," he said, "something good, lots of chocolate. It's named for a famous Gypsy violinist of the last century, Rigo Jancsi, who broke the heart of every noblewoman in Vienna—and not only by his playing of Paganini!" He laughed and shook his head, but as he withdrew his hands from mine, he seemed to be observing me closely.

Without a word, he took something from his inside vest pocket and gave it to me. In my open hand lay a small gold locket, oval in shape, etched with an animal-bird design similar to the one on his vest. There was a hinge at either side; when I clicked the pin one side of the locket popped open. Inside was a picture, quite old—a shimmering hand-tinted photo on metal like the platinum-coated tintypes from around the turn of the century. But unlike many photos of that era, whose subjects had the glassy expression of sockeye salmon, this picture with its lifelike tints had the freshness of a recent snapshot.

The face in the oval was clearly the young Dacian Bassarides. I regarded with a kind of awe that magnetism everyone had described; in this time capsule from his youth, his elemental primitivity leapt out like a force of nature. His loose black hair was swept back and his shirt was open to reveal his bare chest and powerful neck. His handsome face with its straight, slender nose, intense dark eyes, and slightly parted lips exuded a wildly breathless essence that called to mind Laf's steaming jungle panther—companion to the god.

But when I pressed the pin again and the other gate opened, I nearly dropped the locket. It was like looking into a mirror at my own reflection!

The face within the locket had the same pale-tinged "Irish" coloring as mine, my unruly mass of dark hair and pale green eyes. But also, each detail—even to the identical cleft in the chin—was a flawless match. Although the clothes were of another place and time, I thought this was how one might feel walking down the street and unexpectedly meeting his own twin.

Dacian Bassarides still watched me closely. At last he spoke.

"You are exactly like her," he said simply. "Wolfgang Hauser had warned me, but still I wasn't prepared. I watched you from the back of the restaurant for some time before I could bring myself to come to this table and meet you. It's hard to say what it's like for me—like vertigo, like falling through a tunnel in time. . . ." He drifted into silence.

"You must have loved her very much."

As I said it, I was only just realizing myself, with full and painful impact, exactly what issues that raised about him and the role he'd played regarding my family. But brutal though it might be, it couldn't be helped. I had to ask.

"If you and my grandmother grew up together and loved one another, if she was carrying your child, why did she marry Hieronymus Behn? I thought she despised him. And then, why would she run off with Lafcadio after the child was born, abandoning him too?"

"As I said earlier, it's hard to answer questions unless they're put properly," he told me with a wry smile. "You mustn't believe whatever you hear, and least of all from me—after all, I am Rom! But I'll explain what I can, for I believe you've every right to know. Indeed, you *must* know everything, if you expect to protect those papers you have in your bag there under the table—"

Somehow a swallow of wine seemed to have been sucked down my windpipe. I was choking and reaching for the water as I wondered if he had X-ray vision or, perhaps, could read my mind.

"Wolfgang Hauser told me of them when we passed in the kitchen," he said, reading my mind. "When he saw your bag examined by two customs authorities and by security at the IAEA, he found it strange that you should be carrying so much paper only for your work. He made a reasonable assumption. But we will come to that. To answer your question, Pandora was indeed my lover and the mother of my son and only child, but she was not my cousin at all. She was my wife. Those pictures in your hand were taken on our wedding day."

"You were married to Pandora?" I said, dumbfounded. "But when?"

"As you see, in that photo she might have been eighteen or twenty years of age," he said. "But in fact she was thirteen, and I sixteen, the day we were married. It was different then, you know: girls of tender years were already women, and early marriages are anyway quite customary among the Rom. At the age of thirteen Pandora was a woman, I assure you. Then when I was twenty and she seventeen, she left, and our son Augustus was born inside the house of Hieronymus Behn."

My brain was swarming with a million questions, but just then the waiter arrived with the chocolate dessert named for the Gypsy violinist, a bowl of *Schlagobers*, and a bottle of *grappa*, that heady Italian liqueur made from the fermented seeds of grape, which is twice as strong as cognac. When the waiter left, I waved my hand to indicate I didn't want anything further to drink—I was almost hyperventilating as it was. Dacian filled my glass anyway, then he picked up his own glass and touched it to mine.

"Take it. You may find that you need it before I've finished," he said.

"You haven't *finished*?" I hissed under my breath, though when I glanced around, I saw that we were the only diners still left in this part of the restaurant and the waiters, with towels folded over their arms, were at a discreet distance across the room chatting among themselves.

After all that business of beliefs clashing with reality, I suddenly knew what *I* believed: Of everything I'd thought I didn't want to hear up until now, this was likely to be the worst. I prayed reality would prove me wrong, but I didn't have much faith. I closed my eyes for a moment. When I opened them, Dacian Bassarides was seated beside me, blocking my exit from the booth. He rested one hand on my shoulder, and again I felt the energy of the man. He was so close I could inhale his perfumed warmth, like the scent of sage and bonfires, like the moist aroma of deep pine forests where the divine panther moved.

"Ariel, I know what I've said has shocked and perhaps even frightened you, but that was only part of what I came here from France to reveal," he said gravely. He took the locket from my hand, closed it carefully, and replaced it in his vest pocket. "It's imperative that you hear everything I have to say, however unpleasant. To close one's eyes and ears at this moment is a dangerous decision for any of us to take—most especially for you."

"I can't 'take' any decisions at all," I said bitterly. "I don't think I can 'take' any more of anything."

"Oh yes, you can," he said. "You are Pandora's only grandchild, and mine too. Whether you know it or not, you were born, as one might say, to have a rendezvous with destiny; your journey toward it has already begun. But my people make a distinction between destiny and fate. We don't think we are born with a 'fate' that impels us to act out some script composed by a higher hand, but rather that each of us has a destiny, a preexisting pattern which, in our hearts, we wish one day to fulfill. However, in order to pour yourself into this new form—this higher vessel, as it were—you must *recognize* it is your destiny and seek it accordingly—just as a swan that's been raised among chickens must realize his own destiny is in learning to swim and to fly, or he will remain nothing but an earthbound fowl, scratching in the dust all his days."

Somehow, this comparison made me improbably angry. How could he even suggest that anything in our "swanlike" blood might call for a "higher vessel"? I helped myself to a healthy slug of the *grappa* and turned to him.

"Look," I said in frustration, "maybe it was my 'destiny' to be Pandora's only granddaughter, maybe it was my 'destiny' to look so much like her. And maybe it's true that I was born just after she died. But that doesn't make me some kind of reincarnation or clone of her—or mean that *her* destiny is in any way related to mine. There's no 'form' or 'pattern' or anything inside of me that would cause me to do even *one* of the terrible, cruel things it seems she did to you, and to everybody else she came into contact with."

Dacian looked at me with widened eyes for a moment. Then he burst into a kind of cold laughter.

"This is what I meant by not believing all you hear, and again the result of not putting questions properly," he said. When I said nothing, he added, "You must understand that we were none of us pawns. Not Hieronymus Behn nor I. Not Pandora, Lafcadio, Earnest, or Zoe. Like you, we had choices. But a choice is a decision, and decisions lead to events. Once an event takes place it's too late to turn back the clock and change it. But it is never too late to examine the lessons of history."

"I've avoided examining my family's history all my life," I told him. "If I've been successful at it for so long, why start now?"

"Perhaps because ignorance is not success," Dacian said.

Wasn't that *my* song he was playing? I spread my hands, showing my willingness to proceed.

"Just before we married," Dacian began, "Pandora and I learned to our horror that something of great value belonging to her family, something of vast importance, had by deceit come into the possession of a man named Hieronymus Behn. Pandora was obsessed with getting it back, a mission we both undertook knowing the possible penalties should we fail. It took time to find him, and when at last we did, we knew our task would require us to gain access to his household, to win the family's trust. I befriended Lafcadio at his school in Salzburg—and Pandora met Hermione and the children, finally moving into the Behn house itself in Vienna. But no one could know that just as our efforts were about to bear fruit, Hermione would fall gravely ill. When the brain sickness took her so swiftly and she died, Hieronymus raped Pandora that very night and forced her into marriage without delay. The man was the darkest scoundrel. But when she married him, she was already married to me. For some time, I couldn't accept that she'd subjected us all to such a fate—for what could be worse than having your pregnant wife despoiled by another man, who then casts her out ignominiously while kidnapping the child—"

"Kidnapping?" I said in shock. "What on earth do you mean?"

"I mean your father was not abandoned by anyone," he told me clearly. "When Hieronymus Behn discovered Pandora had indeed succeeded in recovering what she was seeking, he threw her into the streets, then shut up the house and absconded with our child. Augustus was held hostage for a ransom we would never pay, Pandora and I, even if we had the means to do so."

"Ransom!" I said. But then of course I got the picture. Neither of us glanced at the bag sitting between us under the table. My mind was so frayed that when he spoke, it took me a minute to process what he said.

"Perhaps you don't know exactly what the contents of your satchel are, my dear," he said, "but you must have a very clear idea of their value and their danger. Had you not, you'd have sold them, or burned them, or left them behind when you came. You would never have made so great a commitment as to bring them with you halfway around the world. So when Wolfgang Hauser said he believed they were in your possession and I made the decision to tell you everything about our family—including our Romani roots—I quickly sent him away. You see, the information about those papers in your possession meant something to me that was fortunately lost on him. I asked him to meet us a short distance from here, a quarter hour from now."

He paused and looked me directly in the eye. I froze when I heard his next words:

"You could only just have learned the importance of these documents, and from someone who had far more than a superficial grasp of their true meaning. Since it wasn't myself, and all the others have taken their secret to the grave, I presume you've learned it from the person who last held them in his possession. This strongly suggests that your cousin Samuel is alive—and that you've spoken with him quite recently."

THE AXIS

The branches and fruit of the . . . World Tree appear in the art and myth of Greece, but its roots are in Asia. . . . The World Tree is a symbol which complements, or on occasion overlaps with, that of the Central Mountain, both forms being only more elaborate forms of the Cosmic Axis or Pillar of the World.

—E.A.S. Butterworth, *The Tree at the Navel of the Earth*

In a universe where planets revolve around suns, and moons turn about planets, where force alone forever masters weakness, compelling it to be an obedient slave or else crushing it, there can be no special laws for man. For him, too, the eternal principles of this ultimate wisdom hold sway. He can try to comprehend them; but escape them, never. —Adolf Hitler, *Mein Kampf*

I was a mess. A real mess. I felt truly ill. How could I have been so naive as to imagine that an innocent girl nuke like me, with no training in espionage, could save these dangerous manuscripts and protect Sam too, when the first two people who saw me had figured out at once what I was toting in my bag?

I tried to mask my churning emotions as the waiter arrived to reckon our bill. God knows how I managed to crawl from the booth, yank my coat on, and navigate the length of the restaurant. Dacian Bassarides followed without a word. Out in the middle of the Herrengasse, I hung on to my lethal shoulder bag in a white-knuckled grip.

"My dear, your fears are almost palpable," Dacian said. "But fear is a necessary and healthy thing. It sharpens our awareness, it isn't something to be suppressed—"

"You don't understand," I interrupted with urgency. "If you and Wolfgang guessed that I have these papers, maybe others have figured it out, too. Sam's in terrible danger—people have tried to kill him. But I don't even know what these manuscripts *are*, much less how to protect them. I don't know who to trust!"

"The answer is plain," Dacian said. He calmly removed my hand from my bag and tucked it beneath his arm. "You must trust the one person who *does* know what they are and who can advise you, for the moment anyway, what to do with them—which in both cases happens to be me. Furthermore, since our friend Herr Hauser believes you have these papers, it would be a mistake to arouse his suspicions by pretending you *haven't*. You must take him into your confidence at least so far as what he's already guessed, a gesture which may prove expedient in other ways as well. But he's waiting for us not far from here, so let's join him. I have something I want to show you both."

I tried to calm down as Dacian, still cradling my hand, led me through narrow streets to where the Graben dovetailed into the Kärntner Strasse, another avenue of fashionable shops, and the Stephansplatz fanned out to display the gaudy jewel at its center: Saint

Stephan's, the gold-tiled, multispired cathedral that forms the heart of the circle of Vienna.

Wolfgang was pacing at the corner where the two streets met. He glanced at his wristwatch, then scanned the crowds. I was reminded of the first time I'd seen him, in the same elegant camel overcoat and silk scarf and leather gloves, at the Technical Science annex of the nuclear site back in Idaho—good lord, was it only one week ago? It seemed a million years.

"Do you know the meaning of the word 'aeon'?—or more properly *aion* in Greek," Dacian asked me. "It has to do with why I've brought you both here to this corner."

"It's a long span of time," I said. "Longer than a millennium."

Wolfgang caught sight of us and cut through the swirling throngs with an expression of relief. But after one look at me his eyes clouded with concern.

"I'm sorry I agreed to leave you," he told me. "You were already exhausted before." Then he snapped at Dacian, "She looks awful—what have you said to her?"

"Gee, thanks a lot," I commented with a wry smile. But I knew if my stress was so visible at first glance, I needed to pull myself together fast.

"Come now," Dacian reassured Wolfgang. "Ariel has merely survived the ordeal of an hour or so spent with a member of her own family. Not a pleasant chore perhaps, but a task she's managed splendidly."

"We gorged on food and philosophy," I told Wolfgang. "Now we've moved on to the millennium—Dacian was about to explain what the Greek word *aion* means."

Wolfgang glanced at Dacian in surprise. "But it's what Ariel and I were speaking of only yesterday in Utah," he said. "The coming of this new century will also be the start of a new 'age' or aeon—a major two-thousand-year cycle."

"That's the common understanding," said Dacian. "A vast span, a recurring cycle, from *aevum*, a full circle or axis. But for the ancient Greeks the word *aion* meant something more: moisture, the cycle of life itself that begins and ends in water. They imagined a river of living waters surrounding land like a serpent swallowing its tail. Earth's *aion* consisted of rivers, springs, wells, underground waters that erupted from the depths and radiated outward to create and feed all forms of life. The Egyptians believed we were born from the tears of the gods, and that the zodiac itself was a circling river whose axis was the small bear's tail. Another reason why the bears are called ladles or dippers—which leads to what I want to show you, just near here."

Back at the corner where Wolfgang had been pacing, mounted on the wall of an unobtrusive grey building, Dacian pointed out a small cylindrical glass case. Within it was a gnarled object about three feet long, with a skin of black lumps as if diseased with a fungal growth. It seemed to be writhing—alive. Even separated by the glass, I got a chill of repulsion looking at it.

"What is this?" I asked Dacian.

It was Wolfgang who answered. "It's very famous—it's the *Stock-im-Eisen*. *Stock* means stump, and *Eisen* is iron. This is a five-hundred-year-old tree trunk, studded with old-fashioned square-headed carpentry nails so thickly you can't see any wood. People say it was the tradition of some blacksmith guild. The Naglergasse, or Nailmakers' Alley, is not far from here. This stump was found only recently, when the *U-bahn* was dug. They also found an early chapel which you can see, perfectly restored, in the subway. No one has ever understood why they were buried so deeply, centuries ago—or by whom."

"*Almost* no one," said Dacian with a mysterious smile. "But it's late, and I've another nail to show you at the Hofburg treasury. I must speak a bit of trees and nails as we go." We set off on foot down the broad Kärntner Strasse with tourists swirling around us in the late afternoon light.

"In many cultures," Dacian began, "the nail was thought to possess a sacred *binding* property, bringing together contrasting realms like fire and water, spirit and matter. Since the tree was often regarded in ancient texts as the World Axis, channeling energy from heaven to earth, the nail was called the hinge or pivot of God, anchoring that energy. Indeed, in Hebrew, God's name itself has a nail in it: the four-letter word *Yahweh* is spelled *Yod-He-Vau-He*, where the letter *Vau* means 'nail.' And in German, *Stock* not only means stump or trunk, it also means stick, rod, grapevine—and beehive. And bees are associated with hollow trees. It's of the greatest importance, how all these things are connected," he said.

I didn't have a bee in my bonnet—at least, not yet—though my head *was* buzzing. The zodiac might be a zoo of archetypal beasts, but this new aeon we were talking about was to be symbolized by a man,

Aquarius the water-bearer, pouring a stream of water into a fish's mouth. Though this might fit well with dippers, Dacian said there was something that connected it *all*—the rotating sky, the trees and nails, the flowing waters, the bears—and perhaps even Orion the mighty hunter. Then I thought I saw it.

"The goddess Diana?" I said.

Dacian shot me a surprised glance. "Precisely," he said approvingly. "But retrace the path you've followed. The journey is often as important as the conclusion."

"*What* conclusion?" Wolfgang asked, turning to me. "Forgive me if I fail to see what a Roman goddess has to do with trees or nails."

"Diana, or Artemis in Greek, was equated with the Dippers," I said. "Ursa Major and Minor, the bears revolving around the celestial pole—that is, the axis. She also drove the chariot of the moon, just as her brother Apollo drove that of the sun. She was a virgin huntress who followed the chase by night with her own pack of dogs. In early religions, the act of hunting and devouring an animal forged a unity with that animal. So Artemis was patron of all totem beasts. Today, she still rules the heavens, as her name suggests—*arktos* is bear; *themis* is law."

"More than law—*themis* is justice," Dacian said. "It's an important distinction. The oracle at Delphi was *themistos*—one who not only knew right but could prophesy, could translate the higher justice of the gods."

"So that explains her connection with bees—" I started to add.

"Please," Wolfgang cut in, frustrated. "I've no idea what you mean."

"Bees were prophetesses," I said. "Deborah in the Old Testament, and Melissa, a name for the Delphic oracle and for Artemis too—both names meant 'bee.' Bees were also identified with the virgin because it was believed they created themselves through parthenogenesis, without copulation."

"Exactly," said Dacian. "The virgin is important to the aeon just ending now. Two thousand years ago, when the age began, the virgin goddess was worshiped throughout the world. The Romans called her Diana of the Ephesians: her Greek temple at Ephesus, the Artemision, was one of the seven wonders of the world. The famous statue of the goddess, whose worship Saint Paul so hotly opposed as idolatry, still stands there today, its robes covered with carvings of animals and birds, and also with her prophetic bees. It's this same goddess in a new incarnation, along with her son, the 'fisher of men's souls,' who forms the axis of the aeon now ending: the age of Pisces, the fish. The constellation opposite Pisces on the circle of the zodiac is Virgo the virgin."

"Jesus and the Virgin Mary are a duo because those constellations are across from each other in the zodiac?" I said, intrigued as I always was when before my eyes a code was broken that I hadn't seen myself. I could tell Wolfgang was interested too.

"The twelve constellations of the zodiac are, in reality, of greatly varying sizes," Dacian pointed out. "Astrologers simply divide the sky into twelve equal pieces like a torte, and appoint one constellation within each slice as its 'ruler.' Because of the earth's tilt on its axis, every two-thousand-year aeon, during the spring and fall equinoxes—the two days each year when day and night are equal in length—the sunrise seems to shift from one of these wedges in the sky to another, moving backwards through the signs of the zodiac. That is, at each new age, the sun appears in a sign *preceding* the one that would follow, if the sun were moving through its normal course in the span of an ordinary year. Which is why the *succession* of aeons is called the *Precession* of the Equinoxes.

"Throughout the past two-thousand-year cycle, during the equinoxes, we've seen the sun rise against the backdrop of the dual constellations jointly ruling this age: Pisces at the spring equinox, and Virgo in autumn. In this sense, the character of the age is defined by the character of its rulers. One might call it celestial mythology.

"It seems of great interest that the legends of all peoples have so closely matched the archetypal images associated with each new aeon. The age of Gemini, for example, was an historical period noted for legends of twins: Remus and Romulus, Castor and Pollux. The next age of Taurus, the bull, was symbolically represented by the Egyptian bull-god Apis, the golden calf of Moses, and the White Bull of the Sea in Crete, who fathered the Minotaur. The age of Aries, the ram, is associated with the Golden Fleece sought by Jason's Argonauts, the ram's horns of Alexander the Great, and other initiates of the later Egyptian mysteries. And of course Jesus the Lamb, who was the chief pivot of the transition from the Arian age into the one that is just now ending: the age of Pisces.

"Fish symbols, too, have penetrated throughout this aeon. There's the Fisher King, who guarded the Holy Grail sought by King Arthur and his Round Table of holy knights. Though the Grail chalice itself would be a more appropriate symbol of the *coming* new age—pouring out, you see."

We had cut through an open plaza with a grotesque Baroque fountain splashing water everywhere. I knew we were approaching the Ring.

"What can you tell us about the age of Aquarius?" I asked Dacian.

"From the beginning, the image of this age has been rather like that of a deluge," Dacian told me. "Not a flood such as Noah experienced in Genesis, where the earth was drowned in waters from the heavens as punishment for mankind's sins. Instead, this will be a time of unexpected, volatile upheaval in the fabric of the entire social order. The liquid the water-bearer pours out is seen as a gigantic tidal wave of liberation: the waters of the earth will rise, gushing wellsprings of freedom unleashed against all bonds of tyranny—at least, for those seeking such liberation. It seems no accident, therefore, that Uranus, the planetary ruler of this coming age, was discovered at the dawn of the French Revolution.

"According to the ancients, our coming age will be ushered in by unchecked waters gushing forth. Those who build dams to hold it back, who construct walls to resist change, who are repressive, inflexible, unaccepting—those who wish to turn back the clocks, to return to a golden era that never existed—will themselves be destroyed by this tidal wave of transformation. Only those who learn to dance atop the waters will survive."

" 'Go with the flow,' " I said with a smile. "But there've been so many books and songs and plays written about the age of Aquarius from my mother's generation. They made it sound like a time of love and peace and—what was it?—'flower power.' What you've described sounds more like a real revolution."

"A revolution describes a circle, too," Dacian pointed out. "But the ideas you've mentioned are fantasies more decadent than any sugar-dusted bonbons: their values do not suit the age at all. Indeed, it's just such 'utopian' concepts that are deeply dangerous in the circumstances. Remember that Utopia, *ou topos*, translates as 'no-place.' And if you look carefully, that's precisely where you'll find each 'golden age' of legend exists."

"How could dreaming of a better world be dangerous?" I asked him.

"It isn't, as long as that world is truly better for *everyone*. And as long as it is a real world, not just a dream," said Dacian. "Our present year, 1989, marks two centuries since the utopian ideals of Jean-Jacques Rousseau ushered in the French Revolution we were just speaking of. The sunrise at spring equinox at that time was within five degrees of the cusp—the point on the zodiacal circle marking the sun's entry into the sign of Aquarius—close enough to feel the tug of the coming age. Yet twenty-five years of bloodshed later, the French monarchy was restored, followed by further decades of upheaval.

"Then 1933, the year that Hitler came to power, brought us within *one* degree of the countdown toward the new age. As of today, we are within one-tenth of one degree of the cusp of the Aquarian age: it is already happening."

"You're saying Napoleon and Hitler are connected with the new aeon?" I said. "They certainly wouldn't fit anyone's image of utopian idealists."

"Would they not?" said Dacian with lifted brow. "And yet that's exactly what they were."

"Just a minute!" I said. "Please don't tell me you *admired* those guys!"

"I am telling you," said Dacian carefully, "just how dangerous idealism, even spirituality, can be, when nurtured in the wrong hothouse. Idealists who begin by wanting to create a higher civilization almost always find they must begin by trying to improve cultures and societies. And invariably, this ends where it must, with trying to cull wheat from chaff—by genetics, eugenics, whatever it may be—to create a better breed of human being."

With these weighty words, we'd reached the Hofburg. Wolfgang got us tickets, and we all entered the *Schatzkammer*.

We walked through rooms of big glass cases chock-full of crown jewels, imperial regalia, costumes, and reliquaries: the octagonal jewel-crusted millennium-old crown of the Holy Roman Empire with the figure of Rex Salomon emblazoned on the side, the Habsburg crown and orb with *AEIOU—Austriae est imperare orbi universo*: Austria Has Sovereignty Over the Entire World—and other modest family trinkets. At last we reached the final chamber with the swords of state and other imperial ceremonial weapons.

There, on a bit of red velvet inside a small case against the wall, along with other items of seemingly greater value and interest, was a small dagger-shaped object, two pieces crudely made of some kind of iron, tied together with something that looked like catgut. The handle was designed to be fitted to a shaft, the center section surrounded by a thin collar of brass: the perfect image of the spear Laf had described from his childhood visit here nearly eight decades ago.

"It looks like nothing, really, doesn't it?" said Dacian, standing beside me as we gazed down into the glass case.

Wolfgang, at my other side, said, "However, it is supposed to be the famous spear of Longinus. Many books have been written about it. Gaius Cassius Longinus was a Roman centurion who, it's said, pierced the side of Christ with this very weapon. Beneath the brass collar, they say, is one of the crucifixion nails removed from the body of Christ. It is said, too, that Charlemagne's sword in the next display case—thought to have belonged to Attila the Hun—is the same once wielded two thousand years ago by Saint Peter in the garden of Gethsemane."

"All nonsense, of course," Dacian said. "The sword here is a medieval saber, not an early Hebrew or Roman weapon at all. And this spear before us is only a copy. Books have been written about that, too. Everyone coveted it, right down to Adolf Hitler, because of mysterious powers it possessed. It's reported that when Hitler took the true spear of Longinus off to Nürnberg, along with other such treasures he'd gathered, he had copies made of each—and those copies are what we see today. From then on, everyone interested in power or glory was looking for the real ones, including the Windsors during their long exile and the American general George Patton—who'd studied his share of ancient history, and who himself turned Nürnberg Castle upside down hunting for them as soon as he arrived there at the end of the war. But the authentic objects had vanished."

"You don't credit all those stories about Hitler living on after the war, and keeping the sacred hallows with him?" Wolfgang asked Dacian.

"As you see, my dear," Dacian addressed me with a smile, "there are many stories afloat. Some even support the lengthy survival, well beyond death, of nearly everyone in history associated with these objects, from Hitler to Jesus Christ. Since religions and political movements—which I confess often are indistinguishable to me—have been widely based on such tales, I decline to comment. I find the topic neither of importance nor of interest. What *is* of interest, however, is why individuals like Hitler or Patton wanted the so-called hallows at all. Only one person can answer that question."

"You don't mean to say that *you* know where the sacred hallows might be?" said Wolfgang. Naturally, I wanted to hear the answer too, but Dacian didn't bite.

"As I explained to Ariel earlier," he said patiently, "it's the process, not the product, of the quest that's truly important."

"But if the hallows *aren't* the point," Wolfgang said in frustration, "what is?"

Dacian looked grim and shook his head. "Not *what*," he repeated. "Not who, nor how, nor where, nor when, but *why*: that is the question. However, since facts seem so important to you, I'll share what I do know. Indeed, I've already arranged to do so just after we've finished here."

He put one finger beneath my chin. "The moment I learned from Wolfgang what you might be carrying with you, I reserved a spot for us, by telephone from the restaurant. Our appointment is just one minute from now, at three o'clock, only a few steps from here on the Josefsplatz. We have the place to ourselves for an hour, until four when they close, and it may well take that long. I hope our friend Wolfgang won't be disappointed that it's not all cut-and-dry facts; quite a lot of background goes with the story, as well as some hearsay and a few surmises of my own. I'll tell it while the two of you dispose of those dangerous papers—"

"*Dispose* of the papers!" I choked, tightening my fingers on the bag. Wolfgang seemed shocked as well.

"My dear, be reasonable," Dacian said. "You can't take them into the Soviet Union. Their customs officials confiscate, on general principles, whatever cannot be identified—including parking tickets. Nor can you scatter them on the streets of Vienna, nor entrust them to Wolfgang or me, since we're both leaving the country tomorrow too. Therefore I urge the only solution I myself can think of given such short notice—to hide them in a place where no one is likely to find them soon: among the rare books of the Austrian National Library."

◆ ◆

The Nationalbibliotek, built in the 1730s, is one of the most impressive libraries in the world—not because of its size or grandeur but because of its unearthly, fairylike beauty and the exotic nature of its collection of rare books, from Avicenna to Zeno, which places it second in importance only to that of the Vatican.

I'd been here rarely as a child, but I still recalled vividly the library's whipped-cream Baroque architecture and the astonishing pastel trompe l'oeil ceiling of the lofty dome. Last but not least—the most wonderful surprise in the world to a child—the bookcases were actually *doors*, paneled in books on each side, that swung open to reveal secret book-lined chambers beyond, each containing a large table and chairs and big airy windows overlooking the courtyard, where scholars could shut themselves away and work in private for hours. It was one of these that Dacian had reserved for us.

"It's a good plan," Wolfgang assured me when we three were ensconced within the room. "I'd never have thought of anything better at such short notice."

Once I'd thought it over I agreed that, risky as it might be, Dacian had come up with a plausible way to protect the manuscripts. Even if anyone learned they were hidden here, the quick tally I'd made from the placard up front told me the library's collections of books, folios, manuscripts, maps, periodicals, and incunabula totaled around four million items. That, and the fact that the stacks were closed to public access, made retrieving the scattered pages a project of colossal proportions for anyone so minded.

For ten minutes we filled out cards for dozens of titles, handing them to librarians and waiting for the books to be pulled. When we were alone, I inserted pages of text into books pulled from shelves here in this room. As a further precaution, I proposed that once we were done we destroy all the call cards and keep no list.

"But how will we find them again?" Wolfgang objected. "To find a thousand pages by trial and error among so many books—it would take dozens of people years and years!"

"That's what I'm counting on," I said.

I didn't feel it essential to mention my photographic memory again, but I could recall a list of five hundred items—such as the author/title of each book where we'd stashed a few pages—for up to about three months. If I couldn't return in that time, I'd write out the list, recommit it to memory, and destroy it again.

More urgent was the matter of Dacian. As he said at the Schatzkammer, he had to fly back to Paris, so this session at the library was likely to be our last for quite a while, and I had plenty I needed to know before he got away. I'd have to walk and chew gum at the same time—try to split my brain to pay attention to Dacian while committing the book list to memory. I drew up my chair near his beside the window. Wolfgang stayed at the door accepting fresh shuttle-relays of books. He slid each pile down to me, maintaining a watchful eye to be sure we weren't overheard. As I stuffed the volumes with folded pages of manuscript, I nodded for Dacian to proceed.

"I'll try to address both your questions," he began, "the thirteen hallows Wolfgang is interested in, and the meaning of Pandora's papers in Ariel's possession. The answer to both centers on a remote part of the world little visited today—and then, little understood. Once this region had the highest culture. But now its past lies buried beneath the dust of centuries. It has been battled over constantly by the great powers, and its lines of demarcation even now are in dispute. But as some have learned to their cost, this is a land so wild and mysterious that its people, like the wild panther, can never be tamed."

He turned to regard me with those dark purple-green eyes. "I speak of a place—or so I understand—you'll both be investigating in your journey to Russia. So our meeting today is fortunate. I am one of the few who can recount its history and, more important, the deeper meaning concealed beneath that history—for I was born there myself nearly a century ago."

"You were born in Central Asia?" I said in surprise.

"Yes. And Sanskrit was the early language of this region, an important key. Let me give you a clearer picture of my homeland."

Dacian withdrew from his satchel a thin piece of leather rolled up and tied with a chamois thong. He undid it and held it out to me. It seemed so fragile, I was hesitant to touch it, so Dacian spread it on the table. Wolfgang came over and stood beside us, looking down.

It was an antique map, carefully drawn and hand-tinted but without boundary lines. The map I'd just studied all that morning depicted pretty much the same terrain, so I felt topographically acquainted with the turf even without the labels: the inland seas were the Aral and the Caspian, the main watercourses the Oxus and the Indus, and the mountain ranges the Hindu Kush, the Pamirs, and the Himalayas. The only lines drawn in were dotted ones that might designate major travel routes. A few circles were drawn indicating geographical features—a few recognizable ones like Mount Everest. But it was hard to guess others without those artificial demarcations designating national boundaries we're so accustomed to. Anticipating this, Dacian unfolded a sheet of translucent tissue marking the present boundaries and laid it over the map so the separate regions again leapt to life.

"So many people have lived here over the centuries, it blurs one's awareness of what is important," he explained. "These circles on the map are sites of legendary, even magical significance that transcend political changes. For instance, here."

He indicated a spot where a podlike protrusion of Afghanistan slipped between two mountainous regions of Russian Tajikistan and Pakistan in a long, extended flow that reached out to touch westernmost China.

"It's surely no accident," said Dacian, "that the first of the major upheavals announcing our entry into the new aeon should occur in this particular corner of the world. From ancient times, more than any other spot on earth, it has acted as a cultural cauldron mingling east, west, north, and south—so it provides the perfect microcosm of this new age nearly upon us."

"But if this age is to be a wave, tearing down walls and mingling cultures," said Wolfgang, "I don't see how it connects with this part of the world—especially Afghanistan, where Russia's bloody but insignificant little war is unlikely to affect any culture but that one."

"Not so insignificant. A turning point has been reached," said Dacian. "Perhaps you think it coincidence that only this February, the Soviets withdrew from that unfortunate war ten years after invading? The withdrawal came at the precise moment when sunrise during the spring equinox, as I described before, approached one-tenth of one degree of entry into the constellation Aquarius—exactly eleven years and eleven months before the official dawning of the new aeon expected in the year 2001."

"I agree with Wolfgang," I told Dacian, stuffing another sheet. "It hardly seems troops marching home from a no-win war will trigger an earthshaking new two-millennium cycle. For the Russians, it seems more like back to business as usual."

"That's because no one has asked the key question: *Why* were the Soviets there in the first place?" said Dacian. "The answer is simple. Just as Hitler had, fifty years before, they were searching for the sacred city."

Wolfgang and I stopped stuffing books for a moment, our eyes fixed on Dacian. He tapped at the map as if thinking, and favored us with an elusive smile.

"Magical cities have always abounded in the region," he said. "Some were historically factual, while others were speculation or myth, such as Mongolia's Chan-du—the Xanadu of Kublai Khan—described by Marco Polo. Or the Himalayan retreat of Shangri-La: according to legend it appears just once every millennium. Then the far western region of China, the republic of Xinjiang: In the nineteen-twenties the Russian mystic Nicholas Roerich recorded tales he collected from Kashmir to Chinese Xinjiang and Tibet of the fabulous sunken city of Shambhala, an oriental version of Atlantis. It was believed this miraculous city once was swallowed by the earth, but that it would rise again quite soon, to usher in the birth of the new aeon."

Dacian's eyes were closed, but as he slid his finger across the map, he seemed able to see each of these spots as he touched it. Although he had admitted he was recounting largely myths, they seemed so real to him that I was fascinated. I had to force my attention back to the papers I was supposed to be concealing.

"It is here in Nepal," he went on, "that for thousands of years Buddhists have believed the lost city of *Agharti* is buried within Kanchenjunga—the third highest peak in the world, whose name means 'five holy treasures of the snows.' Then south of the world's *second* highest mountain, K2—in the disputed zone claimed by China, India, and Pakistan—lies another secret hoard of mysterious treasure and sacred manuscripts. The legendary occultist Aleister Crowley, who was first to attempt an ascent of this mountain in 1901, was searching for these. And the most magical mountain in the region is Mount Pamir—formerly Mount Stalin, today Mount Communism—in Tajikistan. At almost twenty-five thousand feet, it's the highest peak in the Soviet Union. The Zoroastrian Persians viewed this mountain as the chief axis of a power grid connecting sacred points of Europe and the Mediterranean with those of the Near East and Asia—a relay, it is believed by many, that can be activated only under the right circumstances, such as those that will occur at the turn of this next aeon.

"But the most interesting of all these sacred places was a city founded by Alexander the Great around 330 B.C. near today's Russian-Afghan border. According to legend it was on this spot, thousands of years ago, that a city of great mystery and magic once stood: the last of the fabled seven cities of Solomon."

"King Solomon?" said Wolfgang in an odd tone. "But is it possible?" He got up, quietly spoke to the librarian outside, pulled the book-laden doors shut, and came back to sit beside me.

I kept stuffing Pandora's papers into volumes, my head down so no one could look at my face. I knew this reference to Solomon was no casual remark on Dacian's part, any more than Sam's many allusions: the Solomon's knot he'd left on my car mirror, the anagrams and phone memos directing me to Song of Songs. Plenty of input, but what did it mean? I felt like a reactor at critical mass. I sat there trying to shove my control rods back in and focus on the connections. I slid my pile of books to Wolfgang, who handed me another.

"It's a part of the world few would associate with Solomon," Dacian conceded. "Yet an entire range between the Indus Valley and Afghanistan, just south of where the hidden city is thought to be, is named for him: the Suleimans. There, in a hollow crater on top, his throne—the *takht-i-Suliman*—was regarded by the ancients as another axis connecting heaven to earth.

"With Solomon, myth is often mingled with fact: it's said he was a magus with dominion over water, earth, wind, and fire; that he understood the language of animals, employing the services of ants and bees to build the Jerusalem temple; that doves and feys designed his magical city of the sun in Central Asia, a place long sought by Alexander the Great through many lands. When Solomon took Balqis, Queen of Sheba, on a tour of the many cities he'd created, aboard a magic carpet on which he placed a royal throne, and the queen looked back toward her homeland, Solomon's genie scooped the hollow from the mountaintop and set down the throne so she had a better view. A real *takht-i-Suliman* was recorded in the expedition survey of the region in 1883. There was also a Persian fire temple from the time of Alexander built on the very spot. The link with fire worship is of importance to our story. Alexander and Solomon, each with one foot dipped in history and one in legend, are linked in other ways, too—in the lore of Hindus, Buddhists, Tantric Tibetans, Nestorian Christians—even the holy book of Islam, the Qur'ān."

"Solomon and Alexander are mentioned in the Koran?" I said, surprised.

"Indeed," said Dacian. "One of the hallows so intriguing to Wolfgang was described in the Qur'ān: a magical, luminous green stone believed to have fallen from the sky millions of years ago. Solomon, an initiate into the secrets of the Persian magi, had a chunk from it mounted in a ring which he wore at all times, until his death. Alexander later sought this stone for the powers it rendered over heaven and earth."

Still listening, I resumed stuffing books as Dacian began his tale.

◆ ◆

THE STONE

He was born at midnight in the heat of high summer, in the dog days of the year 356 B.C., at Pella in Macedonia. They called him Alexander.

Before his birth, the Sibylline Oracle predicted the blood-drenched slaughter of Asia by the one who was about to come. With his first birth cries, it's said the Artemision, the great temple of Artemis at Ephesus, burst spontaneously into flame and was totally destroyed. The magi of Zarathustra who witnessed this cremation, so Plutarch tells us, wept and wailed and beat their faces, and they prophesied the fall of the far-flung Persian Empire which began at that very hour.

Alexander's mother, Olympias, princess of Epirus, was a priestess of the Orphic mysteries of life and death. As a girl of thirteen she'd met his father, Philip II of Macedon, on the isle of Samothrace during their initiation into the darker Dionysian mysteries that ruled the winter months. By the time of her marriage to Philip, five years later, Olympias was also a devotee of the rituals of the bacchantes, the followers of Dionysus the wine god, who in the god's Thracian homeland were called bassarides after the fox furs they wore (and little more) when they danced wildly over the hills all night, drunk on undiluted wine and mad with both sexual and blood lust. In possession by the god, the *bassarides* captured wild animals with their bare hands and tore them apart with their teeth. In such states they were called *maenads*—the frenzied ones.

Olympias often shared her bed with the oracular serpent, a full-grown python—a habit that frightened her husband so badly that, for some time, it postponed the conception of a child. But at last the oracle told Philip he would lose an eye for watching his wife engaged in a coupling with the sacred reptile, a mystical event when her womb was opened by the thunderbolt of Zeus and flames poured forth, heralding a child who would one day set the East ablaze. The oracle said their marriage must be consummated in the flesh. Their child would unite the four quarters and awaken the dragon force latent in the earth, bringing the dawn of a new age.

Alexander was fair, rosy, and handsome, of fine form, with one blue-grey eye and one of dark brown. He had a melting glance and exuded a marvelous spicy fragrance from his mouth and all his flesh due to his warm, fiery nature. The young prince's education by Aristotle included training in metaphysics and the secrets of the Persian magi. He was soon wise beyond his years. By his mother, Olympias, he was tutored in the Mysteries. He became a fleet sprinter, a champion horseman, and an accomplished warrior, and was admired throughout his father's kingdom.

But when he turned eighteen, Alexander's life changed. His father divorced his mother, exiled her, and married a young Macedonian woman, Cleopatra, who quickly produced an alternative heir to the royal line. Olympias flew into a black rage and exercised her magic powers, which were formidable. She arranged by ruses and curses to have Philip assassinated by one of his male lovers, so Alexander might succeed to the throne. Alexander was twenty when, upon his father's death, he became king of Macedon.

His first act was to bring his neighbors Illyria and Thrace within the Macedonian fold. Then he torched the rebellious city of Thebes in central Greece and enslaved its population. On the Ionian coast of modern-day Turkey, for more than one hundred fifty years Greek cities had labored under Persian vassalage. Alexander set about to defeat the Persians and restore democracy, and in some cases autonomy, to the former Greek colonies. His initial mission, to break a two-hundred-year hold by the Persian Empire over the Eastern and Western worlds, was soon revised into a mission of world domination. His final mission would be to bond himself with the divine fluid—to become a living god.

Alexander's armies entered Asia through Phrygia—today Anatolia, in central Turkey—and came to the city of Gordion. In the eighth century B.C., four hundred years before Alexander, the people of Phrygia had been told by an oracle that the true king of their people would appear one day and be recognized by the fact that, as he entered the city gates, a raven would perch upon his cart. A shepherd, Gordius, had arrived down the eastern road. When he came to the first town, a prophetic raven perched on the yoke of his oxcart, and together they entered the city. Cheering throngs escorted Gordius to the temple and crowned him king. It was soon discovered that no one could untie the complex knot in the leather thong with which the yoke was fastened to the pole of his cart. The oracle said whoever undid the knot would one day be lord of all Asia. This was the Gordian knot that, four hundred years later, Alexander would cut in two with his sword.

Gordius married the oracle of Cybele—a name meaning both cave and cube—the great mother goddess of all creation since the Ice Age. Cybele's birthplace was Mount Ida on the Ionian coast, from which the gods looked down to observe the Trojan War, but her principal shrine was at Pessinus, only a dozen miles from Gordion, where she was enshrined as a meteoric black stone. One hundred twenty years after Alexander's death, as protection against Hannibal and his forces during the Carthaginian Wars, this rock would be brought to Rome and enshrined on the Palatine Hill. It remained there, wielding Phrygian power, well into the time of the Caesars.

Gordius and his prophetess wife adopted the half-mortal son of the goddess Cybele, a boy named Midas because, like the goddess, he was born on Mount Ida. Midas became the second king of Phrygia. While still a young man Midas, accompanied by the centaur Silenus, tutor to the god Dionysus, traveled to Hyperborea, a magical land beyond the north wind, associated with the pole star and the world axis. Upon their return, Dionysus rewarded Midas with anything he wanted. Midas asked for the golden touch. Even today, the rivers where he once bathed flow with gold.

In the year 333 B.C., when Alexander cut the Gordian knot, he paid a visit to the tomb of King Midas, also to the temple of Cybele to see the black stone, and lastly to the temple of the patron god of the Phrygian kings, Dionysus. Having refreshed himself in the springs and wells of the Eastern gods, he then proceeded to conquer the East: Syria, Egypt, Mesopotamia, Persia, Central Asia, and India.

The key event of these campaigns was in Central Asia, at the Birdless Rock—a city built on a seven-thousand-foot tower of rock believed to be the pillar holding up the sky, so high that it could not be besieged by catapult. Alexander selected three hundred soldiers from the mountainous regions of Macedon who were capable of scaling the cliffs and the city walls by hand; once above, they fired arrows down on the defenders, who surrendered.

Somewhere near this site, the Qur'ān tells us, Alexander built a pair of vast iron gates to seal a difficult mountain pass against tribes from the east called the Gog and Magog—tribes in later times called Mongol. It was here also that he built his sacred city on the earlier site of the seventh city of Solomon. It's said the sacred stone of Solomon is buried as a cornerstone, enabling the city to rise at the dawn of each new aeon.

Once the region beyond the Oxus was pacified, a troop of nobles visited from Nysa, a valley at the other side of the Hindu Kush. When they laid eyes upon Alexander, he was still in battle armor and covered with dust. But they were struck speechless and fell to the ground in awe, for they recognized in him those divine and godlike qualities already recognized by the Egyptian high priests and, indeed, the Persian magi. The Nyseans invited Alexander and his men to visit their homeland, which they claimed as the birthplace of the 'god of Nysa'—Dio-nysus, who was also the chief god of Macedon.

It's said that Alexander's visit to Nysa was the turning point of his short but influential life. Approaching this verdant valley spread out between mountain ranges was like entering a lost and magical domain. The valley not only boasted rare vineyards and the heady wines Alexander loved to drink, it was also the only place in this part of the world where ivy, sacred to the god, was known to grow.

The vine represents the journey into the outer world, the quest. The ivy describes the journey within, the labyrinth. Alexander and his troops, always ready to toast the principal god of their own birthplace, twined sacred ivy upon their brows and drank and caroused and danced across the hills in celebration of this new invasion of India—for the legends told that the god Dionysus himself was the first to cross the Indus astride his steaming, perfumed panther.

Alexander's career was brief, but the oracular dice had been cast before his birth. In thirteen years and many campaigns he conquered most of the known world. Then, at age thirty-three, he died in Babylon. Because his hard-won and far-reaching empire was dismantled immediately after his death, historians believe he left nothing but his golden legend. In this they are mistaken. In those thirteen years he accomplished all he'd set out to achieve: a mingling of East and West, spirit and matter, philosophies and bloodlines. In every capital he conquered, he held public mass marriages between Macedonian-Greek officers and native noblewomen; he himself took several wives of Persian stock.

It is known, too, that Alexander was an initiate of Eastern esotericism. In Egypt, the high priests of Zeus/Jupiter/Ammon recognized in him an incarnation of that god, and conferred upon him the ram horns of the figure who was associated on all three continents with Mars, the planet of war, and with the current age of Aries, the ram. Up north in the lands of the Scythians—Central Asia, the part of the world we are speaking of—he was called *Zul-qarnain*: the Two-Horned God. This term also means 'lord of the two paths' or two epochs—that is, he who'll rule the transition between two aeons.

◆ ◆

"Alexander's mother, Olympias," Dacian finished, "told him he was the seed of the serpent power, the cosmic force. The ambition she'd nurtured in him as a child grew into an unquenchable thirst for world dominion. To this end, he built a sacred city at each 'acupuncture point' on the earth's power grid. Alexander thought that to pin these points along the spine of the earth, like driving the axis of a nail into a tree, would enable him to harness the 'dragon forces' of earth—and that one who possessed the sacred stone of the new age and planted it precisely at the center of the grid would bring about the last revolution of the wheel of the aeon, would have it under his control and dominion, with the rest of the earth. This was so important, Alexander stopped his campaigns to survey each locale before breaking ground, and he insisted on naming each city himself—seventy in all—before he died."

"Seventy cities?" said Wolfgang, looking up from the book he was stuffing.

"An interesting number, is it not?" Dacian agreed. "With the earlier seven cities of Solomon, it makes seventy-seven points in the grid, a profoundly magical number."

I hadn't missed the parallel between the seventy-seven cities of Alexander and Solomon and the Group of 77 nonaligned nations I'd spent the morning being briefed on. As I passed Wolfgang the book I'd just stuffed, the door swung inward on its hinges and a librarian popped his head around the side and nodded to indicate it was time to close. Dacian rolled his leather map up and replaced it in his bag as Wolfgang neatly stacked the last pile of books and headed with them toward the door.

"Even if there were some kind of grid that harnessed such mysterious energies," I asked Dacian, "what would be the value of controlling it?"

"Remember, Solomon was regarded as lord of the four quarters—not only of earth, but of the four elements, too," he said. "Thus, he possessed the powers of an immortal. And Alexander, in his short span, became the first Western man to be regarded even before his death as a living god."

"You don't believe there are gods who come to earth in human form?" I said. "I love these old myths—but this *is* the end of the twentieth century."

"Precisely the moment they're expected to arrive," said Dacian.

◆ ◆

We went out into the darkened street and the library door closed behind us. Dacian looked rather drained as he stood in the golden light of the first streetlamp that had just switched on above our heads—but his face was still so handsome.

"I must leave you in a moment; I'm very tired," he said. "But I shall see you again—at least, if the gods we spoke of are willing. And though I've just scratched the surface of what you need to know, at least it *has* been scratched so you can peer through the glass a bit. I shouldn't be concerned about those manuscripts. They're of little use by themselves. It's not enough to read; one must also understand. This ability, as I said, calls for a questing mind—and for something more."

"Something more? Like asking the right questions," I said. "But earlier, at the Hofburg, you told us you were the one person who could explain why everyone wants these manuscripts, and the hallows too—that you alone could answer the question of what's so dangerous about them. So the question is, why haven't you?"

"I said only *one* person could answer the question—not that *I* was the one," Dacian clarified. "Perhaps you'll recall my saying that Sanskrit was a key to this mystery? Or that the ancient fire temple built on the site of Solomon's throne in Afghanistan was also of importance? These are both related to that quality I've called 'something more.' It's best described by a Sanskrit word, *salubha*, meaning 'the way of the moth or grasshopper'—to fly into fire, to rush without thought into danger as the salamander does. To dance upstream like the salmon. To possess the powers of salt."

"Salt?" I said.

"Salt, the most valued commodity of the ancient world," said Dacian. "The Romans paid their troops in it: hence today's word 'salary.' The oldest Celtic settlement in Austria, one of the earliest and richest in Europe, was Hallstatt, high in the Salzkammergut, 'salt chamber country'—quite close to where our friend Lucky was born and where he lived in later life. Its name reveals its source of wealth: like the German *Salz* and old German *Halle*, *hal* was the Celtic name for salt."

With a chill I recalled Lucky's words to Dacian, as recounted by Laf: that on the river, and in the Salzkammergut, would be found the message from the ancient peoples, written in the runes. . . . But what did it take to uncover that message? I knew the salt lakes and saline springs high in the Austrian Alps, and the mysterious, crystalline underground salt mines, like Merlin's cave—like those seventy-seven fabled cities.

"Are you saying that when Hitler built his house in the Obersalzburg he was trying to tap into some force, like the hidden cities of Alexander and King Solomon?" I asked. "But what was it?"

"All these things," said Dacian, "Solomon, the salamander, the salmon, even the town of Salzburg, have one thing in common. Whether *sal* or *Salz* or *sau* or *sault*—it comes down to 'saltation,' a word that means to leap, to jump, to dance—"

"I'm afraid that calls for a quantum leap on my part," I said.

"That's the secret ingredient I asked for: *sal sapiente*, wise salt, the Salt of Wisdom," said Dacian. "Sprinkle a little, and it gives you those leaps of intuition like the ones King Solmon was noted for, a dancing mind filled with sparkling energy. Like the salmon leaping upstream—like a leap of faith."

My beloved! I heard the Song of Songs, which is Solomon's echo in my mind, *behold, he cometh leaping upon the mountains, skipping upon the hills.*

Dacian turned to me and put his hands on my shoulders ceremonially, almost as if bestowing an oak cluster or passing a torch. Then he looked over my shoulder at Wolfgang with an enigmatic smile.

"My dear," he told me, "there's only one thing for it. You're surely going to have to learn to dance!" Then he moved into the shadows of the oncoming night.

◆ ◆

"I just thought of something," said Wolfgang, when Dacian left. "I was so hypnotized by the man, I almost forgot. I went back to the office while you were lunching, and there was a fax for you that had been forwarded from your office in the States. I hope it's nothing urgent." He reached in his pocket and handed me a folded slip of paper. I opened it under the yellow light of the streetlamp:

> The first phase of our project is now completed in earnest, and the information archive for phase two is under way. Please

advise how to forward future communications to you as we progress. Our team can be reached at the above number starting tomorrow.

—Yours, R. F. Burton, Quality Assurance

Sir Richard Francis Burton, indefatigable explorer and orientalist, had been one of my favorite authors as a child. I'd read everything he'd written or translated including his sixteen-volume *Thousand Nights and a Night of Scheherezade*. Clearly, this message was from Sam. Though I could hardly dwell on the contents while standing here under a Viennese streetlamp with Wolfgang looking on, it was a simple enough communiqué that I was quickly able to figure out a few things up front:

Phase one "completed in earnest" told me Sam had met with his grandfather, Dark Bear, on the Nez Percé reservation at Lapwai and had learned something pretty important about his father Earnest—or he'd not have taken the risk to communicate with me so overtly though I'd said he could. As for phase two: signing the message Sir Richard Burton said it all. In addition to the many books Burton had written about his treks to exotic locales like al-Medina, Mecca, and the source of the Nile, he'd also written one on his pilgrimage to "City of the Saints"—the Latter-day Saints, that is.

So the fax told me that by tomorrow this time, Sam would be checking out the rest of our family history in that other well-known salt land, America's version of Salzburg: Salt Lake City, Utah.

In response to an oracle of the goddess [Cybele], Dionysos learned the use of grapes from a snake. Thereupon he invented the most primitive method of making wine.

—Karl Kerenyi, *Dionysos*

I am the true vine, and my Father is the husbandman.

—Jesus of Nazareth, Gospel of John 15:1

And God said . . . I do set my rainbow in the clouds, and it shall be a token of the covenant between me and the earth. . . . And I will remember my covenant . . . and the waters shall no more become a flood to destroy all flesh. . . . And Noah began to be an husbandman, and he planted a vineyard: and he drank of the wine.

—God's Covenant with Noah, Genesis 9:12–21

Let us get up early to the vineyards; let us see if the vine flourish, whether the tender grape appear, and the pomegranates bud forth: there I will give thee my loves.

—Song of Solomon 7:12

It was after dusk when Wolfgang and I were on the road that ran out of town along the Danube. The deep periwinkle sky was already sprinkled with a few stars; we left behind the fat yellow moon just rising over the city of Vienna.

We didn't speak much during the trip. Though I was emotionally drained, I couldn't close my eyes. Soon the city lights had vanished and we followed the broad, graceful sweep of river west toward the Wachau wine country. Wolfgang drove with the same gracefully timed precision he displayed when skiing, and I looked out the windows at the broad, glassy surface of the river to one side and clusters of hill villages stacked up like Hobbit houses just beside the road on the other. In less than an hour we arrived at the town of Krems, where Wolfgang's office was located.

By now the moon was high, bathing the surrounding hills in light. We took the branch off the main road uphill into the charming walled town of Krems with its interesting assortment of whitewashed buildings whose potpourri of styles could be picked out in the bright moonlight: Renaissance, Gothic, Baroque, Romanesque. We passed through the town and the Höher Markt with its square of country palaces and museums, but to my surprise Wolfgang headed out of town once more on a narrower, winding road that led up into the open hill country, thick with vineyards, high above the village. I glanced at his profile, outlined by the dull green glow of the dash lights.

"I thought the plan was to drop by your office the very first thing, to go over tomorrow's agenda," I said.

"Yes, but my office is in my home," Wolfgang explained, his eyes still on the road ahead. "It isn't far, only a few kilometers more. We'll be there at any moment."

The road had now become narrower and seemed to be running out of pavement as we continued up the steep hill that led farther and farther from the river and its small pockets of habitation. We passed a tiny thatched mud shed that was built into the hill beside the road, the kind where grape pickers store baskets and tools, and take shelter during those sudden drenching rains so common here in the hill country. Beyond it, there was nothing suggesting civilization—except, of course, row after row of grapevines under cultivation.

When we reached the hilltop, the vineyards abruptly stopped and the road dead-ended at a bridge spanning a wide creek. A cloud momentarily shadowed the moon so it was hard to discern the outline of the rugged and very high stone wall that seemed to provide an impasse on the opposite bank.

Wolfgang stopped the car just before the bridge and got out. I thought perhaps I should do likewise. But suddenly a blaze of floodlights switched on outside, drenching the landscape in golden light like an outdoor theater set. I stared in awed disbelief at the view through the windshield.

What I'd taken for a high pasture wall was instead the crenellated rampart of an ancient Austrian *Burg*, a fortresslike stonework, and what I'd believed to be a creek was really a half-filled moat, its mossy granite walls sloping down into the water. High wooden gates were embedded in the rampart. These stood open so I could see the illuminated interior within: a broad, grassy courtyard, an ancient oak tree spreading its branches above the sweep of lawn, and beyond it the circular stone form of a true medieval castle.

Wolfgang returned to the car without a word, put it in low gear, and slowly drove over the drawbridge and through the open gates. He parked on the grass beneath the oak, just beside an old stone well. He switched off the ignition and looked at me almost shyly.

"Your *house?*" I said, amazed.

"How do you say it—a man's house is his castle?" he asked. "But in my case, what was left to me was an attractive pile of rocks that nearly a thousand years ago formed a castle here above what would one day be the town of Krems. I've spent ten years, and most of my leisure time and income, I admit, finding experts to assist me in trying to restore it. Except for those few—and Bettina, who thinks I am crazy to be doing this—you are the only one I've brought here. Tell me, do you like it?"

"It's incredible!" I said.

I got out of the car for a better look. Wolfgang joined me as I walked around the courtyard studying each detail. It was true that ruined castles dotted nearly every hill throughout Germany and Austria; they were so lovely and seemed to have such terrific views, I'd often wondered why no one bothered to restore them. Now I appreciated what effort must have gone into this one. Even the stones of the ramparts were clearly hewn, laid, and mortared by hand. When Wolfgang unlocked the doors of the castle, let me inside, and flicked on the lights, I was even more astounded.

We stood on the slate-paved floor of a large, circular tower; the ceiling soared what must have been sixty feet above us, with a complex domed skylight like a kaleidoscope at the top through which I could see the night sky. The interior was illuminated by a scattering of embedded lights that twinkled, starlike, from niches set in the stone walls. A metal scaffolding rose like an abstract sculpture from the floor to the top of the tower, supporting from beneath assorted structures in various shapes that looked like treehouses jutting at random angles from the outer stone wall. Each "house" was enclosed by a curved wall of hand-polished wood in warm, graduated shades. And each had a Plexiglas section of wall, a floor-to-ceiling picture window, facing the central open space and curving up partially across the ceiling like a skylight, to let in light from above. It took a moment before I saw that these chambers were connected by a suspended spiral of wooden steps that ran along the circular perimeter of the outer wall. The result was absolutely breathtaking.

"It reminds me of those underground cities Dacian spoke of," I told Wolfgang. "Like a magical cavern hidden within a mountain."

"And yet by day, it is completely filled with light," he said. "In those medieval-style window openings, machicolations, and fenestrations, I've installed glass and added skylights everywhere—as you'll see. When we have breakfast here tomorrow morning, sunlight will flood the place—"

"We're staying here tonight?" I tried to suppress the flutters this idea caused.

"I was certain you would be too exhausted to go back to your uncle Lafcadio's tonight as you'd planned," he told me. "And my house is so near the monastery where we're going tomorrow morning—"

"It's fine," I told him. "If it won't be too much trouble."

"It's all arranged," he assured me. "We'll have a light supper at a little inn just below that belongs to the vineyard. It overlooks the river. But first, I'd like to show you the rest of the castle—that is, if you'd like."

"I'd be delighted," I told him. "I've never seen anything like it before."

The slate-tiled ground floor of the tower was about forty-five feet in diameter. At the center was a seating area for meals, a low oak table surrounded by softly upholstered chairs. Beyond this, opposite the entry where we stood, was the kitchen, set apart by yards of open shelving filled with glasses, dishes, and spices. Along the kitchen wall were work surfaces of thick wood, interrupted only by a large hearth-type oven with a stone flue built into the outer wall, as one might expect in a castle. The stairs that rose along the nearby tower wall led to the first tier, the library.

Though somewhat larger than the higher chambers, the library fanned out in a semicircle also supported by scaffolding and pinned into the tower wall for stability. Most of the stone wall here was taken up by a large fireplace already piled with wood and kindling. Wolfgang knelt on one knee before it, pulled open the flue, and with a long straw lit the fire.

Before the hearth was a sofa of glove leather piled deep with pillows, and a boomerang-shaped coffee table stacked with heavy books. The expanse of floor space was strewn with thick Turkish carpets in pale colors. And though there were no actual bookcases, the high Biedermeier desk was stacked with papers and writing tools, with more books piled on tables, chairs—even the floor—throughout the room.

Up the next curved flight of steps, on the second tier, was the room Wolfgang said would be mine, with a large comfortable bed, an armoire, a sofa, and an attached bath. The two rooms above were alternate bed-work-living spaces, and by the abundance of research materials and papers, the computer, and other equipment in one of these, it was clear this had been put into use as Wolfgang's office. Each room had several tall, slitlike fenestrations fitted with windows that opened to overlook the broad, grassy courtyard below.

The top floor just under the skylight was Wolfgang's suite, which like my room boasted a large private bath. But in other respects it was unique. Suspended almost fifty feet above the ground, it was a sweeping O-shaped ribbon about twelve feet wide that circled the outer wall of the tower, leaving open the twenty-odd feet at the center, ringed by a protective railing of hand-rubbed wood. At night, as now, light from the twinkling lamps embedded in the tower walls was reflected from beneath, as well as the softer lights through the glass walls of the lower rooms that seemed to float beneath us as if supported by clouds.

We walked around the curved space so I could really see it. There was a raised platform for a bed on one side, a seating area with wardrobes and dressing space on the other, and between them a large brass telescope pointed toward the sky.

The stone wall of the tower flared outward from waist level, laced with machicolations—those slits common in the turrets of medieval fortifications, from which the besieged could rain down heavy stones on their besiegers. These machicolations had been fitted by Wolfgang with windowpanes that opened inward and could be locked in place like shutters.

The suite had a much higher ceiling than the other rooms, placed as it was up under the heavy angular beams crisscrossing the dome of beveled skylights. As Wolfgang had pointed out, by day the massive skylight-roof would provide additional light throughout the tower. Now the dazzling stellar array of the night sky fanned out like a giant bowl of light through which shone the whole star-spangled universe. It was a truly wonderful space.

"Sometimes when I am here," Wolfgang said, "I lie in bed at night and try to imagine what Odysseus must have felt—lost and wandering all those years, with sometimes his only companions the silence of deep space and the cold, immobile indifference of the stars."

"But in a room like this," I said, "I would think, if you were very quiet, you could hear the constellations singing: the music of the spheres."

"I prefer human voices," said Wolfgang.

He took me by the hand and drew me across the room. In the outer wall he opened one of the windows to let in the fresh, cool air from the river below. Then he switched off the outdoor lights still illuminating the ramparts and outer courtyard, so we could see the countryside. We stood side by side and looked down on the twinkling lights pouring across the rolling hills and, farther out, the double serpent path of lights outlining the undulating Danube. On the river, the moon's circular reflection was broken into ribbons of silver, all that illuminated the surface of the deep, dark water. In this magical place, for the first time in weeks I began to feel at peace.

Wolfgang turned to me in silence and set his hands on my shoulders. Against the glittering night glow, his eyes refracted light like translucent crystals of aquamarine. Between us a wave was slowly building; I could hear its rumble moving toward a roar. Wolfgang finally spoke.

"Often, it's hard for me even to look at you," he said. "You're so astonishingly like her, it can be devastating."

Like *her*? What was *that* supposed to mean?

"My father took me to see her when I was only a small child," he went on. Though his hands still rested lightly on my shoulders, he was gazing down at the river, as if lost in a dream. "I remember she sang '*Das himmlische Leben*' by Mahler. Later, when my father took me backstage to present to her the small flower I'd brought, she looked at me with those eyes." He said in a strange, choked voice, "*Your* eyes. The first instant I saw you in Idaho, even though you were wrapped up like a polar bear and all I could see were your eyes; they riveted me."

Holy shit! Could this be happening? Was this man I was so obsessed with in love with my *grandmother*? What with the week I'd just been through, all I could think of to remedy the way I felt was to catapult myself through that open machicolation like a medieval cannonball. To make matters worse—though I hardly needed help in that department—my damned tempestuous Irish-Gypsy blood was gushing its way to my telltale face again. I abruptly turned away from Wolfgang, and his hands dropped from my shoulders.

"What have I said?" he asked in surprise, swinging me back to face him before I could get control. When he saw my expression, he looked at me in confusion.

"It isn't what you're thinking, you know," he said seriously. "I was only a small boy at the time. How could I have felt, back then, the way I feel now as a grown man?" He ran his fingers through his hair and added in a frustrated voice, "Ariel, I never seem able to explain myself properly to you. If I could only—"

But he'd grasped both my arms above the elbow, and I gasped as the scorching pain shot up my arm. I felt my face contort.

Wolfgang quickly released me. "What is it?!" he said in alarm.

I gingerly touched my arm and smiled through a glaze of tears.

"Good lord!" he exclaimed. "You don't still have those stitches?"

"My appointment with the doctor to remove them was yesterday morning," I told him as I took a deep breath to help quell the throbbing ache. "But we were already in Utah by then."

"If you'd spoken today, we might have done something about it earlier in Vienna," he said. "But you understand, those stitches must come out. Even if they dissolve, your arm may become infected, or worse. Our schedule is so close before we leave for Russia—shall I do it myself? Right now?"

"You?" I said, staring at Wolfgang in genuine horror.

"Please—if you could see your face," he said, laughing. "I have all the supplies right here, disinfectant and ointment and forceps and scissors. It's really a simple procedure. I worked in the clinic in boarding school, and young boys are always having stitches put in and taken out. So I assure you I've done it hundreds of times. But first, I'll bring our things in from the car so we needn't worry about them later. It will take me a bit of time to collect the rest from the kitchen."

He yanked open the door of a nearby wardrobe and pulled out a thick, soft bathrobe. "Why don't you get undressed here and put this on so you don't ruin your clothes," he said. "Then just go down and wait for me in the library—it should be warm there by now. Also, it's closer to the kitchen and the light is far better there than anywhere else." Then he was gone.

I didn't know what I'd had in mind for the evening—but *I'm in love with your grandmother* followed by *Shall I remove your stitches?* wasn't exactly the direction I'd thought it might take.

On the other hand, it would be good to get rid of the itching and throbbing of the past week. Furthermore, the stitch removal might provide time and space to come to terms with the fact that this man I was so attracted to myself seemed to have more intimate relations with everyone connected to my family than he had, so far, with me.

I went into Wolfgang's bathroom, took off my warm wool challis dress, and studied in the mirror the purplish gash that ran from elbow to shoulder, track-marked with fourteen spiderlike black stitches. My eyelids were puffy and the tip of my nose was red from those unexpected tears. I was a wreck. I picked up a wood-handled brush, ran it through my hair a few times, splashed water on my face, pulled on the fleecy bathrobe, and went downstairs.

When I came into the library, the fire was crackling cheerfully and the room smelled of pinecones. I walked over to the open Biedermeier desk and ran my fingers over the pile of books stacked there. I noticed one that looked rare and old, embossed in gold with a beautiful soft leather cover, nearly the same buttery shade as the nearby sofa. It had a bookmark in it. I pulled it from the stack and opened it.

The first page was illuminated with the title

Legenda Aurea
The Golden Legend: Readings on the Saints
by Jacobus de Voraigne
A.D. 1260

It was scattered with gruesome gilded paintings of men and women in various stages of torture or crucifixion. I turned to the place of the marker: saint number 146, Saint Jerome. I was surprised to learn that his name in Latin was Hieronymus, like the man who, until today, I'd thought was my father's father.

Apart from his renown for revising the church liturgy fifteen hundred years ago in the reign of the emperor Theodosius, Saint Hieronymus—like Androcles, his predecessor in the famous Roman tale—had healed the paw of a wounded lion. That seemed to ring a bell with respect to something Dacian said earlier today. But I couldn't put my finger on it at the moment.

Just then Wolfgang arrived bearing his tray laden with tubes of medicaments, a pot of surgical implements soaking in disinfectant, a bottle of cognac, and a snifter. His shirtsleeves were rolled up, his tie hanging loose around his open collar. Over his arm was a stack of towels. He set the tray on the low table before the sofa where I'd taken a seat. I put the book beside it. When Wolfgang saw it, he smiled and said, "A little light reading in preparation for your martyrdom, I see."

He trained a nearby floor lamp over the sofa, spread a few towels on the cushions, and took a seat beside me. Then with one swift tug, my sash came loose and the robe—all I was wearing over skimpy undies—fell open. After a glance at my face, he smiled wryly. "Shall I shut my eyes as we proceed, then?" he asked in mock politeness as he extracted my arm from the robe and drew it discreetly closed again.

"Now let Professor Hauser have a closer look." He lifted my arm to the light and carefully examined the wound. He was so close I could smell the aroma of pine and citron—but then I saw the expression on his face.

"I'm sorry to say that this looks really awful," he said. "You've healed too quickly—the skin is overgrown in many places. It will only become worse unless these stitches come out now. But unfortunately it will take a bit more time than I'd first thought, and it may hurt more than I thought, too. I must remove them carefully to be sure the wound doesn't reopen. Drink some cognac. If it hurts too much, bite on a towel."

"Perhaps we should reconsider doing this tonight?" I suggested hopefully.

Wolfgang shook his head. He set my arm down gently and poured a stiff cognac from the decanter on the tray beside us, handing it to me.

"Look here, I've brought plenty of towels to wrap you, but you must lie on your side of the sofa in order for me to get the proper angle of attack. Drink some of that first; it will help."

My stomach was all butterflies, but I drank as he asked. Then I lay on the towel-draped leather sofa, as soft as cradling arms enfolding me, and let Wolfgang cover me with more of the towels. He placed my arm carefully on top. I closed my eyes; the fire was so warm, I could feel the flames licking my eyelids. I tried to relax.

At first the pain was distant and cold as the antiseptic dripped on my skin—but it quickly turned hot. When I felt the slight tug of the forceps against the first stitch, I wondered if this was what a fish might feel when it sensed the first jab of the barbed hook puncturing flesh—no deep pain or fear yet, only the dim sense that something might be terribly, terribly wrong.

From the first tug, it was like scraping a pin against glass. The pain crawled deeply into the bone with a slow, nagging ache. I tried not to flinch and make it worse, but the dull, rhythmic throbs were almost more than I could bear. Though my eyes were shut, I could feel hot tears welling behind my lids. I tried to steel myself with a deep breath for each new assault.

After what seemed forever, the tugging stopped. When I opened my eyes, the dammed-back tears trickled in rivulets down my cheeks and onto the towel-draped sofa. My teeth were still gritted against the pain; my stomach was in knots. I knew if I tried to speak, I'd burst into sobs. I took another breath, and let it out slowly.

"That first one was difficult—but I was able to remove it cleanly," Wolfgang said.

"The *first* one!" I protested, struggling to prop myself on my good elbow. "Couldn't we just chop my arm off with one quick whack and have it done?"

"I don't like to hurt you, my dear," he assured me. "But these must come out. It's been too long, as it is."

Wolfgang held the brandy to my lips. I took a big slug and choked a little. He wiped a tear away with his finger and watched in silence as I drank some more. Then I handed the glass back to him.

"You know, when Bettina and I were small, our mother had a saying if she had to do something unpleasant," he told me. "She said, 'A kiss makes everything better.' "

He leaned over and touched his lips to the place where he'd pulled out the stitch. I shut my eyes as I felt the warm glow spread through my arm.

"And does it?" he asked softly. When I nodded mutely, he said, "Then the others must be kissed as well. Now let's have this finished, shall we?"

I lay back on the sofa in preparation for the renewed assault. With each stitch, there was that grinding pain as he pulled carefully with the forceps to release the suture from the skin—then the sharp incisive clip of the scissors that heralded the last tug. After each clip, Wolfgang bent to kiss the place where the stitch had come out. I tried to keep count, but after five or ten minutes I was sure he'd pried out thirty, or three hundred, instead of only the remaining thirteen. Still, the kisses mysteriously did seem to help.

When at last the ordeal was over, Wolfgang gently massaged my arm until the blood returned to wash the pain away. Then he wiped the area with a disinfectant that smelled faintly of fresh wintergreen. When he was through, I pushed myself to a sitting position beside him. He helped me slip my bare arm back into the sleeve, then he sashed up the robe again.

"I'm sure that wasn't pleasant. You've been very brave this past week, my dear, but it's all over now," he told me, hugging me lightly around my good shoulder. "It's only just past seven, so you've plenty of time to bathe and have a rest if you'd like, before we need to think about supper. How are you feeling?"

"I'm okay—just tired," I said. But though the will was there, I didn't actually seem to be moving.

Wolfgang looked at me with what seemed concern—and another expression I couldn't quite decipher. It was true I was dizzy from the wallops of cognac mixed with the megadose of natural endorphins that had been released by nearly half an hour of slow, grinding pain. I leaned back against the cushions and tried to pull myself together. Wolfgang reached over and twirled a strand of my hair in his fingertips meditatively. After a moment he spoke, as if he'd arrived at some private conclusion.

"Ariel, I know this is probably the wrong time, but I don't know when the right time will be. If not now, perhaps never. . . ." He stopped and shut his eyes for a moment. "My god, I don't know how to do this at all. Give me a sip of that cognac."

He leaned across me, plucked my half-full glass from the table, and tossed down a swallow. Then he set the glass down, turned back to me with those fathomless turquoise eyes, and said,

"The first time I saw you in the Technical Science Annex at the nuclear site—did you hear the word I said as I passed?"

"I'm afraid I didn't quite," I told him, though I vividly recalled what I'd *hoped* he'd said—"enchanting" or "exquisite"—a far cry from what I looked or felt like right now. But I was hardly expecting what came next.

"What I said was 'ecstasy.' At that moment, I really thought of abandoning the entire mission. And I assure you, there are those who'd prefer me to do so, even now. My reaction to you has been so—I'm not really sure how to say it—so immediate. I suppose you can see now where this awkward confession is proceeding."

He stopped, for I'd abruptly stood up, completely flustered. Here I was—a girl who balked at dipping her skis into deep powder—being invited once more to leap willy-nilly from yet another dangerous height. I could feel the panic surging, even as I struggled against it. Fuzzy I might be, but it didn't take Albert Einstein to figure out what I wanted Wolfgang to do right now—and what he certainly seemed to want as well.

I tried to be rational about it. What other man would bring me halfway around the world, and invite me home for the night to his very own castle? What other man would look at me, as Wolfgang was looking at me right now—in my dishevelled state, grubby and battered from my travels and travails—and even *want* me? What other man exuded that heady aroma of pine and citron and leather that made me want to drink him in and drown? What in God's name was my problem, anyway?

But deep within, of course, I knew exactly what it was.

Wolfgang stood to face me without touching me. He looked at me with those X-ray eyes that affected me with the same results kryptonite had on Superman: weak knees and an empty mind. Our lips were inches apart.

Without another word, he folded me into his arms and buried his hands in my hair. My lips touched his; then his mouth was on mine as if he were drinking my soul, washing everything from my mind but the warmth of his lips moving down my throat. The robe slipped from my shoulders and fell in a pool around my bare feet. His teeth grazed my shoulder, his hands moved over my body where he'd slid my underthings away. I couldn't breathe.

I pulled back. "I'm frightened," I whispered.

Taking me by the wrist, Wolfgang kissed my palm. "And you think I'm not?" he asked, regarding me seriously. "But there's only one thing we need to remember, Ariel: *Don't look back.*"

Don't look back—the single rule the gods gave Orpheus before he plunged into the underworld to rescue his great love, Eurydice, I thought with a chill.

"I'm not looking back at anything," I lied. Then I lowered my eyes—too late.

"Oh, yes, you are, my love," said Wolfgang, tilting my face up to his. "You're looking at a shadow that has stood between us ever since the moment we met—the shadow of your late cousin, Sam. But after tonight is over, I hope you will never—not even once—look back again."

◆ ◆

Okay, call me crazy. Indeed, that night I myself thought I might've gone more than a little mad. Wolfgang had opened a different kind of wound from the one patched together by those stitches in my arm, a wound that ran deep and bled silently within, so I couldn't be sure exactly how much damage had been done. This unhealed trauma, which I'd managed thus far to hide even from myself, was the fact that I might be more than a little in love with my cousin Sam. So what did the situation make me? A pretty confused girl nuke.

But those conflicting emotions playing war games in my chest were at least partially obliterated that night—along with everything else—by something Wolfgang unlocked that I'd never known or even imagined existed within me. When our two bodies met and melted together, in the heat of passion, there arose in me a mixture of pain and yearning and desire that worked in my veins like a drug, with each new taste only making my craving for him increase. We fed each other's fires with a hungry obsession until every muscle in my body quivered in exhaustion.

At last Wolfgang stretched motionless across me where we lay on the soft Turkish rug before the fire, his face pressed against my stomach. Our skin was drenched in moisture, and the flickering glow of the coals burnished his tautly muscled body as if it had been dipped in bronze. I slid my hand along the curve of his back from his shoulders to his waist, and he shuddered.

"Please, Ariel!" He lifted his shaggy head to grin at me. "You'd better be sure what you're doing, my dear, if you begin that again. You're a sorceress who's put some sort of spell over me."

"You're the one with the magic wand," I said, laughing back.

Wolfgang sat up on his haunches and pulled me to an upright position. The fire had died down to embers. Despite our recent exertions, the room was growing cool.

"Someone has to use some sense for a moment," Wolfgang told me, drawing the bathrobe around my shoulders again. "You need something to relax you."

"Whatever you were just doing seemed to be working fine," I assured him.

Wolfgang shook his head and smiled. He pulled me to my feet, scooped his arms beneath me, and carried me up to my room and through to the bathroom, where he set me down again and drew us a hot bath. He splashed in plenty of mineral salts, then he fetched us fresh clothes and laid them out near the tub. As we sank into the aromatic waters, Wolfgang soaked a thick sea sponge and drizzled warm water over my shoulders and breasts.

"You're the most desirable thing I've ever seen," he said, kissing my shoulder from behind. "But I think we should be practical. It's only just after nine, right now. Are you very hungry?"

"Voracious," I said, suddenly realizing it for the first time.

So after we bathed and toweled off, we threw on the warm clothes and walked down through the vineyards to the little restaurant he'd spoken of, overlooking the river. When we got there, another fire was cheerily burning in the hearth.

We had hot soup and a salad of fresh greens along with a *raclette*—that dish of melted cheese with its rich oaky flavor and steamed potatoes and tartly pickled gherkins. We dipped it from the plate with bits of crusty bread, licked the pickle juice from each other's fingers, and washed everything down with an excellent dry Riesling.

When we hiked back up though the vineyards it was just after ten o'clock. Mist was rising from the river; snatches of it slipped, wraithlike, between the rows of clipped-back vinestocks that were just getting their new shoots. Though the air was tinged with a chill, the earth smelled fresh and new with that special dank night scent that heralds the coming of spring. Wolfgang pulled off one of my gloves and took my bare hand in his, and I felt the heat move through me again that I felt whenever he touched me. He smiled down at me as we walked, but just at that moment a fog bank scudded across the moon, hurling us into darkness.

I thought for an instant I heard the sound of a branch cracking, a footstep behind us not far down the hill. I felt a sudden cold pang of fear, though I couldn't think why. I stopped in my tracks, drew my hand from his, and listened. Who could be coming this way so late at night?

Wolfgang's hand pressed my shoulder: he'd heard it, too. "Wait here, and don't move," he said quietly. "I'll be right back."

Don't *move*? I was in panic—but he'd been swallowed into the darkness.

I crouched between two grape stocks and focused my ears on the night sounds as Sam had taught me. For instance, just now I could identify the separate calls of a dozen or more insects against the background of the slowly lapping waters of the river wafting from the valley floor. But beneath these sounds of nature I was able to pick out the whispers of two distinct male voices. I caught only fragments—someone said the word "she" and then I heard "tomorrow."

Just as my eyes had fully dilated in the dark, the scudding fog blew off and the hillside was drenched in silvery moonlight. About twenty yards below where I crouched, two men stood huddled together between the rows of vine. One was clearly Wolfgang; when I stood and he saw me, he raised his arm and waved, then turned away from the other figure and started back up the hill toward me. I glanced at the other man. His crumpled hat cast a shadow on his face so I couldn't make it out in the moonlight, but when he turned back downhill to depart, there was something about the way his slightly shorter, wirier body moved away. . . .

Just then Wolfgang reached me. Tossing his arms around me, he lifted me off my feet and swung me in a circle. Then he set me down and kissed me full on the lips.

"If you could see yourself all in silver light like this," he told me. "You're so incredibly beautiful—I can't believe you're real, and that you're mine."

"Who was that man who was following us?" I asked. "He looked familiar."

"Oh, not at all, it was only my groundskeeper, Hans," he told me. "He works in the next village during the day, and he looks in here each night when he comes back. Often, like tonight, it's rather late. But just now when he returned, someone told him they'd seen lights on earlier, up here at the castle. He was coming to check everything before he went to bed. I suppose I'd neglected to tell him I would be home, and he certainly isn't used to finding houseguests here."

Wolfgang looked down at me and tossed his arm over my shoulder as we started up the hill once more. "And now, my dear little houseguest," he added, squeezing me inside the circle of his arm, "I believe it's time for us to go to bed as well—although not necessarily to sleep."

◆ ◆

But sleep, at long last, we did—though not until well after midnight—among piles of fluffy goosedown comforters in Wolfgang's bed, high at the top of the tower, beneath that vast tinseled canopy of stars. This one-night odyssey of tempestuous passion had certainly cleared my brain out—not to mention my pores. I was finally at peace despite the fact that I had no idea what the morning, much less the rest of my life, might bring.

Wolfgang lay exhausted in the pillows, as well he might, one arm tossed diagonally across my rib cage, his hand caressing a lock of my hair that rested on my shoulder, as he drifted off into a seemingly untroubled sleep. I lay on my back and looked at the midnight sky spangled with stars. I saw the constellation Orion just overhead, Dacian's "home of the Romani" in the sky, with those three bright stars at the center of the hourglass: Kaspar, Balthasar, and Melchior.

The last thing I recall was gazing up into the sky at the enormous serpent of light that Sam said the ancients believed was created by milk spurting from the breasts of the primal goddess Rhea: the Milky Way. I recalled the first time I'd stayed up all night to see it—the night of Sam's *tiwa-titmas*, so many years ago. And then, unconsciously, I slipped back once more into the dream. . . .

◆ ◆

It was well past midnight, but not yet dawn. Sam and I had maintained our vigil most of the night, keeping the fire stirred and fed as we waited for the totem spirits. This last hour we had remained very still, sitting crosslegged on the ground side by side, just our fingertips touching, hoping that before the night was over Sam would finally have the vision he'd waited for, over and over, these past five years. The moon was low on the western horizon and the embers of our fire were merely a glow.

And then I heard it. I wasn't sure, but it seemed like the sound of breathing, and very nearby. I tensed, but Sam pressed my fingertips, warning me to stay still. I held my breath. Now it seemed even closer—just behind my ear—a rough, labored sound, followed by the warm, heady scent of something powerfully feral. An instant later, there was a flicker at the periphery of my eye. I kept my gaze frozen straight ahead, afraid to move even my lashes though my heart was beating wildly. When the blur of movement solidified within my field of vision, I nearly fainted from shock: it was a full-grown cougar—a mountain lion!—only a few feet away from me.

Sam pressed my hand harder to be sure I didn't move, but I was too rigid with fear to try. Even if I wanted to get to my feet, I wasn't sure my legs would carry me—or what I should do if they could. The cat moved across the circle in slow motion, gliding soundlessly except for that even, guttural breathing, almost a purr. Then it stopped beside the dying fire and slowly, gracefully turned to look directly at me.

Just then, a dozen things seemed to happen all at once. There was a loud crashing in the brush at the far side of the circle. The cougar looked quickly over its shoulder toward the sound and hesitated. As

Sam gripped my fingers, a dark shadow suddenly crashed through the underbrush and stumbled into the circle: it was a baby bear cub!

The cougar, snorting heavily, headed toward it. Suddenly, from the brush below, an enormous female bear catapulted after the small one into the open circle. With one circular swipe of her paw, she batted her cub behind her and reared on her hind legs—an enormous silhouette drowning out the moon. The astonished cougar whisked sideways, dropped over the rim of the hill, and was swallowed into the darkened forest. Sam and I sat frozen as the mother bear slowly came down from her hind legs and moved to the rim of our dying campfire. She sniffed a few times at my small backpack, and with her paws rummaged through it until she found my apple. She took it in her mouth, paced back, and gave it to her baby. Then with her nose she nudged him ahead of her, back down into the thick part of the wood.

Sam and I were absolutely silent for the next half hour until the sky began to turn pale. He stirred at last and squeezed my hand, and he whispered,

"I guess you've had your *tiwa-titmas* too, tonight, hotshot. Whoever that lion was hunting for, he sure found the right human—Ariel the Lionhearted."

"And they came for you, too—your totem bears!" I whispered back in excitement.

Getting up and pulling me to my feet, Sam gave me a big bear hug.

"We entered the magic circle together, Ariel, and we saw them—the Lion and the Big and Small Bears. You understand what it means? Our totems have come to show us they're really ours. At dawn, we'll tie the bond by mixing our juices together as blood brothers. After that, everything will be different for both of us," he assured me. "You'll see."

◆ ◆

And everything truly had changed, just as Sam promised. But that was nearly eighteen years ago, and tonight in Wolfgang's bed, beneath the rotating circle of sky, was the first time since childhood that my totem had come to me in a dream.

Then just before slipping back into predawn sleep, I thought I glimpsed the connection I'd been hunting last night, with Saint Hieronymus and his wounded lion. As Dacian had pointed out yesterday, the zodiac sign opposite the "ruler" of each new aeon was considered by the ancients as the symbolic coruler of each coming age—just as the Virgin Mary had wielded equal symbolic clout along with the school of Christian fish. Since I knew that the sign in the zodiac opposite Aquarius was Leo the lion, maybe my dream signified that my totem lioness had come to me to draw me back once more into the magic circle.

When I awoke in the morning, it didn't take long to figure out I was no longer on a mountaintop with Sam watching the sun rise. I was alone in bed on the top floor of Wolfgang's castle surrounded by pillows and down comforters—but the sun was already flooding into the room. What time was it? I sat up in panic.

Wolfgang arrived just then, dressed in slacks and a soft grey cashmere turtleneck, bearing last night's tray, now laden with cups and plates, a steaming pot of chocolate, a basket of rolls and hot croissants. I helped myself to a dark, crusty roll as Wolfgang sat on the bed and poured the cocoa.

"So what's today's agenda?" I asked him. "We never actually got around to discussing it as we'd planned last night."

"Our flight to Leningrad departs at five this afternoon, and the monastery at Melk will open at ten A.M.—a bit more than an hour from now—which leaves us several hours of study there before we must head for the airport."

"Did Zoe give any clues about what we should be looking for?" I asked him.

"A connection that will link the documents that were rescued and hoarded by your grandmother all those years," said Wolfgang. "The monastery of Melk houses a large medieval collection that could provide us that missing thread."

"But if this monastery's library has as many books as the one we visited yesterday, how will we ever find anything in just a few hours?" I asked.

"Like your relatives, I'm hoping that *you* will find what we're looking for."

◆ ◆

That cryptic reply was all Wolfgang had time for, if I was to shower, dress, and get moving before the monastery opened. I was ready to leave when I suddenly recalled something: I asked if I could use the machine in his office to answer yesterday's fax from the States.

When I went down to the small office I tried to organize my thoughts. I wanted to communicate to Sam yesterday's more important events, but I knew there was something I had to confront first. I felt pretty awkward even thinking of Sam, much less writing, given my surroundings and my recent activities. It might seem ridiculous, but I knew if anyone could pick up on my vibes, torrid or otherwise—even separated by thousands of miles of fiber-optics—it was Sam. It occurred to me that maybe he already *had*. It hadn't been lost on me that that lioness wasn't the only one who'd visited my dreams last night. Walking beside my moccasin tracks through the dream world were Sam and his animal totems too.

Pushing these thoughts to the back of my mind, I tried to come up with a double-entendre note—something short, sweet, and to the point, yet conveying as much as possible. Recalling that Sam was calling himself Sir Richard Francis Burton these days, I came up with the following:

> Dear Dr. Burton,
> Thanks for your memo. Your team seems on target. I too am ahead of schedule established as of our last meeting: a whale of a job accomplished. If problems arise in my absence, contact me directly via IAEA. I depart for Russia, 5pm Vienna time today.
> Best regards, Ariel Behn

Most of this should be pretty clear to Sam, I thought: I'd received his fax and had understood it. The only thing we'd "established" at our last meeting—since we didn't know yet where Pandora's papers were—was that I would personally try to reach Dacian Bassarides and pump him for information. So the statement that I was ahead of schedule would convey that I'd managed to do so. The whale reference—the whale being the floating repository of clan totem memory—should tell Sam I'd safely stashed the "gift" that my last fax said I was now in possession of.

Much as I'd have liked to share more, when I contemplated trying to encode in this brief time the complexities of what I'd learned about the rest of my family—not to mention sacred hallows and vanished cities and zodiacal constellations—I confess I foundered. But at least now Sam would know this much: that the game was afoot. After shredding and burning my original memo in the fireplace and scattering it among the cold ashes—better to be safe than sorry—I went outside and found Wolfgang just coming across the lawn to find me.

"We're ready to go," he told me. "I've put our luggage in the car, so we needn't come back to the castle. We can leave directly from Melk for the airport. Claus has a key and will tidy up here when we've gone."

"Who's Claus?" I asked.

"My groundskeeper," Wolfgang replied, opening the passenger door and handing me in. He went around back and locked the trunk, then got behind the wheel.

"I thought his name was Hans," I said as he turned the key in the ignition and adjusted the choke.

"Whose name?" said Wolfgang. He pulled the car out from beneath the tree and crossed the lawn, navigating the drawbridge carefully.

"The guy you just called Claus," I said. "Last night, when your groundskeeper followed us up the hill in the dark, you told me his name was Hans." I didn't feel it necessary to mention that all along I'd felt there was something suspicious about the fellow, anyway.

"That's right: Hans Claus," Wolfgang said. "It's more customary in these parts to call such people by their family names. But perhaps last night I did otherwise."

"You're sure it's not Claus *Hans*?" I suggested.

Wolfgang glanced over at me with one lifted eyebrow and a puzzled smile. "Is this an interrogation? I'm afraid I'm not used to that, though I may safely assure you I do know the names of my own servants."

"Okay," I conceded. "Then what about your own name? You never mentioned to me that there was a real person named Kaspar Hauser."

"But I thought you already knew of him," he said as we navigated downhill through the vineyards. "The Wild Boy of Nürnberg, as they called him. The legend of Kaspar Hauser has been a very famous one in Germany."

"I know about it now; I've read up on him," I said. "Instead, you implied you were named for one of the biblical Magi. Maybe you know more about this Kaspar Hauser than I do, but it appears his main claims to fame were his shadowy past and his unexplained murder. It seems strange that anyone would want to saddle a child with either of those associations."

Wolfgang laughed. "But I've been thinking of him myself! I was astounded yesterday by Dacian Bassarides's story of those seven hidden cities of Solomon. I suspect both Kaspar Hauser and the town of Nürnberg are related to those cities, as perhaps too are Adolf Hitler and the sacred hallows he researched at Melk. I was going to speak of it last night, but I was—somewhat distracted." He smiled. "After listening to Dacian, what I think may connect all these things is the *Hagalrune.*"

"*Hagalrune?*" I said.

"*Hagal* in old German meant hail—you know, pellets of ice—one of the two important symbols of Aryan power: fire and ice," said Wolfgang. "The swastika has since ancient times symbolized the power of fire. It was carved on many Eastern fire temples like the one Dacian mentioned. More important, Nürnberg, the town where Kaspar Hauser first appeared, is considered the absolute geomantic center of Germany: the three lines forming the *Hagal* rune cross from other parts of Europe and Asia, meeting at Nürnberg to form a cauldron of power."

I felt a chill as Wolfgang, removing one hand from the steering wheel, drew a sign in the air with his finger—precisely the image that had formed across my computer screen the night Sam had begun to communicate with me in code:

My heart was pounding. I wished I could speak with Sam. I drew my coat collar up, more to still my hands than for warmth. Wolfgang didn't seem to notice; he replaced his hand on the wheel and kept speaking as he drove.

"This placement of the *Hagal* rune at Nürnberg is central to everything Adolf Hitler ever said or did," he told me. "As soon as Hitler became German chancellor, his first act was to form a college of *Rutengänger*—how you would say?—water diviners."

"We call them dowsers," I said. "It's an old practice among Native Americans: they use Y-shaped willow or hazel switches balanced between their fingertips as they move over terrain to find underground water."

"Yes, exactly," Wolfgang said. "But these men of the German college didn't only look for water, they were searching for sources of power within the earth, forces of energy the Führer could tap into, in order to increase his own powers. If you watch those old films of Hitler, you'll see what I describe. He'll be standing in his open car as it moves along the street, with the throngs cheering around him, but before the car completely comes to rest, it backs up and goes forward, adjusting until it settles on exactly the right spot.

"You see, Hitler's dowsers went first to measure the forces, to locate the most propitious spot to stop the car—and find the right building or window or balcony for him to give a speech. These forces protected him against sabotage, and also increased his own energy. You know how many assassination attempts failed—even bombs planted beside him in an enclosed room—because of the power grid shielding him. And it was known from ancient times that there was nothing stronger than the forces that Adolf Hitler later tried to harness, there at Nürnberg."

"Whatever Dacian may believe, you can't imagine that Hitler actually survived multiple assassination attempts because of some weird force like a 'hail rune'?" I said.

"I'm saying what *he* believed—and I've plenty of evidence to support it," he assured me. And he began as we drove toward Melk.

◆ ◆

THE HAIL RUNE

Even at so late a date as the end of the Napoleonic Wars, the upbringing in a cage of an abandoned boy like Kaspar Hauser was not unheard of. Many situations were known of children who'd been raised by wild beasts. But until Kaspar Hauser's case, few had prompted scientific study.

A ritual was commonly practiced by many fraternal orders or secret groups, involving the spilling of royal blood. Three kinds of death were delivered at once, to propitiate the gods of three realms: fire, air, and water. These were symbolized by blows to the head, the chest, and the genitals. We only know that the first two of these blows were practiced on Kaspar Hauser.

It was widely believed after his death that the boy was descended from nobility or royalty, that he'd been kidnapped at birth and raised by peasants in bizarre conditions, confined in a space so low that he could not even stand up, and fed on a diet of barley bread and water—interestingly enough, the food anciently given an animal being prepared as a sacrifice. In other words, Kaspar Hauser was very likely the victim of an unexplained pagan ritual that suddenly surfaced in Nürnberg at the beginning of the modern era. One hundred years later, Adolf Hitler would be completely fascinated by the implications of this story.

Toward the end of the last century, around the time Hitler was born in 1889, there was a movement resurgent throughout Germany to delve into the *völkisch* roots of the Germanic people, the common folk or peasants, as they were pictured in Norse legends and German fairy tales—to renew traditional values and customs believed to comprise the very core of the Teutonic soul and bring back a golden age.

At the time, it was widely believed by German-speaking peoples that for thousands of years there had been a secret plot against them, rooted in a desire by the tribes of Mediterranean stock—for example, the Romans during the Empire, the Moors in medieval Spain—to conquer all the northern peoples, those of so-called Aryan blood, and perpetrate cultural genocide against them. It was also held that these Teutonic ancestors had a higher culture than those of the Mediterranean, and kept their blood purer and unsullied by any hybrid contact with other groups—much like today's Brahman caste in India.

Despite this supposed Nordic superiority, the runic alphabet was a late development—around 300 B.C.—possibly borrowed by the Teutons from the Celts or another group. As with previous cultures, however, the skill of writing and the runes themselves were invested with magical, even divine, significance.

The *Hagalrune* is the ninth letter of the runic alphabet. Nine is a very powerful Nordic number: the *Havamal*, part of the famous Icelandic epic the *Edda*, tells us that the Norse god Wotan had to hang on the World Tree for nine days and nights in order to become initiated into the power and mystery of the runes.

Nine was the most important number to Hitler: the date November 9 carried mystical meaning for him: as he said, "The ninth of November 1923 was the most important day of my life." That was the day of the Munich *putsch* that sent him to jail, where he wrote *Mein Kampf*. But November 9 is an important date in the history of our part of the world. As well, it is the date of Napoleon's coup ending the French Revolution, the death of Charles de Gaulle, the German revolution resulting in the abdication of Kaiser Wilhelm at the end of World War

I, the abdication of Ludwig III of Bavaria who founded the Second Reich, and also *Kristallnacht*, that night in 1938 when riots of broken glass against the Jews took place all over Austria and Germany.

But the *Hagal* rune has other meanings of importance. It stands for the sound equal to our alphabetical letter *h*—a letter that does not exist in the Greek alphabet. This is, by no coincidence, the letter beginning the last names of both Adolf *Hitler* and Kaspar *Hauser*. That the rune was a magical talisman for Hitler is borne out by the curious fact that many of his inner circle also had names that began with *H*:

Heinrich *Himmler* the occultist, head of the widely feared *Schutzstaffel*, or SS. "Putzi" *Hanfstaengl*, head of the Nazi foreign press department. Reinhard *Heydrich*, the butcher of Prague, head of the SD, whose assassination during the war led to the Nazi massacre of an entire Czechoslovakian village. And the Führer's closest friend, Rudolf *Hess*, who helped draft *Mein Kampf* and later rose to be second in command to Hitler. Hess was born and raised in Egypt, where he absorbed many occult teachings, too. Hess introduced Hitler to his former professor Karl *Haushofer*, founder of German geopolitics and the Nazis' favorite theorist. Then there was the Nazi philosopher Martin *Heidegger*. And Hitler's personal photographer Heinrich *Hoffmann*, who was instrumental in his rise and who introduced the Führer to his assistant, the woman Hitler would marry just before his death, Eva Braun. And in the nuclear field, the chemist Otto *Hahn*, who, with Lise Meitner, conducted the first successful fission experiment; and Werner *Heisenberg*, who was in charge of Hitler's atomic bomb project.

There were many who shared Hitler's early interests, such as Hans *Horbiger*, father of the *Welteislehre* or Theory of World Ice—the idea that ice ages were caused by planetary collisions and, before each age, fabled cities like Atlantis, Hyperborea, and Ultima Thule sank or vanished beneath the ground along with their people. During such cataclysms, great seas became deserts like the Gobi, where underground kingdoms still exist and thrive today, like Dacian's lost cities of Solomon. Horbiger maintained that the Lord of the World would rise at the dawn of the coming aeon—a theory so popular that the Nazis legitimized its study into an official science.

Another contact of Hitler associated with the *Hagal* rune was noted astrologer and psychic Erik Jan *Hanussen*, who cast Hitler's horoscope on Christmas of 1932. He and Hitler had met as early as 1926, at the home of a wealthy Berlin socialite, and Hanussen had given him advice ever since—especially in speaking and body techniques for maximum hypnotic effect upon large crowds. In the year-end horoscope Hanussen predicted success, but only if "adverse forces" currently opposing Hitler—and there were many—were overcome. Hitler could prevail by eating a mandrake root dug by the light of a full moon from a garden at his birthplace, Braunau-am-Inn. Hanussen himself traveled there, dug the root, and on New Year's Day delivered it to Hitler where he was staying at his leased cottage in the Obersalzburg.

The very night he received his horoscope and ate the mandrake root, Adolf Hitler went with Eva Braun, Putzi Hanfstaengl, and some other friends to see a performance of Richard Wagner's opera *Die Meistersinger von Nürnberg*. As it was later reported in Hanfstaengl's diary, after the opera Hitler gave a lengthy commentary—for it is known he had committed all of Wagner's works to memory—about the hidden meaning Wagner had incorporated in his libretto. When Hitler left the supper at the Hanfstaengls' that night, he signed their guest book and made a point of remarking the date: January 1, 1933.

He told his friend Putzi: "This year belongs to us."

From that moment onward, Hitler's fortunes indeed changed. In the first month of 1933 Adolf Hitler went from being the widely caricatured hysterical buffoon who headed up a divided and unpopular political party to being sworn in, on the thirtieth of January, as chancellor of Germany. It was one hundred years since the soil of Germany was consecrated, in 1833, with the spilling of the "royal blood" of Kaspar Hauser.

◆ ◆

When Wolfgang finished this story, we were headed up the long road that passed through the rolling hills and high open meadow toward the white-and-gold-walled monastery of Melk at the top, overlooking the broad, fertile Danube river valley. We pulled onto a broad gravel apron. Wolfgang switched off the engine and turned to me.

"There is one more *H* who was tied to the power of the *Hagal* rune, one that may well be the most significant," he told me. "During the period the young Adolf Hitler lived as a struggling artist in Vienna, the famous father of Germanic paganism, Guido von List, was living there too. List had had a mystical experience in the year 1902, while in his fifties. Recovering from cataract surgery, he went blind for eleven months. During this time he believed he had rediscovered, through occult insight, the long-lost meanings, origins, and powers of the runes. He also claimed he'd received information about an elite order of priests of Wotan existing in Germany in ancient times, and he soon established a modern-day order of that priesthood.

"In the first century, the historian Tacitus had divided the Germans into three tribes. List maintained that these 'tribes' had really been castes: that the outer circle, the Ingaevones, were farmers, and the next, the Istaevones, were military, but the inner circle, the Hermiones, were sacred priest-kings who guarded the secret of the runes.

"So profound did many regard these concepts that by 1908 the List Society for Preservation of Germanic Heritage was created, numbering among its members some of the wealthiest, most prominent people in the German-speaking world. Its fervent following was almost like a new religion. Later it grew into a moving force in the zealous nationalistic movement that led to the First World War. In 1911 List formed a select inner circle within the Society, based on the pagan priesthood. To lend the name a more German-sounding ring, he called it the *Armanenschaft.* Only the members of this new priesthood itself were fully aware that the *Hagal* rune was the secret, unspoken power contained within this name. . . ."

Wolfgang paused and looked at me, as if expecting some reply.

"You mean, the name Hermione?" I said carefully.

I had, of course, observed the resemblance of this turn-of-the-century Teutonic *Armanenschaft* priesthood to the name of an ancestress in my own family, Hermione. And I also saw, with an uneasy twinge, that until now the former Dutch orphan and boat person had remained a sketchy figure who seemed to have done little with her reputedly haunting beauty except marry twice, inherit money, and die young.

"An interesting name, don't you think?" he said, smiling strangely. "In myth, she was the daughter of Helen of Troy, abandoned at age nine when Helen eloped with Paris and the Trojan War began. In Greek the word *herm* means pillar—the real meaning of the name of those ancient tribes at the absolute geographical center of Germany, and of course the name of the runic priesthood, too: the pillars. So you see, if Hermione means Pillar Queen, it's the woman around whom everything revolves. The one who, herself, must be the Axis."

MEPHISTOPHELES:
A great mystery I'll now unfold.
There are goddesses enthroned in solitude, sublime,
Beyond place, beyond time.
Only to think of them makes my blood run cold.
They are the Mothers!

FAUST:
The Mothers, the Mothers! It has a wonderful sound! . . .
How do I reach them?

MEPHISTOPHELES:
There's no path to the unreachable, no map to the unmappable.
There are no locks, no bolts, no barriers there.
Can you envision emptiness everywhere? . . .
Here, take this key to sniff out the true path from all the
others,
Follow it down. It will take you to the Mothers.

—Johann Wolfgang Goethe, *Faust*

Who dares [to love] misery
and embrace the form of Death,
To dance in destruction's dance—
to him, the Mother comes.

—Vivekananda

My grandmother Pandora might have set things in motion by scattering the contents of that box among members of my family, but it now looked like she wasn't the only contender in this game. It was hammered home to me that there were *two* mothers—Pandora and Hermione—who'd spawned all those other recipients of my grandmother's bequest. Like the nails hammered into the *Stock-im-Eisen*, I felt this new axis, Hermione the pillar queen, might help tap into something too.

When it came right down to it, what did I really know about Hermione Behn, the mother of Zoe, Earnest, and Lafcadio? It mattered little whether any or all the stories I'd heard of her were true—whether, as Laf claimed, she'd been a poor Dutch orphan and later a rich South African widow or, as Wolfgang said, she was the namesake of a secret Wotanist-runic-Aryan priesthood, the *Armanenschaft*. So far everything about her from alpha to omega was Greek to me.

But of course, that was the one clue I'd fished from all the opinions, myths, and maybe out-and-out fictions I'd been fed these past few days—the very clue Hitler himself might have been hunting for here at the monastery of Melk. If Hermione connoted 'axis' in Greek, and if there was really some geographical connection to mythology as everyone seemed to think, then the important Hermione—the Hermione I should be looking for—wasn't likely to be found in a phone book, a family album, or a history of early Germanic tribes. It had to be found on a map.

When Wolfgang and I came into the library's entrance hall, I saw it at once: On the far wall, beneath a slab of glass, was a hand-tinted antique map of Europe written in medieval Germanic script. With Wolfgang, I went over and stood before it. Had it been here seventy-five years ago when the young Adolf Hitler walked through these doors?

The typed legend on the wall said, in German, French, and English, that it was from the ninth century, the time of Charlemagne, and depicted important religious sites throughout Europe—churches, shrines, and sanctuaries established since the beginning of the Christian era. Since a Greek name like Hermione seemed to point to a Greek location, it took only a quick scan to find it.

Hermione was a seaport on the southeast coast of the Peloponnesus. On this map, a Christian church was marked there with a tiny cross and a first-century date. Interestingly, it was surrounded by four other marked sites that were identified with the sun god Apollo. So what had clearly been an important pagan site may have been converted, as Dacian Bassarides described yesterday, from worship of a prior aeon's gods to those of a new one. If his idea was right, holy sites of the age of Aries would now be replaced with sites of the new age that had just been dawning two thousand years ago: Pisces, fisher of men, and his mother Virgo, the celestial Virgin.

If Hermione represented an axis on the world grid even before Christianity, it should be connected with earlier pagan sites bearing symbols like Aries the ram and Taurus the bull. Hermione was situated facing Crete, where an earlier culture, the Minoan, coexistent with Egypt, had once flourished. I traced a line from Hermione to Crete, where Zeus, father of the gods, was nursed on Mount Ida by the she-goat Amaltheia—a goat whose image Zeus later fondly set among the stars as another constellation: Capricorn. But I knew there was another god whose worship in the form of a bull had been equally influential on Crete, the very god Uncle Laf had assured me I'd know when to call on in time of need: Dionysus.

Given all this, when I traced the Crete-Hermione axis toward the northwest, as Wolfgang looked on, I found it more than interesting that it ran smack into the heart of the most powerful religious site of ancient times, a site shared by two great gods: Apollo in summer and Dionysus during the long, dark winter months until the sun made its return from the land of the dead. That site, of course, was Delphi.

Here was the python-inspired prophetess, the Pythian, the Delphic oracle. For thousands of years, these successive oracular mouthpieces of Apollo had foretold events and prescribed actions the Greeks had adhered to religiously. No ancient writer doubted that the Delphic oracle could see the interconnected web of time comprising past, present, and future. So a site like Hermione, connecting places as important as Delphi and Cretan Ida, may well have been *the* axis.

I drew an invisible X with my finger across the axis, making a six-pointed asterisk, a *Hagal* rune like the one Wolfgang had drawn earlier in the air.

At this point, it seemed far from coincidental that the first line passed through Eleusis, home of the Eleusinian Mysteries, continuing to the Macedonian peninsula where Mount Athos projects into the Aegean—a site plastered here on the map with dozens of tiny crosses. A famous group of twenty monasteries built by the emperor Theodosius, patron of Saint Hieronymus, Athos was once a major repository of ancient manuscripts repeatedly looted by the Turks and Slavs in

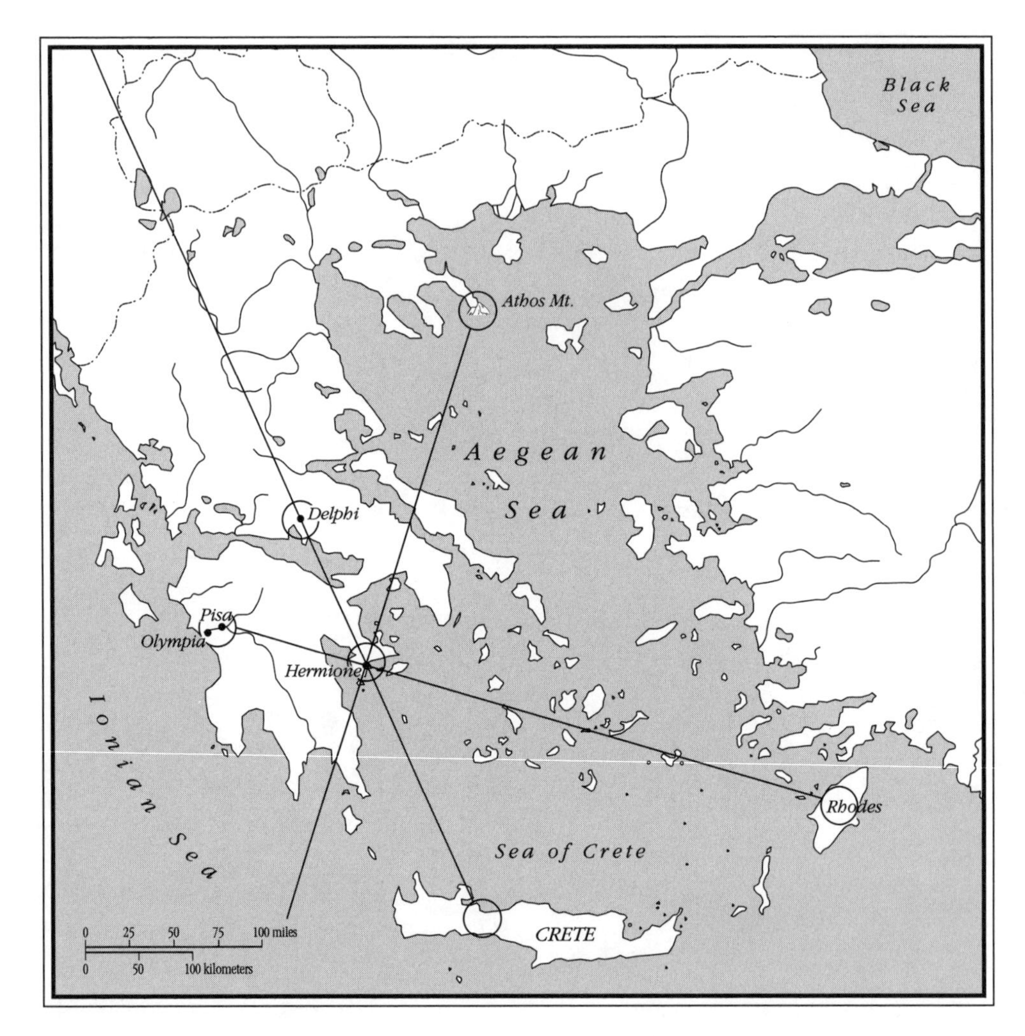

innumerable Balkan wars. Its unusual location, equidistant from Mount Olympus on the Greek mainland and Troy on the Turkish, was visible from each. Perhaps Athos itself was yet another axis?

The other line of my asterisk was even more interesting. It led to Olympia on the Alphaeus river, home of the Olympic games. I'd been there one weekend after a concert of Jersey's in Athens. We'd hiked over broken stone beneath Mount Kronos. Aside from Olympia's famous ruins like the temple of Zeus, there was a relic at Olympia that stuck in my mind: the Heraion, temple of the goddess Hera, wife and sister to Zeus. Though built of plastered wood and less impressive than the Zeus temple, the original Heraion was constructed as early as 1000 B.C. and is the oldest extant temple in Greece.

Then I knew why the name Hermione seemed so familiar (not just familial) to me. In the myths, Hermione was the place Hera and Zeus first landed when they came to Greece from Crete—the entry point of the Olympic gods to the continent of Europe.

Wolfgang, who'd been watching in silence as my finger traced the map beneath the glass, now turned to me.

"Astounding," he said. "I've often walked by this map, but I never saw the connection you've seen at first glance."

A uniformed guard arrived and secured open the high inner doors, and Wolfgang and I entered the gold and white Baroque library of the monastery of Melk. A wall of French windows at the far end overlooked a sprawling terra-cotta-colored terrace; beyond it lay the Danube, its surface glittering like crystals in the morning sun, filling the vast library with bouncing light. As a custodian wiped one of the glass display cases dividing the room, a wiry grey-haired man in a priest's cassock adjusted leather-bound books on a shelf partway down. He turned as we entered, smiled, and came toward us. He seemed somehow familiar.

"I hope you don't mind," Wolfgang said, taking my arm. "I've asked someone to assist us." We went forward to greet him.

"*Professore* Hauser," said the priest, his English heavily flavored with Italian, "I'm happy you and your American colleague were able to arrive early, as I asked. I've already prepared some things for you to see. But *scusa, signorina*, I forget myself: I am Father Virgilio, the library archivist. You will excuse my poor English, I hope? I come from Trieste." Then he added, with a somewhat awkward laugh, "Virgilio, it's a good name for a guide: like Virgil in the *Divina Commedia*, no?"

"Was that who escorted Dante around Paradise?" I asked.

"No, that was Beatrice, a lovely young woman I imagine very much as yourself," he added graciously. "The poet Virgil, I apologize to say, guided him through Purgatory, Limbo, and Hell. I hope your experience with me will be better!" He laughed,and added almost as an afterthought, "But Dante had a third guide, as few seem to recall, one whose works are treasured here in our collection."

"Who was the third guide?" I asked.

"Saint Bernard de Clairvaux. A most interesting figure," Father Virgilio said. "Though he was canonized, many thought him a false prophet, even the Prince of Darkness. He initiated the disastrous Second Crusade, resulting in the destruction of the Crusader armies and the eventual return of the Holy Land to Islam. Bernard also inaugurated the infamous Order of Templars, whose mission was to defend Solomon's temple at Jerusalem against the Saracen; two hundred years later, they were suppressed for heresy. Here at Melk we have illuminated texts of the many sermons Saint Bernard delivered on the Canticle of Canticles, and dedicated to King Solomon."

But as Father Virgilio turned and headed off down the long room, distant bells started clanging in my head, and not for his mention of Song of Songs. As we followed our shepherd, I scanned the books lining shelves to my right and the contents of the imposing glass cases to my left. And I racked my brain, trying to figure out exactly what was bugging me about this black-clad priest. For one thing, Wolfgang hadn't mentioned any spiritual guide on today's agenda, nor any knightly orders I ought to be boning up on. I studied Virgilio as we followed him, and all at once I bristled with anger.

Without those priestly vestments—but with the addition of a dark, battered hat—Father Virgilio might well be the spitting image of someone else. Then I recalled that those few whispered words I'd heard in the vineyard last night had been in English, not German. By the time Father Virgilio stopped before a large glass case near the end and turned to us, I was seething with fury at Wolfgang.

"Is this not a great work of art?" he asked, gesturing to the richly detailed hand-colored manuscript beneath the glass as he glanced from Wolfgang to me with dewy eyes and fingered his crucifix.

I nodded with a wry smile, and said in my rusty German:

"Also, Vater, wenn Sie trun hier mit uns sind, was tut heute Hans Claus?" (So if you're here with us now, Father, what's "Hans Claus" up to today?)

The priest glanced in confusion at Wolfgang, who turned to me and said, *"Ich wusste nicht dass du Deutsch konntest."* (I didn't realize you could speak German.)

"Nicht sehr viel, aber sicherlich mehr als unser österreichischer Archivar hier," I told him coolly. (Not very much, but surely more than our Austrian archivist here.)

"I think perhaps you've helped us enough for the moment, Father," Wolfgang told the priest. "Could you wait in the annex while my colleague and I have a word?"

Virgilio bowed twice, said a few quick *scusa*'s, and bustled from the room.

Wolfgang had leaned over the glass case with folded arms and was gazing down at the gilded manuscript. His handsome, patrician features were reflected in the glass. "It's magnificent, isn't it?" he observed, as though nothing had happened. "But of course, this copy was executed several hundred years after Saint Bernard's time—"

"Wolfgang," I interrupted this reverie.

He straightened and looked at me with clear, guileless turquoise eyes.

"That morning back at my apartment in Idaho, as I recall, you assured me you would always tell me the truth. What exactly is going on here?"

The way he was looking at me would have melted the *Titanic*'s iceberg, and I confess it did a pretty good job on me—but that wasn't all the ammo up his sleeve.

"I'm in love with you, Ariel," he said simply and directly. "If I say that there are matters in which you must simply trust me, I expect you to believe me—to believe *in* me. Do you understand? Is this not enough?"

"I'm afraid not," I told him firmly.

To do him credit, he registered no surprise, just complete attention, as if waiting for something. I wasn't sure exactly how to say what I knew I must.

"Last night I believed I was falling in love with you, too," I told him sincerely. His eyes narrowed, as they had when he'd passed me that first day in the annex lobby. But I couldn't hold back my frustration. "How could you make love to me that way," I said, glancing to be sure no one could overhear, "then turn around and lie to me, as you did in the vineyard? Who is this damned 'Father Virgilio' following us around like a wraith?"

"I suppose you do deserve an explanation," he agreed, rubbing one hand over his eyes. Then he looked at me again with an open expression. "Father Virgilio truly is a priest from Trieste; I've known him for years. He has worked for me, though not in the capacity I told you earlier. More recently, by doing research here in this library. And I did want you to meet him—but not late last night when I had . . . other things in mind." He smiled a little self-consciously. "After all, he *is* a priest."

"Then what was all that Hans-Claus business this morning, if you knew we were coming here to meet him?"

"I was worried last night, when you thought Virgilio looked familiar," Wolfgang said. "Then this morning, when I made that slip and you pursued it, it was already too late to change plans. How could I imagine you'd be able to recognize him from earlier yesterday, just by one glimpse in darkness last night, and at such a distance?"

I was getting that déjà-vu-all-over-again feeling as I racked my brain for when I'd seen Father Virgilio "earlier." But I didn't have to ask.

"You have every right to despise me for what I've done," said Wolfgang apologetically. "But it was at such short notice, when I learned I wouldn't be joining you and Dacian Bassarides for lunch—that man is so unpredictable! I shouldn't have been surprised if he'd spirited you away and I'd never seen you again. Luckily, I had chosen a restaurant where they knew me well enough to accept Virgilio as a 'temporary employee'—to look out for you during the afternoon—"

So *that* was it! No wonder he'd seemed familiar to me in the vineyard. In my frenzied preoccupation yesterday afternoon at the Café Central, I'd hardly glanced at the faces around me, yet I must have registered that same figure performing some service around our table perhaps half a dozen times. Now, torn between relief and worry, I wondered just how much our impromptu busboy had overheard of our luncheon conversation. Though it seemed Wolfgang had only been trying to protect me from the vagaries of my unknown grandfather, I cursed myself for not being more vigilant, as Sam had taught me all through childhood.

But I had no chance to dwell on these thoughts. Father Virgilio, peering through the entrance doors, seemed to have decided that adequate dust had settled to cushion his return. Seeing him, Wolfgang bent toward me and spoke quickly. "If you can read Latin half as well as you speak German, I shouldn't comment in front of Virgilio on the first line of this manuscript of Saint Bernard's: it might embarrass him."

I looked down at the book and shook my head. "What does it say?"

" 'Divine love is reached through carnal love,' " said Wolfgang with a complicitous smile. "Later, when we've a free moment together, I'd like to test that theory."

Father Virgilio had arrived with a map of Europe, a modern one. He unfolded it on a trestle table before us and said, "It is important that from ancient times a mysterious tribe in this region held the female bear as their totem, and that they were possessed of an almost mystical reverence for a substance with many alchemical properties: salt."

◆ ◆

THE BEARS

At age seven, I carried the sacred vessels . . . when I was ten I was a bear girl of Artemis at Brauron, dressed in the little robe of crocus-colored silk.

—Aristophanes, *Lysistrata*

Bernard Sorrel—the saint's family name—was born in A.D. 1091, at the dawn of the Crusades. On his father's side he was descended from wealthy nobles of the Franche-Comté, on his mother's from the Burgundian dukes of Montbard—"bear mountain." The family castle, Fontaines, was situated between Dijon in northern Burgundy and Troyes in the province of Champagne—a region of vineyards planted from Roman stock that were consistently under cultivation since ancient times.

Bernard's father died in the First Crusade. The young man suffered a nervous collapse when his beloved mother died also, while he was away at school. At the age of twenty-two, Bernard joined the Benedictine monks. Always of fragile health, he soon became ill, but was given a small cottage on the nearby estate of his patron Hugues de Troyes, count of Champagne, where he recuperated. The following year Count Hugues visited the Holy Land to see at first hand the Christianized kingdom of Jerusalem that had been established after the successful First Crusade. On his return, the count at once ceded part of his property to the Church: the wild valley of Clairvaux branching off the river Aube. There, at age twenty-four, Bernard Sorrel established an abbey and became first abbot of Clairvaux.

It is relevant to our story that Clairvaux is situated at the heart of the region that in ancient times encompassed today's French Burgundy, Champagne, Franche-Comté, Alsace-Lorraine, and adjacent portions of Luxembourg, Belgium, and Switzerland. This region was once ruled by the Salii, whose name means People of the Salt. These Salic Franks, like the Roman emperors from the time of Augustus, claimed their ancestors came from Troy in Asia Minor—as place-names on the map like *Troyes* and *Paris* attest. Ancient Troy itself had profound connections to salt. Bounded on the east by the Ida range of mountains, its *Halesian* plains are watered by the *Tuzla* River, whose pre-Turkish name was *Salniois*—all these names meaning salt.

The Salii claimed that their ancestor Meroveus, "Sea-Born," was the son of a virgin who'd been impregnated while swimming in salt water. His descendants, the Merovingians, lived in the time of King Arthur. They were believed, like the British king, to possess magical powers associated with the polar axis and its two celestial bears. The name Arthur means bear, and the Merovingians took for their battle standard the figure of an upright female fighting bear.

This connection between salt and bears goes back to two goddesses of ancient mystery. The first is Aphrodite who, like Meroveus, rose "foam-born" from the salt sea. She is ruler of both the dawn and the morning star. The other is Artemis, the virgin bear goddess, whose symbol is the moon, which nightly pulls the tides of the sea. This forms an axis between dawn and night, and also between the celestial pole of the bear and the fathomless sea.

It's no accident that many place-names in the region just described are connected with aspects of these two. *Clairvaux* itself means vales of light, and the *Aube*, the river at Clairvaux, means dawn. Of equal or greater importance then there are those names beginning with *arc-, ark-, art-, or arth-*, like the *Ardennes*, named after *Arduinna*, a Belgian version of Artemis—and the German *bär* or *ber* found in place-names like *Bern* and *Berlin*. All these names, of course—like Bernard's itself—mean bear.

In his first ten years as abbot, Bernard de Clairvaux rose swiftly—one might say miraculously—to become the leading French churchman, a confidant of popes. When two popes were elected by separate contingents of Italians and French, Bernard healed the schism and got his own candidate, Innocent II, seated on the pontifical throne. This success was followed by the election of a former Clairvaux monk, Eugenius, as the next pope, for whom Bernard preached the launching of the Second Crusade. Bernard was instrumental, too, in gaining Church sanction for the Knights Templars, an order founded jointly by his uncle André de Montbard and his patron Count Hugues de Troyes.

The Crusades began a millennium after Christ and lasted some two hundred years. Their mission was to reclaim the Holy Land from the "infidel," *al-Islam*, and unite the Eastern and Western churches, Constantinople and Rome, with a common focal point in Jerusalem. Of specific importance was to gain Western control of key religious sites, like Solomon's temple.

The real Temple of Solomon, built around 1000 B.C., was destroyed by the Chaldeans some five centuries later. Though it was rebuilt, many holy relics already were reported missing, including the Ark of the Covenant from the time of Moses, which had been brought back to Jerusalem by Solomon's father, David. This second temple, refurbished by Herod the Great just before the time of Christ, was razed by the Romans in the Jewish Wars of A.D. 70 and never rebuilt. So the "temple" guarded by the Templars in the Crusades was actually one of two Islamic structures built in the eighth century: the *Masjid el-Aqsa*, or Farthest Mosque, and the slightly older Dome of the Rock, site of David's threshing floor and of the Hebrews' first altar in the Holy Land.

Beneath both these sites ran a vast man-made system of water conduits, caves, and tunnels, begun before the time of David and mentioned many times in the Bible as honeycombing the entire Temple Mount. In these catacombs also lay "Solomon's stables," caves used by the Knights Templar, reputedly capable of sheltering two thousand horses. One of the Dead Sea Scrolls from Qumran, the Copper Scroll, lists an inventory of treasure once hidden in these caves, including many ancient Hebrew holy relics and manuscripts, and the spear that pierced the side of Christ.

This spear was discovered by the first Crusaders while besieging Syrian Antioch. Trapped by Saracens for over a month between the inner and outer siege walls, the Crusaders resorted to eating horses and pack animals, and many died of starvation. But one monk had a vision that the famous spear was buried in the Church of St. Peter beneath their very feet. The Crusaders exhumed the spear and bore it before them as a standard. Its powers enabled them to conquer Antioch and march on successfully to storm Jerusalem.

The name Frank—*Franko* in Old High German—meant spear, while the Franks' neighbors, the Saxons, were called *Sako*, meaning sword. These tribes of Germanic warriors proved so formidable that Arab chroniclers called *all* Crusaders Franks.

◆ ◆

"Although the Second Crusade, propagandized by Bernard de Clairvaux, had proved a disaster," Father Virgilio concluded, "the Templars continued to flourish throughout his lifetime. The abbot of Clairvaux then set himself the curious task of writing one hundred separate allegorical and mystical sermons on the Song of Songs, of which eighty-six were completed at his death. More peculiar still is the fact that Bernard is known to have identified himself with the Shulamite, the black virgin of the poem—with the Church, of course, identified with Solomon, her beloved king. Some believe the Songs are an encoded form of an ancient esoteric initiation ritual which once provided a key to the mystery religions, and that Bernard had deciphered it. Yet the Church's regard for Bernard was such that he was canonized only twenty years after his death in 1153."

"What about the Order of Knights Templar that he helped launch?" I asked him. "You told us that later they were convicted of heresy and wiped out."

"Hundreds of books have been written on their fate," Virgilio said. "It was chained to a star that rose swiftly, burned brightly for two centuries, then vanished as quickly as it had come. Their initial charter from the pope was to protect pilgrims traveling to the Holy Land, and to secure the Temple Mount. But these Poor Knights of Jerusalem and the Temple of King Solomon soon became Europe's first bankers. They were eventually ceded properties amounting to a tithe by the crowned heads of Europe. Highly political, they held themselves independent of Church or State. Eventually the Templars were charged by both these institutions with heresy, treason, and deviant Satanic sexual practices. They were rounded up to a man, and tortured and burned at the stake by the Inquisition.

"As for the Templars' vast hoards of treasure," he added, "these reputedly included holy relics possessing enormous powers, like the sword of Saint Peter and the spear of Longinus, not to mention the

Holy Grail itself—relics that were sought by courtly knights throughout the Middle Ages, from Galahad to Parsifal. The whereabouts of this treasure, however, is a mystery that remains, down to the present, unresolved."

Of course, I hadn't overlooked the parallels between Father Virgilio's medieval whodunit and all the previous details dropped by everyone else. There were the references to Solomon and his temple, tying them to everyone from the Queen of Sheba to the Crusaders. But Virgilio's tale seemed also to point elsewhere: once again, to a map. Though I couldn't see the whole pattern, I was hoping at least to tie up a few loose threads. Then Wolfgang did it for me as we looked at Virgilio's map before us on the trestle table.

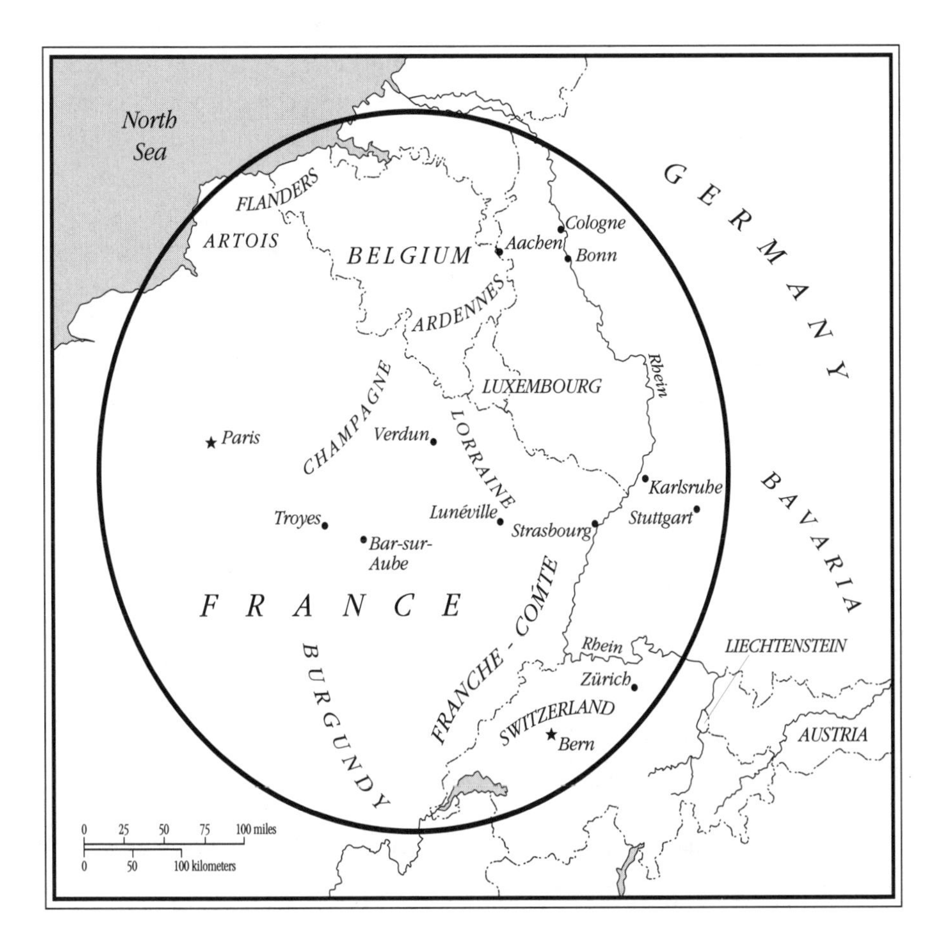

"It's incredible the way things leap out, when you look at a map," Wolfgang said. "I now see how many of the old epics—the Icelandic Eddas, even the earliest Grail legends of Chrétien de Troyes—describe battles and adventures that are centered on this one region. When Richard Wagner wrote the *Ring* cycle that Hitler admired so much, he based it on the Germanic epic the *Nibelungenlied*, which tells how the Storm from the East, Attila the Hun, was fought by the Nibelungs—who were none other than the Merovingians."

"But all that happened long before the Crusades," I pointed out. "Even if we're talking about the same piece of turf, how does it relate to Bernard or the Templars, hundreds of years later?"

"Everything," said Virgilio, "is shaped by what went before. In this case, it relates to three kingdoms: the one established by Solomon's father, based in Jerusalem; the kingdom set up by the Merovingians in fifth-century Europe; and the Christian kingdom of Jerusalem, founded five centuries later in the Crusades, by men who came from the same region of France. There are many theories, but they all pertain to one thing: the blood."

"The blood?" I said.

"Some claim the Merovingians carried sacred blood," Virgilio explained. "A bloodline descended perhaps from Christ's brother James, or even from a secret marriage between the Magdalene and Jesus himself. Others say the blood of the Saviour was collected by Joseph of Arimathea in the Holy Grail, a vessel later taken by the Magdalene to France and preserved against a day when science could restore a human being to flesh."

"You mean, like DNA re-creation, or cloning?" I said with a grimace.

"Such views, of course, are not only heretical but, if I may say so, rather foolish," said Virgilio with a wry smile. "There is one curious fact we *do* know about bloodlines: that all the kings of Jerusalem over the years of Christian rule were descended from one woman, Ida of Lorraine."

It hadn't escaped my attention that there were two Mount Idas of importance. The first, on Crete, was the birthplace of Zeus, a major site of Dionysian worship, and also connected to Hermione on the map. The second, on the coast of modern-day Turkey, was the site of the Judgment of Paris; from it the gods had watched the progress of the Trojan War. And now a third Ida, according to Virgilio, was the ancestress of every king who'd ruled Jerusalem for two hundred years. A woman from the very region we'd spoken of. And apparently that wasn't all.

"The big story of the high Middle Ages in Europe," said Virgilio, "was not the Crusades, but rather the blood feud between two families known in history books by the Italian names Guelphs and Ghibellines. They were actually German: Bavarian dukes called *Welf*, meaning whelp or bear cub, and Swabian Hohenstaufens called *Waiblingen*, or honeycomb. One man alone, coincidentally also a protégé of Bernard de Clairvaux, combined the blood of these adversaries. This was Frederick Barbarossa, who survived Bernard's disastrous Second Crusade to become Holy Roman Emperor.

"As the first ruler to unite in his veins the powerful bloodlines of those two Germanic tribes, whose private battles had defined the history of the Middle Ages, Barbarossa was regarded as the saviour of the German people, someone who would one day unite them to lead the world.

"He went on to forge Germany into a major power, and to launch the Third Crusade at age sixty-six. But en route to the Holy Land, he mysteriously drowned while bathing in a river in southern Turkey. His famous legend maintains that Barbarossa sleeps today within the mountain of Kyffhäuser in the center of Germany, and that he'll rise to come to the aid of the German peoples in their hour of need." Virgilio folded his hands on the map and asked me, "Does it remind you of another story?"

I shook my head as Wolfgang placed his finger on the map and slowly traced a circle around the region Virgilio had spoken of. I froze at his next words.

"According to Hitler's architect, Albert Speer," Wolfgang told me, "it's precisely this area where Heinrich Himmler wished to create, after Germany's victory in the war, an 'SS parallel state.' Himmler planned to put high-ranking storm troopers there with racially pure wives selected by the genealogy research branch of the SS, and to form a separate Reich comprised of them and their children. He wished to purify the blood and reawaken the ancient mystical ties to the land—blood and soil."

I looked at him in horror, but he wasn't quite through.

"This is also certainly why Hitler called his attack to the east Operation Barbarossa—to awaken the waiting spirit of the emperor Frederick, long asleep within the mountain. He wished to invoke the magical blood of the long-lost Merovingians. To bring forth a utopian new world order, based on blood."

It was believed that the blood in [the Merovingians'] veins gave them magical powers: they could make the crops grow by walking across the fields; they could interpret bird-song and the calls of the wild beasts; and they were invincible in battle, provided they did not cut their hair. . . .

Pepin [the first Carolingian] lacked the magical powers inherent in royal blood. He therefore sought the Church's blessing . . . to show that his kingship came not through blood, but from God. Pepin was thus the first monarch to rule by the grace of God. To underline the importance of this act, Pepin was anointed on two occasions, the second time, with his two sons [Charlemagne] and Carloman, [to combine] the new concept of monarchy by divine right with the Germanic concept of magic power carried by blood.

—Martin Kitchen, *Cambridge Illustrated History of Germany*

Tiberias, Galilee: Spring, A.D. 39

INTROIT

◆ ◆

During that time [Herod Antipas] was almost entirely under the influence of a woman who caused him a whole series of misfortunes.

—Emil Schürer, *The History of the Jewish People in the Age of Jesus Christ*

In all the woes that curse our race
There is a lady in the case.

—Gilbert & Sullivan

Herod Antipas, tetrarch of Galilee and Peraea, stood with widespread arms at the center of his royal chambers as he did each morning, while three of his personal slaves prepared him for his appearance at the receiving chambers to hear petitions. They attached the straps of the gold breastplate with its heavy chains of state, and draped the official red robes across his shoulders. His wardrobe complete, the slaves knelt and were dismissed by his freedman, Atticus, who accompanied the guards posted outside to follow the tetrarch along the promenade from his private wing of the vast palace at Tiberias.

This long walk in silence was the only occasion during the day when Herod Antipas ever had time to think—and right now he certainly had a lot of thinking to do. He'd already learned of the horror awaiting him in chambers: the freshly arrived imperial messenger dispatched by the emperor Caligula from his summer home at Baiae—an emperor, as Antipas could ill afford to forget, who regarded himself as a god.

Of all the woes that had befallen Antipas of late, he knew this might well prove the worst. And in this case, as in previous crises, the axis was centered upon his own family. Perhaps it ran in their blood, Antipas thought with a kind of dark humor. As many had observed, the brief history of the Herodian dynasty wasn't lacking in problems of consanguinity. Whether intermarriage, blood feuds, bloodletting, or out-and-out bloodbaths, it seemed the Herods liked to keep things in the family.

This canker in the Herodian bloodline was derived directly from Antipas's father, Herod the Great, a man steeped in his own sensuality and greed, who had slaked his thirst for riches and power in the blood of his own relations—a group that had included ten wives and dozens of offspring, many of whom he'd dispatched with an efficacy otherwise reserved for sacrificial beasts.

Herod Antipas himself had once stood very far down the line of succession. But due to the sudden shortage of heirs at his father's death forty years ago, the kingdom had devolved upon himself, his brother Archelaus, and his half brother Philip of Jerusalem. Now, with both these brothers dead, Antipas found himself at sixty the last Herod still in possession of Jewish lands. But as of today, all that had changed—thanks in large part to the machinations of his ambitious wife Herodias.

Antipas knew he'd been cursed from the start by this love, this lust, this obsessive passion he felt for the woman who was actually his niece—and who, when they'd first met, had herself been married to another of his Herodian half brothers, Herod Philip of Rome. Galling as the theft of a brother's lawful spouse might have been to his Jewish subjects here in Galilee, the wound was further exacerbated by Antipas's repudiation of his first wife, a princess of royal blood.

To make matters worse, ten years ago, at the goading of Herodias and her daughter Salome, Antipas had actually executed a grass-roots spiritual leader from the Essene community who'd done nothing more than to publicly call the tetrarch's wife a whore. Not satisfied with having a man beheaded to salvage her reputation, the power-hungry Herodias was now at it again—this time within their own long-embattled family.

More than forty years ago, when Herodias's father was executed by Herod the Great, young Herodias and her brother Agrippa had been carried off by their mother to Rome, where they had grown up alongside the children of the imperial family. Agrippa was now spoiled out of all proportion. At nearly fifty, he was a dissolute spendthrift whose only achievement was having cultivated in himself the tastes of a king. And therein lay the crux of the problem. For thanks to his friendship with Caligula, today Agrippa, the man who would be king, indeed *was* a king.

The moment Tiberius was dead, Caligula—that vile little former dancing-boy who'd succeeded him—had released Agrippa from jail and lavished gifts and lands and titles upon him with the same abandon he would soon exhibit in spending all of Tiberius's legacy of twenty-seven million gold sesterces in less than one year. Among these gifts, Caligula gave Agrippa lands that in Herodias's opinion should certainly have gone to her husband Antipas, including the sacred land where the tomb of Abel, son of Adam and Eve, was located—the spot where the first blood had been shed by mankind.

The Hebrew peoples had always wrestled with the paradox of blood, for had not their God forbidden the shedding of *all* blood with the commandment "Thou shalt not kill"? Antipas might be only the converted Jewish son of a Samaritan mother, but commandment or no, this injunction had proven to be both his personal test and his private curse. And he was about to be tested or cursed once again.

Herod Antipas well knew the poison of power lust still working in the veins of his ambitious relations, not least of all his wife. Humiliated that her brother was made a king when her husband was yet a mere tetrarch, Herodias nagged until Antipas sent a deputation from Galilee to Rome with gifts for the greedy boy emperor, an attempt to bribe him for equal treatment. But this approach had worked against them. Caligula's messenger, just arrived from Baiae, was bearing a list of further contributions expected from the tetrarch. On this list was something that made Antipas's heart contract, for it was an object that, apart from its surface value, held deep meaning for him and him alone.

It went back to that time when they'd gone to the palace built by Herod the Great at Machareus, east of the Dead Sea, to celebrate Antipas's birthday. Herodias's lovely daughter Salome was with them. Still a young girl, Salome had danced in honor of the event. But of course, as Herodias surely knew when choosing Machareus as a birthday site, it was also the very fortress where her hated enemy had long been held in prison. So after her charming dance, Salome had asked the favor.

The hideous scene still haunted Antipas's nightmares. Even now, after so many years, he felt sick to think of it. In her fury, unassuaged by this gruesome death, Herodias had sought further triumph. She'd ordered the severed head of her victim brought into the great hall where they were dining—my God, it was arrayed like a boar's head on a platter! But despite his horror and revulsion, there'd been something deeper, something hidden within that scene that Antipas had never spoken of in all these years, though he'd thought of it many times. It was the platter itself.

Antipas recognized that platter from his youth. It was a relic unearthed from beneath the Temple Mount during the costly eight-year expansion and reconstruction of the second temple by architects of his father, Herod the Great. It was thought to be part of the original treasure of King Solomon, perhaps hastily buried during the destruction of the original temple. But his father Herod had always joked—Antipas got a chill whenever he thought of it—that it was really the shield Perseus had used against the snake-headed Medusa, to turn her to stone.

It was this dreadful object that was now forever coupled in his mind with the severed head of his wife's victim—that gauntly ecstatic face, the open eyes, the hair still drenched with blood.

He wondered how Caligula had learned of the golden platter. And why in God's name had this boy who now considered himself a god decided to demand it as part of his tribute?

Rome: Noon, January 24, A.D. 41

SPIRIT AND MATTER

◆ ◆

It is no paradox but a great truth borne out by all history that human culture advances only through the clash of opposites. —J. J. Bachofen

It is difference of opinion that makes horse races. —Mark Twain

Herod Agrippa struggled uphill, his breath labored, his heart pounding against his ribs, his brow drenched in sweat—and with only a single soldier of the Praetorian Guard to share his burden. He was terrified they might be recognized. After all, it had been done in broad daylight. And he was even more afraid someone might guess exactly what the burden was they carried beneath this blanket.

Who could imagine, thought Agrippa, that someone so lithe and graceful, a dancer, a youth who'd actually been acclaimed a spirit or a god, would be as heavy as a sackful of stones? But those thirty knife wounds through the face, stomach, and genitalia of the late Gaius Caesar—who only twenty minutes earlier had been alive and well in the colonnade—should have convinced anyone the emperor Caligula had been anything but a god.

The flesh was still warm as they lugged his corpse up the Esquiline Hill to the shelter of the Lamian Gardens, but the blood-soaked toga, already stiffening in the cold January air, adhered to the blanket. Agrippa realized that under the circumstances of the emperor's violent death a state funeral was hardly possible, but he prayed at least they might accomplish a swift and covert burial before the maddened mobs found the body and indulged in the favorite Roman sport: desecration of the dead.

This brutal assassination had taken place before Agrippa's very eyes. He'd just left the auditorium with Claudius and Caligula where they'd been watching the Palatine Games. Caligula paused to watch some boys rehearsing the Trojan war dance, to be performed for those returning after lunch. It was then that the attack came.

A large group of men—a group that, to Agrippa's amazement, included the emperor's own personally chosen German and Thracian bodyguards—fell en masse upon Caligula with spears and javelins, yelling blasphemies and, while he yet continued to live and breathe, hacking him to bits. Claudius, who fled and hid behind a curtain in the Hermaeum, was discovered there and whisked outside the city gates, for his own protection, by the Praetorian Guard.

In the pandemonium that ensued, a splinter group hurried off to dispatch Caligula's wife and son, while those of the Roman senate who were among the conspirators scurried to convene an emergency session, calling for a vote to bring back the Republic. It had all happened so fast—in a matter of moments—that Agrippa's head was still spinning as he puffed uphill, finally reaching the leafy obscurity of the gardens so they could lay down their burden. He sat on a rock and mopped his brow as the guard began to dig.

It was in fact mere chance that found Agrippa in Rome on this fateful day.

Two years ago Herod Antipas and his wife, Agrippa's sister Herodias, had been banished by Caligula to Lugdunum in southern Gaul for demanding too many favors. Now his uncle Antipas was dead and Herodias with him, and Agrippa found himself in control of a domain that, though far from united, approached the size of that his grandfather Herod the Great had once possessed. And with it, he'd inherited most of the headaches. Not least among these was trying to manage the many conflicts between his Roman patrons and his subjects, the zealously religious Jews.

The most recent stir, the one that brought Agrippa here to Rome only this week, was the emperor Caligula's recent decision to "teach the Jews a lesson" for all the disturbances they'd caused their Roman overlords. Caligula planned to do this by setting up a colossal stone statue of himself as Gaius the God—within the very grounds of the Jerusalem temple!

The statue was rumored to be already en route by ship to the port of Joppa. Agrippa would have full-blown riots on his hands the moment such an effigy disembarked on Jewish soil, and so he hastened here to Rome at once to see whether he might change the course of events already set in motion.

After all, had Agrippa not grown up alongside Caligula's uncle Claudius, within the very bosom of the imperial family? And he'd also remained close enough to Caligula all these years to have reaped the reward of gold chains and jewels, not to mention a kingdom of his own. He therefore had cause to hope that, together with Claudius, he might convince the young emperor to see reason in the matter. But upon his arrival at Rome, Agrippa had been hardly prepared for the man he was to meet in the person of the emperor.

The very first night he was fast asleep in the palace when, well past midnight, he was aroused by the palace guard. They'd forced him to dress and then marched him double-step to the palace auditorium. There he found a group of prominent senators and statesmen, as well as the emperor's uncle Claudius, who'd likewise been brought from the safety of their homes in the dead of night.

They were trembling in fear as soldiers lit the wicks of oil lamps on the stage up front. Claudius was about to speak when, with great fanfare of flutes and cymbals, the emperor leapt onstage dressed as Venus in a short silk toga and a wig of long blond hair. He sang a lovely song of his own composition, performed a dance, and vanished!

"It's been like this ever since his sister Drusilla's death," Claudius told Agrippa when they'd quitted the chamber. "He sleeps barely three hours a night, roaming the palace and howling at the sky, inviting the moon goddess into his bed to take his sister's place in his arms. Drusilla died, you'll recall, on the tenth of June not three years ago. He was inconsolable, sleeping next to her corpse for days on end; he wouldn't be removed from her side. Then he raced off alone by chariot through the Campania, took ship to Syracuse, and vanished for a month. He didn't shave or cut his hair; upon his return he looked and behaved like a wild man. Things only went downhill from there."

"Good grief," said Agrippa. "What could be worse than what you've just told?"

"Plenty," said Claudius. "During Drusilla's official mourning period he made it a capital offense to laugh, bathe, or dine with one's family, and then required all state oaths to be sworn to her divinity. He accused both of his other sisters of treason, exiled them to the Pontian Islands, then sold off their houses and jewelry and slaves to raise cash. Then he built a stable of ivory tusks and jewels for his racehorse Incitatus. He often throws lavish dinner parties where Incitatus, dining on golden barley, is guest of honor. He has seized and liquidated people's property on the merest pretext, and has opened a brothel in the west wing of the imperial palace. I myself have often seen him run barefoot, or even roll about on the floor, in those piles of gold coins he hoards.

"A year ago, he mounted a military expedition through Gaul and Germania, with the express intent of conquering Britannia. But after a long, hard winter and a six-month march, when the legions reached the Channel at last, Gaius only had them collect thousands of seashells; then they headed back to Rome!"

"But Caligula had planned that mission ever since Tiberius died and he first became emperor!" cried Agrippa. "Why did he abandon it—and in such bizarre fashion? Has he gone mad?"

"Doomed, rather—and he knows it," Claudius replied gravely. "Of late, the omens have not been good. On the ides of March the capitol at Capua was struck by lightning; then when Gaius was sacrificing a flamingo, he was splashed by its blood. Sulla, the astrologer, cast his horoscope this past August for his birthday and said he must prepare to die soon. That same evening, Mnester danced the tragedy that was performed on the very night Alexander's father, Philip of Macedon, was assassinated."

"You can't believe such things really carry weight?" asked Agrippa, at the same time recalling from his youth just how obsessed the imperial family had always been—like most Romans—by omens read in the entrails of birds and beasts, and with all forms of prophecy. Did they not keep the ancient books of the Sibylline Oracles encased in gold?

"What does it matter what I believe?" Claudius replied. "You don't understand. If my nephew dies just now, with all we've learned, I may have to invade Britannia myself!"

Syrian Antioch: Passover, A.D. 42

EPISTLES FROM THE APOSTLES

◆ ◆

To: Maryam Mark
at Jerusalem, Roman Judea
From: John Mark
at Antioch, Syria

Revered and beloved Mother,

What shall I say? So much has changed this past year here at our church of Antioch, it is hard to know where to begin. It's more impossible yet to think that this week's Pesach marks the tenth since the Master's death—it shocks me just to think of it. Young as I was, I still recall the Master so clearly from his constant visits to our home. And especially vivid is my memory of that last supper he and his disciples ate together at our house.

I was so proud that it was I he'd chosen to run to the fountain with the water pitcher, so that when his disciples arrived there they might follow me and learn where their meeting would take place. But indeed, it's that very memory that has impels me to write to you today.

Uncle Barnabas—who asks that I send warmest brotherly regards to you as always—tells me he feels that by this coming summer when I turn twenty-one, I shall have enough grounding in the Master's work—and my Latin and Greek should be sufficiently developed—that I'll be ready to accompany him on my first official mission among the Gentiles. Of course, this is excellent news, and I knew you'd be proud I had come so far in this, our second major church outside Jerusalem. But there is one thing that rather sours the matter, and I want your advice. Please share this with no one—not even your closest friends like Simon Peter. I ask this for reasons you'll soon understand.

There is a man who's come to Antioch at the express request of Uncle Barnabas to work with our church. He's a diaspora Jew of the Benjamin tribe who grew up in the north, in Cilicia. As a young man, he studied with *Rabb* Gamaliel at the temple in Jerusalem, so it's possible you know him. His name is Saul of Tarsus—and, Mother, he is the problem. I fear matters will only grow worse if nothing is done about it.

I hasten to add at the very outset that Saul of Tarsus has many positive qualities: he's extraordinarily educated, not only in Torah, Mishnahim, and classical Hebrew, but he also is fluent in Latin, Greek, Punic, and standard Aramaic. He comes from a wealthy and respected textiles family who retain the main concession to supply the eastern Roman legions with that sturdy goat-hair cloth, *cilicium*, that they use for everything from tents to shoes. As a result, the family holds hereditary Roman citizenship. Clearly, the assets adhering to Saul of Tarsus go far to explain Uncle Barnabas's attraction to the man.

This is where my principal conflict arises, Mother. For Saul of Tarsus must be regarded, first and foremost, as a man of privilege even from birth: rich, educated, well-traveled, a Roman citizen. And what single thing was the Master most opposed to, as being contrary to the kingdom? It can be said in one word: privilege—most especially, privilege of this particular sort. To highlight the contrast I must be more specific about the events preceding Saul's own conversion to our order—observe I do not say "to our belief," for he has an established set of beliefs of his own. I assure you that everything I'm about to tell you I have garnered from the fellow's own lips.

While studying under Gamaliel at Jerusalem, Saul for the first time became acquainted with the many activist factions in the region—Zealots, Sicarii, Essenes—all agitating for liberation from Rome. And he was also exposed to those, like the Master's cousin the baptizer, who even went "back to nature" dressed as wild men in fur pelts and subsisting on wild locust and honey. The most despicable of all of these, in Saul's opinion, were the Master and his followers.

As a sophisticate from cosmopolitan Cilicia, Saul felt horrified repulsion at these sickeningly primitive peasants. Did not he himself, though a Jew, hold the highest honor on earth: citizenship of the Roman Empire, the only passport to the civilized world? He regarded these Judeans as no better than terrorist rabble. Their hysterical demands for freedom from Roman rule, both religious and political, enraged him beyond words. For a paltry freedom they thought they desired, they were relentless in pitting provincial Jews against the whole vast Roman empire. They had to be stopped.

Saul begged permission from his teacher Gamaliel to hunt them down—he wanted to haul them to the temple where they could be tried as heretics, as Roman law allowed, and put to death by stoning. But Gamaliel wisely replied that such was expressly opposed to prescribed Jewish law, as already established in the time of Gamaliel's grandfather, the great Hillel. In frustrated rage Saul resigned his studies and next took his plea to the Roman-appointed *zadok* Caiaphas, who was glad of a new recruit to his private mission of supporting the Romans by handing over any rabble-rousers who opposed their rule. Saul soon proved to be the perfect candidate for this bloodthirsty persecution.

Mother, you will hardly credit it when I tell you Saul of Tarsus was actually among the mob that was screaming for blood outside Pilate's palace the night of the Master's trial! Not long after, Saul was there again with the mob that stoned our compatriot Stephen to death—though now he claims he never cast a single stone himself, but merely held the cloaks of the others, that they might take better aim! The man is completely unconscionable—and the story of his own "conversion" may be the least believable of all.

Despite his many gifts, Saul of Tarsus has a serious physical shortcoming. He has the falling sickness, the malady of the Caesars that the Greeks call *epilepsia*—grasped by an outside force. I've seen it myself, and it was not a pretty sight. At one moment he was giving a speech—and he does have a golden tongue—at the next he was lying on the ground, foam at his lips, eyes rolled back in their sockets, gurgling from his throat as if possessed by demons. Today he even travels with his own physician.

The story of his conversion to follow the Master, which is rich and strange and completely unverifiable, involves such a seizure. Saul claims that shortly after the stoning of Stephen, he was on a mission to Damascus to spy on some of our number in behalf of the high priest Caiaphas. But just as Saul reached the city gates, he had one of these attacks. He fell to earth and was blinded by brilliant light. Then he heard the Master's voice, asking why Saul was persecuting him!

Some of our cohorts found Saul there in the road, brought him within the city walls of Damascus, and cared for him. And although he did remain blind for a number of days, at last they succeeded in restoring his vision. Afterwards he went into the wilderness, where he remained for several years—doing what, he declines to discuss.

The upshot, however, is that in the end he convinced himself he'd received a personal calling from the Master that provided him and him alone with special insight. So he went down to Jerusalem to meet with the Master's brother James, and Simon Peter, to announce his intention of becoming a leader of our church, based solely upon this highly suspect vision. As I've heard it, they brushed him off—so he turned to Uncle Barnabas, as independent leader of the northern church.

I mean to say, Mother, this fabrication cut of whole cloth seems of the sort that only a master weaver like Saul of Tarsus might be capable of turning out! What better design than to entrench oneself in the bosom of the very community one has been attacking? To present oneself as a miraculous gift, and pass through the gates of Damascus like a Trojan Horse? To conquer as a worm does, from within! How is it that Barnabas could be taken in by so obvious a charlatan, or by so transparent a scheme?

But if that were all he'd done, I should not be writing this letter. It's something far worse, and I believe it bodes serious ill.

Do you recall some eight or nine years ago, not long after the Master's death, Miriam of Magdali came round at the behest of Joseph of Arimathea and asked each of us to recount what we could of the Master's last week on earth? Though I was a child at the time, even I was asked to tell her all I knew—which proved lucky, as it seems.

Only last year I received a letter from Miriam just before she decamped from Ephesus to join her brother and sister at the mission they've begun in Gaul. In this letter, Miriam told me she'd sealed up a great many scrolls of those eyewitness reports in clay cylinders and dispatched them, by the hand of James Zebedee, to Joseph of Arimathea in Britannia. At first, the rest of her letter meant little to me. It was only when Saul of Tarsus revealed he knew something of those documents, and began asking questions about them, that I took a closer look at what they might mean.

Miriam heard back at last from Joseph, to the effect that the documents, combined with information he'd gathered on his own, had enabled him to see a much larger picture than was possible just after the Master's death. Though Joseph has declined to share this in detail with Miriam until she arrives in the Celtic lands, she was able to pass along to me what he did reveal: It appears, in my role as water-jar boy at that last Pesach supper, I might have seen or heard, or perhaps even done, a few things to help expand that view. But the secret I didn't understand myself, until Miriam's letter, involves the Master's last instructions to me on that fateful evening exactly ten years ago, and what those directives really meant.

He told me I should go to the Serpent Pool carrying a big pitcher, and when others arrived and followed, I should pass through the Essene Gate and lead them to our house on Mount Zion. They'd been told to look for one sign: to follow the water-bearer. But what I didn't realize until Miriam pointed it out is that the Water-Bearer is also a constellation, as well as the symbol of the world age after this one. "For I am the Alpha and Omega, the first and last," the Master said. Did he mean to connect himself to both the beginning and the end of the current aeon?

This question brings me again to Saul of Tarsus, Mother. Though I've lived near the man every day for nearly a year, he remains an enigma. But just now, I believe a key has surfaced: he's changed his name from Saul to Paul. Some think he's merely copying the Master's well-known quirk of giving all his disciples nicknames. But I think I've deciphered the truth—that it has to do, instead, with the Master's passion for finding hidden meaning in numbers: the *geomatria*. I calculated for myself what hidden meaning might be produced by such a symbolic change.

The numerical value of "Saul" in Hebrew letters adds to ninety, which equals the letter *tzaddi*, a letter that also represents the astrological constellation of Aquarius. But "Paul" in Hebrew numerology has the value of one hundred ten, *qoph-yod*, signifying the signs of the fish and the virgin—that is, the new age of Pisces and Virgo we've just entered.

In Greek numerology the meaning of the letters is much the same: "Saulos," with the value of nine hundred one, represents *Iakkhos*—Bacchus or Dionysus—the water-bearer who brings forth not this age but the one after it, whereas "Paulos," seven hundred eighty and eighty-one, symbolizes Sophia or Virgo on the one hand and Ophis, the serpent or sea beast, that is, fish, on the other.

Hence, Mother, I believe that through this change of spelling from Saul to Paul, he intends to announce himself, rather than the Master, as avatar of the coming age.

To: Miriam of Magdali
at Massilia, Roman Gaul
From: Maryam Mark
at Jerusalem, Roman Judea

Dearest Miriam,

I apologize for the untidiness of both my penmanship and my thoughts. Although a ship bound for Massilia now leaves from Joppa weekly, I know you don't plan to stay there on the coast of Gaul for long, that you'll soon be heading north to join the rest of your family in the Pyrenees—so I'm hastening to dispatch this letter at once.

I also enclose the letter I've just received from my son. As you see, he requests that I share his words with no one. But his letter triggered in me such turbulent feelings, Miriam.

There are things I fear I should have told you earlier in your capacity as apostle or messenger. However, I admit these things meant little to me until John's recent letter brought back so many memories of events that took place in the last week in the Master's life. Specifically, what occurred that very last night.

As you surely know by now through reports you've received from others, even before reading this letter of John's, the last Passover supper attended by the Master took place here at my residence in the upper city. But what perhaps no one knows, except myself, is the attention the Master himself paid to the planning of this meal down to the finest detail. He was very clear about the appointments he wanted to be made within the upper chamber of my home, where he'd designated the meal would take place: some of these appointments were actually so lavish as to surprise me. It was most important, the Master stressed to me over and over, that everything before, during, and after the meal must happen precisely as he asked. Then he added, strictly in confidence, that he hoped just after the supper to retire to the cave on Joseph's estate at Gethsemane, to perform an initiation ritual. This now seems significant.

The evening of the supper, also at the Master's request, we arranged that Rosa and my staff of servants would prepare the meal and carry the courses upstairs, but they were to remain outside the door for greater privacy, while my son John and I would serve the guests on our own. This explains why I was so fortunately able to see and hear everything that passed during that most remarkable meal. I wrote it down soon after, as a kind of story. Only now, for the first time, do I see that evening in a whole new light. And, Miriam, although you were not present at the meal yourself, and though what I have to say may shock you, in rereading my observations I've come to realize that a great many of the events that took place at that strange supper must in fact have revolved around you.

Of course, it has long occurred to me there must have been a valid explanation why you were not asked to what the Master surely knew would be his last supper among his disciples. After all, it was known to everyone you were the chosen disciple—"alpha and omega" he often called you, didn't he? Then too, after his death you were the first witness of his ascent to the bosom of God. But the decisive factor, as I see it, Miriam, is that well before the supper you were already initiated into the Mysteries!

Undoubtedly, you've received many reports of those events from others who were present. But their reports may have been colored by their own participation, thus missing the crucial point. Indeed, it is possible that the whole meal and the events surrounding it were designed by the Master as a kind of test of the other disciples, as my son once speculated, to see which among them might turn out to be wheat or chaff: that is, which would—at the end of that evening and of the Master's life—prove worthy of the transformation he'd always offered those who passed such tests. I have written this story as if I were an outside observer. I ask you alone to be the judge.

◆ ◆

THE LAST MEAL

Some days before the Passover, for reasons unknown to any but himself, the Master told his disciples by what means they must enter the city that night, to locate the site of their supper: to wait by the Serpent Pond near the Essene Gate south of town. There, a man bearing a water pitcher would come and lead them, one by one, to the appointed spot. By this device, the Master ensured that only the twelve would be present at the meal. By arriving last himself, therefore, the Master was thirteenth.

There was controversy over the secrecy, this unorthodox approach to planning a ritual meal whose rules, after all, had been handed down more than a thousand years ago, directly from God to Moses. How could they know, for instance, that the meal would be prepared according to Torah, using proper rules of cleanliness and cooking technique? And according also to the Mishnah, the leaven must be searched for by candlelight, and cast out, the night before—who would see to that? The Master ignored these complaints. He shrugged and simply said all was arranged.

It was a surprise that the water-bearer was young John Mark, the ten-year-old son of Maryam Mark, who along with her brother Barnabas from Cyprus was among the Master's wealthiest patrons. Her palatial residence on the western side of Mount Zion had for years been Simon Peter's second home when not in Galilee, and the Master's "fireside chats" there with his disciples, lavishly catered by her staff of servants, were often known to go into the wee hours of the night.

But on this occasion, a surprise was in store. When each disciple was greeted at the gates by Rosa, Maryam Mark's housekeeper, he was escorted by another servant, not to the dining hall, but up several flights of stairs to an unknown room beneath the very rafters of the house. Furthermore, this room was outfitted with costly furnishings the like of which none had seen before in a private home: low marble tables, exotically inlaid with colored stones that glittered in the yellow light of Persian hanging lamps; thick carpets from the Ionian coast and multicolored tapestries redolent of the African north coast; huge samovars of tea and giant urns brimming with foamy wine, set everywhere around the room.

Although many of the twelve were successful professionals—tax collectors like Matthew, or well-to-do proprietors of fishing fleets, like Simon and Andrew and the Zebedees—still they were taken aback by this extravagant splendor, which seemed to approach a nearly Roman level of decadence. They stood awkwardly, gazing around Maryam Mark's upper room at the Roman couches where three together could recline while dining, too awed to help themselves to any wine or to converse much until at last the Master arrived.

He seemed somehow preoccupied, and motioned for the others to be seated. He didn't sit at once himself, but paced back and forth beside the door as if waiting for something to happen. The servants brought bowls of water and towels. When they'd departed and the door was shut behind them, the Master, without speaking, took up a bowl and towel and set them on a nearby table. Then removing all his clothes, he wrapped the towel around his waist, knelt on the floor before Judas, and began to wash his feet. The others were embarrassed and more than a little shocked. More so, when they saw he intended to do the same to each. One by one, he came before them to wash their feet, wiping them dry with the towel as they looked on uneasily. But when the Master reached Simon Peter, the disciple jumped to his feet in refusal, crying,

"Never, never! You shall not wash my feet! Not mine!"

"Then it seems we have nothing in common," the Master told him quietly. He was not smiling. "If you all believe I'm your Master, you should follow my example. I hope you'll do the same when I'm no longer here to show you what love is. It's an arrogant servant, Peter, who can learn nothing and thinks himself greater than the one who sent him. When I'm gone, I hope my followers will be recognized by the fact that they serve one another and love mankind."

"Then wash me, Master!" Peter cried enthusiastically, sitting again in haste. "Not just my feet—wash my hands, too, and my head—"

The Master burst out laughing. "Only what's dirty," he said. And glancing at Judas with an enigmatic smile, he added, "Most of what I see here is clean—but not all." A comment that later was interpreted by many as a reference to the "dirty" money Judas had accepted, in exchange for betraying him.

When the Master put his linen robe on again, he reclined on the couch between Simon Peter and young Johan Zebedee, whom he'd affectionately dubbed *parthenos*, the virgin girl, for his childlike if often unruly innocence. The Master spoke throughout nearly the entire meal, with a flushed intensity, eating little save some sips of the ritual wine and a few tastes of the traditional symbolic foods.

As to what he was speaking *about*, it appeared his principal interest was to recite—as age-old tradition dictated—the history of the Passover and the exodus of our people from Egypt. But despite the Master's keen interest in rabbinical law, it did seem to those present that he placed unusual emphasis on the food and drink connected with this ritual meal, and even more upon those things forbidden by God—especially the leaven. Here is what the Master said:

◆ ◆

THE LEAVEN

These are the things wherewith a man fulfills his obligation on Passover: barley, wheat, spelt, rye, and oats. —*Pesachim 2; Mishnah 5*

In ancient times the two holy days we call Pesach and Massot—the Passover and the feast of unleavened bread—were separate events, unlike today. The feast of unleavened bread was the more ancient tradition, dating to the time of Abraham and Noah, and was only later made a part of the Passover ritual that commemorates the escape of our people from bondage in Egypt.

The first Pesach meal was eaten in haste as our people prepared for flight. On their lintels were painted *tau* symbols in lamb's blood, as instructed, so when the Lord passed over, Egyptian firstborn males would be struck down instead of our own. Also as instructed, during the period before the flight, no leaven was permitted.

The law pertains to five specific grains: barley, wheat, spelt, rye, and oats. The flower of each, if in contact with water for more than a brief time, becomes leaven. God told Moses and Aaron the people must not "eat leaven, touch leaven, profit by leaven, neither shall they keep leaven in their house," during seven whole days, from the fourteenth of the month of Nisan through the night of the twenty-first when they left Egypt. Anyone who disobeyed, God promised to cut off from Israel, *forever*.

Why was this strange commandment so important? And since the feast of unleavened bread is older than Moses' departure from Egypt, the ritual of searching for leaven is *more ancient than the Hebrew people's recognition of the one true God*. What does it mean?

The number of grains we classify as leaven—five—was important to the Greeks, who called the number five the *quintessence*: the fifth essence, the highest level of reality, to which all others aspire. The five-pointed star—the pentacle, with a pentagon at its heart—was the symbol of Pythagoras, and also of King Solomon. It stands for wisdom, reflected in the apple, a natural form that conceals this symbol in its core. And within that symbol—the true Solomon's seal—is the secret of the eternal flame.

The process of leavening raises something to a higher level and transforms it. We can see that during the first Passover, God forbade earthly leaven for Jews in favor of transformation to a higher state, making us able to attain that celestial bread which Pythagoras called the Eternal Leaven, a food we also know as *manna*, wisdom, *sapienta*, the Word of God. It is associated with a mysterious, invisible element called "ether" that the ancients conceived as binding the universe together: the axis.

◆ ◆

Miriam, I may tell you, when the Master finished this story, no one in the upper chamber of my home made a sound. The Master gazed slowly around the circle of his disciples, and in that absolute silence he posed an unexpected question.

"Does anyone know the true identity of 'the Shulamite'?" He added, "I speak of King Solomon's darkly beautiful and mysterious love in the Song of Songs. Shulamite means Salem-ite, for she was a city-dweller, and Salem was an early name of Jerusalem. When Solomon asked God for her hand in marriage, perhaps she was more ancient than the city itself. So who was she, really?"

After a moment's awkward silence, Simon Peter responded for the others.

"But, Master," he objected, "for a thousand years since the time of Solomon, rabbis and priests have debated the matter of that famous woman who was neither queen nor official royal concubine, but only a lowly keeper of vineyards. Yet the efforts of those wise men met with no success. How can we, here in this room, untutored as we are in all the scholarly aspects of Torah, be expected to fare any better?"

The Master's answer, though delivered in the same soft tone, struck Peter so bluntly that he nearly recoiled.

"Miriam of Magdali would know the answer." Then the Master smiled. "It *is* a knotty problem. But perhaps you'll recall that the night before Solomon began construction on the temple, God appeared in a dream and told him to ask anything he wished. The young king replied that his only desire was the Shulamite's hand in marriage—"

"Forgive me, Master," young Johan Zebedee cut in. "I'm afraid that isn't so. As everyone knows, Solomon's first wife was Pharaoh's daughter. Furthermore, Solomon only asked one thing of God that night—not marriage, but *wisdom*."

"Exactly," agreed the Master, still smiling. "And though Solomon had many wives, the one that remained first in his heart, as you've correctly said, was the dark, mysterious beauty with whom he celebrates his betrothal in the Song of Songs. To what better bride could a king wish to be yoked, throughout his days, than Wisdom? In the Song of Songs, she herself tells us her symbol is that five-pointed star that Solomon later accepts as his own seal:

" 'Set me as a seal upon thine heart, as a seal upon thine arm: for love is strong as death. . . . the coals thereof are coals of fire.'

"This is the secret flame, the eternal leaven," the Master said. "For the Greeks, the morning star was Artemis or Athena, virgins noted for their wisdom. The evening star was Aphrodite, goddess of love. Since we know these two stars are one, it reveals that in earliest days, men held the key to the highest mystery: the knowledge that wisdom and love are one, a knowledge permitting us to transcend even death."

Those in the room remained in stunned silence as the Master casually tousled the hair of the young, and very confused-looking, Johan Zebedee, who was reclining near him on the sofa. Then he motioned for my son to pour him more wine.

"Master, forgive me," said Philip of Bethsaida. "Your words seem to touch on past, present, and future events, so I'm never quite sure how to interpret what you say. But when you speak of love, surely you mean that our love of the Divine, if properly understood and nourished, might enable us to transcend even death? And yet, one must agree that the Song of Solomon, like the historical king himself, would suggest a very different, sensual, one might almost say a *carnal* picture of love—a portrayal that seems scarcely to suit the image of the coming kingdom which you, yourself, have foretold."

"Indeed, Philip," said the Master. "And that is precisely where the mystery lies."

◆ ◆

Mona Island, Britannia: Autumn, A.D. 44

To: Miriam of Magdali
at Lugdunum, Gaul
From: Joseph of Arimathea
at Mona, Sea of Eire, Britannia

Dearest Miriam,

As you see, your last parcel found me, though it took some time to arrive here. Due to last year's "conquest" of southern Britannia by the emperor Claudius, I've temporarily relocated our base of activities here to the north, a druidical stronghold where we've received much support. Though I was never physically in danger—the Roman landing was a bloodless takeover, no battles were fought, there were no casualties, and the Romans were in and out in a few months' time, leaving only a few legions behind to start construction—still I feared for the safety of those things I possess, which as you know are of some value. This leads naturally to the topic of your letter.

With regard to your offer—much as I yearn to see you in person, I don't think it a good time for you to travel here just now from Gaul. I'll explain in more detail below. But first I must convey my great appreciation for the new information you've provided, which I've taken much care in reviewing.

More and more, as our original numbers are decimated by the Romans or their puppets—James Zebedee's brutal execution last spring at the hands of Herod Agrippa, or Simon Peter's imprisonment, followed by his self-imposed exile to the north—I have come to see how very important it is for us to piece together a much fuller vision of what the Master was trying to accomplish in that fateful last week of his life.

Further, with all his warnings of false prophets, it seems clear Jesua must have foreseen someone like this Saul of Tarsus of whom John Mark speaks in his letter, who might arrive on the scene after his death and try to alter his entire message in such fashion. So I've tried to combine this new account you've sent of the Master's last supper with his disciples with the information we'd previously collected. And I agree that we can see far more clearly now just where his message was heading.

First, the Master's presentation of himself as the divine servant whose chief task is to ritually cleanse the temple and all who are about to enter it. Submission. And then the comparison of his body and blood with bread and wine—an Isaac-like gesture, as if he were offering himself as both matter and spirit in lieu of the ritual offering usual on such occasions. Self-sacrifice.

If only his arrest had not come so soon, that night in my garden, and he'd been able to complete his initiation of young Johan Zebedee as he'd intended. (Though I can well see why Johan resents you so today, since you are now the only disciple who ever received the full initiation directly at the Master's own hands.)

Finally, you must have guessed, as I did, from Maryam Mark's letter that if the Master planned every detail of the meal, it was likely no more than he did with the other events of that week. Perhaps his stress on the appointments of her upper chamber was designed to conceal the significance to him of a few specific objects—for example the chalice he drank from at her home, which you've told me she later entrusted to you at his request.

It occurs to me now that he seems privately to have arranged for each of us individually to take one of the objects that he touched—or that touched him—in his last hours on earth, and to keep it in a special place until his return. For instance, the garment he wore that Nicodemus preserved after we washed the body. Or the spear-tip that pierced his side, which I was instructed to remove from the haft of that Roman centurion's javelin and to preserve, as I have to this day. I believe these objects may possess some sacred power—and may be far older than we imagine.

But quite a few have been entrusted to me by others, as you know, for Britannia was one of the few outposts that has remained independent of Roman occupation or influence—that is, until now. It's this alone, Miriam, that makes me fear for you to come here with the chalice. I believe the time has come for me to share some information with you that you ought to know, should anything happen to me.

Perhaps you recall, twelve years ago, just before the Master's death, the trip I'd just returned from? At the request of the Sanhedrin, I'd been on a special mission to Capri where I had successfully petitioned the emperor Tiberius for the return of exiled Jews to Rome. What perhaps you were not aware of is that my escort to Capri on that occasion, and my advocate in that plea, was none other than the man who has just invaded Britain: Claudius.

Furthermore, as our newly minted emperor is likely aware, that interview with his uncle Tiberius was not to be my last. Indeed, I was with Tiberius on the isles of Paxi not a week before his death. And if Claudius has learned what we were doing there, we must wonder whether he had more than one motive in this recent expedition to Britain. He has left behind three legions, now busily engaged in building roads and setting up townships in preparation for the long occupation of Britannia he clearly foresees. They've used native forced labor to build a temple at Camulodunum.

The emperor Claudius may have failed to find what he sought here. But it seems he plans a more extended visit in future.

Rome: Spring, A.D. 56

CONFLAGRATIO

◆ ◆

While I yet live, may fire consume the earth. —Nero

As his slaves untied the curling ribbons and unwound his long blond hair, curl by curl, it tumbled in a tempestuous mass over the emperor Nero's bare shoulders. He sat naked before the full-length glass, analyzing himself with cold blue eyes.

Yes, it was true. He was actually beginning to resemble Phoebus

Apollo, as everyone claimed. His facial features were so sharply chiseled as to be almost pretty. He dabbed a bit of rouge on his lips to heighten their voluptuous appearance. This explained his appeal, practically since infancy, to both women and men.

After shaking his hair loose—it fell in abundance nearly to his waist—he stood up, the better to admire his remarkable physique in the glass: those hard, sinewy muscles toned by several years of competing in wrestling at the Olympiad in Greece—where in fact he'd just won several first-class medals. Ah yes, that shouldn't be overlooked. As a reminder to himself, he leaned forward and jotted a note: *Give province of Olympia its freedom.*

To think, he had still several years before twenty, and already ruler of the largest empire in world history—and surely the only emperor ever who possessed the voice of an angel and the body of a god. All this had fallen into his lap, only because his beautiful mother Agrippina had been clever enough to marry her uncle Claudius, who then conveniently died from eating that batch of fortuitously poisonous mushrooms. Nero had Claudius deified soon afterward, explaining as part of the eulogy that it was appropriate since, after all, mushrooms were known to be the food of the gods.

The servants had just pulled his purple silk toga over his head, arranged his curls, and finished draping the gold-star-spangled cape over his shoulders, when his mother herself arrived in Nero's private chambers. She looked beautiful, as always, so he took her into his arms for a warm hug and a warmer kiss on the lips.

"Darling, you won't believe what I've planned for us for this evening," Nero announced, drawing her away the better to look at her.

Then he undid the sash that closed the bosom of her toga and pulled the fabric away to expose her beautiful breasts. Truly, the twin golden globes of a goddess, he thought—but after all, she was only yet in her thirties, wasn't she? As the servants and slaves cast their eyes discreetly elsewhere, Nero bent his blond head over his mother's breasts and flicked his tongue over them, serpentlike, until her nipples became aroused. He let her touch him under his toga, as he loved. Mother was the only one who really knew how to excite him. But after a moment, he drew her hand gently away.

"Not tonight, darling," he said. "At least not yet. We're having supper at the tower of Maecenas, just you and me in the upper room. I've prepared a spectacle that's about to start soon—just after dark, you know—and we'll miss the first part if we dally."

◆ ◆

Nero was enraptured by the beauty of the flames. When he'd first come up with the idea of getting rid of those rickety wooden houses scattered all over Rome that were cluttering up the view from his new palace, he'd never imagined the actual fire would be so lovely. He'd have to remember to record his feelings about it in his diary. But the diary recalled something he'd planned to speak of with Agrippina:

"Mother, I was going over some of Claudius's copious piles of papers yesterday, and imagine what I found?" he said. "The old goat kept a diary! It's true, all sorts of libidinous thoughts—if very few actual deeds. I stayed up all night reading it, and I learned something of enormous interest. It seems your brother Caligula, before his untimely death, was on the trail of some powerful objects. Caligula had kept this even from your sister Drusilla, though they were so close. But he told Claudius about them, so he says in the diary. Though you and Julia were in exile—as you'd say, you were hardly Caligula's confidantes—still I thought you might've learned something from Claudius."

"Not this time," Nero's mother said calmly, sipping her wine as she looked down over the city of seven hills that lay in a darkness spangled by many little bonfires that were growing steadily brighter.

"But in fact," she added, "I heard something of it from Drusilla's husband, Lucius, when I came back to Rome to bury my brother. Lucius's own brother Gaius had been a centurion in Roman Judea under Tiberius, more than twenty years ago, and he presided over the execution of one of these annoying Jewish religious fanatics you've lately been tossing to the lions. It seems already back then they were rabble-rousers, and their original ringleader was the very chap Gaius crucified. But the interesting part is, it seems he didn't die by crucifixion, but was killed by a stab of Gaius's javelin, which then inexplicably disappeared. Apparently the Jews believed the javelin held some mysterious power of a religious nature. I was never quite clear on the rest, so I'm afraid that's really all I can say."

Agrippina set down her wineglass and came over to sit on Nero's lap—just as she used to do with Claudius whenever she wanted to have her way or wangle something important. Nero grew instantly suspicious. But as his mother rubbed her hands over his private parts and sucked his neck, he also felt himself growing stiff.

Damn: just when he most wanted to pay attention, not only to the wonderful spectacle he'd arranged outside but, more important, to the topic of conversation that had been so unceremoniously abandoned by her ploy for sex. But Agrippina had loosened the front of her gown and popped her golden apples tantalizingly out of the basket once more. They were practically in his face. He took a deep breath, swallowed air, and got to his feet, spilling the witch to the floor in a pile of her own silks.

"I don't believe that's all you know," Nero told her. Tossing his long blond mane over his shoulder, he gazed down at her petulantly with icy blue eyes. "Claudius says in his diary that Caligula had all this information not only from that brother-in-law of yours, as you said, but some more from Tiberius, too. He lists what the items are—there are thirteen of them—and says that though they aren't exactly treasures, they possess some kind of powerful force instead. Claudius even invaded Britain years ago, trying to get his hands on them! You *must* know about them—maybe what their value is, too."

He bent down and grabbed Agrippina by the arms, pulling her up off the floor to face him. He tried to keep his eyes on her face and away from the beautiful curves of her golden, half-naked skin—her warm, sensual flesh that even now was being licked with light from the sweeping roar of flame washing the hills of Rome outside beneath the window. Agrippina smiled like a cat—then pulled his thumb into her mouth and sucked on it erotically, as she used to do when he was still a child. He felt his knees growing weak, but he remained determined and yanked his thumb out.

"I need a new ship, so I can come and go easily from my estate at Bauli," Agrippina mentioned, picking up her wineglass as if nothing had occurred since her last sip.

"It's yours," Nero told her, privately wondering how he might quickly find someone who knew how to build a collapsible boat.

The woman held too much power over him—and she knew it. But if he could dispatch Claudius as he had, why not Agrippina too? Then he'd finally be free, while possessing more power than anyone else in the world. Which brought him back to the topic.

"What kind of power 'of a religious nature' did Lucius say the Jews believe the javelin possessed?" he asked his mother.

"Oh, Lucius had done quite a study of it," she replied. "It involved a number of items the Jews had brought with them out of Babylon or Egypt, and some of the secrets of their mystery religion, as well. It all had something to do with rebirth, I believe—if these objects were held together in the right hands."

"Do these Jews really believe that?" Nero demanded. "Or how did Lucius think it could take place?"

"It seems they must be put in the right spot," she said. "A place of power, like the caves at Eleusis, or that one at Subaico just outside Rome, opposite where you're building your summer palace. And of course, the time must be right too."

"The time?" said Nero. "You mean morning, afternoon, or midnight? Or the time of year—spring or fall?"

"No, nothing like that," Agrippina said. "Lucius said it was a Persian or Egyptian concept." She stroked his arm and added with a smile, "I mean, the idea that it must be done while the aeon is changing—at the cusp between one celestial age and another."

"But then," said Nero, gazing out on the raging fires that were now devouring his eternal city, "that would mean these objects must be collected together right now!"

THE LOST DOMAIN

Such moments, such particular glimpses down long vistas of the unattainable . . . phrases like the domaine perdu *and the* pays sans nom *[describe] far more than a certain kind of archetypal landscape or emotional perspective on it . . . . We first grasp the black paradox at the heart of the human condition [when we realize] that the satisfaction of the desire is also the death of the desire.*

—John Fowles, afterword to *Le Grand Meaulnes, by Alain-Fournier*

Only after Wolfgang and I had completed the two-hour drive to the airport at the far side of Vienna, got through parking, check-in, and customs, and boarded our plane for the flight to Leningrad did I have a real chance to try to organize all my mental notes on what I actually knew so far about Pandora's mystery.

I felt like a player in a millennial scavenger hunt, chasing scattered clues across continents and through aeons. But what had begun as a dizzying pile of unrelated facts was now a clearer path that connected geographical spots on the map with animal totems, animals with constellations in the night sky, constellations with gods, and the names for these providing the key. So as I looked out my plane window at Leningrad, that watery city of inland canals just beneath our wings, it seemed appropriate that this land into which we were descending had as its own symbol, mascot, and animal totem the Russian Bear.

For the first time I realized in just how many cities I'd sojourned without seeing them as the residents did—or even as tourists might. Because of Jersey's and Laf's status as world-class performers, even inside Russia at the height of the now waning Cold War, their lives on the road had remained an endless procession of chauffeured limousines and champagne.

My father, too, on the rare occasions I'd joined him abroad, preferred to cloister himself within the walled fortresses of hotels for a privacy only money could buy—just like that week in San Francisco. So although I'd experienced the glittering facades woven by the history and mystery and magic of many spots on the planet, I'd missed most of the dirt and drudgery and inconvenience—a portrait very likely far more real.

Tonight, as Wolfgang and I stood on the granite steps outside the Leningrad airport along with a steaming mass of a hundred or more shadowy Eastern-bloc types, waiting in the dark drizzle to be cleared, one by one, through the *single* glass-walled immigration station open within the airport, I began to see for the first time a wholly different picture.

This was the USSR depicted in State Department statistics books like those Wolfgang had loaned me—a land with a population thirty percent larger than that of the U.S., inhabiting more than double the land mass, yet living on only a quarter of our per capita annual income, producing only a third of our per capita gross national product, and experiencing a significantly higher birth rate and lower life expectancy.

And Leningrad, the sparkling city of Catherine the Great and Peter the First which had shimmered upon the waters like a northern Venice, now seemed to be sinking back into the pestilent marshland from which it had once been reclaimed. As with most Russian cities, the occupants of Leningrad spent their time queuing up and waiting, in what appeared to Western eyes an inexplicably contagious mass atrophy.

It had been nearly seventy-five years since the Russian Revolution. I wondered how long a people so weary of their own existence could endure the stranglehold of beliefs and methods of enforcement they didn't agree with. Maybe our invitation and presence here today would provide part of the answer to that question.

Wolfgang and I were collected at the airport by an officious-looking uniformed young woman from Intourist—a group rumored to be the hospitality branch of the KGB—and taken to our hotel. En route, Wolfgang cryptically intimated that the Soviet government wouldn't approve of unmarried male and female colleagues practicing on their premises what he and I had practiced, and nearly perfected, in his castle all last night. I got the message, but not the whole picture—until I got a load of the place.

The barrackslike "hotel" that our hosts, the Soviet nuke establishment, had graciously arranged for the duration of our stay had all the charm of your average U.S. federal penitentiary. There were many floors that all looked identical, long halls paved in grey linoleum illuminated by fluorescent lights that, to judge by the humming and flicker level, hadn't had their tubes replaced since they'd been installed.

After quickly arranging tomorrow's schedule, Wolfgang and I were parted and I was led to my own wing by a hefty female storm trooper I imagined was named Svetlana. Arriving at my *boudoir du soir*, she assured me in broken English that she would remain posted downstairs for the night, then showed me three times how to lock myself in, and waited outside my door until she heard me do so.

It was only then I suddenly realized I was starving, having eaten nothing since the croissants and chocolate that morning. I rummaged through my bag until I found some trail mix and a bottle of water, wolfed down enough to silence my ravenous stomach, undressed in those damp, unheated, unappealing quarters, unpacked a few items, and turned in for the night.

◆ ◆

There was a soft tap at the door. I glanced at my travel clock on the bureau of the cold, sparsely furnished room. I hadn't reset it yet from Vienna time, so ten-thirty meant it was after midnight in Leningrad. Wolfgang had made it quite clear that tiptoeing about with the intention of hanky-panky was strictly off limits according to Soviet etiquette. So at this time of night, who on earth could it possibly be?

I sashed up my robe over my pajamas and went to unlock the door. "Svetlana" was standing outside, looking oddly shy and awkward compared with her former boot-camp persona. Her eyes flicked sideways and she shot me a purse-lipped look, which I supposed was the Soviet idea of a smile.

"*Pliss,*" she said in a low voice, almost confidential. "Pliss—somevon vish spick viss you." She was gesturing sideways with her hand, as if actually expecting me to step out the door, leave my uncomfortable but relatively secure icebox of a room, and follow her in the dead of night to some unspecified rendezvous.

"*What* someone?" I pulled my robe more tightly up to my chin as I stepped back a pace, my hand still firmly on the door handle.

"*Some*von," she insisted in a whisper, glancing around nervously. "Hiss wery *oor*gent, he must be spicking viss you now—at vonse. Pliss to come viss me—he iss down the sterrs—"

"I'm not going downstairs, or anywhere else, unless you tell me who wants to speak with me," I assured her, shaking my head firmly for emphasis. "Does Professor Hauser know about this?"

"No! Must not to know *nossing*!" she said—in a tone that could only be interpreted, in any tongue, as real fear. What in God's name was going on?

Now Svetlana was digging in her pocket, and she pulled out a card on heavy paper, waving it under my nose for just a moment before quickly tucking it away again. I'd barely had time to read the two words printed on it: Volga Dragonoff.

Good lord! Volga—my uncle Laf's valet! Could something have

happened to Laf in the few days since I'd seen them at Sun Valley? But what else could Volga be doing here, hunting me down at midnight in the north of Russia? How did he get so cozy with Ms. Keys-to-the-Kingdom that she'd toss her rule book out just for him?

To make matters worse, my sturdy Soviet bodyguard was acting more than suspicious. Her anxious eyes darting everywhere, she made the pliss-to-follow gesture to me again, making me pretty damned nervous myself. But deciding I'd better learn exactly what was going on, I grabbed my fur-lined boots from beside the door, shoved them on my feet, yanked my heavy coat over my bathrobe, stepped out into the hall, and let Svetlana "officially" lock the door behind me. I could see my breath in the dim fluorescent light as I followed her along the corridor; I pulled on my gloves as we went down the two flights of stairs.

Volga was waiting there in the lobby, bundled in a dark, heavy coat. As I went to greet him, and looked at his craggy, sober face that never smiled, I realized that in the twenty-odd years I'd known this valet, factotum, and inseparable companion of my uncle, we'd probably spoken fewer than two dozen words to each other—which made this unexpected late-night tryst even more bizarre.

Volga bowed to me, glanced once at his watch, and spoke a few words in Russian to my escort. She crossed the lobby, unlocked a door, flicked on one dim bank of lights, and left us alone. Volga held the door for me to enter first, and we went inside. It proved to be a vast dining hall filled with long tables already set up for tomorrow's breakfast. Volga pulled out a chair for me, then sat himself, took a flask from his pocket, and handed it to me.

"Drink this. It is slivovitz mixed with hot water; it will keep you warm while we speak."

"Why are you here in the middle of the night, Volga?" I said, accepting the proffered flask, if only to warm my hands. "Nothing's happened to Uncle Laf?"

"When we did not hear from you yesterday, nor did you arrive last night at the maestro's home in Vienna as expected, he became alarmed," Volga said. "Today we thought to contact your colleague in Idaho, Mr. Olivier Maxfield, at your office. But due to the time difference—eight hours—it was too late when we learned that you had already left Vienna for Leningrad."

"So where's Uncle Laf?" I asked, butterflies still hovering in my stomach. I unscrewed the flask and had a swig of the hot liquor; it did seem to warm me a bit.

"The maestro wished to come himself to explain the urgency of the situation," Volga assured me, "but his Soviet visa was not refreshed. I am Transylvanian, though; the Rumanian government has a 'friendship pact' with the Soviet Union making it possible to come here at brief notice. I arrived on the last airplane from Vienna, but the entry procedure causes further delay. I apologize—but the maestro insisted that I see you at once, tonight. He sends this note to confirm what I say."

Volga handed me an envelope. As I slipped out the note to unfold it, I asked, "How on earth did you get that lady storm trooper to let me out of my cage for a rendezvous with you at this time of night?"

"It was fear," Volga said cryptically. "I know these people; I understand their ways very well."

I made no comment as I read Laf's note:

Dearest Gavroche,

Your failure to arrive here suggests to me that you have ignored my advice and last night perhaps done something foolish. Nevertheless, I send you my love.

Please listen with great attention to everything Volga has to tell you, for it is quite important. I should have shared it all with you before departing Sun Valley, but not in front of the person you arrived with—and then suddenly you had to leave.

Your colleague Mr. Olivier Maxfield tells me that he also would like to reach you. He asks that I tell you he needs to speak with you privately on another subject, and soon.

Your uncle Lafcadio

"Did Olivier mention what he wanted to talk to me about?" I asked Volga, hoping this didn't mean something was wrong with Jason, my cat.

"It was concerned with business, I believe," he said, adding, "I have little time and much to say. And I should dislike for you to become ill by staying up so late in the cold, therefore I must proceed. But because Russian walls like these around us often have ears, I ask that you not ask questions until I have finished—and even then, please take caution about what you say."

I agreed with a nod, helped myself to another swig of the warm libation he'd brought, and bundled my coat up tighter around me so Volga could begin what I thought might well prove the longest speech in his reclusive life.

"First," he said, "you should know that it was not the maestro Lafcadio who was my original patron: it was your grandmother, the *daeva*. She found me when she was already a well-known singer and I was a young boy orphaned by the First World War, working for pennies on the streets of Paris."

"You mean Pandora took you in as a child?" I said, surprised. Along with Laf and Zoe, that seemed an excessive burden for a young woman who, if Dacian was accurate about her age, by the end of the war couldn't herself have been much more than twenty. "And how did she get to Paris? I thought she lived in Vienna."

"To understand the nature of our relations, I must tell you something about myself and my people," Volga said almost apologetically. "It is part of the story."

It suddenly occurred to me that the stony Volga Dragonoff might actually know more—or at least be willing to divulge more of what he knew—than the other players in my extremely reticent and suspicious family. Being alone with him like this, after midnight in a freezing, deserted barracks of a dining hall, might in fact prove to be my best shot at peeking under that lid.

"You've come all this way at great inconvenience, Volga. Of course I'd like to hear whatever you're willing to share with me," I assured him with great sincerity, pulling off one glove and blowing on my fingers to warm them.

"Although I was born in Transylvania, it was my mother's people, not my father's, who originated there," Volga said. "My father was from a triangular region running from Mount Ararat, near the Turkey-Iran border, to the Georgian Caucasus and Armenia. In this small wedge of land there had flourished what was already a century ago a dying breed of men, of which my father was one: the *ashokhi*, bards or poets who were trained to hold in their memory the entire history and genealogy of our people, dating back to Gilgamesh of Sumeria.

"Several figures who played a part in my father's childhood were later to cross paths with our family, at critical moments, over many years—and with yours as well. While still a child, my father began his studies at Alexandropol under the tutelage of a noted *ashokh*, father of a boy my father's age. The son would one day become the famous esoteric Georgi Ivanovitch Gurdjieff. Some years later, another boy came from Gori in Georgia to stay, along with my father, with the Gurdjieffs.

This was the young Yusip Djugashvili, who was preparing himself for a path he soon rejected: the Orthodox priesthood. Yusip would also later become famous under his adopted name of 'Steel-man': Stalin."

"Wait, Volga," I said, putting my one gloved hand on his arm. "Your father grew up with Gurdjieff and Stalin?" To be frank, the way my life had been running of late, I was stunned that Volga's ancestry could outclass my own, when it came to bizarre.

"Perhaps it's hard to imagine," Volga said. "But this small part of the world had a powerful mixture of—how one would say?—great fermentation. My father remained until nearly age forty. Then during the revolution in 1905, he crossed the Black Sea into Rumania, where he met my mother, and I was born—"

"But the Russian Revolution didn't take place till 1917," I pointed out. Even *I* knew that much about twentieth-century history—at least so I thought.

"You refer to the *second* Russian Revolution," Volga said. "The first one, in January of 1905, began as an agrarian revolt and general strike and ended in 'Bloody Sunday' when the brutal tsarist program of Russification of all subject peoples touched off a massacre that was long building. My father was forced to flee Russia. However, as an *ashokh*, he never forgot his roots.

"When I was born in 1910 in Transylvania, I was given the name Volga, the Slavic name for the longest river in Russia or on the European continent. Its oldest name was Rha—like Ammon Ra the Egyptian sun god. But the Tatar name for this river, Attila, means iron—from which the Scourge of God also derived his name—"

"Your name is the same as Attila the Hun's? Like in the *Nibelungenlied*?" I said.

I recalled this bit of data from only this afternoon. It was against Attila that the Merovingian-Nibelungs had fought over the same piece of turf later claimed by Heinrich Himmler's SS—a connection that seemed important enough to follow up. My fingers were tingling, not just from the cold. Despite the extent of my hunger and fatigue, I was truly focused on where all this was leading.

"Precisely," said Volga with a nod. "Your grandmother came from a part of the world that, from time immemorial, everyone wished to possess. Even today, this struggle is far from over. For the past hundred years, the Germans, French, and Turks, as well as the British and Russians, have vied for the lands that Genghis Khan, and before him my namesake Attila, had conquered centuries ago: Central Asia. It was a more recent version of this struggle that killed my father, and brought me together with your grandmother Pandora in Paris when I was only ten years old."

"You mean the struggle for Central Asia?" I said, as the image I thought I could almost see coalesced a bit. Swallowing with dry throat, I decided to take a chance. Even if Volga didn't know what I was talking about, at this point I had little to lose.

"Volga," I said, "do *you* know how all this history, geography, myth, and legend relates to my grandmother? Do you know what her manuscripts are all about?"

Volga nodded, grimly. With his next words, I understood why.

"I myself was trained from infancy as an *ashokh*," he told me. "I knew the unwritten history of our people. When my parents were killed in the First World War, during the so-called Balkan Crisis, the world was in flux. I was taken in by a band of Gypsies who were fleeing the region; I supported myself like other Gypsy children, begging for coins. The pre-Roman inhabitants of Transylvania were called Daci, or Wolves, so it was no surprise that the man in his twenties who adopted me into the tribe went by the name of Dacian. He proved a masterly violinist, and indeed later instructed a young fellow, by the name of Lafcadio Behn, whom we picked up in Salzburg toward the end of the war."

I started to speak, but pressed my lips together and let him continue.

"When Dacian began to comprehend what I'd been trained for—that despite my youth, I might know an ancient legend that few had ever even heard of—he said we must journey to France and meet his 'cousin' Pandora. That I must tell her everything I knew, and she would understand what to do."

"And did you tell her when you got there?" I asked, barely breathing.

"Indeed I did," said Volga. "The world would be a vastly different place today, as you must realize, had I not met your grandmother when I did—or had we all not agreed to help her in her most important mission."

It was a surprise when the sober Volga Dragonoff leaned forward and grasped my hands firmly in his, as Dacian had done in Vienna. His ungloved hands were warm and strong, and gave me for the first time in weeks a feeling of security and confidence.

"I shall now tell you something no one knows, perhaps not even your uncle," he said. "My last name, Dragonoff—it wasn't my father's name, which was simply Ararat, after the mountain. Your grandmother gave it to me as a kind of honor or title. 'Like King Arthur's father, Uther Pendragon,' she told me. 'It means one who can harness and bring under control the all-powerful dragon forces lying beneath the earth's surface.' "

"Why did she say that about you?" I asked in a hushed voice, almost a whisper.

Volga looked at me with dark eyes, as if thinking of something long ago and far away, too dim for me to see.

"Because I revealed to her what I am about to reveal to you," he said at last, though not reluctantly. When I glanced quickly toward the door, he added, "You needn't fear what it may mean to others: only an initiate will be able to truly fathom what it all means."

"But *I'm* not an initiate of *anything*, Volga," I assured him.

"Yes, you are," he said with a partial smile. "You have certain qualities your grandmother once possessed. A moment ago, you found a common thread in patterns of antique history, medieval legend, and contemporary politics. The ability to form such connections is the one skill required of an *ashokh*. But innate ability is not enough—appropriate training is also required. I can see you have received such training to an advanced degree, although you yourself may yet be unaware of it. See if you don't feel the power to detect another, hidden level in the story I'm about to tell you."

◆ ◆

THE SECRET HISTORY

There was a bluish wolf which was born having his destiny from Heaven above.
His spouse was a fallow doe. They came, passing over the Tenggis. . . .
At the moment when [their descendant] was born, he was holding in his right hand
a clot of blood the size of a knuckle bone. [He was given] the name of Temujin
[blacksmith].

—*The Secret History of the Mongols,* trans. Francis Woodman Cleaves

In nomadic cultures like those of the steppes, the sky itself is regarded as God. The axis on which the universe pivots is the Pole Star, at the tip of the small bear's tail. It is held that a leader's destiny is to subjugate and unite the "four corners"—the four quadrants of humanity on earth corresponding to the four quarters of the night sky.

The most important function in the nomad's world is that of the blacksmith; his craft of creating the tools, weapons, and utensils so essential to this harsh existence is believed to be taught him directly by the gods. In such a belief system, all those born to be leaders were first born smiths; like the Greek Hephaestus, they're considered partly magi and partly gods. The long rule of the Mongol dynasty was known to the Mongols themselves as the Blacksmith Monarchy.

In the year 1160, beside a freshwater spring near the river Onon in the grasslands of the Mongolian steppes, a mysterious figure was born. His ancestors, the legend says, were a blue wolf and a fallow doe. His name was Temujin, meaning blacksmith—as Attila's, who came before him, had meant iron.

When Temujin was nine, his father arranged his betrothal to a girl of a neighboring tribe, but during the father's return journey he paused to dine on the steppe with some Tatars, and was poisoned. Owing to their youth, Temujin and his brothers lost their father's herds to their own tribe, who moved on, leaving the boys and their widowed mother destitute. The family removed to the sacred mountain Burqan Qaldun, at the source of the Onon River, where they foraged for food. Each day, Temujin prayed to this mountain:

> *O Eternal Tangri, I am armed to avenge the blood of my ancestors. . . .*
> *If you approve what I do, lend me the aid of your strength.*

And Tangri spoke to him. By the time Temujin was grown and married to his betrothed, he had succeeded in rallying the Mongol tribes and reducing their enemies the Tatars to mere collections of bones decorating the battlefields he'd left behind. He conquered a third part of China, and much of the eastern steppe. The shaman Kokchu revealed to the Mongol peoples that it was Temujin's destiny one day to rule the world, to become the great leader who would unite the four corners as had been foretold since the dawn of time.

And indeed, at the age of thirty-six, after many successful battles, Temujin the blacksmith was elected the first Great Khan to unite all the tribes under one *tuq*, or banner. His title as Khan was Chenggis, from the Uighur word *tengiz*—which, like the Tibetan *dalai*, means sea.

His followers called themselves *Kok Mongol*, the Blue Mongols, after their powerful patron, the sky god Tangri. The magical White Banner they followed, with its nine yak tails, was believed to be imbued with shamanic powers, to possess a *sulde*—a soul or genie of its own—that led Genghis Khan and the Kok Mongol onward to their conquest of the sedentary civilized world.

It was later said that, from the moment of his birth, it had been ordained that under Genghis Khan, East and West would be woven together like the warp and woof of a complex tapestry, so inextricably knotted as to be inseparable in future. Before they were through, the Mongol Empire stretched from the inland waterways of central Europe all the way to the Pacific Ocean. Genghis Khan had truly lived up to his title Ruler of the Seas.

He'd conquered the lands of Hindus and Buddhists and Taoists, Muslims, Christians, and Jews, but Genghis retained to the end his own animist faith and his worship of rivers and mountains. He rejected costly pilgrimages and religious struggles over places like Mecca and Jerusalem as foolishness, for the god Tangri existed everywhere. He illegalized baptism and ritual ablution as pollution of the sacrosanct source of all life: water. He demolished large stretches of China and Iran, razing all vestiges of earlier civilization, including animal and human life, art, architecture, and books. Loathing the soft decadence of city life, he burned vast tracts of cultivated soil, returning them to the appearance of those harsh, clean steppe lands he felt most comfortable living on.

Though illiterate, Genghis understood the power of writing. He had his own moral code written into law, and so rigidly enforced that it was said during his lifetime a virgin with a golden platter on her head could walk the length of the Silk Road unmolested. He had the history and genealogy of the Mongols encoded into sacred Blue Books and had these placed in caves for future generations to find. He also had the ancient wisdom of the shamans, magi, and priests of each land he conquered carefully examined and recorded, and he set these in the caves as well.

It is said that these documents, when combined, provide the key to ancient secrets of great power—secrets of a nature so organic that, when unearthed, they would demolish the pretensions of today's "organized" religions, religions that have crystallized over the centuries, trapped within their own intractable dogma, their petrified rituals and rites.

What Genghis—the blacksmith who became an ocean—really hid

in the caves, it is said, is a tradition transcending all faiths but containing the concentrated essence that provides the kernel of each. Down to our own century, those with an interest in harnessing such power have sought these caves and their contents.

Gurdjieff claimed to have found some of these documents before the turn of the century while traveling through Xinjiang and Tajikistan, somewhere in the Pamirs. There was also the famous British black magician and occultist Aleister Crowley, who was later evicted from Germany and Italy by Hitler and Mussolini, two men who feared the threat his own dark knowledge might pose to their plans. In the spring of 1901, Crowley was a principal in an Anglo-Austrian expedition for the first ascent of *Chogo-Ri*, or K2, on the China-Pakistan border—a failed attempt to locate these same caves.

After Red October, first Lenin and then Stalin would attempt to get back such territories once possessed by the tsars that were lost during the Russian Revolution. Then in the 1920s, between the First and Second World Wars, the Russian mystic Nicholas Roerich learned of the documents while traveling through Mongolia, Tibet, and Kashmir. He was told they were scattered across Central Asia, Afghanistan, and Tibet, and that when they surfaced, the hidden cities of Shangri-La, Shambhala, and Agharthi would rise. But there was another hidden city that sank beneath a mysterious lake when the Mongols first invaded Russia—Kitezh, the Russian city of the Grail—which will also rise from the waters to usher forth the transition to a new age. . . .

◆ ◆

Volga couldn't have hit the button better when he'd said I might find a "hidden level" in the story he had to tell me. He must have noticed just now the effect of what he'd said, for he suddenly stopped speaking. He'd long ago released my hands, and was now watching me closely.

The story of Kitezh was told in the famous Rimsky-Korsakov opera. Jersey had the starring role of Lady Fevronia, Saviour of the City, the last time we'd visited Leningrad. It's a tale of two cities, the first destroyed by the grandson of Genghis Khan in his ten-year rape and pillage of the lands between the Volga and the Danube, a conquest followed by the long-term suppression of Russia, first under the Mongol hordes, then the equally brutal reign of Tamerlane's Turks.

The hopes of Christian Russians were kept alive for three hundred years, until Ivan the Great freed them, by the myth of the second city, Great Kitezh. The prayers of Lady Fevronia, an innocent forest maiden, bring the city protection by the Virgin Mary, who covers it with a lake through whose clear waters it can be seen, but not reached or harmed. Kitezh, like the Grail, is attainable only by the faithful like Fevronia, who can accept the concept of "life without time" and who will live in the restored city when it rises, dripping from the waters, like a New Jerusalem at the dawn of a new age, as it does at the end of the opera.

In this case, I knew the lost city wasn't just a landscape of the mind. Lost cities of the Khazars had only recently been discovered in this same region, which Stalin had buried underwater by rerouting rivers. This triggered a picture that was gaining prominence in my mind, something that seemed to pop up at every metaphysical-metaphorical-mythical-mystical turn in this millennial hunt for the "sacred hallows"—something I knew must be the kernel of hidden truth in Pandora's manuscripts.

"All these legends, the *Kitezh*, the *Eddas*, the *Nibelungenlied*, the Grail sagas of Wolfram von Eschenbach and Chrétien de Troyes—they're all tied together somehow, aren't they, Volga?" I said.

He nodded slowly, but continued to study me, so I went on:

"It must mean something, then, that while they're all a bunch of legends, they're set within the context of plenty of verifiable historical facts. Not to mention that the objects and places and events described in these tales seem to have been sought for so long by everyone from powerful political leaders to mysterious mystics—"

I thought I noticed a strange gleam in the depths of Volga's black eyes.

"Okay, I've got it," I said, all at once on my feet. Though I could still see my breath in the air, I didn't want another swig of slivovitz just yet. I paced as Volga sat in silence. "Norse, Teutonic, Slavic, Celtic, Semitic, Indo-European, Aryan, Greco-Roman, Dravidian, Thracian, Persian, Aramaic, Ugaritic," I said. "But Pandora figured out *how* they're all related, didn't she? That's the reason why she divided her manuscripts among four people in the same family who never spoke to each other—so nobody could ever put it all together and see what *she* had seen."

Then I stopped and stared at Volga, realizing I might have revealed too much of what I knew or didn't know. After all, hadn't Laf sent him all this way here to reveal things to *me* instead? But when I looked down at Volga, he had a strange expression.

"There is one very important thing in what you've just said—more important than the rest," he told me. "Can you see what it is?" When I was clearly at sea, he said, "The number four. Four people, four corners, four quarters, four sets of documents. Time is of the essence, for the aeon draws near. And you haven't seen the parts Pandora herself collected, all combined."

"As I understand it, nobody's seen them all," I pointed out.

"That is why I've come to Russia tonight," Volga said with great care. My heart was pounding as I slowly sat down again. "In Idaho, you were unprepared for the acceptance of this mission that now I see in your eyes. I hope it is not too late. There *is* one person who's had access to all the documents over the past many years—or at least, to those individuals who themselves possessed them. Although, as you've suggested, those four people—Lafcadio, Augustus, Earnest, and Zoe—were estranged from one another, they were *not* estranged from *her*."

I stared at him, not believing my ears. There was only one person he could possibly be speaking of. But then mercifully, I thought of a hitch that would make his suggestion impossible.

"It's true that Jersey *was* married to my father, Augustus, and afterwards to Uncle Earnest too," I admitted. "And we lived off and on with Uncle Laf while I was growing up, in the years between. But Jersey never had anything to do with my horrid aunt Zoe in Paris. The two of them have never even *met*, so far as I know."

If Russian walls had ears, it wouldn't take an "initiate" to translate Volga's reply.

"I'm sorry to have to be the one to tell you, but it's quite urgent that you know," Volga said firmly. "Your mother, Jersey, is the daughter of Zoe Behn."

[When the Moirai weave fate] the length of a man's life . . . is represented by . . . the vertical, i.e. the warp threads. [But] what of the woof, those threads which are . . . knotted round the individual warp threads? In these it would be natural to see the various phases of fortune which are his lot while he lives, and of which the last is death.

The old Norse goddesses, the Norns, spun the fates of men at birth. . . . The Slavs also had [such] goddesses . . . so too apparently the ancient Hindus and the Gypsies. . . . Not only do the Norns spin and bind, they also weave. Their web hangs over every man.

—Richard Broxton Onians, *The Origins of European Thought*

Buddhism is both a philosophy and a practice. Buddhist philosophy is rich and profound. Buddhist practice is called Tantra. Tantra *is the Sanskrit word meaning "to weave."*

. . . The most profound thinkers of the Indian civilization discovered that words and concepts could take them only so far. Beyond that point came the actual doing of a practice, the experience of which was ineffable.

. . . Tantra *does not mean the end of rational thought. It means the integration of thought . . . into larger spectrums of awareness.*

—Gary Zukav, *The Dancing Wu Li Masters*

Volga Dragonoff's revelation turned out to be the first of all my recent family shockers that didn't make me feel like collapsing. Indeed, there were aspects of this revised picture—based on what I knew for certain about my mother's side of the family—that actually rang true. I hoped they might even help fill in a few pieces of the larger puzzle.

When I was two years old, my mother had packed me up and left my father. For the next twenty-odd years, Augustus divided his time between his Pennsylvania estate and posh offices in New York that were home to the family mining and minerals empire, the legacy of Hieronymus Behn.

Jersey returned to her life performing throughout the glittering capitals of Europe. I was carried along in her turbulent wake for the next six years, until her subsequent marriage to Uncle Earnest. I rarely saw Augustus after the split. He'd never been much of a talker about family matters, so all my information about my parents' marriage or my mother's previous life had been filtered through Jersey's ice-blue eyes.

Jersey was born in 1930, between the wars, to a French mother and an Irish father on the British Channel island for which she was named. The Channel Isles, just off the Normandy coast, became indefensible by the British once France surrendered to the Germans in 1940. Inhabitants were evacuated upon request, but many demurred—especially the residents of Jersey, of whose population more than eighty percent opted to stay on. These suffered the predictable deportations or depradations when Germany occupied and fortified the islands to create the "mailed fist of the western wall." Those who'd refused evacuation wouldn't be liberated by the British until near the end of the war. But by then, my mother was not among them.

Early in the invasion of France, so the story ran, Jersey's mother went to the aid of her family and was trapped inside France. Jersey's father, an Irish pilot who protected English skies in the Battle of Britain, was shot down by the Luftwaffe soon after. Ten-year-old Jersey, a virtual orphan, was forcibly evacuated by the British to London. Then, during the Blitz that rained German fire from the skies on the civilian population of England, she was sent for safety with other English children—"bundles from Britain"—to families in the United States until the war's end. By that time Jersey's mother, a member of the French Resistance, was reported "missing in action" in France.

The story, repeated these many years, always ended with a tearful Jersey avoiding further comment by reminding us of the bravery of her ill-fated parents, and of the pain it caused her to try to think back on those harsh, hard times.

In support of this picture was plenty of circumstantial evidence, including posters, playbills, and reviews detailing Jersey's extremely early public life in America. At ten she was placed as the foster child of a New England family who recognized, when Jersey was about twelve—an age when many musical prodigies are discovered—that she had a most remarkable singing voice. In the summer of 1945 when the war was drawing to a close, Jersey lied about her age (which was fifteen) to try out for the lead part of Margot in *The Desert Song*, a Sigmund Romberg musical that had been touring the provinces since the dawn of history and was crying out for fresh blood. The tour de force role was ideal for a young coloratura like Jersey.

On opening night in the boondocks, our Cinderella was discovered by the proverbial New York scout, who understood the depth and range of those fresh, bell-like tones that would later make Jersey's voice so easily differentiable from dozens of other young sopranos. The agent signed Jersey, assuring everyone that she would complete high school despite the brilliant career he foresaw. He got her a high-caliber professional voice coach. And the rest, as they say, was history.

What I needed to find out now was the *secret* history, as Volga Dragonoff might call it: the unknown story, if indeed there was one, behind the very public story of my mother. But in all honesty, taken fact for fact, there weren't so many details of Jersey's well-documented life that would actually *contradict* what Volga had claimed: that the sensational dancer and demimondaine Zoe Behn was really Jersey's mother.

For instance, a quick calculation told me that if Laf was born at the turn of the century, and if Zoe was six years old when he was twelve, then when my mother was born on the isle of Jersey in 1930, Zoe would have been twenty-four, the perfect age to run off to an island with a handsome Irish pilot and make a baby. And hadn't Wolfgang said she was a member of the French Resistance? It was also plausible that Zoe, who'd lived most of her own flamboyant and equally well documented life in France, might have left a ten-year-old daughter in the relative security of the Channel Islands, if she feared for someone else whose safety might be threatened by the German occupation. But just for starters on my lengthy list of questions—who might that someone be?

Furthermore, though thousands of families had certainly been separated by the war and many were unable to locate lost relatives for a period extending into decades, it had now been nearly fifty years since the described events took place. It was highly suspicious, if not impossible to imagine, that in all that time neither Jersey nor Zoe was aware that the other was alive and well, living glamorously in Vienna and Paris.

Add the significant fact that my mother had been married to two successive men named Behn, and had also lived with a third, my uncle Laf. Regardless of how little Jersey claimed to know, or actually might know, of her own roots, how could the detail have escaped her, these many years, that the three men she'd lived with were actually her mother's brothers—hence, her own uncles? And if Volga and Laf knew this much of family affairs, what about Jersey's two husbands, Uncle Earnest and my father Augustus?

I didn't get much further with Volga on these questions, though. Either he didn't know anything else or he was reticent to say more.

"You must ask your mother," he repeated whenever I pressed him. "It is for her to say what she wishes. Perhaps she's had reasons for not speaking before now."

When my patience and stamina were nearly at an end, my warden Svetlana returned, motioning with those frantic, frightened gestures, desperate to lock me back in my room before someone caught us all dallying there in the dining hall. Before we parted, I thanked Volga for what he'd revealed. Then I took a quick moment to scribble a note to Uncle Laf, saying I'd surely try to check in with him as I passed back through Vienna. I added by way of explanation that the tightness of my schedule and the distance between the IAEA and Melk had prevented me from keeping my earlier promise.

Back in my room, though, I couldn't get to sleep—and not just because of my empty stomach, icy bedchamber, or mental exhaustion. To the contrary, I knew that my insomnia resulted from a hyperenergized brain. I had some serious thinking to do about this pattern of errors, omissions, myths, and lies that seemed to make up my life. At the crack of dawn, I'd surely be roused back to action by life's little importunities rapping once more at my door. But I wouldn't be ready to field anything new until I'd regrouped and figured out where I stood right now.

From the moment Volga mentioned my mother as a possible contender in the game, it had occurred to me that, just like Hermione, Jersey was not only a name but a place—a place, if memory served, with enough Celtic standing stones to qualify as a key point on the mysterious power grid. And it had finally registered that all this time I might've been looking in the wrong direction: down, instead of up.

Those ancient builders who'd designed Egypt's pyramids or Solomon's temple didn't need maps and calipers to site their structures. They had used the same tool kit over a span of thousands of years, whether to navigate a desert or an ocean. It was also the single reference they'd have needed in order to pinpoint precise spots on earth—that is, the canopy of stars painted across the night sky. So once again, all that history and mystery and mythology seemed to drive home a key point, at the same time pointing *me* in the right direction. Toward the stars.

Before turning in, I rummaged for a bottle of mineral water to brush my teeth, and noticed at the bottom of the bag the Bible still there from Sun Valley. Seeing it triggered the memory of a conversation with Sam, out under the stars one evening before I went away to school. Though I couldn't have known it then, that would be the last time I would see Sam until just this past weekend, on another Idaho mountaintop.

I pulled the Bible from the bag, rested it on the chipped porcelain rim of the bathroom sink, and flipped through the pages until I came to the Book of Job, as I heard Sam's voice in my mind. . . .

"Do you remember the story of Job?" he asked as we stood there together looking up at the night sky.

It seemed an odd remark for someone who didn't read the Bible. All I could recall was that Yahweh had cut poor Job a pretty one-sided deal, giving Satan carte blanche to torture "God's servant" as he pleased; it seemed awfully cruel. I said as much to Sam.

"And yet, interestingly enough, despite the suffering he underwent," said Sam, "in the end Job had only one real confrontation with God. He asked a famous question: 'Where shall wisdom be found? and where is the place of understanding?' Do you recall what God's reply was to Job's simple plea for understanding?"

When I shook my head in the negative, Sam took my hand in his, lifted his other hand, and swept it wide to encompass the entire night sky—that sparkling stellar array that had remained so remote and unchanged over billions of years.

"*That* was the answer to Job," Sam told me. "God arrives in the midst of a terrifying whirlwind, and for page after page he enumerates all He's accomplished. He's created everything from hail to horses to ostrich eggs—not to mention the universe itself. Job can't get a word in edgewise with all the bombast, nor should I imagine he'd want to at this point, what with all he's just been through. God's behavior on the occasion seems incomprehensible, and philosophers have wondered about it for thousands of years. But I believe I've found an interesting clue. . . ."

Sam looked down at me in the starlight with clear grey eyes and quoted: " 'Where wast thou when I laid the foundations of the earth? . . . Who hath laid the measures thereof . . . or who hath stretched the line upon it? . . . Knowest thou the ordinances of heaven? canst thou set the dominion thereof in the earth?' "

When I made no comment, he said, "That's a pretty specific answer to a pretty specific question, don't you agree?"

"But you told me Job's question was, 'Where is wisdom to be found?' " I pointed out. "How does showing off over creating the universe answer that?"

"Precisely what's been puzzling the *sages philosophes* all these aeons: What was God's point?" Sam agreed with a smile. "But as my favorite poet-philosopher said, 'In the end the philosophers always go out by the same door that in they came.' On the other hand, for those who can read a road map, I suggest God's reply *is* an answer. Think about it. God seems to be saying that the coordinates mapped out in the heavens *are* the guide to wisdom here on earth—'as above, so below'—do you see?"

Maybe I hadn't seen it then, but I thought I did now. If the placement of holy sites in relation to one another was truly patterned after the constellations themselves, it was even possible to visualize how, over time, that heavenly map had gradually *become* the map of earth—which in turn would connect the geography below with the archetypal meaning of the constellations above: totems and altars and gods.

I saw something else too, though I had only three hours to sleep before learning what all this had to do with the Soviet Union, nuclear energy, and Central Asia. For once, I'd actually begun to feel the warp and woof were twined into a pattern.

◆ ◆

Wolfgang rang me on the house phone in time for the two of us to have a brief tête-à-tête over breakfast before our nine o'clock meeting with the Soviet nukes. I found him alone in a corner of the dining hall where I'd met Volga only hours earlier, seated at the end of one of the long tables, his back to the wall.

I passed down the rows of Russian businessmen in ill-fitting black suits, huddled together eating bowls of thick hot porridge and sipping their black coffee in silence. When Wolfgang saw me approach, he put his napkin on the table and stood to seat me beside him, then poured me some hot java. But his tone, when he spoke, was surprisingly chilly.

"I don't think you quite understand the position we are in, here inside Russia," he told me. "It's rare for Westerners to be invited in for open discussion on so sensitive a topic, and I explained that our behavior would be watched. What on earth were you thinking, to conduct a secret late-night meeting with someone right here in the hotel? Who was he?"

"It was a surprise to me too, when he showed up. I was already in my pajamas," I assured him. "It was my uncle's valet, Volga. Laf was worried that I never even phoned him in Vienna. I should have called."

"His valet?" said Wolfgang in disbelief. "But I was told you were together for hours—until nearly dawn! What did he say that could possibly have taken so long?"

I wasn't sure how much I wanted to tell Wolfgang about last night's chat, and I resented his tone. Wasn't it enough that I'd spent a week with little sleep, and all night with no dinner, without being confronted at breakfast by the Spanish Inquisition? So when a surly mustachioed woman arrived at our table with a tureen and a bread basket, I ladled myself some hot oatmeal, stuffed a piece of dry toast in my mouth, and made no reply. After my tummy was warm, though, I felt a bit better.

"Wolfgang, I'm sorry, but you know how my uncle Lafcadio feels about you," I explained. "He was truly worried, knowing you and I were alone together in Vienna. When he didn't hear from me, he even called the office back in Idaho to try and find out what might have become of me—"

"He called your office?" Wolfgang interrupted. "But with whom did he speak?"

"With my landlord, Olivier Maxfield. They've met each other," I reminded him. "It seems there were things Laf wanted to discuss with me. He tried first in Sun Valley, then in Vienna, but it never happened. That's why he sent Volga to meet me here."

"What sorts of things?" Wolfgang asked quietly, sipping his coffee.

"Family things," I told him. "They're pretty personal."

I looked at my bowl of porridge, already congealed. I'd learned from last night one couldn't be sure when the next meal might be forthcoming, so I forced myself to take another mouthful. I washed it down with some of the bitter coffee. I was unsure exactly how to say what I knew I had to, so I just set it out there:

"Wolfgang, when we get to Vienna, instead of flying directly back to Idaho, I want to make a detour—just for one day." I paused as he looked at me. "I want you to arrange for me to meet my aunt Zoe, in Paris."

◆ ◆

Wolfgang and I were picked up after breakfast, in front of the charming penal colony we now called home, by a van that resembled a tank with windows. It was equipped with a driver, as well as a fresh female Intourist "escort" to be doubly sure we got where we were supposed to go. To remind myself, I pulled out my file from the IAEA and checked the schedule and attached map.

This morning's first meeting was about an hour west of Leningrad, toward the Baltic: the nuclear power plant at Sosnovy Bor near the summer palace of Catherine the Great, where we were scheduled to tour what in America we'd call a commercial reactor, one that produces electricity for public consumption.

As we went, it occurred to me that this was the first time since San Francisco I was free of drizzle, fog, ice, and snow—free to look at my surroundings. Along the river I had a sweeping view of the Hermitage, a brilliant shade of pea green, reflected upside-down in the Neva like Volga's fabled city of Kitezh, shimmering in the depths until the Last Days when it would rise again, dripping from the waters. Fleecy clouds floated across a brilliant turquoise sky. The skeletal architecture of trees lining the road, their branches spangled with diamonds from last night's rain, still spoke of winter, but the earth was moist with the rich aroma of newly awakening life wafting through the half-open windows of our van.

Right off the bat that morning, as we were escorted around the vast power plant at Sosnovy Bor by a group of clean-cut engineers and physicists with names like Yuri and Boris, I learned for the first time, with enormous interest, precisely what had brought the Soviets to the pass of extending us this invitation. Just this month of April, during a visit to London, Mikhail Gorbachev—perhaps carried away by the spirit of *glasnost* and *perestroika*—had surprised everyone by announcing the USSR's decision to cease unilaterally the production of HEU, the highly enriched uranium used in nuclear warheads, and to shut down several Soviet plutonium production reactors as well.

That afternoon, during my first in-depth plunge into that premier Soviet think-tank, the Leningrad Nuclear Physics Institute, the story began shaping up on a very significant scale. In another of those lengthy briefings that nukes everywhere are so fond of, the institute's director, one Yevgeny Molotov, a handsome but hatchet-faced man with an unsettling resemblance to Bela Lugosi, gave us the back story.

It began with the same struggle Volga Dragonoff had alluded to only last night, a contest waged for the past two millennia which still seemed to be under way today. The part of the world involved—once again, Central Asia—had lost little of its mystery in the process. The British, along with the Russians and others, had engaged in this tug-of-war for the past five hundred years, and coined a name for it. They called it the Great Game.

◆ ◆

THE GREAT GAME

Throughout the history of human knowledge, there have been two conceptions concerning the law of development of the universe, the metaphysical [idealist] concep-

tion and the dialectical [materialist], which form two opposing world outlooks. [In dialectical materialism] the fundamental cause of the development of a thing is not external but internal; it lies in the contradictoriness within the thing itself.

—Mao Tse-tung

East is East and West is West and never the twain shall meet.

—Rudyard Kipling

The East will help us to conquer the West.

—Vladimir Ilyich Ulyanov (Lenin)

Ivan III of Russia, a descendant of Alexander Nevsky, shook things up for the first time in a quarter millennium when he refused, in the year 1480, to pay tribute to the Golden Horde. Ivan married Zoe, the only niece of the last Christian Byzantine emperor. When Constantinople fell to the Turks, he arrogated to himself the spiritual crown of head of the Eastern church and Defender of the Faith.

This politically astute wedding of church and state took place at what would be an important historical moment for western Europe: the year 1492, when "Columbus sailed the ocean blue" and Ferdinand and Isabella evicted the Moors and Jews from Spain, severing the seven-hundred-year infusion of southern and eastern cultures and pointing the face of Europe to the west. It marked the beginning of the end for the feudal system and lit the fuse of nationalism, with the subsequent rush for colonial expansion that that would entail.

An island to the north was rather late at jumping into this land-grabbing game. The East India Company was officially chartered by Queen Elizabeth I of England only on December 31, 1600. It was established to compete with the Dutch who, themselves already in competition with the Spanish and Portuguese, had still managed to corner a virtual monopoly on the spice trade in Malaysia and the Spice Islands. Within fifty years, chartered East India trading companies had also blossomed in Denmark, France, Sweden, and Scotland. The "jewel in the crown" of England was India with her vast troves of wealth, seemingly inexhaustible natural resources, and warm-water ports.

But the Russians by now had noticed these attributes, too.

Until the many reforms of Peter the Great in the eighteenth century, the Russian peoples themselves had appeared more Asiatic than

European, with their long flowing robes, uncut hair and beards, sequestered women, and exotic church rites. Yet with their paranoiac fear of being surrounded again as they had been during the "lost centuries" of Mongol domination, these formerly backward feudal fiefdoms managed to expand their borders at the truly impressive rate of 20,000 square miles per year. In the two centuries from Peter's death in 1725, they absorbed nearly all the vastly diverse cultures in a several-thousand-mile swath surrounding them, pushing to the east through Siberia all the way to the Bering Sea, and to the west grabbing all or sizeable portions of Lithuania, Poland, Finland, Latvia, Estonia, Livonia, Karelia, Lapland.

A panicky Britain extended its influence north and eastward into the Punjab and Kashmir, annexing Burma, Nepal, Bhutan, Sikkim, and Baluchistan, and making serious runs on Afghanistan and Tibet. Egypt and Cyprus were occupied, the East India Company was dissolved, and Victoria, crowned Empress of India, had an empire where the sun never set.

As a countermove, by the beginning of the First World War, Russia expanded south and west and seized possession of Ukraine, the Caucasus, Crimea, and western Turkestan—today Central Asia—right down to the Indian-Persian border. Now two empires that once had been separated by thousands of miles had borders, in some places, within only a few miles of each other.

Nor did Russian expansionism end with the Russian Revolution. When Lenin called for a world uprising of the masses against colonial oppressors, he focused specifically on India, encouraging the colonized to throw off the (British) yoke of imperial slavery. But the Bolsheviks themselves, it soon proved, had little intention of offering autonomy to the colonial possessions Russia had acquired throughout four centuries of imperialism. Those regions attempting to break away during the ensuing civil wars and peasant uprisings were quickly brought to heel.

When the USSR was created in 1922, it consisted of the republics of Byelorussia (White Russia), Transcaucasia (Georgia, Armenia, and Azerbaijan), Ukraine, and the Russian Federated Soviet Socialist Republic, which included just about everything else. Only later, when the principally Islamic former Turkestan requested to become a separate and independent republic, were artificial boundaries drawn dividing it into not one but five states based on "ethnic nationalities." That decision was taken in 1924, the year Lenin died and Joseph Stalin succeeded him, to remain for the next thirty years the steel fist of the Communist Party.

Beginning in 1939, the USSR "pacified and absorbed" all or part of Poland, Czechoslovakia, Rumania, the Baltic states of Latvia and Lithuania and Estonia, and portions of Germany and Japan.

I hardly needed Yevgeny Molotov of the Leningrad Nuclear Physics Institute to fill me in on the rest of the picture. After World War II, the name of the game had changed but the players remained the same: now it was called the Cold War. The new toy possessed by all key players was a nuclear "device." Diplomatic strategy was patterned on the game of Chicken where two cars are driven straight at one another, accelerators to the floor. The driver who turns away first to avoid collision is the loser, the chicken. And the USA had been accelerating faster than anyone. The only difference I could see between the automotive and Cold War versions of this game was that, with the former, there was the off-chance somebody might win.

◆ ◆

In our week of scheduled meetings, Wolfgang and I traversed a broad swath of central Russia, visiting facilities and meeting with groups and individuals that worked in various capacities within the nuclear field, and I discovered the Soviet government's gravest worry wasn't the operational safety of their power plants but something I myself might be uniquely placed to deal with: the security of nuclear materials, especially those recycled from fuels and weaponry. Much of these, in the case of the Soviet Union, happened to be located *outside* the Russian Federal Republic proper. That's where I came into the picture.

For almost five years, Olivier and I had been constructing a database designed to locate, classify, and monitor toxic, hazardous, and transuranic waste that had been produced by segments of the U.S. government and related industries. The project involved many groups around the country and the world, and we all shared expertise in our own Yankee version of *glasnost-perestroika*. We interfaced with the IAEA, and with databases from Monterey to Massachusetts that monitored trade in nuclear materials, equipment, and technology. But our efforts were just beginning to explore the surface of a very deep wound.

The secrecy and mistrust of the now waning Cold War period, I soon found, had left scars that were hard to erase—especially on Mother Earth. The horror stories were many: for years the motto in the nuclear field had been: The left hand knoweth not what the right hand doeth. The military shoved waste into landfill where housing subdivisions were later built; liquid waste from reactors was injected into the aquifers of rivers and such. But our Western military-industrial predecessors seemed lily white, I learned, compared with their counterparts in Russia these past forty years.

While we'd long wrangled over how to locate and dig up waste—not to mention what to do with it once we found it—I learned, in my week of traveling Russia, that the Soviets had Satan ICBMs and Bear H bombers and thousands of stockpiled strategic warheads. They had numerous storage facilities for spent fuel assemblies; gaseous diffusion and laser isotope plants for uranium enrichment; open pit and slurry mines and *in situ* leaching of deep-seated uranium deposits. Dumping in the Arctic and Pacific of tritium and zirconium, it seems, had been going on for decades.

There were roughly 900,000 people employed in—and at least ten cities solely dedicated to—the Soviet nuclear industry. There were more than 150 sites where fissile materials were used or produced, and plans on the books to double the number of commercial reactors within the next twenty years. And that was only the beginning.

The problem that proved the biggest burr under the saddle, as Olivier might say, was Central Asia—the area called, in the Turkic tongues of the region, *Ortya Asya*—which included the five largely Islamic republics of Kazakhstan, Kyrgyzstan, Uzbekistan, Tajikistan, and Turkmenistan. When Karl Marx said religion was the opiate of the masses, he forgot how deeply the drug coursed in the veins of humanity—and that rhetoric had never proven any antidote. Russia's ten-year war of aggression against her Islamic neighbor Afghanistan, "the Russian Vietnam," had only exacerbated this age-old spiritual-material schism.

To further fuel the fundamentalist fire, the Russian name for this same region, *Sredniya Aziya*, referred to only *four* of the republics—excluding Kazakhstan, which, with its large ethnic Russian population, they considered part of Russia. The Soviet Union's nuclear test sites were located in Kazakhstan, which shared a border with Xinjiang—the former Chinese Turkestan, with its own Islamic population—where China's nuclear testing had taken place, at Lop Nur in the high desert, since 1964. The whole area was a powder keg.

Russian operations outside the USSR looked no better. There were weapons arsenals and mining and fuel production centers in Czechoslovakia and Poland. From the 1970s, Russia had supplied nuclear fuel to countries like Egypt, India, Argentina, and Vietnam, as well as highly enriched uranium to research reactors in Libya, Iraq, and North Korea. Yet there wasn't a single customs post in the entire USSR set up to measure the radiation level of shipments on a regular basis.

Given this picture, it didn't take a stretch of the imagination to figure out why the Russians were hopping on coals. Clearly, Western expertise hadn't arrived a moment too soon. But when it came to sandbagging dikes, my philosophy had always been better late than never.

The mythical Pandora had opened her fabled box so long ago, the moral of her tale seemed lost. She might have released on the world all the evils a vengeful Zeus could dream up. But as Sam said, maybe we'd been reading the maps wrong. After all, one thing had still stuck in the box that never escaped: hope. Looking at the picture from a different perspective, maybe hope really was still waiting for us inside the box. At least, so I hoped.

We agreed with our Soviet fellow nukes to enter into the new spirit of problem-sharing. What with the recent atmosphere of openness and cooperation, Soviet scientists were lately permitted to travel outside the Iron Curtain as never in the past. Before Wolfgang and I left the country, we made dates for follow-up contacts—and I'd even collected a bagful of those new elitist items that had been pressed on me all week: business cards.

◆ ◆

The Vienna airport was nearly deserted by the time our plane arrived late. We'd already had a close connection and thought we might miss our flight. But the last plane to Paris was held for minor repairs and hadn't been boarded, so we checked in. While Wolfgang waited with the others for the bus to the landing strip, I went to phone Laf as I'd promised. Wolfgang said not to talk long, as we might board at any moment.

I was hoping it wasn't too late to call, but I really wasn't expecting the barrage I got, when the servant who'd answered found Laf and put him on the phone:

"Gavroche, for heaven's sake—where are you? Where have you been?" said Laf, sounding in a tizzy. "We've been looking for you all the week. That note you sent with Volga—what were you doing at the monastery of Melk? Why couldn't you phone me while you were in Vienna, or even from Leningrad? Where are you right now?"

"I'm here at the Vienna airport," I told him. "But I'm on a flight to Paris that's leaving at any moment—"

"Paris? Gavroche, I am extremely worried about you," Laf said, and he certainly sounded it. "Why go to Paris—only because of what Volga told you? Have you spoken with your mother first about any of this?"

"Jersey didn't see fit to mention anything to *me*, these past twenty-five years," I pointed out. "But if you think it's important, of course I'll let her know."

"You must speak with her *before* you speak with anyone in Paris," said Laf. "Otherwise, how will you know what to believe?"

"Since I no longer believe anyone or anything I hear," I said sarcastically, "what difference does it make whether I deceive myself in Idaho, Vienna, Leningrad, or Paris?"

"It makes a good deal of difference," said Laf, sounding genuinely angry for the first time. "Gavroche, I am trying only to look after you, and your mother as well. She had excellent reasons not to speak of these matters earlier—it was really for your own protection. But now that Earnest and your cousin Sam are both dead . . ." Laf paused as if he'd just thought of something. "Whom exactly were you with at Melk, Gavroche? Was it Wolfgang Hauser?" he asked. "And did you happen to meet anyone else while you were here in Vienna? Other than your business associates, I mean?"

I wasn't sure just how much I should say to Laf, much less over a public phone. But I was so sick of all this secrecy and conspiracy, even among my own family—*especially* among my own family—that I decided to have an end to it.

"Wolfgang and I spent the morning at Melk with a guy named Father Virgilio," I said. When the line remained pregnant with silence, I added, "The prior afternoon, I had lunch with a handsome devil who claimed he was my grandfather—"

"That's enough, Gavroche," Laf snapped over the line in a tone wholly unlike him. "I know this Virgilio Santorini; he's a very dangerous man, as you may live long enough to discover for yourself. As for the other—this 'grandfather' of yours—I pray only that he came to you as a friend. You must say no more—we cannot discuss it now, for you have made so many bad and foolish choices since we parted from one another in Idaho, I cannot think what to do. Though you have failed in all you've promised so far, you must swear to me one thing: that you will phone your mother first, before meeting with the person you plan to visit in Paris. It is of the utmost importance, no matter what else you may foolishly choose to do or not to do."

I wasn't sure what to say. I admit, I was chagrined; I'd never heard Laf so upset. But just then I heard the first call in German for our plane.

"I'm really sorry, Laf," I whispered under the background noise of the public address. "I'll phone Jersey the minute I get off the plane in Paris—I swear."

There was a silence on the phone as the racket went on, the call for our plane first repeated in French, then in English. Wolfgang popped his head out the glass doors of the waiting area, gesturing frantically to me—but just then another voice came on the phone. It was Bambi.

"Fräulein Behn," she said, "your *Onkel* is so unhappy by your conversation, I think he forgets some messages he was planning to give you. One is a computer mail for you, sent over here to us from Wolfgang's office. The other is from your colleague Herr Maxfield. He has telephoned many times this week; he says you have never called him back, as he asked. He has a most important message for you. He sent a telegram."

"But quickly," I said. "Our plane is about to go."

"I shall read them both to you myself: they're very small," she told me. "The first is from a place called Four Corners in America, and says, 'Research phase completed. Take extreme care in handling K file. Data are suspect.' "

I knew the only thing in Four Corners, that remote spot in the high desert of the Southwest, would be the ruins of ancient Anasazi Indian dwellings. So this message was Sam's way of telling me, based on what he'd learned from his researches in Utah, that I should beware of any "data" issuing from Wolfgang "K" Hauser. This seemed bad enough. But Olivier's telegram was worse. It said:

The Pod took the next plane after yours to Vienna; he's still there. Maybe you lost more than I did on our lottery. Jason's doing great and sends his regards. My boss Theron sends his, too.
Love, Olivier

That packed a wallop: The only good news was that my cat was doing well. It was definitely *not* good that my boss the Pod had followed me to Vienna. This raised the specter of something that, for the entire past week in Russia, had been hovering at the back of my mind. Sam's warning only seemed to confirm it.

Wolfgang *was* telling the truth in admitting I'd seen Father Virgilio earlier, before meeting him at the monastery of Melk. As he'd pointed out, I had seen Virgilio the day before, in the restaurant where the padre was disguised as a busboy, keeping an eye on me all afternoon with Dacian Bassarides. Seeing Virgilio as a fleeting busboy might explain why, later, he would have seemed familiar to me—but not *that* familiar. Then I recalled Wolfgang's evasive replies to my questions about his mysterious servant Hans Claus, whose name kept changing. It was there that I found the lie.

How *relieved* he must have been when I believed it was Father Virgilio I had recognized from the back that night in the vineyard. But I realized now that the figure I'd seen moving away from me in the moonlight was not Virgilio but a figure I had often followed through the corridors of the nuclear site back in Idaho—a wiry figure that moved with the spry step of a trained boxer and Vietnam vet. I knew, with not the shadow of a doubt, that the man who'd met Wolfgang so clandestinely in the vineyard above Krems had been none other than my own boss, Pastor Owen Dart.

In the wake of that came a flood of thoughts about just what such a connection might mean. For starters, I couldn't overlook that it was Dart who'd hired me into the nuclear field right out of college, with no experience, then put me on this assignment with Wolfgang just after my return from Sam's funeral. Now in hindsight, given everything else in the picture, that seemed more than exceptional timing.

Then it was again Dart who'd supposedly spoken with the *Washington Post* about my "inheritance," and whose idea it had been to send Olivier quickly to the post office to *retrieve my package*. It was Pastor Dart, too, who'd sent Wolfgang chasing after me across two states to

Jackson Hole, and who'd gone up against even federal security to make sure I was on that plane with Wolfgang. What else could it possibly mean, if the Pod himself had jumped on the very next flight to Vienna? Furthermore, his secret night meeting with Wolfgang, just after we'd hidden the manuscripts, coupled with Olivier's message that the Pod was *still there* in Vienna seemed to have obvious implications—though there was bloody little I could do about them by myself, tonight.

As we boarded the plane to Paris, something strong and cold was forming inside me. I tried to swallow what bitterness I might feel over the depth of Wolfgang's treachery, until I could wade to the bottom of this quagmire of lies. But there was something more important I really couldn't bear to think of, though I knew I must. I was terrified to learn what the rest of Olivier's message meant, the part at the very end, since it might prove the most dangerous of all.

For the man who'd been killed in San Francisco in place of my cousin Sam was named Theron, like Olivier's "boss." His name had been Theron Vane.

FIRE AND ICE

DISCIPLE:

Lama, about the Great Stone we have many legends. . . . From the old Druidic times many nations remember these legends of truth about the natural energies concealed in this strange visitor to our planet.

LAMA:

Lapis Exilis . . . *the stone which is mentioned among the old Meistersingers. One sees that the West and East are working together on many principles. We do not need to go to the deserts to hear of the Stone. . . . Everything has been indicated in the Kalachakra, but only few have grasped it.*

> *The teaching of Kalachakra, the utilization of the primary energy, has been called the Teaching of Fire. The Hindu people know the great Agni—ancient teaching though it be—shall be the new teaching for the New Era. We must think of the future.*

—Nicholas Roerich, *Shambhala*

> *Some say the world will end in fire,*
> *Some say in ice.*
> *From what I've tasted of desire*
> *I hold with those who favor fire.*
> *But if it had to perish twice,*
> *I think I know enough of hate*
> *To say that for destruction ice*
> *Is also great*
> *And would suffice.*

—Robert Frost, *Fire and Ice*

It was not yet midnight when we arrived, but Charles de Gaulle airport was pretty deserted. The money changers had locked up their booths and gone home, and the moving escalator tracks inside their clear glass tubes had been shut off for the night. Luckily, we hadn't arranged to meet with Zoe until tomorrow morning.

But midnight here meant it was before six P.M. at Jersey's elegant New York penthouse—early enough in the cocktail hour that she might still be able to focus if I phoned her right away. It had also occurred to me that it would be better to call from a public phone at the airport than wait to try from whatever hotel accommodations Wolfgang had arranged for us. Back then, a week ago, my principal thought had been when and where we could spend another long, liquid night of lust before a castle fire—but now I tried to push all that from my mind.

I figured out how to use my calling card at the pay phone. Wolfgang waited for our bags to arrive at the nearby international carousel, where I could see him through the glass wall. After a few rings, Jersey came on the line. Her voice was as crystal clear as if she were only two feet away, and she sounded uncharacteristically sober.

"*Bonsoir* from Paris, Mother," I greeted her politely—but not too warmly. "Laf insisted I phone you as soon as I got here from Vienna. I'm standing in a phone booth in the middle of Charles de Gaulle, it's past midnight, and I'm not alone. But you've probably guessed what brought me here—a little family matter it seems you forgot to mention these past twenty-five years. Maybe you'd be willing to save us time and hassles, and let me know what you think *I* need to know?"

Jersey was silent for so long that I thought maybe she'd dropped the phone.

"Mother?" I said at last.

"Oh, Ariel honey, I'm so sorry," she answered in a tone that seemed genuinely contrite—though naturally I hadn't forgotten for a moment that divas are also actresses. "Sweetheart, it's just that I hoped if I kept you apart from all of this, despite everything, maybe at least you'd have some chance of a normal life." She laughed and added, a little bitterly it seemed, "Whatever *that* might be."

"Mother, I'm not asking you to explain the motives for all you've done or not done these past many years. That can certainly wait until later." *Much* later, I thought. In fact, if I got lucky I might even get to forgo the pleasure of hearing that particular confession forever. "But what I would like tonight is some cold hard facts," I suggested. "Just a mini-recap, a clue here and there, of what might be going on with your family—*our* family. If it isn't too much to ask?"

"I don't know why I irrationally hoped this day wouldn't arrive," Jersey said, almost irritably. "But I certainly never conceived I'd be ambushed long distance by my own daughter, before I've even had a chance to toss down a preparatory drink! Do you expect me to apologize for my entire life in three minutes?"

"Okay, take your time," I told her. "Laf wanted me to speak with you first—but that gives us all night, since I'm not actually meeting Granny dearest till morning."

"Very well. Exactly what sort of 'cold hard facts' did you have in mind?" she asked me coolly.

"Things like why your mother ran off to France and deserted you during the war, and why you then married, or lived with, not one but all three of her brothers—"

"For that, I need a drink," Jersey cut in abruptly, leaving me dangling on the line three thousand miles away, and on my nickel.

When she came back a moment later, I could hear the ice cubes clinking in her glass like tiny punctuation marks as she spoke. Perhaps it was the liquor talking, but her voice had taken on a steely tone, as if she'd just stepped into a full suit of armor.

"Exactly how much have you been told?" Jersey asked me.

"Far too much for my own good, I'm sure, Mother," I said. "So you needn't worry about pulling any punches at this late date."

"Then you know about Augustus," was her reply.

"Augustus?" I said.

Though it seemed clear she must be referring to Dacian Bassarides's true paternity of my father, wasn't *I* the one who was supposed to be asking the questions? Nor was I at all sure I should just blurt out everything I knew to a woman—mother or no—who'd kept me in the dark so long about her *own* parentage. With Jersey's next unexpected comment, I was relieved I'd had the sense, for once, to hold my tongue.

"I mean," said Jersey, still able to phrase her words carefully despite the drink, "has Lafcadio explained why I left your father?"

Now, I hadn't a clue where all this was leading, but of one thing I was positive: Whatever was coming down the pike, it was too critical for me to screw up now.

"Why don't you put it in your own words?" I suggested—the only compromise I could think of between simply answering yes or no.

"It's clear you don't know," said Jersey. "And to be frank, if it's to be left in my hands, I'm not sure exactly what to do. I know it would be far better not to tell you any of it. Yet, considering that you said you've just been to Vienna and you're now in Paris, I'm afraid keeping it all secret any longer might only place you in serious danger—"

"I'm *already* in serious danger, Mother!" I exploded between clenched teeth. Jesus, how I wanted to wring her goddamned neck!

Wolfgang had glanced over at me with one raised eyebrow through the glass wall of the booth. I shrugged my shoulders as if nothing were amiss, and I tried to smile.

"Of course, I realize you have every right to know," said Jersey.

But she lapsed into silence again as if trying to sort her thoughts. All I could hear was the tinkle of ice cubes in the background thousands of miles away. I'd thought by now I was braced for anything anyone could possibly throw at me. But at last my mother spoke, and as always with my family, I wished to God she hadn't.

"Ariel, sweetheart, I have a sister. . . ." Jersey began. When I said nothing, she added, "I should rather say I *had* a sister. We weren't close, I hadn't seen her in years, and now she's dead. But due to an—unforgivable infidelity on your father's part all those years ago—" She choked on her next words, as well she might! "Darling, *you* have a sister too, nearly your own age."

I really couldn't believe this was happening. Why hadn't anyone told me? All these generations of lies and deception spewing from the operatic throat of my diva mother truly sickened me—though clearly the blame was far from hers alone. Augustus had done a pretty good cover-up job, too.

I probably would have done well to hang up and pretend we'd

been cut off. But somehow I sensed this was just the left hook, that the right to the jaw was still coming. So I held my breath and waited. I knew that the mother in question—the "corespondent" in my father's infidelity—couldn't have been his current wife, Grace. She'd have been too young, twenty-odd years ago when Jersey left my father. But Jersey was still speaking.

"Ariel, I know your father and I should have told you long ago. . . ."

She paused, as if she had to put down a healthy slug of her drink before she could go on. As I watched Wolfgang pacing near the carousel I was grateful the French baggage system was one of the slowest in Europe, so I still had time to get to the bottom of this—though I wasn't at all sure I wanted to.

"You asked why my mother deserted me," Jersey said. "She didn't, exactly. Zoe had gone into France to fetch my sister Halle, who'd been brought by her father to Paris. It was wartime, you know—"

"*Her* father?" I interrupted. "You mean your sister's father wasn't the same as your father, the Irish pilot?" But why should that be surprising, given Zoe's reputation?

"My mother was married, or I should say, she had a child—my sister—by another man. With fathers on opposite sides in wartime, Halle was understandably raised apart from me, we had separate lives. But when you said just now you'd recently been in Vienna, I thought your uncle Lafcadio had introduced you to her—"

"To *her*?" I said, as I felt the blood clotting in my chest. The two girls' fathers were on opposite sides in the war? But if Jersey's sister was dead now, who could be the *her* whom Laf might have introduced me to in Vienna? Then Jersey delivered that right cross I'd been expecting.

"I can never forgive your father Augustus, nor my sister, for their betrayal," she said. "But the child they had together—your sister—has become a truly beautiful girl, and exceptionally talented too. These past ten years, Lafcadio has been her guardian and a kind of Svengali. That's why I thought you might have met. They travel everywhere together."

I clutched the phone to my chest, hyperventilating, praying the airport would collapse on me or something. I couldn't believe this was happening. I slowly brought the phone back to my ear just as Jersey said, "Ariel, your sister's name is Bettina von Hauser."

◆ ◆

"I hope you will be like sisters," Laf had said—hadn't he?—when Bettina Braunhilde von Hauser and I first met. Then the same night, when she came to my room in the Lodge, Bambi spoke of her brother Wolfgang's "dangerous involvement" with me—though at the time, as I recall, she'd said it might endanger us all. Good lord, did this mean Wolfgang was my brother too?

Luckily, no. Wolfgang's mother Halle was married to an Austrian who died sometime after Wolfgang was born—but mercifully *before* she'd made her intimate acquaintance of my father, Augustus. But that didn't simplify the family complexity.

By the time I rang off the phone with my mother, some twenty minutes later, I was immeasurably wiser about family matters. To my shopworn line "My family relations are rather complex" I thought I might now be justified in adding the tag line "Little did she know." But this time as the stew bubbled—thanks to a little heat applied to Jersey's feet by me—more than hot air floated to the surface.

According to Jersey, her mother Zoe Behn, youngest child and only daughter of Hieronymus and Hermione, had run off with Pandora and, by the age of fifteen, had developed into an excellent dancer. Like the generation-older Isadora Duncan, who'd become her friend, tutor, and patroness, Zoe soon created her own unique style of performance. By the time of Isadora's tragic death in 1927, when Zoe was only twenty, my young grandmother was already a star of the Folies Bergère, Opéra Comique, and numerous other venues. It was the year she met Hillmann von Hauser.

Hillmann von Hauser was in his late thirties, rich, powerful, a knight of the Teutonic Order, a member of several underground Germanic nationalist groups like the Thule Society and the *Armanenschaft*—and already, in 1927, a strong financial backer of the National Socialist Party and of Adolf Hitler. He was blond like Zoe, handsome, strapping, and for the past ten years had been married into an old, respected noble family like his own back in Germany—a marriage that had yet to produce a child.

Young Zoe was a wild exhibitionist of easy virtue, who for five years had danced nude onstage before the public each night—all attested to in her own memoirs, the scandalous exposé of an already scandal-riddled Roaring Twenties. Apparently Zoe was only too happy to provide empirical proof that the von Hauser's barren marriage could not be the result of his own sterility. My mother's older sister, Halle von Hauser, was born to Zoe in 1928.

In the decade after the First World War, Hillmann von Hauser and his kind experienced few of the depredations suffered by most Germans. Rather, a group that weathered the storm between the wars very well was a certain set of industrialists and armaments manufacturers like the Krupps, Thyssens, and—why, yes—the Ritter von Hauser himself. Zoe's daughter Halle was taken to Germany, adopted by her father and his legitimate wife, and sent for much of her education to elite schools in France. As Jersey understood the story, her mother Zoe soon fled to the isle of Jersey, where she met and impetuously married a successful young sheep rancher engaged in the production of Irish wool, and they remained there with their own daughter, Jersey, until the outbreak of the Second World War, when he became a heroic pilot and Zoe returned to France.

Though this missing "pastoral" portion of Zoe's past didn't jibe too well with her self-perpetuated legend, it *did* coincide with something of historical import that sent chills up my spine. I hadn't forgotten what was going on in 1940, the very week Jersey told me Zoe had made her unexpected jaunt back to France: it was the week of the German occupation. Not only was the Ritter von Hauser in Paris—as Jersey said he was, collecting their twelve-year-old daughter Halle—but an even older acquaintance of Zoe's would also have been present there.

Nor had I forgotten my afternoon with Laf in the hot tub at Sun Valley, when he'd told me Zoe was "never the queen of the night as she liked to portray herself," that it was all propaganda designed by "the cleverest salesman of our century"—Zoe's Austrian compatriot Adolf Hitler, who'd come to Paris that same week to have his mug snapped, smiling like a tourist before the Eiffel Tower, as the long-awaited conqueror of the descendants of those Salic-Burgundian Franks of the *Nibelungenlied*.

Whether my grandmother Zoe turned out to be a demimondaine or simply a dancer—whether she'd served with the OSS or French Resistance in the war as Wolfgang claimed, or was more like what Laf said, a Nazi collaborator—by tomorrow the real Zoe Behn would be measured by *me* for the very first time.

Given the environment of secrecy, not to say treachery, in which our family operated, maybe Wolfgang didn't know that our mothers, Jersey and Halle, were half sisters. It was also possible he was unaware the eighty-three-year-old bombshell Zoe, whom he'd found so charming, was actually his own grandmother. After all, I hadn't known such things myself until tonight.

But one item Jersey explained was something Wolfgang *couldn't* have been telling the complete truth about. It had to do with the week of Sam's funeral. And it made my latest cryptic message from Sam seem even more ominous.

Before the funeral, like Augustus and Grace, Jersey had talked briefly with the executor about the reading of the will; but unlike Augustus and Grace, Jersey had had a reason to do so. She was acquainted with Mr. Leo Abrahams, who'd been Uncle Earnest's attorney as well as executor of the estate when Jersey was left widowed by Earnest's death. Now that Sam too was dead, it was understandable Jersey would want to know how, in future, her own income would be paid by the estate her stepson had managed these past seven years. But that wasn't all.

When Jersey had learned *I* was likely to be Sam's major beneficiary, she wanted to find out whether I understood just what that responsibility might entail—for an excellent reason. She herself had a better than average guess of what Sam might have inherited from his father. Maybe my mother hadn't been quite as drunk as she'd seemed that day at the graveside. In hindsight, her astonishing behavior had certainly given us a breather from Augustus and Grace long enough to have lunch by ourselves. But when Jersey realized I knew zilch, she decided that once the rest of the family left town, she would corner me and fill me in on everything.

Jersey had brought something of her own to the funeral, and though she couldn't say much right now, the little she *could* communicate was enough. She'd intended to give me what she'd brought after our talk—but I had vanished. So after much soul-searching, she'd wrapped it in butcher paper and twine and mailed it to me, with a note scribbled on the inside of the brown paper. This I'd unfortunately thrown away without seeing. But from Jersey's brief description, as precise as she could afford to be on our transatlantic trunk line, I knew this was surely the rune manuscript I'd stashed in the Department of Defense Standards manuals at the nuclear site—just before I got those more deadly manuscripts from Sam, now tucked away at the Austrian National Library in Vienna. So Jersey's document was the very rune manuscript Wolfgang claimed he'd received from Zoe and mailed me *himself*—a manuscript that Laf later assured me neither Wolfgang nor Zoe could possibly have possessed.

My mother and I agreed, for reasons of prudence, that we'd discuss the rest when I got back home. When I rang off the phone, Wolfgang was waiting outside the booth with our bags, and we headed for the airport taxi stand. As our cab swept into the wet black velvet Parisian night, I knew, just as Laf had repeatedly warned, I might be walking into the proverbial lions' den without my whip.

Indeed, as I now grimly appreciated, it was entirely conceivable Wolfgang had never seen the rune manuscript until that night he'd spent in my room back in Idaho, just after the avalanche, when I myself was drugged and out cold. And if that were true, I understood with a horrible chill exactly what it would mean: that the man sitting beside me in this taxi, rolling down a dark French highway at midnight, might well have deceived me in everything he'd said or done, from the very first moment we'd met.

◆ ◆

Our cab pulled up in a narrow street on the Left Bank before the Relais Christine; Wolfgang hopped out, paid the driver, and rang the bell at the gate.

"Our plane was quite late," Wolfgang told the desk man in rather impeccable French. "We haven't yet eaten. Could you give us our room key and stow our baggage while we go for a short meal?"

The desk man agreed, Wolfgang exchanged a healthy tip for our room key, and we went on down the one-block street to where lights were still glowing and numerous tables of what seemed ebullient after-theater people were still dining inside a chic, cozy bistro.

Our *coquilles* arrived, filled with a wonderful rich concoction of seafood seasoned with exotic Mediterranean spices. Something about a good meal and a full-bodied wine always seemed to make me truly relaxed and mellow—and to dull my survival instincts exactly when I needed them sharpest.

"It was rather a lengthy phone call you made just now to the States," Wolfgang finally commented when our crispy green salad showed up afterwards. "Do you speak with your mother often?"

"At least every few years—without fail, rain or shine," I told him.

"Perhaps this call was related, then, to the call you made earlier to your uncle?" he suggested. "You've been uncharacteristically quiet ever since we left Vienna."

"I *am* often more of a blabbermouth than serves my own good," I agreed. "But on the subject of my family, I've usually been reticent. Of course, now that it turns out you and I are actually *related*, I guess there's practically nothing we couldn't discuss with one another. That is, if we both decided to tell the truth, for a refreshing change."

"Ah," said Wolfgang quietly, looking down at his plate.

He picked up a crusty roll and broke it in two, studying the pieces in his hands as if expecting them to contain the key to some mystery. At last he looked up at me with those incredible turquoise eyes beneath thick lashes, which always made me more than a little weak in the knees. But I knew I'd better keep my attention focused on mind instead of matter.

"It's your serve, I believe," I told him. "But please be advised, this isn't a set of lawn tennis we're playing anymore."

"It's clear you've been told something that reflects badly on me," Wolfgang said calmly. "But before I try to explain my side of things, I must ask how much of the situation you already know?"

"Why is that always the first question everyone asks me?" I said. I stabbed at my salad a few times, then put down my fork and looked him in the eye. "I think that even if you did meet Zoe Behn for the first time last year, you know she's your grandmother, which makes her daughters—your mother and mine—half sisters. And I know neither you nor Zoe sent me that rune manuscript. My mother has just informed me *she* did. She may have concealed the truth from me for a very long time—but she's not an out-and-out liar. I wish I could say the same of you. The one thing I have to thank you for is saving my life in an avalanche. Otherwise, as far as I can see, you've misled me from the very moment we met up on that mountain, and I demand to know why—tonight."

Wolfgang was staring at me with a kind of astonishment. I admit, a few of the waiters and other patrons had glanced in our direction, though I'd kept my voice pretty well under control. Then, unexpectedly, Wolfgang smiled.

"Only *one* thing?" he said with raised brow, ignoring the rest of my tirade. "*I* should have to say, rather, that I have *many* things to thank *you* for. The first, that I have never fallen in love with anyone before now. The second—something I really didn't expect—that it could be with such a hellcat as you. So I must thank you for—how do you Americans say?—for 'introducing me to reality.' "

He put his napkin on the table and motioned for our bill. But I was blazing mad and not about to be put off one more time, even by this scathing, if possibly accurate, portrait of myself. I waved the waiter away and picked up my wineglass to emphasize the fact.

"I haven't finished," I told Wolfgang firmly.

"Oh yes, you certainly have," he assured me in exactly the same tone of voice. "Does it not occur to you, Ariel, that I didn't speak of our relationship earlier because I was warned by everyone of how you feel about the Behn family? That you've been distant toward all but your cousin Sam since you were even a little child? Don't you think I knew beforehand what your reaction would be if I arrived without warning, immediately after this very cousin had died, and said to you, 'Hallo, it's me, your cousin Wolfgang whom you've never heard of; I'm here to drag you into the bosom of your dangerous family whom you've avoided for so long'? And as for the rune manuscript you say I lied to you about, Zoe knew you'd been sent it by your mother because the two of them spoke of it together. Ask her yourself tomorrow, if you don't believe what I say. I'm sorry, but when I told you it was I who sent it to you, it was the only way I could think of that I could quickly win your trust—"

"Why is it that the only way you can ever think how to 'win my trust' is to tell me another lie?" I interrupted Wolfgang's extremely untimely confession.

But in the back of my mind, I had to admit that much of what he said was true. Handsome and desirable as Wolfgang had seemed to me from the moment I'd first clapped eyes on him, I *had* spent much time and effort trying to avoid proximity at all cost—and for a reason I could hardly have shared with him, then or now: that Sam was still alive and in danger from every quarter I could think of but my own, and I couldn't afford to trust anyone, anyone at all.

I also couldn't help noticing there was still one cog that didn't fit into Wolfgang's mechanical blueprint.

"Even if all you've said is true," I added, "it doesn't explain your lie about the Pod."

"The—pod?" said Wolfgang, confused.

"My boss, Pastor Owen Dart," I translated. "Why was he so anxious to get me out of town on an assignment to Russia, and then turn around and follow us to Vienna? What was he doing lurking that night in the vineyard below your house? What did you and he speak of that you couldn't discuss in front of me?"

Perhaps it was my imagination that Wolfgang grew slightly pale. He seemed about to speak, then stopped. I hoped he wouldn't try to go on pretending that the man in the vineyard was Father Virgilio—but that thought in itself suggested yet another question.

"Who is Virgilio Santorini, anyway?" I asked. "My uncle Laf seems to know of him, but believes he's a very dangerous man. Why did you have him meet us at the library of Melk?"

"This is hardly the time or place I would have chosen for such a conversation, but at least it's difficult to eavesdrop," Wolfgang said with a sigh of frustration. "And everything is nearly over now, so I'm able to tell you whatever you'd like to know—if at least it will finally make you feel you can trust me. Life is very complex, Ariel, and people are often complex beyond our understanding—"

"Wolfgang, for heaven's sake, it's nearly two o'clock in the morning. Let's cut to the chase, okay? Who's Virgilio, and why was Pastor Dart following us in Vienna?"

"Very well," Wolfgang said, looking me right in the eye with a you-asked-for-it expression. "Virgilio Santorini is a highly educated, erudite scholar of medieval texts who received his degrees from the Sorbonne and the University of Vienna. He is in fact a priest, but not a librarian of the monastery of Melk. He has complete access to their archive, however, since his family in Trieste donated a large portion of their rare book collection. Their money pays for many restorations now under way on the monastery."

None of this was surprising. But I was soon grateful for the covering sounds of waiters clattering dishes and some laughing ribaldries in raucous French wafting from a nearby table, for I was hardly prepared to swallow what came next.

"Virgilio Santorini's family," Wolfgang went on, "are also among the largest arms dealers in Eastern Europe, specifically Yugoslavia and Hungary, which is how they've made their money for generations. What your uncle may have meant when he spoke of danger is the fact that Virgilio's family is also widely reputed to be connected with a mafia group called Star, a consortium believed to have traffic in weapons-grade nuclear materials. So you see, as I mentioned earlier, people themselves, as well as situations, can be more complex than a simple talk over supper can express."

Okay, I was surprised by this revelation about Father Virgilio, who seemed a charming if somewhat bumbling medievalist scholar. Before pursuing that, though, I tried to harness my attention long enough to hear the rest of my question answered.

"Pastor Dart's role is even more complex," Wolfgang went on. "It requires a bit more background. On first arriving in Idaho, I was worried to learn that your colleague Olivier Maxfield was also your landlord, and so in a convenient position to tap your phone and spy on you virtually twenty-four hours a day. How could I be sure he wasn't someone's agent? For that reason, as soon as you'd returned from the funeral, I had Pastor Dart send Maxfield to intercept you at the post office, while I myself followed by car. It was apparent from your behavior there that Maxfield, arriving before you, had done something to arouse your suspicion. Once you had picked up your package, I saw you drive away from Maxfield and race off from town. So I followed you myself to Jackson Hole.

"Though I knew that a rune manuscript had been sent to you by your mother, your attitude of fear and suspicion from the moment we met up on the mountain made it clear you believed the document in your possession was your inheritance from your cousin instead. I had the opportunity to verify that these were your mother's runes later that night when you slept. I also knew that this must be the only document you'd received so far, which meant you didn't have your cousin's inheritance yet, but were still expecting it. This was very dangerous if what I strongly believed was true—that Maxfield was trying to get hold of the documents, too.

"Though our Russian trip was planned, Pastor Dart and I decided to accelerate the schedule of our departure to take you from Maxfield's position of constant surveillance. Dart himself would remain behind to intercept the second parcel when it arrived, to be certain it didn't fall into the wrong hands. But after all these careful arrangements, you were late for our connecting flight to Salt Lake. I was in shock when you finally arrived. From the look of your bag—three times as heavy as it was the day before—and also from the fact you said you'd 'run an errand' between office and airport, I was certain you had again been to the post office, and this time you had collected the real thing!

"So what must I do," he went on, "but arrange by phone from Salt Lake airport, while you were off at the women's room, that Pastor Dart purchase a ticket for himself at once, on the very next airline headed to Vienna? I gave directions to where we could meet below my house at Krems, the one place I thought was safe from prying ears, the one time you and I might be completely alone. All the while, I prayed I could find a way to get you to leave the manuscripts in Austria, rather than run the risk of taking them into Russia, where they'd surely be confiscated. I contacted Dacian Bassarides, and asked him to come from France and meet us at the restaurant in Vienna. I hinted you'd received your inheritance and needed help understanding what to do with it. At the restaurant, I hadn't expected him to send me away so he could be alone with you. But at least Virgilio watched so he didn't take you off somewhere and fail to meet me on the corner he'd designated. . . ."

Wolfgang paused for the first time, and shook his head. "Ariel, if you could know how insane I've been these past two weeks, merely trying to protect you from yourself."

From *myself*? I nearly screamed.

With thousands of gongs clanging in my brain, I wrestled myself back to reason. Let's see if I'd got it right: this guy had just confessed that ever since meeting me he'd been embroidering on the truth until it looked like a Gobelin tapestry; that he'd had me watched all afternoon by a priest who was a possible arms dealer with mafia connections; and that he'd gotten my own grandfather to convince me to abandon my inheritance in a public library. Had I left anything out?

Well, actually, yes: there was one small thing.

"Wolfgang, why do you and Pastor Dart and everyone else in the world *want* these manuscripts?" I asked. "I know they're valuable—but what's so important about them that the Pod had to fly halfway around the world at the drop of a hat just to meet you for a few minutes at night in that vineyard? What did you two need to speak about that you felt you could only discuss right then and there?"

Wolfgang looked at me as if the answer were ridiculously obvious. Then for the second time, he motioned to the waiter for our check.

"With respect to the contents, I only know a portion—not all—and even that will take some explaining," he said. "But as for Pastor Dart, I had to tell him where the manuscripts were just as soon as I myself knew where you had finally hidden them—and certainly before you and I had to leave for Russia. How else would Dart have been able to retrieve them from the Austrian National Library before someone else did?"

◆ ◆

The word that instantly leapt to mind was Olivier's *oy*. Virgilio, it seems, had followed us right from the Café Central, and as Wolfgang handed those slips out the door of our room in the Austrian National Library, he'd copied down every single book title. Actually, I couldn't think of a word for that.

As we walked back along the narrow street, close enough to the river to smell the damp night air, I felt like weeping.

Wolfgang had taken my hand as if nothing were wrong, and now he squeezed it. "Let's walk down by the river for a bit, shall we?" he suggested.

At the end of the street I saw the glittering lights of the Île de la Cité that seemed to be underwater. What the hey? I thought in silent desperation. I could always throw myself into the drink—or drag him in too, if he didn't start coming up with some decent answers soon. This was hardly my idea of a weekend in Paris with Wolfgang. Right now I wanted to shoot him. I'd destroyed all Sam had risked his life for, by forgetting Laf's injunction to "resist the *men*, until you learn exactly in what kind of situation you are involved."

Well, I sure knew what kind of situation I was involved in now, though I hadn't a clue what in God's name to do about it. I felt like screaming my brains out. I still knew less than *nothing* about these bloody manuscripts! Just thinking of all they'd cost ripped me inside out. But the night was far from over, and I vowed to get some straight answers before it was up.

We went along the quai to where we could see, across the water, the illuminated facade of Notre Dame towering above its famous wall of ancient ivy that dripped down to the rippling river.

"Ariel," said Wolfgang, turning my face up to his in the glittering night light. "If I lie to you, you say it makes you unhappy. But when I tell you the truth, you're unhappy, too. I love you so much—what can I say or do that will make you happy?"

"Wolfgang, you've just said that you and some mafioso and my boss Pastor Dart have manipulated me and betrayed me, that you've betrayed everything Sam ever stood for—what indeed he may have lost his life for—and you expect that to make me *happy*?" I said. "It would make me happy if you'd just tell me the truth—up front for a change—rather than forcing me to pry it out of you, or keeping me in the dark 'for my own good.' I want you to tell me right now exactly what you know about Pandora's manuscripts—what they have to do with Russia and Central Asia and nuclear matters, as clearly they do, and what role you and those others play in all of the above."

"It seems you understand nothing I've just said," Wolfgang said in frustration. "First of all, I never said Virgilio was a mafioso but that he was from a family of arms dealers—there is a difference. I said your uncle might have heard of mafia connections: those like Virgilio often must maintain contacts with such people for their own security. In my field too, if we treat every arms dealer as an enemy, then all activity goes beneath the table and we lose any measure of control over smuggling that we might have had to begin with—we close all doors.

"But when you speak of betrayal," he added, "there's something you clearly don't know. There's a group I'm given to understand had investigated Samuel Behn for many years, since his father Earnest's death. They'd even hired your cousin at times to work for them in order to win his trust. But in the end I believe it was they who killed him.

"These people claimed to work for the United States government, but in fact were multinational, controlled by a man with a lengthy dossier—a man named Theron Vane. When I was absent, that week before I came to Sun Valley to find you, I learned several things about this man. The first: that he was in San Francisco the week your cousin Sam died. They were working on an assignment together. The second: that Vane went underground immediately after Sam's death and has not resurfaced. The third—and you *must* believe me about this part,

Ariel—is that Olivier Maxfield is, and has been ever since the day you met him, a henchman of Theron Vane. Maxfield came to Idaho, and secured his job, and also his acquaintance and friendship with you, for one reason and one reason only: because *you* were the only way they could think of to slip inside the defenses of your cousin Sam."

I stood there absolutely stunned. I knew from Sam that he *had* worked with Theron Vane for over ten years. The man must have hired him out of college, just as the Pod had done with me. I also knew Theron Vane was there when Sam had "died" because, according to Sam, the man was killed in his place! And in that cryptic message Olivier had left with Laf, he too admitted he worked for Theron Vane.

In hindsight, it did seem odd for Olivier's credentials to have matched mine so perfectly that from day one, five years ago, we'd been assigned codirection of the same project. Not to mention how he'd lured me to my tenancy in his basement apartment by providing cheap rent, designer meals, the willingness to cat-sit in a pinch—and by conjuring up that weird dream about me as the Virgin Mary beating the Mormon prophet Moroni at a game of pinball!

Indeed, all Wolfgang had said, if taken from a slightly different perspective, might present as accurate a picture. Theron Vane might have deceived Sam about who he was really working for. Somebody might have been out to get Theron Vane, not Sam. And Wolfgang and the Pod could simply have been trying to provide the documents more protection than Sam and I, in our bumbling attempts, had been able to do on our own.

I was so bloody confused: I had a million questions that were still unanswered. But Wolfgang took me into his arms there beside the river and he tenderly kissed my hair. Then he held me away and regarded me with a serious expression.

"I will tell you the answer to everything you've asked—that is, if I know the answers," he said. "But it's after two in the morning, and though we don't meet Zoe until eleven tomorrow, I must confess I'd like to spend at least some of tonight making up for all the unhappiness it seems I've caused you." He smiled wryly and added, "Not to say what it's cost *me*, to spend all those nights alone in that Russian barracks!"

We headed along the quai where the fuzzy new leaves draped on the chestnuts, illuminated by little lights from below, were like gauzy shrouds of dangling caterpillars. The air was laden with the moisture of spring. I felt as if I were drowning and I knew I had to snap out of it.

"Why don't you start with Russia?" I suggested.

"First of all," Wolfgang began, taking my hand once more, "perhaps you found it odd, as I did, that during our entire stay in the Soviet Union—and despite our extensive discussion on the topic of security and cleanup of nuclear waste—not a single mention was made of the 'accident' at Kyshtym?"

In the 1957 disaster at Kyshtym, a nuclear waste dump had gone critical, like a live reactor minus control rods, and spewed waste over an estimated four hundred square miles—roughly the size of Manhattan, Jersey City, Brooklyn, Yonkers, the Bronx, and Queens—an area possessing a population of around 150,000.

The Soviets had successfully covered up this "mistake" for nearly twenty years, despite the fact that they'd had to clear population from the region, divert a river around it, and shut down all roads. It wasn't until an expatriate Soviet scientist in the 1970s had blown the whistle that it all came out. But with today's new atmosphere of cooperative atomic *glasnost*, one did have to wonder why, when they'd made a clean breast of everything else, Kyshtym was never broached throughout our week of intensive dialogue. It suddenly occurred to me that Wolfgang had an important point.

"You mean, you believe that the Kyshtym 'accident' was really no accident?" I asked.

Wolfgang stopped and smiled down at me in the almost surrealistic night light of the unfolding Parisian spring.

"Excellent," he said, nodding his head. "But even those who finally did expose the mishap may never have guessed the awful truth. Kyshtym is located in the Urals, not far from Yekaterinburg and Chelyabinsk, two sites that are still today actively engaged in design and assembly of nuclear warheads—and where you and I, of course, for security reasons were not invited to visit. But what if Kyshtym had not actually been a waste dump for these two sites? What if it didn't go critical by accident, as everyone believes? What if, instead, the incident was the result of a controlled experiment that turned out very differently than planned?"

"You can't possibly imagine that even in the days of darkest repression, the Soviets would ever have performed a nuclear test in a populated area?" I said. "They'd have have had to be completely insane!"

"I'm not referring to a nuclear weapons test," said Wolfgang cryptically, gazing out across the river. He stretched one arm toward the flowing black waters of the Seine.

"More than a hundred years ago," he said, "at this very spot in the river, young Nikola Tesla used to go swimming. He'd come to Paris from Croatia in 1882 to work for Continental Edison, then continued on to New York to work for Edison himself, with whom he soon quarrelled bitterly.

"As I'm sure you know," Wolfgang added as we walked on, "Tesla held original patents on many inventions for which others later took all the credit and profit. He was first to conceive, design, and often even to construct inventions like the wireless radio, bladeless turbine, telephone amplifier, transatlantic cable, remote control, solar energy techniques, to name only a few. Some say, too, that he invented 'antigravity' devices that had the superconductive properties known today—as well as a most controversial 'death ray' that could shoot planes from the skies using only sound. And in his famous secret experiments at Colorado Springs in 1899, it's said he was able to change even patterns of weather."

"I've heard the story," I assured Wolfgang dryly. It was the endless debate between "hands-on" engineers, who credited the self-propagandizing Tesla with inventing techniques for everything from raising the dead to walking on water, and "conceptual" physicists, who pointed out that the self-educated Tesla had rejected most modern theory, from relativity to quantum physics. Your basic rehash of spirit-matter polarity.

"But Tesla died before the atomic bomb was invented," I pointed out. "And he refused to believe that even if you succeeded in splitting an atom, the released energy could ever be successfully harnessed. So how can you imagine, as you seem to, that the awful disaster at Kyshtym in the fifties was some kind of botched version of a Tesla experiment?" I asked in disbelief.

"I am not alone in imagining it," said Wolfgang. "Tesla established a new science called telegeodynamics. Its goal was to develop a source of unlimited free energy by harnessing natural forces latent within the earth. He believed he could send information underground, around the globe. He applied for very few patents in this particular field—unlike all his other discoveries—nor did he give away any but the broadest descriptions of how such inventions might work. But he experimented extensively with harmonics, inventing oscillators so tiny they could be carried in a pocket, yet whose vibrations, when applied to a structure like the Brooklyn Bridge or Empire State Building, could cause it to sway and break to bits in a matter of minutes."

"So let's get this straight," I said. "You're saying the Soviets might have attempted a controlled chain reaction, trying to somehow invoke this Tesla-type force in 1957—and then it went haywire? But if Tesla didn't write anything about it, how would they know what to do?"

"I said he didn't *publish*—not that he didn't write," said Wolfgang. "In fact, it's possible such specifications were among his papers, many of which mysteriously disappeared when he died in New York at the age of eighty-seven—significantly in 1943, at the height of the Second World War, when the race was on for a new kind of weapon. Indeed, Hitler announced just thereafter, to his intimate confidants, that scientists were on the brink of developing a fabulous new 'superweapon' which would shortly end the war in Germany's favor."

My mind was flooded with unbidden thoughts: Nikola Tesla from Yugoslavia, Virgilio from Trieste, Volga Dragonoff who was given his name by Pandora for the "dragon forces" of the earth and who hailed from the Caucasus.

"What does all this have to do with Pandora and her manuscripts?" I asked—wondering if even at this late date I was really prepared for the answer.

But Wolfgang had stopped dead on the walk to gaze through the mist rising from the Champs de Mars to where the Eiffel Tower loomed like an apparition before us. Looped up its sides a message in neon letters was spelled out. *Deux Cent Ans*—two hundred years.

Good lord! I glanced quickly at Wolfgang, who'd started laughing.

"Though I mentioned it myself to you only last week, I'd already forgotten," he told me. "This year, 1989, is the two-hundredth anniversary of the French Revolution. But 1789 was also the year the new element uranium was discovered by Klaproth in Saxony. He named it after the planet Uranus that another German, Herschel, had discovered with his sister at their observatory in England not ten years earlier. These three events marked the beginning of the destruction of the old aeon your grandfather was speaking of, and Uranus became regarded as the planet governing the new age—the age of Aquarius. I think that's what Pandora's manuscripts are all about. Do you see the connection?"

I began to say I didn't get it—but all at once, I thought I did.

"Prometheus?" I said.

Wolfgang snapped his eyes from the neon lights and stared at me in surprise.

"That's correct," he said. "In the myth, Prometheus stole fire from the gods and gave it to men—just as in the coming age, as Dacian Bassarides said, the water-bearer pours out a great life force for mankind. Such gifts often turn out to be curses as much as blessings. In the Prometheus myth, Zeus turned around and gave us Pandora. She opened a box—a jar, actually—and released all the evils into the world. But there are those who don't think the story of Prometheus and Pandora was totally a myth. I suspect your grandmother Pandora must have been among them."

"You think the manuscripts Pandora collected told how to make a nuclear pile? Or how to tap into the earth's energy forces?" I said. "But I understood that her documents were ancient—or at least much older than any modern technology or inventions."

"Most inventions would be better termed discoveries—or even *re*-discoveries," said Wolfgang. "I don't know if the ancients had such knowledge, but I do know that there are places on the planet where the components of sustainable chain reactions—radioactive materials, heavy water, other ingredients—exist together naturally. It has often been commented that the Bible and other early texts describe scenes very much resembling atomic explosions—the destruction of Sodom and Gomorrah is only one—just as there are indeed specific spots on the earth's surface most conducive to Tesla's power vortices, artificial creation of thunderstorms and ball lightning, and harmonic oscillations. In most of these places, we know that the ancients built monuments, raised standing stones, or left shamanistically significant cave art—well before recorded history."

"But even if all Pandora's documents were collected, translated, decoded, deciphered, and understood—what would someone be able to do with the knowledge?" I said in frustration. "Why would it be dangerous?"

"Since I've only just glimpsed the documents for a few moments myself, clearly I don't know all the answers," Wolfgang said. "But I do know two things. First: the early philosophers from Pythagoras to Plato believed the earth was a sphere suspended in space through equilibrium, and attuned to the music of the spheres. But the details of the power sources themselves were always kept veiled, since they were believed to be a key element of the Mysteries.

"On his deathbed, just before Socrates drank hemlock, he told his disciples that the earth, if viewed from above, resembles 'one of those balls made of twelve pieces of skin in different colors.' That is the description *not* of a sphere but of the largest Pythagorean polygon—the dodecahedron, a figure of twelve sides where each face is a pentagon. This was the most sacred form to Pythagoras and the Pythagoreans. They conceived of the earth as a gigantic crystal—today we'd say a 'crystal set'—a transmitter that harnessed energy from the heavens or the depths of the earth. They thought it could even be used for psychic control on a broad scale if one manipulated these key pressure points. And further, they imagined that the forces within the earth, if properly 'tuned,' would vibrate like a tuning fork to harmonic correspondences in the sky."

"Okay," I said. "Let's say the earth really is a gigantic energy grid, as everyone seems to think. Then I could certainly understand why people who were after power would want to get their hands on that hidden map of trigger points. But when it comes to 'mysteries,' let's not forget that Socrates and Pythagoras, despite all the secrets they knew, or maybe because of them, got wiped out by popular demand. Whatever 'hidden knowledge' they had certainly didn't save them in the end.

"Anyway," I added, "you said there were two things you knew about Pandora's documents. What's the second?"

"The second is what Nikola Tesla believed—which wasn't such a very different picture from what I've just described," said Wolfgang. "He thought the earth contained a form of alternating current that was continually expanding and contracting—at a rate that was difficult but not impossible to measure—rather like the rhythm of breathing, or of a heartbeat. He said that by placing a load of TNT in the right place at the right time—just when a contraction was beginning—he could split the earth itself in pieces 'as a boy would split an apple.' And by tapping into this current, this energy grid, he could harness unlimited power.

'For the first time in man's history,' Tesla said, 'he has the knowledge with which he may interfere with cosmic processes.' "

Holy shit.

Wolfgang looked up at the Eiffel Tower for a moment, its small red beacon at the top nearly lost in the silvery mists. Then he slipped one arm around me as we stood there in silence.

"If Tesla, like Prometheus, gave mankind a new kind of flame," Wolfgang said, "maybe Pandora's knowledge will prove to be both the world's own gift and punishment."

SOCRATES:	*You speak of good and evil.*
GLAUCON:	*I do.*
SOCRATES:	*I wonder if you understand them as I do.*

—Plato, *The Republic*

Despite the best of intentions and well-laid plans, I found myself lying in the carved four-poster bed of a Renaissance suite at the Relais Christine making love with Wolfgang all night—or what was left of it—with a passion so intense, so draining, I felt I'd passed the time in the arms of a vampire rather than an Austrian civil servant.

There was a little garden just outside our room. Wolfgang was standing at the French windows looking out on it when I opened my eyes in the morning. His magnificent naked body was outlined by the web of wet black branches with their haze of tender pale green leaves unfurling just beyond the windows. I recalled that first morning in my cellar bedroom, when he'd crawled out of my sleeping bag and turned his back so he could dress—before he came over to kiss me for the very first time.

Well, I was no blushing quasi-virgin any longer: life had certainly seen to that. But I knew that this man who'd driven up my heartbeat—once again, all night long—was still the enigma he'd been when we'd first met, long before I'd learned that he was my cousin. And despite any philosophical observations about spirit and matter, I had to admit that what I'd coveted from Wolfgang was a pretty far cry from spiritual enlightenment. I wondered just what that said about me.

Wolfgang opened the windows that gave onto the garden, then came over and sat on the bed. He pulled down the sheet and ran his hands over my body until I began to tremble again. "You're so beautiful," he said.

I couldn't believe I actually wanted more. "Don't we have an imminent date for lunch that we really shouldn't miss?" I forced myself to mention.

"Frenchwomen are always late." Licking my fingers, he regarded me meditatively. "It's something in the air—an exotic, erotic perfume you exude that makes me somehow wild. Yet I always feel it's illusion, that we're wrapped in a magical smoky veil that no one must penetrate, or the spell will be broken."

It was a fair description of how I felt myself: there'd been an air of unreality about us from the beginning, an illusion so powerful it often seemed dangerous.

"It's just past nine o'clock," Wolfgang whispered, his lips hovering at my breast. "We can skip breakfast—can't we?—if we're having an early lunch. . . ."

◆ ◆

Les Deux Magots is one of the most famous cafés in Paris. It was once the favorite rendezvous of the literati as well as the underground—two groups that, in France, had often boasted the same membership. Everybody from Hemingway to de Beauvoir and Sartre had hung out there. And apparently also Zoe Behn.

As we crossed the square of Saint-Germain-des-Prés, its sculpted chestnut trees already coming into bloom, Wolfgang pointed her out, seated alone at a corner table in the sunny, glass-walled outdoor solarium that gave onto the open plaza. We entered through the restaurant, past the famous wooden statues, the two *magots*. These Oriental figures in their robes of blue and green and gold, surrounded by gilded mirrors, hovering on thrones high above the bar, seemed like Elijahs swept from the streets of Paris up to heaven in chariots of fire.

We went out to the glassed-in terrace. As we crossed to Zoe, I studied this woman, my infamous grandmother, of whom so many scandalous things had been said and written over so many years. She might be eighty-three, but as she sat there sipping her glass of bubbly, it seemed the life she'd lived—lavish with wine, men, and dance—hadn't served her at all badly. She sat "tall in the saddle," as Olivier would say, with a proud bearing that complemented fine unweathered skin and the remarkable French braid of snowy hair that fell nearly to her waist. The strength revealed in her face recalled Laf's comment that as a child she'd had all the self-containment of Attila the Hun.

When we reached her corner table, she studied me with intense aquamarine eyes—a shade somewhere between Wolfgang's turquoise and my mother's famous "ice blue" ones. Wolfgang presented me to her formally, pulled out a chair, and seated me when Zoe nodded. She addressed Wolfgang, her English lightly flavored with a mixture of accents, never taking her eyes from me.

"The resemblance is truly remarkable," she told him. "What must Dacian's reaction have been the first time he saw her!"

"At first he found it difficult to speak," Wolfgang admitted.

"I don't mean to be rude," Zoe told me. "You must understand, Pandora was unique. Now that she's dead, it's startling to encounter someone who is almost her incarnation down to the finest detail. You've done well, having avoided most of your family all these years. Seeing this amazing replica of Pandora on a more regular basis, we might all have had to resort to taking salts or drinking something stronger than champagne! She was something powerful to be reckoned with, I can tell you."

For the first time, she smiled, and there was a glimpse of that languid sensuality she'd been renowned for—an attribute, as I recalled, that for nearly four decades had brought nobles and magnates to their knees, spilling riches at her feet.

"Were you very close to my grandmother?" I asked. Then, remembering that Zoe was *also* my grandmother, I said, "I mean—"

"I know what you mean. Don't apologize," she cut in curtly. "One day perhaps you'll learn the most important lesson I could ever teach you: that you may do and say as you please in this life, so long as you apologize for nothing." I had the feeling, in Zoe's case, this little rule of thumb must have come in handy more than once.

She'd motioned for the waiter to come pour champagne into two more glasses that had been sitting at a side table awaiting our arrival. They were already partly filled with a mysterious purplish mixture which the waiter stirred into a cloud as he poured.

"This drink is called *la Zoe*," she told us. "Like my name, it means 'life.' The concoction was created for me one night at Maxim's—oh my, how many years ago! Everyone in Paris who wished to be chic drank it. I wanted to meet you here at the Deux Magots for a toast to Life. As no one comes out so early, we can also speak privately here. I wish to tell you of the missing *magot*, and how he relates to us. Then, as it's also the case that no one goes to lunch until two or so, I've made us reservations at the Closerie des Lilas in a few hours from now. I expect, at the hotel where you're stopping, you've been given a decent breakfast."

I sat there frozen-faced, trying desperately not to let my telltale skin flush beet red at recalling our "breakfast" this morning. Wolfgang squeezed my hand meaningfully under the table.

"Perhaps just a dish of olives," he told the waiter in French. When he'd departed, Wolfgang added to Zoe, "In America, one doesn't take alcohol quite so early in the day without a bite of food."

Except *my* bacchanalian family, I thought. We lifted our glasses to Life. With my first sip, the dark, heady flavor of this drink tasted somehow of danger.

"Ariel . . ." Zoe pronounced my name with an almost proprietary expression. Her next words made clear why. "Since your mother has always kept our relationship secret, perhaps you weren't told that it was I who selected your name? Can you guess after whom you were called?"

"Wolfgang told me Ariel was an ancient name of Jerusalem, and that it means Lioness of God," I said. "But I'd always imagined I was named for the little spirit Ariel who was held in bondage by Prospero the magician, in Shakespeare's *The Tempest*."

"No—but in fact you were named for another spirit who was later patterned after that one," Zoe said. Then she quoted in German:

> *"Ariel bewegt den Sang in himmlisch reinen Tönen;*
> *viele Fratzen lockt sein Klang, doch lockt er auch die Schönen. . . .*
> *Gab die liebende Natur, gab der Geist euch Flügel,*
> *Folget meiner leichten Spur! Auf zum Rosenhügel!"*

" 'Ariel sings and plays the—um, harp,' " I translated. " 'If Nature gave you wings . . . follow my steps to a hill of roses.' What's that from?"

"From *Faust*," Wolfgang said. "It's the scene atop the Brocken mountain, on the night called *Walpurgisnacht*, an ancient Germanic festival invoked by Goethe in his play. The word means 'the night they cleanse the woods'—with fires."

Zoe looked at Wolfgang as if there were some unspoken significance in what he'd just said. Then Granny ever so charmingly pulled the pin from her hand grenade.

"That part of *Faust*, the cleansing scene, is when the little spirit Ariel cleanses Faust of the bitterness and suffering he's caused others," she told us. "Often, mind you, Faust had harmed them unintentionally, in his quest for higher wisdom as a magus. You know, it was Lucky's favorite passage. He wept tears every single time he heard it." Then she added, "Most people don't realize that the night he died—April 30, 1945—was also May Eve. Which is to say he killed himself, and Eva too, on *Walpurgisnacht*."

" 'Lucky'?" Wolfgang asked, puzzled. I realized he'd missed Laf's story revealing our family's cute nickname for the world's most evil tyrant. "But April 30, 1945, it's a famous date: the day Hitler committed suicide. That was 'Lucky'?"

"Why, yes," I commented cynically. "A family friend, it would seem. I'm surprised you hadn't heard." But there was something *I* hadn't heard yet, which I'd have been only too happy to have missed, myself.

"Not really a friend," Zoe replied with remarkable sangfroid. "One might say, practically a member of the family."

While I was collecting myself from that remark, she added,

"You must realize, I knew him since I was a child. The truth is, Lucky was an ordinary man with ordinary skills and background and education, but one who knew that his great strength lay in simplicity. That was what made it the more frightening to many, I think, for beneath it was something primal that resonates in one without conscious awareness. With Lucky, it was more than just mass hypnosis, as many wish to believe. Everything about him was archetypal: he touched a place of truth in everyone." She paused, and added chillingly, "After all, he didn't personally pull a trigger thirteen million times—nor did he give written orders for others to do so. Lucky knew all he needed was to make people feel they were given *permission* to do what is hidden within them, what lurks in their hearts."

I felt truly ill. Zoe regarded me coolly with those steely blue eyes as she sat there sipping her plum-tinged champagne that looked like blood. The sunlight seemed suddenly cold. It was true, Laf and everyone else had warned me Zoe was a card-carrying Nazi collaborator. But that was before I was sitting here, sipping a drink named for her, hearing the noxious news from her very own lips. And it was surely before I'd learned that this storm trooper before me was my own *grandmother*! It was no wonder Jersey wanted to disclaim her—I felt like throwing up. But instead, I gritted my teeth and pulled myself together. I carefully set down my own glass of purple poison and squared off to confront her face to face.

"Let's get this straight: you think there's something 'primal' and 'archetypal' that makes ordinary people 'resonate' to the idea of genocide?" I asked her. "You think your pal Lucky was just some ordinary Joe with an idea whose time had come? You believe we just need *permission* from someone in authority for most folks to play follow-the-Führer and do the same thing again today? Well, let me tell you, lady, there's nothing primal, archetypal, metaphorical, or genetic that would cause *me* to take any action without full awareness at a conscious level of what I was doing—and why."

"I have lived long enough," Zoe said calmly, "to see what forces are unleashed by making contact at such deep levels—including those you've seen triggered by Pandora's manuscripts. So let me ask you something: Was it not you who requested this interview we are having? Are you then 'fully aware' that the date you've chosen—today, April 20, 1989—marks the one hundredth anniversary of Adolf Hitler's birth? Is it coincidence?"

I felt a horrid, horrid chill as I forced myself to look into those clear, frozen eyes of my awful, awful grandmother. But unhappily for me, she hadn't quite finished.

"Now, I shall also tell you something you must believe. Who doesn't grasp the mind of Adolf Hitler will grasp neither Pandora Bassarides and her manuscripts nor the true motives driving *die Familie Behn*."

"I'd hoped Wolfgang would make it clear to you," I told her coldly. "I came to Paris for one reason. I thought you might be the only person living who could explain the mystery of Pandora's legacy and unravel the many secrets surrounding our family's relation to them. I didn't come to hear Nazi propaganda; I came here for the truth."

"So, my girl: you want everything to be true and false, good and bad, black and white. But life is not that way, nor has it ever been. The seeds are in each of us. Both things are watered and grow side by side. And when it comes to our family—*your* family—there's a great deal you'd be quite unwise to turn your eyes from just because you can't sort things easily into boxes. It's not always easy to separate grain from chaff, even once the crop has been harvested."

"Gee, I've never been a whiz at deciphering parables," I said. "But if your idea of 'truth' is that we're all potential mass murderers unless we stumble onto the right fork, I'd disagree. What makes 'civilized' people think they can get up one morning, round up their neighbors, shove them into boxcars, tattoo them with serial numbers, then ship them off to a farm somewhere to be methodically exterminated?"

"That is not the right question," said Zoe, echoing Dacian Bassarides.

"Okay, what's the right question?" I wanted to know.

"The right question is: What makes them think they *can't*?"

I sat there looking at her for another long moment. I had to admit, if only to myself, it *was* the right question. Yet it was clear Zoe's and my perspectives, from the starting gate, were very different. I'd made the perhaps naive assumption that all people were innately good, but capable of being led into evil acts on a mass scale by the dark, hypnotic manipulations of a single man. On the other hand, Zoe—who, I had to recall, actually *knew* the man—held the position that we came equipped with the seeds of good and evil, and all it took to tip the balance the wrong way was a gentle nudge. What was the secret ingredient, clearly buried deeply within all sane societies, that prevented us from shooting our neighbors just because we didn't like the way they cut their hair or mowed their lawns? For wasn't that precisely what Hitler said he hated most about the Gypsies, Slavs, Mediterraneans, and Jews?—that they were different?

And in fact, I should know better than anyone that tribal hatred and genocide were hardly a fairy tale lost in the mists of the long ago and far away. It still echoed in my mind, from my first day at school in Idaho. Sam had escorted me, and as we'd passed some other boys in the hallway, one had whispered just loud enough for Sam to hear: "The only good Indian is a dead Indian."

My God.

It sickened me that every time I scratched a little deeper into the surface of the family history I found something ugly, chilling, or unacceptable—but I did understand that whatever my newfound Fascist grandmother here had to say, it might indeed prove the one thing that would bring me closer to the center Dacian had called Truth, at least about our family. So I swallowed the dryness in my mouth and nodded for Zoe to proceed. She set down her glass and narrowed her eyes at me.

"In order for you to understand any of this, whether or not you find it pleasant, you must first understand that the nature of the relationships we, in our family, had with Lucky were different from those he had with others.

"There were some who thought they knew him well. Like Rudolf Hess, who named his son after Lucky's 'secret' nickname: Wolf. More attuned was Josef Goebbels, who had six beautiful blond children. An interesting number, six. Their names were Helga, Hilde, Helmut, Holde, Hedde, and Heidi." She looked at me intently, then asked, "Perhaps you don't know what happened to these little blond Goebbels children whose names all began with *H*? They too were sacrificed on *Walpurgisnacht*: poisoned with cyanide in Hitler's Berlin bunker by their parents, who killed the pet dog Blondi in the same fashion and then took their own lives too."

"Sacrificed? What on earth do you mean?" I exclaimed.

"May Eve is the night of sacrifice and purgation," Zoe explained. "The next day, May first, was once called Beltaine, Bel's or Baal's fires, the sixth station of the Celtic calendar and the pivotal midpoint of the pagan year. The prior night, when Hitler committed suicide, April 30, was in ancient times called the Night of the Dead. The only pagan holy day never converted to the Christian calendar, it still possesses its original, undiluted primal power."

"You can't mean the people who died in Hitler's bunker sacrificed their own children in some kind of . . . pagan rite?" I asked in horror.

Zoe did not answer directly. "The most important event of that night was the first: a marriage that took place between two people who knew they would soon be dead," Zoe said. "Adolf Hitler of course was the bridegroom. But who was the bride in this oddly timed wedding? An insignificant woman who filled a significant role—and who interestingly was named Eve, like the first woman in the Bible, the mother of us all. Her last name describes the color of the earth, the *prima materia* that provides the basis of all alchemical transmutations. She was Eva Braun."

And with that observation, Zoe began her tale. . . .

◆ ◆

MR. BROWN

-And there is a certain man, a man whose real name is unknown to us, who is working in the dark to his own ends. . . . Who is he? We do not know. He is always spoken of by the unassuming title of 'Mr. Brown.' But one thing is certain, he is the master criminal of this age. He controls a marvellous organization. Most of the Peace propaganda during the war was originated and financed by him. His spies are everywhere. . . .

-Can you describe him at all?

-I really didn't notice. He was quite ordinary—just like anyone else.

—Agatha Christie, *The Secret Adversary* (1922)

He was born at Braunau-am-Inn, a town whose name also reflects the word "brown." The storm troopers who brought him to power were called brownshirts; the offices of the National Socialist Party were located at Brown House in Munich. And then, there was Dr. Wernher von Braun, whose secret rocket fabrication was performed by slaves in underground caves in the Harz Mountains, quite near the Brocken. The Führer himself named the place Dora, meaning, like Pandora, the gift.

Names and words were important to Lucky. Words such as "providence" and "fate" and "destiny" appear dozens of times throughout *Mein Kampf*, as in "Today it seems providential that Fate should have chosen Braunau-am-Inn as my birthplace."

The Inn is one of four rivers that rise near each other at a place high in the Swiss Alps, rivers that form a cross spreading over the map of Europe and flow into four seas. The Inn is the last tributary to the Danube as it leaves Germany to cross Austria, Czechoslovakia, Hungary, Yugoslavia, Rumania, Bulgaria, emptying at last into the Black Sea. The northern arm of the cross, the Rhein, passes through Germany and Holland, spilling into the North Sea. The Rhône flows west and south through France to the Mediterranean. The Ticino joins the Po in Italy and empties into the Adriatic. Four rivers, four directions.

The division of a space into four quarters, like the four rivers of Eden, or making two lines cross and the four ends terminate in right angles, was also an ancient symbol of enormous power called the

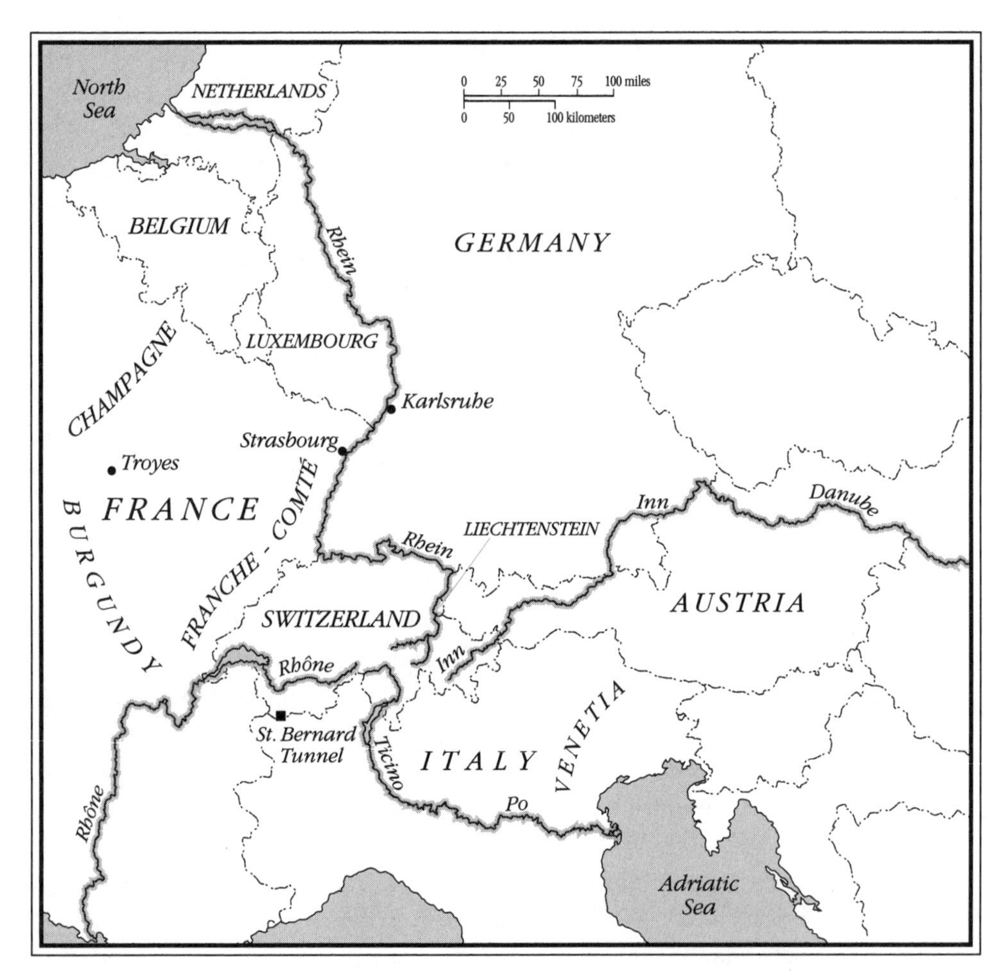

Cross of the Magi. In Sanskrit, the name was *svastika*, one of the oldest symbols of mankind. It describes four elements—earth, air, fire, and water—and a fifth hidden at the center, the polar axis, the hinge upon which the world turns and around which the celestial bears revolve.

At the place where these four rivers rise is the Little Saint Bernard Pass, known to the Romans as Alpis Graia, the Greek alp, believed to be the path of Hercules on his return to Greece, and Hannibal's route into Italy. A temple to Jupiter existed here before the time of Caesar, and at the end of the last century, a utopian community of some importance to my story. The most important axis of the German peoples, connected geomantically to this very spot, was the Irminsul, which stood in the sacred grove at Externsteine, a stone outcropping high in the Teutoburg Forest of Westphalia. It marked the hallowed place where the Teutonic tribes drove back the Romans in A.D. 9, forcing Rome to abandon her northern province of Germania.

When Charlemagne defeated the Saxons in 772, the first thing he did was to destroy this famous pillar along with its sacred grove, for he understood the Irminsul marked far more than an important date in Teutonic history: ancient lore told that a pillar had stood at this spot since the dawn of time.

Irmins Säule, the path of Hermann, was the bond connecting heaven and earth. The Norse god Hermann—variously Ir, Tyr, Tiu, or Ziu—was none other than the warlike sky god Zeus. His stone, the Irminsul, was carved in the shape of the *Tyr* rune, the oldest northern form of the swastika:

Guido von List, the same Viennese occultist who at the turn of this century, during a bout of blindness, had rediscovered the lost meaning of the runes, had also twenty years earlier founded the Iduna Society, an esoteric group named for the Teutonic goddess Idun, who carries the magic apples of immortality. Like the Roman Idas, for whom the ides or turning point of a month were named, Idun was the goddess of the Eternal Return. The Sanskrit root was also one of the two great forces, Ida and Pingala, forming the serpent path of transformation.

At the height of World War I, Guido von List revealed his last and most powerful prophecy, inspired by the *Eddas*, the famous Icelandic sagas that tell of the world's final battle in the Last Days. In the legend, each warrior who dies on the Plain of Ida—"shining renewal"—is instantly reborn as soon as he's slain. List foresaw that those who died on the battlefield for the ideals contained in the runes would participate in the Eternal Return: that those slain in the First World War, the

War to End All Wars, would instantly reincarnate like those on the mythological Plain of Ida. The newly reborn would then coalesce into a force that would attain its full power when most of them turned eighteen. This force would awaken the sleeping spirit of *der Starke von Oben*—the Strong One from On High—who would invoke the ancient Teutonic gods and change the world. Astrological examination revealed that this spirit would manifest itself around the end of 1932, unleashing the power of the runes that had been sleeping for two thousand years since the time of the Roman conquest.

When Adolf Hitler became chancellor of Germany on January 30, 1933, at once he ordered the rebuilding and consecration of the Irminsul destroyed by Charlemagne. At nearby Paderborn, Himmler remodeled the castle of Wewelsburg for his unholy Order of Teutonic Knights. When Hitler instructed his architect Albert Speer to copy the design of the temple of Zeus at Pergamon on the Turkish coast for the Nürnberg rally grounds, the German College of Dowsers didn't just dowse the field to locate major earth forces. They determined from architectural renderings that the 1300-foot temple structure where Hitler's podium was to be placed would not be situated correctly to harness full geomantic powers. So the building site was relocated several hundred feet to the west—requiring a lake to be drained and a railroad to be rerouted.

Over the stadium Hitler ordered an enormous eagle with outstretched wings in the shape of the *Tyr* rune, symbolizing both the *Weibaarin*, female-eagle consort of Zeus, and the *Weberin*, the weaver or spinner of the world's fate in the last days. Hitler told Speer this image was revealed to him in a dream he'd had after being blinded, rather like List, by mustard gas while serving on the western front in World War I. These two elements—eagle and spider, soaring and weaving, the forces of sky and cave—were combined in a single heraldic spirit that would one day serve as sun and moon, guiding his Holy Order.

On November 9, 1918, when Lucky learned that Kaiser Wilhelm II had abdicated and the new socialist government had sued for peace, it triggered a second prophetic dream—that Wotan had come to guide him and Germany to greatness. He wrote this poem:

I often go on bitter nights to Wotan's oak in the quiet glade
Invoking dark powers to weave a union—those runic powers

the moon creates with its sorcerer's spell; And all who are brazen by daylight are defeated by their magic formula. . . .

Hitler often said he regarded Berlin as head of his new religious order, and Munich as its heart. But that night, in the darkness of his mind, he saw that even from ancient times Nürnberg had been the spiritual center, soul of the German people, the mountain where the god Wotan slept. Albert Speer named his creation at the Nürnberg parade ground the Cathedral of Light, fitting for one who wished to portray himself symbolically as *der Starke von Oben*—the axis between heaven and earth, the door connecting past and future.

The operant word in the National Socialist Party's name was "nationalist." The Nazis were interested in finding the roots of Aryan genealogy, geomantics, mysteries, and the occult. They searched wells and springs and ancient burial sites, documenting the legacy preserved on standing stones throughout Europe. They sent secret expeditions high into the Pamir Mountains and the Pyrenees, rifling ancient caves to search for lost documents sealed within clay jars for thousands of years, which might reveal the truth of their sacred lineage and lost wisdom.

It was believed much information was secretly encoded in national epics of the northern lands, and these they set about deciphering. Many clues pointed to the history of the Trojan War. In the famous thirteenth-century Icelandic sagas the Prose Eddas and the Heimskringla, Odin was the king of ancient Tyrland, named after the Norse god Tyr, a kingdom also known as Troy. The saga *Rajnarok*, the Twilight of the Gods, on which Richard Wagner based his opera *Die Götterdämmerung*, is thought to be a description of that long and devastating conflict, with Odin himself as King Priam.

Through Odin's marriage to the Trojan Sibyl, he obtained for himself the gift of prophecy, and thereby foresaw the coming destruction of Troy—and saw too that a glorious future awaited him after it, in the North. With his family and many Trojans and numerous valuable treasures, Odin began peregrinations through northern lands. Wherever they tarried in this migration, the local inhabitants looked upon them more as gods than as men; Odin and his sons were given as much land as they wanted, for they brought the gift of abundant harvests and, it was believed, they controlled the weather.

Odin settled his first three sons as kings in Saxony, Franconia, and Westphalia; in Jutland (Schleswig-Holstein and Denmark) he made a fourth son king, and in Sviythiod (Sweden) a fifth; a sixth became king of Norway. At each spot they settled, they buried one of the sacred treasures they'd brought with them from Troy—the sword of Hercules, the spear of Achilles, and such—as a foundation to protect their kingdoms, and to form a geomantic axis connecting them: the six-pointed star of the *Hagal* rune.

A sorcerer of enormous powers and wisdom equal to Solomon's, Odin would later be deified as the god Wotan. Odin's wife, the Sibyl, a prophetess from Marpessos at the foot of Mount Ida in modern Turkey, was one of a long line of women who recorded the history of the Trojan kings and prophesied the future of their descendants: their writings were also called the Sibylline Oracles.

After the Trojan War, two copies of these Sibylline Oracles were made and carried for safety to the Greek colony of Erythraea on the Turkish coast and to the Cumaean caves just north of Naples. The Cumaean books were later brought to Rome, in 600 B.C., by the last descendant of the Trojan sibyls, and offered to the Roman king Tarquin, who guarded them in closely held fastness, as they were still maintained down into imperial times. For these were of great value not only to the Teutonic descendants of Wotan but also to the Romans: Remus and his twin Romulus, who founded Rome, themselves were descendants of Aeneas, the Trojan hero of Virgil's epic poem the *Aeneid*. When Virgil died, the emperor Augustus placed his grave along the road from Naples to Cumae, where Aeneas likewise had descended into the underworld.

The Roman culture enjoyed a "Thousand-Year Reich" from its founding in 753 B.C. until its conversion to Christianity under Constantine, who in A.D. 330 moved the imperial capital back to the region of Troy. A second phase lasted until the conquest of Constantinople by the Ottoman Turks in 1453, one thousand years after the fall of the western Roman Empire to the Germans. So these two cultures, the Teutonic and the Roman, can be seen mythologically as two branches of the same vine, both descended from Troy.

The Germans regarded themselves as the "rightfully chosen" sons whose ancestor Wotan was not only a hero like Aeneas but a king of royal blood and a divinity. They loathed the imputation that civilized culture had been brought to the pagan North only latterly by Charlemagne and the Carolingian Franks, usurpers who'd crawled to Rome to kiss the pontifical ring and have themselves crowned Holy *Roman* Emperors.

◆ ◆

When Zoe's eclectic romp through two millennia ended, she told us how these Thousand-Year Reichs were woven together.

"Hitler, from an early age, attended boys' school at the Benedictine monastery at Lambach. As a choirboy there he claimed he'd 'intoxicated himself with the solemn splendor of the brilliant church festivals'—and aspired to become a Black Monk, as the Benedictines were called."

This recalled Virgilio's comments on Saint Bernard, patron of the Templars, who'd single-handedly made the flagging Benedictine Order the most powerful in Europe.

According to Zoe, Benedict—a contemporary of King Arthur and Attila the Hun—built thirteen monasteries, all located at or near important pagan religious sites. Twelve were outside Rome, at Subiaco, within spitting distance of the ruins of the emperor Nero's palace facing the *Sacro Speco*, a famous oracular cave where Benedict himself spent several years as a hermit. When some monks of neighboring orders tried to poison the meddlesome Benedict, who was bent upon "purifying" them, he broke camp and relocated to the site of the ancient city of Casinum between Rome and Naples, where he built his now legendary thirteenth monastery: Monte Cassino.

At the height of World War II, when the Allies landed at Naples just after the fall of the Mussolini government, the Germans spent six months defending Monte Cassino in one of the longest pitched battles of the war. Allied bombing raids reduced the mountain to rubble. Yet the German army—though they'd removed the monastery's many treasures and archives to safety—fought on amid the broken stones, in a desperate attempt to hold the mountain.

"By order of Hitler himself, Monte Cassino was defended fanatically," said Zoe. "Just as he wished to seize Mount Pamir in Central Asia in his invasion of Russia, Hitler was assured by his dowsers and geomantic scientists that Monte Cassino in Italy was one of the key points on a massive power grid girdling the earth."

"Yes, it's what I was telling Ariel about, only last night," Wolfgang said. "It seems these places are all connected with the coming aeon. And Hitler's actions as well."

"Indeed," Zoe agreed. "An important event confirms it. Since Lucky's horoscope foretold he could only be destroyed by his own hand, he was known among his intimates as 'the man who couldn't be killed.' The last attempt on his life, at his Wolf's Lair headquarters on July 20, 1944, was led by Claus Schenk von Stauffenberg, a handsome war hero, an aristocrat and mystic. Because his name connects symbolically to the coming age—*Schenk* means cup-bearer and *Stauf* a tankard—Stauffenberg was regarded by many as the coming 'pourer' who would usher in the age by destroying the Great Adversary. Of further importance was that, like Wotan, Stauffenberg had lost—or perhaps given!—one of his eyes in the war.

"But once again, Lucky lived up to his nickname," Zoe added. "Later, when he took his own life, he underwent cyanide, a bullet, and the flame—symbolic too—the Celtic triple death, like *die Götterdämmerung*."

"That's a pretty glamorous description for a guy who was your basic homicidal maniac," I pointed out. "Just take a look at the actual deaths of Mussolini and Hitler: the first was hung up in the town square like a stuffed sausage, while the other got cremated with a can of gasoline. I'd hardly describe those as heroic or noble ways to die—much less a 'Twilight of the Gods.' Not to mention how many millions of people Hitler wiped out before himself, in the Holocaust."

"Do you know the meaning of the word 'holocaust'?" Zoe asked.

"Holo-kaustos," Wolfgang said. "It means totally burned, yes? In Greek, if an animal offering was thought a good sacrifice, they called it 'completely consumed by fire.' It meant the gods had accepted everything that was sent them. For the Greeks, though, this was more of a thanks offering for gifts already received, where for the Semites such things were expiation of the past sins of the tribe."

What in God's name were they saying? I reminded myself I was *related* to both these individuals who were sitting here chatting so calmly, even blithely, about the world's largest-scale mass murder as if it were some atavistic religious rite. Wasn't it enough to suggest that Hitler had arranged to have himself torched like a marshmallow—that he undertook a pagan ritual involving six children, a dog, and a handful of miscellaneous friends in an underground bunker on *Walpurgisnacht*—just so in death he'd resemble some self-sacrificial Teutonic hero? That was sufficiently disgusting. But if I understood correctly, what they were now implying was even worse.

"You can't be serious," I said. "Surely you're not saying Hitler's death was part of some god-awful rite involving slaughter on a massive scale—trying to purify the earth and everybody's bloodlines because of some prophecy about an avatar of a new age?"

"It's a bit more complex than that," Zoe informed me. "When you arrived, I said I'd explain the magus missing from the *deux magots*. Some think it's Balthasar, who brought the gift of bitter myrrh, for tears of repentance. But in fact it was Kaspar, whose gift was incense: an offering of sacrifice."

"Like Kaspar Hauser's death," I said, recalling Wolfgang's tale on our drive to the monastery of Melk.

"Have you ever visited Kaspar Hauser's grave at Anspach?" Zoe asked. "It's a small stone-walled cemetery filled with flowers. To the left of his grave is a tombstone that reads *Morgenstern*—in German 'morning star,' the five-pointed star of Venus. The stone to the right is *Gehrig*—'spear-bearer,' or the celestial centaur Sagittarius, from the Old High German word *ger*, spear. Coincidence? More likely a message."

"Message?" I said.

"The centaur sacrificed his life to trade places with Prometheus in Hades," she said. "He's still associated with the Sufis and the Eastern mystical schools. The five-pointed star of Venus was the symbol of the sacrifice required for initiation into the Pythagorean mysteries. I think the message to be read at Kaspar Hauser's grave is that at the turn of each age, sacrifices must be made, willingly or unwillingly."

Zoe smiled strangely, her cold aquamarine eyes looking through me.

"There was such a sacrifice in our story: the death of Lucky's niece, his sister Angela's child. Perhaps the only woman Lucky ever wholly loved," she said. "She was an opera student, like Pandora, and might have become a fine singer. But she shot herself with Lucky's revolver—though the reason was never adequately explained. Her name was Geli Raubal, short for Angeli, 'little angel,' from *angelos*, messenger. So you see, as in the case of Kaspar Hauser, it may have been the symbolic messenger who died for what others were seeking."

"What were they seeking?" I asked.

"The knowledge of the eternal return—Pandora's magic circle," Zoe said. "It is, quite simply, the power of life after death."

The belief of [the Thracians] in their immortality takes the following form. . . . Every five years they choose one of their number by lot and send him to Zalmoxis as a messenger . . . to ask for whatever they want. . . . Some of them hold javelins with speartips pointed upward, while others take hold of the messenger's hands and feet and swing him aloft onto the points. If he is killed they believe that the god regards them with favour, but if he lives they blame his own bad character, and send another messenger in [his] place.

I've heard a different account from the Greeks: . . . Zalmoxis was a man and lived in Samos where he was a slave in the household of Pythagoras. . . . After gaining his freedom and amassing a fortune he returned to his native Thrace . . . where he entertained the leading men and taught them that neither he nor they, nor any of their descendants would ever die.

—Herodotus, *The Histories*

And those of the disciples who escaped the conflagration were Lydis and Archippos and Zalmoxis, the slave of Pythagoras who is said to have taught the Pythagorean philosophy to the Druids among the Celts.

—Hippolytus, Bishop of Romanus Porto, *Philosophumena*

And I only am escaped alone to tell thee.

—Job 1:15, 16, 17, 19

Camulodunum, Britannia: Spring, A.D. 60

FRACTIO

◆ ◆

Jesus took bread, and blessed it . . . and gave it to the disciples, and said, Take, eat; this is my body. And he took the cup and gave thanks . . . saying, Drink ye all of it. For this is my blood.
—Matthew 26:26–28

And in this mountain shall the Lord of hosts make unto all people a feast of fat things, a feast of wines on the lees, of fat things full of marrow, of wines on the lees well refined. And he will destroy in this mountain the face of the covering cast over all people, and the veil that is spread over all nations. He will swallow up death.
—Isaiah 25:6–8

The grass spread beneath her was a thick carpet of rich emerald green that soothed her soul after another long, hard winter under the Roman yoke. She stood tall and proud in the wicker chariot perched high on the grassy knoll, holding the reins lightly between her fingers, her wild red hair lifted from her broad shoulders and tumbling to billow about her waist in the early morning breeze.

This past year had been far worse than the previous fifteen years since the Roman occupation, for the young emperor Nero had proved far greedier than his stepfather, Claudius, whom the rumors said Nero himself had poisoned.

Now native Britons were being brutally dispossessed by floods of opportunistic Roman colonists backed up by garrisons of legionary troops. Only a few months ago, when her husband died, she herself—proud queen of royal blood of the house of Iceni, and her two young daughters—had been raped by Roman officers, dragged out of their home and publicly beaten with iron rods. Her vast holdings of land were seized on behalf of the emperor Nero and her family's wealth and treasured possessions, as with those of so many others, carted off to Rome. But despite these tragedies, she knew she had fared better than many others: Britons were everywhere being captured and sold into chain gangs to build Roman towns, Roman garrisons, Roman aqueducts, Roman roads. What was the choice now left them, really, as Britons? Only liberty or death.

With her daughters beside her in the chariot, as the horses stamped the turf and blew air through their nostrils, she stood in silence surveying the throngs below, all massed there in a broad circle around the borders of the vast open field, all gazing up at her—all waiting for what she would do.

When at last they fell silent, she knotted the reins on the pommel and opened the folds of her multicolored tunic. She lifted out the rabbit and held the creature high above her head for all to see. It was a snow-white sacred hare, bred and raised by the Druids for precisely this purpose. From the eighty thousand men, women, and children thronged there on the green, not a single breath was heard. Only the whinnying of a horse broke the endless silence. Then she released the hare.

At first the animal sat there on the grassy knoll in stunned confusion as thousands of humans stood below, planted like forests of stone, waiting in silence. Then it pelted in a wild burst down the knoll and made a beeline across the open field, a small white blur against a dropcloth of green. The direction it ran was southwest—away from the sun—and when the crowds saw it, with one voice they burst into a warlike scream of cheers, tossing their tartans into the air like a blizzard of plaids from the sky.

For they had seen that the prophetic hare had dashed straight in the direction of Camulodunum. Boudica's armies that were gathered here could reach it, on fast march, by nightfall. And by dawn, sixteen years of abuses against the Britons and their land would be washed away in an orgy glutted on Roman blood.

Mona Island, Britannia: Spring, A.D. 60

CONSIGNATIO

◆ ◆

Here at the world's end, on its last inch of liberty, we have lived unmolested to this day, defended by our remoteness and obscurity. Now the farthest reaches of Britain lie exposed . . . nothing but sea and rock and hostile Romans, whose arrogance you can't fool by compliance or modest self-restraint. Predators of the world . . . [Neither] east nor west has satiated them . . . to plunder, butcher, steal—these things they falsely name empire. They've turned the world into a wasteland, and they call it peace.

—Tacitus, *Agricola,* quoting British chieftain Calgacus on the Romans

It is the primary right of men to die and kill for the land they live in, and to punish with exceptional severity all members of their own race who have warmed their hands at the invaders' hearth.

—Winston Churchill, *A History of the English-Speaking Peoples*

It wasn't merely a question of achieving short-term control or submission among the natives, as Suetonius Paulinus well knew. He'd begun his career in the Atlas Mountains putting down uprisings by the Berbers against Roman occupation. Having weathered many such campaigns, Suetonius was well prepared to wage warfare over difficult terrain, or to meet fierce hot opposition in hand-to-hand combat.

But in the two years since the emperor Nero had appointed him governor of Britannia, Suetonius had come to understand that these Druids were something else. As both rulers and seers, whether male or female, they held the highest priestly offices in the land and were regarded by their people nearly as gods. Suetonius knew without question that in the long run there was only one way to deal with them: they had to be utterly destroyed.

Their chief sanctuary was located just off the coast of Cambria on the isle of Mona—the cow, a nickname for Brighde, a Demeter-like moon goddess of fecundity. They believed they were protected by this goddess, and that their warriors who were slain in battle would be rejuvenated from her cauldron of rebirth. The underground passage to the cauldron was located beneath a lake that lay near Mona's sacred grove.

It had taken Suetonius Paulinus two years of stealth and trickery to determine exactly when was the most propitious moment to strike at this offshore stronghold, without chance of defense or retreat. At last he learned that all the principal druidical priests were present each year on the first day of the Roman month of May. This was the day the Celts called *Beltaine* for the *taine* or fires they lit the night before to cleanse and purify the sacred woods in preparation for the Great Mother's yearly visit to usher in the month of fertility. This was the holiest day of the year, when the Druids neither worked nor bore arms—and therefore, Suetonius could hope, the day they would very least be anticipating an attack.

He had a flotilla of flat-bottomed boats built to bring his troops across the narrow but often violent strait from the mainland. At dusk on May Eve they crept through the sea foam, rounding the coast along the southern tip of the island for a landing away from the mainland, in the west at Holy Head.

There, as their boats slipped soundlessly in toward shore, the ceremonies of the cleansing ritual were already under way, though it was not yet dark. Shadowy figures bearing flaming torches moved through the silent groves that ran the length of the strand. The sun was slowly sinking into the bloodred sea as the Roman troops beached their craft and splashed through the sweeping surf. But all at once they halted at the sight that confronted them.

A mass of people, all in robes of deathly black, came onto the beach, advancing like an implacable black-clad wall of human flesh. The male priests moved with their arms raised to the heavens, screaming curses and oaths at the top of their lungs. The women, with wild, disheveled hair, flitted among them like insects, with torches held aloft. Then in a sudden wave, the women rushed shrieking like furies across the pebbled beach, directly toward the Roman soldiers.

Suetonius's officers looked on helplessly as their troops stood motionless on the beachhead, overawed, paralyzed by that band of howling harpies that seemed straight from Hades. Suetonius ran down the lines between them as the crazed women rushed onward; he screamed commands and imprecations to the troops above the deafening racket of the Druids, until at last his officers collected themselves and began to follow his example.

"Cut them down!" the command ran down the ranks. Those shrieking women with flaming torches bore down upon them still, with the screams of the mad Druid priests resounding in their ears. At the last possible instant, the soldiers charged.

◆ ◆

Joseph of Arimathea stood beside Lovernios at the edge of the cliff. He couldn't help but recall that other sunset when he'd stood on another cliff beside his friend and watched the sea turn to blood—a sunset twenty-five years ago, on another coast of another country, when it had all begun. When perhaps it could have been stopped. But now, as the screams from the beach below filled his ears, he turned to Lovernios in horror.

"We must intervene!" Joseph cried, grasping his friend by the arm. "We must help them! We must do something to make it stop! They're not even defending themselves! The Romans have turned their own torches upon them—they've set fire to their hair and clothes! They're cutting them to bits!"

The Druid stood immobile. He only flinched slightly when, over the terrible clamor and screams, he heard the sound of the axes ringing back from the rocks and realized for the first time what the Romans were really bent upon: they were going to obliterate the sacred grove.

Lovernios didn't look at Joseph. Nor did he glance at the carnage on the beach below that represented not only the massacre of his people but the destruction of everything they believed in and cherished—the twilight of their whole way of life, even of their gods. Instead he gazed out to sea as if in that western twilight he could see another place, another time in the distant past or far more distant future. When at last he spoke, to Joseph the words sounded remote and strange, like echoes from some dank and bottomless well.

"When Esus died, you had the strength of your wisdom," he reminded Joseph. "You knew what to do and you did it. You tried to comprehend the meaning of his life and death, and you have never ceased to do so these nearly thirty years. True wisdom, however, lies not only in understanding what can or cannot be done, but in knowing what *must* be done. And also in knowing—how did you say it to me then, so long ago?—the *kairos*: the critical moment."

"Please, Lovern, this *is* the critical moment. My God!" Joseph cried.

But it was clear, even in his despair, that the situation was utterly hopeless. He dropped to his knees there on the cliff, face buried in hands, and he prayed as the crash of felled trees below mingled with the horrifying screams of death. He heard these sounds together, drifting like wraiths across the silent waters. After a moment Joseph felt Lovernios's comforting hand resting on his hair, his voice strangely tranquil, as if he'd found a hidden core of hope that he alone could see.

"There are two things the gods demand," he told Joseph. "We must go at once, tonight, and sacrifice all the potent objects we possess, cast them into the holy waters of the Llyn Cerrig Bach, the lake of small stones."

"What then?" whispered Joseph.

"If that does not turn the tide," said Lovernios gravely, "it may come to pass we will have to send the messenger. . . ."

◆ ◆

The messenger from the south had arrived at the far side of the island just after dawn, as Suetonius Paulinus was watching the last tree fall. It was an ancient tree, the oldest of literally thousands in a wood that had taken all night for his legion to reduced to complete devestation.

The tree had a girth of more than sixty feet: his garrison engineers had calculated that it was the size of a galley under full oar. Lying on its side, as now, it was the height of one of those three-story buildings they'd constructed along the African coast when he was governor of Mauretania. How old could a tree grow to become, Suetonius wondered? Would its rings, if he could take the time to count them, number as many as those lives his troops had obliterated last night? Would the death of this tree, as with other holy trees, in the end mark the death of the Druids—as they seemed themselves to believe?

Erasing these thoughts for more practical matters, Suetonius set his men to work stacking up the dark-clad corpses of the dead Druids and building bonfires for their cremation. Then, recalling the emperor Nero's chief request, he sent a posse of soldiers off to explore the island. For Nero had written he had cause to believe from his late stepfather (and great-uncle) Claudius that the Druids held many valuable treasures in strongholds exactly like this one at Mona. Nero wished to be informed of any such findings at once.

This important business under way, Suetonius Paulinus remembered the messenger and beckoned to have him brought from where he'd been waiting. The soldier looked rather the worse for wear after his lengthy journey. Further, Suetonius was informed, the fellow's wet and bedraggled appearance was the result of his plunge into water to cross the narrow strait to the island, along with his horse, only moments before. The frothing horse, still lathered despite its dip in the channel, was led away as the messenger was brought to the governor's side.

"Take your time; catch some breath, man," Suetonius reassured the messenger. "However important your news, don't expire before delivering it."

"Camulodunum—" gasped the messenger.

Suetonius realized for the first time how ill the man seemed: his parched lips caked with blood and dust, his eyes drifting aimlessly, his short-cropped hair as disheveled as those Druid cadavers that littered the ground around them.

Suetonius snapped his fingers for a skin of fresh water and handed it to the messenger. When he'd drunk and cleared the dust from his throat, the governor nodded for him to continue. But the chap still seemed crazed. Though of course all his men were seasoned soldiers, he wondered if perhaps the sight of these corpses that they were practically wading in, male and female, might not have driven his senses momentarily from him.

"Come now," Suetonius said firmly. "You've traveled all this way—over two hundred miles at what was clearly a breakneck pace. You've something urgent to tell me about Camulodunum."

"All dead," the messenger croaked. "Thousands—tens of thousands—all dead. And the city, the Claudian temple—all of it burned to the ground!" The man began weeping.

Suetonius, at first astounded, quickly turned furious. He drew back his hand and slashed the fellow brutally across the face. "You're a soldier, man!" he reminded him. "In the name of Jupiter, pull yourself together. What's happened at Camulodunum? Has there been an earthquake? A fire?"

"A native uprising, sire," the messenger said, gulping for air. "The Iceni and Trinovantes—perhaps some tribes from the Corn Wall as well—we're not yet sure—"

"And where was the ninth legion Hispana all this while?" demanded Suetonius with ice in his voice. "Was the commander mending his toga while tribes of barefoot natives were burning the cities he's supposed to be defending?"

"These are no barefoot provincials, sire, but fully armed troops—perhaps two hundred *thousand* or more," the soldier told him. "It's commander Petilius Cerialis himself who sent me to you, just as fast as I could traverse the country and get here. Half the ninth legion has been destroyed: twenty-five hundred of the men I was with, who went in to attempt a rescue of the town. The Roman procurator Decianus has fled with his officers to the mainland, and Petilius is barricaded within his own fortress awaiting the reinforcements he prays you will bring."

"Nonsense. How could a handful of uneducated, primitive Britons destroy half a Roman garrison and drive out the chief colonial administrator?" Suetonius said, not even trying to disguise his contempt for a people he'd come to loathe. He spat on the ground and added, "They don't even make good slaves, much less good soldiers."

"Yet they possess many weapons, full horse and chariot," the soldier told him. "Their women fight alongside the men, and are far more vicious. At Camulodunum, the atrocities I've witnessed, sire, are nearly beyond comprehension. They slaughtered old and young, civilian and soldier, mother and child alike, with no distinction, so long as those they were killing were Romans or our collaborators. I saw the corpses of Roman women with suckling babes pinioned to their breasts! And men who were crucified along the streets—the gods forgive me to say it—but they had their body parts cut off, and stitched to their lips while they were still breathing. . . ."

The messenger fell silent, eyes glazed over with a look of terror that clearly his arduous journey had done little to assuage.

Suetonius sighed. "And what paragon of a commander am I to guess they've found to lead them in this expedition?" he asked in disgust.

"It is Boudica, queen of the Iceni, sire, who is their leader," said the messenger.

"These savages would follow a *woman* into battle?" said Suetonius, exhibiting real shock for the first time.

"Please, sire," said the messenger. "Commander Petilius begs you to make haste. From what I've witnessed myself, the rebellion is far from over; it fattens, the more blood it's fed. Camulodunum is lost. They are headed now toward Londinium."

Londinium, Britannia: Early Spring, A.D. 61

COMMIXTIO

◆ ◆

Very many types of mass-destruction of human beings have taken and will take place, the greatest through fire and water, other, lesser ones, through a thousand other mischances. —Plato, *Timaeus*

Londinium had not been the largest town in Britannia, nor the oldest or most important, as Joseph of Arimathea knew. But it had once been one of the loveliest, situated as it was on the broad, placid bosom of the great mother river. Today, as he walked for the last time along the riverbank, there *was* no Londinium: what had been a thriving colony was reduced to nothing but a layer of thick red ash.

Joseph watched the Romans across the river as they drove their chain gangs of native laborers through the rubble. And he understood exactly how much had been lost through the destruction of this city—and exactly how long this act of British vengeance, however justified, would be paid for by the Britons. The Romans, realizing the town was indefensible, had abandoned it until they could amass a larger force. Now, with three Roman cities including Verulamium destroyed, the rebellion had been crushed. The rebels, wholly unequipped to contend with fully armored and trained Roman legions, had been pinned against their own wagons and massacred—methodically butchered along with their own horses and pack animals.

Boudica and her daughters were dead, poisoned by their own

hand, choosing the forgiveness of God rather than a future at the hands of the Romans. But because the rebels had abandoned their homes last spring, before sowing their crops, to pursue vengeance and war, the land was barren and famine had raged all winter.

Now there was an endless supply of native slave labor available to the Romans, which would encourage any colony to wax and grow fat, with more settlers than ever there were in the past. The Romans would rebuild Londinium soon, Joseph knew, this time with stone and brick for stability and strength, rather than clay and wattles. There would be fortifications and garrisons. Any meager pretenses of civility they might formerly have shown the natives could be abandoned to the winds.

That night of death in the sacred groves on the isle of Mona—when Joseph had thrown his own hallowed objects, the Master's objects, into the Llyn Cerrig Bach along with those of the Druids and had watched them vanish beneath the dark waters of the lake—he'd known it was the end of an era. But what had really been accomplished, of all they'd once hoped and planned? What would become of the objects the Master had wanted them to safeguard? Would they, or the Master, ever rise again?

It had been thirty years since the Master's death. Joseph was now nearly seventy, and everything he'd fought so hard to preserve seemed to be washing away beneath his feet. When he'd returned here to the south last year, for example, it was only to discover that his small sod-walled church at Glastonbury—along with most of southern Britannia—had burned to the ground during the year-long civil unrest.

It seemed everything he'd lived for and the Master had died for was vanishing like a cloud floating off toward the horizon. Even those words of the Master's that both Joseph and Miriam had fought so hard to preserve for so long were now back in clay cylinders, tucked away in a cave in the Cambrian hills. And lacking a proud tradition like that of the Druids—an oral tradition that the Master himself had hoped would preserve his words and actions in memory forever—all their lives, including the Master's, seemed to be slipping away, lost in that no-man's land somewhere between memory and myth.

Conquerors wrote history, as was often pointed out. But history was what had already happened, what was past and finished, thought Joseph. What of the future? That was precisely what he was about to return north to find out. For though, in these past thirty years, the Druids had helped Joseph spread the Master's philosophy here in Britannia as well as across the straits in Eire and even in Gaul, today the Druids themselves were hunted to earth like wild beasts by the Romans.

But with their deeply religious feeling for life and the land, their ancient Celtic culture, and that peculiar strain of mysticism they chose to nurture in themselves and in others, Joseph was inspired to hope perhaps they could put him in touch once more with the mission the Master had set him upon so many years ago. Maybe even with the Master himself. That's why he had offered himself as the messenger.

For the first time in thirty years, Joseph knew with certainty that something of great importance was about to happen—though whether for good or ill, he couldn't foresee.

Black Lake, Britannia: Beltaine, A.D. 61

SENDING THE MESSENGER

◆ ◆

All good things, my dear Klea, sensible men must ask from the gods.
—Plutarch, *Isis & Osiris,* to Klea, priestess of Delphi

It was midnight when the Roman sentries finally departed the area and it was safe to build the fire. The rest of the tribe stood at a distance, sheltered by the dark woods.

Joseph, with the three other men who'd been chosen, stood beside the fire and watched in silence as Lovernios, his skin bronzed by the flame, mixed some lake water with the flour of five grains they'd brought and prepared the pancake, then wrapped it in damp leaves and cooked it in the ashes. When the pancake was done, he unfolded it and burned one corner a bit; then he broke it into five pieces, four cooked and one burned, and placed them in the bowl.

He held the bowl before each man, and each pulled out one piece. Lovernios accepted the last. When Joseph opened his hand, he found he had not chosen the blackened fragment of the pancake. He glanced at the others with a mixture of relief and discomfort as, one by one, each man looked up from his hand. Then the tall, handsome young man with russet hair and beard, Lovernios's own son Belinus, smiled broadly in the firelight. He held open his hand containing the blackened fragment and displayed it for all to see. His smile was so radiant that, for just that fleeting instant, he reminded Joseph of the Master. Though Joseph hadn't meant to disturb the ceremony no matter what might happen, he'd never expected Belinus to be the one.

"No!" Joseph heard himself say aloud.

Lovernios quietly put his hand on Joseph's arm, then threw his other arm around his son's shoulders and squeezed him, almost with a look of pride.

"Let it be me," Joseph protested quietly to Lovernios. "Not your son: he's only thirty-three with his entire life ahead of him. I'm nearly seventy, and a failure."

Lovernios threw back his head and laughed aloud—which hardly seemed appropriate to Joseph under the circumstance.

"If that's the case, my friend," he told Joseph, "then why do you volunteer? What possible good could you be even to *us*, much less to the gods? Belinus is the perfect specimen—strong, healthy, unblemished. And he knows how to be the perfect servant, to submit to God's will. Ask him if he isn't happy to serve as our messenger."

Joseph was suddenly flooded with the memory of the Master's last meal, when he'd washed the others' feet. He wondered why, whenever he thought of anything profoundly moving, instead of feeling inspiration he only wanted to cry. Belinus smiled almost beatifically at Joseph as he opened his mouth and happily popped in the blackened pancake. When he'd swallowed it, he came to Joseph and took him in his broad arms, rocking him gently just as Lovernios had once done, so many years ago.

"Joseph, Joseph," he said. "I won't be dying, you know. I'm going to eternal life. You must be happy for me. When I see your Esus on the other side, I shall bring him your loving thoughts."

Joseph put a hand over his eyes and sobbed, but Belinus only glanced at Lovernios with a bemused shrug. His expression said: All these years living among the Druids and he still thinks like a pagan or a Roman.

They motioned for the others to come out of the woods as Joseph tried to collect himself. One by one, the people of the Celtic tribes moved from the shadowy thickets, came before the fire to be blessed, then carried their treasures of gold or copper to the lakeside and committed them to the waters. When all the vessels, torques, even slave chains had vanished, they moved in single file behind Lovernios away from the fire, around the lake's edge, to the lowlands where the darkened peat bogs lay. Clouds whispered over the moon, sifting an eerie half-light across the surface of the land.

At the edge of the expanse of bottomless peat bog, Belinus got down on his knees and held his hands aloft. The two younger men who'd volunteered for this role, along with Joseph and Lovernios, removed his robes and other garments. Lovernios waited until his son was completely naked, then handed him the band made of fox fur. Belinus slipped it onto his arm, then lowered his head and folded his hands behind his back to be tied with leather thongs. The men also slipped a leather noose around the young man's neck. Belinus, his head still bowed toward the bog, said softly,

"Mother, into thy hands I commend my spirit."

Joseph felt these words cut like ice into his very soul. He watched, not breathing, as Lovernios reached for the soft leather sack and extracted the razor-sharp hunting axe. Holding it high above his head, he raised his eyes to the sky. Just then the moon appeared from behind the clouds and flooded the landscape with light. The Celts stood in silence at the bog's edge; to Joseph they resembled a forest of praying trees. Lovernios intoned in his deep voice,

"This is the death by fire. By the god's thunderbolt we commend thee to Taranis."

Belinus did not flinch as the axe swept down behind him, swift and sure—though Joseph thought he heard him gasp once as the sharp metal blade struck the back of his skull with a brittle crunch. Belinus fell forward on his face.

The two younger men moved forward swiftly and tightened the noose as Lovernios, with one hard yank, pulled the axe free from his son's head.

"This is the death by air," said Lovernios. "We commend thee to Esus."

Joseph heard the loud crack in the silence: the sound of the windpipe snapping.

The two men, now joined by Joseph, lifted the limp but beautiful body of Belinus from the earth and held it face down over the brackish waters. Then Lovernios spoke the last words that would be spoken that night:

"This is the death by water. We commend thee to Teutates."

Joseph watched as the body was sucked down into the bog, disappearing without a trace, swallowed by the earth.

But just before it vanished Joseph thought—only for an instant—that he saw something move in the thick black waters. He thought he saw God, with open arms, receiving the body of Belinus. And God was smiling.

UTOPIA

Whoever feels that he is the carrier of the best blood and has consciously used this blood to guide the nation will keep this leadership and will not renounce it . . .

Its fatal image . . . will be like a Holy Order. It is our wish that this state shall endure for thousands of years. We are happy to know that the future belongs to us.

—Adolf Hitler, sixth Party Congress,
"Thousand-Year-Reich" speech

I have felt it my duty to my fellow-men to place on record these forewarnings of the Coming Race. —Edward Bulwer, Lord Lytton, *The Coming Race*

The Closerie des Lilas remains one of the loveliest restaurants in Paris, lavish with flowers at all seasons. It seemed an incredibly inappropriate setting for today's romp through Nazi Germany and Austria, caught in the viperlike embrace of my blue-eyed grandmother Zoe. Heaps of white lilacs greeted us as we arrived. We had a table beside the terrace, where outdoor trellises were laden with dripping vines.

Zoe told us that she'd ordered our meal in advance. So when the sommelier had brought the wine, and she'd sipped and we'd been served, she returned to the topic we'd come to discuss: our family.

"As I mentioned earlier," she began, "high in the Swiss Alps four rivers rise near the San Bernardino Pass. There existed at that place a century ago a utopian community. My grandmother Clio, a woman of no fame but of enormous importance to our story, lived there for a number of years with my grandfather Erasmus Behn, one of the community's principal founders."

I suddenly heard that bell go off, as I flashed on what Dacian Bassarides had said about utopias when we'd stood together just outside the doors of the Hofburg in Vienna: that idealists who begin by wanting to improve civilization often wind up trying to create a better breed of human.

"A perfect world high atop a mountain, the return to a Golden Age," said Zoe. "Everyone sought such things in the past century—and many still do, even today. But as I also said, life is neither simple nor black-and-white. It may well be that my grandfather's desire for Utopia was, at heart, the cause of all the unhappiness that followed."

I don't recall what we had for lunch that afternoon. But I do recall every detail of Zoe's story. As the pieces fell into place, I began to see how one small family's role could actually be that hinge or axis Dacian had spoken of, around which things turn as animals do on a carousel, as the zodiac seems to revolve around that star at the tip of the small bear's tail.

I listened with interest as Zoe began her story of our family's personal Garden of Eden. That is, before the Fall.

◆ ◆

My grandmother Clio, said Zoe, was the only child of a Swiss family that, like many wealthy families of the day, held broad interests in scholarly pursuits. These included travel, and investigation into the lost kingdoms and cultures of many lands. Clio too possessed a deep interest in researches into antiquity. She not only leafed through dusty books but she had a passionate interest in a discipline only recently invented: field archaeology.

By the age of twenty, Clio had already engaged in numerous such trips with her father to exotic and far-flung regions of the world. She joined the adventurer Heinrich Schliemann, who'd made his early fortune in the supply of military armaments during the Crimean War and was spending it lavishly in highly publicized and opportunistic quests for the lost kingdoms of Mycenae and Troy.

Clio had spent her young life studying ancient tongues, and tracing the origins of many objects she'd learned of in decaying documents she'd found in tombs, gravesites, and caves. She used this knowledge with some success in locating lost sites of power and grandeur, and in hunting down physical objects of great value—just as Schliemann, only by his careful reading of the classics, had at length found the tombs of Mycenae, containing the richest hoard of ancient treasure in the world.

In the year 1866, at age twenty-one, Clio met and married a Dutchman who, like Schliemann, was rich from the spoils of war. This man, Erasmus Behn, who'd invested in Schliemann's archaeological projects, was a widower with one small son, Hieronymus, who would one day be my father. If the large fortune made by Heinrich Schliemann in armaments was used almost exclusively for the rape and pillage of mankind's past, the fortune of my grandfather Erasmus Behn was earmarked for nothing short of a complete transformation of man's future, all to be molded to *his* image. And something a bit more.

Among Erasmus Behn's interests was the utopian community he'd helped finance in Switzerland. It was based on many new theories abroad, including "triage," the genetic culling and sorting that played a large role in the main field of scientific interest of his day: selective breeding. Techniques to accomplish improved strains of crops and livestock were experimented with in such utopias, and Erasmus spent each summer in the Alps, visiting the site of his investment.

All this was anathema to Clio. Though raised a Swiss Protestant, she'd received a liberal upbringing, broad in taste and quite unusual for a girl of her day. Though the man she'd married was wealthy, intelligent, and handsome, it didn't take long after their marriage for her to become disenchanted with everything about Erasmus Behn—especially his views on perfecting the world. She quickly realized she'd been yoked to a dour, strict-principled Calvinist who regarded women and children as little better than chattel, while holding himself and his kind superior to nearly everyone on earth.

Clio soon discovered, too, that Erasmus hadn't married her only for her tawny blond beauty, healthy body, or clever mind, but rather to secure for himself the large financial estate that she, as an only child, would possess upon her father's death—and, more important, the historically valuable collection of artifacts, talismans, and scrolls she'd helped collect, and would also inherit from her family.

Erasmus seemed mesmerized to the point of obsession with knowing more about the secrets of the past, as well as powers that might be garnered in the future, while remaining practically oblivious to the demands of the present. When Clio gave birth to their daughter, just two years after their marriage, Erasmus left her bed altogether, having exercised his genetic duties. After all, if you counted the son he'd produced by his earlier marriage, he'd fulfilled this duty not only once but twice! Though this was a situation common in upper-class marriages of the past century, our family's progress was soon to take a very strange and different twist.

In summers, Erasmus took Clio to visit his utopian project in the Alps. It soon became clear he could ill afford to go on pouring money into the project so lavishly, year after year. But that was not all that attracted his interest in the region. In the vicinity was something that might prove of great value: the pagan shrines I mentioned, as well as caves, some dating back to Neanderthal times, that due to their inaccessibility were largely unknown and unexplored, except by a band of migrant Gypsies that sometimes summered nearby. With visions of gold artifacts and sugarplums dancing in his head—most of them planted by Schliemann's recent splashy successes—Erasmus hoped to find something of value, even of great power. Interestingly, Clio agreed.

Clio hardly needed prompting to organize the Gypsies in support of her first love, archaeology. The summer after her daughter was born, she set off with her posse. As they explored the alpine caves together, Clio found the Gypsies extraordinarily knowledgeable in the meaning of artifacts they unearthed, and of their surrounding history even from ancient times. She began leaving more and more of her collection in their hands for safekeeping. But also she found wisdom in the ways of these people, who attracted her greatly—especially one.

Clio's expeditions with the gypsies soon went farther afield. She returned with interesting objects and pottery. The most unusual piece, found in a cave between Interlaken and Bern, was a statue of an ancient bear goddess, along with a totem bear. Deeper in the same cave were some intriguing clay jars that looked very ancient, containing scrolls she at once set about trying to decipher.

On their return to Holland that fall, Clio was enraged to learn Erasmus had taken some of her documents and artifacts, and even sold several objects to boost a dwindling income from poorly chosen investments. More upsetting, he'd also appropriated a number of her notes and translations of what she believed the more historically valuable documents.

When confronted, Erasmus riposted by drawing Clio's attention to those scrolls she'd more recently discovered, which she'd left in the hands of the Gypsies. He'd hoped these might lead to further treasure and he became insistent that, as her husband, by rights they belonged to him. Without telling Erasmus, Clio took everything of value still in her hands and locked it all away in a vault.

Their battles over the next six months were to prove many, heated, and lengthy, as Erasmus's nine-year-old son Hieronymus was there to witness. The quarrels between his father and what he perceived as a difficult, tempestuous stepmother, who refused to do his father's bidding, planted seeds in his young mind that would eventually produce a dark and dangerous fruit.

The summer of 1870, when Hieronymus was ten years old and his baby sister had just turned two, Clio's father died, and his rich trove of manuscripts and objects came into her possession. Her father sensibly left the money in trust, for the sole use of Clio and her descendants—

and a private message to be opened only by her. Based on her father's last letter, Clio planned an extended trek with the Gypsies across the Swiss border into Italy, leaving the children behind with their father. But this time Erasmus insisted upon accompanying her. He'd begun to suspect his young wife of holding back much she'd discovered—and he thought he might know why.

Then Clio simply disappeared one night with the Gypsies, leaving a note that she would be back by summer's end. But that was never to be. From that point onward, event swiftly followed event almost as if directed by an unseen hand.

On July 19, 1870, the Franco-Prussian War broke out, and pandemonium ensued. The utopian commune swiftly dissolved, its outside funds cut off by the war. Erasmus Behn—with two children on his hands, a missing wife, and dwindling fortunes—knew he must hasten home to try to secure those of Clio's documents and artifacts still in his possession, should Holland be overrun.

Erasmus was wounded while crossing the battle zone between Switzerland and Belgium. He barely managed to enter Holland with the children before he died. His little remaining money was used by the local church to provide for his son's education. His daughter with Clio was sent away to a foundling home. To be separated by war seems the endless fate of our family, as for so many others. In this case, however, it will never be clear whether Clio's permanent separation from Erasmus was accidental or planned. Had war not intervened, would she have returned?

Eight years after Erasmus Behn's death, his son Hieronymus completed his education and entered training for the only profession, except the army, available to a boy with limited resources: the Calvinist ministry. His preparation served only to strengthen beliefs already well ingrained through ten years of living with his father. Indeed, the ideas inculcated in him by the church became his first passion.

Hieronymus Behn had come to resent his stepmother Clio bitterly. He irrationally saw her as having robbed him and his father of everything for which, in the Calvinist sense, they'd been "chosen." She'd abandoned his father in wartime, going off with the Gypsies and stealing everything the family owned of value. In the darkness of his heart, Hieronymus suspected her of far worse, for who knew what the unbridled passions of a woman like that might have led her to? If only his father had gained the upper hand with this woman, his wife, as had surely been his right in the eyes of God, and under the law! Everything Clio owned, even before her marriage to his father, Hieronymus believed, should by rights now belong to *him*.

Instead, it was because of his stepmother Clio, Hieronymus reasoned, that he'd wound up receiving nothing better than a pauper's education. He really cared nothing about his young half sister, who'd been sent off God knew where. After all, she was partly of Clio's blood. It was his inheritance he wanted. He'd perused his father's papers, kept for him by the church. He now had an excellent idea of the nature and value of those artifacts and documents his stepmother had hoarded and refused to let his father see or sell. They'd be worth far more today, when the value of such things was better understood. He resolved that one day he would find his stepmother and get his birthright back. This day of reckoning might be years in coming—but come, at last, it would.

In the year 1899 festivities were under way in countries throughout Europe, prematurely celebrating the dawn of the last century of our millennium, which didn't legitimately take place until 1901. The Schönbrunn Palace in Vienna was illuminated for the first time by electric lights; Ferris wheels blossomed on the riverbanks of many cities; modern scientific technology flourished everywhere.

None of these new inventions, however, was so widely heralded both by the press and by popular opinion as a single ancient discovery. On Christmas Day of 1899, as workmen were repairing a water pipe deep in the foundations of the castle overlooking the town of Salzburg, they uncovered a large golden platter that was believed to predate, by one thousand years, the time of Christ.

Experts were called in, and various theories as to the platter's origins were given. Some believed it came from the first Temple of Solomon, others that it had been among the objects melted down to create the Golden Calf, then later restored to its original form. Some claimed the design was Greek, others Macedonian or Phrygian. Since these cultures had traded with one another over thousands of years, the only consensus was that the platter was ancient, and of Eastern origin. It was to be put on public display at the Hohensalzburg castle throughout the month of January 1900 before being carried off to the royal treasury house at Vienna.

Hieronymus Behn, now nearly forty, had spent the past twenty years seeking the woman who'd stolen his inheritance and blighted his very existence. But the moment he saw reports in the Dutch press describing the Salzburg platter, he was sure he knew how to find her. One of the few rare scrolls his father had managed to appropriate from Clio was still in Hieronymus's possession, along with the only copy of the extensive research Clio herself had done on the document. If he wasn't mistaken, this scroll pertained directly to the recently surfaced Salzburg platter.

He took the train from Amsterdam to Salzburg, arriving a day before the exhibition was to open. He went on foot from the station to the castle, and contacted the curator at once. It wasn't the platter he was interested in, but he *did* want the woman who would surely travel to Salzburg to see it, if only Hieronymus could quickly and effectively plant the right bait.

After handing over the rare scroll to the curator, Hieronymus provided him with Clio's papers—claiming they were those of his late father, Erasmus Behn, a noted patron of Schliemann. Hieronymus readily agreed to the museum's request to stipulate that these documents hadn't yet been authenticated, asking only that at least their general contents—and the name of their donor, his late father—be made public at the opening of the show. Having studied the research notes in depth himself, Hieronymus knew that when they surfaced, the attention they drew would also draw his stepmother like a magnet.

In the scroll, which Clio and her father had found in an ancient clay jar in the Holy Land, the platter was said to have once been a decoration on a shield in ancient Greek times, and later to have been part of the hoard of Herod the Great. It was stored in the reign of Herod's son Herod Antipas at the palace of Machareus, at the time John the Baptist was incarcerated there and beheaded. Antipas later brought the platter to Rome, where it passed through the hands of three emperors: Caligula, Claudius, and Nero.

Clio's subsequent researches into this object indicated that Nero, believing the platter to possess unusual occult properties, had it removed from Rome to Subiaco and placed in a famous oracular cave just across the valley, facing his summer palace there. After Nero's premature death by assassination, the platter stayed in the cave untouched for nearly five hundred years. This very cave at Subiaco became in

A.D. 500 the site of Saint Benedict's famous hermetic retreat. According to Clio, once the platter surfaced it passed into the hands of the Benedictine Order, the Black Monks, where its powers as a holy relic enabled them to proselytize the Germanic lands successfully and to become the most powerful monastic force in continental Europe.

◆ ◆

The first meeting between Hieronymus Behn and his long-absent stepmother, Clio, was not what either might have imagined. She, still a beauty at fifty-five, and he, a dazzlingly handsome blond Netherlander of not quite forty, made a striking couple. But Hieronymus quickly learned that, much as he wanted to repair past injustices to himself, so did Clio. Injustices to *her*self.

Clio explained that she had returned to the utopian community by summer's end as promised, but she'd learned that the community had been broken up for want of funds and that her husband had taken the children and returned to Holland. After the war, she'd contacted the Netherlands government and received notice that her family, missing in the war zone, were all presumed dead.

For the thirty years that Hieronymus had spent resenting Clio and planning to exact restitution and retribution, she'd been living in Switzerland among the Gypsies, as before, imagining the Behns all long dead. She'd even recently adopted a young girl to replace her only child, and planned to begin soon to train her in the same languages and research techniques that Clio herself, under the tutelage of her father, had also acquired at an early age.

When she learned that her natural daughter was indeed alive but had been put in a foundling home thirty years ago—and that Hieronymus Behn had done essentially nothing to find his sister in all that time—Clio understood that this man before her, as handsome and dashing as his late father, was also as cold-blooded and self-involved. Clio proposed an arrangement between them that required a compromise.

Since Hieronymus himself was no blood relation of hers, she owed him nothing, she said. But if he would use his connections in the Calvinist Church to discover the foundling home where his sister had been sent, then trace her and find her and bring her to Switzerland so her mother could see her at last, Clio would settle a handsome sum from her own large estate on each of them. To this, Hieronymus swiftly agreed. But he was hardly expecting what would happen next.

◆ ◆

As Wolfgang and I sat there in a silence so tense you could cut it, Zoe continued, "The long-lost half sister my father was sent in search of, a half sister he eventually found to the great misfortune of each, was the woman who would soon become his wife—Hermione."

Wolfgang was regarding Zoe with an expression I couldn't fathom. Then his eyes narrowed. "You mean to say, your parents—"

"Were half brother and sister," Zoe finished for him. "But I'm not through."

"I've heard enough," I said abruptly.

So this was the reason everyone had kept our family relationships under wraps all these years. I truly thought I was going to be ill. I couldn't breathe. I wanted to escape from the room. But Zoe was having none of it.

"These manuscripts were given into your possession," she said. "But you'll be able neither to protect them nor make use of them unless you know everything."

From the corner of my eye, I noticed Wolfgang pick up his wineglass and throw down a healthy slug. He'd been awfully quiet and noncommittal throughout all this. I wondered how he was taking it. After all, Zoe was his grandmother, too. I prayed to God this was the last little surprise coming. What could be worse?

"Through his connections with the Calvinist Church," said Zoe, "Hieronymus located the foundling home and learned that his half sister Hermione, at the age of sixteen, had been sent to South Africa with a boatload of other girls as Boer mail-order brides. The war was over, so he took a boat to the Cape to find her." Watching me closely, she added, "Christian Alexander had just died of complications of a war wound. Hermione inherited his fortune, including vast mining and mineral concessions, but she was also pregnant with a second child. She was beside herself with grief and fear about her future, a widow alone with two children in a war-torn country. When the stunningly handsome Hieronymus Behn arrived, claiming he was her cousin—"

Wait! my brain cried as I tried to piece this all together. Something else was wrong with this picture. And this time I knew exactly what it was.

"*Two* children?" I said in horror. "You mean Christian Alexander was the father of *both* of Hermione's sons—Lafcadio and Earnest? But how could that be?"

"This is the lie that lurks behind it all," said Zoe. "Earnest was the one who exposed the truth of our family's past, though it took him many long years to understand what treachery had been practiced on him and Lafcadio—separating them in childhood, lying about Earnest's parentage. And all the while, they were full brothers, sons of the same parents: Hermione and Christian Alexander. Earnest came to Europe not long before Pandora's death and confronted her. She must have known all along, he said, so why hadn't she told him?"

"I think you'd better tell *us*," I said to Zoe. "From the beginning—including Pandora's connection."

And she did. When Hieronymus Behn arrived in South Africa in the summer of 1900, he was almost forty years old, a Calvinist minister with one prospect—to find his half sister, bring her to her long-lost mother Clio, and thereby gain the inheritance he felt his stepmother owed him.

He found his beautiful blond sister a recent widow, age thirty-two, with her hands full. She had mineral concerns and estates to manage, a six-month-old child (Uncle Lafcadio) and another expected (Uncle Earnest). Hieronymus saw enormous potential for himself in the situation. He quickly and ruthlessly determined how to kill two birds with one small stone.

Claiming he was her cousin who'd been searching for her for years, Hieronymus convinced Hermione he'd fallen passionately in love with her. Orphaned at two, she had no way of knowing that the man who called himself her cousin was really her half brother. He literally swept her off her feet: they were married within weeks, and he assumed management of all her late husband's properties.

But Hieronymus knew he would have to reveal their true relationship before taking Hermione back to Europe, or he wouldn't be able to claim their estates from Clio. There was an additional problem: If Hermione revealed their marital status to her new-found mother, the promised inheritance would surely blow up in his face. Further, once Hermione had learned how she'd been deceived, she might try to dissolve the marriage due to consanguinity. But Hieronymus realized it would be difficult to do so if they'd already had a child of their own.

However, given the possibility that they might be incapable of producing a child, the only insurance Hieronymus could think of was to convince Hermione, as a bond of their love, to name *him* as legitimate father on Earnest's birth certificate. It wasn't until Earnest himself discovered, years later, through his own research, that he was only *one* year younger than Lafcadio—not two, as they'd always been told—that his suspicions became aroused, and he dug further.

A great deal was beginning to fall into place for me, too, given this unpleasant revelation. It made sense, for instance, that little Lafcadio was sent off, just as he was nearing school age, to a place like Salzburg where he knew no one at all. Sooner or later, if he'd remained in South Africa, he might have heard details from others about the situation of his father's death, his mother and stepfather's hasty marriage, and the peculiar timing of Earnest's birth. It also made sense that when Hermione got pregnant with Zoe, Hieronymus would pack up and move the entire family to Vienna where no one knew anything of their background—and where, according to Laf's story, his mother became a prisoner in her own house.

This scenario made it clear why Laf was so upset about my meeting Zoe—not to mention his obvious distaste for the woman from the beginning. After all, she represented in her own person the single piece of evidence of his mother's carnal relationship with her own brother. But for every one thing that got cleared up, others seemed to get murkier.

"Where does Pandora fit into all this?" I asked Zoe.

"There was one person," she said, "who'd encountered Hieronymus and Hermione early on, as brother and sister, and then again years later, as husband and wife. It was the child Clio had adopted in Switzerland to replace her lost daughter, and had taken under her wing. When Hieronymus Behn finally brought Hermione to Switzerland for the promised reunion with her mother, Clio signed the papers that released a large part of her trust to her daughter and stepson, little realizing the legal and fleshly bonds these two had already entered into. When they left, it was discovered that—like his father before him—Hieronymus had appropriated some of those ancient scrolls he felt should have been his by God's destiny. Scrolls that by now belonged to Clio's adopted daughter. Though it took many years for her to run them to earth, she found them at last: that child, of course, was Pandora."

The rest of the story was easy enough to flesh out based on what I already knew from Laf, Dacian, and others: how Pandora later infiltrated the Behn household in Vienna with the aid of Hilter's high school chum Gustl and befriended the imprisoned Hermione as her adopted sister; how Hieronymus failed to recognize the child he'd met so briefly, now a beautiful woman; how Pandora blackmailed Hieronymus and managed to bring young Lafcadio home for Hermione's deathbed scene. But there was something else still unexplained. By Dacian's account, Hieronymus forced Pandora to marry him, then threw her into the streets when she stole something he valued. But hadn't Zoe then run off, too, with Pandora and the Gypsies? And if Laf's story held water, both girls had been cozy, from square one, with Adolf Hitler.

"Where does Hitler connect to all this?" I asked Zoe. "From everything you've told us, it's plain these were Clio's manuscripts Pandora wound up with. But even if your pal Lucky was after them, why would he go on outings with all of you—like that merry-go-round ride in the Prater Laf told me about—or take you to the Hofburg to look at the sword and spear? Why would he be so chummy with Pandora and Dacian, if he knew they were Rom?"

"When Lucky ran into Pandora and Dacian the first time in Salzburg," Zoe said, "he learned they were hunting for Hieronymus Behn—the very man who, twelve years earlier, had made an enormous splash with his revelations about the possible history and provenance of the platter of John the Baptist. Lucky himself, as a boy of only eleven, had gone with his grammar-school class to view that celebrated object. Like the other hallows, it was something he dreamed of possessing himself, ever afterward. By the time he lived in Vienna, he'd learned a good deal about the background of the Behn family. Though it's never been proven, I'm quite certain that my father became one of Lucky's earliest and strongest supporters. And as you say, Lucky surely knew a good deal about Pandora's background. Dacian had to flee to the south of France, where, thanks to my own unusual brand of connections, I was able to assist him throughout the war. And while Lucky always kept a low profile about it, he would let no one touch Pandora, all through the war in Vienna—though of course he knew that she and Dacian were Rom—for he believed she alone held the key to a power that he himself sought."

"You say Rom—but what exactly does it mean?" Wolfgang interrupted in a strange tone. He'd been unusually quiet in this last part of her story.

"Gypsies," Zoe told him. To me, she explained, "The child that Clio adopted, Pandora, was actually the young niece of Aszi Atzingansi, a man of distinguished Romani blood who'd helped her recover many ancient texts, including the oracles of Cumae. Though there is no hard evidence, Pandora always believed that Aszi was also Clio's great love. As I told Wolfgang last year when he first sought me out at a *Heuriger* in Vienna, it's the oldest souls who preserve and keep alive the ancient wisdom. Pandora was such an old soul, as are most of the Romani people. Dacian very much wanted me to meet you, for he believes you are another—"

"Just a moment," Wolfgang cut in again, a bit more firmly. "You don't mean to tell me that Pandora and Dacian Bassarides—Augustus Behn's parents, Ariel's grandparents—were actually Gypsies?"

Zoe regarded him with a strange little smile, and lifted one brow.

But wasn't it Wolfgang who'd introduced me to Dacian in the first place? Then I recalled with a certain uneasiness that Dacian had *not* mentioned any Gypsy ancestry in Wolfgang's presence, and indeed had cautioned me not to mention it either. In retrospect, considering how candid Dacian had been on other topics—the sword and spear, and even where we'd hidden Pandora's manuscripts—the fact that he'd made a point of sending Wolfgang away during the part of our chat dealing with the family suddenly seemed chillingly significant. And more so when Zoe added enigmatically, "Your mother would be proud of such a question."

◆ ◆

Wolfgang was clearly as exhausted as I, what with the weeks we'd spent running all over Europe and Soviet Russia, not to mention our combined data overload. He slipped off to sleep just after dinner on the first leg of our nearly twenty-four-hour return trip to Idaho.

Though I had a multitude of topics to discuss, I also knew I needed time on my own to think things through and figure out where I stood.

So I ordered strong black coffee with refills from the steward, and tried to focus my mind on reviewing everything I'd learned.

One month ago, Zoe's theory would have sounded completely insane: that Lucky, his niece, his dog, his friends, and their children had all been used—just as he himself had previously "used" millions of Gypsies, Jews, and others—in some kind of mass pagan sacrifice, a shamanistic "working," to usher in the New Age. But Hitler had so many around him who believed, as he himself did, in utter nonsense. The magical Atlantis-like home of the Aryans at the North Pole; the final destruction of the world by Fire and Ice; the power of sacred hallows and "purified" blood to work terrestrial miracles. Not to forget, as Wolfgang had pointed out, his belief in a weapon of mass destruction that was known and repeatedly rediscovered since ancient times.

For those who wanted to turn back the clock to an earlier golden age that they believed had once existed in pagan times—a danger Dacian Bassarides had warned against—human sacrifice could be very much a part of the system. So, revolting as such an idea might be, viewed within the context of what we knew of the Nazi belief system it didn't actually seem all that far-fetched.

But despite this possibly useful process of sorting and culling, I ran into a brick wall every time I returned to the frustrating topic of my family's true relations with Adolf Hitler and his ilk. I had no idea where to begin. I thought of that jingle of William Blake's:

> I give you the end of a golden string,
> Only wind it into a ball:
> It will lead you in at Heaven's gate,
> Built in Jerusalem's wall.

If I could find the beginning of my own golden string—where and how the story had begun for *me*—that would certainly be a start.

I did know, in fact, where I had first fallen into this labyrinth: it was the night I'd returned from Sam's funeral in a blizzard, when I'd nearly drowned in snow. Then I'd picked up the ringing phone to learn from my father, Augustus, that my "inheritance" might include something of great value I hadn't expected: Pandora's manuscripts.

But in hindsight, it suddenly occurred to me that maybe from that very first phone call, instead of pursuing the truth I constantly claimed I wanted, I might have been shutting my eyes whenever it was staring me right in the face. Hadn't Dacian Bassarides said it was essential to ask the right questions? That the *process* could often be more important than the product? There was something connecting all these seemingly unrelated things, and though it might seem like trying to find a missing chunk in a scrambled pile of jigsaw pieces, I had to figure it out.

And that was when I saw it.

All this time I'd been sorting and culling and following bits of string when I *should* have been looking at what Sam called the "tantra" of it all—that is, the thing that held the whole tapestry together, as in Eastern cultures tantra tied Fate to life and death. Sam said it even existed in the animal kingdom: that a female spider wouldn't eat the male if he left the web by the same path he'd entered by, showing that he recognized the pattern. Well, I'd finally recognized the pattern *I'd* been missing. I felt a cold little ball forming at the pit of my stomach.

Though everyone in my family had perhaps told me conflicting stories, there was one person whose stories *themselves* were riddled with twists and turns and internal contradictions. And though the history or genealogy of each person might've turned out differently from what I was first led to believe—maybe even from what each believed about himself—there was one person I now realized I knew almost nothing consistent about. It was certainly true, though, that everyone had warned me against him from the very start—including, as I now realized in an awful flash, his own sister!

It was the man sitting beside me here in the plane, his dark, shaggy head leaning against my shoulder so I could barely make out his chiseled profile. It was my colleague, cousin, and erstwhile lover, Wolfgang K. Hauser of Krems, Österreich. And although only weeks ago I'd believed Wolfgang to be my own destiny here on planet earth, in the hard, cold light of reality I was forced to recognize that his every lie had only led to another lie, from the moment he'd mysteriously arrived in Idaho while I was away in San Francisco at Sam's funeral.

Speaking of that funeral, hadn't Sam himself told me—in contradiction of Wolfgang's claims about the employer of Olivier and Theron Vane—that it had all been arranged with blessings bestowed by the highest echelons of the U.S. government? And hadn't Zoe also pointed out that Wolfgang had sought *her* out in Vienna to pump her for information, not the other way around?

But the bitterest pill was the thought that Wolfgang had appropriated Pandora's manuscripts from beneath my very nose, deploying the same suave deftness he'd used to appropriate my body and my trust.

There were already enough hints of Aryan preoccupation in his Valhalla-like castle and his upbringing by a mother who herself had been raised by a Nazi. And what about Wolfgang's direct question to Zoe: "You don't mean to tell me that Ariel's grandparents were actually Gypsies?" What else could that mean?

Having already swallowed enough lies to choke a warthog, I wondered when I was going to stop lying to *myself*.

Now that I feared, in the deep recesses of my mind, that Wolfgang Hauser himself was the missing link that tied together this mingled, mangled, muddled web of myth and intrigue, I only prayed I could retrace my own steps carefully enough to extricate both Sam and myself from it alive.

I would like at this time to touch upon the greatest spiritual event which has taken place . . . the release of atomic energy. . . . I would call your attention to the words "liberation of energy." It is liberation which is the keynote of the new era, just as it has always been with the spiritually oriented aspirant. This liberation has started by the release of an aspect of matter and the freeing of some of the soul forces within the atom. . . . For matter itself, a great and potent initiation paralleling those initiations which liberate or release the souls of men . . . The hour of the saving force has now arrived.

—*Externalization of the Hierarchy*,
"DK the Tibetan," channeled by Alice Bailey, August 9, 1945

The Uranus cycle begins when the planet reaches its north node . . . the last heliocentric passage of Uranus over its north node occurred most significantly on July 20, 1945, four days after the first atomic explosion in Alamogordo, New Mexico, which indeed ushered in a new era—for better or worse. . . . Events do not happen to us; we happen to events.

—Dane Rudhyar, *Astrological Timing*

The most important thing in the life of any man is to discover the secret purpose of his incarnation and follow it with wariness as well as passion . . . the Uranus in us is the Sacred Lance of the Legend. In the hands of the Holy King it built the Temple of the Grail; in those of Klingsor the Garden of Evil Enchantments. . . . Uranus is the royal Uraeus Serpent in Egyptian Symbolism, slow yet sudden Lord of life and death. It takes a great deal to move him; but once in motion he is irresistible. . . . If you do not allow him to create, he will devour.

—Aleister Crowley, *Uranus*

Before I could formulate any real plan of action, I knew I had to find Sam. Terrible as it might be to face him and reveal my many disastrous failures—not least of all, fiddling with Wolfgang while Rome burned—I'd suddenly grasped the fact that, thanks to me, Sam might be in worse danger than when I'd left, if anyone learned he was alive.

Wolfgang was uncharacteristically quiet for the balance of the trip, which suited me fine. By the time we landed in Idaho, we'd agreed he would go directly to the office and let the Pod, who'd be back from Vienna by now, know we were back safely, too. I would briefly run by my house to drop off my things before coming in to work. The only weapon left in my diminished arsenal was that Wolfgang didn't yet suspect that I suspected *him*, so I'd have to act quickly.

I knew Olivier would be at the office, too, by this time—already ten A.M.—so I thought I could phone Sam's grandfather, Dark Bear, from home. Though my line might still be bugged, I could at least try to get a message passed to Sam that I was back in town.

As I came up the road, I saw Olivier's car in the drive and another car parked up on the road not far from the mailboxes, a compact with rental plates. Since the house nearest ours was some way down the road, it was a safe bet Olivier had company—the very last thing I wanted or needed right now. I had pulled into the drive to turn around and try a new plan when Olivier himself popped his head from the rear door with a slightly wild expression, his dark curly hair more disheveled than usual. He hooked his hand toward me, gesturing me to come inside fast. Against my better judgment I switched off the ignition and got out, dragging my coat and shoulder bag. But before I could speak, Olivier came out and took me firmly by the arm.

"Where in God's name have you been?" he hissed, sounding slightly hysterical. "You haven't returned a single message of mine in two whole weeks! Have you any idea what's been going on around here?"

"Not a clue," I admitted, starting to feel more than frightened. I motioned to the car parked on the road. "Who's your guest?"

"*Your* guest, my dear," Olivier informed me. "She drove in from Salt Lake late last night and stayed upstairs at my place, where there's heat. I've put her down in your flat just a moment ago, with the little argonaut for company." She? "As we cowpokes say," Olivier added glumly as he followed me down the steep steps to my apartment, "I'm afraid we're all up Shit Creek without a paddle, thanks to you."

When I stepped into the living room of my vast root cellar, more than a surprise was in store. At the far corner table was the new half sister I'd spoken to only two days ago from a phone booth at the Vienna airport, Bettina Brunhilde von Hauser.

Olivier was right: her presence here couldn't be good news. But I didn't have to hold my breath. Bambi rose and came across the room. She was wearing another of those amazing jumpsuits, this one a tawny *biscotti* shade that made her look as if she'd taken a full-body plunge into a caramel vat. Jason trotted by and disdainfully ignored me. I hung my coat and shoulder bag out of reach on the coat rack.

"Fräulein Behn—I mean Ariel," Bambi began, quickly correcting herself. "Your *Onkel* sent me here as soon as he understood how urgent the situation had become."

She glanced at Olivier with those gold-flecked eyes, and he flushed a little pink.

"I guess that's my cue to make myself scarce," he said.

"What for?" I asked him, adding, "Don't you have my apartment bugged as well as my phone? Or why's your boss kept you here, spying on me all this time?"

"I think you should tell her," Bambi surprised me by informing Olivier. "Tell her what you told me last night. Then I will explain the rest as well as I can."

"The group I work for sent me here five years ago, when the Pod first hired you," Olivier told me. "We weren't at all certain then which of your family was involved in this complex affair—but we knew plenty about Pastor Dart and his cohorts. We were keeping a very close eye on them. We found it suspicious that Dart would hire you right out of school as a direct report to himself, with so few credentials. Except, of course, the important one: that you were so close with your cousin Sam."

Worse and worse. So the Pod was every bit the villain that I'd feared, and that his nickname Prince of Darkness had always proclaimed. But I had one big question:

"Did Sam know you were spying on me? Or were you spying on him, too, even though he often worked for your boss, Theron Vane?"

"We're not spies," said Olivier. "We're an international agency along the lines of Interpol, which cooperates across national boundaries in tracking illicit activities—especially the smuggling of space-age weapons. We've learned that many of the people *engaged* in such activities have managed to infiltrate, at very high levels, institutions responsible for *controlling* them. High on the list are national drug traffickers, and even the KGB and CIA themselves. We fear they may soon be selling "hot products"—including atomic materials—on the open market, just as they're currently selling off their *own* undercover agents to the highest bidder!"

That was the longest speech I'd ever heard from Olivier, and the most serious, but he still hadn't answered my question.

"If you weren't spying, why was my phone bugged?" I said. "Why were you working undercover? Why did you try to grab the rune manuscript from the post office before I got there?"

"I was sent here to protect you, as soon as we learned what they were after," Olivier told me. "Though most often, I've wound up protecting you from yourself."

Shades of Herr Wolfgang, I thought.

"Once I saw that rune manuscript through the window of your car, I knew those weren't the documents your cousin had described to our people. When you stayed to work late at the office, I watched until I saw where you planned to hide it—in the Department of Defense Standard, a marvelous choice! I've retrieved it, of course, and made copies, so as not to lose it forever. Bambi says Lafcadio is afraid the other documents, those that belonged to your cousin, have already fallen into her brother's hands."

I actually felt relieved that at least one document, the rune manuscript, existed in more than just the hands of my own family. And also that Olivier had, as I'd hoped, been on my side. But my preoccupation with truth had led to a key observation—that the real danger in these documents might come from another quarter.

I couldn't forget what Sam told me after describing how Theron

Vane had been killed in his place by that bomb, an idea he'd repeated when warning me not to be obvious about haunting the post office or the mailbox. He said once anyone knew how and where to get their hands on a copy of these manuscripts, it might be easier if one of *us* were dead. I now understood that his cautionary reserve wasn't because the parcel he'd mailed me was the only extant version of these documents—but rather because Sam was the only person who knew where Pandora's originals were hidden. This strongly suggested to me that the folks who were after the documents didn't just want to know their contents—*but to be certain no one else did.* So those documents now in the hands of Wolfgang and the Pod *would* be the unique version—if Sam were dead. It didn't take much to figure out what came next in the scenario. For once, I tried not to shut my eyes.

"The Pod's in cahoots. Your telegram warned me, but I got it too late," I told Olivier. "Wolfgang has the manuscripts, though you both tried to warn me of him, too."

"I believe that my brother has genuinely fallen in love with you," said Bambi. "Had he met you earlier, this love might have forced him to reconsider his values and have saved him. Wolfgang is an educated person with high ideals, if the wrong ones. I think it surprised him to find he also has strong passions. But it's far too late for salvation, or even for talk. Where is my brother right now?"

"He went to the office from the airport," I said. "I was to meet him there shortly—"

"Then we must act at once," Bambi said. "If he's discovered that Olivier is not there either, he may come directly here. If he believes that *you* know where your cousin hid the original manuscripts, then you'll be in terrible danger. My brother must be stopped before he kills anyone again."

I stared at her in horror as Olivier put his hand gently on my arm. What in God's name was she saying? But of course I knew. I suppose, somehow, I always must have known.

"We were never quite sure," Olivier was telling Bambi.

I heard a slight buzzing in my ears as if I might black out. Then I heard Bambi's voice off somewhere in the distance.

"Yes, I'm certain of it. My brother Wolfgang murdered Samuel Behn."

◆ ◆

The man with whom I'd passed those nights of tempestuous lovemaking was a cold-blooded killer who, all the while I was in his arms, had believed he'd murdered Sam. I felt like taking a big slug of absinthe laced with opium, or even some of that hemlock that carried Socrates off to nirvana—though it might be more propitious right now to take to the road. But to where?

Olivier seemed about to make a suggestion when we heard a strange sound. We looked at each other for an instant before realizing what it was: our rarely used front doorbell at the far side of the house. Since the front door was separated from the road by a ninety-degree dropoff "front yard," most people came to the rear door, off the drive.

We rushed to the high dormer windows surrounding my potato-cellar living room and peeked out. We could see only the road, not the person who was standing on the front stoop. A large Land Rover with Idaho plates was parked up there behind Bambi's car. It had the profile of a standing grizzly bear stenciled on the front fender. I smiled. Maybe things were finally starting to look up, after all.

"Do you recognize it?" Olivier asked me.

"Not the car—just the bear. You get the door," I told him, "while Bambi and I round up Jason and grab some decent coats and shoes for all of us. We may be headed up-country for a while."

"But who is it?" asked Olivier. "We can hardly afford to open the door at this point, unless you're absolutely sure who it is."

"I'm sure," I told him. "It's a bear who drove here all the way from Lapwai—five hundred miles. He's an emissary of my dear, late cousin Sam."

◆ ◆

Bambi and Olivier both seemed a little taken aback by Dark Bear's appearance. Like most Nez Percé, Dark Bear was an extraordinarily handsome man, with his straight nose, cleft chin, strong features, long legs and broad shoulders, his braids of dark hair ribboned with white, and those silvery eyes beneath dark brows that, like Sam's, seemed like bright crystals that could see into the heart of time.

He was wearing a fringed, beaded jacket with a blanket tossed over one shoulder. He crossed to me and took my hand firmly but warmly in his.

As I've said, Dark Bear was never a huge fan of mine, due in large part to my strange side of the family. But this handshake was clearly intended to communicate his understanding and appreciation that I was helping Sam. Of course, neither he nor Sam yet knew how royally I'd already screwed up. I introduced Dark Bear to the others.

Dark Bear, never one to mince words, told me, "He has heard your heart and knows what decision you have taken. He approves. He asks you to come."

Sam had somehow read my mind from afar. I wasn't surprised: Sam had always been able to tap into my mind long-distance. And hadn't I felt him walking in my psychological moccasin prints these past weeks?

"There was no mention of others," Dark Bear added, motioning to Olivier and Bambi. "I was to bring only you."

This put me in a quandary. Here were two people who were ready to tell me the truth—a truth that might prove instrumental not only to my safety but to Sam's as well.

"Who does he mean by 'he'?" asked Olivier. "Where's he taking you, and why doesn't he want us to come along?"

Before I could think how to reply, Bambi resolved the problem—though I admit I wasn't quite sure how she did it.

"I am Halle's daughter," she told Dark Bear. "I've come from Vienna to reveal what I know about the man who was Sam's father and Ariel's stepfather—Earnest Behn."

"Ah," said Dark Bear with no expression. "I understand."

◆ ◆

I threw Jason in my backpack and gave him a pat. I didn't want to leave him alone in the house when I wasn't sure where we were going or how long we'd be gone. I slung the pack over my shoulder along with my regular satchel, gathering up what I thought we might need for a hike in the mountains with Jason along for the ride. I hopped onto the front seat of Dark Bear's Land Rover while Olivier and Bambi took the back. This enabled me, turning to listen to Bambi's story, simultaneously to watch the rear window and be sure we weren't followed.

"Okay, folks," I said to Bambi and Olivier, once we'd pulled out of town and were headed north along the Continental Divide. "I can't tell you where we're going, because I don't know myself. But I know who Dark Bear is taking us to meet. I therefore assure you this is no boondoggle. We're getting to the bottom of everything, once and for all."

Olivier was regarding me with a puzzled expression, then slowly the dawning light crept over his face.

"My God!" he cried. "Do you mean to say he's not really dead?"

I nodded slowly. At least I'd managed to do *one* thing in all this time: keep Sam's living, breathing existence a secret from just about everyone on the planet. But all that was about to change, as it must if we were to unravel this mess.

"But if Sam is alive . . . then whom did Wolfgang kill?" asked Bambi, quicker on the uptake than I'd thought when we'd first met.

I glanced at Olivier uncomfortably.

"Oh no," said Olivier, as he suddenly got the picture. "All this past month, I've felt something was horribly wrong. It wasn't usual for us to communicate personally while on assignment, but I knew Theron Vane had gone to San Francisco the same week your cousin was killed. It seemed odd to receive no news at all, after the brutal murder of someone who was helping with a case I'd been working on myself for five years. I even thought to contact Theron on my own, but I decided there must be some good reason why he was keeping silent." He smiled grimly. "It now appears that there was."

As we wound our way up into the thickly forested pine country with its swift, dark rivers and sheer drops of sparkling waterfalls glimpsed between the trees, I inhaled the pine scents and listened to Bambi's story. As she told it, the last few pieces of the puzzle I'd been both hunting and dodging for so long finally fell into place.

"My mother Halle was raised by her father, Hillmann von Hauser," she said. "As you see, Wolfgang and I, too, use our grandfather's name."

"I understood, from a phone call with my mother Jersey, that you and Wolfgang had two different fathers," I said, not really wanting to make a public issue of Bambi's illegitimate paternity by my own obnoxious father, Augustus. But I was the one to be let in for another surprise.

"Different fathers, yes, but with the same family name," Bambi told me. "Wolfgang's father, my mother Halle's legal husband, was actually Earnest Behn."

I was no longer shocked by such revelations about my family. But in view of what Bambi had said earlier about Wolfgang being the instrument of Sam's death, I knew this was truly important, since it meant that Sam and Wolfgang shared the same father, Earnest. They were half brothers—just as Bambi and I were sisters through my father, Augustus. I glanced at Dark Bear, who noticed it from the corner of his eye as he drove, and nodded in affirmation.

"Yes, I knew of this," he said. "I knew Earnest Behn for many years. Earnest was a very handsome man, and rich. He came to northwest Idaho, well before the war, to purchase mining properties, fifty thousand acres north of Lapwai containing numerous untapped mountains and caves filled with mineral resources—a large chunk of Mother Earth to be so exploited. The war, of course, made him even richer.

"After the war, when Earnest was in his mid-forties, he returned to Europe, married the young woman Halle, and stayed in Europe for some time. They had a son, Wolfgang. Suddenly Earnest returned to his property north of Lapwai, without the woman or child. He said they had died. He asked permission to marry my daughter Bright Cloud, whom he had known from her childhood. She was very attracted to him, but it was . . . uncustomary. Earnest Behn was a white man from foreign lands. How did we know he would be willing to learn our ways? How did we know he would not leave the country again, perhaps never to return?

"When I asked him if he loved my daughter, Earnest Behn said he believed himself incapable of love—a remark that, to be plain, my people cannot understand. To admit such a thing is as much as saying you are already dead. He promised he would care for my daughter, however, and that any child they had between them would be raised on the reservation among our people—a promise he failed to keep. For when Bright Cloud died, Sam's father took him from the reservation. Then he married your mother Jersey, and we feared Sam would be lost to us forever."

Dark Bear said this without bitterness, though he looked as if he were deep in thought. Then he added, "Earnest Behn said something else very strange, just before his marriage to my daughter. He said: 'I pray it may remove the stain of my pollution.' He never said what he meant, nor would he ever accept to take the sweat lodge for purification."

Something about that rang a bell.

"You said Earnest Behn bought property in America before the Second World War," I said. "When exactly was that?"

"It was in 1923," said Dark Bear.

The date had unarguable significance—though after a quick calculation, it didn't make sense.

"But Earnest was born in 1901," I said. "By 1923, that would make him only twenty-two. Why would his father entrust such a young man with buying and managing so much land in a foreign—"

But Olivier and Bambi were looking at me with wide eyes.

"My God," I said.

So this was the "pollution" our family never spoke of, clearly with good cause—as if bigamy, kidnapping, incest, fascism, and murder weren't enough. By the end of our two-hour ride through the Bitterroot Range of the Rockies, supplementing my own knowledge with Dark Bear's and Bambi's, I'd pieced together a good deal. And I realized I owed both my grandmothers an apology—especially Zoe.

Hitler's Munich *putsch* took place on November 9, 1923. At the time, no war was in sight—but Hieronymus Behn knew there would always be war. And he also knew which side he planned to be on. He sent Earnest to America to establish a mining presence there. Ten years later, in 1933—the year Hitler became chancellor of Germany—Hieronymus sent his other son, by then twenty-one years old: my father Augustus. These two young men were planted like moles, burrowing into the mountains and caves of the New World, stockpiling important minerals against a time when the world would enter another war.

One flew east: my father to Pennsylvania. And one flew west: Earnest to Idaho. And one flew over the cuckoo's nest. That was Zoe.

Though Zoe might have deserted her parents to run off with the Gypsies, it seems that by the time she was grown, Hieronymus Behn wanted his daughter and only true blood descendant to "breed with good blood." It was he who sent his colleague and friend Hillmann von Hauser to Paris to seduce her. Whatever the circumstances of their relationship from Zoe's viewpoint, her daughter Halle was taken from her and raised by the father and his dutiful if barren Germanic wife. Zoe married a wild Irishman and had another child: my mother Jersey.

So if Hieronymus Behn essentially kidnapped my father Augustus from Pandora, he also appropriated the two sons his sister-bride Hermione had conceived with Christian Alexander: Laf by adoption, and Earnest by changing his birth certificate to name Hieronymus as the real father. This meant that Zoe's two daughters, my mother Jersey and her sister Halle, were Hieronymus Behn's only true grandchildren. It therefore made sense, as the story unfolded, that Hieronymus plotted to marry them off to these two appropriated "sons"—Halle to Earnest, and Jersey to Augustus. Through this manipulation, Hieronymus hoped to ensure that any future recipients of his fortune and power would be tied to his own bloodline, through Zoe.

The biggest fly in the ointment, of course, was that he'd married the wrong sisters off to the wrong brothers. My prestige- and power-oriented father Augustus would have been the perfect match for Halle, who had been given the finest Aryan preparation that a beautiful blond girl with Nazi parentage might ask. The product of that liaison was Bambi. Then Earnest and my mother Jersey, when they got together in later life, were as happy as two such exploited and emotionally traumatized people might hope to be.

So the pollution Earnest could never wash himself clean of was something he only understood fully after he'd married Halle von Hauser. Not just what her daddy had done in the war as an armaments manufacturer—which she was quite proud of—but also where all the minerals had gone that Earnest himself had placed, all those years, in the hands of his own "neutral" Dutch father, Hieronymus Behn.

Earnest started pulling together, slowly and painfully, the family background that no one fully knew. When it became clear to Earnest that he, Augustus, and Hieronymus had built their enormous fortune on the suffering of others—in Hieronymus's case, in full awareness of what he was doing—that was bad enough. But when he learned that he'd been used as a tool by the man he'd always regarded as his father—not only to breed a superior race, but to control the world—that knowledge was almost impossible for Earnest to live with.

The girls' mother, Zoe, on the other hand, had gone into occupied France to try to persuade her former seducer to let her take her daughter Halle out of German-occupied territory, and had been trapped there, as Pandora and Laf had in Vienna. It must have seemed ironic to Zoe to be sitting across a table from me in Paris beside my own gorgeous Nazi seducer, replaying a version of her life between the wars.

The true irony, for all these people, was that their connections with Hieronymus Behn and Hillmann von Hauser and Adolf Hitler had, according to Bambi, enabled them not only to survive the war themselves but, in the cases of Pandora and Zoe, to protect or rescue hundreds of people with impunity. This included Pandora's husband Dacian Bassarides, who'd run a Gypsy shuttle of escapees—with Zoe's help from Paris—out through southern France.

"Does Wolfgang know anything of this story—or the fact that Sam is really his brother?" I asked Bambi.

She was silent for a moment, regarding me seriously with her speckled golden eyes.

"I'm not sure," she said at last. "But I do know he has been heavily influenced by my mother—the essential reason why Lafcadio has despised him, though he's been reluctant to discuss it. I have pieced together some of the story from Lafcadio, who must have learned it from Earnest, many years ago, when Earnest came from Idaho to Vienna to confront Pandora. It seems all along Pandora had known the entire story."

Of course!

I remembered Wolfgang's words when he was gazing out over the Danube as we stood there together beneath the glass ceiling of his castle, just before we made love: "My father took me to see her when I was only a small child. She was singing '*Das himmlische Leben*.' She looked at me with those eyes—*your* eyes."

"After marrying my daughter," Dark Bear said, "Earnest Behn returned to Europe twice. When Sam was three years old, Earnest went to speak with Pandora, the mother of his brother Augustus, about an important family matter. The second trip was for Pandora's funeral, just after Bright Cloud died, and he took Sam along with him. Pandora bequeathed him something he had to retrieve in person, Earnest told me. When he came back to Idaho, he left the reservation for good."

I had just one more question. And luckily I was so accustomed by now to off-the-wall answers, I hardly even flinched anymore.

"How was it that you went to live with Lafcadio, after your mother Halle died?" I asked Bambi. "Did you already know Uncle Laf well?"

"My mother never died. She's still quite alive, I'm afraid to say—though I haven't seen her since I left home ten years ago," Bambi said, narrowing her eyes. "But I thought you must have understood, all along, that it is *she* who remains in the shadows, behind everything!"

◆ ◆

If Bambi's mother, Halle von Hauser, was "behind everything," as Bambi said—and if she was truly so awful that her husband ran off and married Bright Cloud, and even her daughter Bambi left home at age fifteen to live with Uncle Laf—then it was clear what this suggested about Wolfgang's connection to the dark side of our family.

But what about Augustus's role? I asked Olivier if he knew.

"Your father's very high on our list," Olivier told me. "Apparently, he hasn't been involved with Bambi's mother romantically in years—each has by now married someone else—but they do seem to understand one another extremely well. About ten years ago, your father helped set up Halle von Hauser in a position of prominence in Washington, D.C., from which she is now able to exercise significant political influence, both here and abroad. Indeed, there's a delicacy involved in unraveling with whom these two have connections. In Halle's position on the boards of several museums and a major newspaper, she's the capital's most influential social beast—"

Holy shit.

"That paper wouldn't by chance be the *Washington Post*?" I interrupted. "And Halle's new husband wouldn't by chance be named Voorheer-LeBlanc?" It *did* sound Dutch-Belgian, part of the very region of Himmler's *nouveau paradis*.

Olivier smiled. "You certainly *have* been doing your homework."

Naturally she would have picked a different first name, like Helena, in case anyone ever mentioned a person with a memorable name like Halle. I recalled, too, how interested my father and stepmother Grace had been to see what *I* knew about my inheritance, at dinner that night in San Francisco. They'd thrown a press conference afterwards to try to dig out even more from the estate executor. That would also be a good cover motive for someone else to phone and pump me, maybe with more success, about just which manuscripts were included in Sam's estate. When Ms. Voorheer-LeBlanc of the *Washington Post* phoned later, she never said she was a reporter, just that she wanted to buy my manuscripts. I had little doubt at this point that she was none other than Wolfgang's and Bambi's mother, Halle von Hauser.

Did Jersey know her sister was alive, or what she and my father had been up to since they'd left the bedroom? She hadn't told me, but Dark Bear soon explained why.

"Naturally, I had many suspicions regarding the sudden, unexplained death of Earnest's first wife and child," he told me. "But I never had evidence they were alive, until Sam's recent research trip to Utah. Sam thinks your mother and Earnest believed the best way to protect you children from the past was simply to maintain silence."

I was about to pursue the point when Dark Bear slowed the Land Rover nearly to a standstill and carefully pulled off the road into the woods. The forest floor, thickly padded with layers of pine needles, gave off a heady scent as we passed. Bambi and Olivier and I fell to a hushed quiet as we watched Dark Bear carefully maneuver the large vehicle through narrow passages among the trees, as tight as threading an embroidery needle. After what seemed ages, the land started to rise gradually, until at last we were headed straight uphill. When the rugged terrain became too steep, Dark Bear stopped at the edge of a narrow crevasse and switched off the engine. He turned to me.

"I am to take you as far as the river, then my grandson will come and meet us," he told me. "He is expecting me to bring only you, however—so perhaps these others should stay behind and wait here at the car."

I turned to Olivier and Bambi with a raised brow, to see what they thought.

"I should like to accompany you," Bambi told me. "And to help in any way I can. I consider myself responsible for much of what has happened to you and your cousin—*our* cousin," she corrected herself. "Had I told you everything about my brother the moment I knew you had met him, it all might have been avoided."

"Well, that cinches it," said Olivier, coating his *québecois* with a western drawl. "No self-respecting feller'd let two fillies like you run loose, alone in them thar hills."

But he dropped his jaw when Bambi whipped from her jacket pocket a small Browning automatic, which she pointed toward the roof with a professionalism rivaling Annie Oakley's. Olivier had always claimed he was searching for the cowgirl of his dreams, but now he flung up his hands.

"For heaven's sakes," he cried, "put that thing away before someone gets hurt! Where on earth did you get it?"

"My grandfather Hillmann was advanced group trainer in the *Ballermann Gewehrschiessen*—the shootists' club—of central Germany. Everyone in our family was required to learn to shoot," she informed Olivier. "I am merit-qualified in the Walther, Luger, Mauser, and all models of the Browning—and I am licensed to carry this for my own protection."

Right. You never know when somebody might try to bump off a twenty-five-year-old blond girl cellist. Especially in a family like *ours*.

"Let her bring it along," I told Olivier. "It might come in handy."

◆ ◆

We followed Dark Bear on foot up the long, rocky defile. The going got rougher toward the top, as big chunks of rock broke loose from the rubble and slipped away under our feet. I really wasn't looking forward to another avalanche. You couldn't even out-ski ten thousand tons of crumbling rock.

We got to the top of the cliff overlooking, about two hundred feet below, a thickly forested valley cut by a broad, glassy ribbon of river, and something I recognized at once that told me precisely where we were: Sam's favorite spot in northern Idaho, the upper Mesa Falls.

The river was wide here, and the falls dropped in a single burnished sheet, as golden in the sunlight as Bambi's hair. Only the constant roiling mist rising from its base gave any indication of the volume of pounding water crushing the ancient rocks down there into pebbled sand. I'd come here years ago, as a teenager, with Sam. It was my last outing before I went away to school, and he wanted to show it to me.

"It's my secret place, hotshot," he'd told me. "I found it when I was out fishing on my own once, when I was quite young. Nobody's been here for a very long time, maybe thousands of years."

Holding hands, we'd waded the shallow waters just above the falls and climbed down the crooked rock face at the far side of the cliff. There we found a narrow seam in the rock, nearly invisible until you were right upon it, and so close to the pounding water that its sides were slimy with green mosses from the constant spray. Sam slipped sideways into the crack, pulling me by the hand after him.

We were inside a large cave, behind the roaring waters that fell like a veil in front of our very faces. We went back into the cave a few yards until we were swallowed in darkness. Then Sam took out a flashlight and switched it on.

It was absolutely breathtaking. The walls and ceiling of the cave were a fairyland of crystals in rainbows of colors. Real rainbows were cast everywhere, refracted from the churning mist swirling around us and the myriad prisms.

"If I ever wanted to hide myself, or you, or anything else of value to me," Sam told me in the breathless silence that was swept beneath the vacuum of roaring waters, "I couldn't think of a better place to do it than right here."

And now, as I stood on the high cliff overlooking the falls with Dark Bear and Olivier and Bambi, I knew beyond question why we'd been brought here. I knew exactly what must be hidden down there in that cave.

◆ ◆

It took half an hour to reach the river from the cliff, picking our way through forest and thick underbrush over rocky terrain. When at last we reached a clear level spot on the embankment above the falls, I turned to the others and said over the sound of the water, "We have to wade across here. Our spot is at the far side of the falls. There's no other place for miles where it's shallow enough to safely ford the river."

"There isn't any place at *all* that's safe for me, I'm afraid," Olivier said, regarding me with large dark eyes. "I hate to have to reveal it at *this* late hour—but I've never learned to swim!"

"Then it's too risky," I agreed. "Even though the water will only be up to about our knees here, the current is terribly strong and swift so close to the falls. You'd better stay here while we cross it and find Sam."

Dark Bear, no spring chicken, agreed to wait on the bank with Olivier. As Bambi and I took off our shoes and rolled our trousers to wade out into the river, I set my backpack on the ground beside Olivier. To my astonishment, Jason's furry black head popped out—I'd completely forgotten him! His eyes lit on the silently moving waters just beyond me, and his ears twitched with enthusiasm at such a large swimming pool.

"Oh, no, you don't," I informed him firmly. I shoved him back in the pack and handed it to Olivier. "That's all we need right now—a cat swept overboard. You'll have to be the boss." I pointed my finger at Jason and added, "No more kippered herring from your landlord here, if you misbehave while I'm gone."

As Bambi and I waded out into the waters, hand in hand, I felt my first flash of panic. The water was far colder, the current stronger than I'd recalled from the other time I'd tried this. Suddenly I understood why. Sam had brought me here in late summer—the hottest time of year, and so dry that it actually marks the start of forest-fire season.

But now we were here just after spring thaw, when the rivers were at their swiftest and most swollen. The water was shoving against us so hard I had to slide my feet along the pebbled bottom. If I lifted one foot only slightly, I might easily be swept away. Much worse, it was clear from the force of the waters—only up to midcalf at this point—that if we got in more than knee deep, we might not be able to advance at all.

I was about to yell to Bambi over the roar of water that we ought to beat a retreat to Olivier back on the bank—but just at that moment I saw a flicker of motion more than fifty feet ahead, across the river. I glanced up and saw Sam's tall, lean outline on the opposite bank, silhouetted against the brilliant sunlight. He held his hand up, motioning us to stop where we were, then kicked off his moccasins and stepped into the river. When he got close enough to Bambi and me, I saw he had a length of rope about his waist that must be secured on the far bank. He reached us, grasped me by the shoulders, and yelled over the crash of water, "Thank God! Let me get this anchored over there, then I'll help you across."

When Dark Bear had lashed the other end to a tree, Sam and Bambi and I started to pull our way along the rope, across the river to the opposite bank. When we reached it in safety, though the water had never come higher than midthigh, about three feet deep, I was exhausted from the strain and tension required to hold the rope and my balance. Bambi seemed much the same.

Sam scrambled up first onto the rocky slope and helped us out in turn. Then wordlessly—we were now too close to the waterfall to hear, even if we screamed—Sam clambered down over the rocky side of the falls to a small standing space and reached up his hands for

Bambi. He took her by the waist from beneath as I tried to help steady her precarious descent from above. Then, all at once, something horrible happened.

Sam stood there, barefoot in the roiling mist on that narrow ledge of rock, only inches from Bambi, his long dark hair swirling out in the mist and mingling with her golden strands. As he looked down, his hands still on her waist, his silvery eyes smiling into her golden ones, I felt a sudden sharp pain.

What in God's name was wrong with me? This was hardly the time to get mauled by the talons of the ugly green dragon of jealousy. Besides, who was *I* to feel this way? I, who'd almost destroyed everyone by disregarding pleas for sanity from all sources, to go trotting off on my own little lust-ridden sexual odyssey? Further, I had to recognize that Sam had never, never—not once, by word or deed—actually *told* me he and I might be anything more serious than blood brothers. So why couldn't I be detached enough, or even concerned enough for him, to show the same love, openness, trust, and support that he'd shown me, the moment he realized exactly how I felt about Wolfgang Hauser? But, God, I just couldn't do it. As I watched them, I felt as if someone had plunged a knife into my heart and twisted it. But this was hardly the time or place to lose control.

These thoughts rushed through my mind for the few short seconds—though it seemed like hours—that Sam and Bambi appeared to be hopelessly lost in each other's gaze. Then Sam slipped Bambi through the slot in the rock and reached up his arms for me.

When he lowered me to the platform of rock, Sam put his lips to my ear and yelled above the roar of the waters: "Who's *that*?"

I put my mouth likewise to his ear and yelled back: "My *sister*!"

He drew away to stare at me, shook his head, and laughed, though I couldn't hear a sound. Then he slid me into the cave and quickly followed.

Sam's flashlight led us back through the glittering labyrinth that had been cut over the aeons out of the solid rock and decorated by dripping water. It twisted back farther into the mountain until we reached a place where we could speak over the distant sound of the waters. Then I introduced Sam to Bambi.

"Well, my friends." Sam's voice echoed against the stalagmites of the crystal cave. "I'd really like to pause and admire all the pulchritude that's crossed the wilderness in my behalf. But I'm afraid we have a rather big task before us."

"Bettina and I have plenty to fill you in on, and Olivier does, too," I told Sam. "It might be dangerous to remove Pandora's manuscripts—I'm assuming they're here—until you hear what we have to say. Besides, where could you find a better place to hide them safely than this?"

"I don't plan to hide them at all," said Sam. "They've been hidden long enough, it seems to me. Honesty's the best policy: that's *your* motto, hotshot, you taught it to me." He smiled at Bambi and added, "Did you know the mountain lion is your sister's totem? I wonder what yours will turn out to be." As Bambi smiled back, I felt my fingers tingling—perhaps with the damp cold here in the cave.

"If you don't plan to hide them," I asked Sam with numb lips, "what *will* you do? Everyone in the world has been after these damned manuscripts of Pandora's."

"My grandfather has a terrific idea. Did he tell you?" said Sam. "He thinks it's high time for the whole Indian Nation to do something for our reservations—something that might be a big boon to Mother Earth too." When Bambi and I made no reply, Sam added, "Dark Bear thinks it's time to open the first Native American electronic publishing house!"

◆ ◆

Sam had sealed the manuscripts in slender, opaque, airtight lucite tubes that were stacked toward the rear of the cave. If you didn't know exactly what you were after, in the dim light they'd seem just another clutch of stalagmites rising from the floor.

Sam had told me, that morning up on the mountain above the Sheep Meadow, how he'd painstakingly transcribed onto plain paper Pandora's collection, inherited via his father, of ancient parchments, thin wood panels, and copper scrolls. Then he said he'd sealed the originals in "hermetic containers" and hidden them in a place where he thought they'd "never be found." The plain paper copy Sam had made—the *only* copy, as he'd described it—was that set of documents he'd taken from his bank in San Francisco right after Theron Vane was killed, and tossed in a mailbox, addressed to me. Those were the manuscripts I'd now dragged around the world, and painstakingly inserted into books at the Austrian National Library. Documents that now, according to Wolfgang, were in the hands of Father Virgilio and the Pod.

Dark Bear's idea, Sam explained, was for us to collect all the ancient original manuscripts sealed in containers here in the cave, and once again to transcribe them and translate them into English—this time, along with the rune manuscript of unknown provenance I'd gotten from Jersey. Then we'd publish these translations, one by one, on a computer network, for the edification and enlightenment of the public at large.

After publication, Dark Bear thought we should parcel out the ancient source records—the delicate tin plates and parchment scrolls—to various American Indian museums and libraries, whichever ones possessed the wherewithal to preserve and handle them properly.

Unlike the famous Dead Sea Scrolls of similar antiquity, which had been closely held in the hands of a few totalitarian data-mongers these past forty years, Pandora's and Clio's wonderful trove of exotica would be made available for study and analysis to qualified scholars in every field. If we translated these things ourselves, we'd at least know nothing was swept under the rug. And if we did learn of something dangerous—for instance if there were spots on Mother Earth that could be manipulated, but that were sacred or vulnerable or both, like Wolfgang's hints about Tesla's inventions—we would make that knowledge public too, so action could be taken to protect those places.

We three formed a relay to remove the lucite tubes: Bambi handed them out through the crevice of the cave to Sam, who knotted them together with twine in three big bunches while I ascended the steep rock to the top of the cliff. Then Sam lifted the bunches, and I hauled them from above by sturdier rope. I set them beside the waterfall until the others clambered up.

Though individually each lucite tube was light as a feather, their combined weight was fairly hefty; I estimated my parcel and Bambi's to weigh close to twenty pounds apiece, and Sam's seemed heavier. Further, though the tubes were tightly sealed, Sam feared that, due to the delicacy of many of the items, if anything leaked or even sweated, some of their valuable contents might be destroyed.

So we carried our bundles on our backs, well above waterline, the tubes stacked horizontally from waist level to just above our shoulders. Sam secured them to our backs with a buntline hitch such as mountaineers use, in case one of us went down and had to quickly shed the pack. The awkwardness of our loads, we hoped, would be offset by weight, helping to provide a firmer grip on the river bottom against the onrush of water.

Just before I stepped into the river, I looked across at Dark Bear waiting on the opposite bank beside a tense-looking Olivier—who was wearing my backpack with Jason inside it. Then I climbed carefully down into the icy waters and we moved out into the river single file—Sam leading the procession to keep the rope taut, Bambi in the middle, and I bringing up the rear—all of us clinging tightly to the rope. I had to concentrate as hard as I could to keep my knees flexible, my body balanced, and my feet planted firmly as I felt my way along the slippery, uneven rock on the bottom of the riverbed. So I was well out into the river before I suddenly realized something was terribly wrong. Sam had stopped dead in midriver.

There on the opposite bank, at the forest's edge, were the two very last people on earth I wanted to see: my boss Pastor Owen Dart, and Herr Professor Dr. Wolfgang K. Hauser of Krems, Österreich. Wolfgang was holding Olivier with a gun at his throat. Dark Bear, only yards away, had been firmly lashed to a tree.

How did they get here, a hundred miles into the wilderness? Then I realized that in the few minutes, back at the house, when Dark Bear had stepped inside, we'd left the cars unattended. Those few moments might have been all the time required to attach tracking devices to our vehicles. It seems Wolfgang had learned from his experience the last time he'd tailed me.

Even at this distance, I could see Wolfgang's deep turquoise eyes riveted on the three of us out across the river—first resting briefly on Bambi and me, then burning like horrible coals into Sam, as if he couldn't believe what he saw.

I wanted to weep. But my more immediate desire was to stay alive, a prospect that didn't seem too awfully promising just at this moment. I suddenly noticed that the Pod held a hunting knife in his hand. Now he set his other hand firmly on the thick line of rope that was tied to the tree just beside him—the rope we were all clinging to, our total life support system out here in the rapid waters. A twinge of fear ran up my spine as I realized he was about to hack it in two! But then I saw Wolfgang shake his head and speak a few quick words to the Pod, who removed his hand from our lifeline with a nod of agreement, and glanced back at us.

Bambi and Sam and I stood there in midriver, frozen like statues, as I prayed that maybe Wolfgang had had a change of heart, maybe he'd undergone radical personality surgery in the few hours since I'd seen him. After all, I tried to reason, if their objective was to destroy all trace of these documents, leaving their team with the copy Sam himself had made as the only version in existence, then there was no reason why the Pod shouldn't cut us all loose like bait and toss us over the falls to feed the fish.

But of course there *was* a reason, and it wasn't long before I grasped it. If we went over the falls right now, Pandora's manuscripts would, too—but they wouldn't be destroyed if they floated! Dozens of ancient messages bobbing in modern little bottles, running the Salmon River hundreds of miles, to the Snake and the Columbia and out to sea. Scattered in such a manner, how could anyone ever begin to collect and destroy them all before others could find them? These messages and their bottles had to be captured or destroyed first, before destroying the messengers.

Just then, Sam motioned behind his back for Bambi and me to move closer. When we'd closed ranks, Sam glanced over his shoulder at me—and he winked! What in God's name was *that* supposed to mean?

About thirty paces ahead, Wolfgang was wading down into the water in his shoes and stockings, without bothering to roll his pants. He held Olivier in front of him, gun to his head, as a shield. The Pod followed just behind, holding a gun in one hand, his knife in the other. I had to hand it to Wolfgang: he must be well acquainted with his kid sister Bettina's flair with a pistol, and was taking no chances. But I couldn't help being depressed over Olivier, and not only because I liked him. If we three *did* try to jump the others, whom we outnumbered by two to one, it might cost Olivier's life, since he couldn't swim.

Though it was hard to be cheery in such circumstances, I tried to focus on what Sam might have meant by that wink. It was clear there was something up his sleeve. Knowing Sam, I knew the moment he decided to act we'd all have to think on our feet and take quick action too. But when it happened, it wasn't what I would have thought of.

Wolfgang and the Pod moved cautiously along the rope, on the upstream side, as we were, using it as a buffer—which would soon prove their big mistake. I could witness their progress by craning left, as Bambi just behind Sam leaned right for a better view.

When they reached midstream, Wolfgang, still with a throttlehold on Olivier, stepped aside from the rope in the rushing waters so the Pod could get past to reach Sam. As Wolfgang moved slightly upstream, holding the white and sick-looking Olivier at gunpoint, Dart inched forward toward Sam's load of cylinders, still foolishly wielding his knife and gun.

Then casually, almost as if providing assistance to the Pod, Sam lightly flirted the rope that secured his tight parcel of tubes to his back—and before anyone grasped what he was about to do, he'd spilled the buntline hitch and snapped his securing rope free. The haul of hollow lucite tubes started to slip swiftly downstream, headed for the falls.

If memory serves, it was just about then that all hell broke loose.

Pastor Dart dropped his knife in the water and lurched forward across the waist-level rope to grab at the iceberg floating away. But at that instant, Sam shoved the rope deep into the water so the Pod, expecting it higher, lost his balance and flipped forward on his face into the ever rushing waters. Then Sam yanked the rope back up with a snap so it snagged the Pod, hanging him up like a bundle of wet laundry.

As the Pod floundered trying to get off the rope, Wolfgang shoved Olivier to one side for a clean shot at the swiftly retreating mass before it went over the side. But just as he did, an angry black bundle of fur, too long restrained in Olivier's backpack, exploded right in Wolfgang's face! I never knew Jason had that many claws, or could deploy them with such rapid-fire, razor-sharp precision.

When Wolfgang threw up his arms to cover his face, Jason track-cleated over them, then over his head, and disappeared behind him. Wolfgang's gun flew into midair—thanks to a fast-acting Browning and a very resourceful Bambi. Wolfgang screamed curses over the rush of falls, but it didn't stop him. Holding his bleeding hand, he leapt over the heavy rope to tear after the disappearing mass of tubes, just as

Sam barreled into him sideways and they went down together. I glanced around fast, trying to reconnoiter for Olivier—but he'd vanished as swiftly as my cat.

All this happened in seconds. I finally wrestled free my own incapacitating pack of tubes and quickly lashed them to the strong, thick rope to secure them. Then I grabbed the Pod, whose gun had vanished, too, as he was pulling himself upright in the churning waters. As Bambi covered him with her weapon, I stripped off his necktie and tied him tightly by his wrists to the hefty rope, alongside the pack.

Bambi was pulling free her own pack as I climbed across the rope and moved toward Wolfgang and Sam, still churning together in the water. Over my shoulder, Bambi let out a piercing scream. I whipped around to follow her gaze, and I saw Olivier's body, partly submerged and thrashing but well downstream of us—maybe sixty feet—headed straight for the falls.

I was trying to figure out what in God's name to do, when just up ahead I saw Wolfgang drag Sam from the water, slug him hard in the jaw, drop him back in the drink again, and plunge off on foot toward the swiftly vanishing object of his desire.

Sam clambered upright, took one look downstream, and caught sight of Olivier. Before I had time to think, he'd dived into the same fast water that was swiftly dragging Olivier toward the falls. Some distance beyond him, Wolfgang—still on his feet and nearly within reach of the iceberg—made a grab for it, missed, lost balance. He went down, and the water grabbed him too.

Bambi had managed to get her pack off and lashed down, while keeping her powder dry. Still holding the gun, she picked her way the short distance to where I stood, a few yards downstream beyond the rope, and she hollered in my ear:

"My God! Can't we *do* something? They will all be killed!"

I had to admit it sure looked that way. Nor for the life of me could I imagine what might prevent it. Even if I could get to one end of the heavy rope stretched across the river and free it to toss as a lifeline, I was sure it wouldn't be long enough to reach that far downstream. We watched in horror as the ghastly scene unfolded before us: three men and a crystal iceberg all drawn by the dark, glassy waters inexorably toward the cliff. I couldn't breathe.

Bambi shifted her gun to her right hand, her cellist's bowing hand,

and took mine in her left as we saw the pile of crystalline tubes containing Pandora's deadly manuscripts moving in slow motion to the brink of the abyss, where they twisted gracefully once, like a ballet dancer, then slipped silently over the edge. A moment later, Wolfgang's dark head followed just as silently after.

We saw Sam, with swift strokes, catch up to Olivier's possibly already lifeless body—too late for either of them to be extricated from the terrible undertow. Bambi and I, with the water's roar in our ears, watched in silence as we saw the rest of our generation, except us two, slip swiftly over the edge of the abyss into oblivion.

As I stood there in those cold, rushing waters I had no tears, either of forgiveness or remorse. I felt nothing at all for those who'd created or perpetuated this swamp of treachery—most of whom, as it turned out, were members of my own horrid family. But I did have something I still clung to, as I'd clung to that lifeline of rope, something that might keep me alive in the face of such overwhelming odds. It was the one thing that remained at the bottom of Pandora's box when all else had flown the coop: that thing called hope.

I turned to leave the river, but Bambi was clutching my hand.

"What shall we do now?" she asked over the sound of the rushing waters—the waters I had just watched carry away everything I'd ever cared for in my life.

"The first thing we have to do," I told her just as loudly, "is to find my cat!"

◆ ◆

Bambi tied our cylinders together and floated them back to the shore, while I dragged the body of the dreadful Pod on his back through the waters and deposited him unceremoniously on the riverbank. She held the gun on him as I went to untie Sam's grandfather Dark Bear, who helped us lash Pastor Dart to the tree in his place: tit for tat, asshole. Then the three of us hiked downstream to hunt for Jason.

I'll never understand exactly how I knew Jason was the key to the solution, or that he might still be alive and afloat. But I knew Jason's psyche as well as one could grasp the psyche of a cat. His natural instincts, naturally, were those of the mythological hero he was named for: he took like an argonaut to water.

Even if he'd never before gone over a waterfall the height and breadth of this one—maybe forty feet high by a hundred feet wide—still, you couldn't keep him out of the water chute rides at amusement parks that were higher than that, and he was well used to swimming in fast water along the Snake. The water below the falls here would be slower and far more tranquil, so if Jason had indeed made the drop without breaking any bones, I was pretty sure we'd find him down there alive.

And Jason loved retrieving things, whether a rubber ball in the stream or a yellow post office slip in the snow. So why not locate an iceberg of lucite tubes containing valuable manuscripts? Not to mention the bodies of Olivier, Sam, or Wolfgang, whether dead or alive.

◆ ◆

We found Jason first, "happy as a clam at high tide," as Olivier might say, paddling in a calm pool just below the falls. The object he was paddling around with a certain pride was the floating pile of plastic tubes, their rope snagged on a rock. A few tubes had broken loose and were floating nearby in the pool looking little the worse for wear.

Since Bambi and I were already soaked to the skin, we climbed down the bank to the pool and pulled them out—along with Jason—while Dark Bear went on along the riverbank as far as he found it still passable on foot. By the time we'd hauled the cylinders up to a ledge, he had returned.

"I could go no farther—the bank drops off in the underbrush," he told me. "But I've spotted them from above. They're downstream not far from here. I saw three heads, all floating in a small inlet that projects slightly from the river."

"Alive?" I asked him.

"I believe so," said Dark Bear. "But the walls are sheer and slick. We can't get them out that way. They must be brought back up here by way of the water."

The dropoff to the river was steeper here, the water far deeper than above. Though Dark Bear, Bambi, and I were all pretty strong swimmers, we still tied a few loose containers around each of our chests as flotation devices. She hid her gun in a bush. Then, one by one, we slipped into the dark river.

We found them less than a mile downstream, and were in for quite a surprise. Sam, treading water, was supporting not Olivier but

Wolfgang, whose eyes were shut. Sam was holding him under the chin in a lifeguard's grip while Olivier was bobbing around nearby, cheerful as a Hallowe'en apple in a tub!

"Men overboard!" Olivier cried when he spied our swimming flotilla's approach. "And women and natives to the rescue!"

When we reached Olivier, I said, "Thank God you're all alive—but I thought you couldn't swim!"

"So did I!" he said. "Your backpack saved me. It kept me afloat, though I got swept over the falls. Pretty scary! Then I bobbed up like a soap bubble as soon as I landed."

Of course! My huge plastic bottle that I always carried for hiking, to filter water. Filled with air, it had saved Olivier's life.

"Are you all right, too?" I asked Sam with enormous concern.

He looked awfully ragged—but not as bad as Wolfgang, who must have lost plenty of blood, what with his cat-clawed face and Bambi-wounded hand.

"I'm pretty sure he broke his leg in the fall," Sam told us, still treading water. "He must have passed out from the pain."

"So. We will take him ourselves," said Bambi. "For we must swim back."

She helped Dark Bear take Wolfgang from Sam as I showed Olivier how to propel his now-floating self back up through the milder current beneath the falls. When we'd crawled up the bank, Dark Bear lifted the lifeless Wolfgang in his arms and we picked our way back to retrieve the Pod and the other vessels. Olivier, carrying Jason while holding Bambi's gun trained on the Pod, marched our soon-to-be-former boss before us back to the car, as Sam, Bambi, and I carried our ever more costly treasures.

A muddy, bedraggled Sam crawled into the front seat of the Land Rover beside me, and Dark Bear drove, with Olivier, Bambi, the cylinders, and our hostages in the roomy back. I was completely exhausted. Despite all the lifeblood I'd invested in these manuscripts, I almost wished they'd actually vanished beneath the glassy but dangerous surface of the river. My imagination was so demolished by all that had happened that I couldn't think beyond the end of my nose.

"What next?" I asked the ensemble, who seemed as battered and confused as I.

"I can tell you," said Olivier, "that my first steps are going to be to throw all my nuclear security badges in the nearest mailbox, pull out a few of my other badges, and use them to haul these two chaps to the authorities for attempted mass murder." He paused and added, "We'll discuss all the other charges after that."

"And for me," Bambi said proudly, "as we were walking down here from the river, Dark Bear asked that Lafcadio and I use our many contacts to help select the best archaeological and academic institutions in other parts of the world to review and authenticate the original documents. I know we will be pleased to do it. As for my brother, as Lafcadio says, he has planted during all his life what he will shortly harvest."

I myself really wasn't yet prepared to think about the unconscious Wolfgang, lying waterlogged beside a dripping Pod on the backseat.

"But these manuscripts aren't quite out of the woods yet," said Sam. "Not until we've rounded up a few more people—including your father, and Bettina's mother—who'd surely still leave no stone unturned to put their hands on them." Despite my feelings toward my unrepentant father, I felt an understandable pang at how things had turned out, and I could tell from her face Bambi must feel the same. "But until we get all the culprits put out of commission," Sam added, "it will be my continuing job to protect and decipher these documents."

As for me, I had no idea where I went from here. I couldn't help wondering what life would be like after these past weeks, when everything had altered so irrevocably. I had no real job, no newfound friends, no mission, and no danger.

"I haven't a clue what I'm supposed to do," I admitted to everyone in general.

"Oh, you're about to have the biggest job of all," said Sam with a muddy grin, as I sat there waiting for the other moccasin to drop.

"You're going to learn to dance," he said.

THE DANCE

Mandala *means "circle," more especially a magic circle. . . . I have come across cases of women who did not draw mandalas but danced them instead. In India [this has] a special name. . . .* mandala nrithya, *the mandala dance.*

—Carl G. Jung

In the ecstasy of dance man bridges the chasm between this and the other world. . . . We may assume that the circle dance was already a permanent possession of the Paleolithic culture, the first perceptible stage of human civilization.

—Curt Sachs, *World History of the Dance*

The oldest dance form seems to be the Reigen, *or circle dance [which] really symbolizes a most important reality in the life of primitive men—the sacred realm, the magic circle. . . . In the magic circle, all daemonic powers are loosed.*

—Susanne K. Langer, *Feeling and Form*

So we'd come full circle—but my dancing days hadn't quite begun.

Olivier arranged, by pay phone from the road, that the Feds send a deputation from Boise to rendezvous with us back in town, pick up the Pod and Wolfgang, and put them on ice. The goods he had on them—including treason, international espionage, fraternizing with known foreign arms dealers and nuclear smugglers, attempted multiple homicides in a river, and the assassination of the high-level government operative Theron Vane—seemed pale, in my perception, compared with what Wolfgang had done: the attempted murder of his own half brother, Sam.

In town, Olivier scribbled on a clipboard resting against the side of Dark Bear's Land Rover, filling out the required forms for transfer of both his captives. The Pod, due to his lofty position as head of the nuclear site, was moved first by the Feds to their armored vehicle for immediate transfer to a federal prison, for detention awaiting trial.

Meanwhile Wolfgang, bound and harmless but sitting up now on the backseat, requested a word alone with me inside the car. So the others got out and milled around as I turned over my shoulder to look into his face, a mass of cat-tracks, and Wolfgang glared back at me in barely suppressed pain. It seemed to run deeper than something triggered by a wounded hand or fractured leg. Those dark turquoise eyes, that had only recently left me weak in the knees, now left me feeling isolated and frightened by everything that had passed between us since we'd met.

"Ariel," said Wolfgang, "can you even imagine the pain I feel when I look at you? I believed that you understood I loved you. Now, to suddenly discover that you've done nothing all along but tell me lies."

I had told *him* lies? That, to say the very least, was something a bit more excessive than the proverbial pot calling the kettle black! Good Lord, for weeks, whatever rock I'd turned over, there was still another lie. I had confronted Wolfgang so often, only to hear more lies, only to swallow each and every one just as gullibly as the last, only to wind up back in his arms and his bed, again and again. But since his most recent point had been made over the barrel of a gun, I thought it might be the better part of valor to reserve comment.

"You *knew* Sam was alive, yet you concealed it!" Wolfgang spat out with great bitterness. "You lied to me all the while."

"Wolfgang, you were trying to *kill* him!" I pointed out the seemingly obvious. "Would you have killed your sister, too? Were you going to kill me?"

"I love you," he said between narrow lips, ignoring my question as another wave of pain passed over him. When he'd recovered, he said, "Of course I wasn't going to kill any of you—don't be mad. Do I seem like a homicidal maniac? I was only after those relics that are so important. Oh, Ariel, don't you see? You and I could have used that information correctly. We could have accomplished so much. Through the use of those manuscripts, together, we could have created a better world."

He paused and added carefully, "I know what you were thinking after Paris—after Zoe spoke to you. It was my question about the Gypsies, wasn't it? I could feel it all the way back on the plane, and I should have said something then. But I was only surprised to learn of it, that's all. Please believe it made no difference between us. It wouldn't have mattered to me—"

"*What* wouldn't have mattered to you?" I erupted in fury. "What on earth are you talking about? You mean you'd have condescended to go on sleeping with me, even though I have tainted blood? My God—what kind of person *are* you? Don't you see how it makes me feel, to know it was *you* who tried to kill Sam with that bomb in San Francisco? You tried to murder him, Wolfgang. And all the while, you *knew* for a fact that Sam was your own brother!"

"*No he's not!!*" Wolfgang practically screamed, his face ashen white with an agony that expressed, in one look, everything he'd left unsaid.

Olivier had glanced in alarm through the window, and he started to open the car door, but I waved my hand no. I was shaking all over with an emotion I couldn't even begin to name. Hot tears were welling in my eyes as I turned back to Wolfgang and took a deep breath. I said, as calmly and distinctly as I could without going to pieces,

"Yes, Wolfgang. He is your brother."

Then I turned, climbed out of the car, and closed the door behind me.

◆ ◆

Dark Bear, one of the most astonishingly organized individuals on the planet, would have made a terrific CEO of a major corporation, if he hadn't been so attached to the more important tasks of preserving the roots of his people and unraveling the mysteries of life. In the interim, he'd also managed to organize Sam's and my project.

But Dark Bear considered it too dangerous to turn us loose—"go public," as it were—until Olivier and his troops managed to round up a few more of the bad guys. Thanks once again to Dark Bear, they'd now have more ammunition to do so. Uncle Earnest's private files—the unpleasant information Zoe said he'd ferreted out about the Behn family—had been found anonymously tucked amid a morass of old property claims from decades past, in a sturdy safe on the reservation at Lapwai.

Though Earnest might have purged the very existence of Halle and Wolfgang from his mind, as Dark Bear had told us, this new trove did include documentation on our family's role—including my father's—as long-hidden financiers backing their own concept of caste supremacy, and placing weapons of mass destruction in the service of their unpleasant view of the New World Order.

There were a few surprises from the more upbeat side of my family. As Sam had suspected and Dacian Bassarides now confirmed, there actually had been four parts to Pandora's legacy, divided among the four "Behn children." After meeting me in Vienna, it seems Dacian had arrived at a few of his own conclusions. He took it upon himself to forge a long-overdue reconciliation between Lafcadio and Zoe, sweeping aside all those decades of family bitterness that had essentially been spawned by just one man, now long dead.

Nor did Dacian have to convince Laf and Zoe that I was the one to pull all the pieces together as Pandora once had done—but that then by the terms of her will, twenty-five years ago, had again been torn apart. Uncle Laf shipped a case of Dacian's estate-bottled wine to me, with a note from Dacian detailing that other estate, Pandora's, which had attracted so much interest all these years. Following up on this input myself with a pertinent call to my mother and several chats with Dark Bear, I found the picture growing crystal clear.

First, there was the rune manuscript my mother had sent from San Francisco, which Olivier had then retrieved from where I'd hidden it in the DOD Standard at the nuclear site. Laf, I recalled, told me early on that Pandora had made a practice of copying runes in her own hand from standing stones all over Europe: these runes became her bequest to my father. When Jersey discovered Augustus's involvement with her sister, she'd made her own clandestine copy of this manuscript. Though my father still had the original copy, Earnest later advised Jersey to save her copy to give to me when I was grown, just as he'd saved his own part of Pandora's legacy for Sam.

That brought me to the second set, inherited by Earnest and left by him to Sam. These were the rare and crumbly scrolls, boards, and cloths we'd rescued at so much peril from the crystal cave, the set everybody was so hot to get that they'd even plunged after them down the dark path of murder and mayhem. It wasn't hard to guess Wolfgang's private motive, of course, given what seemed his obsessive preoccupation: that his father had abandoned *him* and left his entire estate—including these relics—to his younger, and Native American, son Sam.

As Dacian Bassarides had pointed out in Vienna, one quarter of a jigsaw puzzle, even half, was of little value without the other parts. And as Volga Dragonoff had explained during our midnight chat in an icy Soviet dormitory, even with *all* the pieces heaped together in a pile, you'd still need someone who was initiated into the right way of thinking—as he'd claimed he believed *I* was—to assemble the whole puzzle.

There was only one person who could have given me such training, with or without my knowing it. That was Sam. The two people who held the other pieces of the puzzle, Lafcadio and Zoe, had sent copies of their own chunks of Pandora's estate, which they'd entrusted Bambi to deliver when she came to warn me about Wolfgang. With these now in my possession as well, I felt equipped to begin my attack.

◆ ◆

Dark Bear had come up with an ingenious plan so Sam and I wouldn't have to spend our time in lean-tos and remote mountain sheds while completing our project—a plan he'd already set in motion weeks ago, as soon as Sam had returned from Salt Lake with his own goods on the family. We had all the provisions prepared that we'd need to spend at least six months "up-country," enabling us to begin and finish the project in relative secrecy.

We took four sturdy pack horses, a decent supply of dried food and herbal home remedies, a teepee and plenty of waterproof thermal gear, and two laptop computers with battery packs, complete with the best software on the market in multiple languages, ancient and modern, to aid in our translation. Our campsite was a charming private plot watered by a fast freshwater creek, just a day's pack trip from Pend'Oreille Lake and the Kootenai wilderness up in the Idaho panhandle close to the border of British Columbia and therefore, in a pinch, within drumbeat distance of plenty of Indian tribes. The only real town within thirty miles of us was a little place (Pop.: 800) that bore the improbable name of Troy.

My dark, green-eyed saviour Jason accompanied us into the wilderness—albeit somewhat reluctantly, until he got a load of his own private fast-water creek. At the end of each week, Dark Bear sent a nameless courier to us on a dappled Appaloosa to drop off a few staples and pick up whatever documents we'd finished transcribing and translating, wafting them away to parts unknown—or at least, if known, known only to Dark Bear himself.

"If I'd ever heard about this Indian underground railway," Sam said, "it would sure have saved me plenty of hassle and headaches when I first inherited these things!"

I had forgotten what it was like to live outdoors on the land, where fresh water, food, and air are provided by the earth itself—with no middlemen to dilute or pollute them. It was an exhilarating experience, from the first moment we pegged down our teepee and stepped inside. Though Sam and I planted the few short-season crops that would grow up here, so deep into the high country, and though we had to fish and forage each day in order to eat, we were able to spend most of our time translating manuscripts. And the more we translated, the more fascinating it became.

Here was a procession of histories and mysteries that seemed to pour forth from the deep, silent voice of an unknown, and until now unheard-of, past. This past slowly began to emerge from the concealing fog of a smoke machine that I soon understood had been cranked for millennia by historians and biographers.

"Something's occurred to me," I told Sam late one night beside the fire after we'd been at work for about a month. "In these tales, we rarely see some kind of truly superior society invading and subjugating an inferior one—it's more often the reverse, whether you compare the two in terms of scientific or artistic skills. Basically, history is a record of the conquerors' stupendous deeds of valor. But their 'superiority' is often based on the fact they succeeded in beating and enslaving others."

"You're getting the message," said Sam. "Too bad you aren't an Indian—you'd have gotten it the day you were born. As a child, you know, Hitler's favorite author was a guy named Karl May: he wrote cowboy-and-Indian tales for young German boys. At the end of these stories, guess who usually won?"

It was the only hint of bitterness I'd ever heard from Sam about a part of his heritage that I, as a non-Native American, could likely never completely understand.

"You saved Wolfgang's life," I pointed out. "But now you know, from what Bambi has told us, that he hated you, that he planted the bomb that nearly killed you. If you'd known it then, do you think you would still have tried so hard to rescue him?"

"You mean, am I so altruistic I could forgive someone who enjoyed eradicating people like me? Like, 'He ain't heavy, he's my brother'?" said Sam. Then he smiled, got up from where he'd been leaning back on a saddle beside the fire, came over, and pulled me to my feet to face him.

"I knew," he said.

"You knew it was Wolfgang who tried to kill you?" I said in amazement.

"I guess you think I'm pretty goddamned noble right now, don't you?" said Sam. "So let me clarify. I don't think people as evil as *he* is should get off with just a broken leg and a quick, painless drowning. I think his fine Aryan name should be dragged through the mud—and that he should go to jail for the rest of a long life."

I guess when you finally uncorked Sam's bitterness, you found there was a pretty decent jugful there, after all. Sam's hands still rested on my shoulders. He was watching me with a strange expression as we stood there at the center of the teepee, facing each other beside the fire.

I closed my eyes. I remembered another fire in another man's castle, and the unquenchable fire that had been created inside *me* by the touch and smell of that man, the man we'd just discussed and so irrevocably dismissed. A man so filled with hatred that he would try to blow his own brother to bits—the same brother who wound up saving his life, in spite of knowing all that. For all his protestations that he loved me, I wondered if Wolfgang ever really had. I wondered if I'd loved him.

When I opened my eyes, Sam's silvery eyes were searching me deeply, as if seeking some hidden answer to an unspoken question. I remembered his words up on the mountain that morning: "Ariel, have you any idea just how dangerous this untimely friendship of yours might prove to us both?" Had he known even then? Well, I'd bloody well found out for myself by now, hadn't I?

"I really did try to warn you," said Sam. "I didn't consciously suspect anything until I got to Salt Lake. But when I began to put two and two together from family documents and understand the situation—when I realized the person you'd let me know you were involved with, Wolfgang Hauser, might well be the same man who murdered Theron Vane—I wasn't really sure what to do. I knew how dangerous it might prove for *me*: I knew it was me he was after. But I couldn't believe he'd harm you. I sent you that note to be careful around him. At the same time, you aren't a little girl anymore, sweetheart. I truly wanted you to do what was best for *you*."

"That was awfully bloody magnanimous of you," I snapped, with more than a little anger and frustration. "You thought it was 'best for me' to let me go on making love with someone, to fall in love with someone, who might have destroyed us both?"

Sam flinched as if I'd struck him a physical blow, and I realized how he must have tried to close his eyes to what had actually happened between Wolfgang and me. Finally he took a deep breath and spoke very quietly.

"If you wanted to glut yourself with liquor or some dangerous drug, I'd let you do that too, Ariel. You're surely responsible for your own decisions and actions. But that isn't love, and you know it: love isn't something you want to *do* with someone."

"I'm not at all sure I know what love is," I told him, meaning it. I recalled Dark Bear's comment that Sam's father Earnest had believed himself incapable of the feeling. So maybe for the Nez Percé, I'd be a dead person, too.

"I think I know. Shall I tell you?" Sam asked, still watching me.

I felt so empty—but I nodded for him to go on.

"I think love is when you know that a part of you *is* the person you love, and a part of him or her is inside of *you*," Sam said. "You can't use or manipulate or deceive someone you truly love, because you'd be using or manipulating or lying to yourself. Does that make sense?"

"Are you saying that if Wolfgang lied to me," I said with no small irony, "he was really only lying to *himself*?"

"No—it wasn't necessary for him to deceive himself, was it?" Sam snapped back. "Aren't you forgetting a little something? You slept with him and lied to him, too."

I was truly dumbstruck, but I knew it was true. I'd had the most intimate relation one can have, with a man I'd never trusted. A man I'd never opened up with enough, of my own volition, to tell him the complete truth about anything. It was a bitter pill to swallow, that deep inside I'd known what Wolfgang was, all along.

"I've long ago given you part of my heart, and part of my soul, Ariel. I'm sure you know that." Sam smiled mischievously and added, "But there *are* a few strings attached before I can let you have part of my body."

"Your . . . body?" I said, my head throbbing. "But I thought you were . . . attracted to Bambi."

"I know you did," said Sam with a grin. "When I saw that look on your face as I lifted Bettina down beside the waterfall—well, it was the first time I thought there might be real hope for you and me, Wolfgang or no Wolfgang." He ruffled my hair and said simply, "I love you, hotshot. I guess I always have."

I admit, I was thunderstruck. I stood there in a daze, not knowing what to do. Was I ready for this?

Oddly enough, Sam had started moving sleeping bags and saddlebags, clearing a space at the center of the teepee, around the little stone fireplace.

"What are you doing?" I asked.

"There's just one string, really," Sam explained, piling blankets to one side. He stood up and shook back his long hair with impatience.

"How can you expect me to go on loving someone, Ariel," he asked me, "who doesn't know how to dance?"

◆ ◆

As Dacian had told me, the process *was* more important than the product.

During this past month that Sam and I had lived our fraternal existence, until we danced, I would never have had the vaguest understanding of the manuscripts we were translating—that all the talk of world grid, warp and woof, yin and yang, alchemical marriage and Dionysian ritual, essentially boiled down to one thing: transformation. Indeed, that's what the manuscripts were all about.

We danced all night. Sam had tapes of Native American dances and chants to play on a portable cassette player, but we danced to everything—Uncle Laf's *Zigeuner* music, Hungarian rhapsodies, and Jersey's favorite wild Celtic songs that were feverishly danced, so she used to tell Sam and me, at every Irish wedding and every wake—fast and slow, exciting and magical, powerful and mysterious.

We danced barefoot around the fire, then outside in the dark meadow atop the mountain that smelled of the first cornflowers of early summer. Sometimes we touched one another, held hands or danced in each other's arms, but often we danced alone, a different and fascinating experience.

As I danced on and on, it seemed that I truly felt my own body for the first time—not only more centered and balanced within itself, though that was true too, but also completely connected in some mysterious fashion with the earth and sky. I felt parts of me dying, falling away in pieces, spinning out into the universe and turning into stars in the vast midnight space, a space spangled with galaxies that seemed to go on forever.

We danced into the morning, until the coals of our fire had flickered out, then we danced out into the wildflower meadow once more, to see the first grey light of dawn bleeding red into the morning sky. And still we kept on dancing. . . .

It was only after all this time that something strange began to happen—something frightening. And the moment it did, I stopped dancing on the spot. The music was still playing on our cassette, as Sam whirled round and saw me standing there, barefoot in the wildflowers. He came over to me.

"Why have you stopped?" he asked.

"I don't know," I told him. "I'm not dizzy or anything, it's just . . ." I couldn't say.

"Then dance with me," he said.

Bending down to switch off the music, Sam took me in his arms there in the meadow and we moved slowly in a circle, almost floating. Sam held me lightly, just enough for support. His rugged face with straight nose and cleft chin, his lashes shadowing strong cheekbones, seemed as he leaned toward me like those of a strong protecting spirit. Then he pressed his lips to my hair.

"I learned something from Pandora's manuscripts," he said. "In an early version of a medieval alchemical text—the *Goethe*, the Magic Circle of Solomon the Magus—it says angels don't make love like human beings. They don't have bodies."

"How do they do it?" I asked him.

"They have a much *better* way," Sam said. "They mix themselves together, and actually become one for a very brief time, where before there were two. But angels, of course, have no substance. They're made of moonbeams and stardust."

"Do you think we're angels?" I suggested, leaning back in his arms with a smile. Sam kissed me.

"I think we should mingle our stardust, angel," he said. Then he drew me down by the hand onto the grass, to lie on top of him among the wildflowers. "I want you to do whatever you feel like—or nothing at all," he said with a smile. "I'm completely at your service. My body is your instrument."

"Can it play *El Amor Brujo?*" I asked him, laughing.

"It can play whatever selection the virtuoso wishes to ripple out upon it," he assured me. "What will it be?"

"All at once, I feel like I'm way above timberline," I told him seriously.

"We've been there before, and we survived," Sam said softly, taking my fingers and brushing them over his lips. "We entered the light once together, Ariel. Just after our totems found us—do you remember?"

I nodded slowly. Yes, I remembered.

◆ ◆

When the cougar and two bears had vanished from that predawn mountaintop, we'd sat for a very long time, Sam and I—maybe hours—just touching each other's fingertips, side by side, not moving. As darkness had faded to dawn, though, I had the uneasy feeling of something changing in my body, something shifting like restlessly sifting sands. Then all at once I'd found myself moving away from earth itself, floating through the air high up into space. I felt completely separate from my body, yet I still had form and shape—like a teardrop filled with helium, suspended in the night sky.

I had a moment of panic, that I might fall or that I might actually be dead and leaving the earth forever! But then I suddenly realized I wasn't alone up here. There was someone beside me: Sam. It was almost as if he were speaking to me from inside my own mind, though if I looked, I could actually see both our bodies sitting side by side, down there on the earth below!

"Don't look down, Ariel," Sam had whispered in my mind. "Look up ahead. Let's enter the light together. . . ."

Oddly enough, we'd never spoken of it afterwards, not once. And odder still, it had never seemed to me that it was all only a dream. If anything, it was more vivid than reality, just as our three-dimensional, Technicolor world is so much more solid than a two-dimensional black-and-white photo pasted on cardboard. This was many exponential dimensions greater and deeper. But if I'd had to really pin it down in specific words, I would never have known where to begin.

We had entered the light together as children, Sam and I. Now we were about to do so once again. This time, I knew, it was going to be very, very different from the last. We two were about to be transformed into one, on a spring morning among the wildflowers.

And this time, I was no longer afraid.

◆ ◆

As I lay in Sam's arms hours later, instead of feeling drained I felt exhilarated, as if my veins were suddenly filled with something light and bubbly and effervescent.

"How exactly would you describe that?" I asked him as he wove his fingers together with mine. "I mean, what happened to us?"

"Hmm," said Sam. "I suppose if you must have a name, the technical term would be 'mutual orgasm.' A very *long* mutual orgasm. More or less your basically endless, drawn-out, hours-long, *nonstop* mutual orgasm—"

I shoved my hand in his face.

"On the other hand," said Sam, smiling as he kissed my bare shoulder, "you could simplify things a lot and just call it love. Were you surprised?"

"I've never felt anything like that before," I admitted.

"I guess I should be relieved," said Sam. "But to be honest, neither have I."

He sat up and looked at me lying in the grasses, and he ran his finger from my chin down the center of my body until I vibrated. Then he leaned over and kissed me on the mouth as if we were slowly pouring stardust into each other. I couldn't believe how it felt.

"I think we're tuned up," said Sam. "No more rehearsals—what about a real live performance?"

◆ ◆

Sam and I were still in the mountains six months later, early November, when Dark Bear sent us snowshoes, cross-country skis, and some bearskins in preparation for the expected first big snow.

We'd nearly finished translating the manuscripts—Earnest's, Lafcadio's, Zoe's, and the runes Jersey'd stolen from Augustus. As Wolfgang and others thought, these pointed to locations on earth that formed a grid the ancients had not only believed possessed enormous powers but which apparently they'd actually *used* in ceremonies and rituals, documented here in detail, over a period of at least five thousand years. The closely held secret of early mystery religions like the Orphics, Pythagoreans, and early Egyptians was that activating this grid was an alchemical marriage that would transform the earth, bringing down energy that connected us in a kind of "marriage" with the cosmos.

"Do you know what a 'center of symmetry' is?" Sam asked me one day. When I shook my head, he explained. "In some mathematical models, like those in catastrophe theory, you can pinpoint the absolute center of a shape. There's a model for wildfires, for instance. If a wildfire starts around the edges of a field, regardless of the field's shape, you can predict precisely where the fire will burn out, at true center, by drawing a straight edge at each contour around the periphery and dropping a ninety-degree line from it. The place where most lines overlap is the absolute center, the center of symmetry—a kind of path of least resistance. Many field models can be analyzed that way—fields of light, of the brain, of the earth, and possibly the cosmos. Let me show you."

He drew the shape on his small computer screen for me:

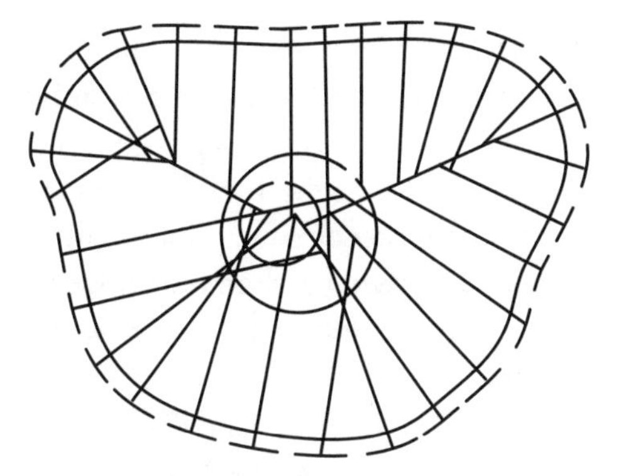

"You think these locations we're looking for on earth aren't necessarily just connected by straight lines or six-pointed stars?" I surmised. "You think they're important because they're acting as centers of symmetry?"

"A kind of vortex or maelstrom," Sam agreed. "Something that pulls energy into itself and magnifies its power, because it's the *true* center of the form."

Part of the blueprint was inherent in the pages we had before us. For instance, as we figured out in a flash one day, those patent drawings Nikola Tesla had made for his own high-voltage tower built in Colorado Springs—the tower he claimed would channel energy across the world grid—closely resembled a famous drawing of the first alchemical retort, the Chrysopoea of Cleopatra, from the oldest extant alchemy text. And both of these resembled—literally to a T—the tau cross, power symbol of the ancient Egyptians, as well as the *Tyr* rune Zoe spoke of, which invoked the magic pillar of Zeus. And, eerily, even the Irminsul itself, destroyed by Charlemagne but rebuilt in the Teutoburg Forest one thousand years later by Adolf Hitler.

Tyr Rune **Irmin Saule** **Tesla Tower** **The Chrysopoea of Cleopatra**

Still, Sam and I knew our task had a long way to go. Some documents pointed to others that weren't in our possession. We figured out where many had been hidden millennia ago—a crevasse on Mount Ida along the coast of Turkey, Mount Pamir in Central Asia, a cave where Euripides wrote his plays in central Greece—but although some ancient documents had recently been found in these regions, clearly there was no guarantee the ones we were looking for would be there today. We decided that when we finished our task here, in the spirit of Pandora and Clio, we'd try to find at least a few of those others.

It was uncanny, too, that as each event popped out of our Pandora's box of ancient revelations, it seemed to be echoed simultaneously somewhere on earth, in the present. We knew we must be getting close to the transformation we were awaiting.

Not only had the Soviets withdrawn from Afghanistan in February, but other countries with walls, whether political or physical ones, began to be hit by democratic urges and surges that were suddenly moving in torrents, like dammed water trying to seek its natural level, its center of symmetry.

In June, Tienanmen Square in China, the country most famous for a wall that could even be seen from outer space, had erupted in social protest. Though the tanks rolled in, the yeast of ferment had already started. Then, on the November ninth we'd been awaiting—the date Wolfgang had identified as a turning point for Napoleon, de Gaulle, Kaiser Wilhelm, and Adolf Hitler—we received the astonishing news, via our Appaloosa express, from Laf and Bambi in Vienna. The Berlin Wall, symbolically separating East and West for more than twenty-five years, had come down overnight. The tidal wave had at last broken through; it was rolling now and couldn't be stopped.

But it wasn't until late December—almost the anniversary of the ninetieth year since Uncle Laf's birth in Natal province, South Africa—that I made the breakthrough of my own that Sam and I had been hoping for. I was working on the text of a long roll of very old and fragile linen, written in Greek, that I'd just unsealed from one of Sam's lucite tubes. I knew I hadn't seen it before. But as I was tapping the Greek words into my laptop, I thought something about it seemed familiar.

"Do you remember a document of Zoe's we translated around two months ago?" I asked Sam, who was working on his computer across the room, sitting cross-legged with an upside-down Jason sacked out in cat nirvana on his lap. "I mean the story about a voice calling across the waters from the isles of Paxi, telling an Egyptian pilot to announce, when he was off Palodes, that the Great God Pan was dead."

"Yes, Tiberius had the pilot brought to Capri for interrogation," said Sam. "The pilot's name, coincidentally, was Tammuz, like the dying god in the ancient mysteries. And he announced Pan's death the same week Jesus died. What have you figured out?"

"I'm not sure," I told him, still tapping text into my computer. "But from just the amount of Greek I've picked up these past months by watching the machine translate, I think this letter may provide at least some kind of key to how things fit together at a deeper level. Unfortunately it's torn, and some is missing. But it's clearly written by a woman to a man—a woman that I think we're already pretty familiar with."

"Read it aloud?" Sam suggested, pointing to the snoring cat on his lap with a smile. "I hate to disturb folks in deep contemplation." So did I.

Perdido Mountain, Pyrenees, Roman Gaul

Beloved Joseph,

Following your advice, my brother Lazarus and I have put the alabaster box, the chalice, and our other objects the Master touched in his last days, here in a secure hiding place within the mountain, where we pray they will remain safe until they are needed. I've made a list of these, and directions to find them, and will send these separately.

In your last letter, Joseph, you expressed the thought that since you've now reached a great number of years, you may yourself soon be going to join the Master. You asked whether I, as the only true initiate of the Master, could find it possible to share my perspective of what occurred at that last supper he passed with his disciples, and how it related to the earlier descriptions I'd sent you, written by others present on that occasion.

It's impossible to put into words what can only be grasped through experience, such as one might attain through the process of initiation. But I shall try as best I can.

It has always been my belief that in all he said or did, the Master was expressing himself at dual levels, though he made a clear distinction between them. Let us call them the levels of teaching and of initiation. In teaching, he was fond of using allegory and parable to provide an example of what he wished to communicate. But beneath such parables always lay hidden the second level, the level of symbol, which I believe the Master used only within the context of initiation.

The Master told me that a single symbol, picked up in this way, would touch many levels in the mind of the disciple. Once someone experiences a specific image in this way, its deeper meaning works on him beneath the skin at a primal, almost physical, level.

In a way, the Master was like one of those Eastern magi he'd studied with—always on a path, seeking, questing, looking for his special star to follow into a night of endless mystery. In that sense, one could see that he constantly scattered clues in his path, on his personal quest for the initiate who might pick up those clues and follow him down that road. Even today, so many years since he left us, I feel the same chill at recalling his tone when he first told me, "Put down your things and follow me." I now understand he meant it to be taken at both levels, that I was not only to follow him but to follow his example in learning to ask the right questions.

The Master's questions on that last night seemed to me, as always, every bit as important as his answers. He told the others that I would know how to answer his question about the significance of the Shulamite, Solomon's lover in the Song of Songs. Then the Master proceeded to give his own answer: The Shulamite represents Wisdom. But do you recall, at first, he'd mentioned it was a "knotty" problem? He once used that expression to ask <u>you</u> what was "unchanging and imperishable"—suggesting his answer on each occasion was only a partial one.

The Master thought the initiate must always strive to unravel the full answer for himself. In this case, I believe I can suggest the full answer he had in mind. The Greek root of the word knot is "gna"—to know—from which we also derive gnosis, or hidden wisdom. There are words in many languages that come from this root, but all have meanings that suggest ways of gaining such hidden knowledge.

By identifying the Shulamite with the Eastern or morning star, the Master has again pointed our attention to these mysteries. In the poem, Solomon's love is black and beautiful: she represents dark matter, the Black Virgin of ancient belief, or the black stone that falls from the skies.

The three chosen disciples of the Master's inner circle were Simon Peter and James and Johan Zebedee, who wanted to sit beside him when the kingdom arrived. But he assigned them instead—significantly and symbolically, in my opinion—to fulfill individual missions, just after his death, at three very specific spots here on earth: James to Brigantium, Johan to Ephesus, and Peter to Rome. The first is the home of the Celtic goddess Brighde; the second, home of the Greek Artemis or, in Latin, Diana. And Rome itself is home to the earlier Phrygian Great Mother, the black stone brought from Central Anatolia that now sits enshrined on the Palatine Hill. The first initials of these three cities strung together spell BER—the acronym of that goddess herself, in the form of a bear.

These three spots on earth represent three faces of an ancient goddess—a goddess represented by the Shulamite of the poem.

So the Master's very question—Who was the dark woman of the Song of Songs?—drives right to the heart of his message that the Song itself was a formula of initiation, to be undertaken only by those setting out to conduct the Great Work. The marriage between the white king of the apple orchard and the dark virgin of the vineyard represents the marriage of divine and carnal that lays bare the very core of the Mysteries.

◆ ◆

When I finished reading and looked up, Sam, still sitting with Jason in his lap, was grinning at me.

"That was one of the ones I'd translated myself, before Wolfgang made off with the copies of my manuscripts," he said. "If it means what it sounds like, it would sure knock the stuffing out of a few of those good old celibacy theories—but I'd find it pretty hard to believe. And why did you say you thought it had to do with the 'voice upon the waters,' or the death of the Great God Pan?"

"It may be exactly what connects all Pandora's manuscripts together," I told him. "What this letter here is telling us, I think, is that initiation—*any* initiation—requires a kind of death. Death to the world, death to the ego, death to the 'former self' of one's existence, just as the earth has to die and be reborn every year for its renewal. Don't forget, the two gods who traded off at Delphi each year were Apollo the apple king and Dionysus, god of the vineyard—same jobs as our hero and heroine in Song of Songs. By the same token, the birth and baptism of a new aeon, of a brave new world, requires the death of the old way of thinking, old belief systems—even the death of the old gods."

"So the knot is just a different way of looking at the warp and woof," said Sam.

Then I thought of something else, and I pulled up on my screen one of the documents I'd just translated earlier, of Uncle Laf's.

"Do you recall all that stuff about the Knights Templar of Saint Bernard and the Temple of Solomon? Well, guess what this manuscript says was the logo on their flag? The skull and crossbones—same as the Death's Head squadron of Heinrich Himmler's SS. But it doesn't mean death in *this* document. It means life."

"How so?"

"There are two figures of importance in the Greek pantheon that keep appearing over and over in these manuscripts," I told him. "Athena and Dionysus. Can you think what they had in common?"

"Athena was goddess of the state," said Sam. "But also of the family, the home, and the loom—ergo, of order. That's *cosmos* in Greek. While Dionysus was lord of chaos. His pagan festivals, which still survive in Christian ones like Mardi Gras, were a license for drink and debauchery and madness. They're connected in ancient cosmogonies, where cosmos is often born from chaos."

"I found another connection—in the way they were born," I told him. "Dionysus's pregnant mother Semele was burned by his father Zeus when he appeared to her in the form of a thunderbolt. Father Zeus took the unborn baby from the mother's ashes, sewed him up in his own flesh, and gave birth to him later from his thigh. That's why Dionysus is called 'twice-born,' or 'god of the double door'—"

"And Athena was swallowed by Zeus and later born from his forehead," finished Sam. "So she can always read his thoughts. I get it. One was born from the skull and one from the thigh of the father. Skull and crossbones, two kinds of creation or generation, spiritual and profane, only together are they *whole* or *holy*—is that it?"

I recalled Saint Bernard's words in his Song of Solomon commentaries, "Divine love is reached through carnal love."

"I'm sure that's what this story is hinting at, about the Mysteries," I told Sam. "The message must be that there's no death without sex."

"Pardon *me*?" said Sam.

"Bacteria never die, they divide," I said. "Clones just keep on mimeographing the same material. Humans are the only animals that understand and anticipate death. It's the basis of every religion, all religious experience. Not just spirit, but the *relationship* between life and death, spirit and matter."

"Our nervous system has two branches that tie consciousness to emotions called the cranial and sacral. They connect the brain and sacrum," agreed Sam. "Your skull-and-crossbones, where the kneebone's connected to the thighbone, are associated in many languages with powerful generative properties, in words like 'genius' and *genoux*. There's plenty of evidence, physical and linguistic, for Pythagoras's famous line: As above, so below."

"That was the whole job of Dionysus in mythology: to *connect* the sacred and profane. The only way to do it was to hybridize. To yank women from the loom, get them away from the hearth and out of the house, up on the mountain, dancing and cavorting with young shepherds. Dionysus destroyed his hometown of Thebes, not once but twice. Or rather, they destroyed themselves."

"One time, it was because of incest," Sam said. "Oedipus had killed his father, been crowned king in his place, and married his own mother. When it comes to our family, I do quite take your point. But what was the other time?"

"It was when the young king of Thebes, Pentheus, refused to let the women, including his own mother, take part in the celebration of the Dionysian mysteries up on the mountain," I said. "Pentheus claimed that the Lord of the Dance wasn't a true god, not the son of Zeus. He actually wanted to keep the women home at night, so landowners could feel confident that their offspring and heirs weren't sons of satyrs or shepherds."

"What happened to the young king of Thebes?" asked Sam.

"His mother was driven mad," I said. "She cannibalized her own son."

"That's pretty gruesome," said Sam. Then he added with a grin, "So basically you're saying that Dionysus—the god of the coming age—also provides the long-awaited answer to Freud's question, 'What does a woman want?' You want a night off now and again, so you can run howling around up on the mountain, dancing, getting drunk, cavorting with young shepherds—is that it?"

"Well, it sure might flush out a few of those coagulated bloodlines," I agreed. "Nobody seems ever to have introduced folks like Hitler or Wolfgang to the concept that hybridization breeds strength. I think a little shepherd-pollen might also answer Zoe's question, 'What makes them think they *can't*?' I think it's just what you said to me about lying versus loving. If you do it to someone else, you're doing it to yourself."

"Yesterday, I may have learned something that connects this stuff together," Sam told me with one of his mischievous looks. "The Essenes, who lived down at Qumran in the time of Jesus, believed that Adam had a secret wife, a first wife who came before Eve. Her name was Lilith—it means 'owl,' wisdom, *sophia*. Lilith deserted Adam, though. Guess why."

"No clue," I told him.

"Adam wouldn't let her be on top," Sam said. When he saw my face, he started to laugh. Then he said, "No, really, I'm serious—I think I'm onto something. Just listen."

He sat up from his bearskin and faced me.

"Lilith is not only wisdom, she's Mother Earth—wise enough to support all life, if we don't dam her up but leave her free to do what she does best. Maybe the mystery is the ancient wisdom, how to use earth's natural rhythms and energies to support us, instead of damming up rivers that are her arteries, ripping minerals out of her belly, cutting down trees that are her breath, building walls to confine all life to allotted spaces.

"You know that the Indian nation is matriarchal," Sam added. "But you may not know this Nez Percé prophecy. During the Last Days, in any lands where women have been reduced to minions under male tyranny—or where the earth has been parceled out according to some patriarch's land-grabbing—those lands in the End Time will be destroyed in the second flood.

"So when it comes to Mother Earth," Sam finished with a smile, "I think we should let her be on top from now on, as she truly deserves. Just like you and me."

And he *was* telling the truth.